RUNE SEEKER

1

RUNE SEEKER INCLUDES:

RUNE SEEKER

1

J.M. CLARKE

C.J. THOMPSON

RUNE SEEKER
Published by Vault
In association with Aethon Books

ISBN 978-1-63849-324-2 (hardcover)

First AETHON: Vault Edition: Spring 2026

Printed in the United States of America.
1st Printing.

Aethon Books
www.aethonbooks.com

Vault Storyworks
www.vaultstoryworks.com

Cover art by Antti Hakosaari. Book design by Steve Beaulieu and Adam Cahoon. Title type design by Steve Beaulieu. Print formatting by Kevin G. Summers, Adam Cahoon, and Rikki Midnight.

AETHON: Vault books are published by Vault Storyworks LLC in association with Aethon Books LLC. "Aethon", the Aethon Logo, "Vault", the Vault logo, and the "AETHON: Vault" logos are copyright and trademark Aethon Books, LLC and Vault Storyworks LLC.

RUNE SEEKER

1

1

EVERFAIL

HIRAL took a deep breath as he stared at the stylized sun on the heavy door in front of him. The same sun tattooed on the center of his chest; both the symbol and source of a Shaper's power. *His* power, if he managed to pass the test…

No. No, he couldn't think like that. He *would* pass this time. He had to.

"You're nervous." The gravelly voice of his teacher and sponsor, Loan, came from behind him. "You always roll your right foot and stand on the edge of it when you're thinking too much."

Hiral snapped the sole of his foot back down on the ground, the thin wooden sandal of his ceremonial outfit clapping on the stone.

"Nothing wrong with thinking," he said to his mentor without turning. "You always tell me to visualize. I'm *visualizing*."

"I tell you to visualize success. Shaping. Forging your will and the energy granted to you by the sun to bring your tattoos to life. This, what you're doing now, is visualizing *failing*." Loan's comforting hand dropped onto Hiral's shoulder.

Hiral took another deep breath, letting it flow out of his lungs along with the building anxiety. Loan was right; Hiral *was* nervous.

"I know you want to, so go ahead and take a look at your status window. I can practically see your fingers itching," Loan said.

"I…" Hiral started. Would it make a difference? He knew what it said. What it always said. But, then again, if it *had* changed—finally—then maybe it would ease his nerves. "Just give me a second."

Hiral reached his hand up to the sun on his chest and pushed gently on it, the warmth of the solar energy flowing through his body focusing on that spot. "Do you want me to share the window?" he asked Loan.

"No need. It will be your turn any minute now."

Hiral nodded and pulled on the only magic he could use, his status window, and the information sprang to life in front of his eyes like he was reading from a luminescent blue page.

Name: Hiral Dorin
Race: Maker
Class: *Unavailable*

Attributes
Strength *(Str)* – 18 (0)
Endurance *(End)* – 18 (0)
Dexterity *(Dex)* – 20 (0)
Intelligence *(Int)* – 18 (0)
Wisdom *(Wis)* – 18 (0)
Attunement *(Atn)* – 18 (0)

Solar Energy Processing
Absorption Rate: S-Rank
Capacity: S-Rank
Output Rate: *Unavailable*

Abilities – Tattoos
Herald of Peace (Head, Left) – Unavailable
Herald of War (Head, Right) – Unavailable
Perfect Sense (Ear, Left) – Unavailable
The Crowd as One (Ear, Right) – Unavailable
Equilibrium (Neck) – Unavailable
Wings of Anella (Shoulders, Both) – Unavailable
Spear of Clouds (Spine) – Unavailable
Way of Shadow (Chest, Left) – Unavailable
Way of Light (Chest, Right) – Unavailable
Banner of Courage (Bicep, Left) – Unavailable
Banner of Despair (Bicep, Right) – Unavailable
Touch of the Primal (Abdomen, Left) – Unavailable
Abode of Asinef (Abdomen, Right) – Unavailable
Dagger of Sath (Forearm, Left) – Unavailable
Dagger of En (Forearm, Right) – Unavailable
The Pack (Thigh, Left) – Unavailable
Waters of Frey (Thigh, Right) – Unavailable
Path of Butterflies (Calf, Left) – Unavailable
Disc of Passage (Calf, Right) – Unavailable

Well, the constant training had paid off, with his *Str* and *Dex* both increasing by a point—that was no surprise, really. His eyes continued down the page until he found what he was looking for. Output Rate: Unavailable.

"No change to my output rate." Hiral withdrew the power fueling the status window, and the page vanished. "I'm sure it's wrong, though. I mean, I can open my status window, so there has to be *some* output."

But, when had a status window ever been wrong? *No, don't think like that. It has to be.*

"Remember your training," Loan said, having had this discussion dozens of times in the past. He added a squeeze of Hiral's shoulder. "You work harder than anybody else. Practice longer. Your mind is sharper than any of the other initiates and ninety percent of the full Shapers. Present company excluded, of course."

"I'm also ten years senior to any of the other initiates, and older than many full Shapers. Present company excluded." Despite his words, he found himself quirking a smile back at his mentor.

Meridian Lines spanned the towering older man's cheeks and forehead, running back across his shaved head and then down his neck to vanish beneath the loose robes he wore today. Due to years of Shaping, the lines had a faint luminescence to them against his dark skin. Those same lines glowed where they showed on his arms and the backs of his hands, their power feeding the intricate and similarly shining tattoos that covered him from head to toe.

If Hiral passed the test, mastered his power, that was what he would look like in a few years. Sure, he was leaner than his teacher—the man, like most Shapers, was almost as wide as he was tall, with arms as thick as Hiral's legs— and, while the tattoos covering Loan's seven-foot-tall body glowed with the energy he absorbed from the sun, Hiral's were noticeably dark. Not for long, though. This time, he'd...

"You didn't shave your head." Loan's words interrupted Hiral's thoughts, and the older man glanced at the unruly mop on Hiral's scalp.

"I..." Hiral started, but a gong sounded from the opposite side of the door, catching the rest of his excuse in this throat and setting his heart thumping like a drum in his chest.

"Breathe," Loan said with another squeeze of Hiral's shoulder. "Let's go."

Hiral nodded at his teacher, and the bigger man let go of Hiral's shoulder and stepped in front of him. He then put both hands on the heavy stone doors and leaned into them, legs bracing.

Muscles bunched on Loan's back between the wide strips of cloth that crisscrossed his upper half, Meridian Lines flaring as he called on his sun-granted strength. With the power of the Meridian Lines, and being mid-B-Rank, Loan had to have close to 160 *Str*—almost ten times what Hiral had, or more. A grinding along the stone floor accompanied a gentle grunt escaping the man's lips, and a gap split down the middle of the doors, bright sunlight piercing the darker room.

The huge doors, symbolic in the strength required to open them, parted to reveal the open-air testing stadium. A warm, sun-drenched breeze rushed into the opening and over Hiral's skin, his body instinctively reaching for the light and pulling some of that power into his core. While he couldn't output any of that power—yet—drawing it in was just as easy as breathing.

"Come," Loan said, taking his hands off the thick blocks of stone pretending to be doors.

He strode toward the center of the stadium, where seven equally massive Shapers stood waiting along with six much smaller initiates. Barely more than children, the oldest possibly ten years old, if that, they were almost comical beside the huge, sun-powered Shapers.

Years of pulling on the sun's energy had made the Shapers' physiques legendary. Each in the B-Rank and standing seven feet tall on average, their corded muscles bunched and flexed with every breath. Like Loan, their Meridian Lines glowed faintly from long use, though their individual tattoos varied widely, giving each of them unique strengths.

"You've got to be kidding," one of the women said when her eyes fell on Hiral stepping into the stadium. "This is a waste of our time." She focused her ire on Loan and crossed her arms.

"Jukil is right; we're done," the man beside her said, turning his attention to the six initiates.

Each of the children stood tall and proud where they lined up, none with more than the sun on their chests and the Meridian Lines running straight up to circle the base of their throats and connect to their shoulders. No tattoos to shape beyond the simple daggers on their inner forearms, and no intricate system of Meridian Lines stretching out across the rest of their body to strengthen their limbs.

Judging by a quick look, those tattooed daggers couldn't be higher than C-Rank. None of the children would ever be powerful or influential Shapers— but if they passed the test, at least they *would be* Shapers. As for Hiral...

No. Stop thinking like that.

Still, compared to the full set of Meridian Lines connecting Hiral from scalp to toes, and the multitude of S-Rank tattoos painstakingly etched into his skin, they were practically naked. And yet... and yet *they* looked at *him* with pity and disdain. They didn't hide their smirks, and the one on the left end even went so far as to elbow his neighbor and whisper, "The Everfail."

"Hush, now," the eldest of the Shapers said quietly, turning a quick glance on the children. Though her skin stretched and sagged from her almost two hundred years, her tattoos glowed the most fiercely of all. "Though you may have passed the physical test of giving shape to one of your tattoos, you are far from Shapers if you believe behavior like that to be acceptable." Her eyes turned toward Jukil and the man beside her, as if reminding them of the same fact.

Jukil had the decency to look abashed, until her eyes settled on Hiral again. "Well, what are you waiting for? Let's get this over with." She jabbed her finger toward the center of the stadium.

Hiral let the bite in her words roll off him like the warm breeze. Her attitude wasn't anything new. She'd been the same—no, worse—the year before. This time... this time, he would prove her wrong. He'd show them all he could do it, that he could pass...

"Your *tenth* attempt," one of the Shapers said. "Nine times, over nine years, you've come before us, and been unable to shape even the smallest thing. Not the **Daggers of EnSath** on your wrists, the **Wings of Anella** on your shoulder blades, neither of the **Ways of Light** or **Shadow** nor the **Waters of Frey**, or the…"

"Vule," the eldest Shaper said softly.

The Shaper who'd been listing off Hiral's past attempts gave a small bow of his head to the elder. "No offense intended, Ilrolik. I'm merely curious as to why this initiate, this… man…"

"Everfail," one of the children snickered, but straightened at a sharp look from Ilrolik.

"As to why he thinks this, his tenth test, will be any different," Vule went on as if the child hadn't spoken at all.

Hiral waited for a small nod of Ilrolik's head before he answered. "I've trained extensively for the year since my last test, and my father has finished the last of the tattoos on my…"

"**The Spear of Clouds** is finished?" one of the quiet Shapers interrupted. "Truly?"

"… Yes," Hiral said slowly. "He finished it within the last pass, and the bandages came off…"

"Yes, yes, yes, you heal slowly," the not-so-quiet-anymore Shaper said, striding out from the rest and right up to Hiral. "We know. Just show us the spear."

"I wasn't planning on shaping the spear…" Hiral said, and the Shaper waved a quick hand to dismiss the thought.

"Of course you weren't. Nobody has been able to shape it in thousands of passes, despite how many hopefuls have it inked. The odds of you bringing out more than a puff of light in the vague shape of the spear is so small, I would never…" He trailed off at a slight cough from Ilrolik. "Ahem, yes. Let's see it, then."

"I don't… This isn't why I'm here…" Hiral said, looking at the man.

"Please humor us," Ilrolik said, coming up beside the other Shaper. "Your father's work is masterful, and to finally see his rendition of the S-Ranked **Spear of Clouds** is a treat for us. We will proceed with your test after that."

Hiral's eyes went to Loan, and the man gave a small nod as he and the other Shapers walked over and encircled Hiral.

"As usual," Loan said, "Master Dorin's work is exceptional. It took my breath away the first time I saw it. Hiral, if you would…" He gestured to the wide swaths of cloth over Hiral's shoulders.

Even the initiates crept over as Hiral slid the shoulders of the ceremonial robe down his arms so they hung loosely by the tight belt around his waist.

"Well, where…?" Vule started to ask, but the gasp from one of the Shapers behind Hiral had the whole group moving around behind him. Predictably, there were twelve more sharp intakes of breath as the others joined the first.

Hiral stayed perfectly still as their eyes became glued to the spear tattooed up the length of his spine. The less he moved, the sooner this would all be over so he could take the test.

"The detail… Amazing," Jukil said in barely a whisper, and fingers traced down Hiral's back.

"Master Dorin has truly outdone himself with this," Ilrolik said. "His work is usually so small, but the scope of this has allowed for unprecedented detail. The spear almost looks like it could shape itself with the faintest application of power."

"There has never been a more perfect version of the **Spear of Clouds**, I'd dare say," Loan agreed. "Other than the original, I would imagine. Though, since none of us has ever actually *seen* it, perhaps my statement holds some truth."

"It does… It does," Ilrolik said as more fingers ran along Hiral's back.

"My test?" he asked, turning to face the semicircle of gawkers.

"Such a waste," Jukil said with a shake of her head. "If Master Dorin is capable of this, I should go talk to him about getting…"

"It'd do you no better," Vule quickly interrupted. "You don't have the Solar Absorption Rate or Capacity necessary to shape a tattoo of that Rank. None of us do, other than…"

All eyes turned to Hiral, more than half the people scowling out of jealousy, the other half out of disappointment.

"Next year, he'll have the **Emperor's Greatsword** tattooed…" Vule started, trailing off at Ilrolik's hand on his shoulder.

"Let us begin your test, Hiral," the old Shaper said.

"And, just in case you forgot what it is you're trying to do," Vule said, and nodded at the six young initiates, most of them less than half Hiral's age. "Shape," he commanded them.

Almost as one, the six children touched the dagger tattoos on the insides of the left forearms with the fingers of their right hands. The suns on their chests glowed faintly, and as they pulled their right hands away, glowing light— almost like smoke—flowed from their dagger tattoos for several seconds before solidifying into life-size versions of the weapons. None of their Output Rates could be higher than E-Rank with how long the shaping took, but that was still infinitely higher than Hiral's.

"Well done, initiates," Vule said before turning his attention back to Hiral. "The minimum expected of a Shaper. Nine times you have…" He stopped with a glance at Ilrolik, then started again fresh. "Your turn."

Hiral nodded and took a deep breath, focusing on the solar energy stored within his body. It flowed through him like a raging river, the S-Rank power—his potential—just waiting to be tapped and shaped. All he had to do was draw it through the tattoo of his choice to prove to them he could be a Shaper.

The **Spear of Clouds** running the length of his spine—the weapon said to have separated the ground from the sky itself—was too much for him at this point. As much as he hated to admit it, it was beyond him for the moment, as were most of his other tattoos. Sure, they were all technically S-Rank, but with the level of detail his father had put into them, they should more likely be classified above that.

No, like the other initiates in front of him, Hiral's best bet—and biggest chance of success—lay in the first tattoos he'd received: the daggers on his forearms.

With another deep breath, he moved the fingers of his right hand to the tattoo of a dagger on the inside of his left forearm. Unlike the simple things held in the hands of the initiates, daggers that looked like things of simple metal, the tattoo on his wrist was a weapon seemingly made of water. Blade and hilt both.

It was one of a pair, with the other sitting on his right wrist. Together, the **Daggers of EnSath** were said to have slain a beast of fire threatening to burn the world to cinders. Beautiful. Powerful. Deadly.

The wall between Hiral and his dreams.

"The same tattoo you tried in your first test?" Vule asked.

"Back to basics," Hiral said, not really paying attention to what his mouth was saying as he instead focused on pulling the solar energy in his body out through the tattoo.

Nothing happened.

Stomach flipping at the memory of all his past failures, Hiral pushed it back down and focused harder on the tattoo. The energy was *there*, waiting for him to call on it, just like when he used the status window. So he called as hard as he could, pushing his will and everything he had into shaping the dagger.

Still nothing.

"Whenever you're ready…" Vule said, and Hiral glanced up to see the Shaper focused on cleaning the dirt out from under his fingernails.

"Just… visualizing…" Hiral said, and spared a look at Loan.

The man gave Hiral a nod of encouragement, but there was a tightness around his eyes. Unlike the other Shapers, Loan wanted Hiral to pass… but he didn't really believe it any more likely than the others.

All the more reason Hiral couldn't fail. He lowered his eyes to focus on the one thing he needed to do.

Come on, he practically screamed in his mind at the energy in his body. It was everywhere in him, in every muscle and bone. It was so much a part of him, it practically glowed, but never once came when he called, like something was blocking it.

If the solar energy in his body was a river, then there was a dam obstructing it somewhere, and that meant one thing—he needed to rip it right down.

More focus. More pulling. His fingers drove into the skin of his wrist as he willed the energy to come through. His eyes squeezed shut as something wet and warm ran down his wrist.

"Hiral," Loan said quietly, but Hiral blocked out his words. It was… It was right there… literally on the tips of his fingers…

A flash behind his eyes hit him at the same time a jolt of searing pain ripped through his body and dropped him straight to the ground.

His head bounced off the warm stone as darkness clouded his sight from all sides and a single child's voice filled his ears.

"…Everfail…"

2
DEFINITELY NEXT YEAR

HIRAL groaned as sensations overcame the darkness, and his eyes flickered open. Pain—or was it the memory of pain?—shot through his body, and then faded away almost as quickly. What in the Fallen's names had happened?

"You're awake." Loan's voice drifted over to Hiral's ears, and the large man shortly followed, leaning over to look at Hiral's face. Fingers thicker than sausages pried Hiral's eyes wide, and Loan looked at each long and hard before finally leaning out of Hiral's line of sight. "Bring up your status window, and let's see if any lasting damage was done."

Lasting… damage? Still, Hiral didn't say anything, pulling up the window for Loan with a thought.

"Hrm, your attributes look fine, though I really wonder about these intelligence and wisdom scores after that stunt. And this—what's this down here?" Loan pointed at a notification near the bottom of Hiral's window.

Overcharge attempt: Unsuccessful
Debuff applied: System Shock
System Shock: No class abilities can be used for one hour
(174 seconds remaining)

"No class abilities can be…?" Hiral started, then barked out a short laugh. He didn't even have a class for abilities.

"This isn't something to laugh about, Hiral," Loan said, more seriously than Hiral would've expected. "I've heard of others triggering this *Overcharge*. It maximizes Solar Output for a brief moment, but comes with risks. At best, nothing happens. More likely, people suffer this debuff, and their internal solar pathways are shut down so they can't be damaged further. At the worst, though, well, people completely lose their ability to utilize Solar Energy.

"And before you wonder if that's maybe what happened to you, they can't even use their status window anymore. Try to avoid doing that again."

Hiral nodded, but mention of the Solar Output Rate turned his attention to that section of his status window. He'd felt *something* when he *Overcharged*, but apparently, it wasn't enough.

Output Rate: Unavailable

"Go ahead and close the window," Loan instructed, and Hiral followed suit, more than happy to ignore those cursed words while his eyes refocused on his surroundings.

The ceiling of the room told him he wasn't in the testing arena anymore, and the cot beneath him was uncomfortably familiar. Back in Loan's training compound?

Hiral turned to the question that'd been rattling around his head since he opened his eyes—the one he couldn't work up the nerve to voice. "Did I pass?"

A second of silence, then two... three...

"No," Loan finally said. "I thought you'd had it. *Something* stirred inside of you, obviously the **Overcharge**, and your eyes flashed like your power was finally coming out..."

"And then?" Hiral asked when Loan didn't seem like he'd continue on his own.

"Then you collapsed, blood coming out of your ears, and your body shaking in seizure. Even Vule looked worried." Loan chuckled, then caught himself as Hiral squeezed his eyes shut. "I'm sorry, Hiral. Can you move?"

Despite what had happened, Hiral swung his legs off the cot and pulled himself up to a sitting position. The room spun for a second, but quickly settled, and he ran his hand through his hair. A good thing he hadn't cut it after all.

"How do you feel?" Loan asked, seated across the small room in his large wooden chair.

Hiral's eyes settled on his bandage-wrapped wrist, the red of blood soaking lightly through. "I failed. Again," he said quietly, something in his chest contracting so much, it felt like his whole body would collapse on itself.

Everfail. The whisper in a childlike voice echoed in his ears over and over, and he saw the other initiates laughing at him as he closed his eyes. Another year. Another fiasco while other... children... half his age succeeded where he failed. Another embarrassment. Another shame to his family.

He leaned forward, elbows on his knees, and dropped his hands into his face. Ten times. *Ten.* Ten years, and he hadn't been able to shape a single thing. Not once. What was *wrong* with him?

"What will you do?" Loan asked softly. The same thing he'd asked last year. And the year before that.

Hiral squeezed his eyes shut as hard as he could, the tops of his fingers digging into his scalp under his hair, and he took a deep breath. Holding the air in his lungs, he squeezed *everything*, pushing all his frustration to its peak... and then let it *all* out with his breath.

Raising his head, he looked at Loan. "I'll try again next year."

The expression on Loan's face didn't shift even a little. "You're sure?"

"Something was different this time," Hiral said. "I *felt* something. I'm getting closer to a breakthrough. I'll get it next time."

"Hiral, the blood coming out of places it wasn't supposed to is what was different. Are you sure you should keep pushing…?"

"Yes," Hiral interrupted. "If I give up now, what will the last ten years have meant? They'll all have been nothing but a waste. I *have* to succeed or… or…" Hiral trailed off and looked away from his teacher.

"Do you want to find another instructor?" Loan asked evenly.

Hiral shook his head immediately. "No. You've stood by me all this time. The problem isn't you. It's me. Besides, nobody else would take me on as a student," he added, only half-joking.

"Hiral, maybe…" Loan cut off as the door to the room cracked open and Hiral's father poked his head in.

"I heard voices," the man said, opening the door all the way and stepping in.

"Elezad," Loan said, using Hiral's father's first name.

With a small nod to Loan, Elezad came over to crouch in front of Hiral. He took Hiral's right hand in his, putting a thumb over Hiral's wrist and nodding in time with the heartbeat he felt. Then he turned his attention to his son's left wrist and the bandages there. "The dagger failed you again. I'm sorry."

"It's not… You didn't… You don't have to be… You saw?" Hiral started and stopped until he finally got a question out.

"Of course I did. I wouldn't miss your testing."

"Did Mom…?"

Elezad's eyes drifted to the side, then back toward Hiral. "Your mother had important work she couldn't get away from today."

"I understand," Hiral said, the words somehow stinging despite him knowing they were coming. His mother hadn't come to a test since he'd failed his first. Why would she have come to this one? It was better, really. One less person for him to embarrass. It'd be bad enough when word of his tenth failure left the testing grounds.

Who was he kidding? It was likely already all over the island and probably all the way down to the Nomads by now.

"Let me take a look at your Meridian Lines; maybe I made a mistake somewhere when I was inking them," Elezad said, turning over Hiral's arm. Starting with the circle on the back of Hiral's hand, Elezad followed the thumb-thick line up to the circular node on Hiral's elbow, then continued up the connecting line toward Hiral's shoulder.

"Dad," Hiral said, trying to pull his arm away from his father's grip, but the man was always surprisingly strong for an Artist. "You've checked my Meridian Lines every year. You didn't make any mistakes when you inked me. Even the Shapers at the test marveled at the work you do. You're the best there is. There is nothing wrong with my tattoos."

"Mmm, your mother might disagree with part of that. Did I hear you say you'll be trying again next year?" Elezad glanced back down at Hiral's bloody wrist.

"Yes," Hiral said simply, meeting his father's eyes.

"You could come work with me, you know," Elezad said predictably. "You don't *have* to be a Shaper."

"I can't be an Artist. Can't take that class," Hiral said, pulling his wrist back and crossing his arms to hide the bandage. "You know my blood doesn't mix with the ink. I can't do what you do."

"Maybe the test was wrong," Elezad said. "Being an Artist would explain why you can't shape."

Hiral looked across the bare skin of his father's arms. Toned from hard work, yes, and with the same Meridian Lines all Makers had, but completely bereft of any other tattoos. His father, the most skilled Artist in the city, like any Artist, couldn't shape tattoos into reality—the two classes were mutually exclusive.

But at least *he* had a reason he couldn't shape. Unlike Hiral, who was just a failure. He couldn't shape. Couldn't inscribe. Couldn't even pass the same test nine-year-olds were breezing through.

Everfail indeed.

"I'll try again next year," Hiral said, mainly to drown out the echoing children's voices in his head. "And the year after that, if I have to, until I pass. I will be a Shaper. It's what I was meant to be."

Elezad opened his mouth to speak, then closed it again, stood up, and put his hand on Hiral's shoulder. "And I'll be in the stands watching until you do. Loan"—Elezad turned to the Shaper—"you'll keep working with him?"

"I will," Loan said. "Once he cracks the wall holding him back, he'll make them all regret their words."

Nobody in the room needed to specify who "they" were. *Everybody.*

"Well, how about we go find something to eat, then? You must be hungry," Elezad said, breaking the dark silence.

"How long was I unconscious?" Hiral asked instead of answering.

"About an hour," Loan said. "You sure you're feeling okay? We cleaned you up, but without knowing what *caused* that…"

"An hour? Fallen's balls," he cursed, then coughed at the glare from his father. "I have to get over to the port."

"The port?" Elezad asked.

"Work," Hiral said, pushing himself to his feet smoothly. His limbs were stiff, and despite what he'd told the others, the pain wasn't completely gone. Good thing he'd become so good at faking he was okay over the last ten years. "Scheduled for a trade run down to the Nomads."

"Arty would understand if you didn't make it today," Elezad said. "I know this new place that just opened up. Been smelling the bread every morning on my way to the studio."

"Dad," Hiral said evenly, "nobody other than Arty will hire me. If I lose this job, what am I going to do until I become a Shaper? Besides, it… it'll distract me. I need that right now. And you—if you've been here for the hour waiting for me to wake up, you must have clients lining up at your door. Do you *really* think Yanna would appreciate you coming back any later than you already are?"

Elezad winced at his receptionist's name, but nodded. "You make a good point. Look, fine, you win. But I'm bringing bread home tonight to go with dinner, so don't you dare fill up on some port-market junk food."

"I'm going to work, Dad, not to shop," Hiral said. He turned to Loan and gave a bow. "I'm sorry I let you down again. Thank you for continuing to support me long after anybody else would've given up on me."

Loan coughed, the sound muffled like he'd put his hand in front of his mouth, then cleared his throat. "When I took you on as a student, it was because I saw the potential in you. Not just the potential the Measure saw when they put that crystal in your chest and your status window came up for the first time." He touched his own chest, where his crystal was embedded under his sun tattoo. "You had a look in your eyes—still do—that spoke to me. Something I don't see in a lot of initiates.

"Most of the children who walk through my doors act like they are entitled to become Shapers, just because the Measure and their status window said they had a little bit of potential when they were born. Even though only about one in ten of the people who come take the test actually have what it takes, they all *assume* they are that one.

"Not you, though," Loan continued. "You told me you'd earn your place among the Shapers, and work as hard as you needed to. Even if it's turned out to be a bit harder than either of us expected, it hasn't changed my opinion of you. I know you'll succeed, and I'll be there with you when you do."

"Just to rub it in Vule's face?" Hiral wisecracked to keep down the emotions bubbling in his chest. He could break down later, both at his own failure and the undeserved support, but for now, he had to keep it together. Keep faking. For them… and himself.

"Might be part of it," Loan said, his voice a little hoarse, and he coughed into his hand again. "Didn't you say you had work to get to? The port isn't close, even for somebody with your dexterity, and you can't be planning to go down to the Nomads dressed like that?"

Hiral straightened and looked at his arms, the Meridian Lines and tattoos still dark against his skin, then shook his head. No, no, he *definitely* couldn't go down looking like that.

"You're right. I need to get home and change first," Hiral said to the two men, his father so *normal-sized* compared to the gigantic Shaper. "If you'll excuse me…"

"Go on, then," Loan said, his big thumb running along the bottom of one of his eyes.

"I'll see you at home," Elezad said, obviously not planning to leave with Hiral.

"Don't keep Yanna waiting any longer than you need to," Hiral said, but ducked out the door before his father could respond. He put his hand on the knob and gently pulled it closed as his father's whispered words crept out behind him.

"Do you think he has a chance at it next year?"

Hiral closed the door before he could hear Loan's answer, then ran away from there as quickly as his legs would carry him.

3

TIME TRIAL

HIRAL checked up and down the hall—clear in both directions—then opened the door and slipped in before anybody noticed him. Quickly closing the door, he leaned back against it and gently banged his head. Once, twice, three times.

He'd only told a partial lie to Loan and his father—he *did* need to get to the port for work, but not quite as soon as he'd suggested. He still had a couple of hours before Arty was expecting him, and after the test, he needed to vent some frustration. It was *that* or collapse in a corner and completely shut down.

Why couldn't he just *do* it like everybody else could? Why did he have to be the *Everfail*? Why was he broken?

Hiral pushed off from the door and walked down the narrow hall, pounding the bottom of his fist against the stone wall every few steps. He'd worked so hard. Trained every day. Read all the books and done every exercise he and Loan could think of. And it *still* hadn't been enough.

Twenty feet—and an endless stream of internal insults—later, Hiral exited the hallway into what looked like a small waiting room. A crystal sat on a pedestal in the middle of the room, a plain wall beyond it.

Looking at the pedestal, he almost turned around and left again. He'd planned to have a class the next time he came here, but… apparently, that wasn't in the cards this year.

"Nothing for it, then," he mumbled to himself with a sigh, then stepped forward and put his hand against the crystal. Luckily, it didn't require an input of solar energy. Otherwise, he wouldn't have been able to use the interface, even though the **System Shock** debuff had faded.

Not even a second later, a blue screen similar to Hiral's status window materialized in the air above the pedestal.

Fallen Reach Training Room – Time Trial
Difficulty – E-Rank

Top Scores
Hiral Dorin: 1:01
Hiral Dorin: 1:02
Hiral Dorin: 1:03

15

Attempt Time Trial?
Yes / No

Hiral scratched at his cheek while he looked at his previous times. So close to breaking the one-minute mark, and he'd hoped having the stat boosts from his Meridian Lines after getting his class would make the difference. If any Shapers actually came down to the training room, one of them would've shattered his records without even really trying. It was only because they all preferred sparring up in the Amphitheatre that Hiral's name was on there at all.

"Ah, whatever," Hiral said, tapping the *Yes* icon hanging in the air.

Fallen Reach Training Room – Time Trial selected
Choose Difficulty – Low / Medium / High

Hiral tapped *High*, and the blue window faded at the same time blue energy swirled in front of him like some kind of doorway. He rolled his wrist a few times to make sure the injury and bandage didn't get in the way—little tight, he could deal with it—then stepped through the portal into the next room. As soon as he passed through, the portal closed, and another blue window popped up to his left.

Begin? – Yes

The lack of a *No* option always made Hiral chuckle, but he took a moment to check out the course ahead of him before he hit *Yes* while he took his sandals off. As always, the first hundred feet had triangular islands suspended above water, and then a slowly spinning disc immediately after. When he'd first done the course, he'd had to leap onto each triangle and grab the top, and then—only after catching his balance again—leap to the next and repeat. Then again, he'd only had 10 *Dex* at the time.

Still, falling meant swimming, and there was no way he'd crack one minute if he got wet. Even with his higher *Dex* of 20, he couldn't get cocky now.

The moving disc would have three opponents to defeat, generated somehow by the *Training Room* itself, and then a new path would open. His best times had come when the three enemies were thin but fast. The ones who carried stupidly large shields always ruined his run, even though they opened the easier of the two paths.

Hiral took a deep breath, blew it back out slowly, and repeated the process twice more. At least the familiarity of the *Training Room* helped keep his mind off the test. Of course, as soon as he realized that…

He slapped the *Yes* button before his brain could get in his way, then dashed straight ahead as soon as a glowing blue *Begin* appeared in the air. Ten feet, and he was up to a full sprint. Fifteen, and he changed his angle slightly. Twenty feet, and he leapt from the platform to the first triangular island ahead and to the right, his foot barely hitting the incline before he pushed off toward the next slanted island three feet ahead and to his left.

Left, right, left, right, left, right, he bounded back and forth between the triangular islands, his feet only touching them long enough for his leg to bend and then spring him off again. With his high *Dex* and hundreds of times running the obstacle course, almost all of his momentum kept him racing forward. A handful of seconds later, he was halfway to the spinning disc, and three red icons appeared in the air above it.

Fallen's luck. Red means shields.

Nothing to do but keep going, Hiral bounded back and forth between the islands until he leapt from the final one to the spinning disc. Tucking into a roll to absorb some momentum as soon as he landed, Hiral popped to his feet at the same time three red humanoid constructs of solid light started appearing with shields as tall as they were. A couple good hits were enough to bring them down—they didn't have much health, if he could get around the shields—but the shields themselves completely negated any damage they blocked.

I need to try something different.

Hiral moved in the second it took the opponents to fully solidify, darting toward the one on his left, then swept out and around the shield. Suddenly behind the red shield-bearer, he could *probably* land enough blows to bring it down from that angle, but there was another idea he needed to try. Instead of lashing out with a kick to a vulnerable flank, he instead rushed in and wrapped his arms around the shield-bearer's waist, then hauled up with all his 18 *Str*.

Far lighter than expected, Hiral's opponent went up and over as he bridged his back, slamming the red head to the stone with an echoing crack. Knowing the other two would already be moving, Hiral gave a gentle push, and the momentum of the shield-bearer's legs carried it over the edge of the disc to fall into the water.

Ah, no, if it isn't…

One of the red icons above the disc vanished at the same time he kicked up to his feet.

Wait, did it vanish because of the damage I did, or because it fell into the water? That could mean…

Hiral spun to face the other two, who were already shield-rushing straight at him. He'd learned the hard way they could shove him right off the disc if they hit him, so he'd always fought them near the center of the spinning platform. But it was time for a new plan.

Bending his knees, Hiral set his feet and forced himself to be patient as the shield-bearers charged. They moved fast, but it still felt like it took them an eternity to corner him on the edge of the platform, and then they both twisted their shields so they held them horizontally instead of vertically. The move exposed their heads—it'd still take more than a single blow to put them down—but also completely cut off any escape routes along the disc.

Suddenly with nowhere to go, Hiral took a step back, the heel of his left foot hanging off the edge of the platform. The shield-bearers charged in, intent on pushing him over the side even if they went with him. When they came so close Hiral could touch the shields if he reached out, he bent his knees and then leapt straight up, hands extended for the shield-bearers' shoulders.

Feet just *barely* clearing the rushing shields, Hiral pushed himself off the shoulders toward the center of the disc. That slight nudge was all his opponents needed, and they went tumbling into the water. Still, his landing wasn't as graceful as it could've been, and he stumbled and fell to his hands and knees, losing precious seconds while he twisted to look at the red icons hovering above him.

Both winked out.

With no time to waste, Hiral pushed himself to his feet and spun to orient himself, eyes peeled for the path that would open…

There!

He was on the wrong side of the disc, but that gave him a chance to build up speed as a wall on one side of the hall lifted to reveal a narrow balance beam. Fifty feet long, and only as wide as the palm of Hiral's hand, it was still no match for his *Dex*, and he vaulted onto it without hesitation, ran along it as easily as a normal floor, and then jumped to the next platform without slowing.

As soon as he landed, however, he paused to peer down into what would be best described as a moving, jigsaw-puzzle pit. Blocks all along the twenty-foot depths of the pit moved back and forth, sliding along one wall, and then hovering across the opening to sink into the opposite. Originally designed for racers to leap down block by block, Hiral instead waited for the familiar pattern, and then simply jumped into the middle of the pit.

Arms tight at his side, and through a space not much wider than his shoulders, Hiral dropped straight between the shifting blocks to land on the next platform below, crouching down to absorb some of the impact, then launching forward like a sprinter. The long hallway, bare by all appearances, stretched a good two hundred feet ahead of him, but he immediately went over to run along the right wall.

No sooner than he'd covered fifteen feet, arm-thick poles rotated out of the wall on his left, reaching just past the middle of the hall—but not quite far enough to whack Hiral. One, two, three, four poles swung out at varying heights, and then Hiral dove forward over another bar that rose out of the floor and went from wall to wall at shin height.

Easily clearing the tripping bar, Hiral tucked his shoulder and rolled under another bar that dropped from the ceiling. Up and to his feet again, he only lost half a step, then ran against the left wall as more bars swung out from the right toward the center of the hall.

Part of him would've felt guilty at the way he almost *cheated* by memorizing the movements of the **Time Trial**, except he'd also gained just as many mental stat point increases from the training as he had physical. If anything, he was *supposed to* learn and memorize the course's obstacles to get the best time.

Two more shifts from side to side, a quick jaunt of hopping, and one final tuck-and-roll got him to the end of the tunnel. Sliding under the last bar, Hiral popped to his feet as three blue icons appeared in the center of the walled room.

Not even waiting for the three thin constructs to form, he dashed at where he *knew* one would emerge. The instant its outline appeared, he skidded to a stop and launched a quick barrage of blows—kidney punch, liver punch, right hook across the blue jaw—and the construct was gone. Shifting his weight, Hiral spun around on his lead foot, bringing his left arm up just in time to catch a high kick aimed for the side of his head on his bandages.

Because of his 18 **Str** and **End**, he didn't even budge from the impact. Instead, he leaned his weight on his back foot and raised his right foot, narrowly evading the sweeping kick from the other blue construct he knew was coming. Like he was just stepping over the low kick, Hiral dropped his foot back to the ground as soon as it was past, simultaneously reaching up and hooking the high-kicking leg as it tried to retract.

Turning as he grabbed the leg, a shoulder-bump to the blue fighter stole its balance, and then Hiral hauled in the other direction. With a solid grip on the leg, his **Str** was more than enough to lift it completely off its one foot, and he swung it around to slam into its partner. The two blue bodies crashed to the floor in a tangle of limbs, and Hiral dove on top of them in a flurry of punches that first dispelled the top fighter, and then the bottom one almost immediately after.

Lacking even the time to take a deep breath, Hiral was back on his feet and sprinting toward a wall just now raising. Before it reached the ceiling, he was already in the air, leaping for the two bars attached to the wall above another water-filled hallway. His lead foot touched down perfectly on the lower of the bars, about the same level as the floor he'd just left, while his hand reached out to barely touch the bar at shoulder height.

Just inches from the wall, and no wider than the balance beam had been, Hiral quick-stepped along the lower bar, using his hand as a guide and nothing more. When he reached the end of the fifteen-foot path, he leapt across the eight-foot hall to more bars on the other wall.

Faster!

Hiral devoured the fifteen feet on this bar and sprang across the hall to the next set, bare feet slapping with each step. Five feet before the end, he eased up on his mad sprint and focused on the coming trial. The horizonal bars coming weren't a challenge by themselves, but he'd learned the hard way that if he jumped to them with too much momentum, it'd mess up his rhythm and slow him down in the long run.

Step, step, leap, and Hiral caught the first horizontal bar with his right hand, his forward momentum swinging his legs well above the water below. Still, he'd hit them with a bit too much speed, and his only chance was to... *reach!*

Hiral extended his left arm past the next bar and instead reached for the bar after that, just barely snagging it with his fingers. Without a full grip on it, it'd be a risk to let go with his right hand, but to have any hope of breaking one minute, he'd need to take a chance and trust his **End**.

Here goes. He let go with his right hand, letting his inertia swing him around on the fingers of his left hand, while he brought his right back around and reached for the next bar. *So close... Got it!* With a secure grip, Hiral fell into his usual powerful rhythm to swing from bar to bar.

Almost there. Only the rope left...

Fifteen bars in total, barely a few seconds to get across them all, and Hiral reached for the last one while snapping his legs forward. Up and outward he sailed across the three feet of empty air to catch the rope hanging down through the last vertical part of the course. By the time he'd gotten here during the first hundred runs or so of the **Time Trial**, his arms had been burning to the point the fifty-foot climb seemed almost impossible. Today, he barely noticed it as he tucked his feet around the rope and began the hand-over-hand climb.

What's the time? Am I going to make it?

Hiral pulled himself up in what felt like record time, a small swing and jump getting him back onto solid ground before he lunged out and tapped on the floating blue **Finish** hanging in the air. Leaning forward and taking deep breaths, he waited the prerequisite six seconds before he got the result. It was almost as though whoever had designed the **Time Trial** wanted to add a small flare of drama.

Fallen Reach Time Trial: Complete
New Record

Hiral's breath caught at the mention of a new record, but then he blew out the air in his lungs with an annoyed sigh.

Time: 1:00

Well, he *had* improved his time, but just like the Shaper test, it wasn't enough. His new time, along with his old, hovered in front of him, along with a new prompt.

Try Again / Exit

Hiral ran his hands through his hair while he breathed out. He'd made progress, but it still felt like he'd failed again, and the child's mocking voice flitted through his mind over and over.

Everfail… Everfail… Everfail…

He slapped his hand on the ***Try Again*** button, and another portal opened up to where he'd started his last run.

"I *will* do this," he grumbled, then started the course all over again.

4

WHAT'S WRONG WITH ME?

H IRAL put his hands on his knees, then leaned back against the wall in the shade of his home's overhanging roof as he sucked in air. Sure, maybe he hadn't *needed* to sprint all the way home after two hours of running the obstacle course, but as soon as he'd left the ***Time Trial*** and the first set of eyes fell on his tattoos, then his small size, the whispers had started.

No Shaper had as many tattoos as he did without being almost seven feet tall from their constant use of the energy gifted by the sun. Only one person in the entire city, on the entire island, fit his description.

"Everfail," he whispered to himself as he shook his head, eyes landing on the tattoos covering his sweat-sheened skin.

Fallen's balls, even the fact he was *sweating* with that many tattoos made him stand out. Sure, his ***End*** was higher than most E-Rankers because of his constant training, even without a class, but a Shaper with that many tattoos would be at least D-Rank, with three times the ***End*** stat. Sweating and out of breath? No way.

He hadn't even gotten a sub-minute run for all his trouble. He'd managed to tie his best time twice more, but the rest of the runs were abysmal, despite him having figured out the best way to deal with the red shield-bearers when they popped up. Maybe after his work with Arty, he'd hit it up again. Or, maybe he should wait a few passes? That was a question for later. He *did* actually need to get to work now.

He couldn't go to the port dressed like this, with everybody watching him. Whispering. Time to lose the ceremonial outfit and put on something a little less… revealing.

Then he had to get to work. He hadn't been lying when he said nobody else would hire him. He couldn't afford to lose this job… even if there really wasn't any good reason Arty had hired him in the first place.

"He's just taking pity on me," Hiral told himself for the hundredth time, then straightened and walked around to the back door of the building, still sucking in air through his teeth.

The stitch in his side ached like somebody had stuck their hand in and ripped something out, and he rubbed his abdomen as he scanned the wide backyard to make sure his mother wasn't out there tending to her hobby garden. When he thankfully didn't see her, he scooted around to quietly push the door open.

"You're terrible at being sneaky," his younger sister said as he peeked his head in. "The deep breathing right outside the studio window… I thought some creeper had come looking for me while I was home alone."

"Hey, Nat," Hiral said, carefully stepping through the door and looking around.

"Mom's not home, if that's who you're looking for," Nat said from where she leaned against the studio doorframe, arms crossed. "Nobody but you and me."

Hiral let out a sigh of relief. One less thing for him to deal with right now.

"You… you don't look like you're in the mood for celebrating," Nat said, and Hiral looked up to find concern in her eyes. She stepped away from the wall and came over to wrap her arms around his chest.

Even though she was only three years younger than him, she was small for her age, and her head settled just below his chin. "Want to talk about it?" she asked, ignoring how damp he had to be against the side of her face.

"You can probably guess," he said, fighting to keep the bitterness out of his voice.

"I'm sorry I couldn't make it. I had a test in class, and I…"

"It's okay," Hiral said, and gave her a hug. "Your classes are important. You're going to be the next Master Dorin, if even half of what I'm hearing is true."

Nat stepped back out of the hug, blushing, and shook her head. "It's not like that."

Hiral mussed his little sister's hair, almost as long as his own. "Don't sell yourself short just because I had a rough day. I need some good news before I get cleaned up and head to work. How did your test go?"

"Good, I think," Nat said, walking upstairs with him as she talked. "Won't have the results until later today, but it was just a messaging tattoo. They wanted us to do the **Bird of Twittering**. That bird is so *boring*, though, and there are too many limits on how long the message can be. So, I decided to do…"

"*Two Minds as One*?" Hiral interrupted, and Nat blushed again. "Nat, that's an A-Rank tattoo for a test that was calling for a D-Rank. If you didn't do it perfectly, they can't even give you partial marks."

"I *did* do it perfectly," she said as they got to the door to Hiral's room. "Better than perfectly. You should've seen it."

Hiral smiled at his little sister. He couldn't help it. She was just so… perfect. Everything their parents could want in a child. Smart and determined, which was why she was a level 17 E-Rank Artist—just three levels shy of breaking through to D-Rank, even at her age. Not to mention she was funny and, judging by the number of boys who came by looking for her, pretty as well.

And somehow, Hiral couldn't begrudge her for it even on his worst day of the year, because she dropped everything she was doing to check on him.

"Dad's bringing home bread tonight to go with dinner from some new shop that opened up. Will you have the results by then?" Hiral asked her.

"I should," Nat said.

"Perfect. I've got work, but I should be back by then. There's a cake shop at the port. I'll grab something to celebrate you passing your test!"

Nat smiled up at him, eyes practically sparkling—the girl *loved* cake—but then a shadow passed over her face and the smile vanished. "Maybe we shouldn't. It's not a big deal. Just a small test…"

Hiral forced a smile on his own face, as easy as putting on a pair of pants. "Don't be silly. You deserve this. Look, I've got to get ready for work, but I promise I'll be back for dinner," he said, putting his hand on the doorknob to his room.

"Hiral," Nat said quietly, "do you want me to ink a lower-Rank tattoo on you? Do you think it would help you… I mean, you know, next year?"

Hiral's fingers tightened around the doorknob, but he managed to keep the smile on his face. "I appreciate the offer, Nat, I really do, but if you put anything less than S-Rank on my body, it would lower the potency of *all* my tattoos. All of Mom and Dad's hard work would be gone. All tattoos share the potency of the weakest tattoo—isn't that the third tenet of being an Artist?"

"I know, but what's the point of having S-Rank and above tattoos if you can't…" Nat snapped her mouth shut before the words could come out.

"If I can't use them anyway?" Hiral finished her sentence with the smile still on his face. "Can't use them… *yet*," he said, and mussed her hair again. "Yet. I'll get there. Have a little faith in your big brother, okay?"

"How can you stay so positive?" she asked, her voice quiet.

"Same way you got to level seventeen," Hiral said with a wink. "Hard work!"

"I'm almost level eighteen," she said, a hint of pride in her eyes. "And that's kind of thanks to you. That tip about practicing without using my Meridian Line bonuses was a winner. Gets me more experience for every tattoo I do, and makes leveling easy. Almost feels like cheating. How'd you figure that out anyway?"

"Just an educated guess based on some reading I'd done," he said. "Anyway, I should get changed. I have to get going."

She held his eyes for a few long seconds, searching for… something… then finally nodded. "Yeah, but you know, if you change your mind about…" She trailed off.

"I know just who to talk to. Now, go get back to whatever you stopped doing to make sure I wasn't a crying wreck."

"You *do* ugly cry when you get going."

"Learned that from you," he shot back.

"Bleh." She stuck out her tongue and then forced a smile onto her face. She wasn't quite as good at it as Hiral was, but she was trying… for his sake.

He waited until she went back down the stairs before he opened the door and ducked into his quiet room. The blackout curtains were still in place, leaving him shrouded in darkness as he closed the door and then leaned against it for support.

"Ten… times…" He breathed out, his chest clenching again as he had a moment to himself, with nobody to maintain a strong face for. Sliding down to the floor, Hiral dropped his head into his hands and struggled for breath.

He'd told Loan and his father he'd keep going until he passed, but… could he really do that? Hadn't he worked hard enough? Suffered enough? What else could he possibly do? What would it take to make his status window change?

"I've tried everything," he whispered, tears of anger finally bursting out from behind his eyes and running down his cheeks in a rush. "Why am I such a failure? What is *wrong* with me?" He drove his fingers into his scalp beneath the hair. The pain was a distant thing compared to the emotions ripping apart his chest from the inside.

Hiral's heart hammered against his ribs, pounding like it wanted to get out, while the rest of his body shivered like he was under a lake of freezing water. The air he managed to suck in between his teeth barely filled his lungs, and he was already trying to breathe in more before the last breath even left. Faster and faster he gulped in air, but it didn't seem to be doing anything, and darkness deeper than the room around him clawed at his vision.

Despair and rage warred within him; one telling him to give up and the other driving him back to the *Training Room*. He imagined obliterating those light constructs over and over again, until he either passed the test or broke himself in the effort. Then he would stand before all who'd doubted him, with a new tattoo of the *Emperor's Greatsword* blazing in his hands—just like they mocked. What would they say then? What would they…

Hiral tried to focus on that image, but it slipped away. After all, he *had* destroyed the constructs in the *Training Room;* enough of them to fill an entire army. And if that hadn't helped for ten tests, how would it help for eleven?

He couldn't do it… Just couldn't…

A door closed somewhere downstairs—probably the front door, from the sound of it—and Hiral forced his lungs to stop their spasmed gasping. Who was it?

The bottom stair creaked; somebody starting up to the second level. If it was his other, youngest sister, Milly, she'd come right to his room to ask how he'd done on the test. Wouldn't even knock.

He couldn't let her see him like this!

Somehow, his need to *appear* okay snapped him out of the downward spiral enough to push himself to his feet. Another creak—that'd be the middle landing—and Hiral staggered away from the wall toward his small bathroom. She'd come barging in, but if he was in the shower, even *she* would leave him alone. Probably.

Legs heavy and hands still shaking, Hiral shouldered his bathroom door open, then kicked it closed with the heel of his foot. Without even pulling the ceremonial robes off, he stumbled into the small, enclosed corner of the room and passed his hand over the flat crystal embedded in the wall. Streams of hot water came gushing out of the ceiling above him.

"Hiral, you in here?" Milly called from inside his room. "Oh, you're in the shower? Come find me when you're done."

Hiral held his breath, waiting, just in case, to see if she'd come in anyway. She didn't quite get how privacy worked. Well, at least not anybody's other than her own. When the bathroom door stayed closed, Hiral finally leaned his head back and let the hot water flow over him.

Was he broken? Would he *ever* be able to shape anything, or was he really... Everfail? And if he was, then what? What would he build from his life?

The falling water didn't seem to have the answer.

5

BEST (?) FRIEND

❝ …THEN you snuck out of the house so you didn't have to face Milly?"

Gauto roared with laughter, slapping Hiral on the back. "Why are you so afraid of your sister?"

Hiral glared at his best friend, though maybe *best* and *friend* were both overstatements at the moment, and ground his teeth. "You know *very well* why I didn't want to talk to her. Do you remember what she did the third year when I didn't pass? Six years old, and she marched over and challenged one of the presiding Shapers to a match in the Amphitheatre of the Sun!"

"Yeah, I remember that. Didn't you end up having to take her place?" Gauto asked.

Hiral scowled at the memory of stepping into the Amphitheatre against a full Shaper. A *master*, B-Rank Shaper, no less. Right after his third failure, to boot. Embarrassing was an understatement. "Yes, and… it …didn't go well…" Hiral snarled enough that a couple walking past him did a double take. Actually, *didn't go well* was also an understatement; he'd gotten beaten so badly, the Shaper wouldn't have even gotten class experience for it.

"So? That was years ago…"

"She's done it three more times since then. Thinks it's funny," Hiral deadpanned.

"Last year *was* kind of entertaining," Gauto said, his fingers stroking the patchy scruff on his chin. Having a full, sagely beard to fit his new job at the Academy just wasn't in the cards for him. "Venix chased you around the arena for a good fifteen minutes. If you'd had your Meridian Lines strengthening you, you would've wiped the floor with him. Still, the fact you have more dexterity than he does—and he's C-Rank—is kind of impressive."

Hiral glanced down at the back of his hand, though the glove and sleeve hid his tattoos from sight. Those, along with the hooded coat he wore, were generally enough to keep people from recognizing him on the street. "Without the lines to harden and strengthen me like the full Shapers have, staying out of the way is the best I can do. Most of them put all their points into strength and endurance, so they're pretty slow."

"Well, if you ask me, it *did* make for a more entertaining match than most of the ones we get. Those Shapers tend to just stand there and take turns hitting each other. First one to fall loses."

"Like I said, strength and endurance," Hiral said. "When your skin is practically indestructible and you have the strength of almost twenty average people, it does kind of make you cocky. On the other hand… Shapers who *avoid* getting hit are seen as cowards…"

Gauto glanced at Hiral, but didn't say anything. The implication was obvious.

Hiral, for his part, forced himself to look around. Anything to take his mind off the test. Like always, the day was beautiful, the sun directly above the city, and people crowded the streets. Midway between the Academy where Gauto worked and the port where Hiral was headed, small stalls of goods lined the streets.

They offered baked goods that made Hiral's mouth water, small toys for children, quills brought up from the Nomads for the Artists—though a quick glance showed their low quality—and a dozen other things. If he couldn't find what he was looking for in the port when he came back from work, he'd definitely be able to find something for Nat's celebration in the warren of shops.

"When you come back up from your business with Arty, why don't you come by the Academy?" Gauto asked, finally breaking the silence. "Lika and Professor Itone would love to see you. The professor asks me at least once a week if I've been able to convince you to join us. He says you'd make a fantastic Academic."

"What did you tell him?" Hiral asked.

"That I'd be thrilled if you joined!" Gauto chuckled. "You've got the head for it, Hiral. Your attributes are way above average, even compared to somebody who has a class. I don't know why you'd ever want to be a Shaper."

"You took the test too," Hiral pointed out. "Three times."

"And that's when I learned where my true calling was. Turned my attention to academia, and I've never been happier."

"Or chubbier," Hiral said, gently elbowing Gauto in his soft side.

"We can't all be toned perfection like you," Gauto said, eying Hiral up and down. "Though nobody would ever know, with all the layers you wear."

"Stops people from noticing me," Hiral said, though he'd told his friend that more than once, and pulled his hood lower around his face. Like always, the day was warm under the constant sunlight, but at least he wasn't the only one in the street dressed like that.

"The only benefit I can see from all the work you do to join the Shapers is how much the ladies would appreciate your toned body under their fingers."

"Not going to happen," Hiral said, forcing the smile back on his face. "Most girls won't even talk to me once they realize who I am, let alone touch me. They think my inability to shape is contagious."

"You're harder on yourself than anybody else is," Gauto said.

"Maybe. Anyway, back to your original point, I'm not ready to join the Academy yet," he said, choking off his own words. Yet? *Yet!?* Was he really *considering* a future that didn't involve the Shapers? No, it was just the depression after the latest failure. He'd get it next year.

… Which was the same thing he'd told himself last year…

No, he only had one chance at a class, and he needed to pass the Shaper test to get the one he wanted.

"You have the stats for it," Gauto said. "You enjoy the puzzle of figuring things out. I mean, come on, you love *testing* more than I do. You remember that time we tested how much we could magnify sunlight before it burned even a Shaper's body?"

"We were twelve, Gauto. And the result was us getting *chased* by said Shaper halfway across the city." Hiral chuckled. *Why am I always getting chased by Shapers…?*

"Yeah, but I remember the smile on your face the whole way. Okay… something more recent, then? Last year, when we started my thesis on the strength attribute relative to the force of a punch? It *should've* been a linear relationship…"

"No, I knew it wouldn't be," Hiral corrected. "Rank reinforces the body in ways outside of just plain stats—I'm sure that's where we're seeing the change. Not to mention our natural attributes that aren't modified by Meridian Lines; I'm *sure* they also factor in differently. What we need to do is…" Hiral trailed off when he saw the huge grin on his friend's face.

"See? That's what I mean. You're an Academic at heart, Hiral," Gauto said, though his voice softened.

"I *admit,* some of what Academics do interests me. But being a Shaper has been my dream since I was a kid."

"So you can fight in the Amphitheatre?" Gauto asked. "Sure, there's *fame* there… but also head trauma."

"Not for that, and you know it. *That* isn't what Shapers are meant for. Shapers are supposed to be protectors. Explorers."

"What are you going to protect us from up here? A sunburn. Not that we *can* burn with anything less than eight-times magnification." Gauto chuckled again, obviously remembering the large magnifying glass they'd set up over the sleeping Shaper.

"I've got the **Disc of Passage**," Hiral said. "If I could use it, I could go… anywhere. And I could take you with me. Think of what we could learn. And it's not just that. I've put so much work into passing the Shaper tests. Not just me either. Loan, my dad. My sisters. You. You've all supported me for… so long…" He had to force the last part out.

"You think giving up would be letting us down," Gauto said, and it wasn't a question. "It wouldn't be. You're too smart to believe anything else."

"Yeah, part of me knows that."

"Ah. It's not just us. It's *them*," Gauto said, reading into Hiral's silence. "You want to prove them all wrong. The doubters."

"I… do…" Hiral admitted, his fist clenching at his side. "Gauto, I enjoy the research with you because it's a challenge. I like pushing myself. Testing my limits. I've trained with Master Loan every day for years. How to move, how to fight… for when I finally become a Shaper. I *want* that challenge too. I need to know how far I can go… and… this…" he said, gesturing his hands up and down himself, "…this isn't enough."

"I've seen you train," Gauto said, a twinkle in his eye. "So, when you finally get your class, I *hope* you do spend a few days in the Amphitheatre. You're going to be a terror, and that's a show I'll happily pay to see."

"I've got a few scores to settle, don't I?"

"I don't think *a few* is usually counted in the dozens, but yeah, something like that," Gauto said. "Anyway, at least come by and take a look at our newest discovery when you come back up?"

"What did you find?" Hiral asked, happy to move the conversation along. His friend was only looking out for him—he always had—but it was still hard to talk about.

"Some old rooms *underground*. Like a catacomb or something under the city," Gauto said, the excitement of it infecting his voice.

"Rooms? Underground? How in the Fallen's names did you get approval to dig?"

"We didn't," Gauto said. "Somebody was doing renovations on their home in the east end of the city. Floor gave out from the work, and they found the secret room underneath. Called us right away."

"The floor gave out? That's unusual… but, was the room empty?" Catacombs under the city? Amazing! How had they stayed hidden all this time?

"No," Gauto said, his eyebrows doing a little dance up and down his forehead.

"You're going to make me ask, aren't you?"

"I'm going to make you come *see* if you want to know."

"Not interested," Hiral lied, but he had a lot of practice making people believe what he said, and Gauto's eyes widened.

"Come on!"

"Nope. Busy," Hiral said. "Some moldy old pickle jars aren't worth the time."

"They aren't… pickle jars…" Gauto said, clearly insulted by the mundaneness of it. "Weapons, Hiral. *Crystal* weapons."

That got Hiral's attention, and even he couldn't keep his true feelings off his face.

"Crystal?" Hiral asked. "Like...?" He pointed at the nearby pearly white tower, then up its height to the large crystal that sat at its top three hundred feet up. The crystal that grew brighter as Hiral watched, then suddenly went dark as if all the light inside drained out.

Wait... If the crystal did that, it meant it was...

Hiral blinked and looked at the narrow tower, barely wider than his spread arms from fingertips to fingertips, then at his friend. "That *is* Lusco's Tower, isn't it?"

Gauto looked from Hiral to the deep-red crystal at the top of the tower and back again. "Speaking of head trauma... did you hit your noggin during the test?" Gauto pointed to another barely visible tower ahead of them, its crystal glittering in the sunlight high above the buildings. "That's Bellina's Tower there, Lusco's"—he gestured at the tower near them, then turned and pointed at a third, exactly three miles behind them—"and that's Pallidis'. You know where we are now? What day it is? Do you remember the fifty chips you owe me?"

"I don't owe you any money," Hiral snapped, eyes glued to the tower crystal. "So, the time is...?"

"A few minutes past fifth pulse," Gauto said.

"Fallen's balls, I'm going to be late!" Hiral said. "I'll drop by the Academy if I have time."

"Make sure you do." Gauto said as Hiral dashed off. "And not just to see the crystal weapons. I want you to double-check the numbers on another project for me. I think the island might be slowing down..."

Then he was gone, Gauto's words lost to the noise of the market. Hiral shoved his way through the crowd. All thoughts of mysterious underground caverns and crystal weapons fled his mind as he focused entirely on weaving his way through the crowd. Sure, if he'd had Meridian Line-induced strength, he could've barreled through without slowing down. It was what most Shapers would've done.

And left a dozen broken bones and Fallen knows how many bruises behind.

Instead, his lack of a sun-powered body, his sister's ill-thought-out challenges, *and* his 20 *natural* **Dex** had taught him something, and he weaved through the constantly moving throng of people like an expert dancer.

A turn of an ankle there meant the person was about to change direction, and Hiral twisted around in perfect time with them, sweeping by so only their clothes barely touched. Another quick sidestep brought him between an arguing couple, but he was gone before the surprise even left their mouths, ducking low under an emphatic gesture, then picking up speed as he found some open ground.

Three strides brought him to a full sprint while the people ahead of him shifted forward and back into two solid lines, which could only mean…

Hiral vaulted up and over the cart as it was pushed out into the street, his legs just an inch above the carefully piled fruit, then touched down and turned for a quick apology. The small shriek of surprise from ahead was his only warning as he turned his attention around, where a small child, maybe five years old, suddenly moved in front of him.

Again, while a real Shaper probably would've simply gone through the child and then blamed the kid for not moving, Hiral instead kicked off his lead foot into a high cartwheel. His eyes met the child's as he sailed over, their faces close enough their noses almost touched. Then his feet were on the ground again, and he was running off. This time, he didn't try to turn around to apologize, and his own words were lost to the wind as he ducked behind one of the stalls and ran through the clearer space against the wall.

Several annoyed barkers shouted after him, but they paid him little heed other than that. Few people tried to steal, with Shaper justice being what it was. A left turn down a side alley, another twist around an intimate embrace, then it was clear running.

Good thing, too. If he wasn't at the port in the next fifteen minutes, Arty might well leave without him.

That or he'd yell, and Fallen knew which was worse.

6

THE CITY THAT CHASES THE SUN

"WHAT took you so long?" Arty yelled at Hiral. "We were just about to leave!" He dramatically pointed at the pier.

The *empty* pier.

Hiral raised an eyebrow at the excitable merchant, and Arty squinted his eyes.

"Glasses… glasses… glasses…" the man muttered as he rifled through the pockets of his knee-length jacket. "There," he said, finally pulling the pair of glasses out and putting them on. A second look at the pier, a few blinks, then he turned his attention to a large pile of boxes near the end of the dock.

"Why aren't we ready to leave?" he shouted at the three hulking Shapers.

"You told us to wait for…" the one in the front, Shaper Fual, started.

"Told you that ages ago," Arty shouted. "Get the platform out and loaded up."

"Sure, sure," Fual said, strolling out along the pier and then stopping at the end.

Large tattoos covered his body from head to toe, though his Meridian Lines weren't naturally luminescent from long use, and one tattoo in particular on his upper-right chest began to gently glow as he reached up and touched it. From a distance, it looked like little more than a large square filling with the light flowing out of Fual's fingertips.

The *Platform of Movement*, a lesser C-Rank version of the *Disc of Passage* Hiral had on his right calf. Had he been able to shape, he'd have been the one carrying them down to the Nomads under the city.

While Hiral watched, one second stretched into two. Three. Four. Five. Fual had never been the fastest Shaper. C-Rank Output Rate at the highest. More and more light worked its way through the intricate details that made up the tattoo until, finally, something *snapped* into place and the color went from a bright white to a warm glow.

Nodding to himself, Fual pulled his hand away from the tattoo, a streamer of liquid light like a plasma flare trailing behind and connecting to the tattoo. He looked over at Arty. "Right here?"

"Of course right there," Arty snapped back. "Same place as always!"

Fual nodded again, then jerked his arm out, the tether of light growing taut in an instant and pulling the glowing tattoo off his chest. In less than a heartbeat, the hand-sized block of light grew into a floating platform of heavy stone bricks, forty feet by forty feet, perfectly level except for the small pillar in the center he would use to direct its movement.

"Ready to be loaded up," Fual said, stepping off the wooden dock and onto the platform.

"I can see that! So, what are you all waiting for?" He gestured at the other two Shapers leaning against the pile of boxes.

Without a word, the towering man and woman effortlessly began moving crates as big as Hiral, and likely twice as heavy.

"Just about to leave?" Hiral asked with an effort to keep the sarcasm out of his voice.

"*Just* is relative. Obviously," Arty snapped. "Are you going to help or stand there?"

"Let me get my stuff from my locker?"

"Pah, you're fine the way you are. We're just going down to make an exchange with Caaven for quills. You won't need your weapons."

"I'm supposed to be a *guard*," Hiral said. "What good is a guard without weapons?"

The skin around Arty's eyes tightened, and he stepped in closer to Hiral. "Didn't go well today, then?" he asked quietly.

Hiral forced the smile back onto his face. "Almost had it this time. Next year for sure," he said, repeating his mantra.

"Do you need the day? Those lugs can manage. Not much use when it comes to thinking, but they can lift a box like nobody's business."

"They can also hear a pin drop from forty feet away," Shaper Jenno shouted in her deep voice.

"Should be lifting instead of listening," Arty said without turning.

"Nah, I'm fine," Hiral said, only stealing a glance at the Shapers.

If they hadn't heard about his test, well, they knew the result now. If he took Arty up on the offer, as appealing as it was, that'd just make it look like he was running away. Shapers respected facing things head on. He'd do that here.

"Well, we won't be there long anyway. Should just be a quick down and back. Few hours, tops. Assuming the crates ever get loaded," he added, turning back to the working Shapers.

For their part, the towering trio ignored the mouthy merchant and his usual behavior. Really, Arty wasn't a bad guy, and he paid well for people to put up with him. While his class was technically an Artist, he'd branched out into the merchant field to acquire some of the highest-quality quills in the city from the Nomads below. Without those quills, it would be impossible for Artists like Hiral's father to do their best work. Or any work at all, really.

"Last time we went down, Caaven only had a half-order, and not his usual quality," Hiral said. "You think he'll have what we need this time?"

"He'd better," Arty said while glaring at the three Shapers. "I've got customers practically beating down my door looking for new quills. You know, if we could find a way to use a quill more than once, we wouldn't have this problem."

"Or if we could harvest them anywhere but from the backs of some very particular animals only found in specific dungeons on the surface," Hiral added. "Hasn't anybody tried breeding them?"

"They die quickly outside of their natural habitat. Something about the dungeons… I can't believe we call them that—they're caves!—is important to their lifecycle. Maybe you should bring some of your friends from the Academy, see if they can't figure it out."

"Ah, the Nomads wouldn't let us go on a dungeon run with them," Hiral said. "What did they say, proprietary information?"

"Proprietary price-gouging, if you ask me," Arty seethed. "If we don't know where the dungeons are ourselves, we can't send some of our own muscle-heads down to clean the place out."

"Muscle-heads that can still hear you," Shaper Jenno called, a massive crate on each shoulder.

"Bah," Arty said with a wave, and pointed at the rest of the crates. "Seriously, Hiral, I'd pay good chips to get a look at one of these *dungeons* where the Quillbacks live. There must be a reason the Nomads call them *dungeons* instead of caves, and what's so special about them that the Quillbacks can only live there? The surface is such a mysterious place."

"Mysterious and dangerous," Hiral amended, walking over to the edge of the pier with Arty as his eyes scanned the horizon for the distant, ever-present storm-wall. Just over one hundred miles away, surrounding the city in a perfect circle, the churning gray clouds poured torrential rain on the ground that slowly scrolled past nine miles below the city. "What do you think it's like down there? I mean, really like."

"Our ancestors left for a reason, Hiral," Arty said, but he also looked down at the distant landscape. "Built an entire floating island that circles the world to follow the sun for a reason. It must've been a *good* one to go to all that trouble. I'm more than happy to stay up here where it's safe."

"And where you can make enough chips to feed your hoarding hobby," Shaper Jenno said as she walked past with two more huge crates.

"It's not *hoarding*. It's *collecting*, and you wouldn't understand," Arty said. "They're works of art," he added, only loud enough for Hiral to hear.

Hiral nodded, but wasn't really paying attention to the exchange. The ground below them was so *green*, with a valley over that way, wide forests blanketing the rest until the terrain changed drastically to towering mountains ahead. The highest peak still didn't reach even close to the main island, but the

Nomads' trailing islands would flow right between them as the city moved in that direction along the EnSath River.

"Do the Nomads ever talk about the river?" Hiral asked Arty. "About why the city always follows its path around and around the world?"

"Some stories that are little more than superstition, if you ask me," Arty said. "I think the Academy's theory is more likely."

Hiral nodded again. "Path of least resistance. It's the only passage through the mountains ahead, and others."

"A few more minutes and we'll be ready to go," Shaper Jenno said on another pass. "Anything else in the warehouse?"

"No, everything was already out here and waiting to go," Arty said.

"Got it. We'll let you know when it's done."

"I'm going to go grab the weapons," Hiral said. "I know we're just going down to Caaven's island, not the surface or anything, but at least let me look like I'm doing my job."

"You're there as much for your eye for quills as anything else," Arty said.

"Multitasking so you keep me around," Hiral said, backing away from the edge of the pier, then spinning on his heel and jogging back to the warehouse.

He nodded at a few of the workers inside—they knew him from his years working for Arty and generally kept the gossip to a minimum when he was around—but didn't slow until he got to his locker.

A quick wave of his hand past the crystal sensor, and the door popped open to reveal the few belongings he left there—his weapons among them.

The sigh escaped his lips before he could stop it, and Hiral shook his head. Last time he'd hung these up, it had been with the hopes he'd never need them again. That he'd pass the test today.

"Looks like you're stuck with me a little longer," he whispered to the sheathed swords before slipping them over his shoulders and securing the belt across his chest. A quick check to make sure nothing rubbed the wrong way, then he stepped back and closed the locker door.

"You'll get it next time," a voice said from where the door had just been, and Hiral nearly jumped out of his skin.

"Fallen's knickers in a knot," Hiral cursed. "You scared me, Nanilly."

"Sorry," the older woman said quietly. "I wanted to catch you before you went down with Arty. You can do it; I know you can."

"Thanks, Nanilly," Hiral said, his breathing back under control after the startle. "Yeah, I've got it next year for sure. Just you watch."

Nanilly nodded but didn't say anything else, and Hiral gave her a small wave before he jogged back out of the building.

Sure, he talked a good game, but what was he going to do differently next time? Maybe it was time to pay the Academy another visit. He'd checked before about anybody with his… condition, but maybe he'd missed it? Or maybe he could find something else to help him along. That was how he'd figured out that training without using the Meridian Lines improved experience and attribute gains.

"We're ready to go, Hiral—get over here," Arty called from where he stood beside Shaper Fual on the platform.

"Sorry, coming," Hiral called back, putting the Academy out of his mind until he got back.

7

NOMADS

THE platform pulled away from the pier without even a shudder, and then arched out slightly from the island to avoid clipping any of the other piers. Hiral, meanwhile, stepped up to the edge of the platform so the crates didn't obscure his view, and simply enjoyed his favorite part of going down to the Nomads.

Up in the city of Fallen Reach itself, the scale of the island *floating in the sky* was completely lost, and Hiral's eyes traced down along the rock underneath. Like something had reached into the ground and scooped an upside-down mountain out, then tossed it into the air, the image of the floating island still defied reason, no matter how many times he'd seen it.

Even though the city occupied about half of the island's thirty-mile surface diameter, the mile-deep bottom completely filled Hiral's sight as the platform gently descended. Dropping below the outer edge, his eyes naturally turned to the spiraling mist that stretched from the island all the way to the river nine miles below. Hundreds and hundreds of feet across, the source of all water on the island, it looked like a thick wall of almost impenetrable fog even from fifteen miles away.

Then, there, trailing near the back-most point of the island, the numerous smaller Nomad islands followed like some kind of comet's tail, though the highest of their islands was only about three-quarters of the way up.

That highest island, where the elders of the Nomads resided, was also the only Nomad island directly under Fallen Reach. Dozens of other islands of varying smaller sizes followed behind, connected by huge roots that lashed them to the largest island in the front of the pack.

"Looks like they lost one of the smaller islands from the back," Arty said, coming up to stand beside Hiral.

Hiral did some quick math in his head, then nodded. "It's been almost a full rotation since they lost the last one. Good thing we're coming up on the Needle Mountains soon. They should be able to find another one there."

Arty's mouth made a thin line in response.

"You don't agree?" Hiral asked.

"Needle Mountains live up to their name," Arty said, pointing toward the mountain range as the platform continued its decent. "Narrow and sharp, more like giant stone tree trunks than actual mountains, it's harder for them to find something large enough to make into an island. Has to have the right composition to get caught up in Fallen Reach's magic too, even if they manage to connect it to the others."

"Huh, hadn't thought of that," Hiral said. "You know, now that you mention it, I don't think I've ever been down to the Nomads with you while we're passing over the Needles. Why is that?"

"No quills while we're in the Needles," Arty said. "If there are even any dungeons down there, the Nomads don't go. Too hard to get back up to their own islands since they can't reliably climb the Needles."

Hiral looked from Arty back to the Needles. Fallen Reach moved at a constant, never-changing three miles per hour, and the edge of the Needles was just visible outside the storm wall, which meant about one hundred miles away. Three cycles and they'd be there. "So, you're saying that if Caaven doesn't have any quills for us, we won't have a chance to get more before we come out the other side of the mountains?"

"Longer than that," Arty said. "The Sea of White is on the other side. It'll be at least thirty cycles until the next dungeon. And after the last short shipment, well, we're running out of stock as it is."

"So, why'd we load so much onto the platform?" Shaper Jenno asked.

"Caaven is good for it," Arty said, shivering and rubbing his arms. "We've been trading for years, and they rely on what we're bringing down just as much as we rely on the quills they provide. And why in the Fallen's names is it so cold?"

"Ah, sorry," Shaper Fual said, running his hand across one of the crystals on the pillar in the center of the platform. "There, I turned up the protection magic to keep the cold out a bit more."

Hiral looked, only slightly enviously, at the control pillar. The disc on his right calf would take care of environmental conditions automatically, as well as move *much* faster than the platform. If only he could shape it. On the whole island, there were only a dozen people or so who had the disc and could activate it. Being in that crowd… well, that'd show everybody. Prove them all wrong.

Though, technically, they weren't wrong… yet.

"Looks like Caaven is already waiting for us," Arty said, gesturing with his chin to the third island, his hands still rubbing up and down his arms despite the cold being held back. "Watch out for the kites on our right, Fual."

"See them," Shaper Fual said, shifting the direction of the platform to avoid the kites transporting Nomads between islands. "Why don't they just walk like normal people?"

Hiral raised his eyebrow at the Shaper. "We're not walking, and it would take forever to follow the roots from one island to another."

"Those kites are dangerous," Shaper Fual went on. "How do they even control where they're going without magic?"

"You complain about the same thing every time," Shaper Jenno piped up. "Why don't you just *ask* one of them this time?"

"Me, an Islander, talk to one of those filthy Buggers? No, thank you. I might catch something." Shaper Fual's chin rose higher with each word. "Uh, no offense, Arty."

"It's fine," Arty said. "Thinking like that is why I can trade with the Nomads without much competition. Keep the Bugger talk to yourself while we're down there. The hives they farm are important to them."

"I know, I know," Shaper Fual said. "But seriously, how can they spend so much time around bugs almost as big as Hiral? And *eating* them? Just… yuck."

"They're just livestock, like our cattle," Arty said without turning, his hand going up into the air to wave at somebody on the nearby island. "Now, really, enough. Time to get down to business."

"I don't see a lot of crates there waiting for us," Hiral said, looking from Caaven waving back to the cleared-off area for the platform.

"Depending on the wind, they get spray from the mist," Arty said. "Probably have the crates inside to keep the goods dry. Probably."

"Probably," Hiral agreed, but he scrolled his gaze along the edge of the island.

There seemed to be a bit a commotion further down, half a dozen people with… Wait… weren't those the suits they used to go down to the surface? If what he knew about dungeon runs was true, they'd barely have time to get down and back before the last island reached the Needles.

"Caaven, my friend," Arty shouted as the platform gently settled down on the island. "How've you been?"

"Arty, it's good to see you," Caaven replied, but the hand he held up in greeting was the only open part about his body language. His other hand was held in a fist, and there was an unusual tightness to his shoulders. The man didn't have good news.

And from the way Arty's hand dropped to his side, he saw it too.

"Things haven't improved?" Arty asked.

Caaven shook his head, his other hand balling into a fist at his side as well. "I am afraid not. We are still waiting for the harvesting party to return."

"To return?" Arty asked. "Shouldn't they have been back a cycle ago?"

"Two," Caaven said.

"Any idea what happened?" Arty asked, genuine concern in his voice as he stepped off the platform and walked up to Caaven.

Hiral quickly joined him, though the three Shapers stayed firmly in place on the platform.

"None. It should've been an easy trip," Caaven said, his voice cracking with the words.

"Your niece is part of the party, isn't she?" Arty reached out to put a hand on the other man's shoulder.

"One of them," Caaven said, his head turning briefly to look at the group of people preparing the kite-like suits further down the edge of the island. "The other is planning something stupid."

"But, just because they aren't back yet, that could mean a few things, right? Maybe they just had to make for another jump point?"

"That's one of the possibilities," Caaven said. "The one we're hoping for. The other possibility is that they're…"

"Where's the dungeon they went to?" Hiral asked as the man trailed off, unable to finish his sentence.

"Almost directly below us," Caaven said, and it was a testament to just how worried he was that he answered Hiral's question so quickly.

"So, there's still time for them to get back to the islands before we've passed," Hiral said. "There's still hope."

"Thank you," Caaven said with a grateful nod. "Now if I could just convince Seena of that. Fool girl is insisting to go looking for her sister. I've tried to stop her and the others, but they'll be ready to go within the hour."

"If they go…" Arty started.

"They risk not making it back in time, I know. It's cutting it too close, and that's if things go perfectly."

"The party that went to the dungeon, what Rank were they?" Arty asked.

"All High-E-Rank. Close to breaking through to D."

"Why didn't you send anybody of a higher Rank?" Hiral asked. "Somebody with more experience?"

"It's only an E-Rank area—this is how we do things," Caaven answered. Then his eyes widened, like he realized he shouldn't have spoken so frankly.

"What classes did they have?" Arty pressed on.

Caaven looked off to the side, then back to Arty. "You know I can't talk about that. I've already said more than I should in my worry. Please forget most of what you've heard."

Hiral glanced at Arty, then back at Caaven. In those few sentences, they'd learned more about these so-called dungeons than the Nomads had revealed in years.

"Arty, I know this is a lot to ask," Caaven said, but his eyes went to the platform behind the merchant. "I can't stop Seena and the others from going down, so I was hoping you could perhaps take them on your…"

But Arty was already shaking his head. "Afraid not. The **Platforms of Movement** don't have the range to make the trip. It can go maybe four miles before it needs to stop. We'd get halfway to the ground, then fall the rest of the way. It wouldn't help anybody. If we had a ***Disc of Passage***, maybe we could talk about it." Arty then coughed, apparently remembering what Hiral had tattooed on his leg.

"I… I see," Caaven said, not even looking in Hiral's direction.

With the layers he wore down to see the Nomads every time, they didn't even know he was trying to be a Shaper. They thought he was an Artist like Arty, which was fine by Hiral. All Makers—or Islanders, as the Nomads called them—had the Meridian Lines, so it wasn't possible to tell Artists apart from Shapers by their faces alone.

"So, there's nothing you can do to help?" Caaven asked, a hint of desperation clear in his voice. The look on his face told it all; he was terrified of not losing just one niece, but two.

Arty shook his head again. "I wish I could," the merchant said, not even mentioning the quills that were supposed to be part of the deal.

"I see," Caaven said, slightly deflating. "Thank you for at least entertaining my offer."

"Of course."

Caaven looked at the girl who had to be his niece further along the edge, then back toward a house near the small warehouse. "About… the other reason I asked you to come today," he said with a sigh of resignation, his face lowered. "Did you bring your tools?"

Tools? What tools would Arty need? He was an Artist…

"Uh, why don't we talk about it in your home?" Arty said, throwing quick glances from Hiral to the Shapers on the platform. "Talk… about… the quills you were referring to," he said again, throwing a painfully obvious wink in Caaven's direction.

Caaven's eyebrows bunched up, and his mouth made a little O shape as he looked at Hiral. "Right, the quills," he said. "I'll just be inside with Evenyn… so she can talk to you about the… *quills*," he finished, giving his own version of the painfully obvious wink.

Arty winced and nodded. "Right, right. I'll be along in a few minutes." He watched as Caaven retreated back to his home. "Let's you and me go for a walk," Arty said, putting his arm over Hiral's shoulder and leading him in the direction of the party getting ready to go to the surface.

"What was that all about?" Hiral asked.

"Well," he started, but then looked back at the Shapers again. "Should be far enough, even with their stupid hearing," he muttered.

"Far enough for what? What do you need your tools for? You can't tattoo Nomads."

"Tattoo… no. More of a… glyph. Something much simpler than a tattoo," Arty said sheepishly.

"A glyph?" Hiral asked. "Wait, Evenyn is Caaven's wife. You're not doing a *Glyph of Fertility,* are you? Those are *illegal!*"

"Shhhh," Arty said, throwing more looks back at the Shapers, though none of them seemed to have heard Hiral. "They're illegal in Fallen Reach because of the side effects they have on Makers. On our *race.* Nomads are a different race—Growers, they call themselves. The glyph doesn't have the same risks to them. It's safe."

"You're sure? How?" Hiral asked, but the look on Arty's face told it all. "Oh, this isn't your first time."

"It's how I got the trade contracts in the first place," Arty admitted. "Look, you've got to keep this to yourself. Even if it's safe for Growers, the Council in Fallen Reach won't think the same. I'd lose more than my merchant's license, if you catch my drift. Might get to see the surface after all… while falling the nine miles to get there."

Hiral rubbed the bridge of his nose, but nodded. Arty wasn't exaggerating. Council law wasn't often invoked… mainly because of how seriously they took it. "I won't rat you out. But I'm not going to go in with you and watch you do it."

"Good, because you're not invited. Besides, I've got something better for you to do," Arty said, a small wave of relief washing over him.

"Oh? Am I going to like it?" He suspected he knew the answer.

"Depends how much you like talking to girls your own age," Arty said. "Go talk to that Seena girl, see if you can't find out a bit more about the dungeons. We may not be back here for a year, but the more we know…"

"Fine," Hiral said. If he was honest with himself, he *was* pretty curious about the dungeons.

"Good, I'll come find you when I'm done. Try to stay out of trouble."

"Out of the pair of us, I'm not the one who gets into trouble," Hiral said before spinning on his heel and starting over toward the small group getting their equipment ready to jump off the island.

8

THE FALL

HIRAL approached the small group working on checking bags, some of the kites they used to go between islands, and even a few weapons. It consisted of four young men and a young woman who had to be Seena, unless the child playing around the group—she couldn't have been more than five—was actually the secret leader of the party.

"Hi," Hiral said as he walked up to them, his hand up. "Anything I can do to help?"

A few turned their heads in his direction, took in his Islander clothes, and then went back to what they were doing.

"Your face is funny-looking," a small voice said from beside him, and Hiral looked down to find the child standing in front of him, a kite almost as big as she was in her hand.

"I get that a lot," Hiral said. He crouched down in front of the girl, then scrunched up his nose, squeezed his eyes shut, and stuck out his tongue.

"Hehe, not *that* kind of funny-looking, silly," she said. When Hiral opened his eyes again to look at her, she reached out and poked him in the cheek, right where his Meridian Line was. "Did somebody draw on you?"

"Kind of," Hiral said. "Everybody has these where I'm from. Well, everybody older than ten or twelve."

"Oooooh," she said, tilting her head up to look at Fallen Reach high above them, where the sun just glinted over the edge like a horizon. "You're from up there?"

"I sure am."

"Is it hot, so close to the sun?"

"We're not actually *that* much closer."

"Yeah, you are," she said, pointing up. "Way closer."

"Ah, okay, good point," he said instead of arguing about it. "But, no, it's not really hotter. It's actually *cooler* the higher up you go, but the magic of the island keeps it comfortable. Same as here." He then took a good look at the girl's clothes. And the clothes of the group preparing to go down. They were just as layered up as Hiral was. And they weren't the only ones. Everybody he saw was dressed for cool weather.

There *wasn't* any magic here to keep the temperature constant. How had he never noticed before? Ah, because he was too caught up in himself to think about it, most likely.

"We don't use magic for that, silly," the girl said, confirming what Hiral was just figuring out. "It's for growing stuff!" she added proudly, pointing to a green fence that started about a hundred feet away, then continued off into the distance.

Considering how high up they were, a wall around the edge made sense, except in areas like the port.

"Come on, Favela, don't bother him," the woman around Hiral's age said, coming over and putting her hands on the young girl's shoulders.

"She's not bothering me," Hiral said. "She's actually teaching me quite a lot. You must be Seena, right? Ah, sorry, I'm Hiral."

The woman's eyes narrowed at him, but she gave a single nod. "Go play, Favela, but stay away from the edge or I'll take your kite away from you."

"No, it's mine," Favela said, clutching the kite closer to her chest. "You said it was."

"And it will be… as long as you stay away from the edge," the woman replied, staring at Favela until the younger girl nodded. "Good, now off you go."

"She really wasn't bothering me," Hiral said.

"I know. Now, how do you know my name?"

"So, you are Seena, then?" Hiral asked, then waited until the woman nodded. "I'm here with Arty to trade with Caaven. He said something happened to your sister. I'm sorry…"

"Nothing happened to her. She just decided to stop and look at something shiny. Gets distracted easily," Seena said defensively.

"You're probably right," Hiral said. "But, if that was all you were worried about, would you really be getting ready to go down to the surface yourself?"

Seena glared at him for a moment while chewing on her bottom lip. "She also trips and falls a lot," she finally said. "I'm just going to help."

"But, from what I understand, it's pretty risky. You could miss making it back up."

"We'll make it. We've done it before in less time," she said, looking back at the four men quickly getting their equipment in order.

"Are the dungeons really that dangerous?" Hiral asked, his eyes on a pair of spears. "I thought I heard something about you not killing the Quillbacks to get their quills?"

"Quillbacks aren't the only thing down there," Seena said, part of the worry over her sister seeping out into her words, but she quickly turned her head toward the edge. "Hey! Favela, what did I say about getting too close to the edge?"

"But the wind is better here for the kite," Favela whined, the kite a few feet above her and climbing.

"You'll lose it to that wind," Seena said.

"No I won't. I have a good grip. See?" Favela showed the thick kite string looped over and over around her wrist and hand.

"Doesn't matter—it's not safe over there. Come back here before you…" Seena started, but cut off as a gust of wind whooshed by her like it had a mind of its own and yanked the kite high into the air with a sound like a whip.

And then everything happened all at once.

"Favela!" Seena screamed.

Instincts Hiral didn't know he had kicked in, and he dashed forward. Even with 20 **Dex**, though, he wasn't fast enough, and the *good grip* Favela had on her kite hauled the girl right up into the air with it as it went.

Up… and out over the edge.

Favela's eyes opened wide in shock as her feet sailed away from solid ground, the kite still pulling her up.

Could he make it? Grab her before she dropped?

The gust of wind faded, and then Favela was gone.

No! No, no, no!

Hiral changed the angle of his dash, just slightly, grabbed one of the kites used to go between islands, then sprinted hard for the edge. A quick glance told him there were straps that looked like they were meant to go around his wrists while he held on to the kite with both hands.

He didn't have time for those.

Or for both hands.

With one hand wrapped as tight around the main shaft of the large kite as 18 **Str** would allow, Hiral ignored his mind telling him this was a stupid idea and leapt off the edge of the island.

Already hundreds of feet below him, Favela's face was a mask of shock and fear as she looked back up at the sky, arms and legs flailing, the ground miles below. Miles that would vanish all too quickly, and that was assuming Hiral wanted to reach the surface, which he certainly did *not*. Not like this.

"I'm coming!" he shouted, all his focus on the girl below him.

He tucked the kite against his side like a shield as he dove down, cutting the air like a knife. The wind whistled in his ears, slashed at his eyes as tears flew away, and tried to rip the kite from his hand. Body rigid, Hiral hurtled downward, each small shift of his body or gust of wind threatening to take him off course.

The girl screamed, her voice reaching Hiral's ears in strange, alternating waves as he raced down toward her, the hood over his head snapping back and his hair whipping in the wind. And, somehow, her kite was nowhere to be seen.

Of course she let go of it now.

Squeezing his right hand as tight as he could around his kite's shaft, Hiral extended his left hand out toward Favela, though she was still more than a hundred feet away. The small shift changed the angle of the kite, and suddenly, Hiral was barreling off to the side, whipping out wide from where he needed to be to catch her.

His fall devoured distance like a starving man, islands coming into view in his peripheral vision and then gone again bare seconds later. He'd closed half the distance to Favela, but was now fifty feet out too wide. Her arms and legs still flailed as she fell, increasing her wind resistance, and if Hiral didn't do something *now,* he'd shoot past her.

Muscles in his abdomen tensing, Hiral twisted ever so slightly, the kite at his side cutting the air and dragging him back across to where he needed to be so hard, he almost got whiplash. But at least he'd… No… his momentum took him too far in the wrong direction! He'd overshot where he'd needed to be *and* cut the vertical distance between them in half.

He needed to change the angle again… but that would only do the same thing he'd just done, whipping him past. He couldn't get back directly above her—he just didn't have the practice or control—so he'd need to snag her on the way by.

Yeah, sure, no problem.

…Everfail… a child's voice seemed to echo on the wind. What was he thinking? He couldn't do this. He couldn't even pass a children's test. What had made him jump off the Fallen's arse-end of an island in the first place?

"Funny-face!" Favela's voice somehow broke through the wind whipping past his ears, and Hiral forced himself to look at her. At her wide eyes and face full of fear.

That was why he'd jumped without thinking. She simply didn't deserve to die like this.

"I'm coming, Favela," Hiral shouted, though whether she could hear him or not was impossible to tell. So he stretched his hand in her direction, fingers wide like he was reaching for her, and her hand reached toward him.

Maybe he *couldn't* do this. Just like he couldn't pass the test to be a Shaper.

But that had never stopped him from trying before, and it wasn't going to stop him *now*.

Hiral twisted the kite in his hand, the drag in the air practically flipping him over as it shot him toward Favela. Spinning, once, twice, round and round, Hiral's eyes never left that small hand reaching for him.

At fifteen feet away, the wind gusted and tried to yank him off course. He pulled the kite closer and snapped back toward Favela.

At ten feet, he was upside-down, hand stretched out and eyes watering from forcing them to stay open.

At five feet, Favela's lips moved to form *Funny-face*.

Reeeeeeeaaaaaach, he pleaded with his hand as the wind swirled around them like a living thing, threatening to pull them apart. His fingers brushed again something—skin, cold from the wind—but then slipped past.

No! He'd missed. He...

Something dragged on his sleeve; Favela's small hand had somehow found a grip, and Hiral twisted his body around under hers, using the wide side of the kite to slow his descent so that she practically fell into his chest.

"I've got you," he said, snaking his left hand around her wrist and pulling her into him. "Put your arms around my neck. Go on, hurry, I've got you," he coaxed until she let go of his hand and wrapped her small arms around him.

More islands whizzed past the corners of his eyes. How far had they fallen? How many islands were left? Ah, it didn't matter; he was going to make this happen!

"This is going to be bumpy," he said. "But no matter what, *do not* let go. Okay? Can you do that?"

Favela's small head nodded against his neck, and Hiral made sure he had as good a grip on her with his left hand as he could. With her small body snug to his, he turned his attention to his death-grip on the kite. It all came down to this.

Would his 18 **Str** be enough to hold on? If he'd had his Meridian Lines, it would be no question. If he'd had a class, no question.

He didn't have either of those things. All he had was one little girl counting on him to save her life.

"Here we go." Hiral took a breath and leaned toward the top of the kite so that it tipped forward and they were rocketing straight down, headfirst, again.

Then, before his brain could tell him how colossally stupid this was, Hiral pushed the kite out from his body at the same time he pointed the nose away at an angle.

Pain lanced through his arm as the kite caught the wind under it with a terrifying *SNAP*. His arm? The kite? All of the above? The questions fled his mind as his legs whipped down and around, Favela screaming against his neck at the sudden jerk and twist. Then came more pain, like his fingers coming out of all their joints at once.

Hiral grunted through the agony, focusing all his effort on those digits despite the pain. Everything hinged on them holding on. He *would* hold on, even if it meant they'd need to cut his fingers away from the kite later.

His body swung back the other way, Favela's arms still tight around his neck, the whooshing wind battering against his face, and his legs trailing weakly behind… but …that was it.

That was it!?

Hiral forced his eyes open—when had he closed them?—and looked around. The sky stretched out around him, the distant storm-wall gray and angry, but the rolling landscape beneath him comparatively peaceful.

And far closer than he was comfortable with. They'd already fallen *miles*.

Tearing his eyes from the scenery, Hiral spotted the trailing islands—several were still below him, but not for long. He wasn't falling at the same speed he had been before—more gliding now—but they were still moving fast and losing altitude.

"Almost there," Hiral said, forcing his aching arm to pull on the kite to try and turn it.

Come on, come on. Nothing happened. If he didn't change the angle of their flight—just a little, that was all it would take—he'd still miss the islands and end up Fallen-knows-where.

"You've gotta lean more," Favela said, and he glanced down to see her small face looking up at him. "My Da always talks about leaning."

"I'm leaning as much as I can here," Hiral said, and didn't mention it was taking everything he had just to hold on.

"I can lean too," Favela said, shifting her weight in his arm to his left.

Like some kind of magic, *it actually worked*. The kite gently arched around toward the nearest island, and Favela centered herself as soon as Hiral told her they were on track again.

"You're a natural," Hiral said to her, and her tear-streaked face beamed up at him.

He—no, *they*—had done it. They were going to make it back to the island. All that stood between them and solid ground was a bit of open air and…

Fallen's balls.

A huge green wall.

9

ACHIEVEMENT UNLOCKED?!

"Hold on," was all Hiral had time to say as they raced toward the wall. How strong would it be? Would they bust through or splatter against the surface? Favela... She was in front! He needed to shield her somehow, needed to...

The wall was *right there*, and Hiral did the only thing he could, hauling his legs up in a vain attempt to go over the wall he clearly was heading straight for. It was never going to work. His mind ran through the vectors in the split second before he hit, and he braced for the flight-ending impact...

That didn't come.

Huh?

Hiral glanced down as his legs barely passed over the top of the wall, which somehow looked *shorter*—what in the...?—but he didn't have time to dwell. Ahead of him, the island was barely more than a thin strip of land, more like a bridge covered in thick grass than an actual island. They were going to overshoot it!

Already halfway across and with the far edge coming up fast, Hiral tried to let go of the kite—his only real choice—except his fingers didn't respond.

What is it with kites and not letting go today?

He looked down at Favela. "You need to let go. Now!"

"No!" she said, shaking her head and then burying it in his neck.

Fallen's balls, he didn't have time to argue or fight with her. The edge wasn't more than seventy feet away, so he focused again on his hand. He'd held so tight, and for so long, that the joints screamed in protest as he asked them to unlock.

Come on. Come on.

Fifty feet, and the first finger came off.

Almost there.

Thirty feet, and the second came off.

He wasn't going to make...

The other two fingers completely gave up, and Hiral's stomach jumped into his throat as he fell. Instinct kicked in again as he wrapped his now free arm around Favela's head and tucked his left shoulder to protect her from the worst of it.

Still, this was going to hurt.

Hiral closed his eyes as the green grass raced up to meet him, then clenched his jaw. His shoulder hit first, but the collision didn't shatter every bone. Instead of flipping and rolling, it was like he was digging into some kind of... cushion? Still, with the momentum they'd built up, the slide—or maybe it was a skid— went on for long seconds until they finally came to a stop, and he felt something almost spongey under him.

"Favela? You okay?" he asked as he opened his eyes, finding himself half-buried in what looked like some kind of super-thick moss. But wasn't it grass...?

"My hand kind of hurts," she said, and looked toward where her arm was between Hiral and the thick moss.

"I'm sorry," he said, shifting a bit and then pulling them into a sitting position in the middle of the long, earthy divot created by their... landing. "Let me see it?"

The young girl gingerly pulled one arm from around his neck, though the other stayed firmly in place, and showed him where her forearm and hand had been badly scraped. The fact that she wasn't bawling her eyes out was actually pretty impressive.

"Can you move your fingers? Your wrist?" he asked. Nothing looked obviously broken, but better to be safe than sorry.

Favela winced, but she made a small fist and turned her wrist without too much problem.

"You're such a brave girl," he said, putting his right hand—which didn't hurt much, all things considered—on her head and gently rubbing it.

There was movement around them as well. Mainly people rushing over to see what in the Fallen's names had just happened, but it was the sudden blue screen that popped up in front of Hiral's eyes that grabbed his attention. His status window? No, that wasn't it, but it was similar.

Congratulations. Achievement unlocked - Terminal
You achieved Terminal Velocity without meeting a Terminal End.
Please access a Dungeon Interface
to unlock class-specific reward.

Huh? Dungeon interface? Class-specific reward? What were *either* of those things? And he didn't even *have* a class!

"Hey, you two okay?" a woman asked, dragging Hiral's attention away from the strange prompt, which immediately vanished. "Oh, dear, look at your arm. Come here, let me take care of that."

"No!" Favela said, wrapping the arm back around Hiral's neck and burying her face against his chest.

"Uh, she's probably just a bit…" Hiral started, then looked at the faces very intently staring at him. Or rather, at the Meridian Lines on his face, most likely. Luckily, Favela's arms would probably be covering the tattoos on the sides of his neck, but there was no hiding he was from Fallen Reach.

"Why… *exactly*… does an Islander have one of our kids?" a man asked, coming over to stand beside the woman who'd offered to look at Favela's arm. "Just what do you think you're doing?"

"…was he going to do to her?" another asked.

"Can't be anything good," said another.

"Is he kidnapping her?" another voice asked.

"No, he was *saving* her," a familiar voice shouted, and Seena pushed her way through the gathering crowd. "Being *really* stupid, but saving her," she amended as she crouched down in front of Hiral. "Hey, Favela, how're you doing?"

"How did you get here so quickly?" Hiral asked, but then caught a glimpse of the **Platform of Movement** through the break in the crowd as Arty and Caaven also rushed over to join them. "Ah, never mind."

"Funny-face saved me," Favela said, pulling her head away from Hiral enough to look at Seena.

"He did," Seena said before turning to Hiral. "Doesn't look like she's letting go any time soon. Can you stand?"

"Yeah, I think so. The landing really wasn't as bad as it looked thanks to this…" He trailed off as he eyed the ankle-high grass all around him. Did he… imagine… the moss?

"Give me your hand," Seena said, standing up and offering her arm.

"Yeah, thanks," Hiral said. Making sure he wouldn't drop Favela, he took Seena's hand and let her pull him to his feet. *Huh, didn't even strain her—she must have a decent* **Str**.

"You *idiot*. What would I have told your father, or—Fallen's rutting toenails—your *mother*, if something had happened to you?" Arty fumed as he stormed up to Hiral. "I leave you alone for five minutes, *five minutes*, and then somebody comes in screaming you jumped off the island! What did I say about trouble?"

"Wasn't like I planned it," Hiral said.

"Nobody *plans* getting into trouble," Arty said, but then took a breath and seemed to visibly calm down. "Are you okay? Anything broken?" the man asked while Caaven joined the group of Nomads and quickly explained that *no*, Hiral was not kidnapping the girl.

"Nothing broken," Hiral said.

"Your sword is all dirty, though," Favela offered, giggling.

"Oh?" Hiral said as he turned his head to look at the hilt over his shoulder, dirty with earth and moss. Okay, so at least he wasn't imagining *that*.

"Come on, let's get back up to Caaven's," Arty said, and gestured back to the platform. "We can talk on the way. Starting with how you ever thought that was a good idea."

"I didn't think," Hiral said as they walked, Seena falling in on his other side. "Kind of just… acted."

"You have no idea how lucky you are," Seena said quietly. "The kind of kite you grabbed wasn't meant to be used like that. How it didn't burst apart under the strain, I'll never understand. Or you, doing that with one hand… What level are you anyway?"

"Ah… that's a bit complicated," Hiral said as they got on the platform, and Shaper Jenno stepped up in front of him, her head a solid foot above Hiral's.

"That was impressive." Jenno gave him a quick pat on the shoulder, then went back to stand beside Shaper Fual.

"Impressively stupid," Arty said.

"Okay, I get it!" Hiral deadpanned. "It all worked out in the end, though, right?"

"It did," Caaven said, joining the others as Shaper Fual lifted the platform into the air. "Really, we can't thank you enough for what you did. With the missing party, everybody was distracted from what they should've been paying attention to." The man spared a small glance at Seena. "An accident like this never should've happened.

"How can we thank you for saving Favela?" Caaven finished, putting his hand on the young girl's head. By the smile she gave him, they were pretty close.

"I…" Hiral started, but the memory of the strange blue prompt flashed through his memory. Of the mention of a class. A dungeon interface, huh? What if *that* could help figure out what was wrong with him? Well, there was one place he could probably find something like that. "I want to go with Seena to help find her sister.

"I want to go to the surface."

10
THIS MAKES US EVEN

"I'm sorry, you want to *what*?" Arty asked at the same time Seena spoke up. "What? Why?"

Caaven and the Shapers just stood there with their mouths open, like that was the craziest thing they'd heard all day. Well, aside from when somebody had told them Hiral had jumped off a perfectly good island.

"You're going to go find Mommy?" Favela asked from Hiral's arms, and he looked down at the little girl.

"Mommy?" he asked. "Is your mother…?"

"Aunty Seena's sister," Favela said, which explained why Seena had been babysitting, and why Caaven seemed so familiar with her.

"Well, then, I guess I am." He looked back up at the others. "Maybe," he amended.

"If you'll excuse us, I need a moment with my idiot apprentice in my office," Arty said.

"We're on a platform—what office?" Shaper Jenno asked.

"Fine, then behind those crates we didn't unload yet. Happy?"

She just shrugged.

"Apprentice?" Hiral mouthed at Arty, but the merchant pointed at the slightly secluded part of the platform that was apparently now his *office*.

"Come here, Favela," Caaven said. "Come to your grandpa and let them talk."

"Do I have to?" she asked, but she was looking at Hiral.

"Just for a few minutes, okay? I'll be right back. Promise," Hiral told her.

"You're not going to jump off the side again, are you?" she asked him, her face serious.

"Not unless you are," he said, which somehow seemed to satisfy her, and she let Caaven take her into his arms. No sooner was she out of his hands than Hiral pulled his hood back up to hide the tattoos on his neck.

"Look at your arm, little one," Caaven said while Hiral followed Arty over to the merchant's *office*. "Grammy will get you fixed right up when we get back home. Does it hurt?"

As soon as he'd joined the man, Arty started, "First you jump off the island, and now you want to go down to the surface? Is this your rebellious stage or something? What's gotten into you?"

"I'd like to know that too," Seena said, rounding the crates to join the two men.

"You didn't knock," Arty said testily.

"No door," Seena responded. "And if he's really considering coming down with us, I need to be part of this conversation. You know it'll be up to me to allow it or not."

"And you're considering it?" Hiral asked.

"You've gotten into a *small* amount of my good graces by hurling yourself off the island to save my niece. Doesn't mean I'm going to say yes without knowing why. And the truth. Because by the look on his face"—she pointed at Arty—"this isn't something the two of you planned ahead of time. Unless you're way better actors than I'm giving you credit for."

"We most certainly didn't plan this," Arty said. "So, Hiral, out with it."

Hiral turned his head back toward where the others stood on the far side of the crates. Shapers would probably hear what he said, but he didn't want to lie to Arty. And Seena had a right to know. When he turned back to the others, Arty seemed to figure out what was going through Hiral's head, and the man pulled a flat crystal out of his jacket.

"Here, this should help," he said, running his thumb across the top of the crystal. A small flash of solar energy passed into it before ballooning out to surround the three of them in what looked like a huge soap bubble. "They can't hear us now."

"What... what is *that*?" Hiral asked.

"Part of my collection," Arty said. "But enough about that; it'll only last a few minutes at most. Say your piece. And"—he looked at Seena—"just tell us what's on your mind. If she's related to Caaven, she can be trusted."

Hiral looked down at his right hand and flexed his fingers in and out while he figured out how much to tell them. The pain and stiffness were already mostly gone from his grip on the kite, but he shook his head. He was just procrastinating.

"After the... uh... trip between islands, I got a strange notification. A blue one, like my status window. You have those—status windows, I mean. Right, Seena?"

"Yes, but ours are green. So?" she asked.

Hiral nodded. He didn't know much about Nomad classes, but at least there was that similarity. "Right, when I landed on the other island..."

"Crashed, you mean," Arty pointed out.

"When I *landed*, I got a notification that said something about an achievement being unlocked, whatever that means. I've never seen or heard anything like it before."

"A notification for an achievement?" Arty said. "That's a new one to me… but apparently not to our Nomad friend. What aren't you telling us, Seena?"

Hiral looked at the girl, and yeah, she was acting totally squirrely. Still, she looked between the two men and seemed to come to some kind of internal decision.

"Look, I probably shouldn't tell you this. We kind of keep it close to our chests, but…" She looked at Arty. "Caaven trusts you, and if you can promise to keep it secret, I'll explain what I know."

"Why would you need to keep it secret?" Hiral asked, but it was Arty who answered.

"Because it has something to do with the dungeons and where they find Quillbacks. If there is something *else* special there, the Nomads are worried we'll muscle in instead of trading. Am I right?"

Seena nodded.

"It's fine, we won't tell," Arty said. "Despite some… opinions between the Islanders and the Nomads, I'm one of the ones who believes we need each other. There is too much trade that happens between us for one to last long without the other. And I don't plan on interrupting business. Hiral?"

"If it will help explain what I saw, and you let me go down with you," Hiral said to Seena, "I can keep a secret."

Seena looked at the two of them, as if weighing the sincerity of their words. Thankfully, whatever she saw seemed to be enough—like she'd said, jumping off the island to save her niece probably helped—and she nodded at them.

"Achievement notifications, we don't talk about much because they happen so rarely, and only when we're within about six or seven miles of a dungeon," she said. "For you to have gotten it, we must be almost directly above it, which means we need to leave as soon as we get back up."

"So, what's this class-specific reward it talked about?" Hiral asked. *And will it help me figure out how to actually get a class?*

Seena shook her head. "We don't know. Nobody's been able to find a dungeon interface. I mean, we *thought* we knew what it was, but we haven't been able to activate it, so we're figuring the interfaces must be deeper in the dungeons."

"Deeper? You haven't completely explored them?" Arty asked.

Another shake of Seena's head. "The Quillbacks are always in the outer part of the dungeon, and we're pretty sure there is another *inner* part, but we haven't been able to get into it. We're missing something, but we don't know what it is."

"How many achievements have you gotten, Seena?" Hiral asked.

"Just two, and I've made almost forty trips to the surface. They aren't common, but they also aren't showing up on my status window. If that's your only reason for coming down… well, I don't know if we can help you."

"I'd still like to try. The opportunity for a class… uh… reward… is too much to pass up," Hiral said, and barely fought down the wince at what he'd almost said.

Seena didn't seem to see anything wrong with it, but looking at Arty's face, the older merchant had caught on to what Hiral was after.

"I'd like Hiral to go down with you as well," Arty finally said. "If you need any more convincing, consider it repayment for me leaving my products for trade with you on good faith." He pointed at the crates on the platform.

"There's a risk, you know," Seena said, looking Hiral in the eye. "A big one. There's a good chance we'll be racing to catch the last island, and I'll be honest with you—if you fall behind, you're on your own. I'm not risking my own neck or anybody else's for you."

"I understand," Hiral said immediately. "I won't slow you down. Or, if I do, I give you my permission to leave me behind."

"This class reward is that important to you?" Seena asked.

"It is," Hiral said. "And, if I can help you find Favela's mother, then everybody wins."

Seena crossed her arms, and one finger started tapping just above her elbow while she considered. "Fine, you can come. We probably have about an hour's worth of prep to do before we jump. You've got that long to get up to speed on how our wingsuits work. Just throwing it out there, but I give you a fifty-fifty chance to faceplant from seven miles up."

"I'll take those odds," Hiral said.

"They really aren't *good* odds," Arty said.

"Better than I've had in a while," Hiral said, and Arty scrunched up his lips and nodded.

"But, again, this achievement thing, whether it works or not… it doesn't make it back up to Fallen Reach, right?" Seena asked.

"It stays with your people," Arty said.

"I'll keep it hidden on my status window if we figure out how to make it work," Hiral said.

Seena shrugged. "I really don't get why this is so important to you. We haven't figured it out in years; I don't know why you think it'll be any different for you."

"I know, but I have to try," Hiral said.

"Fine," Seena said, looking over as the platform crested the edge of the island next to Caaven's house. "Looks like we're here. Like I said, you have about an hour to learn how to jump and not die. Usually, people train for weeks before they do it."

"Weeks?" Arty asked. "And he has an hour."

"All the time I can spare. Last chance to back out."

"I'll figure it out," Hiral said.

"Good enough," she said. "Oh, and even though I am trusting you both with this, I am going to explain our agreement to Caaven. If word of dungeons being connected to achievements gets out, that's the end of the trade agreement."

"I make good on my word," Arty said somewhat defensively.

"You do, which is the only reason I've even agreed to all this. My uncle thinks quite a lot of you, for an Islander, and I trust his judgment." Seena turned to Hiral. "I'll find somebody to teach you how to jump the *proper* way, and then I've got to get ready myself. I'll see you in about an hour."

"Thank you for letting me come with you," Hiral said.

"Thank you for saving Favela, but this makes us even," Seena said.

"More than even," Hiral agreed.

"Good. I don't like owing people. And for what it's worth, I actually hope you don't die."

"Me too," Hiral said as the platform settled down on the ground where he would very shortly be jumping off again.

11

THE FALL 2

Hiral looked down at the wing-like thing extending the length of this arm and connecting down his chest, leg, and finally finishing at his ankle. More of the strange fabric ran up the inside of his legs, connecting there as well. It was kind of like a large insect wing, the material surprisingly smooth between his fingers. Oh, and it was as big as he was.

"So, this will let me fly?" Hiral said to his *instructor*—in the loosest possible use of the word.

"Glide, not fly," the man, Nivian, said. "Your platform can fly"—he pointed to the unloaded ***Platform of Movement***—"but we don't have those."

"Like the kite, then?"

The man gave a huffing laugh, then shrugged and nodded. "Something like that. I've told you how to control your direction in the air, and how to deploy the 'chute when it's time to slow down. No time to practice, but do you have any questions?"

Hiral ran his hand along the cord that would *apparently* release some kind of—what did Nivian call it?—parachute to slow him down when they got close to their destination. Assuming they didn't rig it to fail and keep their secret about the dungeons safe. No, Seena didn't seem like that kind of person; she'd looked genuinely thankful Hiral had saved Favela. That, and Arty still knew. If something happened to Hiral… Well, if he was being honest with himself, Arty would probably keep the secret anyway.

"No questions," Hiral finally said. "I'm ready to go when you are."

"You putting on a brave front, or you actually ready to do this?" Nivian said, his own wingsuit getting checked by another member of Seena's party.

"Would you think less of me if I said both?" Hiral asked. "Last time I jumped, well, I didn't exactly *think* before doing it. Now that I've had an hour to consider how far the ground actually is, yeah, I'm a bit nervous."

"Being nervous is fine. Lots can go wrong on a jump, but hold your body rigid like I told you—you seem to have the stats for it—and you'll do just fine. We put your weapons in that narrow pack along your back. Can't risk them creating drag in the air, but you sure you need to take them? Any added weight creates more risk."

"You said the surface is dangerous," Hiral said, and waited for the man to nod. "And from what I've seen, you're carrying weapons down with you too. I want to do my part when we get down there, and these are what I've got."

"Are you any good in a fight?" Nivian asked seriously.

Hiral looked at the three Shapers on the platform. "Nothing like them, if that's what you're asking."

Nivian huffed again, but this one wasn't a laugh. More like a dismissive grunt. "Good. People with power like them; they don't know how to work as a party. Only think about themselves and don't have anybody's back."

"I've got your back, if you'll let me," Hiral said. What… what would it be like to actually be needed? To be *wanted*? To be part of something like a party?

Nivian shook his head. "Seena might trust you for what you did, but that doesn't mean the rest of us do. I don't agree with you coming down, not one bit, but she's the party leader, and I'll follow her instructions. You just keep out of our way, and hopefully, we'll all make it back in one piece."

"Ah, right. I won't get in your way," Hiral said.

Who was he kidding? He wasn't part of the group. He was a tag-along. Well, whatever—if it got him his class, it would be worth it. And, no matter what Nivian said, Hiral *would* do what he could to watch their backs.

"Enough flirting, boys," Seena said as she walked over, moving naturally in her own wingsuit despite the extra fabric. "Last chance to drop out," she said to Hiral, then seemed to think about the words. "Maybe not the best expression, considering what we're about to do."

"No, I'm in, no matter what happens," Hiral responded.

Seena tapped her foot, looking from Hiral to the rest of her party spread out behind him. If they had any further opinions about him accompanying them, they kept it to themselves. "Alright. It's go-time. We're already behind schedule, so we're heading to the Greenvine landing zone."

"Greenvine?" Nivian asked. "That's… not an easy landing zone. Even for regular jumpers."

Seena looked at Hiral, though she answered Nivian. "It's our only chance if we want to make it back in time. Let's go." She turned and strode over to the edge of the island.

"Hiral, don't come back dead," Arty said from where he stood with Caaven. "I *really* don't want to have to explain that to your parents. This is going to be bad enough."

"Sorry to leave that to you, Arty. I'll be back as soon as I can." Hiral pulled on some round goggles Seena had provided for him, then walked over to join her at the edge of the island.

"You know the agreement. Keep up or get left behind," she said as the other four members of her party joined them.

"I know," Hiral said. "And no matter what happens, I hope you find your sister."

"We'll find her—you can count on that," Seena said, the breeze swirling around them again like it had when it had lifted Favela off the side.

Looking down, wow, the ground was a *long* way away, and Hiral's stomach did a flip just at the thought of stepping off the island. Way easier to do when he wasn't thinking about it. Maybe he should just…

Hiral leapt forward, like he was diving into the water headfirst, before his brain could try and talk him out of what he was doing. Faint voices shouted in surprise behind him, but it was all he could do to strain to remember what Nivian had explained to him.

Arms and legs wide out, rigid… That was what Nivian had said, and Hiral extended his arms and legs spread-eagle. The fabric out to his sides billowed immediately, threatening to pull his arms back in their sockets, but it wasn't anything he couldn't handle with his stats, and he kept his limbs spread. More tension built between his ankles, and he could only assume the fabric was catching the air like it was supposed to. He sure didn't seem to be falling *quite* as fast as he had the first time.

So, where am I supposed to go now? Maaaaaybe I shouldn't have jumped first…

Movement to his right, and Hiral turned his head, pushing out a breath of relief despite the wind pressure. Seena had caught up to him, and even with the goggles on her face, he could make out a look of disbelief. Or maybe it was annoyance.

Likely both.

She shook her head at him slightly as four other bodies plummeted past them, their arms and legs tight to their bodies. The same way he'd chased Favela. Seena looked at the four pulling away from them, back to Hiral, then tucked her arms and legs in and leaned forward, quickly speeding away from Hiral.

She *had* said they needed to hurry, so Hiral followed her lead and brought his arms against his body and put his legs together. Leaning forward, the wind built against his skin and flapped his hair around madly. Away from the island, he noticed something he hadn't when he was diving after Favela: the air was noticeably colder, and it was even a bit harder to catch his breath.

Without at least solid E-Rank stats, it would be quite uncomfortable— maybe even enough to make a person pass out. Without the time spent in the ***Training Room***, Hiral wouldn't have been in any shape to keep up with the others.

But, even without his class, he *did* manage to stay on their tails, changing the position of his body as those ahead of him did. ***Int*** and ***Wis*** stat increases from learning the ***Time Trial*** paid off as he quickly copied how the people ahead of him moved and shifted. Arms came out to change his trajectory, then tucked back in to pick up speed again, and they continued their controlled fall.

And, since he wasn't trying to catch Favela—or, kind of, not *die* like last time—he had the chance to really take in the scenery below as it rushed up to meet him. They seemed to be aiming for a slightly rocky area on one side of the woods that nestled up against the EnSath River. Imposing cliffs flanked where the river had long ago carved out the land, its vast and rushing waters whitecapped as it tumbled between the stone.

How many millions of gallons of water is that? I wonder if anybody has ever measured it? The speed. The volume… The… And that right there is why Gauto thinks I should be an Academic.

Far to his right, but not as far as he'd like, the numerous peaks of the Needle Mountains reached toward the sky, while the river charged between them. That was the path Fallen Reach would take, and just from looking, Hiral spotted what had to be the last spot where it would be possible to make the jump to one of the Nomads' islands as it passed.

The thick mountain, so different from the Needle Peaks, was easily as tall as the mountain range, but wide and rugged, where the Needles were little more than smooth, towering spikes. The near side looked possible to climb; maybe that was even a path up—or it could just be his imagination—and then there was a flat plateau in the perfect place to make the jump over the river.

It was miles ahead of where Hiral was, maybe halfway to the storm-wall. Fifteen or twenty hours were all they had before the islands passed over it.

Which meant he didn't have time to be sightseeing!

Just as he turned his attention back to the five people falling beneath him, they gently extended their arms and legs, letting the air catch in the fabric wings. Hiral followed suit. No sooner had he done that than the smallest of the group—Seena, probably—extended her arms a little further, creating more drag and allowing Hiral to catch up to her.

Pulling up beside him, she turned her head to look at him, then looked pointedly at the rocky area, which was now much closer. After his best attempt at nodding, she clenched her fist and pointed one finger at his chest.

What could she…? Ah, the rope for the parachute. It must almost be time.

He did his best to nod again, and she opened her hand so he could clearly see all her fingers. Then she pulled her thumb in. A second passed and she pulled another finger in. Another second, a third finger…

A countdown!

One more nod.

She held up two fingers and changed the angle of her body so she drifted away from him, then she only had one finger left.

Hiral's hand opened and closed, a little numb from the cold but still working. He brought his arm in to grab the rope as Seena made a fist again. The drag created by the air resisted his movement, but his *Str* was more than up to the task, and he yanked on the rope barely a second after Seena did.

Something happened on his back, and there was a jerk on his shoulders that kicked his legs out under him and pulled him into an upright position. Looking quickly over at Seena, he saw her grab a pair of dangling ropes from the compact parachute above her, then found his own and grabbed on.

Below them, four more green parachutes had been deployed. All at once, they curved to the left. Off to his right, Seena pulled down on her left rope, and she tilted and dipped after the others.

Makes sense. Pull left to go left.

Hiral did just that, though it took a little more finesse to pull the *right* amount. Still, with only a few quick adjustments, he had the parachute under control, and followed the other five as they angled in toward a small clearing on top of the rocky area.

Suddenly, the ground was so very close, racing by beneath his feet. Uneven rocks made for treacherous footing, but the first of the group touched down with a kind of hopping run, keeping them ahead of the others who also landed. Hiral, not quite as familiar with the process, watched closely but still soared past the back two people as he struggled to balance speed against height.

As he passed the third person without his feet touching the ground, he very quickly noticed the *end* of their landing area.

The solid rock wall.

12

PERSONAL INTERFACE MAGIC

HIRAL's feet stretched for the ground speeding by. He pulled on both ropes, trying to drop those last few inches, but he still passed the fourth person. The wall wasn't more than ten feet in front of the fifth and final person, but they'd had twice that distance to land and get their momentum under control. Out of options, he pulled down *hard* on both ropes. The edges of the parachute collapsed in, and he dropped like a rock.

Feet churning, he hit the ground at practically a sprint—far too close to the wall—and hop-skipped from one stone to the next while trying to slow down. If it'd been flat ground, he could've done it no problem, but the lay of the rocks meant he had to keep aiming for the next secure foothold, or he'd faceplant.

One step, two steps, three… He wasn't going to stop in time…

Something yanked hard on his back, so much so that one of his feet kept going so that the sole of his boot hit the stone wall and helped absorb the last of his forward inertia. But thankfully, that was the worst of it, and he settled his leg under himself while he turned around to catch of glimpse of Seena and Nivian holding on to the back of his wingsuit before his parachute dropped down to envelop them.

A minute of struggling with the fabric to free them, and then everybody sort of just looked at him.

"Thanks," he said. "Landing was harder than it looked."

Two of the five in the back gave each other a look, but it was Nivian who spoke. "You sure you've never used a wingsuit before?"

"Never," Hiral said. "Couldn't you tell by the landing that almost involved me being smeared on the rock?" He thumbed over his shoulder.

"You must've put points in **Int** and **Wis** to pick it up that quickly. You were practically a natural."

Hiral considered the words while the others slid their parachute-packs off their shoulders and began to take off the wingsuits. "Wait," he said to Nivian. "You expected me to do worse than that?"

"Much worse," Nivian said.

Hiral opened his mouth to ask just how much worse, but Seena shook her head and pointed at his tangled parachute on the ground.

"The wingsuit and the parachute should fit in the pack, even if it's messy," she said. "Get it in and make sure it's closed well. We'll store them nearby to get picked up next rotation."

"If we leave them here, how will we get back to the islands?" Hiral asked.

"We store wingsuits at all the jump points," Seena said. "Now, pack."

"Sure," Hiral said, following the instructions. He took off the wingsuit, careful to keep his tattoos covered. Since he couldn't use them, he just didn't want to deal with the questions, and that wasn't even including Nivian's opinion of the Shapers. With the suit off, he then went to work on getting it all in the pack. It was a tight fit, all bunched up like it was, but he got it all in only a minute after Seena finished hers. "What now?"

"Now we go find my sister and her party," Seena said, pulling out three pieces of wood from another small pack and assembling them into some kind of staff about as tall as she was.

The only other person who seemed to have a weapon was one guy with a spear, though the guy next to him looked like he had small blades on his joints. *Nivian and the other guy don't seem to have weapons. Wait... that other guy...*

Hiral paused, looking at the fifth member of the Nomad party, then back to Nivian again. *A second Nivian? Did I hit my head on the way down...?*

"Wule is my twin brother," Nivian said, the confusion on Hiral's face evident.

"The good-looking twin," Wule added.

"More like the scrawny one," Nivian said, and the man had a point. While their faces were almost identical, their actual bodies couldn't be more different, with Nivian *solid* and Wule... average?

"How did I not notice this before?" Hiral asked.

"Not enough points in attunement?" Wule joked.

"I... My attunement is decent..." Hiral started.

"More likely the whole jumping-off-an-island-again thing," Nivian said.

"Guys, not important right now," Seena snapped, both Wule and Nivian jerking upright and the grins vanishing from their faces like they'd never been there. "You can debate who has the bigger nose later. You all ready?"

"Just about," Nivian mumbled with a small bob of his head.

She's definitely the party leader, just like she said.

Then she looked at Hiral, one eyebrow slowly climbing toward her hairline.

"Ready!" he said, grabbing his harness from his pack and slinging it over his shoulders.

His two short-swords went in the sheaths, the hilts just barely poking up above his shoulders, and he did a couple of quick checks to make sure they drew smoothly.

"What sort of merchant's apprentice carries swords?" asked one of the Nomads Hiral didn't know—the one with the spear.

"Technically not his apprentice," Hiral said. "Guard. And appraiser, I guess."

"Appraiser?" the man asked.

"For the quills," Hiral answered while Nivian stuffed the packs in a small nearby cleft in the rocks.

Deep enough to keep the rain out, but narrow enough nothing too big would call it home. Actually, that brought up the question of what else besides Quillbacks lived on the surface.

"Ah. Makes sense since that's the main thing he trades for," the man said before tapping himself on the chest. "I'm Yanily, by the way. You can use those? The swords, I mean."

"Only ever used them in training. Against people. Not against… What… what exactly are we going to run into down here?"

"Hopefully nothing, if we keep *quiet* and move quickly," Seena said, joining the pair. "As soon as Nivian is…"

"Done," Nivian said, joining them.

"Okay, let's get a couple of things straight before we move. First off, since you actually survived the jump… Everybody, this is Hiral. You all saw him save Favela, which is why I agreed to let him come."

"Really didn't think I was going to make it, did you?" Hiral asked.

"She had odds set at eighty-twenty against," Yanily said. "Don't worry, I bet on you making it. And now I'm going to clean up when we get back. Woo, drinks on me."

The other four glared at Yanily—which meant they'd all actually bet *against* him surviving. Great start.

"Moving on," Seena said quickly. "First off, everything I tell you falls within the bounds of the agreement with Arty and bringing you to the dungeon. Meaning, you can't share anything you learn."

"You sure we can trust him? Just because we know he survived the jump doesn't mean anybody up above does," Wule said.

"Uh…" Hiral started and took a step back, but it was Seena who spoke up.

"I've chosen to trust him." She didn't even bat an eyelash at the casual murder conversation.

"Okay, just making sure," Wule said.

"Now, where was I? Right. The goal is to *avoid* fighting if we can. Normally, we fight for the class experience and to improve our **PIM**, but…"

"**PIM**?" Hiral interrupted.

"Personal Interface Magic," Seena said. "Your tattoo line things. We have something similar, but it takes the form of roots that run through our body. From what we know, they function the same way. Enhance our stats, let us use abilities like how your Shapers turn their tattoos into objects. Can you do anything like that?"

Hiral just shook his head.

"No problem. We move in six-person teams because our ancestors said something about dungeons only letting six people in. We've never run into the issue, but that's still how we build our teams. Because of this, we've got roles to make our parties more efficient. With me so far?"

"Where's your usual sixth?" Hiral asked.

"Wife was in labor. I couldn't ask him to come on such a risky mission with a little one on the way." Seena waited for Hiral to nod before continuing. "Nivian is our tank. Means he gets our enemy's attention and keeps it on him. Wule"— she pointed at the man who'd suggested murdering Hiral and lying about it— "who you've been introduced to, is our healer. Pretty self-explanatory, that one."

Note to self: Don't get injured.

"Yanily and Vix are our heavy hitters. Dungeon terminology would be *damager dealers*, which is fitting."

Yanily had his spear, which had been assembled similarly to Seena's staff, while the one named Vix was the last member. He strapped on a pair of clawed knuckles to go along with the short blades on his knees, elbows, and heels.

"I got classified as support," Seena continued. "Our sixth *was* a scout and damage dealer, but I'm not expecting you to do that. Like I said, we're avoiding fights…"

"But I'm so close to hitting level nineteen," Yanily whined, tapping the butt of his spear on the ground.

"Avoiding fights. That said, if we don't have a choice, just let us handle it. I'm sure you'd like the experience and all, but more likely than not, you'd get in the way," Seena told Hiral bluntly.

…Everfail…

"Yeah, you're probably right," Hiral said, forcing himself not to wince at the implication. She *was* likely correct, though. If their—what did she call it?— **PIM** was similar to his Meridian Lines, Yanily at level 18 would have 54 more attribute points to distribute. Sure, Hiral's base stats were high because of his training, but he just couldn't compete with **PIM**-enhanced stats on top of base attributes if they trained like he did. "But, if I see an opportunity to help, or if one of you needs me… I'm not standing by and doing nothing."

"Only a few things around this dungeon pose much of a threat to us—it's only E-Rank, after all—and anything we can't tackle, we avoid or run from," Seena said with a shrug.

"How far is the dungeon from here?" Hiral asked, moving on.

"Less than a mile, and there's a path straight there. Won't take long. Anybody else have any questions? Did I forget anything?"

"Did you bring lunch, Nivian?" Yanily asked.

"Anything *important*?" Seena asked flatly.

"Sandwiches in my pack," Nivian said quietly, and Yanily gave him a not-so-subtle thumbs-up.

"Anything else?" Seena asked, staring at Yanily like she was daring him to speak again.

Five heads shook in the negative, and Seena pointed down the path with her staff. "Nivian, take the lead. Without Julka here, keep your eyes open. Usual order. Hiral, you're in the back."

"Watch and learn, Mr. Appraiser," Yanily said good-naturedly.

13

A BALANCED PARTY

JUST a few minutes later, the small group stood clustered around a large track in the dirt path, the five Nomads looking distinctly concerned.

"Yanily, this feels like something I should learn about," Hiral said. "What made this track?"

"Well…" Yanily started, scratching at his chin while looking down at the mark in the ground. It was easily two feet long but relatively narrow, with what looked like two clawed toes at the front, and one at the heel. Strangest, though, was how… straight it all appeared. Everything about it was angular and symmetrical, kind of like if somebody was wearing a giant metal boot. "We don't exactly know," Yanily finally finished.

"If you don't know, why do you all look so upset to find it here?" Hiral asked, looking where a second print led into the woods perpendicular to the path. Unless the thing—whatever it was—was really small with big feet, it did an unnaturally good job of moving through the trees. There was barely any sign at all that something had passed.

"We've never seen what makes the track," Seena took over. "But we've all seen the track itself, and been taught to avoid it."

"How does that even work?" Hiral asked.

"We've been dungeon-diving for generations, since our ancestors found the dungeons and figured out what your people would trade for the quills. Over the years, they learned things about the surface, and these things were passed on to us in lessons from generation to generation. Somewhere way back, somebody found these tracks and something *very bad* happened. Bad enough we were all taught to get straight back up to the islands if we ever found a fresh one."

"Is this one fresh?"

Vix crouched down and poked at the dirt in the deep part of the track, then a little at the sides. "I'm no Julka—I wish he was here—but I'd say this is fresh. Rain would've washed the track out if it happened before the clouds passed. So, at the most, it's about thirty hours old. At the worst, five minutes?"

"You can't be a little more accurate than that?" Nivian asked, positioning himself between the group and the treeline where the tracks led.

There was a small almost-pulse of energy, and then thick, thorn-covered vines grew out of the palms of his hands. On his left arm, the vine curled around in a circular pattern to form into a large shield on his arm, while the one from his right hand lengthened into what could only be a spined whip.

And that's why he didn't bring a weapon with him. Must be an ability of some kind. I wonder how… No…stop. No time for testing or measurements.

"No," Vix said in response to Nivian's question. "I hit things, and I'm guessing here based on the things Julka always says."

"What's the call, Seena?" Wule asked.

"Nothing's changed. The plan was always to get back up to the islands as quick as we could. This is just more incentive. For now, we continue to the dungeon, find my sister's group, and then keep going."

"What if…?" Yanily started.

"It didn't," Seena said, cutting him off.

"Yeah, probably, but what…?"

"It didn't. They didn't run into this thing. My sister probably found the tracks like we did, then hurried to the dungeon. We'll either find her party there or on the path to the jump point." Her words completely shut down any further argument.

Hiral watched the group, Seena especially, as the discussion happened. She spoke firmly, and even though he didn't know her well, he had a *lot* of experience covering up his feelings. Seena was doing the same thing. That twitch of her eye. The way her lips tightened, and how her knuckles whitened around the staff. She was putting on a strong front, but there were cracks in it.

"Then we should get to the dungeon to find them, just in case these tracks got made after they passed," Hiral said.

The four men all looked at him, then to Seena, who finally nodded.

More quick bursts of energy pulsed out from the two damage dealers, with Yanily's spear taking on a green hue, while Vix's image seemed to blur at the edges.

Their abilities are very fast to activate. I wonder if they're as strong as a Shaper's?

"Hiral is right," Seena said. "Let's get moving again, and pick up the pace, Nivian. This isn't a stroll with your grandmother."

"You've met Nivian's grammy, haven't you, Seena? She'd leave us in the dust," Yanily said, but Nivian was already moving to the front of the group and jogging down the path.

"I'll leave you in the dust too, if you don't stop yammering," Nivian called back, and the other Nomads quickly fell in line, with Hiral once again in the back.

He took one last look at the track—it really was strange. *What could've made it?*

"Hiral, don't fall behind," Seena called, and he looked up to see her waving him along.

"Right, coming." He jogged after the group, quickly catching up to Seena without much effort. Even with classes and Seena's instructions, Nivian was keeping it at a reasonable pace.

"You must've spent your points pretty evenly," Seena said as they jogged, though her eyes were constantly on the trees on their left. "Picked up the wingsuit just by watching us, and you don't seem to be having any problem physically keeping up. I heard most Islanders spent their points on strength and **End**."

"The Shapers do," Hiral said. "The big guys with all the tattoos. Using your dungeon terminology, I'd say all of them would be tanks. Or damage dealers, I guess? Their training usually involves taking turns dishing out as much damage as possible with another Shaper. They *literally* take turns. Toss a chip to decide who goes first. First one to fall loses."

"They hit each other until one of them falls down?" Seena asked. "No actual fighting? Or tactics? Abilities? Why would they even…?"

"There are whole tournaments based around the matches. Most of the city turns up to watch the B-Rankers go at it. Even if they don't, they can probably hear the impacts coming from the Amphitheatre of the Sun."

"Even though it sounds a bit…mundane that they just stand there and hit each other, it sure would be something else to see a pair of B-Rankers go at it."

"It's not always just pairs. They've been doing this new thing recently where they have a circle, and each Shaper hits the person on their right. When somebody hits the ground, the circle shrinks and continues until just one is left standing."

"I bet there are all kinds of back-room dealings to get the best spot in the circle, right? To be by the weakest people," Seena said as the group crested a small hill, and then started down at an angle toward the base of what looked like another cliff facing away from them.

"Just the opposite, in a way," Hiral said, doing his best to get a lay of the land. The dungeon had to be close. "It's actually seen as cowardly, which is related to why they just *take* the hits instead of actually fighting. The *best* spots are to the right of the strongest people, so they can prove how tough they are."

"Why do I feel like your Shapers get brain damage a lot?" Seena said with a shake of her head.

Hiral chuckled. "Maybe more than they'd like to admit. But don't say that too loudly; they all have *really* good hearing."

"All this talk about what Shapers can do, but you haven't actually mentioned what your class is."

"Neither have you," Hiral pointed out. "Unless *support* is a class?"

"It's not," Seena said, but then looked to her left as the group rounded a curve in the path. "It's just how the dungeon generally refers to my class."

"Was it the dungeon interface that said you're support?" Hiral asked.

"No, like I said before, we haven't been able to figure out how to make the interfaces work. The classifications are another thing passed down generation to generation. We have this… I guess it's a list… of our classes, and where they fit into the dungeon categories. Tanks, healers, damage dealers, support, and scouts. We build our parties around a balance of these."

"Because you were taught that was the best way to build a party?" Hiral asked, and Seena nodded.

"Every party has to have at least one tank and one healer, but after that, it's up to the people themselves. We went pretty diverse, and I think we've been successful because of it. My sister's party, though…" She winced slightly at the mention of her sister. "Her group is a tank, a healer, and four damage dealers. That's what works for them, but I think we've progressed faster than them because we're more balanced."

"Do your lists talk about any of the Islander classes, or just the… uh …the Growers?" Hiral asked, deciding to call them by their proper name instead of Fallen Reach's name of Nomads.

"Just us Growers, but, look, maybe we should pick this up later. Something's up," Seena said as they came upon the rest of the party looking distinctly on edge. "Another one of those tracks?"

"No, something else," Nivian said. "Animals have gone quiet."

Animals?

Hiral listened, but he didn't hear anything… which would make sense, based on what Nivian had *just* said. But, had there been animal noises before? *Yeah, yeah, maybe there were. So, why did they go quiet?*

"Anybody got anything?" she asked as the other Growers spread out slightly along the path.

"Looks like another track over here, but not the same as the last one we saw," Nivian said.

He still had his shield on his arm, and his whip coiled in his other hand. *Like a Shaper's tattoo, it must only cost solar energy to manifest the item. Does it also have special abilities like the tattoos do that cost further solar energy?*

"Anything you recognize?" Seena asked, and Nivian crouched down to get a closer look, then groaned.

"Troblins," he said, getting to his feet and backing toward the group.

"Troblins?" Hiral asked.

"Humanoids, little taller than waist height," Seena explained. "Bark-like skin. Not terribly smart, but they use weapons and hunt in packs. Individually around level twelve in E-Rank. Never seen one in D-Rank, so that's pretty reliable. Depending on the pack size, they can be a challenge, even for our party."

"They have this **Pile On** tactic they use," Yanily added. "Maybe even an ability. Somehow, they all pick one target and then do everything they can to mob them."

"If they go after Nivian, it's easy for us. We just pick them off from behind," Seena said. "But, if they go after somebody else, it's a lot more difficult."

"And my usual abilities to get an opponent to focus on me can't override the **Pile On** mentality," Nivian said.

"They are also *really* nasty," Vix said. "Evil little monsters that've been known to try and *eat* people they **Pile On**. You get a chance to kill one of these things, you do it."

"You should be staying out of the fight," Seena reminded him. "But, if it comes to it, Vix is right. Don't hesitate with these things. Can you do that? Can you *kill* something?"

Hiral's hand went to one of the swords over his shoulder, and he forced himself to nod. "I'll do what I have to."

He may not have passed the Shapers' test, but he'd been training for more than ten years to be able to end fights decisively. Unlike the Amphitheatre fights he'd explained to Seena, Loan had trained him to take advantage of his mobility and skill. When he finally passed the Shaper test, he *would* prove to the others how wrong they'd been to doubt him.

This was just another kind of training. *And it's kind of exciting.*

"Buffs?" Wule asked, ignoring the small exchange between Hiral and Seena.

"Give us **Nature's Bulwark**," Seena said before looking at Hiral. "All of us."

Wule seemed like he'd question it for a moment, but then nodded and held his hand out in front of himself, palm up. With another pulse of energy—activating an ability—his palm opened up for a small green plant stem to grow out of it. The plant grew and twisted around itself until it was about six inches long, then a silver flower with petals like small shields budded and opened at the end of it. The second the petals fully spread, there was another, stronger pulse of energy. Hiral got a blue notification before the plant immediately withered and turned to dust.

You have been buffed by Nature's Bulwark.
Reduces damage taken by 10% for 180 minutes.

"Wow," Hiral said, feeling something like his skin hardening from the ability. It didn't seem to slow him down or restrict his movements, which meant he could still stay mobile. But, on the off chance something hit him, a straight-up reduction of damage by 10% was pretty great.

"Impressive, isn't it?" Yanily asked, waggling his eyebrows. "Wule's got a couple of strong buffs on top of his heals."

"Buffs increase your attributes or abilities," Seena explained. "Debuffs do the opposite."

"It is impressive," Hiral said, and gave a nod of thanks to Seena for the quick explanation of the terms. "There are tattoos the Shapers use that are stronger, but they're personal only. You did the whole group with that one ability?" he asked Wule.

Wule gave Seena a quick look, and she nodded at him. "My abilities are called spells, but yes. I can do up to twelve people with my buffs and one of my heals. The other heals are single-target, though—they only affect one person at a time."

"And they are close range," Seena added. "So make sure you get close to Wule if you get hurt."

"Or be like me, and don't get hurt," Vix said, still kind of blurry around the edges.

"A stiff breeze would knock you out," Yanily said.

"If it could hit me," Vix responded.

"Enough," Seena quickly interrupted. "Standard formation. If we run into the Troblins before we reach the safety of the dungeon, let Nivian get their attention so they use **Pile On** on him. Then hit them hard and fast."

"Oh yeah, level nineteen, here I come," Yanily said, and tossed Hiral a wink. "Don't worry, you'll get experience from this since you're with us."

Dismissing the buff notification still hovering in front of him with a thought—though it still left a small blue shield icon in the corner of his vision—Hiral reached over his shoulders and drew his twin swords.

The two weapons weren't much compared to the powers of the Shapers' tattoos, but they'd have to do, and he fell into place behind the others as they continued down the path.

"How big are these Troblin packs usually?" Hiral asked from behind Seena.

She and Wule were spread slightly behind Nivian, with Vix and Yanily hanging on the sides a bit further back, almost like an arrowhead formation.

"If we're lucky, no more of them than us," Seena said.

"And if we're unlucky, five-to-one odds," Yanily said.

Five to one, and level twelve? Compared to Hiral's level *zero*? It would be much better if it was a small pack. *Much, much better.*

"Dungeon isn't far," Nivian said. "Maybe we missed them."

"Maybe," Hiral answered as he scanned the bushes on his right. He paused on a pair of vibrant green, practically glowing orbs. Orbs that *blinked*. Orbs that were joined by a dozen more pairs almost exactly like them. "Or maybe not."

14

FIRST ENCOUNTER WITH TROBLINKIND

H IRAL instinctively backpedalled as *something* burst out of the bush in a rush, knobby brown limbs swinging some kind of weighted club in an overhead chop. Up and over the thick end came, then *thwacked* into the ground where Hiral had been a second before. The creature scowled at Hiral as if it was annoyed he'd had the audacity to avoid it.

"Troblins!" Nivian shouted, more of the rough-skinned creatures charging out from both sides.

Their crude weapons wailed at the party of Growers, who seamlessly collapsed into a circle to protect each other's backs.

A circle Hiral was on the *outside* of.

But he didn't have time to worry about that—the Troblin in front of him was already recovering from where it had missed its swing, whipping the weapon around from the side for a second go at it. Some kind of guttural growl escaped its lipless mouth past teeth like thorns, its breath smelling like a pile of earthy dirt, and it stepped forward...

Directly into Hiral's straight kick, which smashed its flat-nosed face. Wood *crunched* beneath his heel, and the Troblin flipped over backwards so violently, it actually landed on its chest.

This is level twelve? It's so slow.

Hiral shook the disbelief out of his head and reversed the blade in his right hand into an upside-down grip. Then, as the Troblin pushed itself up to wobbly hands and knees, he stepped in and drove his sword into the creature's wood-skinned back. The natural armor of the bark-like skin held for the briefest part of a second, but it apparently wasn't nearly strong enough to deflect Hiral's attack.

The masterwork blade punched straight through the Troblin's back and out its chest, green blood splashing to the ground as the thing howled in pain. Howled, but didn't die. Its right arm swung the weighted club around to try to catch Hiral in the legs. From that position, and with only one hand on the weapon, the swing was so slow, Hiral nimbly jumped back to evade it, but was forced to leave his sword embedded in the Troblin's torso.

Growling like a feral animal and dripping blood from its face and chest, the Troblin once again took its weapon in both hands, struggled to his feet, and charged at Hiral.

The chest wound looks bad, but I must not have hit anything vital. Its **End** *is probably a bit above average if I was able to punch through it, but not kill it,* he analyzed as he dodged one swing and then the next. Out flicked his sword to parry a blow and test the creature's **Str**—*can't be higher than ten*—and then he stepped around the next swing and brought his sword down in a vicious arc, cleanly separating the arm at the elbow.

Another howl of pain, more spewing of green blood, and the Troblin staggered forward, but still didn't fall. *Yeah,* **End** *must be its highest attribute— maybe twelve.* **Dex** *is abysmal, somewhere in the range of five to eight.* With enough information from the Troblin in front of him, Hiral darted in, spun past a weak punch from the creature, and grabbed the hilt of his weapon driven through the creature's back.

Twist. Twist. Pull. He ripped the sword free and then kicked the Troblin in the ass, sending it stumbling to the ground. As green pooled around its chest, it didn't rise again.

No way a level twelve Shaper would die this easily. Are creatures on the surface weaker, even though they're the same level?

Hiral snapped his wrist to flick the green blood from his blade since he didn't have an immediate answer to his own question, then turned his attention back to the melee. A dozen or so Troblins surrounded the Grower party, half that number again dead on the ground around them already.

Wooden armor, eerily similar to the Troblins' skin, covered Nivian from head to toe, and his whip lashed out like a living thing, constantly moving. While the individual hits didn't seem to do much damage, every Troblin caught by the thorns roared in pain and turned hate-filled eyes on the tank. Behind him, Wule and Seena glowed green, though Hiral couldn't immediately tell what they were doing despite the small pulses of solar energy that signaled they were using abilities—or spells, or whatever they called them. Covering their backs, Yanily and Vix moved like greased lightning, darting in and out of the Troblin ranks and leaving green blood in their wakes.

While the bulk of the enemies was focused on the Grower party, another trio emerged from the woods, something about the one in the middle different from the others. Where most of the Troblins carried weighted clubs or crude blades and wore little more than a loincloth, this one had a staff similar to Seena's and sported a wolf's-head hat. Like Hiral had done, this strange Troblin looked from where most of the Troblins faced off against the Growers, and then turned its attention to Hiral.

Mouth twisting into a lipless, cruel smile, the Troblin lifted a hand to point at Hiral, and a blue notification appeared in front of him.

You have been afflicted with the Lesser Target debuff.
Lesser Target: Enemies will focus on you.

You have been afflicted with the Pile On debuff.
Pile On: Suffer slightly increased stacking damage for every creature beyond one attacking you.

Hiral blinked at the notification, then quickly dismissed it as he looked at the Troblins *all* suddenly turning in his direction. And it wasn't just the ones around the Growers, but more rushing out of the trees to join them. At least twenty, including the strange Troblin that had apparently used **Lesser Target** on him.

Twenty Troblins, each increasing damage by even a *slight* amount, could get pretty dangerous pretty quickly, despite his decent **End**.

"They used **Pile On** on Hiral!" Seena shouted as the mass of Troblins rushed toward him like a wave.

What do I do?

He could run—he *had* to be faster with his 20 **Dex**—but what if more came out of the woods behind him? He'd just be getting further away from the party, and he was sure going to need their help. No, running wasn't the answer. The **Pile On** debuff didn't matter if he didn't get hit, and he'd already proven he could take a single Troblin on. So, Hiral readied his swords and instead charged at the rushing horde of creatures.

Still, this could go very poorly.

Blue notifications sprang to life out of the corner of Hiral's eye as he met the rush of Troblins, but he didn't have time to read them. The first swinging club went for his knees to bring him to the ground, but he pivoted on his lead foot around the attack. Trailing leg coming up at the same time, he spun it over a second weapon, then brought the back of his heel down on a third Troblin with a satisfying crunch that dropped it to the ground.

More movement to his left forced him to dive as soon as his foot touched down, dodging a chopping swing and then rolling under another so close he felt the wind across the back of his neck. Shoulder, back, roll, and he sprang to his feet, both blades lashing out as he rose in a spin. Green blood sprayed in a circle around him as the nearest Troblins fell away from the attack, but more immediately filled the gap.

Bringing his weapons back in close, Hiral moved from offense to defense, parrying aside club after club. Luckily for him, the Troblins' low **Str** meant that, even two-handed, there wasn't a lot of *oomph* behind the swings if he caught the attack properly. Still, there were too many, and though he parried and parried and parried, one got through.

Pain shot up through his hip as the weighted end of a club slammed into it, and a flashing blue notification popped up in front of Hiral's eyes.

You have been afflicted with the Staggering Blow debuff.
Staggering Blow: Reduces Dex by 5 for 1 minute.

The notification vanished almost as quickly as it appeared, but the debuff lingered. The pain lanced through Hiral's hip with every movement, slowing his reaction speed and numbing his leg. For such a small creature and the low *Str* Hiral estimated they had, that blow *hurt*.

Of course. The **Pile On** *debuff. Stacking damage for everyone attacking me if they manage to land a blow. A couple more hits and it won't be the Troblins dying here.*

Redoubling his efforts, Hiral slashed his sword across the face of the Troblin that had hit him. The splash of blood luckily got in the eyes of its nearby comrade, allowing Hiral to mule-kick backwards. The Troblins were so tight around him, he practically couldn't miss, but the power of his kick tossed his unfortunate target toppling straight back to the ground in a tangle with several other Troblins. With a second of breathing room at his back, Hiral launched forward.

Another swinging club came in at his right, so Hiral twisted left and snaked his sword around the attack, pushing it further out with its own momentum. Off balance from the maneuver, the attacking Troblin stumbled into the path of one of its allies and took a crude axe to the face. Green blood burst outward as the Troblin's head nearly exploded.

Critical hit?

Hiral didn't have time to dwell on it, already moving in the other direction as the now headless Troblin fell into the path of the rush from that side.

Stab, parry, slash. His swords worked in quick unison on the small creature directly in front of him, only scoring shallow wounds—but still enough to drive it back—and then he stepped forward on his good leg and leapt over it. Slow to react, the Troblins continued to push toward the center of the circle where he'd just been, while Hiral quick-stepped from head to head, then finally cleared the rush.

Suddenly at the back of the group, Hiral spun around and struck low, hamstringing the nearest pair of Troblins, then turned again to rush away from the mob. Pain lancing up his leg from the overuse turned the *rush* into more of a *stumble*, but Yanily and Vix passed him in a flash as he moved, hitting the pile of Troblins like whirling dervishes.

Yanily's spear moved like a striking serpent, the shaft and blade seemingly defying the laws of being a *solid object* to slip around defenses in a constant stream of blood-drawing stabs. Troblin after Troblin fell in a straight line as the man pushed forward. Vix, on the other hand, danced around the outside of the ring, never slowing as he punched, kneed, and kicked his way past.

All the while, the Troblins basically ignored the two men carving them up, pushing and shoving to get past them and back after Hiral. But then Nivian was there too, his whip snapping in between Yanily and the constantly moving Vix. Glowing green eyes turned to him for the briefest heartbeat, but then the effects of *Lesser Target* took over, and they focused their gaze back on Hiral.

"Can't believe you're still alive—again," Seena said, coming up beside Hiral and raising her staff.

Green light pulsed out of her at the same time Hiral felt a surge of solar energy, and small roots instantly grew out of the ground at the Troblins' feet. The roots weren't thick or tall, but they wrapped around ankles and feet, slowing or tripping the small monsters and making them even easier targets for the damage dealers.

"Me neither," Hiral said, glancing at the three small red icons beside the blue one he could still see in the corner of his eyes. *Are those because of* **Pile On**, *Lesser Target, and* **Staggering Blow***?*

"Wule, can you…?" Seena asked as the other man stepped up beside Hiral as well.

"Are you sure?" he asked.

"Yes, I'm sure. He's part of our party, treat him like one. Please." Another pulse of Seena's green light caused dozens of small… splinters… to appear in the air before her.

"Fine," Wule said as the splinters shot out to embed themselves in any soft Troblin parts they could find. "I'm going to heal you now. Do you have any *debuffs* other than **Pile On**?"

"Something called *Lesser Target* and *Staggering Blow*," Hiral said, swords still at the ready, though Nivian, Yanily, and Vix had things well in hand. "Seena, there was a Troblin dressed differently than the others. It was the one who gave me that **Pile On** debuff."

"What did it…?" she started to ask. "Oh, wolf's head for a hat? Got it. Vix, new target." She pulsed again with green light.

Vix's head immediately turned to look at the strange Troblin, and then the man practically vanished from sight. Appearing beside the Troblin a heartbeat later, Vix ignored the two guards it had with it and laid into it with a vicious combo of punches and knees. The poor monster didn't have a chance, and it dropped to the ground in a bloody mess before its allies even had a chance to react—but even that didn't save them from Vix's follow up.

Whatever the strange Troblin was, its death had an immediate effect on the battle. Two of the red icons vanished from Hiral's vision, and the remaining Troblins all paused and stumbled, like somebody had punched them in the face. Already getting routed by the party, the creatures' sudden stupor spelled the end of the attack, and the last bark-skinned creature quickly fell.

At the same time, there was a pulse of solar energy from Wule, and warmth flowed into Hiral's body, quickly sweeping down and gathering at his hip.

You have been healed by Nature's Mending.
Nature's Mending: Recovers minor injuries, and removes minor debuffs.

Staggering Blow has been removed.

Hiral let out a breath as the pain in his side faded, then shifted a little back and forth to make sure it was completely gone.

"Thanks, Wule," Hiral said. "That's a great ability. Er, spell. Whatever."

"It's a mid-Rank spell, and it has a cooldown of ten seconds, so try not to swim in Troblins again," Wule said. "It also doesn't mend broken bones."

"That cooldown isn't too bad," Hiral said. "Some tattoos have *much* longer cooldowns between abilities."

"You two can talk shop later," Seena said. "How'd we do?" she called ahead to the other three sweeping through the Troblins to make sure they were all dead.

"Didn't *quite* hit nineteen," Yanily said. "Maybe one Troblin short."

Seena rolled her eyes but didn't comment. "Anybody injured? Vix? Nivian? Okay, Wule, can you see to them too? Great. Yanily, you check the bodies for anything valuable; Hiral, you're with me. Two minutes and we're heading to the dungeon." She gestured for Hiral to follow her over to the strange Troblin.

Hiral almost missed the gesture; his eyes were on some flashing notifications that had started popping up during the fight, but had stayed oddly out of the way. He felt like he could pull them out and look at them if he wanted to, but...

"You're probably seeing experience notifications," Seena said. "This is your first *real* fight, right?"

"Oh, is that what those are?" Hiral asked.

"Yeah. Our **PIMs** automatically keep them minimized during combat so they don't distract us. You only see the important notifications, and I'm not sure if you noticed or not, but you don't even really need to *read* them. They pop up, yeah, but somehow your mind knows what they say without taking the time for your eyes to really register all the words." Seena crouched down at the strange Troblin as they got to it.

"So much I don't know about the **PIM**," Hiral said, "but I can ask those questions later. What was this guy?"

"No idea," Seena said. "First time I've seen one of these. Let's see, based on the experience notification, this was a *Troblin Shaman*. You said it debuffed you?"

"Yeah, two debuffs. **Lesser Target** and **Pile On.** I think one may have caused the other."

"Something like that. I have a *Target* spell myself—no *Lesser* part, though. It's what I used to let Vix know what I wanted him to kill. It probably combines with *Pile On* to make the Troblins frenzy like they did. By the way, seriously, good job staying alive. I've only ever seen Vix move like you do. You have some kind of movement-based class?"

"Uh…" Hiral started.

"Nothing of value at all on these guys, and no way I'm doing more than *looking*," Yanily said, coming over to join them. "From a distance. If they keep their stuff under their loincloths, well, they can keep keeping it."

"That's fair—they don't usually have much," Seena said, but grabbed the wolf's-head hat. "Taking this, though. Okay," she called, turning back to the rest of the group, "let's get to that dungeon. We've wasted enough time here."

15

ENTER DUNGEON?

H IRAL pulled up the minimized notifications as he walked.

Level 12 Troblin Warrior defeated. Class experience gained.
No class found.
Experience held in escrow until class enabled.

There were twenty-three of those, ranging in level from 10 to 12, plus the one for the level 13 *Troblin Shaman*, but it looked like Hiral wouldn't benefit from any of the experience until he got his class. Just another thing he was held back from…

He shook his head before he let himself fall down the usual pit of self-pity, then forced his face back to normal.

"Those Troblins were all level ten plus, but why did they seem so… weak?" Hiral asked, the group moving quickly but keeping an eye out for more Troblin ambushes.

"We call anything we fight down here on the surface *monsters*," Seena said from beside him. "Monster levels don't seem to be equivalent to *PIM* and class levels. Don't know why. Anyway, since the level doesn't necessarily describe how tough a fight will be, we also use something we call *CR*, or *Challenge Rating*."

"Okay, and what *CR* would the Troblins have?" Hiral asked.

"Individually, around three or four. We usually add about half a *CR* per extra Troblin beyond one. So, that group we fought would've been around a *CR* of fifteen or sixteen. I might even put it up to seventeen because of the *Shaman*. I think that's why we got slightly above-average experience for each one."

Slightly above average? They must've gotten some kind of numerical value for each monster defeat.

"If the group of us ran into an individual Troblin, we wouldn't get any experience for killing it. They are just too weak for us to learn anything. Oh, and we figure the experience points we get—strange, aren't they?—are actually just the way the *PIM* measures what we learn from the encounter, along with the solar energy we absorb."

"Solar energy?" Hiral asked.

"Didn't you feel it with each Troblin we killed? Like a small burst of energy rushing into you? Ah, maybe you didn't notice it in the heat of the moment.

But, our **PIM**s absorb some of the energy of the monsters we defeat on the surface, which speeds up our growth."

"Wow, no wonder you don't want to share much about the dungeons with Islanders," Hiral said.

If Shapers knew they could speed up leveling by coming down and killing monsters, they'd be all over it. What took decades of training could be accomplished in years or less. Nobody in Fallen Reach had achieved A-Rank in forever—would fighting on the surface let them get through that bottleneck?

If he brought this knowledge back to the Island, he would...

No, he couldn't do that. Not just because of what he'd agreed to, but because if he could finally get a class from the dungeon interface *and* come down to the surface again to fight, he could pass all the Shapers up in Fallen Reach without them ever knowing how.

Heh, how would they feel if suddenly I was the first A-Rank in forever?

"Yes, so don't forget our agreement," Seena said, oblivious to Hiral's internal dialogue.

"You don't have to worry about that," Hiral said. "The secret is safe with me."

"Good."

"Can I ask a couple of other questions, though?"

Seena took a quick look at her surroundings and then at the others in the party. "Sure. We'll be at the dungeon in a couple of minutes, so you have until then."

"How high do **CRs** get?" Hiral asked.

"We do them by Rank. So those Troblins were E-Rank, **CR** seventeen. I've never seen anything above **CR** twenty-five for normal monsters, and we couldn't handle that kind of thing without a full party on the top of their game. D-Rank is quite a bit stronger than E, though, so that E-Rank **CR** twenty-five is about the same as a D-Rank **CR** five or so."

"Makes sense, I guess," Hiral said. "You mentioned *normal* monsters? Is there some other kind?"

"We've run into what are labelled as **Elite** monsters as well. Their **CR** is always way higher than their actual level, but we don't actually know they are **Elite** until we get the experience notification." Seena shrugged. "Still, when something seems particularly tough, we usually assume it's an **Elite**."

"Are there more **Elites** in the dungeons?" Hiral asked.

"Uh..." Seena started, and looked away from Hiral. "You know, it'll be easier to show you than explain. And since we're just about there, let's end the questions for now." She pointed at something on the opposite side of Hiral.

Hiral followed where she pointed to the base of a cliff, expecting to find a large cave, or maybe a small crack they would have to squeeze through. Instead, a carved archway sat nestled in the stone, easily twelve feet tall and seven feet wide. Some kind of symbols were carved into the stone arch from the base all the way to the top, but Hiral couldn't read them. Then again... something about them was familiar. Where had he seen...?

"Normally, dungeons are safe areas. Things like Troblins can't enter, for some reason," Seena said, apparently for Hiral's benefit, but then she looked at the rest of the group. "But that *other* track we saw back on the path, I don't know if it applies to that. Be ready for anything when we go in there."

"Follow me," Nivian said, lifting his shield in front of him. He headed through the archway, Wule close behind, then Yanily and Vix, and finally Seena.

Hiral took one last look at the archway. Something about those symbols— like runes or something—seemed familiar. And the ones on the left looked like mirrored versions of the ones on the right. Were they actually the same, or did it mean something that they were reversed?

This is exactly the kind of thing Gauto would love. And who am I kidding? I wish I could figure it out... Maybe if I can come back to the surface.

"Hiral, you coming?" Seena called from inside.

Hiral pushed his curiosity aside and followed them in. As soon as he passed through the archway, a sensation like dipping underwater passed across his skin, but faded almost as fast.

What was that?

A short hallway, then around a corner, and he'd caught up to where he found them standing.

Standing and staring at the floor littered with dozens of quill-covered corpses, all of them broken and bloody.

"Are those... Quillbacks?" Hiral asked, eying the animals. Each of them would probably stand up to past his knees, and that wasn't even including the forearm-length quills protruding from their backs. They didn't have much in the way of mouths, just short and stubby maws with flat teeth, small ears, and large eyes. Not hunters themselves, from the looks of things.

"They are," Seena said while all five of the Growers eyed the blood-soaked room.

"I thought you didn't kill them to harvest the quills," Hiral said, taking a step closer to a group of corpses off to his right.

From a quick look, all the best quills had been ruined by whatever had killed the animals. There may be a few salvageable ones if the party gave him the time to search, but it wouldn't be a quick process.

"We don't," Seena confirmed. "Killing them ruins the quills. There's a trick to getting them... and this wasn't it."

"Your sister's party didn't do this," Nivian said, as if Seena needed to hear it, "and they aren't here. Only Quillbacks. What do you want to do?"

"Could they have gone deeper into the dungeon?" Hiral asked, looking past the sea of dead animals, only to find a solid wall. "Er, is there even a *deeper?*"

"We think so," Seena said, half-distracted, "but we've never been able to get in. Only these outer rooms where we've found Quillbacks and other animals. Our ancestors *said* there was something more, but as to where it is or how to access it, we don't know."

"Ah, that's why you didn't want to talk about **Elites**," Hiral said, his eyes raking across the room for *anything* that looked like it could be a dungeon interface.

Besides the animal bodies, there also seemed to be what could only be described as nests—piles of sticks, leaves, and other debris that had to have come from outside the dungeon. Was this *really* a dungeon? He hadn't gotten a notification or anything when he'd passed the arch, other than that strange sensation across his skin.

What, did I expect it would be like the training room up on Fallen Reach? Yes, I guess I did, somehow.

"Three minutes," Seena said to the group, snapping Hiral out of his own head. "Look around, see if you can figure out what did this, or if there is any sign of my sister's party. After that, we're heading for the jump point. If they aren't here, that's where they're going, and I'd like to catch up."

The other Growers nodded or voiced a quick affirmative, then spread out to search the room.

"What can I do to help?" Hiral asked. "What am I looking for?"

Seena took a deep breath, then pointed to the far side of the room. "We *think* the dungeon interface is a pedestal on the far side of the room, but we've never gotten it to work. That's what you're here for. Go take a look, but don't get your hopes up."

Hiral's gaze snapped to where she pointed, but he reined in his enthusiasm and looked back at her. At the disappointment and worry over not finding her sister there. "Are you sure? I can help…"

"The others know what they're looking for, and I'm going to search too. It's fine. Do what you came here to do; we're leaving in a few minutes."

"Right, thanks." He quickly picked his way through the carnage.

The room itself was only two hundred feet across or so, and almost perfectly round from the looks of things. *Not natural. Maybe it actually is the dungeon.*

Getting to the other side, he found what had to be the pedestal Seena was referring to. It wasn't much to look at, half-buried by one of the nests, but it was waist height and… yes… it had one of the control crystals embedded in the top. *This better not turn on a shower over my head.*

Hiral waved his hand over the crystal and waited for something to happen, or for a notification to appear. Nothing. Another wave of his hand. Still nothing.

Is it out of solar energy? No, that can't be right. The crystals embedded in the city don't need any external power from us to activate. Maybe the nest is getting in the way...

With that in mind, he tossed aside the branches and leaves, clearing a space around the pedestal. There was another slightly raised area, only a few inches above the ground and about two feet wide, but this one didn't have an embedded crystal in it. *Just a natural part of the cavern? But it's too perfectly round too.* Now branch-free, Hiral waved his hand across the crystal yet again.

Still nothing.

Fallen's balls. What's wrong with this?

"I told you," Seena said before coming up to stand beside him. "We've had generations of people trying to figure it out, but nothing. This might not even be the interface or whatever either."

Hiral pointed at the crystal. "I think it really is. I don't know if you have these, but Fallen Reach has them all over. We use crystals like this to control all kinds of things in the city."

"Do you know how they work?" Seena asked, a brief hunger in her eyes.

He shrugged. "No. Kind of like you and your ancestors talking about tracks and dungeons, these crystals have been there as long as we've been in Fallen Reach, and they just sort of... work."

"How do you use them?"

"Just wave your hand over them like this," Hiral said, passing his hand above the crystal again. He jumped to the side as light sprang out of the slightly raised patch of floor to his left. "What in the...?" he started at the same time Seena cursed and moved, but then he recognized the way the light formed into a humanoid shape.

It was just like the red and blue opponents up in the *Time Trial*, except this one was *much* more detailed. Where the *Time Trial* only used two colors, this image had *every* color, and even mixed several of them.

Within seconds, the nearly perfect image of an older man stood in front of them, his hands calmly clasped in front of him.

"Welcome, challengers, to the ***Splitfang Keep Dungeon***. Please choose an option," the image said, and a blue notification window sprang up beside him.

Tutorial
Enter Dungeon
Help

"What... what did you do?" Seena asked Hiral while he stared at the lifelike image of the man.

"I..." Hiral started.

"What's this?" Nivian asked as he came over to join them, the others quickly following behind.

"No idea," Seena said. "But it looks like Hiral here managed to get the dungeon interface working."

"Are you kidding?" Wule said. "It only works for Islanders?"

But Hiral was already shaking his head. "No, I don't think so. I tried a couple of times, and it didn't work until Seena came over and stood beside me." He glanced down to find faint circles of light around their feet. Blue for Hiral and green for Seena. *Didn't she say her status window was green?* And, on the pedestal beside the crystal, glowing blue and green dots. *Looks like there are two more dots too, though they aren't lit up.*

"Do we have time for this?" Nivian asked. "We've got to catch up with Seeyela's party."

"If we got it turned on, maybe my sister's party did too?" Seena offered.

"It might be able to tell us itself, actually," Hiral said before selecting **Help**. The blue window vanished, and the image of the man shimmered slightly and was replaced by another version of him with his arms crossed.

"Is it recording yet?" the image asked. "Oh? Oh, it is? Well, why didn't you say something?" He straightened his face and dropped his hands back down to clasp in front of himself again. "Please ask your questions."

"Who are you?" Vix asked before Hiral could speak up.

The image smiled. "I am Dr. Gulabi Benza, Director of Dungeon Construction."

"Are you real?" Vix quickly followed up.

"Of course not. I'm a hologram," the image of Dr. Benza snapped, then looked off to the side. "What? Why should I be patient? That was a stupid question. Sure, sure, whatever. Edit it out later."

Hiral quickly held up a hand to forestall any further questions from Vix, then spoke up himself. "Can you show us the top clear times for **Splitfang Keep**?"

The image of Dr. Benza shimmered quickly, then he gestured to his side, where a notification window appeared.

Splitfang Keep – Dungeon
E-Rank
Top Clear Times
XXX : --:--
YYY : --:--
ZZZ : --:--
Close Window

"Looks like nobody has cleared the dungeon yet," Hiral said, rubbing his chin. *This dungeon is E-Rank, like they'd said. So, even if they've never gotten in before—assuming they're telling the truth—then their ancestors must've. How else would they know the Rank? But... no clear times. Do they reset after a certain amount of time, or has nobody ever cleared it?*

"Nobody has cleared it?" Seena asked, echoing Hiral's thoughts. "Does that mean my sister's party...?" She trailed off, her voice cracking at the implication.

"Not necessarily," Hiral said, swiping the notification window closed. Dr. Benza shimmered again and took up his hands-in-front pose. "Has anybody entered *Splitfang Keep*?" Hiral asked.

Another image shimmer. "No. The dungeon is available for a party to enter and is not on cooldown," Dr. Benza said, before shimmering back to his starting pose.

"What does *on cooldown* mean?"

"Please refer to the *Tutorial* for questions on dungeon mechanics," Dr. Benza replied, his face looking somewhat... impatient.

"My guess would be they aren't here," Hiral said. "But let me test one more thing quickly."

Before the others could object, Hiral took several steps back until the blue circle around his feet faded. The blue dot on the pedestal and Dr. Benza flickered out at the same time.

"What happened? Where did it go?" Seena asked.

"Nivian, stand where I was, and wave your hand over the crystal there," Hiral instructed, and after a nod from Seena—she really was the party leader—Nivian did as told.

Nothing happened.

Hiral tested the next possibility. "Seena, can you try the crystal too?"

Still nothing.

"Kind of what I expected," Hiral said before walking up to stand beside Nivian and Seena. "One more time, Seena, please."

This time, when Seena waved her hand over the crystal, the image of Dr. Benza sprang to life again.

"Welcome, challengers, to the *Splitfang Keep Dungeon*. Please choose an option," the image said, and a blue notification window sprang up beside him.

Tutorial
Enter Dungeon
Help

Hiral pointed down at the ground so the others saw the colored circles on the floor, then to the matching dots on the pedestal. "For whatever reason, it looks like it takes representatives from both our peoples to activate it, though I have no idea why. And, based on the dots there, I wonder if there are two more races..."

"Why would the pedestal need Growers and Makers together?" Yanily asked.

"No idea. Probably an answer in that *Tutorial* there, but…" Hiral trailed off.

"But we don't have time. We need to go," Seena filled in. "Hiral, I'd love to find out more about this, just as much as you, but we simply don't have time if Seeyela and the others aren't here. We'll come back next rotation, and you can come with us.

"Let's head to the jump point," she said to the others, though her eyes lingered on the strange image right in front of her. Another quick grimace and she turned away, then took two steps toward the exit. "You coming?" she asked Hiral.

Instead of answering Seena, he spoke to the image. "*Help.*" He waited until the status window vanished and the image shifted. "I've got a class reward I'd like to claim from an achievement—how can I do this?"

The image predictably shimmered. "Class rewards can only be claimed from the dungeon interface found within a dungeon after clearing it. Rewards cannot be issued by access interfaces, such as this one. Please enter and complete the dungeon to claim your reward, along with the usual dungeon loot."

"Loot?" Hiral asked before he could stop himself.

"Please refer to the *Tutorial* for questions on dungeon mechanics," Dr. Benza replied, his face again looking impatient.

"Hiral, now or never," Seena called back.

Hiral didn't turn around to face her, his eyes glued to the strange image. Could he clear an E-Rank dungeon by himself? He could go in and try while Seena went looking for her sister. He probably wouldn't be able to get back up to the city until it came around next rotation, even if he made it through. Would it be an obstacle course like the *Time Trial*?

Who was he kidding? Even if he made it through, nobody survived on the surface once the rains came. It would be suicide to go in… but at least maybe he'd finally get his class.

And what good is a class, idiot, if I'm dead?

"Coming," Hiral called, forcefully tearing his eyes from the image. "Thank you for staying close so I could ask my questions," he said quietly to her, and noticed the others were already over by the exit.

"You had about three more seconds before I left anyway," Seena said. "We'll be back. Now that we know *how* to access an interface… well, it's time to find out what's actually in those dungeons."

"Loot, apparently," Hiral said as he and Seena exited the cave. "Whatever *loot* means."

16

TRY GIVING IT A SANDWICH

THEY left the cave the same way they came in, all of them pausing only briefly to look at the oncoming storm-wall. Less than fifteen hours until it was on them, but they'd gotten to the dungeon pretty quickly.

"How far is the jump point?" Hiral asked, looking up at the islands floating high above.

"Almost fifty miles," Seena said. "I hope your endurance holds up."

"Me too," Hiral mumbled as the group turned from the storm and started up a different path than they'd arrived from.

Nivian set a faster pace, though Seena told everybody to keep their eyes open for any sign of her sister's party. Or more Troblins. If Hiral had possessed any real expertise with tracking, he would've done the same, but his mind was stuck on the dungeon, replaying over and over the things the strange image had said.

To get his achievement award, he'd need to get *into* the dungeon and clear it, but that still didn't actually guarantee he'd get a class. Would he get to the end only to get turned down there too? Or, would that interface at least give him some idea what was wrong with him? Sure, it would be great if it handed a class over to him, but even a hint as to where he was going wrong would be enough.

Something. Anything to get him on the right track.

And Seena had said they'd be coming back, and they'd *need* him—or another Maker—if they wanted to access the dungeon.

*Why does it need a Grower and a Maker both present to activate that interface? What could possibly be the reasoning for it? And that's not even getting into what the dungeon actually is, and how it connects to our **PIM**s. Why did somebody go to all the trouble to build something like that?*

The questions rattled around in Hiral's head nonstop as the hours and miles passed, his high base **End** enabling him to keep up with the E-Ranked growers. It was actually Wule who slowed down first, and Hiral pulled himself out of his own head and looked at his surroundings for the first time.

Still in the forest, but the trees had gotten bigger. Not just the width of their trunks, which would take at least two or three people wrapping their arms around to touch each other's hands, but also their height. The rigidly straight trees stretched hundreds of feet in the air, and seemed to have some kind of needles instead of leaves on their branches.

"We'll take a few-minute break here," Seena said, also breathing more heavily. "We're making good time, and we're probably halfway there, so drink some water and…"

She cut off as something *cracked* in the woods, like a branch breaking, and the entire party turned in that direction.

"Could it be…?" Yanily started, but cut off as Wule put a hand on his shoulder and gently shook his head.

Nivian's thorny whip and shield grew from his hands after a brief pulse of energy, and that seemed to be some kind of signal for the others. Weapons came out and Wule buffed the party with a quick ***Nature's Bulwark***, while Hiral drew the pair of swords from over his shoulders.

"Standard formation," Seena said, sidestepping in beside Wule, who stood directly behind Nivian.

Vix and Yanily took up positions on the outside of the small triangle, and Hiral moved in behind the group to stay out of their way. It sure *felt* cowardly, but he'd cause more harm than good if he interrupted their teamwork.

Another branch *cracked* from the same side of the small path, this time much closer, and the group shifted slightly to make sure Nivian was at the front.

"Speak up if you get an eye on whatever it is," Seena instructed. "We know what we can take, even without Julka. Like more Troblins. But, if it's not something that goes down quickly, I'll slow it with ***Snaring Roots***, and then we're running. Getting to the jump point is more important than a bit of experience."

"So close to level nineteen," Yanily whined quietly, though he eventually nodded.

All eyes stayed on the woods, the air still and humid on the forest floor, and everything stiflingly quiet. *Were there animal sounds before? Birds? Anything? I don't remember. Maybe after the first Troblin ambush.*

Another *crack* came, like something heavy stepped on a branch, and there was movement between the trees.

"There," Nivian said as something rounded one of the large trees.

Taller than any of the party members by at least solid foot, the thing was all hard lines and sharp edges, with the light between the branches reflecting off its polished surface. Three arms—no, four, with one of them broken off just below the elbow. Walking on two legs, it had a body seemingly made of solid crystal and a faceless head that turned in their direction.

Turned in *Hiral's* direction.

Even without eyes, he could feel it looking at him, like the others hardly mattered.

"Look at its feet," Vix hissed, and Hiral did.

Like the rest of the body, the feet were angular and rigid as the thing took a step forward. Two toes on the front, and one on the back—this was the thing that'd made the track on the path before. The thing they'd been told to avoid at all costs.

"Plan?" Yanily asked, his spear angled toward the crystal monster in a ready position.

"Move up the road, slowly," Seena said. "Maybe it's not interested in us."

"Not our usual luck," Wule said dryly, but they moved down the road as a group, shifting to keep all eyes on the monster as it took another step forward.

"Nivian, throw it a sandwich or something to keep it busy," Yanily hissed out of the side of his mouth.

"It's not a dog, Yan," Nivian said quietly.

"Doesn't even have a mouth…" Vix added.

"Would you all just shut up?" Seena snapped in a whisper, turning her attention back to the monster. "Good monster. Good boy." She spoke like she was trying to calm a wild animal, though she still held her staff in front of her. "Keep moving."

"*She's* treating it like a dog," Yanily said. "Try the sandwich."

"I'm *not*…" Nivian started, only to cut off at another glare from Seena.

The group shifted a bit more, and the monster's gaze followed them. Its body turned again in their direction as it took its next step.

Crack. Another branch broke beneath its foot, and everybody jumped at the sudden noise.

"Pretty sure it's interested in us," Nivian said, the thing not more than thirty feet from them. "Fight or flight?"

"Sandwich!" Yanily insisted.

Everybody ignored him.

"How fast do you think it is?" Wule asked.

"Faster than you," Vix said.

Even with the rough terrain off the side of the path, Vix was probably right. Sure, it was moving slowly and steadily now, but there was an atmosphere of coiled tension around it. Like it was waiting to explode into motion.

"Flight," Seena said, apparently sensing the same thing. "On my mark…" She raised her staff, and there was a pulse of solar energy from her.

The roots hadn't even sprouted an inch from the ground before the crystal monster sprang forward, covering the thirty feet in the blink of an eye.

"Look out!" somebody screamed, and the thing was on them.

Nivian's shield came out of nowhere to block the thing's leading hand, which had its palm open as though reaching for something, but the tight-wound vine blasted apart at the slightest touch, and its fingers wrapped around his arm. Then Nivian was in the air, tossed aside like a children's toy—if the child could throw a grown man fifteen feet with barely a shrug.

Wule and Seena reflexively stepped back, while Hiral rushed between them to delay the monster, and Vix and Yanily came in from the sides. Another of the monster's hands shifted toward Yanily, almost too fast to see, and there was a shimmer like a soap bubble bursting. Everything on the ground in a wide cone in front of the hand, including Yanily, shot backwards, leaving a widening scar in the ground. The poor Grower hurtled through the underbrush.

A grunt—he must've hit something—and he was gone.

Vix came in hard from the other side, fists *pack, pack, packing* as he landed a trio of blows against the crystal skin, then quick-stepped back as the head turned toward him. Form blurred from the buff he gave himself, he sprinted right to try and circle around behind the monster, but the third hand came up like it was reaching for him, even though he was ten feet away.

A brief look of confusion passed across Vix's face, and then he lunged ahead, like something had grabbed him by the shirt and pulled.

Hiral leapt forward, colliding with Vix and throwing them both to the ground as the monster's fist sailed through the air right where Vix would've gone. They hit the dirt and rolled apart, Hiral being the first to his feet. He spun around just in time to see the monster's open palm reaching for him.

The same palm that'd blasted Nivian's shield into little pieces.

Even with his 20 **Dex**, he was too slow, the thing in front of him moving infinitely faster. Somehow, his mind had time to tell him there was no way this thing could be E-Rank, or even D, for that matter. It had to be C-Rank or above, which meant it was way out of their league.

And then the hand was just inches in front of his chest, palm glowing from some kind of symbol etched into the crystal.

Another one of those strange runes…?

Hiral braced for the contact—there wasn't anything else he could do—but the ground erupted in a shower of dirt and forest debris as the hand reached for him. Thick roots, like large spikes as wide as Hiral's leg, pin-cushioned the monster, and though none of them were able to pierce its crystal skin, they did a good job of stopping its movement.

For the moment.

"Run. Run now!" Seena shouted, releasing another pulse of energy as smaller roots grew out of the large spikes to further entangle the monster.

Hiral looked at the head, which gave him the feeling the monster was gazing into his soul, then dashed past the immobile creature and ran toward where Yanily had been hurled.

The spearman was already coming out of the woods, one arm over Nivian's shoulder. With a quick glance back at the trapped crystal monster, the party fled down the path as fast as they could.

17

WHAT COULD BE WORSE THAN TROBLINS? OH...

H IRAL looked back as they ran. "How long do you think that will hold it?"
"Not nearly long enough," Seena said. "Let's just hope we aren't worth the trouble to chase."

"Do monsters usually give chase?" Hiral asked as he looked over at Yanily, who half-limped along with Nivian's help. Nothing *looked* broken, but he was obviously hurt.

"They all seem to have territory they won't go outside," Seena said, also looking back over her shoulder. "If we can get far enough away, that thing should lose interest."

"Should?"

"Should," Seena reaffirmed, though there wasn't much confidence in her voice.

"We need to stop for a second," Wule spoke up. "Give me a chance to heal Yanily. We'll move faster if Nivian isn't carrying him the entire way."

"Really think we should keep going," Vix said. "That thing took us apart in short order."

"All the more reason to have Yanily in his best shape," Wule countered.

"Could just leave him as bait. We don't have to be faster than the monster, just faster than Yan."

"I'll remember that," Yanily said.

"No, you won't. You don't even remember what you had for breakfast," Vix replied.

"Uh... I had..." Yanily started, looking at Nivian for support.

"Seena?" Nivian asked to interrupt the banter, but he hadn't slowed, and neither had Yanily.

"How bad is it, Yanily?" Seena asked.

"I can keep going," the man said.

"Could you keep going *faster* if Wule healed you?"

"Yes," he said immediately. "I don't think anything's broken. I just hit the tree funny."

"Just hit the tree funny, he says," Vix deadpanned. "Like it happens every day."

"One spell," Seena said, slowing to a stop. "Make it a good one, Wule."

"I should really take a look and see how bad…" Wule started, but then he looked at Seena's face. "Right. One spell," he mumbled, a plant growing out of the palm of his hand. This one was a green so vibrant, it practically glowed, and the flower that bloomed was a deep blood red. With his other hand, Wule reached out and touched Yanily's shoulder, and energy pulsed from the flower before it turned to dust. "How are you feeling?"

Yanily winced, more like he was expecting pain than actually feeling it, then nodded. "Yeah, much better."

"Hey, guys," Vix said, something about the catch in his voice making everybody turn toward him and get ready for a fight. But it wasn't a crystal monster charging down the path after them—no, he was holding some kind of pouch in his hands.

"What… Where…where did you find that?" Seena asked, rushing over and grabbing the bag out of his hand.

Hiral looked at Nivian and raised an eyebrow.

"It's her sister's," Nivian said. "I think it was a birthday gift or something from Seena."

"A bit in the woods over here," Vix said, and started off the path.

Hiral looked back down the path they'd come from and *almost* asked if they had time for this. But if it was a clue about Seeyela's location, well, that was exactly the reason they were there in the first place.

But, why did it seem like that monster was interested in me? Because I'm the weakest? Or was it all just my imagination?

"More stuff over here," Yanily said from a bit deeper in the woods, the rest of the party apparently having spread out to look around while Hiral was lost in thought. "Hey, I know this spear. This is Balyo's."

"What is their stuff doing here…?" Nivian asked as Hiral jogged in to meet up with the rest of the group.

All five of the Growers were moving through the random smattering of equipment strewn about the forest floor. More weapons, a couple other packs, and some bloodied bandages, which got a worried look from Wule and Seena both.

"They must be around here somewhere, right?" Seena asked with a lilt in her voice, looking around. She put her hands up her to mouth like she was going to shout, but Hiral clamped his hand onto her wrist.

"Wait," he said.

"We don't have time to wait," Wule snapped.

"I know, but think about it for a second. This stuff, it's all in one place. Like it's been *dumped* here. Your sister and her party wouldn't do that, right? This obviously isn't some kind of camp site, which means somebody else threw this stuff here."

"So? That's all the more reason we need to find them," Seena said, pulling on her arm, but Hiral didn't let go.

"Look, I'm not as familiar with the surface as you—obviously—and I don't know a lot about the monsters you usually encounter down here. But how many of them are *thinkers*? That spear looks like it's decent quality. If this was Troblins or something, wouldn't they have taken the weapon?" He gently let go of Seena's wrist.

"Yeah, they would've," Seena said, looking at the spear in Yanily's hand and calming down a bit from her earlier excitement.

"Would they leave the stuff so they could move faster to get to the jump point?" Hiral asked. The Growers looked at each other, then shook their heads. "So, that means they ran into something strong enough to capture them, and not need their equipment. What lives in these woods that fits that description?"

Again, the Growers looked at each other.

"Nothing," Seena said finally. "At least, nothing we know of. Like I said, everything around here *should* be E-Rank. That's the only reason we're allowed to come down here. If there were higher-Rank monsters, we would send higher-Rank parties."

"Other than that crystal thing," Hiral reminded them, once again glancing back the way they'd come. No sign of it. Maybe it had lost interest, like Seena said it would. "Any chance it could've done this?"

"That's the first time we've actually seen one of those things in forever," Wule said. "We didn't even know what made the tracks until a few minutes ago. If anybody had seen it, they would've shared that information with everybody else right away."

"If they'd survived the encounter," Hiral said, only to immediately regret his words when he saw Seena look at the pouch in her hands. "I'm sorry," he said quietly.

"No, you're right, but I also think you're wrong," Seena said. "That… thing… we ran into, it didn't seem keen on capturing us. I think something else did this."

Yeah, it seemed keen on getting to me… but I'm glad nobody else noticed that.

"Any D- or C-Rank areas nearby?" Hiral asked, instead of dwelling on the strange crystal monster. "Any monsters that could've come from there?"

"Hey, guys," Vix interrupted, "I think there might be a trail here…" He pointed at the ground where, yeah, it *looked* like several people may've walked.

"We're following it, right?" Yanily asked, dropping the other spear to the ground and putting both hands on his own.

"We're following it," Seena confirmed.

"Any other tracks? Like the two-toed-and-made-out-of-crystal kind?" Nivian asked.

"No, at least not that I can see. These all look the same to me," Vix said.

"So, either their captors didn't leave tracks, or the tracks are similar enough to our own we don't notice," Hiral said. "Right?"

"Sounds about right. Means they're humanoid," Seena said. "About our size. Rules out of a lot of things."

"What's the worst thing it could be, around here?" Hiral asked.

"Duggers," Nivian said immediately.

"And they are…?"

"Like Troblins' big, angry brothers. D-Rank, but usually hundreds of miles back the way we came. Never seen any around here."

"Individually, they'd be a D-Rank *CR* of seven or eight. In a group, well, they travel in packs of five or six," Seena added.

"Not something we can take, then," Hiral said, and the Growers shook their heads.

"They aren't real fast, though, or smart," Seena said. "If we can distract them, get Seeyela and the others away, we can make a run for it."

"That's the plan, then," Nivian said. "We find the Duggers, distract them, rescue Seeyela and her party, then we bolt. Get to the jump point as quick as we can."

"How fast are they?" Hiral asked.

"Dexterity in the high teens, probably," Vix said. "Pretty slow."

"For you, maybe," Yanily said. "That'd catch the rest of us."

"Then I guess it's me and Vix on distraction duty," Hiral said, the chance at finally being *needed* shushing the part of his brain screaming this was a bad idea.

"Duggers don't like *stuff*, which would explain why my sister's equipment is still here," Seena said. "They *do* like slaves, though. Probably why they took the whole party instead of killing them. But they also have a nasty temper. You're going to need to piss them off to get them to chase you."

"I'll figure something out," Hiral said.

"*We'll* figure something out, you mean," Vix said as he came over and put his arm over Hiral's shoulder. "Don't listen to what Nivian says about you when you're not looking. You're not bad for an Islander," he said in his usual flat tone.

"What does he say about me when I'm not looking?"

"Just told you not to worry about it."

"Enough," Seena said. "Hiral, can you find your way back to the path?"

"Yes," Hiral said without hesitation. "I've got a pretty good memory, and an eye for things. I won't get lost."

"He figured out the wingsuit pretty quick—I'd believe it," Yanily piped up.

"Okay, then that's the plan. Vix and Hiral, piss off the Duggers and get them to chase you. While you lead them away, we'll get my sister and her party away from there. The path we were on leads right to the jump point, though it's still a few miles from here. We'll meet there."

"Hey, why didn't you ask if I could find the path again?" Vix asked.

"Focus," Seena said. "Let's go."

With that, the party moved forward, following the trail while Hiral tried to figure out the best way to get these Dugger creatures to chase him. Insulting their mothers probably wouldn't do anything. Stabbing one in the face? Though, if they were D-Rank like Seena was saying, would he even be able to injure one? Or would his sword just bounce off harmlessly?

Well, he'd have to…

Nivian held up a fist from his lead position of the group, causing everybody to pause and drop into a crouch, then pointed at the side of his head.

What is he…? Oh!

Hiral focused on his hearing and… there… Yes, voices. Somebody was talking.

Do Duggers have conversations?

The party stayed silent, moving up through the underbrush between the wide trees until they came upon a small clearing. There in the middle, in a circle, were what had to be Seeyela and her party, wrists tied behind their backs. Most of them just looked to have mild injuries, but at least one appeared to be unconscious, while another's arm was *definitely* not supposed to bend that way.

And there, past the prisoners, were their captors. Seena had been wrong, so *very* wrong about what the worst thing could've been. Hiral found his breath caught in his throat as he looked at the five towering, tattooed Shapers.

18

A DESPERATE RESCUE

HIRAL'S brain stalled out for a second as he looked at the group of Shapers talking on one end of the clearing, but he held a hand out to the five Grower heads that quickly turned accusing looks in his direction.

"Wait," he mouthed to them while he patted the air. "Just wait. Please."

What are Shapers doing down here? And why do they have Seeyela and her party? Did they rescue them from the Duggers? No… who am I kidding? They obviously captured the Growers all on their own. But, why?

Nivian, Vix, Yanily, and Wule all turned their attention to Seena, but she stared *hard* at Hiral, weighing him and his possible involvement.

"I have no idea," he mouthed while pointing at the chatting Shapers, whose words carried clearly as if they didn't care whether the captured Growers heard them or not. Worse still, they were all Shapers Hiral recognized—a group of popular C-Rank fighters from the Amphitheatre of the Sun.

This wasn't a group Seena's party had *any* chance against in a fight. Hiral held his hand up to form a "C," then pointed at the Shapers. "C-Rank," he mouthed, and made the same shape with his hand again.

Seena's eyes widened a little as she understood, and she glanced back to her sister's captured party.

Please don't do anything stupid.

Seena turned back to Hiral and mouthed, "Make this right."

Hiral nodded—make this right? How in the Fallen's ratty socks was he supposed to do that?—and focused on what the Shapers were talking about.

"Just leave them tied up," Shaper Hizix said. "The rains will take care of them for us."

"Stop wussing out," another Shaper, Gunimat, said. "If we want to be sure, we should kill them now, ourselves."

"Guni is right," Shaper Hadeval added. "It's the only way to be sure."

"But they're people," Hizix countered.

"People with bad luck," Hadeval said. "They saw us. We can't let that get back up to the islands."

"And besides, they aren't *really* people. They're just Buggers," Shaper Madizon said with a shrug of her wide, tattooed shoulders. "It's almost like a mercy."

"A mer… mercy?" Hizix asked. "How can you even say that? Maybe… maybe they can tell us how to harvest the quills properly? We can ask them… again."

Hadeval pointed at the Grower with the broken arm. "If they didn't talk after that…"

"We'll figure out how to harvest the quills on our own with a bit more practice," a new voice said, and a much smaller man stepped out of the trees near the Shapers, two more tattooed women beside him. "Just kill them and get it over with. We need to get back up to the city before anybody catches on these Buggers are missing and decides to send somebody down looking."

Unlike the Shapers, the new man wore a long robe that completely covered everything from his neck down, leaving only his head and hands bare. The Meridian Lines peeking beyond his cuffs and on his face glowed faintly, signaling long years of their use, but he wouldn't have any tattoos hidden beneath the fabric.

An Artist, like Hiral's father.

They'd come down looking to harvest quills on their own, to cut the Nomads out of the trade cycle, which meant they were the ones who'd killed the Quillbacks in the dungeon.

Do they know about the dungeons, then? The interface? Or did they just think it was some kind of cave?

"Sir," Hizix said, stepping toward the Artist, "this isn't what we came down here for. To kill Nomads, I mean. It's not what we signed up for."

"Just shut up, Hizix, okay?" Gunimat said. "When did you get all soft on Buggers? It doesn't matter what we signed up for. Our employer is asking us to do something, and paying well for it. So, we do it."

Hizix opened his mouth as if to say something else, but the other Shapers just looked at him, and his shoulders shrank as if he'd given up. "Fine. Whatever. Let's just get back up to the city before the rains get here."

"About time," the Artist said before looking at one of the two women beside him. "Get our transport ready."

"Yessir," she said, putting her hand up to her shoulder and the ***Disc of Passage*** tattoo there.

Fallen's balls, that's Shaper Velina. She's B-Rank! This is way, way, way out of our league. But, if we don't do anything… if I don't do something… they're going to kill Seeyela and her party. What can I do to stop them, though…?

Hiral tore his eyes away from Shaper Velina as she began the process of shaping the ***Disc of Passage***—it would take at least several seconds—and focused on the other Shapers and the surrounding trees. There had to be *something* he could do.

There was no way he could fight them, but maybe, like the original plan, some kind of distraction?

A branch *cracked* somewhere off in the woods, and Hiral caught the flash of reflected light between the trees to his right.

Oh, this probably isn't the best idea.

Then he was up and running toward the Shapers, only sparing the briefest second to gesture to the Growers to stay down. Hopefully, they would trust him long enough for this to work.

"Thank the Fallen you're here," Hiral shouted as he burst into the small clearing, his high **Dex** making it so he passed through the underbrush with barely a whisper. "I thought I was going to be trapped down here with the rains coming."

Seven Shapers and the Artist snapped their attention in his direction, tattoos shaping into weapons and Meridian Lines flaring with power at his surprise appearance.

"What in the…?" Shaper Gunimat said.

"Is that… Everfail?" another voice whispered, but it carried clearly enough for the question to reach Hiral's ears.

Despite the words, he forced himself to pretend he didn't hear it, and he walked past the group of Grower prisoners without even looking at them.

"You have to take me back up to Fallen Reach with you," Hiral said, continuing on toward the left side of the clearing, putting himself on one side of the Shaper group. He gestured with his hands as he talked to keep their attention on him. "Man, I can't believe how lucky I am."

"What… what are you doing here?" Shaper Hadeval asked. "*How* are you here?"

"I'll explain on the way back up," Hiral said, but Shaper Velina had faltered in her shaping of the **Disc of Passage** at his surprise entrance. "I really, really thought I was going to be stuck down here."

"No, I think it's best you explain now," the Artist said. "You're obviously from Fallen Reach with those Meridian Lines, but who…?" His eyes narrowed. "You're the Dorin kid. The useless one."

Hiral couldn't stop himself from wincing at the comment, but the Artist continued as if he didn't even notice.

"Just kill him too. As much as I hate to do Dorin any favors…" the Artist said, like he had a bad taste in his mouth, before turning back to Shaper Velina. "Well, where's our transport?"

"K-kill…?" Hiral asked, and he didn't have to fake the surprise in his voice at how casually the Artist had just ordered that. From the looks on the Shapers' faces, they were just as shocked… except they all hardened very quickly, other than Hizix. "Woah, woah, woah," Hiral said, holding up his hands and stepping back.

"Sorry, Everfail—not your lucky day either, it seems," Shaper Hadeval said as he took a step in Hiral's direction.

"Pretty sure this is a mercy too," Shaper Madizon said, also stepping forward.

Hiral's eyes went from Shaper to Shaper, four of the towering men and women stalking in his direction while he scrambled backwards. "Hey, what is this? I'm one of you!"

"Nah, you've never been one of us, Everfail," Madizon said.

"Too bad it wasn't someone who could put up a bit more of a fight," Gunimat said. "Would've been kind of fun to let loose down here where there aren't any rules."

"Let loose all you want on this one," Madizon said, continuing to advance on Hiral. "Just don't expect anything back. Though, I hear he is kind of good at running away."

"What do you say, Everfail?" Shaper Gunimat asked, his hand shaping a simple sword from the tattoo on his opposite arm. "You going to make this fun for us? Put up a fight? Try to run away?"

Hiral backed up another step, the edge of the clearing right at his heels, and seriously considered just running away. With his **Dex**, he could probably do it. That *had* been the original plan anyway. But as flames danced on Shaper Hadeval's palms from the **Way of Fire** tattoo, and as Madizon shaped a large bow, he realized they'd just cut him down as soon as he turned his back.

Instead of dashing into the trees and hoping they missed their opening salvo, he reached up over his shoulders and drew his two swords. "We don't have to do this," he said slowly. "I'm sure you're just *joking*. Right? A big joke we can all laugh about on the way back to Fallen Reach. One you can tell all your friends when we get there…"

"Oh, don't worry—we'll laugh about this, alright," Hadeval said, the flames roiling in his hands.

Even though the **Way of Fire** was a B-Rank tattoo, with Hadeval only being C-Rank, he wouldn't be able to use its full potential. Still, considering Hiral was basically *no-Rank* with no class, it'd probably still turn his bones to ash if it hit him. That wasn't even considering the C-Rank weapons the others had shaped.

This… yup… Definitely a bad idea.

"Fine, how do you want to do this, then?" Hiral asked, dropping into a fighting stance with one blade pointed at the Shapers and the other held defensively. "One at a time, or do you all need to come at me at once?"

"All at…? Is he kidding right now?" Hadeval asked.

"It's a good question. I mean, who gets to enjoy this? Should we draw lots or something?" Gunimat asked.

Hiral spared a glance behind the group of Shapers, another flash of reflected light catching his attention, but also made sure not to look at the captured Growers at all. *That's it. Keep talking.*

"Stop talking," the Artist said, frustration clear in his voice. "No drawing lots. Hadeval, burn him. Burn him so badly nobody will ever recognize who he was, even if they find the body."

Hadeval's mouth split in a wide grin. "You got it, boss."

Oh, Fallen's...

The bushes behind the Shapers parted as the three-armed crystal monster stepped into the clearing, its gaze firmly on Hiral. It began stalking toward him at the same time Shaper Velina's *Disc of Passage* manifested directly in front of it. Velina was the first to notice it, and she opened her mouth to say something, but the monster reached out with one of its hands, palm glowing, and grabbed the edge of the floating, thirty-foot-diameter disc.

Like it had been carved into thousands of small, perfectly equal cubes, the disc exploded apart with a sound like tearing paper, and enough force to shoot Velina into the underbrush like an arrow.

Everybody jumped at the sudden sound, the Shapers spinning around to find the crystal monster stepping through the haze of solar energy left by the thousands of cubes dissipating.

"What is *that*?" Madizon asked.

"Who cares?" the Artist shouted back. "Kill it!"

Hiral momentarily forgotten, Hadeval hurled a head-sized ball of flame at the approaching monster. Another of the creature's hands came up, palm glowing again, and suddenly, the fire rebounded like it'd hit something. Right back into Hadeval's chest.

The seven-foot Shaper cursed and fell back, the flames in his hands winking out as he lost control of the magic due to the pain. Even before he hit the ground, Madizon was moving toward the monster, but not of her own volition. No, she flew through the air like she'd been yanked, only to collide with a crystal haymaker punch.

Folding over the fist at the impact, the Shaper let out a pained grunt, blood erupting from her mouth. The monster's follow-through hurled her into the trees. Sounds of breaking wood and branches spelled out her path, until a very solid *thump* signaled the end of her flight.

"What are you doing?" the Artist shouted from far too close to the monster, though it seemed to be ignoring him.

Why?

No time to really get answers to his questions, Hiral bolted toward the captured Growers while the rest of the Shapers charged at the crystal monster.

Seena and the others were already to the group by the time he arrived, helping them to their feet and leading them into the woods.

Good. They have it taken care of.

With that part of it done, all that was left was to escape… and hope the Shapers didn't follow them.

Hiral glanced back toward the melee—another of the Shapers was on the ground, Gunimat this time, while Hadeval was back up. It was Hizix, though, that caught Hiral's attention. The man was looking right at him. Their eyes met. Hizix held his two-handed sword in a white-knuckled grip, but he made a small, sharp shake of his head—just one, to the side—and then turned and charged at the crystal monster.

He's letting us go.

Not wanting to waste the generosity—or the opportunity—Hiral took one last look at the strange crystal monster taking apart the group of C- and B-Rank Shapers, then charged into the forest after the Growers.

19

TRUST

I T didn't take Hiral long to catch up to the others; the injured caused them to move more slowly, and he ran up join Seena. She had one of the four women from the other Grower party—her sister, by the resemblance—beside her, and both of them immediately turned their heads at his arrival.

"You won't take us back…" the sister started.

"What was *that* all about?" Seena asked at the same time, then had to put herself between Hiral and Seeyela as the sister lunged at him. "Slow down. He's not with them. I don't think, at least. He's about to *explain* things very clearly right now."

"I don't *know*," Hiral said, but Nivian and one of the new additions joined them as they continued moving through the woods, the sounds of the fight echoing behind them.

"Explanations will have to wait," Nivian said. "We need to get further away before any of those Islanders come after us. And we're already making too much noise."

WHAM. Something shook again behind them, reminding them that everything from that clearing was well beyond their Rank, and the group continued on in silence.

They found the path a few minutes later, but still kept moving, their voices silent until almost an hour of hard-pressed running later, the injured and barely conscious Grower finally needed a break. He'd pushed on valiantly, only pausing for the most minor of healings, but his body was at its limit, desperately needing a rest.

From the looks on everybody's faces, he wasn't the only one. The woman with the broken arm grimaced like she was barely holding the pain back.

"Now," Seeyela said sternly, looking from Seena to Hiral, the uninjured members of the other Grower party shifting so they could watch, "explain. Why do you have an Islander with you? Do you know what *they* were doing down here?"

"He saved Favela's life," Seena answered after a second's thought, and the mention of her daughter seemed to pause whatever Seeyela was going to say next. "She was playing too close to the edge of the island. It's a long story, but she… fell…"

"How… how could you let…?" Seeyela started.

"I'm sorry, but we can talk about *that* later. The rest of it is this: Hiral jumped off and saved her. In return for that, he asked to come down to the surface with us to look for you. He got an achievement notification while he was saving Favela, and it mentioned the dungeon interface. Instead of letting him go back up to Fallen Reach and start talking about it there, I thought it was best to bring him down with us."

Seeyela groaned at the mention of the dungeon interface. "Favela is alright?"

"She's fine," Seena said. "Honestly, I think she's a little taken by Hiral here. She wouldn't let him go after he saved her."

"She's usually such a good judge of character too," Seeyela said.

Ouch.

"So, what does he know about the Islanders who attacked us? The ones who killed the Quillbacks?" Seeyela went on, her voice rising.

"*He* is right here," Hiral said before Seena could speak for him. "And, look, I get why you don't trust me. I wouldn't, if I was in your shoes. Er, boots… or whatever those things you're wearing are." He gestured at her feet with both hands. "But, really, I have no idea what those Shapers were doing down here. You're saying they're the ones who killed the Quillbacks we saw back at the dungeon?"

Seeyela narrowed her eyes and looked at Seena. "You took him to the dungeon?"

"We checked there first for you, of course," Seena said, no hint of apology on her face.

"Whatever," Seeyela said. "Yes. They killed the Quillbacks. *Were* killing them when we walked in. As soon as we saw what was happening, we got out of there. They caught up to us in the woods before we could get to the jump point. Started questioning us about how to harvest the quills. None too gently, I might add." She nodded toward the Grower with the broken arm. "Why do you look familiar?"

"Hrm?" Hiral half-asked, his brain running through what it could mean for Shapers to be on the surface. "I work with Arty, who trades with your uncle."

"So," Seeyela said, standing straighter, "the two people who know the most about the quills. And, when we come down to the surface to harvest them. You *are* involved, aren't you?"

"Yes, obviously," Hiral snapped back. "Because *that's* why I'm down on the surface now, surrounded by a group of hostile Nomads who are considering whether or not to string me up from the closest tree or bury me under it. Just stop accusing me for a second and think about things.

"One of the Shapers had a ***Disc of Passage*** tattoo, and she was B-Rank. The disc tattoo isn't common; there are maybe half a dozen people who have them and can use them. But! If they had access to it, watching your people come down to the surface wouldn't be a challenge at all. The disc has a lot of functions, one of which makes it practically invisible to anybody looking. Bends light around it... but the details don't matter.

"Yes, people from Fallen Reach were down here, and I'm sorry about what happened to you, but I'm not apologizing because I was involved in it. Maybe you saw the part where they were ready to kill me just as quickly as you?"

"And, as for Arty—your uncle's trust of him aside—he makes his living off trading with your family," Hiral went on, partially thinking out loud. "Shapers coming down and undermining that business would be the last thing he wants. No, if anything, we're the people you can trust the most."

"That's convenient," Seeyela said.

"It is," Seena said back. "And, honestly, that's all I think it is. We can talk to Uncle Caav when we get back up to the islands to see what he has to say. You know Arty has always been good to us. And I don't just mean the trading."

"It's true," Hiral said. "The fertility glyphs he does for you could get him into a *lot* of trouble on Fallen Reach. They're very illegal in the city. He's risking his neck every time he does one."

Seena and her sister looked at each other, and Seeyela's hands instinctively went to her stomach.

Ah. So not just Caaven's wife.

"Okay, let's say for a minute I believe you're on the level. Where do we go from here?" Seeyela asked.

"How about to the jump point?" Yanily offered. "Wule and Cal got Fitch awake and walking. Picoli says her broken arm won't slow her down, and we're literally running out of time here." He pointed back along the path toward where the top of the storm-wall could just be seen.

"It could be dangerous," Hiral said. "If they've actually been watching your patterns when you harvest, they could go to the jump point ahead of us on the disc."

"Do you have a better suggestion?" Seena asked, though there wasn't contempt in her voice. It was a legitimate question.

Hiral opened his mouth to answer, then shook his head. "No, I don't. It's the *only* way back up?"

"It's the only jump point that'll get us to the islands between here and the Needle Mountains," Seeyela said.

"And there's really no way to climb the Needles?" Hiral asked.

"None," Seena said.

"Then I guess we don't have any choice but to risk it," Hiral said with a shrug.

"Anybody else? Open to suggestions here," Seena said, turning her attention to the other Growers, but they all shook their heads. "That settles it, then. We're continuing to the jump point, and hoping we get there first."

"Do you think those Islanders actually even made it out of that clearing?" Vix asked. "Last I looked, they didn't seem to be doing any better than we did against that crystal thing."

"They were all at least C-Rank," Hiral said. "The monster caught them off guard, but do you really think it could've taken down five C-Rank Shapers, and one or two B-Ranks?"

Vix shrugged. "Just saying what I saw. You tell me if they could take that thing or not."

"Actually, that's not a bad idea," Seena said, but she stood up again. "While we move, Hiral, tell us everything you can about those Islanders and what they might be capable of. I'm really hoping they don't know about the jump point, but if they do, it's better we have an idea what we're getting into."

"Assuming he's willing to sell his friends out like that," Seeyela said, also standing.

"Not my friends. They were planning on killing me too," Hiral reminded her. "And yes, I'll tell you what I know. How far is it from here now?"

"Just a couple hours, and we're cutting it close. Everybody ready to go?" Seena asked, and the others nodded at her. "Great. Let's go home."

20

RACE TO THE JUMP POINT

❝ ...AND that's all the tattoos I *know* they have," Hiral said, two hours later. "Problem is, there could be more. In fact, I *guarantee* there are more."

The group had slowed from a jog to a steady walk, the best the injured Growers could keep up. And, really, everybody was pushing their limits anyway.

"That's... that's already enough to worry about," Vix said, his eyes wide after the details Hiral had given them.

Can't say I blame them. Shaper magic is powerful, which is probably why so many of them have superiority complexes.

"I don't know what we can do against half of that," Nivian said. "Correction: I don't know what we can do against *most* of that. Maybe one of them, we could slow down enough to... I don't know, get a few people suited up and jumping. But a full group, with all those abilities on hand, at C- or B-Rank? We're in trouble."

"We're only in trouble if they're actually waiting for us," Seena pointed out. "There's still the chance that crystal thing hurt them enough to make them have better things to do than worry about us."

"Hope the reverse is true too," Yanily said. "That's twice we ran into it. I'd rather not a third after seeing what it can do to a B-Rank."

"It's been a few hours since then. At this point, I think we're pretty much okay..." Wule said, only for the ground to shake so violently, it sent most of the Growers stumbling to the ground.

Thanks to his high *Dex*, Hiral managed to keep his feet, and he quick-stepped to the side of the path and used a thick tree to help balance himself.

"What is that?" he shouted over the rumbling.

"No idea," Seena shouted back, but it was all over a moment later, other than the distant sound of falling rocks.

"Does that happen on the surface often?" Hiral asked, walking over and offering Seena a hand to help her to her feet. "I think I read about something called an earthquake?"

Just a quick look at her sister, then Seena took Hiral's hand and stood up. "Never when I've been down here. Sis?"

"First time for me," Seeyela said. "Everybody okay?"

"No worse than we were five minutes ago," Nivian said. "But, that sound… it came from ahead of us."

"Ahead… The mountain?" Hiral asked, suddenly running through the tattoo inventory he'd shared with them again in his head. "The **Way of Earth**. It's a tattoo that doesn't get used much, because we have to be so careful with the ground up in Fallen Reach. Down here, though? It could be very… dangerous."

"How dangerous?" Seena asked.

"Depends. How obvious is the path up to the jump point?"

Seena closed her eyes and rubbed the bridge of her nose. "To somebody flying? Very."

"Let's hope I'm wrong, then."

"Let's," Seena agreed, and the group went back to a fast jog along the path.

The forest quickly grew sparser after that, the green cover breaking apart to reveal blue sky directly above and needle-like mountains just ahead. Faint dust hung in the air, sparkling slightly, and coated the branches on both sides of the path. Rounding a corner, then cresting a small hill in the path, the group got their first good look at the mountain they needed to climb to reach the jump point.

Well, would've needed to climb… had there still been a path.

It almost looked like the entire side of the mountain had come down in a wide avalanche, piles and piles of stones and boulders towering fifty or sixty feet in the air. And, beyond them, a sheer cliff face so perfectly smooth it couldn't *possibly* be natural.

"Sons of bitches," Seena cursed.

Half of the Growers just stood staring dumbfounded at the destruction. The *other* half turned on Hiral.

"The **Way of Earth**," he said with a shake of his head. "One of the B-Rank Shapers must've used it. I don't think C-Rank could've achieved this."

"What does it matter what *Rank* they were? They've killed us," one of Seeyela's group said.

None of them had bothered to introduce themselves to Hiral, and he still didn't know any names other than Seeyela, Picoli, or Fitch, but that didn't make the woman any more *wrong*.

"Is there another way up?" Hiral asked Seena, ignoring the unnamed Grower.

"Maybe, on the far side of the mountain," she said, looking at her sister. "Do you think we could make it?"

Seeyela was already shaking her head. "No. There might've been another path, once, but this is the only one we've used for generations. Besides, if those Islanders went to all the trouble of collapsing this path, you can bet they looked to see if there were more. Right, Hiral?"

"They had an Artist with them," Hiral said, as if that answered the question. From the looks on their faces, it didn't. "The Shapers—the ones with the tattoos—they don't put many points into their mental attributes, focusing entirely on raw power. If the group was *just* Shapers, I'd say there was a chance another path might be intact.

"With an Artist, though? No. They almost entirely put their attribute points into their mental stats to improve their craft. They need higher mental stats, attunement especially, to craft higher-rank tattoos. It was probably his idea in the first place to do this." Hiral gestured weakly at the sheared-off mountain.

"So, they really *did* kill us," Vix said, dropping down to sit on the ground, his gaze locked on the unclimbable mountain.

Hiral's eyes, at the same time, drifted up, up, up, past the floating Nomad islands miles above in the sky, to Fallen Reach. It was already well past the jump point, the spiraling mist below it leaving a curtain of moisture in its wake. It was kind of beautiful, in a way, like the water was carrying the floating island along through the sky.

And carrying it *away* from Hiral and the others.

Guess I missed dinner, and breakfast. Bet Nat is pissed I didn't get the cake like I promised. No, that's not fair. She's actually going to miss me. At least Mom will be happy...

"When I told you you might die, this wasn't exactly what I meant," Seena said quietly from beside him, snapping him out of his spiraling inner conversation.

"Yeah, I expected a much more dramatic and sudden ending to this trip," Hiral said, and quietly slapped one hand down on the other. "I'm sorry it turned out this way."

"Me too," Seena said. "It's too bad too—for more than the obvious reasons, I mean. We finally figured out how to access the dungeon interfaces. Generations and generations, we've been in the dark about it, and all we had to do was bring an Islander with us."

"Not a lot of trust between our two peoples," Hiral said.

"It's hard to trust Islanders, Hiral, when you're literally *above* us. When Fallen Reach blocks sunlight from the only *safe* islands we have. All the others, the ones that actually get sunlight, could fail at any time. Sure, they usually last a few years, but not always. Let's not even talk about some of the things we trade for that we *need*." The anger in her words didn't sound directed at Hiral specifically.

"It's no different for us," Hiral said, and had to pat the air to stop Seena from immediately objecting. "Really. *Everything* revolves around the quills. Without them, no tattoos. No Meridian Lines. And... up until today, I thought the only way to get those quills was to trade with your people. Though, I guess that's still true since that group"—he vaguely waved his hand up toward the sky—"didn't actually succeed."

"No, but they'll keep trying. And when they finally *do* get it right, everything changes. You Islanders 'put up' with us tagging along behind Fallen Reach, siphoning off some of the magic that keeps it afloat, because we can provide the quills. Once that's gone, all those half-buried hostilities between us may not stay so buried. And, if it came to a fight, up there…"

Hiral couldn't do anything but nod. Seena was right, in a fashion. That *was* how a lot of Islanders felt. Baseless racism, but it didn't change the reality of it. If the people of Fallen Reach didn't need the Nomads—the Growers—how far would they go to get rid of them? Most barely acknowledged their existence, turning a purposely blind eye to where the quills came from.

"If I'd made it back up, I could've talked to my father and Arty. Seen if they knew anything about this, and found out if it was sanctioned by the Council."

"And if it was? Sanctioned, I mean. Would you have been able to change it?"

"It's not the first time Islanders have come down to try and harvest the quills," Seeyela said, coming over to join them. "But it *is* the first time they've attacked us like this. Maybe I should be surprised it took somebody this long to have the stones to do it, but frankly, I'm just too pissed." At this, she turned that familiar glare on Hiral.

"You and me both," Hiral said. "But, I can't believe the Council would sanction this. I just can't. My father is on the Council, and he's always supported the quill trade. Says it makes us better people to need to rely on somebody else. Keeps us… humble."

"Hah," Seeyela barked, and even Seena was chuckling. "*Humble* is never a word I would've used to describe an Islander."

"Well, until I met Hiral, at least," Seena said. "For an Islander, he's not *too* bad."

"Does leave us the question of what we're going to do with you, though, doesn't it?" Seeyela said, meeting his eyes. "Maybe Seena's group thinks of you the same way she does, but my party… we're not so trusting. Not after what happened to us. Not after…" She pointed at the mountain.

"That's an easy answer, actually," Hiral said. "I… think I know exactly what we should do."

"Oh, yes, very humble," Seeyela said flatly to her sister, but then turned back to Hiral again. "Do tell. What should we do now that we basically have a death sentence? The rains will be on us within a few hours, and then…"

"Are you planning to give up?" Hiral asked, and both Seena and Seeyela gave him the insulted looks he expected. "Then, as I see it, we just need to find a way to survive until the islands pass by again."

"*Just* survive, he says," Seeyela said to her sister. "Like it's that easy. Maybe you missed the part where *nobody* has ever survived to see another rotation?"

Hiral looked at Seena and smiled. "Pretty sure we already did something today that nobody else has ever done before. What's one more?"

Seeyela looked between the two of them, her eyes narrowing. "Obviously, there is some kind of inside joke here, and I'm not a big fan of seeing that between my little sister and an Islander. For the moment, I'm going to put that aside so you can tell us what your big plan is."

"We need to go back to the dungeon," Hiral said simply.

21

THE BEST PLAN WE HAVE

"Say what?" Seeyela asked.

"The dungeon," Hiral repeated. "Look, we need to survive the rains long enough for the islands to pass by here again, right? Or, well, technically, I guess we'd need to find a different jump point. Is there another one close?"

"There are a couple," Seena said. "Back that way, though. Other side of the dungeon."

"That works even better," Hiral said. "Seena told me you all believe there's a second area to the dungeon or something, right? Something beyond the interface we found where the Quillbacks were. When we got the interface working, there was that option of *enter dungeon*, or something like that. I figure…"

"Wait. You did what?" Seeyela interrupted. "You got the dungeon interface to work? How?"

Hiral looked from Seeyela to Seena, then gestured at her with both hands. "Thinking she won't believe *me*, so why don't you tell her?"

"The interface activated as soon as we had a Grower and an Islander close enough to it. Like it needed one of each of us to turn on," Seena said. "I don't even know how that makes sense, but it's the best we can figure."

"What did it do? The interface, I mean. What was in the dungeon? What was it like?" Seeyela's questions came rapid-fire.

"Uh, we were kind of busy looking for your late ass, so we didn't exactly hang around once we figured out you weren't there," Seena said flatly.

"My *late ass*? Well, excuse me for getting jumped by a group of crazy Islanders," Seeyela said.

"You know, that brings up a question I had," Hiral interrupted. "Considering you were late enough it warranted sending down a search party for you, how long did the Shapers have you held captive? I think I heard Caaven say you were a couple passes behind schedule?" He turned to Seena with that last part.

"They didn't have us for that long, actually," Seeyela said. "We ran into them, I'd say, twenty or twenty-five hours ago in the dungeon. As soon as we saw them, we bolted. They gave chase. Figured we'd be too easy to spot if we went straight to the jump point. Spent almost the entire time trying to escape them in the forest, but they finally got the drop on us after we thought we'd lost them.

"But back to the important topic, what do you think the dungeon can do for us?" Seeyela asked, a new kind of energy getting her to shift from foot to foot.

Instead of answering, Hiral looked back the way they'd come, specifically at the top of the storm-wall. How close was it to the dungeon? Could they get back first? "Do you know why the rains are so dangerous? Is the water poisonous?" he asked.

"Does he always answer a question with a question?" Seeyela asked Seena.

"Nah, this is new, and kind of annoying, but I think I see where he's going with it," Seena said. "You want us to hide in the dungeon until the city comes by again, don't you?"

Hiral tapped his nose and then pointed at Seena. "That's exactly what I was thinking."

"We don't even know what's in the dungeon," Seeyela pointed out. "But," she continued as Hiral opened his mouth, "if we're going to die anyway, what's the harm? Could be fun."

"Did I hear right?" Nivian asked, coming over with Yanily and Vix to join them. "We're going back to the dungeon? *Toward* the rain? For fun?"

"It's an option. Sis, you want to get your party in on this conversation?" Seena asked.

Seeyela stood and looked over at her party, who'd already started in her direction. "Cal, how're Picoli and Fitch doing?"

"Picoli's arm was broken, badly," the woman, Cal said matter-of-factly. "I used my long cooldown heal on her, so it's mended. Still, she won't be at a hundred percent until she gets some legit rest. Assuming we live that long. Fitch is back to normal, thanks to Wule removing his debuffs."

"Picoli, how're you feeling?" Seeyela asked the woman with the bound arm.

"If we get into a fight, I'll carry my weight; you can count on that," Picoli said.

One of the two men from the party walked up to Picoli and gently elbowed her in the stomach. "You're carrying a bit extra there already."

The scowl she gave him could've melted iron, but he gave her a wink and walked over to stand beside Cal.

"You did good," he said to the healer quietly, and she blushed at his words.

"We're talking about going back to the dungeon and trying to wait out the rains there," Seeyela said, interrupting the banter. "Seems Seena and the Islander here figured out a way to get the interface working, so we might actually have a way inside. Any objections?"

Every head turned to look at the top of the gray clouds. Lightning flashed within, and the soft *thoom* of thunder reached their ears.

"Can we get back to the dungeon in time?" the man who'd elbowed Picoli asked.

"Maybe, Lonil. It'll be up to Picoli, I think," Seeyela said. "You said you'd carry your weight, but you know we won't leave you behind. Tell me honestly, can you keep up, or should we find somewhere closer?"

"If they really *can* get us into the dungeon, and that's a chance for us to survive, then we have to go for it," Picoli said. "I'll keep up. I promise."

"That settles it, then. We're running." Seeyela looked at Hiral. "*You* better be able to keep up too."

"Won't be a problem," Hiral said, looking from Grower to Grower.

He'd half-thought they would fall into a depression after losing their way back up to the Islands. That, or a murderous rampage blaming him for their situation. Was it their style of training that gave them the mental fortitude to carry on? Their mental stats? For him, it was the slim chance at getting a class. Somehow, that made the whole being trapped down on the surface—and the ninety-nine percent chance of death—seem more bearable.

"We should stop and grab their gear on the way back, if we're going into the dungeon," Nivian suggested.

"Good idea," Seena said. "I think I remember around where it was. Shouldn't be hard to find."

"What are we waiting for, then? An invitation?" Seeyela said. She started back the way they'd come, leaving the shattered mountain path behind. Her party was after her barely a second later.

"I really hope you two can get the dungeon interface to work again," Wule said.

"Even if we can't, the Quillbacks survived somehow, right?" Hiral said. "If nothing else, we can set up camp in that room."

"You honestly think none of the other people who've been stranded down here before didn't think of that?" Wule asked.

Hiral opened his mouth to respond, but the man had a point. A good one. So, he just shrugged instead. "We'll get the interface working again."

"As of right now, it's our best chance—come on," Seena said, and when the rest of her party nodded their agreement, they jogged after Seeyela and the others.

That *jog* quickly sped up to a full-on run, though not a sprint, as they spotted the other party already quite a distance down the path. Seeyela hadn't been joking when she asked if Picoli would be able to keep up.

She was setting a hard pace. And they'd need it if they had any hope of getting to the dungeon in time.

"Hey, you never answered my question about the rain," Hiral said as they settled into a comfortable marathon pace. "Is it poisonous or something?"

"We don't think so," Seena said. "We eat food from the surface. Fruits, vegetables, even some animals we hunt. If the rainwater was poisonous, it would make those things poison too, right?"

"Makes sense," Hiral agreed. "If it's not poison, though, then what do you think it is? Why do the histories of both our peoples *insist* the rains are so dangerous? Why does nobody survive getting stranded on the surface? Is it just because we can't collect solar energy? I don't think I ever read anything about that being fatal…"

"Our best guess?" Seena said as Hiral trailed off. "Something comes out in the rain. Some kind of alpha predator or something. A… what did they call it, Wule?"

"Nocturnal hunter," Wule offered. "Something that hunts in the dark. At *night*."

Hiral almost missed a step at the mention of the word. Night. In his entire life, he'd never been without the sun. It wasn't just the rain, or the lack of sunlight to power… well, tattoos he couldn't use anyway… that'd be problems, but they would also be completely in the dark. How in the Fallen's names would they even *see*?

"I think he's starting to get it," Yanily said. "Going to be pretty different than having the sun directly above you all the time, isn't it?"

"Yeah," Hiral said. "I… didn't really consider it. I mean, I did, but not *really* really. Do you guys know anything about what happens at… night?" Even saying the word felt foreign on his tongue.

Day. Night. Darkness. Concepts he'd read about, but never honestly put much thought into. Why would he? He was never supposed to be on the surface in the first place.

Then again, the things he could *learn*… if he lived long enough.

Okay, maybe I shouldn't tell Gauto when I see him that I was excited about this. He'll really try to make me into an Academic again.

"None of us are really ready for this," Seena said quietly from beside him, while the others fell into a comfortable rhythm further back. "We've been taught a bit about what we can eat, where we can find water, that kind of thing. But, really? The strongest advice has *always* been to not get stranded down on the surface. Nobody survives."

"We don't know what happens to them. Most of them vanish completely, but we've found a few… parts… of people in the past."

"That's why you think it's some kind of predator?" Hiral asked.

"Yeah. When we find somebody in pieces, we rule out natural causes pretty quickly. Everybody is keeping their chins up, but I wanted to make sure you knew how bad the odds are."

"Worse than me surviving my jump down to the surface?"

"Much worse," Seena said.

"Well, none of the others before had a way into the dungeon, right? That's got to give us an advantage."

"It does, and hope too," Seena said. Then she looked at him, looked away, looked back, and looked away again.

"Something else on your mind?" he asked.

"Yeah. Thanks for helping save my sister and her party. I don't think we could've done it without your distraction. Fighting against C- and B-Rank, we would've been wiped out almost immediately. How did you know that crystal thing would go after them? Or that it was even there?"

"Honestly? I gambled. Spotted a reflection off the crystal in the woods. Hoped they'd attack it if it showed up because they didn't know what it was."

"Well, the gamble paid off. We got my sister back. And now I owe you again," Seena said with a shake of her head. "Did I mention I don't like owing people?"

Hiral looked around at the trees as they sped down the path. "Somehow, over the coming... what do we even call them now? Pulses, passes, and rotations won't make sense down here without the city. Well, whatever, I'm sure you'll have plenty of chances to pay me back between now and when we get back up to the islands."

"You really think we're going to make it back? Or are you just trying to be positive?" Seena watched his eyes even as they ran along the uneven path.

Her dexterity must be pretty decent.

"Oh, I'm totally just trying to be positive," Hiral said with a small laugh. "But," he went on before she could interrupt, "I *do* think we have a chance. You said something about the *safety* of the dungeon, and the fact it had that strange light-guy... There's more to it than just a place for Quillbacks to build nests."

"It's true," Seena said. "Troblins and other monsters seem like they *can't* pass the archways leading into the dungeons. The Quillbacks actually aren't aggressive—even though you wouldn't want to try to pet one—so we make camp inside sometimes. No real food there, though, but who knows what we'll find in the second area?"

"**Splitfang Keep** didn't really sound like a garden," Hiral pointed out.

"No, but it's something. Anyway, thanks again. I need to catch up to my sister and make sure she knows where her party's gear is. Knowing her, she has no idea. I'm frankly surprised we're even going in the right direction." Seena chuckled. "I'll talk to you later, after we get their stuff."

"Sure thing. I've got a lot to think about anyway."

"Sounds good—just don't get too caught up in your own head. Like you said, those Islanders down here aren't your fault, even if Seeyela and the others don't *quite* get that yet. They'll come around, though." She gave him a pat on the shoulder and picked up the pace to catch her sister.

Hiral half-watched her go, but he was already falling into his own thoughts. This was it. They were going to get into the dungeon and get to the interface at the end.

*I know I shouldn't let myself get excited. The interface didn't say anything about giving me a class, but... I can't help it. And, if this works, I've got the **Disc of Passage** tattoo. I can get us all back.*

Hiral glanced up and over his shoulder as he ran, the tall treetops blocking the sky, but that didn't stop his imagination from filling in an image of him riding the disc back up to the islands. Back up to proving them all wrong.

His father would finally stop worrying he'd made a mistake with Hiral's Meridian Lines. Nat could stop feeling sorry she was succeeding while he failed. Gauto... Gauto would still want him to be an Academic, but maybe he could split his time between training and studying. It wasn't like he had any interest fighting in the Amphitheatre anyway. And besides, it would be a shame to let the base mental stats he'd worked so hard to improve go to waste.

Loan would get the credit he deserved for working with Hiral all those years, and maybe, *just maybe*, Milly would stop charging into his room without knocking.

Hah. Who am I kidding? That'd be an even bigger miracle than me getting a class.

The smile didn't leave Hiral's lips as he ran, and he daydreamed about his return until they found the other party's equipment several hours later.

22
ROUND 2

HIRAL watched as Seeyela and her party gathered up their equipment, only the occasional dirty look shooting his way as they found something broken or torn.

"Wow, they're really holding a grudge, huh?" Yanily said from where he stood beside Hiral, leaning casually on his spear. "Ooooh, that was Balyo's favorite spear too."

"How well do you know Seeyela's party?" Hiral asked.

"Seeyela is five or six rotations older than Seena—I always forget which—so we've actually been training together almost as long as I can remember. Big sis was always watching over little sis, if you know what I mean. Made her kind of like a big sister to our whole party, I guess.

"You probably don't know, but we pick our parties pretty young, after we get an idea where our classes and abilities lean. I practically grew up with those two." Yanily pointed at the two sisters. "Had a crush on Seeyela most of my life too, until she met Trev. Ah, Trev is her husband. He's in a different party, D-Rank."

"Do Growers have a lot of different classes?" Hiral asked.

"Not exactly. There are only six, but the abilities within them can vary a lot. Take Wule and Cal, for example. Wule can cure debuffs, which Cal can't, but Cal can do broken bones, even though they're the same class. Balyo and I are Spear Wardens, so our abilities focus on spears. But that's about where the similarities end. We use different abilities, and have different strengths and weaknesses."

"Wow. Up in Fallen Reach, we only have three classes. Shapers—those big, tattooed folks. Artists—they're the ones who actually ink the tattoos. Lastly, there are Academics, but that one is kind of a catch-all class for people who don't have the affinities to be either a Shaper or Artist. Ah, that's not actually a fair way to put it. The Academics do a lot for the city, and it's not like they're washouts or something."

"Only three classes? That's insane," Yanily said, and it certainly was when Hiral really thought about it.

Odd—why didn't I ever read anything about Grower classes?

Another dirty look in his direction answered his question.

Right. Growers and Makers don't much get along.

"So, which of the three are you?" Yanily asked. "You can't be one of those Shaper folks, unless you just need to drink more milk. Though, now that I look at you, you've got something on your earlobe there. It's small… but…"

"Just decoration," Hiral said quickly, his hand going up to his ear to rub the **Perfect Sense** tattoo there.

"Oh, man, you guys do those things for decoration too?" Yanily asked, thankfully already past the topic of class.

"Yes, but it doesn't give me any abilities like it would a Shaper," Hiral said, the words painfully true.

"Gotcha, gotcha. Do Shapers have any abilities other than the tattoos?"

"Nope," Hiral said. "Their tattoos are their abilities, or magic, or whatever you want to call it. Well, their Meridian Lines—their **PIM**—boosts their physical stats by quite a bit too, I guess."

"But, let me get this straight… Those big guys, the Shapers—they actually have to get the tattoos put on their bodies by that other class you mentioned? The…"

"The Artists," Hiral finished for Yanily. "You got it right. They're really dependent on each other. Shapers have no abilities unless an Artist tattoos them, using a special ink made with the Artist's own blood, and drawn with a Quillback quill."

"So, if there were no Artists, there'd be no Shapers?" Yanily asked.

"Correct, but, looks like they're ready to go," Hiral said, pointing at the other party grouping up. "After we get things figured out with the dungeon, we should talk more about this. I'm really curious to hear about some of the other Grower classes."

"Sure, but only if you're treating me to lunch," Yanily said, and patted Hiral on the shoulder. "Nivian is playing hard to get with the sandwiches," he added in a whisper.

"Uh, right after you show me what we can actually eat down here…" Hiral deadpanned.

"Deal!" Yanily said, and then the pair walked over to join the rest.

"Got everything?" Seena asked, another *thoom* of thunder echoing overhead. Everybody looked up at the darker sky. The storm-wall had to be getting close.

"Everything worth getting," Seeyela said. "Those Islanders did a number on our gear, but it looks like it was almost random. Either way, we can't waste any more time here."

With that, the group filed back out to the path, then turned left to start toward the dungeon, only for everybody to stop dead in their tracks.

There, directly ahead of them in the middle of the path, stood the three-armed crystal monster *again*. Small cracks spiderwebbed out of half a dozen impact points, but it appeared otherwise unharmed.

"You've got to be kidding me," somebody whispered.

"Isn't that the thing that fought the Islanders? The *C-* and *B-Rank* Islanders?" another asked.

Hiral, near the back of the group, looked at the monster's face and, just like before, felt its gaze look right back at him.

"Guys, I think…" he began.

"Seeyela, what do we do?" the woman named Cal asked over Hiral's comment.

"We…" Seeyela started, but the monster made the decision for them, suddenly rushing forward. "Tanks!"

Nivian and Lonil dashed to intercept, the thorny shield and whip appearing in Nivian's hands, while Lonil's skin turned stony gray, and the man grew two feet taller in a heartbeat.

Like it would do them any good.

The monster charged in between them without slowing, twin backhands sweeping out and tossing them aside like playthings. The two tanks crashed into the woods on opposite sides of the path at the same time Yanily, Vix, Balyo, and Hiral raced up to meet it.

Yanily hit it straight on, spear flashing as he *thrust, thrust, thrust*, each attack accompanied by a small burst of solar energy, the shaft and blade bending while he sought openings. Balyo, on the other hand, darted out to the side and planted her feet, her spear held ready to thrust and solar energy building in the blade. That just left Vix and Hiral, who circled around opposite Balyo. The monster turned with them while it completely ignored Yanily's assault.

"I'll get its attention," Hiral shouted, though he *already* had it, and skidded to a stop while Vix continued and circled so they had it surrounded. No sooner had his feet stopped moving than Hiral lunged forward, blades a blur in each hand as he struck.

Tink… tink… tink, tink, tink. His swords bounced off the crystal monster not even bothering to defend itself, and suddenly, three hands reached for him, palms glowing. The memory of Velina's exploding **Disc of Passage**—and the way the monster had tossed around the other Shapers—had Hiral scrambling backwards at the same time Vix and Yanily hit the monster from both sides.

Solar energy pulsed with every strike, but the monster stepped forward to follow Hiral despite the twin barrages.

"Clear!" Balyo shouted behind the monster, and Yanily and Vix immediately backed off.

Oh, this can't be good.

Even though Hiral couldn't see Balyo behind the monster, the sudden *rush* of solar energy clearly meant something big was coming. Well, it wasn't like his attacks were doing anything anyway, so Hiral spun to the side and leapt away—just in time. A giant spear of light slammed into the monster's back.

The force of the impact added to Hiral's own leap, and he flew uncontrollably through the air, pinballed off one tree, then another, before hitting the ground in a bouncing, rolling heap.

"Ugh," he groaned, pushing himself up to his hands and knees, broken branches and leaves cracking with each movement, his swords both lost in the flight, and his body aching. The ground tilted sideways—no, that was Hiral tilting—but his shoulder hit a nearby tree, and he somehow stayed upright. Mostly upright. "That hurt," he mumbled, though his **End** had taken the worst of it. He shifted so he could look back the way he'd come.

Man, that attack was way stronger than E-Rank. Did the monster...?

Forty feet away, the monster stalked toward him like nothing had happened. Vix danced in on its side, his form a blur as he landed blow after blow after blow, constantly moving, never slowing. He might as well have been standing still for how casually the monster slapped him aside.

Fallen's balls.

Thirty feet. Hiral used the tree at his side for support as he pulled himself to his feet, but he wasn't in any shape to fight *or* run.

Too bad. That thing isn't going to give me the chance to catch my breath.

"Come on, then," Hiral shouted as he charged—mostly stumbled—forward, three glowing palms rising as if to catch him.

Twenty feet, and a black-and-red ball of sparking energy appeared beside the monster. Nearby trees creaked and leaned toward the head-sized ball, and debris from the forest floor shot up to get sucked into it. Even the monster momentarily paused. Then one of its hands simply slapped the ball of energy, and it exploded in a shower of perfectly symmetrical cubes of energy before dissipating. Just like the **Disc of Passage**.

But that maneuver had taken the monster's attention off Hiral, and he leapt as it turned back to focus on him.

"Hyaaa!" he shouted, snapping his hip around in the air as he put his entire 18 **Str** into the spinning kick.

Heel colliding *perfectly* with the side of the monster's face, Hiral's other foot met its chest. He let his knee bend, then kicked off back the way he'd come in an acrobatic flip that would get him safely out of range.

Except, as soon as he landed, two hands struck out like serpents and closed around his forearms like a vise. With unbelievable strength, the monster pulled his arms out to his sides so quickly, it almost popped his shoulders out of their joints, and then the third hand lifted between them.

Hiral looked down at the palm, at the glowing rune etched into the crystal. That… that was the same hand that had made the **Disc of Passage** explode.

What will happen to me if…?

The monster pushed its palm against the center of Hiral's chest, right over his central Meridian Node. A brief, slicing line of pain ran straight down his center. There was a pull on his arms, and then the monster ripped him in two.

23

FOUNDATIONAL SPLIT

HIRAL screamed as the monster tore him apart, his two halves going in opposite directions, only to get tossed to the side while the crystal face gazed down at him.

Wait—if he'd just been torn in half, why was he still looking straight up at the monster in front of him. The pain…? It was still there… but not as bad.

What in the Fallen's names is going on?

Hiral's gaze dropped down to where the monster's hand was pressed against him, his coat and shirt simply gone to reveal his bare chest. His… *completely* bare chest. No Meridian Lines stretched up to pass over his shoulders. *No tattoos.*

What… what… what!?

Shoulders aching, he lifted his arms, which were likewise bereft of any line or tattoo. No, that wasn't completely true. There was something on his forearms, where the **Daggers of EnSath** had been—where the monster's hands had grabbed him. Runes, like they'd been etched directly into his skin and infused with a yellow, liquid light.

"Welcome… home… Brother…" the monster in front of him said, the voice raspy and weak, and it pulled its hand away from his chest. More of that yellow light trailed from its palm, sticky and viscous, like glowing snot, connecting to where Hiral's central Meridian Node had been. *Had been.*

The black circle was still there, but instead of being solidly filled, there was instead another yellow rune glowing within it.

"What did you…?" Hiral started to ask, but then his status window appeared in front of his eyes, shivering and crackling.

Is it broken…? The crackling got worse, the words and numbers in it twisting and changing with every beat of his pounding heart. The edges frayed, and everything faded away until only one line was left.

Race: Maker

The screen flickered, and *Maker* vanished from the line while the window snapped from blue to yellow. Another flicker, and Hiral couldn't turn away from the new word that spelled out letter by letter.

Race: B
Race: Bu
Race: Bui
Race: Buil
Race: Build
Race: Builde
Race: Builder

As soon as the word *Builder* finished, the screen flashed yellow, and more streamers of light burst out of Hiral's chest. Spiraling out of the strange rune, they twisted around his chest, ran down his legs, and out across his arms in a double-helix pattern just an inch above his skin. Around and around they went, until they stretched from the tips of his toes, to the ends of his fingers, to the top of his head. And, Hiral noted as he studied the strange light, they weren't just *lines* of yellow light, but an entire *script*, written so small and densely it looked like a solid line from a distance.

"Artificer…" the crystal monster said, and clenched its hand closed, cutting off the snot-like light connected to Hiral's chest, which *snapped* the hovering sentences of light tight against his skin.

New pain flooded through Hiral's body as the light burned itself into his skin, and he dropped straight down to his knees. He *tried* to look at his new, yellow status window, where words and numbers appeared on the page at random, but the pain was just too much, and he squeezed his eyes closed.

It went on and on, digging deeper past his skin and searing him through his muscle and all the way down to his bones. Inside his bones, even, like it was hollowing them out and filling them back up again with something new. It flowed out along all the same paths as his solar energy, and even with his eyelids closed, more and more of the strange runic script flitted past his eyes.

And then the light seared the runes into his eyes as well.

Hiral clawed at his own face as he toppled sideways to the ground, his voice little more than raw, primal sounds of pain. The light found his tongue, his teeth, the roof of his mouth, and then there was silence. Darkness. Peace.

He lay twitching on the ground, his body weak and used, small branches and rocks digging into his skin, leaves sticking to his face from his own tears.

"Ooooh, he's not looking so good," a voice said from in front of him—one Hiral almost recognized.

"Yes, the process does not seem to have occurred without certain… consequences," another voice said, this one similar in tone, but different in cadence.

"What… happened…?" Hiral asked, forcing his eyes open. He found two silhouettes standing over him.

"Can't say we have a good answer for you," the silhouette on the left said, its features resolving as Hiral stared at it. A bald man with Meridian Lines and tattoos—so, a Shaper—but wait… Only on his right side?

"It will be up to you to determine the cause and ultimate ramifications of what has transpired," the silhouette on the right said. This one looked almost identical to the first, except he only had tattoos and Meridian Lines on his *left* side.

And… and they looked familiar. Which also explained why he knew the voices.

They looked just like *Hiral*.

"Ah, he's figuring something out!" the ones with the tattoos on his right said.

"He is," Left agreed.

"Hiral! Hiral, are you okay?" Seena's voice called from somewhere off to the side, and more shapes rushed along the nearby path. "What are…?" She trailed off, and the approaching footsteps slowed.

"It doesn't look like it's moving," Yanily said, and Hiral turned his attention past his strange doubles to the hulking shape of the monster beyond. "What did you do to it, Hiral?"

"And why are there three of you?" Seena added, carefully sidestepping the tattooed twins standing in front of Hiral.

"And, the most important question," Vix said. "What happened to your hair?"

"I didn't… I don't… my hair?" Hiral pushed himself up to a seated position, then ran his hand across his head. His *bald* head.

When he looked up at his two twins, they simultaneously pointed at their own bald heads and nodded.

"We look better like this," Right said.

"It was getting into mullet territory, honestly," Left said. "This is for the best. I see Seena agrees with the assessment."

Hiral looked at Seena, who blushed a little and looked away from him. "I wasn't going to say anything. Thought maybe it was Island fashion, but it was…"

"Not a flattering look," Yanily finished.

"Gee, thanks," Hiral said, but his attention was back on his doubles. They really did look *exactly* like him, other than each having *half* of his tattoos. Like they'd split right down the middle. No, that wasn't entirely true—neither of them had the central Meridian Node he had in the center of his chest.

But, besides that, there were the **Daggers of EnSath** on their wrists, the **Way of Light** on Right's chest, and the **Way of Shadow** on Left's. As he went through his memorized inventory of tattoos, he quickly found them exactly where they should be on Left and Right.

Why?

"Help me up?" he asked, and extended his hands to Left and Right, who immediately took them and went to pull him up. However, instead of lifting him to his feet, they instead *dissolved* into streamers of solar energy that bled into Hiral's hands.

Within seconds, the strange double-helix script faded from Hiral's skin, and the black of his Meridian Lines and tattoos rose to the surface, like bruises forming in high speed.

"Whoa, whoa, whoa," Seena said, and all the assembled Growers took a collective step back, as if he'd absorb them as well with a touch. "Maybe you should stay where you are until we figure out what is going on?"

"Yeah…" Hiral agreed, looking down at his familiarly tattooed hands.

"What class did you say you had?" Yanily asked evenly.

"That's just it, I… I don't have a class," Hiral said, the pain of the words somehow muted by the strangeness of whatever was going on. "But, when that crystal thing touched me, something happened to my status window, like it was broken."

At the mention of the touch from the monster possibly causing the strangeness, the Growers put an extra step between themselves and the frozen, crystal creature. All the nervousness left them oddly spread out on the road, but their eyes were on Hiral.

"Maybe you should check your status window again now?" Seena suggested, taking a breath and then stepping in closer to Hiral again. "And," she added, looking back at the others before turning to Hiral again, "maybe it would all make us feel better if you shared it with us."

Hiral blinked at the forwardness of the request. On Fallen Reach, *asking* to see somebody's status window was like asking them to take off their clothes. Then again, given everything that had happened in the last three minutes, it was pretty fair.

"Sure," Hiral said, pushing aside his natural resistance to the request.

He pulled up his status window for all to see. The first thing that stood out was that it was *blue* again, but Hiral's eyes quickly went to where his *Race* was listed.

Race: Builder

"Not sure what you're talking about; you have a class listed on your status window," Yanily said. "Looks funny, though. Why is it so…faint?"

What!? A class!?

Hiral's eyes dropped from his strange race notation to the line below.

Class: Runic Artificer

"His *Race* is the same way, and why is Maker crossed out?" Seeyela asked, coming closer so she could see the Window as well.

"Same with… Wow, that's a *long list* of—what are those? Abilities?" Wule asked while he tapped his own chin in thought.

"Tattoos, I think. Look there," Nivian said.

But Hiral was only half-listening, his eyes completely glued to that class line.

I've done it! I have a class. Finally!

…somehow.

But why is it grayed out?

"…al. Hey, Hiral, you listening to us?" Seena was saying, and there was a hand waving in front of his face.

"Sorry," he said. "I'm listening now."

"Do you know what's going on?" she asked.

"I have no idea. The monster did something to me when it touched my central Meridian Node, I think. My tattoos have always been listed as unavailable like this—because I couldn't use them—so I guess my race and class have to be the same way."

Typical. I have a class, but I can't use it?

"Looks like you've got one ability that isn't unavailable. Down here." Wule pointed beneath the list of tattoos. "***Foundational Split.***"

"What does that do, Hiral?" Seena asked.

"I don't know. I didn't have that before." Hiral gestured for Seena to back up a bit, and he got to his feet. Considering how weak he'd felt a few minutes before, he was feeling pretty good now. "Let's find out."

"Wait, are you sure that's a good…?" she started, but it was already too late.

Hiral instinctively pushed his solar energy into activating the ability.

The strange rune etched into his Meridian Node glowed a blinding yellow, and then it was like all his skin peeled off in opposite directions. Meridian Lines and tattoos both lifted off his flesh, glowing solar energy coalescing beneath into the shape of his arms, then expanding further to create the sides of his chest, his legs… all of him… until two virtual copies of him stepped *out of* his own body.

The nearby Growers understandably leapt back in alarm as Left and Right solidified, their own blue status windows hovering in front of them.

24
LEFT AND RIGHT

"**A**RE you real?" Hiral asked Left and Right.

"That's somewhat rude," Left said.

"Ah, give him a break—this hasn't been a normal day for him," Right said. "But yeah, we're real." He poked Hiral in the bare chest.

"Hiral, your status window… It changed," Seena said, and Hiral forced his eyes from Left and Right to look.

It was *yellow* again.

And his race and class weren't grayed out anymore! But all his tattoos were gone, instead replaced by a *Runes* category, which only listed three.

> *Runes:*
> * **Rune of Separation – Primary**
> * **Rune of Rejection – Right forearm**
> * **Rune of Attraction – Left forearm**

Hiral looked down at his arm, and yes—there, between the returned, glowing, double-helix pattern, was the strange yellow rune again.

So, these runes must be some kind of abilities.

"Hrm, you're only level six? You've got good base stats, though," Vix said.

"Level…?" Hiral asked, already *really* tired of feeling surprised every time somebody opened their mouth.

Vix was right, though. Apparently, he was a level 6 Runic Artificer—whatever that was—and even had 18 unspent attribute points to allocate.

How am I level six? Oh, it must be that experience in escrow I got from fighting the Troblins. Nice!

"Okay, this is all fun and creepy that the Islander is apparently multiplying, but we *do* need to get a move on if we want to get back to the dungeon before the rains reach us," Seeyela said, though she also looked at the crystal monster. "We sure this thing isn't going to start moving again?"

"Not sure at all," Yanily said.

"And I don't want to try my luck a second time," Balyo said. "My strongest attack didn't even scratch it, and it was a perfect setup for a kill shot. If this thing was *trying*, it could've ended all of us."

"But it was after Hiral, wasn't it?" Seena put the pieces together. "That's how you knew it would come for you when we ran into those other Islanders."

"I didn't *know*," Hiral said, "though I did *suspect*. It acted funny the first time we ran into it."

"You're all still talking, and we still aren't moving," Seeyela said. "We can talk about this all we want when we get to the dungeon. Come on, chop chop," she said, clapping her hands together. "I assume you two are coming with us?" she asked Left and Right.

"We go where he goes, whether we want to or not," Right said.

"Wonderful. What should we call you? Hiral Number Two and Hiral Number Three?"

They both pulled up and looked at their own status windows.

"Apparently, I'm Right," Right said.

"And I'm Left," Left added.

Then they both looked at Hiral and spoke in unison. "You actually named us Left and Right?"

"Uh…" Hiral said, but stopped when Seeyela scowled. "We can talk about it more later, like Seeyela was saying."

"Lead on," Right said, and held out his hand as if gesturing down the path.

"Thanks," Hiral said. "You're very polite."

"And you aren't?" Right asked. "We're just you, you know. More or less."

"What do you mean, more or less?" Hiral asked as the whole group warily kept an eye on the monster while they moved around and past it. They all even gave it one last look before they rounded a corner in the path, then picked their pace back up to a steady run.

"What Right is trying to say is that we aren't *copies* of you," Left explained. "Well, not exact copies. Right is your more physical aspects, while I am your more mental. For example, though we are both level six, as you are, and have unspent attribute points, I can only put mine into my mental stats."

"And I can only put mine into strength, dexterity, or endurance," Right said. "I am going to be so buff."

"You have your own attribute points to spend?" Hiral asked, and quickly pulled up his own status window. It was tempting to allocate those 18 points he had, but maybe it would be better to hold off spending them until he knew what his class actually *did*.

"We do. Do you have any preference how you would like us to spend them?" Left asked.

"Can either of you use your tattoos?" Hiral asked immediately.

"Not me," Right said. "Just the Meridian Line on my right arm… and only below the elbow." He held out the aforementioned limb, and the Meridian Line up to his elbow glowed faintly, but everything above was completely dark.

"I can only use the **Dagger of Sath**," Left said, touching the tattoo with his right hand and instantly shaping the liquid dagger into existence.

"You know," Seena said from where she ran in front of Hiral, though she didn't turn, "it's *really* odd to hear you having a conversation with yourself. All your voices sound exactly the same, so without *knowing* there were three of you behind me, I'd just think you were completely crazy."

"I'm not entirely sure that's not the case," Hiral said. "This is… wild."

"Which… which one of you is the *real* Hiral?"

Hiral opened his mouth to answer, but the question kind of slapped him in the face as he thought about it.

What… what if I'm a copy too? Left and Right seem to have their own thoughts… but am I still me?

"Right and I are the copies," Left answered, as if reading Hiral's mind. "We are the results of his new ability—direct manifestations of his solar energy—given shape and form, much like how Shapers utilize their tattoos."

"You are?" Hiral said. "But I can't use tattoos."

"Because you are, apparently, not a Maker—you're a Builder," Left said. "Nevertheless, we are your solar energy. If you look at your status window, you should notice your current amount of energy is greatly reduced."

"Huh, you're right. It says I've only got about a third of my maximum," Hiral said.

"Correct. We have the other two-thirds," Left said. "However, we cannot absorb solar energy, so we are completely reliant on you for that. Our solar absorption rates are *unavailable*."

"What's your absorption rate, Hiral?" Seena asked.

"S-Rank," Hiral said offhandedly while he looked at his status window. But, even with the glowing yellow screen in front of him, he couldn't miss the eleven Grower heads snapping around in his direction.

"It's *what*?" Seena asked.

"You're kidding!" Yanily said, at the same time Vix cursed.

"Uh, yeah," Hiral said. "But my solar output rate has always been *unavailable*. I've never been able to use my tattoos. Never."

"What does it say now?" Seeyela asked. "Your output."

"Let me check…" Hiral glanced down to find that line, and then even his eyes widened. "Also… S-Rank."

"You've got S-Rank absorption *and* output?" Seena asked, her head constantly turning back to look at him as she ran. "Wait… your capacity, it's not…"

"It is," Hiral said quietly. "What's yours?"

"I've got the highest capacity in the party—well, me and Wule—and we're both only B-Rank in that," Seena said.

"Same here," Cal said.

"How is that even *fair?*" Yanily asked.

"Sorry?" Hiral half-apologized.

"What are you even doing working as Arty's apprentice?" Seena asked, her eyes still wide. "With S-Rank *anything*, shouldn't you be getting groomed to be… I don't know… somebody special? There's maybe one Elder who has an S-Rank ability, and other than that, A-Rank is the highest."

"I had no output rate," Hiral said. "None. I'm not kidding. Until a few minutes ago, my absorption and capacity rates didn't mean anything, because I couldn't use any of the solar energy I had."

"But those tattoos—you had them all hidden under your clothes this whole time?" Seena asked, and there was a bit of an edge to the question.

"Well…" Hiral said.

"Hey, guys, the rest of the questions are going to have to wait," Lonil called from the front of the group, slowing to a stop. "We're not going to make it to the dungeon in time."

Seeyela continued up to join her party's tank, then stopped beside him. "You're sure?"

"Yeah, I've got a pretty good idea where we are now, and look." He pointed through a break in the canopy at the roiling storm-wall flashing with barely contained lightning. "I think the rains are already there, and we're still an hour away, even if we push."

"Damnit, I thought we could make it," Seeyela said.

"I'm sorry, it's my fault," Picoli said. "I slowed you down."

"No, you didn't. It was always a long shot."

"So, what do we do now? We can't just give up," Hiral said.

"Nobody said anything about giving up," Seeyela said.

"We figure the storm is most violent right at the edges, where the magic from Fallen Reach holds it at bay," Seena explained. "If we can survive that part of it, we… hope… the rains beyond are less severe."

"They have to be," Wule said. "Otherwise, there wouldn't be any trees left standing. Or animals…"

"Seena, do you think you can manage something?" Seeyela asked.

"Maybe? But I don't know if I can create anything sturdy enough."

"If I may?" Left said. "You're considering using your ability to quickly grow thick roots to create a shelter to attempt to blunt the worst of the weather?"

"Yeah," Seena said.

"As Wule mentioned, the trees survive, so I suggest we use one or more of them as the storm-side wall of the shelter, to take the brunt when the storm reaches us. If we could find several trees close together, that would work even better."

The Growers all looked at each other.

"It's a good idea," Seeyela said. "Split up, look for something like that, and let Seena know as soon as you find it. How long do you think we have until the storm reaches us, Lonil?"

"An hour or so," he said.

"I'd like at least fifteen minutes to make sure I have time to build something strong enough," Seena said. "The ability has a one-minute cooldown. This isn't what it's meant for."

"You heard her, folks. Get to it," Seeyela said, and the Growers all took one last look at the storm-wall, then split up and headed into the surrounding woods.

"And us?" Right asked Hiral.

"Same as them. Let's find a big tree. Good idea, Left."

"Thank you," Left said. He and Right also headed into the woods.

That just left Hiral on the path looking up at the intimidating clouds. Even if they survived the storm-wall hitting them, they'd still have to travel at least an hour, probably two, through the dark and rain to reach the dungeon.

Two hours… and they still didn't know what in the rains was so dangerous.

First, survive the storm-wall.

25
RAIN & DARKNESS

THE group stood just off to the side of a pair of large trees that naturally grew close together, and the dome of thick roots built by Seena's ability. Not far ahead of them, maybe two hundred feet, the storm-wall hammered the ground with torrential water more akin to a waterfall than rain.

Rain that fell *straight down*.

It was like a literal, solid wall of water, not a single drop daring to fall closer than the collective mass of the others. Still, the wall inched forward, nearer to Hiral and the Growers, lightning flashing through the clouds above, a deep darkness overtaking the land.

"You sure we need to worry about wind?" Hiral asked, practically shouting to be heard over the pounding rain and thunder overhead.

"That's what we were taught," Seena shouted back.

"Doesn't look like there's any wind," Nivian said. "Maybe we should skip the shelter and just take our chances heading for the dungeon right now?"

"Even if there's no wind," Seeyela shouted, "that much rain is a risk. If we got separated, we'd never find each other. Better to stay under cover until the worst of it has passed."

"Will the *worst* even pass? Or will this go on until the island comes back around?" Nivian asked.

"It will pass," Hiral said. "If it didn't, wouldn't the whole world be under water?"

"Is this thing going to be waterproof?" Cal asked. "We're not going to drown in there with that much rain, are we?"

"I'm going to set up a pair of **Gravity Wells** to pull the worst of the rain *away* from the dome, but we'll still get wet," Seeyela said.

"**Gravity Wells**?" Hiral asked Seena.

"Sis specializes in gravity magic. You saw it against that crystal thing," Seena explained quickly, then pointed inside the dome as the next series of lightning flashes showed the approaching wall of water noticeably closer. "Okay, everybody in. I need to get this sealed up."

"Left, Right," Hiral said, holding out his hands to the two doubles. "Best I take you two back in so it's not too crowded in there."

The two tattooed versions of Hiral reached out and took his hands without question.

"We'll be ready when you need us," Right said.

"Thanks," Hiral said before pulling on the solar energy stored in their bodies. Almost instantly, the flesh and muscle of the copies vanished in streams of glowing energy that flowed into Hiral, his double helix disappearing and the Meridian Lines and tattoos again rising to the surface of his skin. A quick glance at his status window showed his solar energy capacity back at ninety-seven percent.

Hrm. A minor loss of energy. For having them out? I'll have to experiment to see what it costs to maintain them.

"Actually," Seena interrupted from where she stood. "You should keep them – uh, get them back – out. I'm guessing that rain isn't going to be toasty warm, which means it'll get cold in here. More bodies means more body *heat*."

"Assuming they generate heat…?"

"Only one way to find out," Hiral said, pushing power into *Foundational Split*. Solar smoke peeled off of him, his tattoos and Meridian Lines vanishing with it, to form into his doubles at his sides.

"We produce heat, in case you were wondering," Left said as soon as they formed.

"Want to cuddle?" Right asked Vix, and the other man just rolled his eyes.

"In you two go before you get me in trouble." Hiral shooed the doubles in with a shake of his own head.

"You seem pretty comfortable with that now," Yanily said as he passed Hiral into the shelter.

"Feels natural," Hiral said, ducking into the dome as well.

"That's how most abilities are," Yanily said. "You *really* didn't have a class before this? And no abilities?"

"Really," Hiral said, unslinging his sword harness from his shoulders and looping it around his wrist so it didn't hit the low roof.

"Then, that fight with the Troblins. All that was… what?"

"Training. Years and years of training. You guys must all have base stats similar to mine, right?"

"Hah," Yanily practically barked, drawing the attention of the other Growers in the shelter as Seeyela stepped inside, a red glow now coming from outside. "Hiral here thinks we have the same base stats."

"Nivian has, what, an eleven endurance," Vix said. "My base dexterity is twelve. Does anybody have a thirteen?"

"My strength is twelve," Balyo said. "Highest base stat for our party. If you count the bonuses from our *PIMs*, then we have higher, but base? Nope."

"Seriously, Hiral, what's going on with you?" Yanily asked. "Twenty dexterity, and eighteen in everything else?"

"Training nonstop," Hiral said with a shrug. "Since I didn't have a *PIM*, I had to do it all with just my base stats, but the work paid off by increasing them.

Most other people don't bother with it because it's just faster to level up and get the bonuses from their Meridian Lines. Since I didn't have that option…"

"Then, your S-Rank solar attributes. What are you?" Yanily said, gently punching Hiral in the shoulder.

"The laughingstock of Fallen Reach?" Hiral said. "I am—was?—basically the weakest person on the island because I couldn't get a class."

"If you're the weakest, I'd hate to meet the strong ones," Yanily said, giving Hiral another playful punch in the shoulder at the same time Seena entered the dome.

"Ready?" Picoli asked Seena, who nodded. "Okay, I'll do what I can for light. It won't be much, though."

"Anything will be better than standing in the dark," Seeyela said. "Do what you can."

"Sure," Picoli said, and there was a pulse of solar energy as small balls of light materialized. They were kind of like fireflies, except they didn't flit around, instead settling near the ceiling. "Try not to touch them; they'll still do their full damage even if they aren't moving."

"How long will they last?" Seeyela asked.

"A few minutes, but they don't cost much energy. I'll just recast the ability when they fade."

"These are normally a ranged-attack ability," Yanily quickly explained to Hiral. "**Light Darts** or something."

"Ah, thanks," Hiral said.

"Stay on that side over there until I'm done," Seena pointed, and everybody crowded against the wall opposite the opening—Right making another cuddle-comment to Vix at the same time. Then, with a pulse of solar energy and a gesture from her staff, spear-like roots erupted from the ground and filled in the empty space. "Oh… wow…" she said again, her eyes wide but her gaze drifting off into space.

"What's up, Seena?" Seeyela asked. "You finished? Is there a problem?"

"Oh… no. I got an achievement notification. Let me finish this up first, though." More minor pulses of solar energy radiated from Seena as dozens of smaller roots grew out of the large spikes to fill in any empty spaces.

It took a few minutes, but soon enough, Seena turned from her work with a sheen of sweat on her skin and a smile on the face. "That's the best I can do, but it should keep us dry," she said closer to a normal tone, the sealed shelter somewhat muting the hammering sound of rain.

"How quickly can you tear it down if we have to get out of here in rush?" Lonil asked.

"Instantly," Seena said. "I can dispel the ability if I need to—otherwise, it will last for ten minutes per level, so three hours."

"Which means we need to hope the worst of the rain will be past us in three hours, or this whole process will have been a waste of time," Picoli said.

"If it's not past us in three hours, that would mean the storm-wall is almost nine miles deep," Hiral said. "If it's *that* big, then we have much larger problems to worry about."

"Nine miles?" Vix asked as the intensity of the hammering rain outside inched ever closer. "How do you figure that?"

"Fallen Reach moves at around three miles per hour," Hiral said. "The Towers of the Fallen—we use them to keep track of time up in the city—are exactly three miles apart, and each pulse follows the previous by exactly one hour. The pulses are markers of time during the day, like how fifth pulse is around when a lot of people eat lunch. That kind of thing."

"Right. We see the pulses under the island," Seena said. "They make the Great Mist light up for a split second every hour. Do you know why that is?"

"There are a few different theories, such as that being the reason the Great Mist rises up from the EnSath River to Fallen Reach, providing water for us. That one never quite made sense to me, though, because wouldn't that mean there would only be water every hour? Anyway, back to the original topic... Since the storm-wall follows the city exactly one hundred miles out—always— then that means the storm has to move at the same speed."

"Well, we don't know what else is in the rain and dark," Seeyela said. "So, I don't want us waiting the full three hours if we don't have to. The sooner we get to the dungeon, the sooner we're safe."

"Assuming the Islander here can open the dungeon like he says he can," Fitch said.

"Now, now, Fitch—no need for that," Seena said. "My whole party saw the dungeon interface open up. We'll figure it out."

"You better," Fitch said, leaning against one of the shelter walls and crossing his arms, though his right hand rested on the sword pommel at his waist.

Seeyela held up a hand to Fitch and Seena before either could say another word. Another pat of the air when they both opened their mouths, and they settled for silence.

"Good," Seeyela said. "Seena, you said something about an achievement?"

"Oh, right!" Seena said, her eyes widening in excitement. "Here, I minimized the notification, but let me share it with you all." A second later, a green status window appeared in the air.

> *Achievement Unlocked: Outside the Box*
> *Skill: Spearing Roots has mutated*
> *due to unconventional and repeated use.*
> *Please access a Dungeon Interface*
> *to unlock class-specific reward.*

"Oh, wow," Wule said. "You got an achievement for building the shelter?"

"Looks that way," Seena said. "Sis, did you get one for the ***Gravity Wells***?"

"No, but I only created two of them," Seeyela said, her eyes scrolling through the floating text again. "This is good to know, though. We can find out what it does as soon as we get to the dungeon."

Seena was already shaking her head. "No, we tried last time. Seems there is another dungeon interface that unlocks when we clear the dungeon or something. The outside interface said we needed the inside one to get achievement rewards."

"Clear? Whatever that means. Well, we can…" Seeyela stopped as the sound of the rain changed, and she reached out and put the tips of her fingers against the shelter's wall. "It's here, the storm-wall," she said a second later.

The group stilled, only their heads moving as they looked up at the ceiling as one, the noise building in intensity as the line of rain crawled across the shelter's roof. Thunder *thoomed* above, so loud, it sounded like the sky itself was cracking, and the ground shuddered beneath their feet.

"I can't believe the rain is this heavy even with the ***Gravity Wells***," Cal said.

"It means they're getting overwhelmed by the sheer amount of water already," Seeyela answered, her eyes—like everybody else's—scrolling across the ceiling of the shelter.

Thoom, thooooom, THOOOOOOM. The thunder continued, reverberating through the thick roots of the shelter along with the rain pounding on the wood. Those closest to the walls instinctively took a step toward the center of the shelter, and within minutes, the heavy rain beat against the entire dome.

"Is… that… it?" Yanily shouted between echoing peals of thunder.

Then a new sound joined the constant thrumming of rain and titanic *thooms* of thunder. It started as a whistle, low in pitch at first, but quickly building.

"What's that?" Vix shouted.

"Do you feel it?" Cal asked, lifting her hands in front of her, palms out. "There's… a… Yes, there." She stepped toward the wall and moved her hands in the air until she found whatever it was she was looking for. "A breeze… here…"

That breeze, and the whistle accompanying it, continued to build, the sound of the rain on the surface of the shelter shifting along with it. The consistent and constant sound of a heavy shower gave way to something more like waves crashing against the shore.

The shelter shook in alternation between the booming thunder and the slashing rain and wind hitting it from all sides.

"We've got water over here!" Wule had to shout for the others to notice him pointing at a rapid series of drips falling from the roof.

Another few seconds, and that *dripping* became a steady stream. And it wasn't the only one. Half a dozen more fell on the ground, shoulders, and heads within seconds.

All around them, the wood grew damp, water running through even the smallest cracks to drip to the ground, the already-damp earth soaking up the moisture in short order. Within minutes, mud was forming around their boots, and the air felt heavy with moisture.

"It's getting colder," Balyo said. "You all feel that?"

"Right, don't even," Hiral warned.

Nivian put his hand under one of the falling streams of water and nodded. "The rain is colder than I expected, but it's not ice-cold or anything. Still, I wouldn't want to stay out in it too long if we don't have to."

"We'll get a fire started as soon as we get to the dungeon," Seeyela said. "There is plenty of wood outside the entrance… even though it'll all be soaked."

"Those Quillback nests should burn pretty well," Hiral pointed out.

Seeyela nodded but didn't say anything else, and the group went back to watching the rain seeping through the cracks. They huddled closer together for warmth as the temperature in the shelter continued to drop, and this time, Hiral wasn't excluded from the circle. Even without moving around much, the mud at their feet quickly churned into a soppy mess.

The party fell into tense silence, listening to cold rain pound against their shelter. Minutes passed, and each heartbeat seemed to stretch on into eternity, letting Hiral's mind begin to wander.

He eyed the rain leaking through the cracks, watching it pool into the mud below. The faint light of his new runes reflected in those pools, drawing his eyes to the symbols. Now that he had a moment to examine them, he felt both excitement and bitterness.

The excitement came from finally having power to call his own, even if it was different than what he'd hoped for.

The bitterness came from realizing he'd wasted years of his life. People had called him Everfail for not being able to power his tattoos, but how could he? He wasn't even a Maker! Asking him to summon the *Daggers of EnSath* was like trying to teach a Troblin to fly with wings it didn't have.

Where would he be now if he'd known he was a 'Builder' ten years ago? How much time would he have had to learn how to use his runes? Would he have been called Everfail at all?

The bitterness threatened to turn into anger, and he shook it off: there were more important things to think about right now—like exploring his new options.

He called up his *status window*:

Runes:
- **Rune of Separation – Primary**
- **Rune of Rejection – Right forearm**
- **Rune of Attraction – Left forearm**

Hiral didn't know how long the rain would pound against their shelter—he could only keep track of time by how many instances Picoli recast her *Light Dart* ability—and if he just sat there thinking about the past, he'd probably drive himself crazy.

Better to test and get a handle on these new abilities before he had to use them in combat.

First was the *Rune of Separation*, but he already knew what that did. *It apparently makes cuddly doubles.* That left just *Rejection* and *Attraction.* Were they some kind of weird social runes? No, that didn't make sense: he'd seen enough bad dates to know you didn't need an ability to cause rejection... just the title of Everfail.

So, what could those abilities do?

Only one way to find out—testing! Carefully and quietly. Fixing his eyes on the nearest stream of falling water, he subtly raised a hand and poured a touch of solar energy into *Rejection.*

Almost like a switch flicking, the falling water jerked away from him to splash against the side of the shelter. A quick look around—nobody seemed to have noticed—and he focused more on his solar energy into the rune. Controlling it, carefully, and he had what seemed to be a weak, conical wave of force pushing away from his hand. *So, a quick burst from a short charge of solar energy, or a weaker, constant force if I keep streaming energy in. Makes sense. And, just like what the crystal monster did. Maybe...*

Next was *Attraction*, and he started to push energy into it...

"Achoo!" Yanily sneezed nearby, startling Hiral and making him dump solar energy into the rune all at once...

...which immediately splashed him in the face.

"Is someone playing with the water?" Balyo asked from behind him.

Only a series of grunts and a murmured "No" answered her. Hiral—wisely, from the tone of Balyo's voice—chose to keep his mouth shut as cold water dripped down his chin.

"Well, whoever it was, stop it. We're going to be soaked enough as it is," Seeyela said.

"Yeah, *Yanily*," Vix said.

"I sneezed!" Yanily countered.

"Just don't do it again," Seena said.

"Yes, boss," the spearman pouted.

Okay, maybe that's enough experiments for now. Don't want Balyo using me for spear practice. Anyway, what did I learn from that? Push and pull, just like the crystal monster, which isn't surprising. It'd be great if these runes were as powerful as the monster's abilities, but I don't know if I'll be that lucky. Still, they should be stronger if I put more solar energy into them. Maybe they could knock back a charging enemy or pull one off balance.

Not directly powerful like a tattoo would be, but they could be *very* tactically useful.

He would have given a lot to have the **Training Room** nearby; he could have tested his runes on the force constructs all he wanted. Instead, he was down on the surface in the dark and rain with—as far as he knew—no way for any of his group to restore their solar power.

The only chance he'd have to test his runes for combat would be in *actual* combat, and he could only hope he'd use them properly. *And preferably not* **Attract** *something into my own face again.* With that reminder, Hiral sat tight, visualizing different ways to use his abilities while counting the times the light went out and shone again inside the shelter.

It wasn't until after around the tenth time Picoli recast her **Light Dart** ability that the sound of the hammering rain seemed to begin letting up. After an eleventh recast, the water falling through the cracks in the shelter had returned to intermittent drips, and the thunder finally sounded like it wasn't directly overhead.

"I think it's almost time to move," Seeyela said. "Picoli, can you keep your darts moving with us?"

"Sure, but they'll be pretty obvious to anybody—or anything—watching."

"We'll have to take that risk. We need to be able to see. That's… something we're going to need to figure out if we want to survive down here." At Seeyela's words, the Growers all seemed to realize how much they'd taken something *simple* like sunlight for granted.

Which leads to another question.

"How are we going to restore any solar energy we use?" Hiral asked, and the Growers shared another look.

"One problem at a time," Seeyela said. "First, let's get to the dungeon. Seena, can you open a door for us?"

"Sure," Seena said.

She took a deep breath, then waved her hand in front of the last section of shelter she'd created. The thick roots vanished as if they'd never existed.

Steady rain fell in the small pool of illumination from inside the shelter, the fallen leaves on the ground reflecting with a light sheen.

"So, who's first?" Yanily asked.

26
AMBUSH!

HIRAL quickly reabsorbed his doubles then stepped out into the rain behind Nivian and Lonil, the steady stream of water cold on his bare shoulders. At some point soon, he'd need to figure out a replacement for the clothes he'd lost to the crystal monster.

Though I guess it saved me the trouble of a haircut.

Still, the rain wasn't so bad—the shower back at home fell about as hard, and his **End** would make the cold bearable. It was the *dark* that was the bigger problem. Even though he remembered what the woods around them looked like, it was almost pitch black to his eyes. The few things he could see from the light spilling out of the shelter seemed warped. Sinister. Like there were new depths to things that only came out at night. Add in the way the shadows moved as things passed in front of the light source, and Hiral's head was constantly turning at some new, imagined threat.

"This isn't so bad," Yanily said, following Hiral out of the shelter. "Maybe Hiral has the right idea, though. Clothes are going to be soaked through here in no time."

"This is *not* another one of your silly plans to try and get Balyo naked, is it?" Wule asked dryly.

"I'm nothing if not a man of opportunity," Yanily said, and turned back to the shelter as the others emerged from it.

"Not the time, Yan," Seena said. "We're not going to be able to move as fast like this. Running is too risky, even on the path."

"It'll be a muddy mess anyway," Nivian said. "It's going to take longer to get to the dungeon then we planned."

"Then we'd best get a move on," Seeyela said. "Picoli, if you could."

"Right," the woman said, more **Light Darts** appearing in the air around them. "Oh," she said suddenly, her eyes widening, "I just got an achievement like Seena did. Same one, I think. **Outside the Box**."

"Ability mutation and a class-specific reward?" Seena asked.

"Yeah, from the dungeon interface."

"Those ability mutations might help address our light and shelter issues if they get abilities similar to how they've been using them," Hiral said, and both Seena and Picoli nodded at that, obviously thinking along the same lines.

"They would," Seeyela agreed. "Picoli, can you spread your darts out a bit more? Good. Lonil, you've got the lead. Vix and Fitch behind him. Then Wule, Picoli, and Cal. Rest behind them, with Nivian bringing up the rear. I want everybody keeping an eye out for *anything* out of place. The mud and dark are going to be bad enough, but if we have Troblins jumping us as well, we need to be ready for them. Questions?"

Nobody voiced a concern, and the group moved out. Hiral settled into step beside Seena, one of his swords drawn and ready in case they ran into trouble.

"You okay with your sister taking charge of your party like that?" Hiral asked quietly.

"When more than one party gets together—usually two, three max—we call it a raid group. Seeyela is always the raid leader for us, so we're used to working with her."

"Raid? What's that?"

"Honestly, no idea." Seena chuckled, her eyes sweeping along the edge of the light as they got back to the path. "Another one of those terms passed down from our ancestors. Like *party*, actually. We don't do much as raid groups other than train together from time to time. It's helpful since we all have a pretty good idea what each other are capable of, but as you can guess, the Quillback harvesting doesn't require eighteen people."

"Why aren't you the raid leader?"

"She's the older sister. More experience, though she's only a level higher than me. Her whole group took some time off when she had Favela, and, on top of that, my party made a lot of progress this year hunting things like Troblins around the dungeons."

"Why's that?"

"Caaven wanted us to try something new. Dedicated harvest parties escorted by a combat party to keep them safe. The people in the harvest party have abilities better suited for dealing with the Quillbacks more… peacefully. While they did that, we scoured the area clear of threats. Since we weren't harvesting, we had more time to hunt."

"Seems like a solid plan," Hiral said, scanning the side of the path. With the oppressive darkness, the mud squelching every step, and the rain still falling, even his 18 **Atn** was pushed to the limit to detect anything further than a few feet away. The logical part of his brain knew his senses weren't useless, but they felt limited. The shadows constantly moving with every step sure didn't help either. "Does Seeyela's party have a scout like… what was his name?"

"Julka," Seena said. "And, no. They're more focused on damage, other than Cal and Lonil. Maybe Picoli would be the closest, but I don't think she's put a lot into her attunement. You're probably the best we've got. Why, you notice something?"

"I'm…" Hiral trailed off as another shadow on the side of the road moved. *What was that? My imagination again?*

"Hiral?" Seena asked.

"It was nothing," Hiral said, but kept his eyes moving.

Was the sound of the rain different? It had been consistently pattering against the leaves. Now, was there less of that? Or was he just overanalyzing things? It could simply be that they'd reached a part of the woods with less leaves, and more rain was directly hitting the ground. That would also explain that earthy smell.

Earthy… smell. It wasn't the same as in the shelter when the ground got wet, or what he'd smelled since they left. It was… warmer.

Another shadow moved along the left side of the path, and this time, Hiral was *sure* it wasn't just a trick of the light.

The shadow had moved in the opposite direction.

"Troblins," Hiral said quietly to Seena.

"You're sure?" she asked, an edge to her voice.

"I'm sure," Hiral said while he searched for the telltale green eyes. In the dark like this, they'd be practically glowing, wouldn't they?

"We've got incoming," Seena said, her voice raised so the others could hear her over the falling rain.

As soon as her words registered, the group tightened up, condensing around Wule and Cal, and all eyes turned out toward the surrounding trees.

"Where?" Seeyela asked.

"Hiral?" Seena spoke up.

"I saw movement over there," Hiral said, pointing one sword toward the trees while he drew the other. If the Troblins saw the group was ready for a fight, maybe they'd back off.

"I don't see anything," Fitch said. "The Islander making stuff up?"

"The Islander is standing right here, and isn't making stuff up," Hiral said evenly, his eyes scanning across the edge of the light. "There!" He pointed as a hint of green blinked between some leaves.

"Picoli, darts," Seeyela ordered, and the other woman sent a trio of glowing *Light Darts* into the woods with a gesture.

As soon as the firefly-like balls of light reached the treeline, a dozen pairs of glowing green eyes stared back at the party.

"Their eyes *reflect* light," Hiral said as realization struck him. "More darts!"

"I'll do what I…" Picoli started.

"Behind us," Nivian shouted as the treeline on both sides of the path burst outward in a rush of Troblins.

A dozen. Two dozen. Three. They poured out of the bushes and swarmed at the clustered party in the middle of the path, the same weighted clubs and crude axes held in knobby hands.

"Hit 'em!" Seeyela shouted.

The two parties took a step forward, lashing out with weapons and abilities in a staccato of pulsing of solar energy.

Light Darts that'd been used to guide them suddenly launched out and buried themselves in Troblin bodies, the small, glowing balls burning whatever they struck. Individually, the hits weren't enough to bring a Troblin down, but rarely did only one find its mark. Four Troblins hit the ground before the horde even reached the group.

The downside was that it got noticeably *darker*.

No choice but to trust they know what they're doing, and do my own part.

Hiral's skin hardened as he got the **Nature's Bulwark** notification, and he also stepped toward the nearest pair of Troblins. Out went his sword, twisting around and catching a heavy club as it missed him, then a snap of his wrist pulled the weapon out of the Troblin's hands. The small monster stumbled forward, off balance, and Hiral slammed his heel into its exposed chest, instantly sending it rocketing back into the other creatures behind it.

No sooner had his foot come down than he pivoted out of the way of a swinging axe, the stone head cutting the air where his knee had been. He followed up with a quick thrust of the sword in his right hand. Green blood, almost florescent in the dark, trailed behind his arcing blade, and then he hit the same creature again with the weapon in his other hand.

Two down.

Hiral ignored the notifications popping up in the corner of his vision as the party behind him cut through the Troblin ranks, instead lashing out at another monster filling the space in front of him. *Parry, stab, slash.* He dropped it to the ground, then snapped his hip around to catch a distracted Troblin in the back of its head with a kick.

The stunned creature dropped its guard and staggered forward, right into Yanily's biting spear. Green blood exploded out of its back as the spearhead drove straight through its chest and out the other side, then Yanily shifted his foot and hauled the spear sideways. Using the Troblin body almost like a club, the Grower slammed it into three more of its kind. The whole group tangled and fell to the ground.

Just in time for arm-thick root-spikes to shoot out of the earth and impale each of them half a dozen times.

"Watch out for one of those *Shamans*," Seena called. "Hiral, you see any?"

"No. Need more light," he shouted back while one sword parried aside an axe, and his other sword punched through a glowing Troblin eye.

"Picoli, we've got the damage covered—keep your darts on light duty," Seeyela shouted.

"Understood," she said, and Hiral felt more than saw a shift of the Growers behind him.

She must be moving in closer to Wule and Cal.

Almost immediately, the **Light Darts** that'd been used offensively again took position above the group, spreading out along the path to light up the area thirty feet in each direction.

"Hiral?" Seena asked again.

"I'm looking," he told her, dropping another Troblin to the ground with a pair of swords through its chest while his eyes checked the horde for another wolf's-head hat.

No, it wouldn't be part of the horde. Last time, it was hanging back to direct the **Pile On**. *It's going to be looking for a weak link...*

Hiral turned to the side, narrowly evading a vertical club that splashed into the mud at his feet, then backhanded the Troblin in the face with the pommel of his sword. The blow didn't kill the creature, but it did stagger it back to delay the others behind it. That gave Hiral the seconds he needed to scan further back along the path, and then around to the head of the party, where Lonil's towering, stony form battered aside Troblin after Troblin like they were nothing more than misbehaving children.

Off to the right, a trio of pulsing red spheres dominated the field, sucking in any Troblins unfortunate to get too close—and doing Fallen knew what to them. There was a kind of *pop* when the Troblins hit the sphere, then nothing. No *Shaman* in their right mind would be anywhere near those things.

To the left? Vix and Fitch had things under control near the front, while Balyo and Yanily controlled things closer to the back. Seena seemed to be filling in the gaps while slowing and herding Troblin movements with her abilities, streaming the enemy straight to Nivian, who held the line in the rear.

Hiral's gaze trailed down the path where they'd come from, but there was no sign of a *Shaman* in that direction. The forest was too dense on both sides for anything to be able to see the conflict from more than a foot or two further in. Which meant the best place for a *Shaman* to direct the Troblins would be directly ahead, somewhere past Lonil. Hiral focused his attention in that direction.

Where? Where...? There!

"Found one!" Hiral said.

"Then what are you waiting for?" Seena shot back.

"Uh... right," Hiral said. "Yanily, I'm leaving. Cover me."

"Eh? You're what...?" Yanily said as Hiral arced his blade through the Troblin he'd backhanded a moment before, then spun on his feet and dashed through the Grower party.

He darted between a surprised Wule and Cal, then stretched his hands forward and activated his **Foundational Split** ability. Lonil, Fitch, and Vix formed a solid wall protecting the two healers from the frontal assault, but it'd be almost impossible to go through them *and* the wave of Troblins. So, Hiral needed another option.

Good thing he had *two*.

Right and Left burst out ahead of him at the same time the double-helix pattern wrapped his limbs, then slid to a stop in the mud and interlocked their hands as they turned sideways. Without slowing, Hiral leapt from the muddy path, his feet perfectly finding the cupped hands of his two doubles, and they launched him up and over the backs of the Grower frontline.

Soaring from the combined 36 **Str** of his doubles, Hiral easily cleared the six-deep mass of Troblin bodies, landed, and ducked his shoulder into a roll through the mud to absorb his momentum right in front of the surprised *Shaman*. Blades sweeping out as he rose in a spin, he caught the *Shaman* across its chest—along with one of the two guards—then dove to the side as the other guard swung its club.

A spike of pain lanced up Hiral's thigh, as he wasn't *quite* fast enough, but the **Nature's Bulwark** buff had taken most of the bite out of the hit. Hiral rolled again to get his feet back under him, boots sliding in the slick mud. One guard and the *Shaman* staggered from his earlier attack as he turned back to the trio, but the other guard was already rushing at him with its weapon held high, green energy wrapping in glowing bands around its biceps.

Up came both of Hiral's swords to catch the descending club in the X formed by his blades, but a stunning amount of strength had Hiral dropping to a knee beneath the weight of the strike. Surprised by the power of the Troblin's blow, Hiral was too slow to avoid the kick it launched into his lowered chest.

Air blasted out of his lungs as he toppled backwards, his years of training taking over and getting him to roll yet *again* through the mud—just in time to avoid the club that smashed down right where his head should've been.

Muddy path gave way to the bushy side of the road as Hiral made it as far as his knees, the Troblin guard with the glowing green bands around its arms charging after him. Parrying hadn't worked so well before, but instinct pulled Hiral's right hand up, and he pushed solar energy into the **Rune of Rejection** on his forearm. A lot more solar power than when he'd experimented with it in the shelter.

A concussive, conical *push* exploded out of his hand, along with his sword, blasting the rain aside and slamming his sword into—and through—the rushing Troblin. Green eyes widened in surprise as the guard's chest vanished in a spray of blood that covered the other guard and *Shaman*, who were also tossed to the ground by the wave of force.

He wasn't sure who was more stunned in that moment—himself or the *Shaman*. That had been a *lot* more powerful than when he'd used it before.

"Fallen's balls," Hiral cursed in surprise, but he pushed himself to his feet and rushed at the *Shaman*. The knockback likely hadn't killed it, and this was his chance to finish it off.

Three lightning-quick strides later, Hiral arrived at the *Shaman* just as it was sitting up. A single, merciless sweep of his remaining sword separated its head from its shoulders. Another quick stab took care of the still-stunned guard, and Hiral turned his attention back to the main force.

He needn't have bothered; the two Grower parties had already gone through the bulk of their enemies, almost casually finishing off the stragglers who refused to retreat. And there, beside Lonil, were Left and Right, fighting their way past the last line of Troblins to join Hiral.

"Nice trick with the rune," Right said, green blood soaking the glowing Meridian Line on his right fist and forearm. "Was half-wondering if you'd try those out."

"It would be prudent to test the limits of your new abilities while outside of combat," Left added, the liquid **Dagger of Sath** glowing a soft blue in his hand.

"Haven't exactly had the chance," Hiral said flatly.

"True," Left conceded.

"Thanks for your help getting over the Troblins, though. I wasn't sure that would work, or that you'd know what I needed."

"We're you," Right said. "Of course we knew your crazy plan."

"Hiral… and… uh… other Hirals, is it really okay to call you guys Left and Right?" Seena asked, coming to join the three of them.

"It's fine," Right said. "We can't change it now—it's what our status windows say."

"Which reminds me," Left said. "We should spend our attribute points. It will make the next fight that much easier."

"Sure, in just a minute," Hiral said. Left had a good point, but first… "Everybody okay?" he asked Seena.

"Yes, thanks to your warning and taking care of the *Shaman*. We didn't even have to deal with a **Pile On**," Seena said. "And Left and Right here—they aren't just for show, are they?"

"What do you mean?" Hiral asked.

"They move just like you do. As soon as they joined Lonil at the front there, it was pretty much over. They're strong."

"Like I said, we're you," Right said, like that explained everything.

"That ability is seriously overpowered," Yanily said, joining them. "And guess who hit level nineteen from that last fight? That's right. This guy."

"Which is good," Seena said, apparently not as excited as Yanily was hoping, from the look on his face. "I've never seen a group of Troblins that big, and we've still got a long way to go. I'm not looking forward to whatever other surprises are waiting for us."

27

SPENDING STAT POINTS

HIRAL walked near the back of the group as they set out again, one of his swords in his left hand, while the other—the broken one—waited in the sheath over his shoulder. The ***Rune of Rejection*** had done quite the number on it—not when it'd gone through the Troblin's chest, but when it had smashed into a thick tree after that. Oh, well, at least he'd learned from the encounter.

Now, since Right and Left had the same *Atn* he did, they walked at his side, and it made sense to keep them out to watch for more ambushes. In the meantime…

"So, you both have attribute points to spend?" Hiral asked, his own yellow status window open, but out of the way, as he walked. From the fight with the Troblins, he'd also gained three more levels, bringing him to level 9.

That was fast. Up in Fallen Reach, it would've taken months or years to gain that many levels. Maybe because I was so low-level compared to the Troblins?

"Yes, we each have twenty-seven points to spend," Left said.

"But, like I said before, I can't put any points into intelligence, wisdom, or attunement," Right said.

"While I am the opposite. I can't put points into strength, dexterity, or endurance," Left said.

"So, you got Meridian Lines, which are like the physical aspect of a Shaper's power, and the physical stats," Hiral said to Right. "While you," he said to Left, "got the mental stats and the ability to uses the tattoos."

"Tattoos rely on mental stats to determine their potency," Left said.

"They do," Hiral agreed. "Even though most Shapers *still* focus on strength and endurance. Kind of like Right, I guess. Anyway, do you have any suggestions how to spend the attribute points, then, Left?"

"As we only have three attributes to choose from, I suggest we balance each one out. At E-Rank, we gain three points per level, so one per stat per level. As we reach D-Rank and above, where we gain additional stats per level, we can decide if we want to focus more, or continue on a balanced approach."

"Hrm… Balanced isn't usually how Shapers spend their stat points. Hey, Seena," Hiral said to the woman listening in while they walked. The rain was such a constant by this point that they'd all sort of tuned it out, even though they were soaked through. "How do Growers spend their attribute points?"

"I think we're a bit different," Seena said, stepping in closer to actually be part of the conversation now that she was invited. "At E-Rank, we get three points, like you do, but one of them always goes to wisdom. We can spend the other two points however we like."

"Wisdom? Really?" Hiral asked. "And one of your three points always goes into that?"

"Yeah," Seena said. "Wisdom is the base stat for a lot of our abilities. You know, determines durability and potency in a lot of ways, stuff like that. People like Yanily or Vix, they'll also put their free points into the physical stats to help with their damage abilities."

"My main damage ability is **Reed Spear Style**," Yanily said, joining in the conversation from the other side. "It uses wisdom, strength, and dexterity to do more damage, so I have to balance all three. Kind of a pain, really. Balyo only needs wisdom and strength."

"Vix is wisdom and dexterity," Seena said, "but Nivian over there puts most of his free points into endurance to make him tougher. I had no idea Islanders had control over all their level-up points. Is it the same at D-Rank and above?"

"Yup," Hiral said. "All of the Maker classes—Shapers, Artists, and Academics—have full control over where they place their stats. Still, Shapers almost always put all their stats into strength and endurance."

"Tanks," Seena said.

"I guess so," Hiral said. "Artists are attunement, first and foremost, then usually intelligence, wisdom, and endurance, in that order. Academics tend to focus on either intelligence or wisdom."

"What about your…uh…new race? Any idea what… What is your race called again?"

"Builder, apparently," Hiral said, glancing at his status window. "I don't know. I haven't checked to see how the points worked since I'd just assumed it was the same as Makers. Figured I'd wait until I knew more about my class."

"Can't hurt to go in and check, can it?" Seena said.

"You're right," Hiral said as he mentally focused on the available attribute points he had to spend. No sooner had he done that than a new window opened with just his attributes on it, and his 27 available points dropped immediately to 9. "What in the Fallen's names?"

"What's wrong?" Seena asked.

"Eighteen of my attribute points vanished," Hiral said, but when he looked at the numbers, that wasn't true. "Never mind… it auto-spent them. Here, look." He shared his attribute window.

Str: 18 (0)
Dex: 20 (9)
End: 18 (0)
Int: 18 (0)
Wis: 18 (0)
Atn: 18 (9)

"Looks like your class is dexterity- and attunement-focused. Maybe you're a scout after all?" Seena asked.

"Maybe?" Hiral said. "Attunement is used for a lot of things other than just perception up in Fallen Reach, but... I guess that'll at least be useful to spot more ambushes."

He looked up and down the path. It definitely wasn't his imagination; the darkness seemed pushed back a little, the sounds clearer, and the smells separate and individually flowing into his nose.

"What are you going to do with the other nine points?" Seena asked.

"Same plan as before—hold on to them for the time being until I know more about the class. Either way, I guess the extra dexterity and attunement won't hurt." Inwardly, he was a little disappointed he didn't get to choose how to build his stats out.

Oh, well. Maybe it's better this way. Now I'm not sitting on all the points and waiting.

"Right, Left, you okay with the plan of balancing your stats until we at least get to D-Rank?" Hiral asked them, and both men nodded. "Great, let's do that."

"And... done," Right said, flexing his arms.

"Also done," Left said. "I'll go join Lonil at the front to help keep an eye out, if that's okay with you."

"Definitely. Thanks, Left," Hiral said, and the tattooed double jogged ahead to the front of the group, quickly falling into conversation with Lonil and Vix.

Fitch, though, to Hiral's newly improved **Atn**, looked less than impressed to have the new company.

"Feeling stronger, Right?" Hiral asked his double.

"And faster and tougher," Right answered. "Should help with any more Troblins we run into."

"Not like you had a lot of trouble with them in the first place," Seena said. "What does that Meridian Line of yours do, anyway?"

"I'll let you field that one, Hiral," Right said. "I'm going to go keep Nivian company."

"Uh... sure," Hiral said, watching Right slow his pace until he was at the back of the group. "Anyway, Meridian Lines primarily act as the conduit for our stat points—our **PIMs,** you called them? However, they can also be infused with solar energy to magnify physical stats only. Basically, they make Shapers even stronger and tougher."

"Wow, the tattoo magic you Islanders use sounds simple, but pretty strong," Seena said.

"Yes. We're lucky those Shapers from earlier didn't take me seriously enough to really *try*."

"Also means that crystal thing that survived them was *super* strong," Yanily said. "I still think we got cheated not getting any experience from it."

"Pretty sure we didn't defeat it," Seena said. "Frankly, I'm just happy we survived. And I guess Hiral got a class out of it too. Can't believe you didn't have one this whole time."

"Sorry," Hiral said.

"Nah, it's fine. I don't think I would've wanted to talk about it if I was in your shoes."

"Thanks. Guess this means getting to the dungeon interface doesn't have the same meaning now." Hiral shrugged.

"It does for the rest of us, though," Seena said, tilting her head back so the rain splashed against her face in the faint light from the *Light Darts*. "I really don't think the Troblins are the worst of what's in this rain. Even a group that big wouldn't explain why none of our parties have *ever* survived getting stranded down here. No, we still need to get into that dungeon."

"You're right," Hiral said. "Oh, that reminds me. When I was fighting that *Shaman*, one of his guards seemed to use some kind of ability. These green bands of energy wrapped around his arms, and I think they boosted his strength. His attacks were much stronger than the others."

"A Troblin used an ability?" Seena asked, her raised eyebrows clearly indicating that was news to her. "I... I guess that makes sense, considering they use *Pile On*, but I've never seen or heard of what you're describing. We'll have to warn the others to keep an eye out for it, or anything else new."

"Do you think it's connected to the rains?" Hiral asked. "The ability was somewhat powerful, but like you said before, I don't think it would be enough to explain why nobody survived the surface."

"Could be. Also could've been a unique Troblin. Like one of those *Elites* I told you about before. Did you see any mention of it in your notifications?"

"No, I think it was just called a *Troblin Guard*. Level thirteen, I think, like the *Shaman*."

"Either way, good to know it's not just the *Shaman*s who can use abilities," Seena said.

"I guess so," Hiral agreed. "Hey, it looks like Lonil and Left stopped."

The others quickly caught up to those in the lead, and it was pretty clear why they'd stopped moving. The path naturally dipped down into something like a valley before rising up again somewhere in the darkness. Except that valley was now a lake, filled with water as far as they could see in the limited light.

28

A NEW FOE

"I'm not keen on trying to swim," Yanily said from beside Hiral.

"And I don't think it'll drain anytime soon," Hiral said, watching the rain pitter-pattering into the surface of the newly formed lake. "Is there a way around it?"

"Probably?" Vix said. "But it's always only been a path before. Maybe through the woods somewhere?"

"Without the sun to act as a reference point, we risk getting completely lost," Wule said. "No guarantees we'll find our way back to the path, or to the dungeon."

"Can't we follow the edge of the lake around until we find the path on the other side?" Left offered.

"Assuming it's actually a lake," Lonil said.

"It is," Hiral said, crouching down by the waterline. "Look, the water isn't moving, like a river would. For now, it's all just right here."

"You know, I don't think we're that far from the dungeon, if this is the part of the path I think it is," Nivian said. "Maybe another mile past where the path rises on the other side."

"And how far is that from here?" Hiral asked, trying to remember this part from earlier.

"Not that far, on a dry, sunny day," Nivian said. "Five hundred feet, maybe."

"Still don't want to swim it," Yanily said.

"We're going around, like Left suggested," Seeyela finally stated. "And since he's the one who came up with the idea, we'll go left in his honor."

The others chuckled slightly, then started around the edge of the lake, the water on their right.

"Hiral, keep an eye on the woods," Seeyela said. "I'm sure Troblins would love to find us with our backs against the water and nowhere to go."

"Sure," Hiral said, though he motioned to Left for the double to join him for a moment while they walked.

"Yes?" Left asked.

"I'll watch the woods, you keep an eye on the water," Hiral suggested.

"You think there might be something in the newly formed lake," Left said, and it wasn't a question.

"I have no idea," Hiral answered. "Better safe than sorry."

"Understood," Left said, making his way back to the front of the line as the group moved.

As they walked, they found it wasn't just trees on one side of them, with many of the mammoth trunks extending up from within the lake itself. The water rippled as the rain fell, but so far, nothing stirred on land or from within the dark depths. The **Light Darts** wound their way above the group and through the trees, tossing shadows as they passed behind branches and trunks, but didn't reveal anything looking to make lunch out of the group.

Around thirty minutes later, Left called out from the front, "I see the path."

"That wasn't so bad," Yanily said as everybody moved out from the woods and back onto the path, which continued to the left before vanishing into the water a few feet away on the right. "There wasn't even a…"

SPLASH. Something hit the water directly out from them. Something *big*, as large ripples washed up on the shore.

"You had to say something," Balyo said, lifting her spear and pointing it toward the water.

"We're not staying to find out what that was," Seeyela said, another *SPLASH* sounding off to their right. "Let's go. Dungeon, come on, come on."

The group all gave one last look over their shoulders, then continued up the path away from the lake, the mud squelching and slipping with every step. While the rain wasn't as heavy as it had been at the storm-wall, it was constant and never-ending, turning the ground into a quagmire of sucking sludge.

"What do you think that was, back there at the lake?" Yanily asked Hiral a few minutes later, the water long gone from their small pool of light.

"Why are you asking *me*?" Hiral asked just as a branch high above them and off to their left snapped.

Hiral didn't even get a chance to look in response to the sound before more branches started snapping, faster and faster, closer and closer to the ground, as if something was falling. Then a muffled *thump* hit the ground somewhere off to their side.

"You all heard that too?" Cal asked, but every head turning in the same direction answered the question.

"Yeah," Seeyela said, snapping her head around in the opposite direction as the same branch-cracking thump pattern repeated itself somewhere deeper in the woods to their right. Then came a third somewhere behind them. "Keep moving," Seeyela instructed, even repeating herself when Lonil didn't get going quickly enough for her liking.

"There's more," Hiral said, his ears perking as the distant sounds of more branches breaking reached him. "Three—no, four—more." He stopped at a much closer sound. "Careful, straight ahead!" he warned, just as a branch directly ahead snapped far above.

Left must've heard it too, because he grabbed Lonil and hauled the man backwards, toppling through Vix and Fitch, but possibly saving the tank's life as *something* big thumped into the ground right where they'd been standing.

"What do you think you're doing…?" Fitch cursed from the bottom of the pile, half-submerged in mud, while the others rushed forward to help them up.

"Everybody okay?" Seena asked, helping pull Left to his feet while Yanily and Seeyela helped Lonil up.

Vix and Fitch were back up only a few seconds after that, though Fitch was staring daggers at Left.

"Yeah, I'm fine, thanks to Left," Lonil said. "What… what *is* that?"

All eyes turned on the strange mass ahead of them.

Easily twice the size of any of them, it was some kind of bulbous brown sac—almost like it was made out of wood, but far too *moist* for that.

"Doesn't… doesn't that look like those strange growths on the trees we see sometimes?" Vix asked, taking a step closer to the lump, then quickly jumping back as something within the sac stirred.

Another shift—something inside the sac clearly moving—and then five finger-length claws pierced the material, the sound like tearing cloth rising above the falling rain. Within seconds, a lizard big enough for a person to ride ripped its way from the cocoon, foot-long spines protruding in a ring around its throat, across its skull, and then down its wide back and long tail.

Easily twenty feet long as it unfurled itself, it turned to look at the group and opened its huge mouth to reveal row upon row of sharp teeth. A deep kind of *croak* boomed out of its throat. Its head rotated ninety degrees, and it launched itself forward.

Lonil was the fastest to react, his body hardening into stone in a heartbeat, and he leapt in front of the party as the lizard struck. Its maw closed around the tank's torso like a vise. He grunted in pain, his feet sliding back through the mud from the lizard's rocketing momentum, and the rest of the party barely managed to dive aside to get out of the way.

Fifteen feet further back, the lizard found enough purchase in the slick mud to finally come to a stop. Tail lashing for balance, it thrashed its head side to side, flailing poor Lonil about like a ragdoll.

"Get him out!" Seeyela shouted as a red sphere appeared right above the lizard's back.

Unlike the Troblins who'd been sucked into the **Gravity Well** and annihilated, the lizard didn't even notice the ability or its pull. While the rain in the air got sucked into the sphere, along with mud from the ground, the lizard ignored the force and continued to shake Lonil around madly.

"Damnit," Seeyela swore. She snapped her fingers, and the **Gravity Well** erupted like a bubble bursting.

Water exploded in a tight circle with enough force to ripple across the lizard's spines and bend its legs, the mud around it in a ten-foot circle flattening out. But, still, it didn't let go of Lonil, though it did turn its head slightly to the side so it could see them from one large, unblinking eye.

Without waiting to see what the rest of the party would do, Hiral darted forward and found the spined tail already sweeping in his direction like it knew he was coming. One more step, his foot somehow finding purchase on the slick ground, and he kicked up and to the left to flip over the powerful appendage that swung underneath him. No sooner had he landed than the tail was already coming back, and even with his newly improved **Dex**, he'd never be able to jump it again.

Instead, letting his instincts take over, he reached out his left hand toward one of the trees along the side of the path and activated his **Rune of Attraction**. Like he'd been yanked by a giant hand, Hiral hauled himself out of the way as the tail came back, twisting in the air just enough to hit the tree feet-first and bending his knees to absorb the impact. Gravity took over a second later, and he dropped to the ground as Yanily slipped past the tail thanks to Hiral's distraction.

Spear dancing and bending like a reed in the wind, Yanily laid into the side of the lizard, his lightning-quick strikes ringing off the thick spines and scales like a drum.

"Heavily armored," Yanily shouted before the lizard spun supernaturally fast, its tail whipping around and colliding with his chest to hurl him backwards. He hit the ground just in front of Hiral, the leathers on his chest torn and blood seeping through. "Ow," he muttered, but was already sitting up.

Lonil hung dazed from the lizard's mouth, and while some blood ran from between the sharp teeth, it didn't look nearly as bad as it could've been. *Snap.* Nivian's thorned whip slapped into the lizard's snout, and while the weapon didn't leave any lasting damage, the lizard's eyes narrowed as it looked at the other tank.

More than happy to have the monster's attention, Nivian charged straight at it, his whip snapping out a second and third time to make sure its attention stayed firmly on him.

A rumbling growl rolled up the lizard's throat, and it half-spit, half-coughed Lonil out of its mouth to flop to the ground, then sprang forward, jaw snapping.

Having seen the move once already, Nivian was mostly ready for it, his shield quickly growing in size as he planted it between the lizard's closing jaws. The thorny shield gave a worrying creak as it bent under the strength of the powerful maw, and Nivian's feet slid several feet back in the mud, but he held his ground. Then, bracing his shield with his other arm as well, solar energy pulsed from the man, and the thorns on the shield doubled in length.

That clearly pissed the lizard off. Another booming *croak* belched out of its throat, and its clawed feet scrabbled at the ground.

"Vix! Fitch!" Nivian shouted along with a huge pulse of solar energy, and the men appeared as if by magic beside him.

Without missing a beat, they each cut to the sides of the wide jaws stuck on Nivian's shield and laid into the forward shoulders. Blows landed as fast as the falling rain drops, but neither damage dealer seemed to be able to punch through the tough scales.

"Set it up for Balyo," Seena shouted, obviously seeing the same thing. "Right side."

"She always gets the easy jobs," Yanily grunted, back on his feet. "C'mon, Hiral. We've gotta distract it again."

"I've got… another idea. Just let me test something out," Hiral said as he remembered how Balyo had hit the crystal monster before. If that kind of blow was enough to put the lizard down, they'd be fine. But, on the other hand, if it wasn't enough to finish it off, they needed to already be thinking about the next move—the spines and scales simply looked to be *that* tough. "Just make sure you aren't between me and the lizard."

"Uh… sure… whatever," Yanily said, no time to spare as the others launched themselves at the lizard to keep its attention while Balyo swung around to the opposite side and began to gather solar energy in her spear.

"Seeyela, can you give me a couple of those *Gravity Wells* right above it?" Hiral shouted at the woman.

"Why? It didn't work before," she said.

"I know, but I need it to be lighter," Hiral said. "Trust me on this, okay? Right, I want you to hit in the chin at same time Balyo attacks. Got it? As hard as you can."

"I don't think it has a glass jaw, but sure," Right said, also focusing his solar energy in the Meridian Lines of his right fist.

"Left, I need you to get Lonil out of there," Hiral said.

"Already on it," the tattooed double shouted, darting in and narrowly avoiding a swinging claw, then grabbing Lonil's hand and dragging him out of harm's way.

So far, so good.

As soon as the red *Gravity Wells* began to appear above the lizard's back, Hiral ducked around behind the tree he'd pulled himself toward before.

"I hope this works," he muttered, bracing himself against the trunk as best he could with his right arm and leg, then extending his left hand toward the lizard. Now he just needed to wait for the right moment.

Light Darts zipped in and struck the lizard like stinging insects, their energy flaring with each impact but doing little more than heating the tough scales. A wild slash of the front claw managed to catch Fitch in the thigh, and the man staggered back with blood running down his leg from the three gashes.

"Balyo? How long?" Nivian shouted, legs spread as he fought against the lizard trying to thrash its head around like it had with Lonil. His shield gave another desperate creak at the same time Vix ducked back in for another barrage.

SNAP. The shield cracked in two, Nivian barely getting his arm out before he lost it to the lizard's teeth, while the monster whipped its head to the side. The sudden jerking movement caught Vix completely unprepared, and the batting blow hurled him off to the side to crash into the bushes.

"Ready!" Balyo finally said, her solar energy peaking and her spear glowing like an earth-bound sun.

"Right!" Hiral shouted at the same time.

"On it!" Right shouted back, dashing in, grabbing Nivian's shoulder with one hand, and hauling him back while sweeping his right hand down, under, and up.

Glowing energy trailed the Meridian Lines of Right's punch, the force of it carving a divot in the mud at his feet, while Balyo set herself and lunged forward, her spearhead suddenly bigger than she was.

Now! Hiral shouted in his own head, flooding his **Rune of Attraction** with as much solar energy as he could.

The two titanic blows hit the lizard at almost exactly the same time, Right's uppercut catching it square in the jaw as the lizard's head swung back from hitting Vix and lifting its front half from the ground with the aid of the **Gravity Wells**. Balyo's spear strike simultaneously slammed into it from the side, crunching scales and spines with a horrific grinding sound, but still not *quite* punching right through.

But, there, hanging in the air, Hiral's **Rune of Attraction** latched on to the lizard. If the monster had been on the ground, or if Hiral hadn't had himself braced against the tree, *he* probably would've shot straight toward a spiny end. Instead, however, the lizard lurched through the air, twisting from the impacts of the two blows, to collide heavily with the tree right in front of Hiral.

The entire five-foot-wide trunk shook from the crash, something *snapping* as the lizard's tail and back legs bent awkwardly, and Hiral toppled backwards.

Still, thanks to his 29 modified **Dex**, he was back on his feet a second later. He rounded the tree opposite the twitching tail to find the beast pinned to the trunk by its own spines. The front legs still lashed out and clawed for purchase, but hanging the way it was, it wouldn't be able to pull itself free.

"Wow," Seena said as most of the others rushed over, though Cal and Wule were moving to look after the wounded.

"The belly scales don't look as strong as the others," Seeyela pointed out. "Balyo, you got enough for one more?"

"You bet I do," the woman said, setting her feet and gathering her solar energy again.

Six seconds later, her energy peaked, and she drove her powerful spear straight into the lizard's exposed stomach. Unlike the scales and spines lining the top of it, these softer scales put up almost no resistance, and Balyo's spear nearly cut the lizard in two.

"Good job, everybody," Seeyela said. "Let's make sure…" She trailed off as another lizard's bellowing *croaks* echoed from somewhere deeper in the woods.

Then a second. A third. A fourth. A fifth.

From all around them.

29
JUST KEEP RUNNING

THE group moved faster than was *safe*, their feet slipping in the slick mud every second or third step. The rain was pounding down on their heads, having picked up again, and their legs were leaden from the constant running. Even Hiral, with his 18 **End**, was getting close to his limit after the chaotic day, and he wasn't even one of the injured. Worse, the throaty *croaks* continued to hound them, echoing off the trees all around.

"That sounded closer," Yanily said, nearly falling with the words until Hiral snagged his arm to keep him upright.

"All the more reason to stay on your feet," Hiral said, though he smiled to let Yanily know he was only half-joking.

"Not all of us have twenty-nine dexterity," Yanily responded with a chuckle, but another bellowing *croak* wiped the grin off his face. "How many of them are there? Where did they all come from?"

"I count at least thirteen, unless they're moving around a lot, based on where the calls are coming from," Hiral said. "As for the other question, I don't know. I thought lizards liked the sun, not the rain. And hiding up at the *tops* of trees? Something is messed up here."

"Thirteen is twelve more than we can handle," Seeyela said from the head of the group.

Lonil was closer to the middle due to his injuries. Wule and Cal had done their best to patch him up, but it would take more time than they had to get him back to one hundred percent after the mauling he'd taken.

Near Lonil, Vix wasn't doing much better, the man leaning heavily on Right as they ran. Even Fitch, usually the most vocal about Hiral's presence, leaned occasionally on Left as he half-limped. They'd mostly closed up the claw marks on his leg, but he ran like it still hurt, and the rest of the party spread around the injured to insulate them from any further attacks.

So far, they'd managed to stay ahead of the lizards—if the monsters were even interested in them—but they weren't out of the woods yet. Literally.

"Nivian, any idea where we are?" Seena asked.

"Sorry, it all looks the same in this rain," he said, putting a hand above his eyes as he tried to get a better look around them.

"It's fine—keep moving," Seena said as the familiar crack of breaking branches sounded off to their left.

Snap, SNap, SNAp, SNAP. The breaking branches tracked the falling lizard, so Hiral threw out his right hand and activated the **Rune of Rejection**. A conical wave of force blasted the rain to intercept the falling lizard sac, slapping it away to pinball off one tree, another, and then finally a third before it *thumped* to the ground somewhere further in the woods.

"That won't do more than slow it down, probably," Hiral said, picking up the pace to catch up with the Growers who'd gotten ahead.

Croooooooooak, croak, croak, croak, croak. The noises echoed behind them, somehow piercing the muffling rain. But they were all *behind* the party now.

"I see something," Seeyela said from her lead position. "Rocks, I think. It's the dungeon!"

That simple statement reinvigorated the tired limbs of the runners, and they threw their last surge of strength into their flight as they left the woods. Like Seeyela had said, the muddy path led down the side of a rocky cliff, around a bend, and then *right* there was the archway, the runes etched in the stone glowing softly.

"Never been happier to see a dungeon entrance, even if the glowing writing is kind of creepy," Cal said while Nivian turned to watch their backs.

The injured went in first, and Hiral stopped beside Seena. "Didn't you say something about only six people being able to go into a dungeon at once?" he asked her.

"We haven't had the problem here, but after what we saw from the interface earlier, I'm thinking that rule of six might apply to the inner dungeon. This, out here, where the Quillbacks are... That might not actually even be the dungeon. But we'll find out soon, won't we?" Her voice held nervous excitement despite the fatigue.

"Getting a good sleep might be a better idea first," Nivian said. "Looks like it's just us left. You two go first. I'll be right behind you."

"Right," Seena said, patting Nivian on the shoulder and heading through the arch. Hiral followed after her, and Nivian was quick on his heels.

As before, there was a strange rippling sensation that ran over Hiral's flesh as he passed the archway, along with a noticeable increase in temperature. A soft light emanated from ahead.

"Might not even need a fire," Nivian said behind Hiral, apparently noticing the same things.

Hiral rounded the familiar corner to the Quillback nesting area, and found the scene much the same as they'd left it—except this time, the walls were softly glowing. No, it wasn't the walls, not exactly. Thin roots growing along the walls gave off the soft yellow light.

"I think this is sunlight…" Wule said just off to the right of the door, his hand held up near one of the glowing lines. "Weak… but enough that it's slowly restoring my solar energy."

"That solves one of my biggest worries, then," Seeyela said. "Cal, Wule, think you two can take a look at the injured?"

"Should we pull up the interface? Get in the dungeon first?" Fitch asked, though he had one hand on his injured thigh. "Assuming the Islander can even do it."

"I don't think we should," Hiral said, looking toward the pedestal.

"Oh, here we go," Fitch said. "Time for the excuses after dragging us all the way through the forest and dealing with those… things."

"*Giant Horned Lizard*, to be exact," Yanily said. "And the experience for beating it was pretty good, even with two parties."

"That's not the point," Fitch snapped. "The Islander is backing out of doing what he said he could."

"Fitch, cool it," Seena said. "My whole party saw the dungeon interface open. You calling us all liars?"

"He must've tricked you all, somehow," Fitch said. "I bet…"

"Fitch," Seeyela said, gently putting a hand on his shoulder, "why don't we *ask* Hiral why he doesn't think we should open the interface?"

"I…" Fitch started, only to finally nod, cross his arms, and look at Hiral.

"I was just thinking," Hiral started, "based on what Seena was saying, that maybe there's a second area to this dungeon, and the idea of *clearing* it—it may not be friendly. We probably want to be in the best shape we can before we face it. Your parties are organized around things you call tanks and healers, which tells me there is something to fight in the dungeons. Or am I totally wrong in my thinking?"

Seena and Seeyela looked at each other, and then both nodded. "It's a good point, and you're not the only one who's thinking it," Seena said. "We're lucky this room has some light and a way to regain our solar energy, so let's take advantage of it. We're still going to set up a watch, and I want us to sleep on the far side of the room, just in case anything *can* get inside here.

"As soon as we're rested, we'll open up the interface again, see what that tutorial or whatever has to say, and then enter the dungeon. If it's a place we can stay until the islands come around again, we'll figure out what we need for supplies and get started on that. If it isn't… well… we'll deal with that if it comes to it.

"Any objections or questions?" she asked, eyes landing firmly on Fitch.

The man glared at Hiral, but finally turned around and limped toward the far side of the room. "Let the Islander and his copies take first watch, then."

"That's fine with me," Hiral said to Seena quietly. "We can keep an eye on the entrance, and I'd like to test out these runes a bit."

"Works for me. Wake me and Yanily in a couple hours, and we'll take over," Seena said.

"We will?" Yanily asked.

"Yes, we will," Seena deadpanned back, following in the same direction Fitch and the others had gone.

"You're going to take my advice?" Left asked as he and Right joined Hiral.

"It was *good* advice—why wouldn't I?" Hiral asked, sitting down on one of the few clear sections of floor. They'd have to do something about the Quillback bodies if they planned to stay. "How much solar energy do you two have left?"

"I used a lot against the Horned Lizard," Right said. "Fifteen percent left."

"Twenty-two percent here," Left said.

"Do you two need to sleep?" Hiral asked, suddenly unsure of their needs.

"Not exactly," Left said. "I don't believe we *can* sleep, but we will need to rest as part of you at some point. We are mostly made of solar energy, after all."

"Okay, then let's run some tests and see what we can do with these runes, then we'll merge back up when Seena and Yanily take over. I'm recovering solar energy pretty quickly, so we should get back to full before we go inside the dungeon."

"Sounds like a plan. What's the first test?" Left asked.

"That depends," Hiral said, looking between his two doubles. "Who wants to be a target?"

30
ENTER DUNGEON!

S EVERAL hours later, after everybody had a chance to get a good sleep and recover their solar energy—and the injured were back in fighting shape—the group approached the interface.

"Shall we?" Seena asked Hiral.

The two of them stepped forward, circles of light forming under their feet. This time, to match Hiral's status window, a yellow circle followed him, and he motioned for Left and Right to come closer as well.

"Hrm, no circles for them. I thought maybe the interface would count them as Makers," he said.

"Just means you still need us to get into the dungeon," Seena said with a wink. "Now, get this thing started. I think my sister will pace a hole in the floor if we make her wait any longer."

"That, or Fitch will glare a hole into the back of my head," Hiral said just for Seena's ears.

"He'll come around, don't worry."

"I guess, though I don't know what he has against me."

"He... has his reasons," Seena said quietly.

From the look on her face, she wasn't going to go into those reasons now, so Hiral waved his hand over the activation crystal.

Like last time, Dr. Benza appeared on the pedestal off to the side.

"Welcome, challengers, to the *Splitfang Keep Dungeon*. Please choose an option," the image said, and a blue notification window sprang up beside him.

Tutorial
Enter Dungeon
Help

"Well, I'll be..." Seeyela said. She stepped forward, her hand passing through the hanging image of Dr. Benza. "You really did get it working."

"What? How?" Fitch asked, moving closer. "How did you do it?"

"Wasn't me alone," Hiral said. "Seems like it needs more than just Growers or Makers—or Builders, I guess. For some reason, the dungeon needs at least two of us to get it started up."

179

"What should we do first?" Seeyela asked, standing close to the three options hanging in the air.

"Dr. Benza, *Tutorial*, please," Hiral said.

The image of the doctor shimmered briefly. "Accessing *PIMs*. Access complete," Dr. Benza said, his voice oddly flat. "No dungeon clears detected. Introductory *Tutorial* loaded. Please complete further dungeons to access more advanced *Tutorials*.

"Welcome, challengers, to the *Splitfang Keep Dungeon*," Dr. Benza continued, his voice more normal. "As this is your first dungeon attempt, I will enlighten you to the most basic... basics of the dungeon." Again, he looked off to the side. "Whatever, we can edit that later. Can I continue? Thank you.

"Now, then, assuming we don't have any further interruptions, I shall continue," Dr. Benza went on.

"Who's he talking to?" Cal asked quietly.

"No idea," Yanily said.

"Shush and listen," Seena scolded.

"The Dynamic Understanding and Navigation Growth Epoch Operating Nodes—or dungeons, for short—are snapshots of a time and place on this world, complete with its usual residents and associated dangers. Upon selecting *Enter Dungeon*, a portal will open, allowing a party of up to six members limited access to this space. From the moment the portal opens, you will have three hours to successfully clear the dungeon and claim the associated rewards from our vault.

"Should you fail to complete the dungeon within the given time, you will be forcibly ejected and made to restart from the beginning, if you choose to challenge the dungeon again. While"—the image of Dr. Benza shimmered— "*Splitfang Keep*"—the image shifted again—"is graded as Mid-E-Rank"— another image shift—"you need to be aware that injury and death are very real possibilities within the dungeon.

"Extensive studies have shown that true danger promotes exponential growth in... What? What do you mean they aren't interested in the *science* behind it?" Dr. Benza looked off to the side again. "You want me to just wave my hands and say, *oh, it's magic?* Well, of course it's magic! We literally named the system the *Personal Interface Magic*, but the science behind why it works is very... Oh, fine. Whatever. I'll skip the science. Plebs.

"Ahem, where was I in the script? Right there? Thank you." Dr. Benza looked ahead again. "However, if you survive the trials of the dungeon and overcome the enemies, you will be rewarded with unique items we believe will aid you in your battle against the *Enemy*."

"Who's the *Enemy*?" Yanily asked. "Troblins?"

"Probably your interruptions. Shush," Seena scolded a second time.

"This unique equipment will only be awarded to each party member the first time they clear the dungeon, and the dungeon can only be cleared three times per person. Now, regardless of whether the dungeon is cleared or not, after three hours, it will reset to its base state. All creatures will live again. Any damage done to structures will vanish as if it never happened, and all progress will be lost.

"Don't worry, though. Completing"—the image shimmered—"*Splitfang Keep*"—another image shimmer—"will also unlock access to the other two dungeons in the area." Another shimmer. "*The Mire* and *Splitfang Throne*.

"Further, successful completion of all three regional dungeons will unlock access to the local *Asylum,* where up to eighteen party members may seek sanctuary from the *Enemy.* Please be advised, however, that no more than eighteen people may occupy the *Asylum* at any one time. You are encouraged to stay only as long as needed so the next group in need can move through the area.

"That brings us to the end of this *Tutorial.* Should you require further information, please complete more dungeons and proceed to the next interface. Note, the *Help* section of this interface has only been uploaded with information pertaining to details found within this *Tutorial.*

"Thank you for choosing…" Dr. Benza looked off to the side again and shrugged. "What? I thought it would be funny. Fine. You can edit that out too!" He stamped his foot and walked off to the side, vanishing from the platform, only for his image to shimmer back into its standing position a second later.

"Anybody have any idea what just happened?" Lonil asked.

"Dr. Benza," Hiral said. "*Help.*" The image on the pedestal shifted slightly. "Dr. Benza, how many parties can enter the dungeon at one time?"

"Up to three parties may enter at once, after which point a cooldown of three hours will begin before the next party may enter," Dr. Benza answered. "However, once a party enters, the entry portal will close, and the only methods of exit will be to clear the dungeon or wait out the three hours."

"So, we can all go in at the same time, if we want to," Seena said with a nod to her sister. "What do you think?"

"We might want to have one party go first, see what it's all about, then report back to the other group?" Seeyela suggested. "Reduce the risk."

"Let me guess, you want your party to go in?" Seena asked.

"We are the more experienced group," Seeyela said.

"And we're the more balanced one," Seena said. "Less injured too," she added, glancing toward Lonil, Fitch, and Picoli.

"I'm fine now," Lonil said.

"Cal fixed up my arm, and after the rest, I'm ready for whatever the dungeon wants to throw at us," Picoli said.

"Me too," Fitch piped in. "And the Islander shouldn't go in if it's risky. We need him to access the other dungeons after we clear this one."

"Wait, what?" Hiral said. "You expect me to just wait outside while you guys go in?"

"It might be the safer play," Cal said. "Keeps him out of danger."

"Or puts me in more, because I don't have the same opportunity as you all do to get stronger," Hiral pointed out.

"We'll keep him safe," Seena said.

"I'm not sure it's your choice," Seeyela said. "This affects all of us."

"It is *very much* my choice," Seena said, stepping toward her older sister. "He's in my party."

"Now, now, now," Picoli said, stepping in between the sisters before the conversation turned tense. "You both bring up good points. What do the rest of you think?"

"It's safer for all of us if Hiral comes in with us," Nivian said. "We can keep him safe, and it means we're also not short a party member. Less risk to the whole party. Also, if we're going to be stuck down here on the surface until the islands come around again, we *all* need to be strong enough to survive."

"Nivian's right," Balyo said. "We barely handled that lizard-thing. We *all* need whatever this dungeon has to offer to make us stronger. Experience and… uh… what did he call them? Unique items?"

The other Growers looked from one another, but Balyo seemed to have made a good point, and none of them spoke up.

"So, it's settled—both parties go in at the same time," Seena said, crossing her arms like she was daring her sister to correct her.

"And see who gets the faster clear time," Yanily added with a wink.

Seeyela looked at her party, and Fitch in particular, before she turned back to Seena. "Fine. Both at the same time. But! This is *not* a race." She directed that last statement at Yanily. "We have three hours to clear this dungeon, so I want us to move slowly and safely. Better to get ejected and restart it than get seriously injured or worse."

"Agreed," Seena said, uncrossing her arms when it seemed the argument was over. "Anything else we should ask this guy before we go in?" She thumbed toward Dr. Benza.

"If I may?" Hiral asked, and when Seena nodded, he turned his attention back to the image. "Dr. Benza, what are the difficulties of the three dungeons in this region?"

"**Splitfang Keep** is Mid-E-Rank, while **The Mire** and **Splitfang Throne** are High-E-Rank," Dr. Benza said.

"And how can we find **The Mire** and **Splitfang Throne**?"

"Upon clearing **Splitfang Keep**, your **PIM** will be upgraded to illuminate a path and show you to the next dungeon," Dr. Benza said.

*A **PIM** upgrade, huh? How's that going to work?*

"Does every region have three dungeons and an *Asylum*?"

"Yes."

"How long can we stay in an *Asylum*?" Hiral asked.

"There is no time restriction on an *Asylum*, however, only eighteen people may be present at any one time."

"Why is that?"

"Eighteen is the maximum number of people that *may* pass under the *Enemy's* notice, though six is the recommended and safer number. Any more than that is almost guaranteed to bring the *Enemy*."

"Who is the *Enemy*?" Hiral asked.

Dr. Benza's image shifted. "Information on the *Enemy* is not present in this interface. Please clear more dungeons to unlock advanced **Tutorial** and **Help** information."

"Really feels like the important stuff is getting held back," Vix said, and several of the other Growers nodded their agreement.

"Dr. Benza, what are **PIMs**?" Seena asked.

"*Personal Interface Magic* systems. Please clear more dungeons for further information."

"Why do we need to clear more dungeons? Why can't you just *tell* us?" Yanily asked.

"Access and dungeon interfaces have limited storage capacity, and information is uploaded based on initial **PIM** scans. Dungeon clears will update your **PIM** so the next scan will upload information you haven't already been told."

"I don't understand what half those words mean, but I think I get it," Wule said, tapping the center of his chest.

"Yeah, the doctor here doesn't have a very good memory," Yanily said.

"Not what I meant," Wule deadpanned.

"Either way, we need to clear this dungeon and then get to the next one if we want to learn more," Seena said. "And, since it sounds like we can't stay in the dungeon for more than a few hours, that *Asylum* he was talking about sounds like our best bet to survive until the islands come around again. Anybody get anything different from all that?"

"I think you covered the important stuff," Seeyela said.

"One more question, if you don't mind," Hiral said, and Seeyela gestured to proceed. "Dr. Benza, is there cooldown before a party can enter the dungeon again after clearing it?"

"The dungeon will reset after being cleared and exited, at which point the party may enter again," the image answered.

"Sounds like we *could* go back in right away, but we probably shouldn't," Hiral said. "Good chance to talk about it if we decide to clear it again for… experience, I guess?"

"Hey, if it gets us all closer to level twenty, or D-Rank, why wouldn't we?" Yanily asked.

"You're such an experience junkie," Vix said.

"Experience is life," Yanily said with a smile. "So, let's get in there and see what this dungeon is all about."

"Yeah, let's. You all ready?" Seena asked, and everybody nodded.

"Seeyela, your party should actually go first, just in case you can't access the interface after I go in," Hiral said, and the party leader nodded.

"Dr. Benza, **Enter Dungeon**," she said.

A ball of blue energy appeared in the air in front of her, quickly spiraling open until a portal led into another plain-looking room.

"That's kind of neat," Balyo said, walking around the portal. "This side is… uh… closed, I guess."

"It's just like the portal I found up in Fallen Reach," Hiral said. "I'd always assumed it was just a fancy door into the next room, but… maybe not…"

"Fancy door or not, follow me," Seeyela said. She took a deep breath, then strode straight through the portal. Testament to her party's trust in her, they followed her in without another word, and the portal spiraled closed a second later.

"Our turn next," Seena said.

"One second," Hiral said, waving Left and Right closer. "You should probably come in with me." He held out his hands, and his doubles grasped his arms to vanish in a puff of solar energy that flowed back into his body. "Just in case they counted as people when we entered," he explained.

"Good thinking. You get a chance to figure out your abilities last night?" Seena asked.

"I did, and as an added bonus, it seems I get a third of their stats added to mine when we're all together," Hiral said, pulling up his status window to show them the extra 3 points in all of his stats. "It's not a lot, but every little bit helps."

"Enough showing off—let's get in there and clear this thing before Balyo's party does," Yanily said.

"I'm… actually with Yanily on this one," Nivian said almost sheepishly.

Seena chuckled, then turned and faced the interface. "Dr. Benza, **Enter Dungeon**."

31

SPLITFANG KEEP

T HE portal closed behind them as the last person, Hiral, passed through it, and the six party members stood in the enclosed room.

"What do we do now?" Wule asked.

A blue window popped into existence as if in answer to his question.

Splitfang Keep – Dungeon
E-Rank
Top Clear Times
XXX : --:--
YYY : --:--
ZZZ : --:--

Attempt Dungeon?
Yes / No

"Everybody ready?" Seena asked, and when they all nodded, she tapped the hanging blue *Yes*.

The room vanished in a puff of what looked like solar energy, and the group was left standing in the middle of a small clearing, huge trees encircling them on all sides.

"We're back outside?" Nivian asked, his thorny shield and whip growing out of his hands, and bark-like armor appearing on top of his skin.

"I don't think so," Wule said, pointing straight up toward the canopy. "It's sunny out."

"There's a path," Hiral said as he gestured ahead of them, the space between the bushes and trees conspicuous in its uniqueness. "Do we follow it?"

"Looks like the way we're supposed to go," Vix said. "Could also be a trap."

"Since we can clear the dungeon, that suggests there is a definite end to it," Hiral said. "Especially if it's like the *Time Trial* I did back up in Fallen Reach. Following the path is likely the quickest way to that end."

"Nivian, out front. Usual formation. Hiral, can you call out Left and Right?" Seena asked as the rest of the group got into position.

"Let's find out," Hiral said, and activated *Foundational Split*.

Solar energy—along with his tattoos—peeled off his body, and Left and Right formed at his sides.

"Looks like we're ready," he said.

"Not quite," Wule said, then **Nature's Bulwark** enveloped everybody. "*Now* we're ready."

Seena, staff in one hand, tapped Nivian on the shoulder, and the tank led them down the path.

The trees towered above them on both sides, but the forest was eerily quiet all around them. No animal sounds. No breeze. Not even insects. The leaves on the nearby bushes hung completely still unless somebody from the party brushed up against them.

"We sure there is anything in here?" Wule asked quietly.

"Something ahead," Nivian answered almost immediately, and the party crept up to the edge of another break in the woods, where they collectively stopped for their jaws to drop.

Directly in front of them stood a massive yet squat tree, easily several hundred feet wide and maybe half that tall. Thick branches twisted and wrapped around themselves, forming what could only be described as a thick-walled building, a single ramp leading from the ground up to the only visible entrance. Rope bridges ran along the outskirts and seemed to connect smaller satellite buildings to the main one.

Two notable structures stood out alongside the main building. The first looked to be some kind of platform, though what was on it was impossible to tell from the angle. It definitely wasn't another building, so maybe a garden of some kind? The other had the unmistakable look of a smokehouse, with three chimneys puffing gray smoke into the air above, and even from a distance, the faint smell of barbeque could be detected.

Then, above it all, the tree's thick canopy completely blotted out the sun with layer upon layer of foliage that draped the entire building in shadows, swallowing even the rising smoke.

"So that's **Splitfang Keep**," Yanily said.

"Shhh. Movement," Seena said, and led the group off the path and into the bushes. "Up there, on the walkways."

"Troblins," Yanily said immediately.

"Why are there Troblins here?" Nivian asked back.

"Where do they usually live?" Hiral asked, and that got a strange look from the Growers.

"I... have no idea," Seena said. "We've never found anything even resembling a Troblin camp. It's always been encounters with them on or around the paths."

"So, this..." Hiral said, subtly gesturing toward the massive keep, "...could be the kind of thing they live in?"

"I had no idea they were so... advanced. Always assumed they were basically feral little bastards," Vix said.

Thinking about something else he'd been told about Troblins, Hiral's eyes drifted up to the smokehouse. "Didn't you say they sometimes tried to *eat* the people they **Piled On**?"

"Yeah, so what…?" Yanily started, but then all eyes went to the smokehouse. "Oh… yuck."

"Yup, time to kill some Troblins," Seena said flatly.

"Plan, boss?" Nivian asked, watching as a group of three Troblin sentries walked a circuit along the rope pathways.

"Only one way in, from the looks of things," Seena said. "We can expect reinforcements as soon as we get noticed, so it's going to be a slog. Thoughts on what our goal should be?"

"The platform and the smokehouse for sure," Hiral said. "The objective is to clear the dungeon, right? Until we know exactly what that means, we should assume it means defeating all the Troblins present."

"From the looks of the walkways, we can get to both of those places without going into the main building," Wule said, pointing at the connecting bridges.

"I count three patrols, moving pretty consistently," Vix said. "They're spread out enough, I think, that we can take one down before the next notices us. Might even be able to move around and pick the others off after we down the first."

"I don't like the looks of all those bridges and overhangs," Seena said. "We don't have anybody like Picoli who could deal with things from a distance."

"I might be able to help with that," Hiral said. "If it comes to it."

"Your runes?"

"Yeah. May not be able to kill the Troblins, but I think I could at least buy some time."

"Good enough. Okay, then, here's what we're doing. As soon as that first patrol passes, we're going to sweep up behind and take it out. Then move around and deal with the other two. From there, I think the smokehouse is the most accessible target. After that, we'll decide if we want to move to the platform or drive into the keep itself. All depends how much attention we get before then."

"The patrols are only groups of three," Vix said. "We could probably take them all on at once if we needed to."

"We don't *need* to, so let's take it a bit slow and make sure we don't take any unnecessary risks," Seena said, making sure she looked at Vix and Yanily both while she spoke.

"Does anybody else see that green band of energy around the patrollers' arms?" Hiral asked. "I think that's the same as the *Shaman's* guard."

"I don't see anything," Nivian said.

"I see it, and agree with Hiral," Left said. "It looks almost identical."

"Twenty-nine attunement," Wule said. "We should trust their eyes for this. That means they'll hit harder, right?"

"Assuming it's the same, yes," Hiral said.

"First patrol is just about to pass. We going?" Vix asked.

"We're going," Seena said, and gave Nivian another tap on his shoulder.

The tank immediately ducked out into the main clearing and made a beeline for the ramp up.

Odd that's unguarded, now that I look at it.

As if his thoughts were a signal, four Troblins rushed out from somewhere under the ramp, heavy axes in their hands, and took up position in front of the incline.

"Hard and fast," Seena ordered, skidding to a stop. She began to build solar energy while Nivian lowered his head, raised his shield, and charged right toward the group.

Nivian seemed to stretch and blur, closing the seventy-five feet between the party and the Troblins in the blink of an eye. Out snapped his whip, catching the shoulder of the closest Troblin, and the monster turned furious eyes in his direction, immediately breaking formation and stepping forward. But Nivian basically ignored it, bull-rushing right past and slamming his shield into the next Troblin. Seemingly surrounded as he shoved the monster to the ground under his thorny shield, a massive burst of solar energy pulsed out of him, and suddenly, Vix and Yanily were right there with him.

Caught off guard by not one, but three Growers right in their midst, another Troblin fell back to a barrage of spear strikes while Vix jump-kicked the other square in the face, staggering it.

"They're tough," Yanily said, his spear tearing off a chunk of bark-like skin, but doing little more than superficial damage. Like it wasn't leaking green blood to run down its legs, the Troblin got its axe in position to deflect the next strike.

There was still also the matter of the provoked Troblin bearing down on Nivian's back. The man was still on top of the other Troblin as he ground his shield into the monster's face.

Not quite as fast as whatever Nivian did to pull Vix and Yanily over, Hiral and Right still sprinted with their 30 **Dex**—which had been earned after reaching level 10 from the lizard—and closed the distance just seconds later. Hiral slid to a stop while Right continued on, snapping out his left arm and activating his **Rune of Attraction**.

The Troblin, with its attention firmly on Nivian, jerked back so violently, it left its axe behind. It flew through the air until Right intercepted it with a glowing haymaker in the small of its back. *CRACK.* The Troblin crumpled the wrong way around Right's fist, the back of its head actually slapping into its heels before the momentum of the punch tossed it aside. It didn't get back up.

Vix, meanwhile, dodged away from a sweeping axe strike, then came back in with his own uppercut, clapping the Troblin's jaw shut and staggering the creature back. Like some kind of prize fighter, the thing wiped glowing green blood from its mouth with the back of its hand, then stepped forward to take the fight back up.

Until four **Spearing Roots** drove their way through its chest and back.

Still, it didn't fall—despite coughing up blood—and hacked into one of the roots with its axe.

Vix blurred around the side of it and then hammered blow after blow into the back of its unprotected head. A few seconds of that, and the axe finally fell from the Troblin's dead fingers. That just left the one under Nivian, and the one engaged with Yanily.

With Left already on his way to back up the spear user, Hiral and Right headed for the tank just as the Troblin underneath him somehow managed to toss the bigger man aside.

With green bands glowing fiercely around its arms, and blood oozing from dozens of wounds on its upper half, the monster found its feet at the same time Nivian did.

"Stubborn bastard won't die," Nivian said, snapping his whip out to lash across the Troblin's chest, like it needed to hate him more.

"Let's motivate it, then," Right said, bolting out to the far side while Hiral went straight until he was opposite Right.

"Do what you've got to," Nivian said, another lash drawing green blood along the Troblin's shoulder.

"Now!" Hiral said.

Right dashed in as Hiral threw out his right hand and activated his **Rune of Rejection**.

Focused just on the Troblin, there was no shockwave or torn ground, but the monster shot sideways, directly away from Hiral—and straight into Right's punch. They'd misjudged the angle this time, though, and instead of bending the Troblin around the punch, it ricocheted off Right's fist to hit the ground and bounce once, twice, three times.

And it began to push itself up…

Nivian's foot slammed down on its back at the same time he looped his thorned whip around its throat. Then he pulled.

Hiral looked away—that Troblin was done for, whether it knew it or not yet—and turned his attention to the last monster standing. He needn't have bothered.

Yanily's spear drove into the Troblin's side, blowing a hole right through where a person's kidney would be, at the same time Left brought his **Dagger of Sath** around. The liquid blade, trailing a stream of water, slammed into the side of the Troblin's neck, then exploded out the other side with enough force to send the head cartwheeling in the air before hitting the ground.

"Ooooooh," Yanily said, his face scrunching up. He stepped in and patted Left on the shoulder. "Nice! I mean, I could've handled it on my own. But, nice!"

"Well done, everybody. Any injuries?" Seena asked.

"Just my pride," Vix said. "These things either know how to take a hit, or I'm wearing my kiddie gloves."

Nivian's eyes seemed to glaze over for a second as he looked at something. "Check your notifications. These are *Elites*. Still only level fourteen, but that explains why they were so tough."

"And this is a Mid-E-Rank dungeon," Wule said.

"Good thing reinforcements didn't arrive, but we'll have to assume there are more in hiding. Either way, we should take a minute and then get…" Seena cut off as a blue notification window appeared in the air in front of them.

Dynamic Quest
The Ritual of Summoning has begun!
Time until completion: 10 minutes.
Stop the ritual or face the consequences.

32

DYNAMIC QUEST

"T HE *Ritual of Summoning*? What is that?" Nivian asked.

"Something *bad*, from the sounds of things," Seena said.

"Then we should probably stop it," Hiral said, looking up the ramp at the keep. "Hey, was there purple light there before?" He pointed at the area that looked like a platform higher up.

"Not that I remember," Seena said.

"There wasn't," Left confirmed. "I suspect that's where we'll find this ritual."

"Change of plans, boss?" Wule asked.

"Yes. Let's have *Nature's Blade*. These things are too tough to go easy on them," Seena said.

Wule nodded and held up his hand. Another plant grew out of his palm, this one with petals shaped like swords.

You have been buffed by Nature's Blade.
Increases damage inflicted by 10% for 570 seconds.

"Nice," Hiral said before looking at Left and Right. They nodded to indicate they'd also received the buff. *Very nice.*

"Uh, fair warning, Hiral—this may look pretty creepy, but it's effective," Seena said, and a thorny vine similar to Nivian's whip grew out of her hand. This one only got to be about six inches long before the woman pulsed with solar energy, and the vine turned to dust.

Almost immediately, there was a tickle on the back of Hiral's shoulders, and he got another buff notification.

You have been buffed by Lashing Vines.
Vines will make independent attacks to enemies
within range for 570 seconds.

"Vines?" Hiral asked, only to notice six-foot-long thorned vines hanging from the backs of everybody's shoulders. A quick glance confirmed he also had the new appendages. "Yeah. Creepy."

"Nine and a half minutes left," Nivian said. "We need to move."

"Heading for the platform will take us *into* the path of the patrols instead of sneaking up behind them," Vix pointed out.

"Nothing we can do about it. Nivian, let's hit that first group," Seena said, tapping Nivian's shoulder. The tank barrelled up the ramp with the others close behind. "Hiral, watch the…"

"Already on it," Hiral said, his eyes scanning the rope bridges crossing above them.

"Incoming!" Nivian shouted as they crested the top of the ramp, and the man cut a hard right straight into three surprised-looking Troblins.

Vix and Yanily were already moving to engage, the distance apparently too close to make the strange teleport ability worth the cost, but movement above caught Hiral's attention.

Two Troblins, one on each side of the path, emerged from concealed doors, something like crossbows in their hands, and rushed to the edge of the balconies to get a better shot.

"Right, catapult," Hiral said, dropping to a knee and cupping his hands.

"I hate this idea!" Right said, but the man rushed over and put his foot in Hiral's hands.

As soon as the foot was in place, Hiral *heaved* and poured solar energy into his **Rune of Rejection**.

"Haaaaaaaaaaaaate!" Right repeated as he shot into the air toward the Troblin on the left, arms and legs flailing.

Hiral didn't wait to see if his double made the jump—*he's pretty durable either way*—and instead spun to face the Troblin on the right as it took aim at Seena and Wule. His left hand snapped out, and power flooded into his **Rune of Attraction** at the same time the Troblin squeezed the trigger. The crossbow *twanged*, but the sudden yank off the side of the balcony ruined the creature's aim, and the bolt buried itself in the wooden wall instead of the side of Seena's head. The Troblin hit the ground a heartbeat later.

Still, the twenty-foot fall wasn't enough to finish the creature off, and despite one of its arms clearly bending in the wrong direction, it got to its feet.

"I've got this," Left said, rushing past Hiral with his **Dagger of Sath** already swinging.

Shockingly fast, the Troblin got its mangled crossbow up to intercept the dagger, a chunk of wood flying away at the impact, but then the two **Lashing Vines** on Left's shoulders activated. They cracked like whips as they struck the monster, the thorns tearing bark-like flesh and leaving lines of green blood in their wake, but doing only mild damage. The distraction they provided, though, gave Left an opening to bury his blade where the Troblin's neck met its shoulder.

More blood spattered into the air, leaving the Troblin staggering back in pain and fear, which let Left rip the weapon free. Finally, the injuries were too much for the creature, and it fell back against the wall and slumped to the ground, where it lay unmoving.

Just to be safe, Hiral kicked the crossbow away from its still hand, then ran up the last half of the ramp to join the rest of the group, where Yanily was burying his spear in the final prone Troblin as he arrived.

"Hated that plan," Right said as he also caught up, a line of leaking solar energy from the bare left side of his chest.

"You okay?" Hiral asked.

"Good enough," Right said, poking the wound and wincing. "No idea why I can feel pain, though."

"Stay close, everybody," Wule said, a plant with blood drop-like leaves growing from his palm.

As soon as the flower reached maturity, a wave of refreshing energy pulsed out from the healer and across the entire party, Right's wounded chest closed up as Hiral watched.

"Thanks," Nivian said as he rubbed at his hip, where dried blood stained his broken wood armor. "Those little bastards hit *hard*."

"Good to keep moving?" Seena asked. "Eight and a half minutes now."

"Let's go," Nivian said. "Which way?"

Hiral took quick stock of the massive main building to their left, and the treehouse-like connections ahead, then pointed to an angled rope bridge ahead and to the left. "There. That will take us to the second level of the keep, and from there, we can cross over to the platform above us."

"Nivian," Seena said, adding the familiar tap on his shoulder, and the tank was off.

The party raced down the walkway, eyes peeled for more secret doors, then turned and ran up the rope bridge, the whole thing swinging as they piled on.

"Careful," Nivian said, forced to slow or risk tumbling off, but the now familiar sound of a secret door opening at the top of the bridge had Seena tapping his shoulder rapidly.

Nivian's shield came up just in time as a Troblin reached the top of the bridge, crossbow in hand and firing without taking aim, though the bolt still *thunked* into Nivian's shield. Two more Troblins joined it a second later, their axes swinging solidly into the bridge supports.

"Can't you move any faster?" Yanily yelled from the back, though a resounding *thunk* told the party Nivian's shield had just caught another crossbow bolt.

"We need to stop those axe users!" Seena shouted, beginning to gather solar energy.

*Her **Spearing Roots** will take too long.*

Spinning in place, Hiral ducked under the rope railing of the bridge and jumped clear. No sooner had his feet left the wooden planks than he pointed at the ground ten feet below him and engaged his *Rune of Rejection*.

Shooting straight up like he was caught in a geyser, Hiral cleared the level where the Troblins struck their second blow against the bridge supports, then reached out with his left hand and used his *Rune of Attraction*. He jerked to the side so hard, he almost popped his shoulder out of joint, but the maneuver whipped him straight over the three surprised Troblins, his *Lashing Vines* striking the two axe wielders on the way by as an added bonus.

Then he hit the wall with a resounding *crunch* and dropped to the floor.

Ouch.

The world tilted. He struggled to draw in a breath, but movement to the side reminded him he didn't have time to lie on the ground, even if his body refused to move.

Good thing he had two other bodies to work with. Hiral cancelled his summons of Left and Right. He lost the solar energy he'd invested in them—he'd only given them ten percent each before—then immediately activated *Foundational Split* again.

Left and Right burst out of him and charged the approaching Troblins while Hiral got himself up to his hands and knees. His lungs still felt like hollow pits in his chest, but with the aid of the wall at his side, he pulled himself to his feet and then leaned his back against the rough-grained wood.

I really need to find a new shirt.

Left and Right fought with the axe wielders, deftly dodging the heavier weapons and scoring their own hits, though these Troblins looked even bulkier than the last ones. Thankfully, Nivian burst off the ramp at that point, actually getting *under* the crossbow-wielding Troblin and lifting it on top of his shield. From there, he simply tossed it over the side to *crack* on the ground somewhere below, then lashed out with his thorn whip to get the attention of one of the others.

The axe-wielding Troblin twisted at the infuriating pain, then took two slashes from Right's *Lashing Vines*—*the ability lasted through getting absorbed and resummoned?*—and a right hook that spun it in place like a top. When it finally got its feet under it properly, it took a staggering step straight into Yanily's spear. The first strike tore out the side of its abdomen, while the second, third, and fourth rapid blows cratered the bark-like armor on its chest.

That just left one more—and between Vix, Left, and a swarm of splinter-like projectiles from Seena, it toppled to the ground a bloody mess.

"Are you crazy?" Seena shouted at Hiral as she ran over.

"I knew… you'd… back me up," he said, forcing the words out as he finally caught his breath. "Besides, I had them." He pointed at Left and Right.

"And what if more Troblins were waiting where we couldn't see? Or came to cut the bridge and separated you from us?" The anger on her face shoved him against the wall like physical pressure.

But there was more than just anger on her face. There was worry there too. *She was worried about me…?*

"I… I'm sorry," he said. "You're right. It was reckless of me… but it was all I could come with on the spot to make sure they didn't cut the bridge."

Some of that fury drained from her shoulders. "Damn right it was reckless," she hissed. "But if you realize *that*, it's a start. When we get out of here, we all need to work together and practice as a team. We're not used to you, and you're not used to us. That needs to change. You're a member of this party now, and I won't lose you. Understood?"

"Understood," Hiral said.

"Six minutes," Vix said. "Looks like one more bridge, though that purple light is getting stronger."

"It's giving me the willies," Yanily added.

"I'm ready when you are," Hiral said, standing straight up without the aid of the wall, but not moving a step until Seena stopped glaring at him.

"No more being reckless," she said, but then her face softened. "You sure you're okay?"

"Just got the wind knocked out of me. I'm good."

Seena gave him a look, like she was trying to tell if he was just faking it, but finally seemed satisfied with whatever she saw. "Buffs are still good. Nivian…"

"Actually," Hiral interrupted, "let me and Right go first. We can get up there faster, and if more Troblins are waiting to cut the bridge…"

Seena narrowed her eyes at him.

"Not trying to be reckless," he said, holding his hands up defensively in front of himself. "You'll all be right behind me, right?"

"Right. I get it, go," Seena said after a moment's consideration.

Without another word, Hiral dashed toward and up the final rope bridge, Right on his heels. Energy gathered in his **Rune of Rejection** in preparation as he crested the edge of the platform, but he needn't have bothered—there weren't any Troblins waiting for them.

Instead, in the middle of the platform, what had to be six *Troblin Shamans* sat bathed in smoky purple light in a wide circle, all facing inward. In the center of the group sat another, larger pillar of the same ominous light, and within it, two eyes almost as big as a person looked at Hiral.

33
THE RITUAL OF SUMMONING

T HE rest of the Grower party filed onto the platform behind him, all eyes on the purple pillar *looking back* at them.

"Wild guess here, but that's what we need to stop," Yanily said.

"Just six *Shamans*?" Hiral asked, checking out the rest of the platform.

At about a hundred feet square, there wasn't much more to it. No other Troblins. No buildings. No places for more secret doors, unless they came out of the floor itself. Just the seated *Shamans* chanting at the central pillar.

Okay, maybe the thing in the glowing pillar of evil doesn't qualify as a "just."

"Five minutes," Vix said.

"They aren't even paying attention to us," Wule said.

"Start with the closest one—there, Nivian," Seena said, pointing at a *Shaman* on the left. "Watch out for any tricks; this seems too easy." Then she turned her attention to the closest *Shaman* on their right and began channeling solar energy.

"Left, keep an eye out on the bridge behind us," Hiral instructed, and his double went to the edge of the platform.

"Here I go," Nivian called, snapping out his whip. The spiked weapon lashed through the air, cutting through the purple light like it was just smoke, and tore into the *Shaman's* shoulder.

If the *Shaman* felt the usual anger toward Nivian—or even pain from the strike—it didn't show it.

It didn't shift. Didn't stir. Didn't stop chanting.

Nivian looked at his twin, shrugged, and tried again. Another trail of blood formed next to the first, but the *Shaman* showed no sign of even noticing.

At that moment, Seena's **Spearing Roots** burst from the platform and impaled the *Troblin Shaman* on the right, lifting it clear off the ground to hang limply in the air.

"Its lips are still moving…" Hiral said, his eyes wide as he looked at the obviously fatal damage, but the energy flowing from the *Shaman* weakened, growing so faint, it was barely there.

Did she do it? Then, something moved within the pillar of purple smoke— just shadows at first, until two forms burst out and launched themselves at Seena.

Humanoid, mostly, they seemed made from the writhing purple smoke, their hands with wicked claws on their too-long arms, and torn, bat-like wings on their backs. A streamer of the smoky purple light connected their heads to the pillar, and a circular maw and eyes made them look like they were constantly screaming.

And they were *fast*!

The first lashed out at Seena before anybody even had a chance to react, its claws slashing across her chest. The leather armor she wore seemed to absorb some of the damage, but blood blossomed near her collarbone, and she fell back with a shout of pain.

The second smoke monster darted left then right around its compatriot, bearing down on Seena even as she fell to the wood flooring of the platform, completely defenseless. Its clawed hands went out wide, and then drove in with inhuman speed.

Crack. Wood splintered as Hiral yanked Seena out of the way—just barely—with his **Rune of Attraction**, and then Nivian slammed into the smoke monster from the side, shield first. The pair tumbled to the ground, the smoke monster more solid than it first looked, but Nivian had learned from rushing the Troblins. He quickly rolled off before it could get around his shield or toss him off balance. Out lashed his whip, scoring one hit, then two, in quick succession across the monster's side and strange wing.

Hiral, meanwhile, ran forward to Seena, Wule arriving a split second later. "Are you okay?" he asked her, and Seena touched her hand to the blood running down her armor and grimaced.

"I'll take care of her," Wule said.

"Okay," Hiral replied, getting to his feet.

Yanily had already moved to aid Nivian, his spear lashing out in a flurry, and he scored two solid hits. That still left the other monster, but Vix and Right firmly had its attention.

The two pugilists danced in and out, deftly—and narrowly—evading the creature's claws while throwing punches and kicks at every opening, while the vines from their shoulders struck like snapping serpents. Each time the monster turned its attention to Vix, Right would slide in and hit it with a staggering combo, getting its attention, which let Vix slip in on the other side and score a combo of his own. Both men fed off each other's momentum, working their way around the monster that never had enough time to focus on one of them without getting punished for it.

Lines of thin smoke streamed from both monsters in short order, but they refused to fall, and the timer continued to tick down. Apparently feeling the pressure, Yanily charged after the first monster as it lunged at Nivian.

But the lunge was a feint. The monster twisted around like it didn't have a bone in its body, and it was suddenly within Yanily's guard.

The spearman tried to get his weapon between himself and the monster, but he wasn't fast enough, and the claws came across—one, two. Blood splashed from four gashes across his thigh, and the second claw caught his wrist. Taking the hits from the vines on Yanily's shoulders, the monster twisted and pulled, lifting Yanily from the ground, and hurled him straight into Vix's unsuspecting back.

The two Growers went to the ground in a heap, the second monster turning its full attention on Right, while the first lunged at the prone and defenseless pair. Up went its claw, holding it for a moment as if savoring it, and then down for the coup de grace like a lightning bolt.

Hiral's feet skidded along the wooden flooring as he slid between the monster and the fallen Growers, his sword up just in time to catch the falling claw. Still, the blow came with enough force that it drove him to his knee, and then a snap of the monster's waist smashed a kick into his exposed side.

"Ooof," he grunted, the air getting blasted from his lungs for a second time in short order.

His *Lashing Vines* scored a pair of hits on the smoke monster before he was tossed aside. He rolled with the force, though it still sent him a good ten feet, and scrambled to his feet to prepare for a follow-up attack.

Except the monster had turned its attention back to Vix and Yanily, who were just now pulling themselves apart. Again, its claw went into the air, preparing to strike, but Nivian's whip caught its wrist like it had a mind of its own. Around and around the whip wrapped the arm, thorns digging deep into the hazy flesh and drawing streamers of smoke.

The creature turned its attention back on the tank, anger simmering in the solid black eyes.

Then half a dozen *Spearing Roots* drove straight into it. Three struck it in the chest, one in the leg, another the arm, and the final one directly through its round mouth. Pinned and unable to move, the opening gave Vix and Yanily the chance they needed to get their feet under them.

"Get the other one," Seena shouted, and a pulse of solar energy rippled off her.

All at once, something seemed to flash in Yanily's, Vix's, and Right's eyes, their focus turning toward the remaining smoke monster.

It tried to turn as it sensed Vix and Yanily coming from behind, but Right dove in at the moment's distraction, punches landing like a staccato drum across its torso. His vines lashed across its arm and face, and as soon as it looked back in his direction, a spear punched through its shoulder from behind. Held for a heartbeat like that, Vix swept its legs out from under it, bringing it to its back on the ground while the spear tore out of its shoulder.

The second it landed on the wooden floor, Right brought his glowing fist up and then down directly on the creature's face. The head exploded like a popped balloon, the limbs and body of the monster tensing straight, twitching, and then falling still.

Then, just like that, both monsters completely vanished.

All eyes turned to the *Shaman* hanging still on the **Spearing Roots** from earlier.

"Left, I need you to…" Hiral started, and then trailed off as the roots vanished.

The *Shaman* was once again sitting in place, its body clear of injuries.

"What in the…?" Nivian said. "Should we kill one of the other ones?"

"Hold up, let's think about this. We have…" Seena said, her eyes glancing to the side. "Three minutes. Wule, see to Yanily."

"Got it, boss," Wule said, hurrying over to the spearman.

"We *must* have to kill the *Shaman*s here to stop this ritual," Vix said.

"I don't want to fight ten more of those things," Nivian said. "We had a hard enough time with two."

"We know what's coming with the next one," Yanily said, his thigh wound closing up as Wule healed him.

"But it's not just the *next* one," Seena said. "This first one is fine again. No, there must be something more to it. I killed this one, the energy got weaker, then a few seconds later, those monsters came out of the pillar."

"Are they an illusion?" Wule asked. "Is only one of them real?"

"Sure didn't feel like an illusion," Yanily said, poking at the bloody armor on his thigh.

"Troblins!" Left shouted, and Hiral turned to see him pointing down the bridge toward where they'd just come from. "More secret doors. At least a dozen of them."

"Of course there are," Yanily said.

"We can't fight a *dozen* of those *and* figure this out," Wule said. "Boss?"

Hiral looked from the six *Shaman*s to the edge of the platform where the bridge connected. Wule was right. How could they…?

"Six *Shaman*s. Six party members. We need to kill them all at the same time," Seena said. "That has to be it. The energy got weaker, and then there was a delay between when I killed it and when the monsters came out."

"And if you're wrong? If we kill them all at once and we get twelve of those things?" Vix asked.

"I'm not wrong," Seena said, steel in her voice. "I'm sure of it."

"I'm willing to give it a try," Yanily said, glancing somewhat nervously at the pillar.

"I don't think I can do enough damage to kill one as fast as you guys," Wule said.

"That's okay," Hiral said. "Left and Right, take Wule's spot and mine."

"What are you going to do?" Seena asked, but the Growers were already moving to take positions around the sitting *Shaman*s.

They really do *trust her absolutely.*

"What do you think? Hold off the other Troblins," Hiral said as he passed Left. "Go on."

Left gave him a look that seemed to say, "Are you sure?" but he didn't speak up, and instead ran over to one of the Troblins.

"Everybody, my *Spearing Roots* will be your cue to go," Seena instructed behind Hiral as he took up position ten feet back from the bridge, the first Troblins already on the platform and glaring at him. "Nivian, you got something to do this with?"

"I'm good," Nivian called.

"Less than two minutes now!" Vix shouted.

"Shouldn't you be on the bridge to block them?" Wule asked from beside Hiral. "I'll keep you healed up. If it's only one or two of them at a time, it shouldn't be a problem."

"I've got a better idea," Hiral said as the next pair of Troblins crested the bridge and stepped onto the platform.

"What's that?" Wule asked, stepping back as two more Troblins joined the first group.

"Just wait a second," Hiral said, a seventh and eighth Troblin making it to the platform.

The eight sets of eyes settled on Hiral, and the group of monsters charged at him as more ran off the bridge.

"Got you," Hiral said, flooding power into his *Rune of Rejection*.

The cone of concussive force hit the gathered Troblins like a bowling ball, tossing them into the air and hurling them off the side of the platform in a chorus of surprised, breathy shrieks.

Two more Troblins peeked over the lip of the platform, obviously wondering what had just happened, and Hiral hit them with a wave from his *Rune of Rejection* as well.

"I guess that works," Wule admitted.

"NOW!" Seena shouted, and Hiral glanced back to see her *Spearing Roots* punch through the seated *Shaman* she'd impaled before.

At the same time, the other five laid into their unmoving *Shamans* as well. Yanily, Vix, Right, and Left made short work of theirs with decisive blows.

Nivian, without any such powerful attacks, simply reached into the purple light and grabbed the *Shaman's* head. Then he twisted it so violently, it almost came off.

The smoky purple light coming from the *Shamans'* bodies flickered and weakened, and all the Growers quickly circled around, gathering as something moved within the shadowy pillar.

"It didn't work!" Yanily said, leveling his spear at where he expected a dozen murderous smoke monsters to burst out of.

"Wait!" Seena said, holding her hand out to the side, though Nivian had his shield back in position, and Wule rushed to join the group.

Hiral, meanwhile, glanced at the bridge up to the platform.

No more Troblins coming up. For now. He turned back to the ritual.

Another flicker, the smoky trails from the *Shamans* vanished, and something within the central pillar roared its clear displeasure. Exploding upwards, the purple energy washed across the underside of the canopy above while the thing inside wailed loud enough to shake the entire tree. Hundreds of leaves rained down all around.

Hiral put his hands to his ears as the cacophony continued, long seconds passing as the timer continued to tick down.

Under a minute!

And then, all at once, it stopped.

The pillar of purple energy vanished with a *pop*, and a blue screen appeared in front of Hiral.

> **Dynamic Quest Complete**
> **The Ritual of Summoning has been thwarted.**
> *Congratulations. Achievement unlocked –*
> *Unsullied and Unsummoned*
> *You prevented an ancient evil from*
> *being summoned into the world (for 3 hours).*
> **Please access a Dungeon Interface to unlock class-specific reward.**

"Did you all just get a… dynamic quest complete notice? Along with an achievement?" Hiral asked, and by the glazed-over looks on their faces, he had his answer.

"What is a quest?" Yanily asked. "I mean, I know what the word is… but… why are our **PIMs** giving us quests?"

"So, those aren't normal?" Hiral asked.

"First one I've ever seen," Seena said, but she had a smile on her face. "And, everybody, good job. Hiral, Troblins?"

Hiral jogged cautiously to the edge of the platform—the Troblins had used crossbows, after all—and looked over the side. Bodies littered the ground far below, where he'd tossed them with his rune, but other than that…

"Clear for now," Hiral said. "Looks like we've got a minute to take a breather."

34

WHAT'S A MID-BOSS?

WULE moved around the party, patching up any injuries that lingered after the battle, while Hiral pulled Left and Right back into himself to restore their solar energy.

"What's next, boss?" Yanily asked from where he sat to recover, and all heads turned to Seena.

Even Vix, who was on watch near the bridge, looked over at the question.

"Smokehouse," Seena said without hesitation. "I think we should save the keep for last."

"You don't think more Troblins will come out of there when we hit the smokehouse?" Nivian asked. "Hiral definitely had the terrain advantage here— good job on that, by the way—but it would've been way tougher without that."

"Actually hoping we can draw a few more out on the way over to the smokehouse," she said. "Will make it easier when it's time to go into the keep. Did any of you notice the tag on the smoke monsters in your experience notifications?"

"*(Mid-Boss) Infernal Smoke 1*?" Hiral asked, checking his notifications. "What's a *Mid-Boss*?"

"Guessing a difficulty tier above *Elite*," Seena said. "Those things were tough. And since it's labeled *mid*, I'm guessing there is some kind of *End-Boss*-type enemy here."

"And you think it's in the keep," Nivian said, nodding. "Okay, smokehouse it is."

"Great," Yanily said, clapping his hands together and standing. "I still need most of the level to hit twenty, so let's get to it."

"Slow down there," Seena interrupted. "How's everybody doing on solar energy?"

"Eighty percent here," Wule said. "It's sunny, but I'm absorbing energy slower than I expected."

"Seventy-five for me," Nivian said. "The *Swarm Tactics* I used at that first ramp is pretty costly."

"Almost full," Yanily said, and Vix chimed in with a "Me too."

"Hiral? You've been using those runes of yours constantly," Seena noted.

"Oh, I'm back to full," Hiral said, and activated *Foundational Split*.

"S-Rank absorption right there," Wule said with a shake of his head and a chuckle.

"I'm almost back to eighty myself. Vix, you spot the best path to take?" Seena asked, turning her attention to the man by the edge of the platform.

"Pretty straightforward," Vix replied. "Down this bridge, along the keep's balcony, then two more bridges and we're there."

"How many places for secret doors?" Nivian asked.

"About a million on the keep balcony, then we can expect them at each of the bridge crossroads," Vix said.

"Do you really think Troblins have buildings like this?" Wule asked quietly.

"Maybe Dr. Benza will tell us when we clear this place," Hiral said.

"Either way, it's a question for later. Wule, give us **Nature's Blade** again," Seena said, and she recast **Lashing Vines** to replace the ability that had faded while they recovered.

"You got it," Wule said, and the familiar pulse of energy strengthened Hiral's limbs. "Bulwark should last until we clear the dungeon, one way or another."

"Then we're ready," Seena said. "Nivian, take the lead again. Hiral, can I ask you and Right to cover the back in case we have more doors opening behind us?"

"For sure," Hiral said, and the group moved back down the bridge to the balcony running along the outside of the keep.

"So far, so good," Nivian said as they cleared the rope bridge, their feet back on solid ground, and then moved along the wide balcony.

The solid-looking wall on their right towered at least fifteen feet up before wooden crenellations protruded from there, indicating a third level, while a low parapet overlooked the lower levels on their left.

"Don't see any secret doors," Yanily said from his usual position on the right of the triangle formation.

"If you could see them, they wouldn't be *secret*," Vix said.

"Good point," Yanily agreed.

"Just be on your guard," Nivian said. "You never know when..."

A secret door twenty feet ahead of them slid open, and a group of five Troblins burst out—two with large wooden shields in the front, two more with crossbows behind, and then a *Shaman* with the familiar wolf's-head cap.

"See!" Nivian said as the shield-bearing Troblins *thumped* their spiked shields to the ground, though it looked like they had small wheels on the bottom.

"What are they doing with those?" Vix asked, but it was the crossbow-Troblins behind that acted first, ducking out to the side of the shield wall to pull their triggers.

Nivian's form blurred as he darted left and right in quick succession—*thunk thunk*—to catch the two bolts before they struck Wule and Seena. The shield-bearing Troblins began to rush forward, the small wheels rolling along the wooden floor.

"Less talking, more killing," Seena shouted, solar energy building in her staff. "Yanily, the *Shaman* is yours."

"Sure, and how do I get to him with those two in the way?" he asked.

"Leave it to me," Seena said, her solar energy pulsing and small ***Snaring Roots*** growing out of the wooden floor to tangle in the wheels of the shields.

Almost comically, the bottoms of the shields abruptly stopped while the tops kept going. The momentum of the Troblins carried them up and over to flip past their shields and hit the ground with a painful *thump*. Behind them, the crossbow-Troblins looked surprised at their sudden exposure, but one of them had already reloaded its weapon, and lifted it to fire.

Not so fast!

Hiral focused on the crossbow and activated his ***Rune of Attraction***. The weapon snapped out of the Troblin's hands and soared straight toward Hiral. With his now 30 ***Dex*** and ***Atn***, snagging the weapon out of the air was almost too easy, and he spun as he caught it to steal its inertia, then leveled it and pulled the trigger.

The Troblin, who was still staring at its empty hands in shock, took the bolt square in the chest and fell back with a yelp of pain. The other, just now getting its bolt loaded, looked over at its fallen ally, then back toward the Grower party—just in time for Vix to clock it in the chin with a rising knee.

Going to the ground on top of the Troblin, Vix laid into the creature with a barrage of spiked punches—the poor monster underneath him was ill-equipped to deal with such close-quarters combat—while Yanily dashed by.

"Left, Right, get those shield guys," Hiral said, but his doubles were already on it, clashing with the closest Troblins as they began to rise.

Even without their shields, these Troblins had much thicker bark-skin than the others, and they each managed to get to their feet despite the blows raining down on them.

That was as far as they got, though. Nivian shield-bashed one straight in the face, and Seena impaled the other on a ***Spearing Root***. The mop-up only took a few more seconds after that, and then the whole party turned its attention to the final remaining *Shaman*.

"What took you guys so long?" Yanily asked, leaning casually on his spear skewering the twitching *Shaman* to the floor, his ***Lashing Vines*** still randomly whipping the creature.

"Form back up," Seena ordered. "Who knows when more will pop out of a secret door."

Yanily ripped his spear free in a spray of blood, then jogged back over to join the party's formation as it continued to move along the balcony.

"Just the one ambush?" Wule asked as they reached the base of the next bridge without any other trouble appearing from within the wall on their side.

"I'm sure we'll find more trouble as soon as we get up there," Yanily pointed out.

"Probably before," Seena said. "Hiral, you want to go first again?"

"Yes. Right, let's go," Hiral said, sliding around the others and then sprinting up the rope bridge, the sway doing nothing to slow him down.

As soon as they reached the top of the bridge—little more than a three-foot-wide platform ringing the large tree and connected bridges—Troblins swarmed around from both sides.

"Troblins," Hiral shouted in warning to the group behind him, simultaneously pointing to the right for his double to intercept the Troblins in that direction.

Knowing he had to slow them before they reached the bridge supports, Hiral darted straight for the axe-wielding Troblin directly in front of him. Faster than it could have expected, he got within its guard, catching the haft of the weapon it awkwardly swung at him in his left hand, then brought the palm of his right hand down and under the Troblin's chest.

Solar energy flooded through the **Rune of Rejection** on his arm, and the resulting wave burst from his hand and tossed the Troblin up and off the side of the balcony. Ripping the axe free from the monster as it flew away, Hiral brought the weapon across as he stepped in, slamming it into the shoulder of the next Troblin in line. Green blood gushed down the creature's arm, and it staggered to the side to collide with the ally beside it, but there were still three more behind that pair.

Six, just on this side!

Using the momentary confusion of the ones stumbling in the front, Hiral took a step in and delivered a straight kick. While his **Lashing Vines** slapped at the Troblins next to him, his foot connected with a heavily armored Troblin's chest, but did little more than make the thing take a single step back. On his right, the Troblin with the axe buried in its shoulder was already ignoring the vines and finding its balance—with the help of its "ally" shoving it away—and Hiral had no choice but to retreat or get surrounded.

Reaching out with his left hand as he backpedalled, he activated his **Rune of Attraction** at the Troblin in the very back, then spun and ducked low, getting his shoulder under the stumbling creature beside him. Weight settling on his back, Hiral straightened and continued his turn, flipping the Troblin up, over, and right off the balcony, while the one he'd pulled on jerked into the two in front of it, throwing them all off balance.

That just left the one beside him, which ignored the pair of lashes it received from Hiral's vines, then lunged at him, swinging its axe with its hand right next to the head of the weapon. The grip made the weapon usable in such close quarters, at the cost of stealing most of its power. Still, the edge of the blade sliced open Hiral's upper arm as he brought it in to block, and Hiral quick-stepped away just in time to avoid an immediate backswing, though it left him with his heels to the edge.

Seeing an opening, bands of green energy wrapped around the Troblin's arms as it took its axe in both hands and raised the weapon to attack. It took a step toward Hiral, at which point Yanily rushed in from its left, his spear lashing across the Troblin's entire exposed side. Leg, chest, and shoulder were ruined in short order, and the creature stumbled at the same time Nivian's whip snapped past.

Like it was a living thing, the whip tore back and forth in the air, slashing into one, two, then all three Troblins and drawing their attention from Hiral to the tank. Nivian wasted no time, withdrawing his weapon and moving forward to kick the fallen Troblin from the ground. He lifted it from the balcony and launched it at the closest standing monster.

Completely ignoring the fact it was one of its *friends*, the lead Troblin slammed into the flying body with its axe, driving it straight down to the wooden balcony as green bands of energy wrapped its arms. The body bounced, then *cracked* as the furious Troblin stomped down on top of it and stepped over, intent on reaching Nivian. Hiral *yanked* the fresh corpse with his **Rune of Attraction**.

Sweeping the feet out from under the advancing Troblin, the corpse shot toward Hiral, only to rebound right back as he activated his **Rune of Rejection**. The Troblin-projectile zipped over the lead monster as it fell to collide with the two behind it, the whole group toppling to the ground in a heap.

A raspy growl escaped the Troblin's lipless mouth as it pushed itself to its feet, eyes still focused on Nivian, only for its head to snap forward when Vix came in from behind. With Right beside him, the pair tore into the backs of the three Troblins, and Yanily danced in from the front.

"And that's that," Yanily said a short moment later, the last of the Troblin corpses toppling over the side of the balcony.

"How'd you take care of that side so fast?" Hiral asked as Right came over to join him.

"Was only two over there," Right said, leaning in to inspect Hiral's injured arm. "You okay?"

"Nothing I can't fix. Hold still," Wule said, and refreshing energy washed through Hiral's body, the wound closing and sealing in a blink.

You have been healed by Nature's Regrowth
Minor wounds and damage repaired.

"Thanks," Hiral said. "Any idea where all those Troblins came from?"

"I think there's a secret door on the back of this tree trunk," Vix said while he ran his hand along the bark of the wide tree. "Can't find it for the life of me, though."

"One more bridge, then we're at the smokehouse," Nivian said. "We ready to move?"

"Hey," Seena said to Hiral as she joined him, though she was looking at the top of the next bridge, "how'd you do that?"

"Do what?" Hiral asked.

"The way you fought them. It's like you knew what they were going to do. You didn't even draw your sword."

"Ah. I think it's the boosted attunement," Hiral said. "I could just sort of *feel* where they all were. That, combined with my higher dexterity, let me react to the things I saw out of the corner of my eyes, or maybe heard? I honestly don't know; that went way better than it had any right to."

"So, you're saying I need to put points in my attunement if I want to take full advantage of building my dexterity?" Vix asked, slapping the tree and finally giving up on finding the secret door.

"Seems like a lot of synergy there," Hiral replied with a shrug.

"When we get out of this dungeon, we're all going to have a chat about how we can work better together as a party," Seena said.

Hiral blinked and looked at her. That was the second time she'd said something like that. *Does she really mean it?* "I… I'm really part of the party?" he asked, something clenching in his chest at the question. He'd always been on the outside—always the *Everfail*—up in Fallen Reach.

Seena raised an eyebrow at Hiral, then glanced at the other Growers. "Well, yeah, of course you are. What did you think?"

"That we were just keeping you around to get into the dungeons?" Yanily asked, and Nivian punched him in the shoulder.

"You didn't have to *say it*," Nivian said.

"Let me make it clear," Seena said, glaring at Yanily. "You're a member of the party. It's that simple. We can talk more about the *why* when we get out of here, but it's not because you can get us into dungeons. Okay?"

Hiral just nodded, words somehow difficult at that moment.

They actually… valued… his contribution?

Wow.

"Enough huggy-feely stuff," Vix said. "Buffs are still good. Smokehouse?"

"You good to go first again?" Seena asked Hiral.

"For sure," he said. "Right, you get the bigger group of Troblins next time."

"Meh," Right said, but it was the double leading the charge up the next rope bridge.

Like they'd seen from the entrance, the large smokehouse dominated the level, its three chimneys spouting gray smoke and the smell of barbeque wafting through the air. No windows decorated the building's walls, and the only obvious way in was a single heavy door.

"You feel that heat?" Right asked, the rest of the group filing onto the platform behind them.

"If it's that hot out here, I can only imagine what it's like inside," Hiral said.

"Says the guy who doesn't even have a shirt on," Yanily said.

"It's where we have to go," Seena said. "Nivian, open that door, and let's go see what these Troblins are having for lunch."

"Somehow I don't think we really want to know…" Yanily muttered.

35

DON'T STAND IN THE FIRE!

A BLAST of hot air buffeted the group as Nivian opened the door, the smell of charred meat crawling up Hiral's nose and down his throat. And, underneath it, something else. Something more… raw… and far less appetizing. The scent of it brought the image of a bloody carcass to mind, maggots and rot taking hold, the body bloated from sitting in the sun too long.

"Ugh, that… that is *awful*," Yanily said. "No amount of cooking will make it better."

"What do you see, Nivian?" Seena asked, the tank still occupying the doorway.

"Nothing good," Nivian said, but he moved further into the building to give the others space to follow.

Metal clanked as Hiral stepped in, and he looked down to find some kind of grating covering the floor—the heat of it already working its way through his boots—and glowing coals beneath. Those coals were the only source of light in the building, but it was more than enough to make out the dozens and dozens of hanging slabs of meat.

Meat that was once people, with the red glow from the floor elongating wounds, highlighting disfigurement, and drawing caricature-like expressions across them.

Hand-sized hooks dangled from chains where the meat had already been taken, while others punched through torsos or legs to suspend the bodies. Smoke coiled around arms that hung limply, the skin on the hands sizzling and bubbling where they rested too long on the metal grating, while heads lolled lifelessly to the side. Men. Women. Children. Age, gender, and size didn't seem to matter—there were bodies of all kinds. And some of them already had pieces carved out of them, like somebody—or something—had gone around testing if the meat had been cooked long enough.

"Don't like this place," Wule said quietly, a chain rattling somewhere ahead and to the left, and the group pulled in tighter to keep a watch in all directions.

"What was that?" Yanily asked, dancing from foot to foot as the heat from the floor penetrated the soles of their boots.

"Can't be anything good," Vix answered, his arm over his mouth to make breathing easier.

A chain off to their right *clinked*.

"Hard to see anything with the bodies and the smoke," Seena said. "Hiral?"

"Not much better for me," Hiral said. "But… wait… I hear something. Footsteps on the metal. Not boots, I don't think."

"How could anybody be in here without something on their feet?" Nivian asked.

Something passed through the smoke ahead of them, the gray fog swirling and chasing it before it vanished again.

"Look, we can't just stand here. We're going to need to… uh…" Seena trailed off.

"Tell me you weren't going to say we need to smoke it out?" Hiral deadpanned.

"Maybe," Seena admitted. "But since *you* already said it… Yeah. That."

"How?"

Suddenly, there was a *woof* and a *flash* from the other end of the building, and all heads turned in that direction.

"What was…?" Wule started.

Woof. Flash. A five-by-five pillar of fire leapt from the floor.

"…that?" Wule finished.

Woof. Flash. Another five-by-five pillar of fire leapt from the floor, but this one was closer.

Dynamic Quest
You've been marked as ingredients for the next meal.
Survive.

"At least the objective is simple," Yanily said as another *woof* and *flash* lit up the room, this one only ten feet away.

"It's getting closer," Nivian said as a red glow enveloped the party.

They all looked down at the same time to see the coals flaring.

"Don't stand in the fire!" Vix shouted, and the party scattered in opposite directions as a *woof-flash* sent another five-by-five pillar of flame erupting from right where they'd been standing.

Hiral pushed through the smoke as the heat seared his back, bumping into something that *squelched* uncomfortably at his touch and stuck to his hands when he pushed it away. He spun around the slab that swung back, then twisted immediately to avoid a second. *Woof,* and a *flash* lit up the smoke that had somehow grown so thick, it was more like soup. He struggled to see anything other than vague shapes. Movement to his left made him twist, sword coming out of the sheath on his back, but there was nothing there.

"Guys?" he asked quietly.

His only reply was a *woof-flash*, this time from somewhere behind him. Had he gotten turned around? Where were the others?

The patter of running feet to his right forced Hiral to spin, the hanging slabs rocking gently back and forth as if something had bumped them, but there was no sign of whatever that was. The clinking of chains came from his right again, opposite the way the running had gone. Hiral twisted that way, sword at the ready. Still nothing.

There was another *woof-flash* somewhere far ahead, lighting up the smoke and a dozen silhouettes—one of them carrying a large cleaver. The flash ended, the shapes vanished, and there it was again—the barely audible running across the metal grating.

What the hell was that? A Troblin? But it was as tall as I am. Taller.

Something clinked to Hiral's left, followed by a *woof-flash* directly in front of him. He turned and staggered back, face scorched by the heat and eyes blinded by the sudden light. He lifted his sword in front of him and swung, panic taking hold in his chest as a sense of impending doom settled on his shoulders. Movement behind him and smoke pulling across his skin caused him to whip around, pushing energy into his *Rune of Rejection*. Chains clamored and clanked as their slabs rocked back and forth from the push, but the sound of running didn't stop.

Where? Where?

Hiral took a step forward, the heat uncomfortable on the sole of his foot. Then he dove ahead, rolling on the metal grating and burning his shoulder and back. The skin sizzled, and a *woof* burst from where he'd just been. Heat washed over him in a wave as he stumbled back to his feet and tried to force his mind away from the pain across his back. Lines of it crisscrossed his skin, his imagination filling in what his still-blind eyes couldn't see.

Debuff applied: Searing Pain
Searing Pain: Mounting pain grows exponentially until removed.
Suffer -1 temporary attribute point every 3 seconds,
to a maximum of -10.

The notification appeared and vanished in a heartbeat, but the meaning of the words sank directly into his mind. A debuff. A bad one.

And there's no duration listed…?

His flesh felt tight, and the pain—oh, the pain—made him reach his empty hand toward his back. And it just kept getting worse, like the smoke was digging its way into the charred skin, burrowing deeper. Into his muscles, bones, and organs.

He couldn't think straight, his feet stumbling forward as if they were trying to escape the constant agony at his back, his hands opening and closing. His sword clanged to the ground somewhere on the metal grate, but his feet kept moving. He needed to get away from the pain. Get rid of it somewhere. Somehow.

How long? How long will it last? Will it ever stop? Wule? Wule can do something about it!

But how was Hiral going to find the healer in the smoke when all he could see were spots from the flash? No, he'd never find him. Not like this. And the pain just kept getting worse, like hundreds of burning coals were rolling across his back, melting his skin, and tearing strips off at the same time. Did he even have any flesh left on his back?

Have to get rid of it. Rid of it. Rid of it. Rid of it, his mind repeated over and over, the words bubbling and boiling until his head was ready to explode.

"RID OF IT!" he shouted as the pattering of feet came straight for him.

Barely thinking, Hiral lifted his hand, throwing his solar energy and his pain into his *Rune of Rejection*, and the energy burst forth.

Something in front of Hiral screamed as blessed relief from the agonizing pain washed over him like cold water.

Hiral blinked his eyes, even the spots lessening as his mind cleared, and saw *something* hobble away as another *woof-flash* lit up the room beyond. A yellow notification appeared.

Debuff removed: Searing Pain

Huh?

Hiral looked around. The smoke was still too thick to see more than a few feet, but it wasn't affecting his breathing. Yes, he could… taste… the foulness in the air, but it wasn't filling his lungs or suffocating him. No, that wasn't entirely true—there was *some* smoke in the air, just not as much as what his eyes were telling him was there.

*It's some kind of ability. And… if my **Rune of Rejection** was able to expel the debuff from my body, I wonder…*

Hiral held up his left hand, concentrating on just the smoke, and focused solar energy into his *Rune of Attraction.* Instead of a single burst of power, he fed a thread of constant power to the rune, the smoke around him shifting as he pulled. It started small—nothing more than a flow of smoke, like it was moving toward an open window—but it built and built as it swirled around the upraised palm of his hand.

Faster and faster, like he was at the center of a whirlpool, the smoke whipped around him and gathered above. It grew larger by the second. The size of an orange. A watermelon. A dog. A horse.

And then the room was clear of smoke, the Grower party spread out and disoriented amongst the hanging slabs of meat. That *something else* stood not ten feet away from Nivian.

Roughly seven feet tall, even hunched over and emaciated, it had the same bark-like skin of a Troblin, though it was cracked and burned like it had been charred over and over. It held a long cleaver in its right hand, and what looked like a large thighbone in its other. It had no nose on its hairless head, its two-inch-long, needle-like teeth overlapped each other, and one eye glowed green while the other was a burning red. Its shoulders twisted and twitched, as if it was trying to get something off its back, and a breathy hiss escaped its lipless mouth.

*I somehow gave it my **Searing Pain** debuff!*

"Seena!" Hiral shouted. "*Target* that!"

The woman, who'd also noticed the nearby enemy, didn't bother responding with words, and a pulse of solar energy instead rippled out of her. Something passed over Hiral's eyes—a red outline appearing around the ***Troblin Butcher***—and from the way the other Growers' heads snapped around, they were all benefitting from the ability as well.

You have been buffed by: Target
Object of the Target Debuff cannot hide from your eyes
for 190 seconds
You inflict 15% more damage to object
of the Target Debuff for 190 seconds

With that done, Hiral released his hold on the smoke above his hand, and the whole ball of it fell down around him like it had weight, then seeped between the grates on the floor. More of the smoke did seem to be leaking out of the ***Butcher***, but it couldn't hide from their eyes with the ***Target*** debuff on it.

No, the game of cat and mouse was over. But who knew how long the debuff would last, or what other tricks the monster had up its sleeve? Hiral and the Growers all charged forward.

36

BUTCHERING THE BUTCHER

N IVIAN, using his movement ability, was the first to get to the *Troblin Butcher*. His whip lashed back and forth in a quick one-two combo that got deflected by the monster's cleaver, and then it was right in front of him, a backhand swing from the large bone *slamming* into his shield. The impact sent a shockwave through the air, rattling the hanging slabs of meat all around, and tossed Nivian back to hit the ground.

The man rolled once, then twice before getting his hands and feet under himself. Armor smoking across his arms and back, he looked down at his left hand and the angry burns on his palm, already shaking it like he was trying to toss off the pain from the burn.

"It's a debuff! From getting burned by the metal grating," Hiral shouted at Wule. "You need to remove it. It's *bad*."

"On it," Wule replied, energy already concentrating in his palm as he rushed to Nivian's side.

Too bad the *Butcher* noticed the same thing. The tall creature lumbered forward and lifted its cleaver high into the air.

Familiar energy pulsed from Seena, *Spearing Roots* taking shape on the floor, but the heat from the metal and coals turned the wood to ash even before the ability could strike the monster. It brought its weapon down like a headsman's axe toward the healer.

CLANG. Yanily slid in front of Wule—not a second too soon—to catch the descending weapon on his spear. Still, the power of the blow drove him straight to his knees, and the *Butcher* leaned down over him. *Sniiiiiiiiiff*. The monster sucked in Yanily's scent even though it didn't have a nose.

"Bet I smell better than you do…" Yanily gasped, the strain of keeping the cleaver at bay evident in his voice.

Then, quick as lightning, the *Butcher* stood up straight and pulled its cleaver away. Yanily overbalanced forward at the sudden movement, then shot backwards as the *Butcher*'s shin connected with his chest in a vicious kick.

Wule, having trusted in Yanily to cover him, reached Nivian, and green light pulsed out of him to wash over the tank. Nivian's eyes cleared almost immediately, and he sprang up and around Wule to intercept the descending cleaver with his shield. Stronger than the spearman, Nivian managed to keep his feet—barely—but the **Butcher** was already winding up with the heavy bone in his other hand.

Whomp. Right's glowing fist hit the grotesque Troblin hard enough in the side to bend it around the blow, and caused the swinging bone to whiff over Nivian.

The thing growled, cleaver grinding against Nivian's shield as it pulled away, then backhanded a swing at the tattooed double.

Right ducked under the blade, sidestepped the swinging bone that followed, then darted back to evade the cleaver as it came across again. The Troblin wasn't done yet, though. It charged forward, weapons swinging in wide arcs that kept Right moving, but also not giving the man an opening to counter or truly escape.

Alone, he wouldn't have been able to keep dodging for long—the Troblin was obviously no novice in a fight—but Right *wasn't* by himself.

As the **Butcher** wound up for another powerful swing, Vix ducked into the opening from a blind spot, fists blurring in a focused combo. One, two, three, four, five times he lashed out, spiked knuckles coming away bloodier with each blow as he tore into the **Butcher**'s thigh.

The Troblin roared in outrage and pain, turning its attention from Right to Vix, and lifted the bone-club straight up to smite the stinging Grower. Down came the powerful blow, whistling through the air, only to *miss* as Hiral pulled it out wide with his **Rune of Attraction**. Right dashed back in as the grating shook from the blow, his own fists pounding into the Troblin's exposed lower back, each punch sounding like he was beating a drum.

Another backhand swing forced both Right and Vix back, but not before their **Lashing Vines** each scored a pair of hits, and a thorned whip snapped in to leave a bloody line on the Troblin's chest.

Nivian followed up the whipping attack with one more, then charged in, shield leading. The Troblin actually looked away from the rushing tank, turning its attention to the more dangerous pugilists on each side of it—until **Spearing Roots** burst out of Nivian's shield. Then, sliding in behind Nivian, Hiral added to the tank's momentum with his **Rune of Rejection**, practically launching the man forward like a giant ballista bolt.

The air seemed to snap from Nivian's sudden acceleration, and the Troblin—with arms out to its sides to ward off Vix and Right—took the viciously spiked shield square in the chest.

The monster roared, pushed back from the impact but not falling—until Left slid in behind it and brought his liquid dagger across the back of both its knees in one fluid motion. The strength left its legs, and the Troblin toppled backwards. Nivian rode it down the whole way and leaned on his shield to drive the spikes even deeper.

A resounding *thud* rang out as the **Butcher** hit the metal grating, quickly followed by the sizzling of its bark-like skin. Weapons fell from its fingers as it frenziedly tried to get Nivian off it, the pain from the debuff maddening its eyes, its long nails scratching at the tank's back.

To his credit, Nivian ignored the gouging wounds despite the **Butcher** tearing through his armor and the flesh underneath.

"Just. Die," Nivian grunted, burying his head behind his shield to protect it, leaning down as hard as he could on the Troblin's chest.

"I can help with that," Yanily said, suddenly standing right by the Troblin's head.

He drove his spear straight down. The metal spear blade pierced directly through one of the Troblin's frantic eyes—as well as the metal grating underneath—and the monster's hands froze. A twitch of the thing's whole body, and its limbs fell limp to the floor, the skin sizzling not even a second later.

"Maybe do the other eye too, just to be sure," Vix said, hands on his knees as he took deep breaths.

Dynamic Quest Complete
You have not been made into lunch.
Congratulations. Achievement unlocked –
Just the Right Amount of Heat
You withstood the heat and stayed in the kitchen.
Please access a Dungeon Interface
to unlock class-specific reward.

"Uh, or maybe we're good," Vix amended, everybody's eyes flashing past the notification that popped up.

"How about we just get out of here?" Wule said, shuffling from one foot to the other.

"Yeah, it's *really* hot in here," Right agreed.

"Okay, but I want everybody on the look out for more Troblins when we get out there," Senna said. "Who knows what's waiting for us outside?"

She offered a hand and helped Nivian pull himself off the **Butcher**. The shield didn't seem to want to come out, producing a wet, sucking sound every time he yanked on it—until Seena dispelled the roots with a wave of her hand.

"Thanks," Nivian said. "I didn't know you could do that."

"Me neither, until I tried," Seena said with a shrug. "I'm just glad it worked."

"I think we all are," Hiral said, and the group moved toward the only exit out.

After Seena gave Nivian the familiar tap on the shoulder, the tank led the group back outside, each of them taking a wonderful breath of fresh air even as their heads swivelled for threats.

"Looks clear," Hiral said, the platform around the building and the bridge leading up to it empty of enemies.

"That may not last," Seena said. "Wule, can you patch us up while we catch our breath?"

"Sure—everybody mind sticking close?" Wule asked, and the Grower group moved in together.

There, Hiral picked out wounds and injuries he hadn't noticed in the thick of the fight. Vix had a nasty gash across his chest, Yanily struggled to breathe, Seena had burns on her left arm, Nivian had tears across his back, and even Left and Right were leaking solar energy.

Just how much damage did that Troblin do while the room was filled with smoke?

"That was a tough monster," Yanily said, as if reading Hiral's thoughts.

"Another **Mid-Boss**, according to the notification," Nivian said. "Quite a bit of experience from it, though."

At the comment, Hiral checked his own notifications, and couldn't help but smile at the fact he'd even gained two more levels, putting him at 14 now.

"Did you two level as well?" he asked Left and Right, and they both nodded.

"Spend the points the same as before?" Right asked.

"Please," Hiral said at the same time a wave of refreshing energy washed out of Wule, healing Left's and Right's wounds. "Done? Okay, let's merge back up to restore your solar energy." He pulled his doubles back into himself with a touch.

Energy filled his body as his tattoos and Meridian Lines reformed across his skin. While he couldn't access his runes or the powers of the tattoos and the lines while merged, having a third of the stat bonuses from Left and Right was noticeable on top of his base stats *and* what he was getting from his own **PIM**.

Having the stats at least offsets not being able to use any abilities if I get caught flatfooted.

"Hey, Hiral, where's your sword?" Seena asked, and Hiral glanced over his shoulder to find the empty sheath.

"Uh… I dropped it inside there… somewhere…" he said, eyeing the smokehouse.

"You dropped it? Your only weapon? In there?"

"I was debuffed and going mad with pain," Hiral said flatly. "Ask Nivian how bad it was."

"It was *bad*," Nivian said. "Like one of your sister's lectures, bad."

"Ooooh," Seena said, wincing.

"Says the guy whose had a crush on Seeyela since he was old enough to pick flowers," Wule said, poking his twin brother in the shoulder with every word.

"You're such a gossip," Nivian said.

"One of us has to be," Wule said with a chuckle.

"Well, you going to go back for it?" Seena asked, ignoring the back and forth between the brothers.

Hiral peered through the door at the smoke still clouding the room, lit up by a *woof-flash*.

"No, I don't think I will," Hiral said. "Could be a good test to see if objects get forcibly ejected as well, and I don't know if I could find it in there anyway. I was pretty turned around when I dropped it."

"You might need it," Seena pointed out. "We've still got the keep to clear, and I have a feeling there might be something labeled as a **Boss** in there."

"You want my backup dagger?" Yanily offered, holding out the sheathed weapon. "I'm not very good with it anyway. All my abilities need a spear to work."

"Thanks," Hiral said, taking the dagger and strapping it around his waist.

Seena shrugged. "Suit yourself, I guess. You've been doing pretty well with those runes anyway. Okay, folks. Five minutes to regain some solar energy, rebuff, and then we're finishing this dungeon."

"We haven't even been in here twenty minutes," Vix said. "I think we're doing pretty well."

"Don't get cocky," Seena said. "Both **Mid-Bosses** were strong. Stay focused until we're out. I've already seen more of our blood today than I have in the last year."

Yanily poked at his bloody thigh armor, the tears in it from the smoke monster cutting clear through to the skin beneath. "I really didn't expect to have trouble with Troblins. Last time we struggled in a fight with them was, what, ten levels ago?"

"Something like that," Vix said. "Since we're sitting here for a couple more minutes, Dr. Benza said we could clear the dungeon up to three times. Are we going to do that? I can think of a few ways we could do this better next time."

"I'm always open to more experience," Yanily said. "Unless the keep gives a *huuuuuge* amount, I don't think I'll hit twenty even clearing this place twice more."

"Really?" Hiral said. "I've gotten, what, four levels since we started in here?"

"That makes you, what, around fifteen now?" Wule asked.

"Fourteen," Hiral clarified.

"Yeah, you're getting more experience per kill because of your level, and the experience required to the next level is a *lot* lower. Given what we're getting here per fight, you'll probably slow down pretty dramatically around seventeen, if not sooner."

"Seventeen, huh? Still, not bad."

"What're your dexterity and attunement at now, then?" Vix asked.

"Uh, when Left and Right are out, my dexterity is thirty-four, and my attunement is thirty-two," Hiral said.

"You're still not spending the free points, huh?" Seena asked.

"Not yet," Hiral said. "Dexterity and attunement have a really interesting interaction, but I want to learn a bit more about my class still."

"Fair," Seena said. "And that's enough time. Let's buff and clear out this dungeon. Just the keep left."

"I *think* the entrance to the keep is actually up there on the third level," Vix said, pointing almost directly across from them.

"Looks like it, but, uh… doesn't that kind of make no sense from a design perspective?" Yanily asked. "Who wants to climb up or down three floors every time they go in or out?"

"Probably secret entrances down on the first level," Seena said. "Maybe we can find one from the inside after we clear it out. Might make it easier to get in next time we enter."

"Which means the entrance we *can* see is probably a trap," Hiral pointed out, and the Growers all groaned.

37

IT'S A TRAP!

"Y UP, definitely a trap," Nivian said a few short minutes later as the group rounded the corner on the second level of the keep, secret doors opening ahead and behind them.

Dozens of Troblins flooded out, green eyes glowing and weighted clubs waving over their heads.

"That's a *lot* of Troblins," Vix said, tapping Right on the arm. The two of them took up the defensive line at the back of the group.

"No green bands of energy around their arms or legs, so no buffs," Hiral said. "And is it just me, or are they smaller?"

"Doesn't change the fact it's still a *lot* of them," Vix emphasized. "Here they come!"

"Bet you wish you had your sword now," Left said. The **Dagger of Sath** appeared in his hand, and he moved up with Yanily to work beside Nivian.

"Keep moving forward," Seena ordered while gathering solar energy.

The first wave of Troblins crashed into them from both sides. Hiral moved back to support Vix and Right, though he didn't draw Yanily's knife yet, despite Left's snarky comment. Instead, he hit the central Troblin with a burst from his **Rune of Rejection**, sending it staggering back into the others behind it, which gave the pugilists an opening to lash out. Two Troblins fell to two punches, their heads practically exploding like watermelons from the blows, and Right and Vix jumped back as if expecting some kind of trick.

"They're *soft*," Yanily shouted from the front. "Like normal, not-in-a-dungeon Troblins."

"Still a lot of them!" Vix said.

"So you keep saying," Right said from beside him.

"I think it's a very pertinent point," Vix said, tearing out a Troblin's throat with the blade on the back of his heel as he hit it with a spinning kick, then seamlessly flowing into an elbow-and-knee combo to drop the next. "Even if they *are* really soft."

"What does *soft* even mean?" Right said, dropping one, then two Troblins in quick succession with punches of his own.

"Don't they kind of feel like hitting rotten fruit?" Vix asked, bringing his fists together on both sides of a Troblin head. A head which promptly geysered blood and gore straight up. "See?"

"Just yuck, guys," Hiral said, shifting to his left and tossing out another wave from his rune. Three Troblins tumbled back, tangling with twice as many more, and even knocking one over the low crenellation.

"Right, Vix, Hiral, fall back!" Seena shouted.

All three leapt toward the Grower party as a wall of **Spearing Roots** burst out of the floor and into the lead line of Troblins. Green blood ran down the five-foot-tall, porcupine-like wall, more Troblins throwing themselves at the spikes despite the danger.

"That'll hold them for a minute or two at least," Seena said. "Help Nivian and the others punch through the ones in the front. We need to get to that door."

"You got it, boss," Vix said. He only needed two quick steps, then he vaulted over the tank to lay into the surprised Troblins all around him.

"If you even *think* of tossing me with your rune…" Right threatened, and Hiral held up his hands to try and calm his own double.

"Didn't even cross my mind," Hiral lied.

"I know when you're lying—you realize that, don't you?" Right asked, but then he joined Vix and the other damage dealers to push through the throng of Troblins.

"I don't think they're **Elites**," Nivian said, his whip snapping back and forth to keep the focus on him.

"Still takes a hit or two to put them down, though," Wule said. "At this rate, we won't get through to the door before the ones in the back catch us."

"So? They're like a free, all-you-can-eat experience buffet," Yanily said. "And I'm ready for seconds! Wooooo!"

Yanily's spear lashed out over and over as he slowly advanced. Still, for every Troblin taking a fatal wound, there were two more rushing out of another secret door further back.

"We're going to get overwhelmed," Seena said. "Hiral, can you do something about the press?"

"I don't think I can do anything permanent, but I might be able to get us some room to make a run for the door," he said.

"That's exactly what I'm looking for," Seena said, then shouted, "When Hiral makes a hole for us, get to that door."

"One hole coming up," Hiral said, the energy already gathering in his rune.

Yellow light poured out of his arm as he filled it with more power than he ever had, and at the point it began to actually *hurt*, he stepped up beside Nivian and thrust his hand out.

The shockwave rolled out in an instant, tossing every Troblin within a thirty-foot cone to the ground and opening a narrow gap through the mass.

"Go, go, go," Nivian shouted, leading the charge with the rest of the party behind him, everybody taking pot shots at the prone Troblins as they went. Even the *Lashing Vines* were having a field day.

Green blood painted the wall and floor as the group moved. Hiral tossed another wave of *Rejection* as they progressed, and then they were in front of the only obvious door, the mass of Troblins *behind* them.

"Figure out the door," Seena ordered, releasing the solar energy she'd been gathering into another wall of *Spearing Roots*.

Judging by the Troblins literally crawling over the corpses of their allies back at the first wall, this one would only slow them for a minute or two at most.

We need to get inside.

"Yanily, Nivian, do what you can to stop them from getting over the wall," she went on, and the tank and spearman moved into position to strike between the spikes.

"What about me?" Hiral asked. "My rune could push them back off…"

"You have the highest attunement; take a look to see if you can figure out a way through the door," Seena instructed.

"Left, help me out," Hiral said, going over to where the large doors were. "What do you think it could be? A secret switch? A lock? Maybe a pressure panel or a crystal…" He ran his hands along the wall, peering at the floor in front of the doors.

The open doors.

"Huh?" he asked, looking at where Left had one hand on each door and had pushed them apart. "How? Where was the switch?"

"It wasn't locked," Left said. He threw the doors wide open, then walked in. "Looks like we can brace it from the inside, though. Everybody in!"

"Wow, you got it open that fast?" Seena asked. "I'm impressed. Let's go, guys."

"Uh… well… you know," Hiral said before following Seena.

Nivian and Yanily were the last ones in, their weapons coated with green blood, and then Right and Left pushed the doors closed.

"There's wood there to use as a brace," Left said, pointing off to the side at something more akin to a log than a piece of wood.

"I'll get it," Nivian said as something slammed into the door from the outside.

"Hurry it up," Left and Right both said at the same time, leaning into the door. "They're not strong, but…" Both heads turned toward Vix.

"…there's a lot of them…" Vix said flatly.

"This should hold them," Nivian said, sliding the four-foot length of wood into the braces built into the door. As soon as it was secure, the three stepped back from the door, which barely moved as the Troblins outside pounded on it.

"I wonder why it wasn't already locked. How would we have gotten in?" Wule asked.

"Gotten in… *to where*… exactly? What is this place?" Yanily asked, looking at the dark hallway leading further into the building. "Are those stairs?"

"Maybe? I can't see a thing," Seena said.

"There's a torch… I think… on the wall here," Wule said, moving in the direction in which he'd pointed. He jumped back as something on the wall burst alight in purple flame.

"What…?" Nivian said, but more points erupted in purple flame in two lines.

The first went around the room they were in, a dozen torches coming to life, and then both lines ran along opposite sides of the hallway leading down the stairs.

"Pretty sure that's not normal," Vix said.

"Has anything here really been normal?" Hiral asked. "It doesn't go too far… I guess that's the first floor at the bottom there."

"We're not going to be able to regenerate solar energy in here," Seena said, the pounding continuing at the door. "And I don't want to trust that to stop all those Troblins from getting in. We've got no choice but to go forward. Don't be surprised if something ambushes us on the way down."

"Rebuff?" Wule asked. "Less than half the duration left on both buffs."

"Good idea," Seena said.

A pulse of energy blossomed out from her a second later, and the timer refreshed on **Lashing Vines**. Wule followed it up at the same time with **Nature's Blade,** and then Seena pointed at the stairs, tapping the tank on the shoulder.

"Nivian, you're up."

"Got it, boss," Nivian said, starting down the stairs. "Keep your eyes peeled. Who knows where they're going to jump out of this time."

"Even if they do, they're not going to have an easier time fighting on these stairs than we are," Right said. "Maybe even worse with their lower dexterity."

He's right. Sure, they might get the drop on us, but we've definitely got the stat advantage. But… what if there aren't secret doors? What if it's something else? Oh…

"Guys, it's a traaaaaa…"

Hiral's words trailed off as the stairs beneath his feet angled down—all of them—and suddenly, the whole group was sliding recklessly down a steep ramp, a line of spears rising out of the floor at the bottom. With no time to really consider what he was doing, Hiral slammed his right hand down on the surprisingly slick wood and thought of the party. Then, with their images firmly in mind, he pushed the power from his *Rune of Rejection* into the ramp beneath his fingertips.

Seena screamed, along with several others—none of them very manly—and the whole group popped off the floor just in time to go sailing over the line of spears.

A quick succession of *thumps* sounded, and then Hiral also hit the floor, his momentum sliding him along the grainy wood. The impact, really, hadn't been that bad, and he was already pushing himself to his feet along with the others.

"I take it you did something?" Seena asked him, but that was all she had time for.

Purple torches burst to life and spread along the walls, lighting up the hundred-foot square room. In the middle, another ring of torches burst to life, and the largest Troblin Hiral had ever seen—or even imagined—got to his feet.

The thing wasn't much taller than the *Butcher*—maybe eight feet to its seven—but where the *Butcher* was emaciated and wiry, this thing was a hulking monster. With arms almost as big as Hiral's chest, muscles so massive and rippling, they cracked the bark-like skin covering them, legs like tree trunks, and shoulders that looked like they could carry the entire keep, this Troblin redefined the word *monster*.

"This... my... keep..." the Troblin breathed, the words sounding strange coming from its lipless mouth. "Me... duke... You... dead."

Dynamic Quest
*You've been accused of trespassing and selfishly evading
the Slide and Spear trap.
Defeat the Eloquent Duke of Splitfang
Keep to clear the dungeon.*

38

ELOQUENT AND ENRAGED

"THAT was eloquent?" Yanily asked.

"Practically a poet," Vix said. "Nivian, you can go first."

"Gee, thank you," Nivian said, but he had his shield up and his whip cocked back to strike.

"Looks like doors between the torches along the walls," Hiral said, scanning the room for more traps. "Might be reinforcements."

"Seriously? The duke here isn't a high enough *CR* on his own?" Seena asked. "Bah, whatever. If we kill him fast enough, reinforcements won't matter."

"Now… fight. Now… die…" the *Troblin Duke* said, heaving a *massive* battle axe off its back.

The thing had to be as tall as Hiral was, and likely weighed even more. The notched blade was balanced by a thick spike on the back of the haft, and most of it seemed to be wrapped in leather strips that looked uncomfortably like Grower skin.

"Hit him hard and fast," Seena said, tapping Nivian on his shoulder, and the tank blurred and seemed to stretch out as he used his movement ability.

A second later, Nivian dashed into the ring of purple torches, skidding to a stop ten feet from the *Troblin Duke*, and lashed out with his whip. Thorny barbs tore the boss's skin as the thing stepped forward, then swung its axe up and over in a vicious arc. With its long arms and the naturally large weapon, Nivian was forced to dive aside before the axe crashed into the ground right where he'd been standing.

The impact from the axe caused a shockwave that shredded the floor in an outward cone another ten feet long, and then the duke effortlessly ripped its weapon free—which pulled a ten-foot section of floor up with it. Wood chunks flew into the air, and the Troblin swung his meaty fist around in a wide sweep, slapping the debris and transforming it into a barrage of rocketing projectiles.

Hiral's *Rune of Rejection* turned aside most of the dangerous shards—just barely in time—but he wasn't able to get all of them. Wule took an arrow-like splinter in the thigh, while Left threw himself in front of Seena and got skewered by a spear of wood through the gut.

The double toppled to the ground, solar energy leaking out of his wound like glowing smoke. He wrapped his fingers around the spike as if to pull it out. "Aaaagh," he grimaced, his whole body twitching from even the slightest movement of the foreign object in his stomach. "That... hurts..."

"I'll take care of Left," Hiral said to Seena as he ran over to his double.

Seena nodded despite the look of guilt on her face, and solar energy began to gather inside her at the same time Vix and Yanily vanished.

Must've gotten pulled up by Nivian's **Swarm Tactics**.

"Not sure if this'll work, but let's try," Hiral said, reaching out his hand to touch Left's shoulder.

"No! Wait," Left tried to warn Hiral, but he'd already begun the process to pull his double back in.

The wood clattered to the ground as Left vanished in a puff of solar energy that flowed back into Hiral.

It worked...

All thought left Hiral's mind as agonizing pain shot through his abdomen, and he dropped to his knees, then fell face-first to the ground. His hand went to his stomach, where his fingers were greeted by warm, thick liquid and a hole where his skin should be smooth and complete.

"Ugh," he groaned, forcing his watery eyes open. Red stained his hand and the left side of his stomach, more of his blood bubbling out from the wound every time he shifted.

"Hold on, Hiral. Hold on," Wule said, the sound of more wood clunking to the floor near Hiral's head. "It's not as bad as it looks."

"Sure... feels... like... it... is..." Hiral groaned, his bloody right hand opening and closing while he held the tattooed left over the injury.

"Really, it's not," Wule reassured him, and refreshing energy washed across his body, then gathered at his stomach.

You have been healed by Nature's Regrowth
Minor wounds and damage repaired.

"Oh... that didn't feel *minor*," Hiral said, but the pain from his stomach was surprisingly gone. A glance down at his abdomen showed it still covered in blood, but the hole had vanished.

"The wound wasn't as big as what Left had," Wule said, offering his hand to help Hiral to his feet—which Hiral gratefully took, legs still shaky from the echo of pain. "If I had to guess, and I am, I'd say it was about a third of the size."

"Great. So, I take their injuries back into me when I take their solar energy. Good to know." Even as Hiral spoke, the ground shook under his feet. "The others?"

"Still alive—for now," Wule said. "But that duke monster isn't slowing down."

Hiral looked to the center of the room, where the party battled it out against the *Troblin Duke*. It was obviously a contest of tight margins. None of the Growers looked to be injured, while the Troblin had half a dozen small wounds. Still, the duke's weapon came terrifyingly close—and was getting closer—with each swing.

It was learning their patterns, even after only a few seconds of battle, and all it would take was one hit of the massive weapon to do some serious damage. *Definitely more than minor.*

On top of its ability to learn, Hiral watched as Yanily scored a clean hit with his spear, and the weapon barely penetrated the thick hide by more than an inch. Green blood dribbled out of the wound, but it obviously wasn't slowing the Troblin down. If anything, the duke's counterattack cut even closer as Yanily narrowly ducked under the backhand swing that sailed over two of the burning torches. The sheer velocity of the blow snuffed them out.

Hiral activated his **Foundational Split** ability, and Left pulled away from his body, the double's stomach thankfully whole and intact.

"That wasn't very smart," Left reprimanded Hiral.

"I didn't know, but we can argue about it later. They need our help," Hiral said. "Go for the legs. Anything to slow it down."

"Got it," Left said, shaping the **Dagger of Sath** with a touch to his left wrist and sprinting toward the duke.

Hiral was right behind him, not even bothering to draw Yanily's knife—the small weapon probably wouldn't even cut the duke's skin—and instead pushed solar energy into his **Rune of Attraction.** As the Troblin's axe came up and over to slash down at Right, Hiral gave a tug on the weapon, pulling it just wide, while the double darted in and landed a pair of strong blows on the monster's hip. The two hits didn't seem to do much other than get the duke's attention, and it ripped its axe free of the shattered floor to try and backhand the pugilist.

Right, while not quite as agile as Hiral, was still pretty damn fast, and ducked under the blow to come in and land another pair of hits on the same hip. With his fist glowing, the second of the two punches packed enough oomph to actually stagger the duke back, and then Left was there behind it, **Dagger of Sath** slashing for the back of its thighs.

A push with the **Rune of Rejection** forced the Troblin back yet another step, closer to the ring of torches, and Vix and Yanily came at it from the side opposite Left and Right. Yanily's spear blurred as he poured solar energy into his strikes, the weapon somehow dancing around the duke's arm as it brought it up to block, which gave Vix the opening to slide around behind it.

Like Yanily, Vix's individual hits did little damage—barely more than scratches—but the precision of his repeated blows finally opened a more serious wound on the Troblin's lower back.

"You… annoying…" the **Troblin Duke** roared, sweeping its axe around again, but the Growers had all learned how it liked its horizontal cuts, and ducked underneath.

231

The great axe ripped through nothing but air, though it snuffed out two more torches as it passed, and then the Troblin stumbled under another push from Hiral's *Rune of Rejection*.

Straight into a barrage of *Spearing Roots*.

"We've almost got it," Seena shouted, *Snaring Roots* growing out of her spears to try and latch onto the *Troblin Duke*. "Don't let up!"

One swing from the duke's axe shattered the *Spearing Roots* like kindling—leaving some of the spikes embedded in its skin—but that bought the other Growers a brief opening. Right and Vix continued to pummel the same spots they'd been focused on, while Left worked on the backs of the legs, and Yanily—with his longer reach—aimed his blows higher. Hiral activated his runes, one after the other, to keep the wild axe swipes from connecting with the Growers. A pulse of energy emerged from Seena, suddenly outlining the duke in red.

> **You have been buffed by: Target**
> **Object of the Target Debuff cannot hide**
> **from your eyes for 190 seconds**
> *You inflict 15% more damage to object*
> *of Target Debuff for 190 seconds*

Nivian, meanwhile, was the one who got the duke's attention with a snapping whip that caught the creature across the eye. The monster's head snapped back in pain or shock, another great roar escaping its lipless mouth, then it brought its axe down unbelievably fast.

Hiral pulled on the axe, just barely in time to make sure it didn't strike anybody directly, but the shockwave from it hitting the floor threw all those around it hurtling through the air and outside the ring of torches.

"Now... me... angry!" the *Troblin Duke* screamed, its axe sweeping back and forth as it snuffed out the remaining torches immediately around it.

What's it doing? Trying to make it so we can't see it? Won't work with ***Target*** *up... and yet...*

"ANGRY!" the duke screamed again, and suddenly, jets of purple flame burst out of the numerous wounds dotting its body. At the same time, previously unseen etchings along the edge of the axe's blade burned to life, the crude script giving off a sinister aura, like the axe itself had intent.

> **Dynamic Quest: Update**
> *The Eloquent Duke has absorbed forbidden magic*
> *and grown stronger as a result.*
> **Defeat the Enraged Eloquent Duke of Splitfang Keep**
> **to clear the dungeon.**

"What does *enraged* mean?" Nivian asked a heartbeat before the duke exploded into motion, purple flames erupting from its back and launching it forward.

Up and over came the axe, trailing its own tail of purple flame like a descending comet. It slammed into Nivian's shield hard enough to crater the wood floor as it drove the man to his knees beneath the blow. Not even giving Nivian a chance to catch his breath, the duke snapped his free hand around to grab the edge of the shield, completely ignoring the sharp thorns digging into his palm, then hauled the tank into the air so abruptly, his feet left the ground.

"Look out!" Seena tried to warn, but it was too late.

The duke swung Nivian like a flail straight into Vix.

Hiral poured power into his **Rune of Attraction**, but he was no match for the **Troblin Duke's** sheer strength, and Nivian and Vix collided with a grunt of pain from both parties. Releasing its hold on the shield at the moment of impact, the duke let the two Growers go tumbling along the ground, then *leapt* into the air—clearly defying all physics with the speed and height of the jump—toward Right.

Purple flames dangled behind the leaping Troblin, like streamers in the wind, then suddenly condensed, hurtling the duke at Right with a *whoosh* of sudden speed. Right, still finding his feet from the earlier shockwave, poured solar energy into the Meridian Lines of his right hand, then cocked his fist back for a counterblow.

It won't be enough!

There was no way Right would be able to deflect the attack, and trading hits would result in Right getting annihilated, so Hiral did the only thing he could think of: He cancelled his **Foundational Split**.

WHAAAAAAM. The **Troblin Duke** hit the ground hard enough to shake the entire keep, a column of purple flame exploding up to scorch the roof, and Right was simply *gone*. Waves of heat radiated across the room, and no solar energy passed into Hiral to bolster his own stores, though his tattoos appeared on the right side of his body.

Did it work?

Hiral checked his status window quickly to find his *Solar Capacity* at a measly twenty-one percent, then put half of it into **Foundational Split**. Right peeled off him a second later, intact and uninjured, but the **Troblin Duke** turned its attention on them, purple flames licking the wreckage of the floor.

"You got its attention," Right said grimly.

"Yup, I did," Hiral said, but something about the scene caught his attention. Several of the glyphs on the Troblin's axe weren't glowing anymore. And... and four of the torches in the circle at the center of the room were burning again.

What does that mean?

233

The **Troblin Duke** didn't give him the time to figure out the answer to the question, planting its feet and sweeping the axe around.

No way it can reach me from that far…

A crescent of purple flame peeled off the axe like a tidal wave ten feet tall and thirty feet wide, racing toward Hiral and Right.

Slipping immediately in front of Right, Hiral poured as much power into his **Rune of Rejection** as he could in the split second before impact, then focused the narrow force straight ahead of him. He didn't try anything fancy, or to stop the entire wave. Instead, he created a wedge of **Rejection**, just wide enough to part the roiling flames as they rolled over him.

Sinister heat bombarded him from all around, whispers in the fire clawing at his ears and promising him a myriad of different—but equally horrible—deaths. Then it was past, a cone of wood starting at Hiral and extending behind him amidst a charred and smoking floor.

And, most importantly, a fifth torch was burning again.

"There's a limit to how many times he can use the flames," Hiral shouted. "Look at the circle of torches!"

Seven more torches remained unlit. All they needed to do was survive that long, and then the duke should power back down. Simple… really…

The duke's good eye narrowed at Hiral, apparently understanding his words, and purple flames danced within it.

Now it was just a question of whether they *could* survive that long.

39

BOSS BATTLE

A touch on his back, then Hiral and the *Troblin Duke* moved at the same time, Hiral's high *Dex* rocketing him forward while the duke's purple flames launched it ahead. *Six torches left.* Relying on the combination of his *Dex* and *Atn*, Hiral dropped to his knees as the axe swung for his neck, sliding through the ashes of the charred wood and barely avoiding getting beheaded.

Yanily's dagger came out in a fluid motion to drive into the floor and slow Hiral's momentum as he twisted around and pushed power into his *Foundational Split*. Right exploded out of him—having been reabsorbed a moment before—and Hiral gave him an extra burst of speed with this *Rune of Rejection*.

Right's glowing fist crunched into the duke's spine with enough force to push the monster forward another step, while Hiral reached for the Troblin's head and yanked with his *Rune of Attraction*. Vastly outweighed by the hulking beast, it was Hiral who shot into the air, twisting as he went to dropkick the duke in the face mid-turn. With his respectable 18 *Str*—and the aid of his rune—Hiral hit the monster hard enough to keep its attention, then immediately pushed off with his *Rune of Rejection* and flipped in the air to land on his feet.

Then he dove out of the way, as the *Troblin Duke* had already recovered and resumed swinging. Huge, sweeping arcs from the axe tore great gouges in the floor as the monster chased Hiral, and he flipped, ducked, and dodged, doing everything he could to stay a step ahead of the brute.

Can't keep this up forever. C'mon, use your flames.

Around came the axe again—another horizontal chop which Hiral easily ducked under—but then the purple flames burst out of the opposite side of the weapon. Completely arresting the axe's swing in an instant, the eruption of fire also shot the weapon back toward Hiral, vicious balancing spike aimed right for his chest.

Hiral pushed on it with his *Rune of Rejection*, the meeting of the two forces lifting Hiral off the ground in the opposite direction, but it wouldn't be fast enough. The axe *would* catch him, and it came around with vicious intent, only to get intercepted as *Spearing Roots* burst out of the ground right in front of the sweeping arm.

Though the roots didn't have enough power to punch through the ***Troblin Duke's*** hide on their own, the mighty swing and jet-like force of the purple flames more than made up for it. Green blood and shredded skin flew into the air as the roots struck the arm at the perfect angle, tearing through muscle and lodging in bone before the roots broke under the weight of the swing.

Roaring in outrage, the Troblin turned its attention to Seena, and its whole arm burst into purple flame.

Four torches left. Hiral hit the ground, then rolled to his feet.

A shower of splinters flashed between Seena and the duke, though most of them got incinerated by the flaming right arm, and the few that made it through seemed to bounce off its tough hide.

Yanily charged in from its side. Instead of his usual barrage of lightning-quick spear strikes, the man set his feet and seemingly put all this strength into a blow aimed where Vix had focused his assault.

The spear-blade plunged into the open wound all the way up to the haft before purple flames billowed back out in response, washing over Yanily and driving the man back with a scream of pain. He batted at his face with still-burning hands as he fell, one of the four remaining torches flaring back to life. The spear haft practically disintegrated into ash.

But, there in the wound, the spear blade remained, and the ***Troblin Duke*** clawed at it with too-big hands, trying to get a hold of it to rip it out.

That distraction gave Vix the chance he needed, and the man charged in to leap into the air. One foot found the Troblin's wrist, and he used it as a steppingstone to gain more height, bringing his bladed knee straight for the duke's face as he reached for the back of the monster's head with his hands. Midair, three afterimages appeared behind Vix at the same time he drove his knee into the duke's nose, blood gushing out and bone crunching. Then the first afterimage caught up, merging again with Vix, but slamming its knee into the Troblin's face like a jackhammer.

The other two afterimages chained in short order, exactly following Vix's path to each deliver blows with multiplying force, the third and final one striking so hard, it blew the Troblin's head out of Vix's grasp.

Hiral yanked Vix back with his ***Rune of Attraction*** as the Troblin swung blindly, pulling the man out of danger to land safely on the ground a few feet back. No sooner had Vix landed than Nivian rushed past, shield lowered, to slam into the Troblin's side—right where Yanily's broken spear was lodged. Another roar of pain from the duke, and its left leg faltered, dropping it to one knee, which lined up its bloody face for a Meridian-enhanced right cross.

Whomp. The ***Troblin Duke*** listed to the side, using the axe to keep itself upright, and Left seamlessly flowed in, the ***Dagger of Sath*** coming around in a complete circle to slice across the monster's throat. Green blood gushed down the duke's neck and across its chest like a waterfall, but then its eye flared a deep purple, and flames glowed under skin that seemed as thin as paper.

The power it's gathering… It's going to explode! And everybody is too close!

Thinking back to the smokehouse, then to the ramp leading down to the duke's room, Hiral concentrated on the purple flames licking out of the duke's wounds and pushed half of his remaining solar energy into his ***Rune of Attraction.***

Please be enough.

As purple flame spewed out of the ***Troblin Duke***, Hiral grabbed on to it with his rune before it could cascade outwards, pulling it all into a tight spiral that raced right for him. Unlike with the smoke, he wouldn't be able to gather it safely in his palm—it was moving too fast—so he put all his remaining energy into his ***Rune of Rejection.***

Just feet in front of him, his rune hit the gushing fire at enough of an angle to send the majority of it careening past him. Small licks of flame still lashed him as it passed, singeing his left side, and then the full force of the blast struck the wall somewhere behind him. The wave of power lifted him from his feet and threw him forward, straight toward the ***Troblin Duke***, who lifted its head to look at him.

The final three torches relit at the same time Hiral hit the ground, the ***Troblin Duke*** almost deflating as the enraging energy left it, its skin hanging from a body bereft of muscle. The still-standing Growers didn't hesitate to strike, laying into the monster with everything they had left. Bones *snapped* with every blow from Vix and Right, while Nivian's whip tore off great strips of flesh where the thorns caught. But it was Left who finished it off, his dagger again finding the Duke's throat, and this time removing the head cleanly from the neck.

As head and body fell in separate directions to hit the floor, a blue notification sprang to life in front of Hiral's eyes.

Dynamic Quest Complete
You have defeated the Eloquent Troblin Duke
Congratulations. Achievement unlocked –
Hazards of the Duke
You proved actions speak louder than words.
Please access a Dungeon Interface
to unlock class-specific reward.

As soon as Hiral's brain processed the words, the notification vanished, only to be replaced by another immediately.

Splitfang Keep: Complete
New Record
Time: 31:23
Congratulations. Achievement Unlocked –
The Trouble with Troblins
You have dealt with the Troblin keep and its inhabitants.
Please access a Dungeon Interface
to unlock class-specific reward.
Time until Splitfang Keep instance closure: 59:59

We did it!

Hiral closed the notification to see to the others, but yet another one popped up in front of his face before he could even take a step.

Congratulations. Achievement Unlocked – My First Dungeon
You have completed your first dungeon.
Please access a Dungeon Interface to unlock class-specific
reward.

40

FIRST REWARDS

HIRAL closed the window with a thought and braced for another one, but it didn't come, so he ran over to join the others gathered around Yanily.

"How is he?" Hiral asked.

"Hurting," Yanily said, though he gave Hiral a thumbs-up. "We did it, and got a new record! Means we beat Seeyela."

"Stop moving until I finish healing you," Wule interrupted. "These injuries are nothing to joke about."

"He's got Hiral's hairstyle now," Vix pointed out, and Yanily's eyes widened a second before he winced again.

"My… my hair?" Yanily asked.

"Went *fwoosh* when you ate a faceful of purple fire," Vix said.

"*Fwoosh?*" Yanily asked, tentatively reaching his hand for his head, only for Wule to slap it away.

"What did I just say?" Wule scolded him.

"Obviously, he's fine," Seena said, but there was relief on her face.

"I'm not fine! My hair!" Yanily said.

Hiral looked at him and nodded his understanding.

Seena rolled her eyes and shook her head, then smiled. "Yanily's hair aside, good job, everybody. That was definitely more difficult than I expected for E-Rank."

"Way more difficult," Nivian said. "My arm is killing me from blocking that monster's axe."

"Honestly surprised he didn't cut you in two," Yanily said from where he lay on the ground, but his flesh was a healthier pink from Wule's healing.

"C'mon," Hiral said, offering his hand, then pulling Yanily to his feet. "Us bald guys gotta stick together."

"I'm not *bald*. I'm… follically challenged. Besides, it'll grow back." Yanily looked at Wule. "It'll grow back? Right?"

"Uh…" Wule said, looking everywhere but at Yanily. "How about we find that dungeon interface? We've got a whole mess of achievement rewards to collect."

"There's something in the center of those torches where the duke was," Vix said.

"The torches that are still burning," Hiral pointed out, looking at the other purple torches around the room. "We're sure that's the end of the Troblins? More aren't going to come running out of those suspiciously placed hallways?"

That question made everybody pause.

"No… we aren't sure at all. Stay on guard, folks," Seena instructed.

"I'm not going to be much good until we get out of here and I can grab a back-up spear from one of our supply stashes," Yanily said.

"Here," Hiral said, returning Yanily's knife to him.

"Not exactly the same, but thanks," Yanily said, then the whole group moved up to the circle of purple torches.

"I'm going first, aren't I?" Nivian asked.

"Yup," Vix said. "Give him the shoulder tap."

"Do you *need* the shoulder tap?" Seena asked Nivian.

"No, I don't need the… whatever," Nivian huffed.

He entered the circle of torches, his shield back up at the ready. Nothing changed and no more monsters burst into the room, so the rest of the group followed him in and up to a pedestal at the center of the ring.

"Looks the same as outside the dungeon," Hiral said, spotting the crystal and waving his hand over it. However, instead of an image of Dr. Benza appearing, every torch in the room simultaneously blinked out, plunging the party into absolute darkness.

"What?" somebody asked, and then the torches burst back to life, this time in shades of green and yellow. Six chests of various sizes sat spaced around the inside edge of the torches, while one larger and plainer one appeared next to the pedestal, though Hiral was too busy preparing for another ambush to pay them much mind.

When nothing immediately attacked the group, though, their eyes began turning to the strange containers.

Hrm. One chest in front of those two yellow torches, and the rest in front of green torches of various shades. Connected to our races? And this big one in the middle? What's it for?

"Is this the *loot* Dr. Benza was talking about?" Seena asked, nodding her chin toward the largest chest.

"I guess so," Hiral said. "He did say something about unique equipment the first time we completed the dungeon. Should we open the chests?"

"We've only got fifty-five minutes until we're forced out, so yes, let's open the juicy equipment chests," Yanily said as he rubbed his hands together in front of a very long and narrow chest. "I mean, I've never been very good at guessing presents, but even I know what *this* is. And I can't wait."

"It could be a fishing rod," Vix said, and Yanily's jaw almost hit the floor.

"No. No way," Yanily said, shaking his head. "It's a spear. It *has* to be."

"It *could* be," Vix said flatly. "It *could* also be a fishing rod."

"Don't make me hurt you," Yanily said, alternating his glare between Vix and the uniquely shaped chest.

"Not much threat without a spear… or fishing rod…" Vix mumbled.

"You think it's safe?" Wule asked.

"I do," Hiral said, stepping up and crouching at the chest in front of the yellow torches. "Dr. Benza seemed to be saying the point of these dungeons is to help us grow, and the equipment will help us against the *Enemy*, whoever that is."

"Well, I'm guessing the *fishing rod* chest is for Yanily," Seena said, her lips quirking, "and the one in front of the yellow torches is for Hiral. What about the rest of us?"

"Match your status window color to the two torches in front of the chest," Hiral said.

"Huh, he's right," Nivian said. "My green is a bit different than this one… and this one…" he said, walking around the ring. "I think this one matches."

"This one is mine," Vix said in front of another, and Seena and Wule quickly found their own as well.

"Doesn't look like Left and Right get chests," Seena said, looking at the two doubles.

"Sorry, guys," Hiral said.

"It makes sense," Left said. "This dungeon was designed for six people, and although we have status windows, we are not technically people."

"People or not, I don't know if we would've gotten through without you," Nivian said before glancing over at Seena. "Uh, I mean, of course a strong party of six people would have no problem getting through…"

"I'm sure my sister and her party are fine," Seena said.

"Still, let's get our loot and get out there," Hiral said. "I'm sure she'll be worried about us as well, if we take too long."

"What about this big one in the middle?" Right asked. "Should we open it first?"

"Yeah, why don't you do that?" Hiral offered.

"Aw, c'mon, how come they get to open something?" Yanily whined, but his mouth snapped closed at a look from Seena.

"There are packs in here," Left said, peering into the now opened chest. "Six, unsurprisingly."

"What's in them?" Hiral asked, though his eyes were glued to the smaller chest in front of him.

"Seriously, they get to open *something else* too?" Yanily whispered.

"Hrm. Food," Left said, "along with some other supplies and necessities. I see a couple of tents, light blankets, and clothing, though I don't recognize the material."

"Tents sure would be useful, considering the rain," Wule said.

"So would a fishing rod," Vix pointed out.

"It's not a fishing rod!" Yanily snapped. "At least, it better not be, considering what this dungeon cost me."

"Your hair?" Vix asked.

"My spear!" Yanily said, then whispered, "And my hair."

"Either way, the stuff in that big chest is going to be really useful. We didn't have a lot of supplies in the cave with us," Seena said. "Still, I'm kind of curious what's in these smaller chests. Maybe we should have Left and Right open…"

"C'mon!" Yanily said, but Seena was chuckling. "Jeez, can I open it now? Please?" Yanily asked, practically salivating at the chest in front of him.

"You're such a kid sometimes," Seena said.

"Sometimes?" Vix asked quietly.

"Go ahead, open these up and let's see what we've got," Seena said, reaching down to lift the top of the chest open.

Not wanting to wait any longer for his own either, Hiral turned his back to the others and flipped his chest open to find a pair of strange, foot-long crystal objects resting on two crystal plates. The devices were somewhat cylindrical with what looked like handles on one end, complete with a trigger.

What are these? Kind of like hand-crossbows.

As soon as he reached into the chest and touched one of the objects, a notification window popped up in front of him.

> **Runic Hand-Cannons: Impact**
> **RHCs project the power of the contained rune.**
> **Range and Damage (if applicable) based on user's combined Dex and Atn.**
> **Impact: Projects focused, concussive force.**

They're weapons? Nice. And what are these?

Hiral's hand touched the plates the **RHCs** rested on, and though he didn't get a pop-up notification for them, he instantly understood the weapons would use solar energy to bond to the plates, kind of like a sheath. Likewise, the plates would also use solar energy to attach to his skin or clothing.

That's convenient.

Hiral lifted the two **RHCs** and their plates out of the chest as he turned to see what the others had found.

"Awwwww, yeah," Yanily said, lifting a spear out of the chest in front of him. "Told you it wasn't a fishing rod. Kind of creepy-looking, but whatever; it has an *amazing* ability."

Hiral looked at the weapon in Yanily's hand, and the man wasn't kidding— the spear radiated a sinister aura. The haft looked to be made of charred wood, black as night and cracked, while the blade glinted with a familiar purple sheen.

There were even crude etchings extending from the haft all the way to the tip of the serrated blade.

"Yanily wins the prize for the spookiest-looking item," Seena said, holding what appeared to be a vine-wrought tiara in her hands. "What did everybody else get?"

"Should we call you princess-boss now?" Wule asked, holding up a two-foot-long rod of solid ice. "Ah, it gives me some attack options," he said as if in explanation.

"Shush, you," Seena said, but she still slipped the tiara on her head. "Speeds up the… uh… cast time of my abilities. Reduces cooldown by a lot too. What about you, Vix?"

"Bracers," he said, holding up the paired leather items. "Apparently gives my punches a range of ten feet?"

"If your arms go all wiggly and long, you'll take the spookiest item crown," Seena said, then looked at Nivian. "You?"

"An amulet," Nivian said, holding up what looked like a simple flower with its stem twisted around. "It adds my strength, dexterity, and endurance to give me some kind of additional armor effect. Looks like it stacks with my **Bark Armor** too."

"Oh, nice," Seena said. "Hiral?"

"They're called **Runic Hand Cannons**. Ranged weapons, from what I can tell," Hiral said.

"Isn't your class called something like that?" Wule asked.

"Runic Artificer, yeah. These must be connected. I'm going to take a closer look at them when we get out. They seem *really* interesting, and there's another rune in there."

He held one of the plates to the side of his right thigh and pushed some solar energy into it. The plate immediately adhered in place, and there was practically no weight to it despite the **RHC** being attached too. The other went on his left thigh a second later, and then he turned his attention to the dungeon interface, along with everybody else.

"How do we get these achievement rewards?" Yanily asked, though he was taking practice stabs with his spear in the opposite direction.

"Just wave your hand over the crystal, I think," Hiral said. "Why don't one of you go first, just to make sure it works for somebody other than me?"

"I say we should let Nivian go first," Wule said, looking at his twin, who took a step *back*.

"Why? You think it's going to explode or something?" Nivian asked warily.

"What? No," Wule said. "I actually meant the opposite."

"Oh, you think *I'm* going to explode?" Nivian asked.

Wule walked over and gently punched his brother in the shoulder. "You always go first into the dangerous situations. Figured you should get to go first for some of the good stuff too."

"Oh," Nivian said, nodding. "Thanks, Wule. Is that okay with everybody else?"

"All yours," Seena said, gesturing with both hands toward the panel, and Nivian walked over to it and waved his hand.

"Sure hope it *doesn't* explode," Wule whispered loud enough for everybody to hear.

"You…" Nivian growled. He hopped back from the interface, his eyes wide. "Oh, uh, achievement rewards." Then his eyes opened even further. "Wow, that's a *lot* of achievement notifications. You guys may want to get started."

"How many?" Seena asked.

"A bunch. Can't tell how many, exactly, since they're hidden behind each other," Nivian explained, and one by one, the party members went over and waved their hands above the crystal.

Time Records
Achievement Rewards
Rank Evolution
Exit Dungeon

As much as Hiral wanted to get his class-specific rewards—*Still can't believe I have a class after all this time!*—he instead focused on the top option and said, "**Time Records**."

Splitfang Keep Clear Times
Party (Seena) – 31:23
Party (Seeyela) – 35:58

"Your sister's party also cleared the dungeon," Hiral said.

"**Time Records**," Seena said immediately, and a tension in her shoulders relaxed as she saw the clear notification. "Good thinking, Hiral. Thanks."

"No problem," Hiral said as the clear times vanished and the original menu reappeared. "*Achievement Rewards*."

Hiral instinctively stepped back as a barrage of status windows cascaded in front him, and out of the corner of his eyes, he saw he wasn't the only one.

Achievement: Terminal
Class Reward: Ability (Active) – Terminal
Terminal (Active) – Once per 24 hours, you may initiate an ability or item at its maximum rank for up to 180 seconds.
Note: Utilizing Ability – Terminal (Active) risks the Debuff – System Shock.
System Shock: No class abilities can be used for one hour.

Okay, so that must be similar to what I almost did by accident during my Shaper test. Same debuff too. Maximum rank, though? That could be handy— though I don't know if the risk would be worth it in the middle of a fight. Let's see what's next.

Hiral pulled up his status window, noticing **Terminal** was now listed under his abilities, then closed the first achievement window to look at the next.

Achievement: Unsullied and Unsummoned
Class Reward: Class Modification – Infernal Conjuration
Infernal Conjuration – Conjured items or creatures
gain the Infernal characteristic.

Infernal? What in the Fallen's names does that mean? Wait… conjured creatures?

Hiral's head turned toward Left and Right, and memories of the purple smoke monsters sprang to mind.

"What? Do I have something on my face?" Right asked.

"Ah, never mind. We can talk about it later," Hiral said, dismissing that particular notification window. Another popped into focus to replace it immediately.

Achievement: Just the Right Amount of Heat
Class Reward: Class Modification – Gourmand
Gourmand – Consuming food or drink will now add limited buffs.
Note: Strength of buffs dependent
on ingredient quality and preparation.

Er, wow. We can get buffs just by eating? That could be pretty powerful.

Hiral double-checked his status window to see both class modifications were listed under a special section of his abilities, then closed the notification window.

Achievement: Hazards of the Duke
Class Reward: Ability – Eloquent (self buff) (1 hour cooldown)
Class Reward: Ability – Enraged (self buff) (1 hour cooldown)
Eloquent (self buff) – Increase all mental attributes
by 50% for 180 seconds.
Note: After Eloquent (self buff) fades, all mental attributes
are reduced by 50% for 180 seconds.
Enraged (self buff) – Increase all physical attributes
by 50% for 180 seconds.
Note: After Enraged (self buff) fades, all physical attributes are
reduced by 50% for 180 seconds.

Fifty percent? To all stats for three minutes? Another really powerful ability… unless the fight lasts longer than that. That's worth testing out, though. Looks like just two more after this.

With a thought, the notification window vanished and the next one popped into focus.

> **Achievement: The Trouble with Troblins**
> **Reward: Class Modification – Racial Growth**
> *Racial Growth – By defeating multiple creatures of the same type,*
> *you gain stacking bonuses to damage and damage reduction in*
> *future encounters.*
> *Racial Growth: Troblins – Level 1 Achieved – 5% bonus*
> *Racial Growth: Troblins – Level 2 – 0/10*

Okay, so if we kill ten more Troblins, we'll get another bonus when fighting Troblins? Handy. I wonder how high it goes—and if it's the same number of monsters for each type. Fighting ten of those lizards would be much tougher than ten Troblins. Only one way to find out, but first, one more notification.

Hiral closed the current window to bring up the last.

> **Achievement: My First Dungeon**
> **Reward: Class Modification: View – E-Rank (constant)**
> *View – You gain additional information through your PIM when*
> *looking at objects or creatures.*
> *Note: View is upgradable to provide more information.*

Additional information? What kind of information?

Hiral finally closed the last of the notifications and looked up to find Seena staring at him.

"Your last name is Dorin?" she asked at the same time he saw a name floating above her head in green script.

"And yours is Aliside?" he asked. "And you're High-E-Rank. So, name and level?"

"Yeah. You're Mid-E-Rank still?" she asked.

A quick look at his status window, and Hiral nodded. "Hit level fifteen, but I guess *high* must be from sixteen on?"

"Mid is the biggest category," Seena confirmed. "Everybody get their achievement rewards?" she asked the group at large, and a wide-eyed party looked back at her.

"Class modifications, abilities… This was a major haul," Yanily said. "Why didn't we do this sooner?"

"No Islander in our party," Vix pointed out.

"Well, yes," Yanily agreed before shuffling over to stand beside Vix. "So, buddy, what did you get?"

"We can compare what we got when we get out," Seena said, holding up her hand to forestall Vix from answering. "In fact, we're going to make a point of it. If you guys got anything like I did, it's going to change how we fight. How we fight *together*.

"We can run this dungeon twice more, from what Dr. Benza said, and I intend to use those runs to fine-tune what we can do and our teamwork. First, though, let's get out of here before Seeyela starts worrying."

Yanily winced, then looked at Vix. "Yeah, Vix. Let's get out of here and *then* talk about the nifty stuff we got."

Vix glared at the spearman, but wisely kept his mouth shut, and Seena swept her hand over the interface crystal.

"***Exit Dungeon***," she said.

41

EXIT DUNGEON

HIRAL stepped out of the portal behind Seena, a pack over his shoulder, and into the room with the Quillback corpses to find Seeyela and her party already waiting for them.

"What took you so long?" Seeyela asked, looking up from similar packs arranged neatly on the floor. She was obviously relieved to see her sister in one piece. "And what happened to Yanily's head?"

"Figured it'd be easier than dealing with wet hair in all that rain," Yanily said, one hand running across the smooth skin of his scalp and his spear gesturing toward the exit.

"*Troblin Duke* burned him," Seena said more seriously. "How'd you do? Any troubles?"

"The duke was a beast," Seeyela said, "but we managed to take him down without anybody losing their hair. Did you manage to stop the summoning ritual or whatever it was called? We took a wrong turn, so we didn't get there in time."

"We got through it with a minute to spare. What did it summon?"

"Some kind of giant, winged purple smoke monster that took up the entire platform. It couldn't move from there, but it harassed us the rest of the time by throwing these balls of smoke that made it feel like we were walking through mud. Burned like a weak acid too."

"That sounds like a pain in the ass," Seena said.

"Was… until I figured out my *Gravity Wells* could intercept them if I put one between us and the platform. Went a lot more smoothly after that," Seeyela said.

"And the *Butcher*?" Nivian asked.

"He nicked Picoli pretty badly with that cleaver of his, and Balyo got caught by the fire trap," Seeyela started.

"Don't stand in fire," Vix said to Balyo, and she just rolled her eyes.

"But again, *Gravity Well* took care of the smoke," Seeyela finished as if she hadn't been interrupted. "Once we could see the *Butcher*, things didn't go so well for him."

"That ability is wildly unfair," Yanily said.

"Can't disagree," Seeyela said with a chuckle. "And it's even better with one of the achievements I got—and this staff." She held up a staff somewhat similar to Yanily's spear. Charred-wood haft, but instead of a purple blade on the end, it had a crystal with purple flames dancing within.

"We should compare notes before we go back in again," Seena said. "There's a trick to the summoning ritual."

"Aw, you don't have to tell her," Yanily said. "They might beat our clear time."

"I'd rather *that* than my sister getting killed," Seena deadpanned.

"Fair," Yanily admitted, walking over to Balyo and the spear she was holding beside her. "Hey, what you got there?"

"I'll show you mine if you show me yours," she said, holding out a spear with a sky-blue haft and a blade that looked like a lightning bolt. It even had arcs of electricity dancing across the metal, but somehow Yanily's eyes were locked on the woman.

"I thought you'd never ask," he said, then glanced around the room. "But, maybe we should find somewhere a bit more private? We've got these tents…"

Balyo cuffed Yanily across his shiny scalp with an echoing *fwap*. "I meant the spears!"

"Oh. Yeah," Yanily said, rubbing at his head. "Totally what I was talking about too. Take a look at this…"

Hiral shook his head and focused back on the others. Fitch, despite the glare he was still throwing in Hiral's direction, had a new sword, vines like a bramblebush in place of a crosspiece. Lonil had a primal-looking stone club beside him, while Cal was shining a simple metal rod. That just left Picoli leaning on a new staff, the head of it blurring like something was there, but out of focus.

Oh, that hurts to look at. Hiral turned away, hands rubbing at his eyes. *Still, it looks like everybody left with a new piece of equipment. I wonder how strong it all is.*

"…your thoughts?" Seena was asking her sister as Hiral tuned back in.

"Probably the same as you," Seeyela said. "We clear this dungeon twice more for experience and practice, then move on to finding—what did they call those other two places?"

"*The Mire* and *The Troblin Throne*," Hiral filled in.

"Well, if this place had the Eloquent Duke, how much you wanna bet we'll find the Kinky *King* at the throne?" Yanily asked.

"Keep your fetishes out of the dungeons," Vix said.

"Isn't that *exactly* where they're supposed to be?" Yanily asked, his face far too neutral.

"Back on point, you two," Seena said. "I agree with my sister, though. Let's use this place as a chance to improve ourselves. If this was Mid-E-Rank, *and* this difficult, we need to be better prepared for the next two dungeons."

"Do we really even need to clear them?" Cal asked, joining Seeyela and Seena. "I mean, why don't we just stay here? We've got some food from the dungeon, we're out of the rain. Why do we *have to* go to the other dungeons?"

"Cal has a point," Lonil said. "Don't get me wrong—I'll go wherever you say we should, Seeyela, but we're safe here. Why don't we just at least consider staying here until the islands come around again?"

"Do you actually think we're safe here?" Wule asked, looking around the room *still* full of bloody and broken Quillback bodies.

"C'mon, Wule, we know what happened to the Quillbacks, and those people are gone," Lonil said. "They returned to Fallen Reach after making sure to strand us down here."

"Bastards," Fitch said, and the look he gave Hiral made sure who he included in that statement.

"I'm not talking about the Islanders," Wule said. "You all know it as well as I do—nobody who stays on the surface survives. And you can't possibly tell me we're the first people *ever* to think about staying here, in this cave."

"And there is the issue of the *Enemy* Dr. Benza mentioned," Hiral added. "He seemed to make it pretty clear the only safe place from them... him... her... whoever or whatever they are, was the *Asylum*. If we continue on Wule's train of thought, that *Asylum* could be the differentiating factor."

"Differentiating? Look at you, using all those big words," Yanily said. "But, jokes aside, I agree with Hiral."

"You just want more dungeons and more experience," Balyo said.

"Damn straight I do. Didn't you all notice we got *bonus experience* for clearing the dungeon? And we can get that eight more times. I'll be level twenty in no time! Do you know how long it would take to get to D-Rank without these dungeons? *Years*."

"I think you're the closest to twenty from our party," Seena said. "You think you'll get it after running this dungeon twice more? The interface had an evolution option to get to D-Rank. Could be useful to use it before we move on, if that's what we decide to do."

"I think I'll be a bit short, unless we change up what we do next time we go in," Yanily said. "We'd have to find a lot more Troblins to kill for me to hit twenty otherwise."

"And we still haven't decided if we're moving on," Cal said. "Sure, there's the issue of this mysterious *Enemy*, but do we even know if it's still around? Or, at least, if it's still around *here*?"

"Waiting here would mean we'd need to survive for a full rotation," Nivian said. "We came back to this dungeon partially because we thought we might be able to stay in *there*. We can't. Sure, we can clear out this cave, and we got some food and other supplies from clearing the dungeon. Maybe we'll even get more the next time we clear it, but it won't be enough to last the whole time.

"One way or another, we're going back out in the rain."

"We know this area," Balyo said. "We know where we can find food."

"And those Horny Tree Lizards?" Yanily asked.

"Horned... not horny..." Vix said. "At least... I hope not. The surface is terrifying."

"Horned... or horny... lizards, Yanily actually has a point," Seena said. "We *knew* the area, before the rains arrived. Already we've dealt with lizards we've never seen and Troblins using buffs outside of the dungeon. Before yesterday, can any of you tell me even one time either of those things happened?"

The Growers all looked at each other, but none of them immediately spoke up.

"We don't *know* if it's connected," Cal said, but even she didn't have any certainty in her voice.

"I think we can safely assume it is, Caleon," Seeyela said.

"Wouldn't that just be another reason we shouldn't go?" Cal asked. "You said it yourself—we don't know what's out there. Here... we know what's here. And the islands pass close, so we can get home as soon as they come around again."

"Assuming those lizards—or something worse—don't find their way in here," Wule said. "We know Troblins and some of the monsters we've seen around the other dungeons wouldn't come into these entry areas, but that doesn't mean the lizards won't."

"Or the *Enemy*," Hiral reiterated.

"Enough with this *Enemy* shit," Fitch said. "We don't know if it's real, or if we can even trust this Dr. Benza. For all we know, these... these images of him could be from so far in the past the *Enemy* is nothing more than dust now."

"I'm sure it's real," Hiral said. "And I'm sure we should worry about it."

"How can you be sure?" Fitch asked.

"Do you think Fallen Reach occurred *naturally*? Somebody built an entire floating island, more than thirty miles long, not counting your Grower islands. Why do you think they did that? To get a better suntan?" Hiral wasn't *quite* able to keep his sarcasm in check. "No. They built it to *escape* something. This *Enemy* would be my guess as to what that something is.

"And if it's powerful enough to scare a civilization capable of creating Fallen Reach, well, I think we should be scared too. I don't know about you, but I'd much rather assume it's still around and be careful than assume it's *not* and regret it."

"And your suggestion is...?" Seena prompted.

"To clear all three dungeons and unlock this *Asylum* place. Maybe we'll find safety there, like Dr. Benza was saying. And we might even get some answers."

"Look, I get it, going out there isn't safe," Seena added, coming over to stand beside Hiral. "But neither is staying here. If we move and clear the other dungeons, not only do we open the *Asylum*, but we also get stronger along the way. More capable to protect ourselves. *That,* at least, is a guarantee."

"You know we're with you, boss," Nivian said, turning his attention to Seeyela and her party.

"We'll take a vote," Seeyela said to her people. "Decide whether you think it would be better to try and stick it out here, or go with Seena's party. But! We aren't going to take the vote *now.* I want everybody to think about it good and hard before making the decision."

"When will we vote?" Balyo asked.

"After we clear the dungeon twice more," Seeyela said.

"And before that," Seena spoke up, looking right at Yanily, "we're going to talk about our new abilities and how we can improve on our last run. Don't expect to go back in today, and maybe not even tomorrow.

"We've got some training to do."

"But first," Yanily interrupted, "we get buffs for eating now. So, what's for dinner?"

42

NEW RUNES

HIRAL looked up from where he sat studying the **RHCs** to see how Left and Right were doing. The two sparred with Vix and Nivian, while Balyo and Yanily practiced spear forms nearby. Fitch was by himself doing sword katas, and Lonil was learning how to swing his new heavy club around. Still, Hiral's eyes kept going back to Left and Right as they trailed purple smoke from many of their movements.

Infernal Conjuration, eh?

Over the last six hours since they'd cleared the dungeon, the party had spent a lot of time discussing the abilities they'd gotten from the achievements and how they could incorporate them into strategies. Interestingly enough, even though they'd all gotten the same achievements in the dungeons—and some before, such as *Terminal*—the abilities they'd gained didn't turn out to all be identical. Hiral and Seena, for example, had both gained *Infernal Conjuration*, imbuing Left and Right—along with many of Seena's abilities— with additional effects.

Seena's roots gained a new damage type—the purple flame—as did Left and Right, though Hiral's copies also now trailed purple smoke when they moved, if they chose to. The smoke, like Seeyela had mentioned, had very minor slowing and acidic effects that didn't affect the doubles or those they considered allies. During sparring, if the doubles concentrated, the smoke would hinder their opponent, so that implied it was at least somewhat under their control.

On the other hand, Vix had gained the ability to do significant extra damage to conjured items or creatures from the achievement **Unsullied and Unsummoned**. And Wule, who got possibly the most interesting ability, could summon a pair of solar energy lanterns that would follow him around, acting like batteries until he used their energy. Each gave him an extra twenty percent solar energy capacity.

The abilities from the dungeon had really given the party a lot more flexibility, and would make the next run they planned for the following... whatever they were going to call it after they slept... much easier. In the meantime, Seena had conjured a barricade in the entry to the cave to help prevent unwanted visitors—after they'd taken a quick look outside.

Just like Dr. Benza had said, there was now a clear path for them to follow, glowing roots marking the trail for them to take to the next dungeon. Even more interesting, those plants in particular gave off faint solar energy which the party could absorb to restore spent energy. It was slow going, not even as strong as the Quillback room, but it was certainly better than nothing. Especially since they didn't know how far the next dungeon was.

Still, those were problems for later, and after moving all the corpses to one corner of the room—they didn't want to risk leaving them outside and attracting predators—everybody focused on training and practicing with their new abilities.

Well, almost everybody. Hiral had been sitting against the wall, studying the **RHCs** for the last hour.

"Figure anything out?" Seena asked, coming over to slide down the wall and sit beside him.

"I think I'm close," Hiral said, lifting one of the **RHCs** up in both hands to show her. "See this rune in here?" He pointed with his left hand at what looked like a crystal slide with the rune etched into it. "This is the **Rune of Impact**, from what I can tell. And, you see how there are three slots here? I think the slot this rune is in is the primary slot. It determines what happens when I pull the trigger. You know, a trigger like a crossbow.

"Anyway, when I tested it out by moving the rune slide into other slots, nothing happened when I pulled the trigger."

"So, what are the other slots for, then?" Seena asked, looking closely at the **RHC**.

"I *think* they modify the primary effect," Hiral said.

"Modify? How?"

"Not entirely sure. I'll need more runes to figure it out."

"More runes? What about the ones on your arms?" Seena shifted her attention to the two visible runes on Hiral's forearms. "Er, you know, Hiral, this is the first time I've really gotten a chance to look at them, but don't both runes look the same?"

"They're inverted versions of each other," Hiral said. "**Rejection** and **Attraction**. Like two sides of the same coin, or a mirror image."

"So, if you flip the rune in here upside-down, does that mean it has a different effect?" Seena pointed again at the **RHC**.

"No, the runes seem to have an absolute orientation, so no matter how you hold it, it's still the same rune," Hiral said, though the question sent his mind down a different path. "You make an interesting point, though." He pulled the **Rune of Impact** slide out of the **RHC** and held it up to his eye. "If this is anything like the runes I have, that would mean there must be a mirror image."

"What would the opposite of impact be?" Seena asked.

Great question. Rejection and attraction. Are they opposites? Kind of, but not exactly. They're definitely related, though. What would be like that for impact? What is impact? The collision of two forces or objects. What's the key there?

Collision. Kind of like rejection.

But collision and rejection don't always happen when two forces or objects meet. Like when I pour water into a larger bucket of water. Or when armor gets struck. Sure, there's impact there, but if the armor is good enough, it protects the person wearing the armor. Why? If it's a hard armor, it rejects the blow. Deflects it. But what about padded armor? It doesn't reject the attack.

It absorbs it.

As soon as the thought solidified in Hiral's mind, scripts of solar energy flowed from the double-helix patterns on his arms to consolidate on his biceps. Yellow energy flared—Seena even had to look away from the bright light—and the power built and built as the scripts swirled into a larger shape. Then, all at once, the light flashed. Hiral's solar capacity dropped to zero in an instant, and his previously bare biceps now held two new runes.

"What...?" Seena started to ask, but a flash and *Whoa* from across the room had both their heads snapping to the commotion.

Blue light billowed out of Left's and Right's upper arms, so bright, it forced everybody to turn away or cover their eyes, then flashed once, and the doubles were gone.

"Hiral...?" Seena asked beside him, and the other Grower heads turned in his direction as well.

"Everything okay?" Yanily asked.

"I think so," Hiral said, opening his status window even though he suspected what he'd find. "I've got two new runes. The **Rune of Impact** and the **Rune of Absorption**." He looked down at his right bicep, though the rune was gone, and his tattoos had returned.

"What happened to Left and Right?" Nivian asked.

"That part... I'm not sure about," Hiral said. "But I'm *completely* out of solar energy, so it'll be a few minutes before I can bring them back to find out."

"Completely out and *only* a few minutes? Overpowered S-Rank absorption," Yanily said. "Well, let us know when you're ready. Balyo, let's get back at it."

The spearwoman shrugged, then fell back in beside Yanily, and the two resumed their spear forms.

"You okay?" Seena asked.

"Yeah," Hiral said. "Guess it answers a question I had, though."

"What's that?"

"How I would learn new runes. The dungeon abilities I got from the achievements didn't give me runes, so I was a little worried I'd never learn any more. I guess I need some kind of... insights... into them. When I understood the concepts of impact and absorption, the runes just manifested on their own. I guess that's how I get new abilities.

"I mean, Shapers need Artists to give them the new tattoos, so I was really hoping that wasn't the case for runes. Actually, how do Growers learn new abilities?"

"Evolution," Seena said. "Not the kind like when we go from E-Rank to D-Rank, but from challenging ourselves. Kind of like, if we *need* an ability to overcome a particular situation, we'll spontaneously learn it."

"Okay, now *that* sounds overpowered."

"It *would* be," Seena laughed, "if it was consistent. We can't control when or why it'll happen. All we can do is keep putting ourselves into more challenging situations to try and force an ability evolution, as it's called.

"Though, I guess it's not really an evolution. We get a *new* ability, not a modification to an existing ability like we got from the dungeon achievements. Or like the mutation where I can use my **Spearing Roots** to create walls. More like my **Target** ability. I got that from one fight where Yanily just *would not* hit the right Troblin. It was driving me absolutely crazy, and then, boom—new ability."

"Wow. Sounds like Yanily needs to be annoying more often," Hiral joked.

"Oh, he's annoying plenty often enough as it is."

"I can see that. Still, it's so interesting. Uh… not Yanily. The magic. All the **PIMs** are different. I wonder what the fourth race is, and how they learn abilities," Hiral mused out loud while he slid the rune-slider back into his **RHC**.

"Fourth race? Oh, from how the dungeon interface had a fourth light that didn't glow? You think there really is one?"

"I think there *was* one, at least. Now? I don't know. I don't even know how many other Builders are out there."

"Growers. Makers. Builders. Strangely… appropriate race names," Seena said. "You think Dr. Benza can explain more about it after we clear the other two dungeons?"

"I was really hoping he'd be able to explain more *now*. We cleared this dungeon, after all, but it was still all the same information when I tried asking after we got out." Hiral threw a dirty look toward the interface.

"He wants us to keep pushing ourselves. Keep getting stronger," Seena said. "We can only do that by moving on to the next dungeon."

"So we can deal with the *Enemy* he's talking about. Well, talking *around*," Hiral amended. "Do you think we'll have an easier time the second run through **Splitfang Keep**?"

"Much easier. Partly because of all the new abilities we got, but more so because now we know what we're up against. Assuming nothing changes."

"I don't think it will. Dr. Benza said something about it being a snapshot, and things resetting. I'm sure the Troblins will all have the same abilities and hide in the same spots."

"That'd be a relief. Anyway, back to your—what did you call them? Cannons? Now that you figured out new runes, can you do anything to them?"

"No. I'm not sure why, but I know the runes I have aren't the right kind to be put in those support slots. I'm not complaining, though. I've learned so much in the last few hours, not to mention since we came to the surface. I have a class. You can't even imagine how big a deal that is."

"What was it like, not having one?" Seena asked.

"Horrible. And I'm not exaggerating. I was the only person above the age of ten without one. People thought something was wrong with me. Like I was sick or broken or something. Worthless. Even my own mother wouldn't talk to me."

"How did you deal with it?"

"By dreaming of the looks on their faces when I finally got my class. When I proved them all wrong."

"Can Makers choose their class?" Seena asked. "For reference, Growers can't. It sort of comes naturally to us around our eighth or ninth birthday. Tenth at the latest. Like our abilities, it's kind of spontaneous. But, I see you've got all these tattoos." She pointed at Hiral's tattooed arm, since he'd reabsorbed Right and Left.

"Yeah, I was trying to become a Shaper, like those… uh…" Hiral trailed off; the issue of the people who'd captured Seeyela's party was still a bit embarrassing.

"I know what Shapers are," Seena said flatly. "Caaven's niece, remember? I've been around enough when Arty came down to trade, though I wasn't sure about you until this last time."

"Oh, you mean when I threw myself off the island? Twice?" Hiral laughed.

"Kind of stands out," Seena agreed with a chuckle. "Shaper?"

"Yeah. Both of my parents are Artists. Two of the best on the whole island, actually. They started doing my Meridian Lines and tattoos even before I was old enough to take the Shaper test. Oh, there's a test you have to pass that grants you the class. You have to"—he touched the dagger on his left forearm then pulled his hand away—"shape something. It's simple, really, if you can do it. I… uh… failed it ten times.

"Anybody who can't do it ends up as an Artist or Academic. Not that either is a bad class," Hiral quickly amended.

"Why didn't you become one of those two, then?"

"Couldn't be an Artist. There's a test for that too. Uh… which I also failed…" Hiral said, and of course his brain whispered *Everfail* in a child's voice for him. "Artists need to be able to mix their blood with a special pigment used for the tattoos. My blood didn't work. And I didn't want to give up and become an Academic.

"Looking back, I bet I couldn't have passed that test either. Seems like I was trying to get a class for the wrong race."

"Were you… adopted… Hiral?" Seena asked.

"I've been wondering the same thing myself." Hiral chuckled. "But, no, I'm pretty sure those are my actual sisters. Uh, I've got two younger sisters. Way smarter and more gifted than me, but totally related. And I remember them since they were babies. I don't know how to explain the race thing. I just don't. Another thing I want to ask Dr. Benza."

"Sounds like you have a long list," Seena said.

"And getting longer."

"Something I don't get," Seena said, scratching at her knee as she sat beside him. "Two things, actually. One, why do you guys even have tests? And two—if this is too personal, you don't have to answer, but—why didn't you give up on being a Shaper? Why'd you keep trying?"

"The test is only once a year, like a rite of passage, and it's a big celebration when people succeed. I think it's mainly just an excuse for *that*. As for your second question, it's not too personal. Stubbornness, I guess? My father suggested I skip the test some years, but I couldn't bring myself to do it. I kept asking myself, 'What if this is the year I get it?' And then I worried I'd have to keep waiting."

"Spoiler, I never got it," Hiral said, forcing himself to chuckle. Oddly, it wasn't quite as easy as he'd expected, even though he had a class. The pain was still there… like part of him thought this was a dream, and he'd wake up classless all over again. "That… and, if I'm being honest with myself, I knew if I skipped a year, I don't think I would've been able to go back later."

"Why did you? What made you want to be a Shaper so much?"

"At first, it was because the Measure suggested I should be," Hiral said.

"The Measure?"

"Ah, it's where we get tested when we're born, and our crystals get embedded in our chests," Hiral said, tapping the center of his chest. "I guess where we get our **PIM**. Since I had the high solar energy scores, everybody assumed I'd be a great Shaper someday. Maybe some of their hopes rubbed off on me. Parents put a lot of effort into my tattoos because of that.

"As time went on, well, I didn't want to let everybody down. Then… that turned into proving them all wrong when they changed their minds so quickly about me. I went from being the once-in-ten-generations prodigy to… the Everfail practically overnight.

"I… just couldn't let it end like that," Hiral said quietly.

"I don't think I could've kept going," Seena said.

"You'd be surprised how far stubbornness and anger will get you. So, Makers have three class choices. Shapers, Artists, and Academics. What's it like for Growers?"

"Six classes," Seena said, mercifully going along with the topic shift. "First, you've got Spear Wardens—or just Wardens, as most people call them—like Yanily and Balyo. I'm not exactly sure why, but the spear is a kind of special weapon for our people. We all learn how to use one, at least basically, starting around when we're five or six."

"Another thing passed down from your ancestors?" Hiral asked.

"Yup," Seena said with a nod. "And when people have a talent for it, they tend to become Spear Wardens. It's a strong combat class, and the only one focused on a single weapon."

"What about Fitch and Vix?"

"They're both class number two. That's right, they actually have the same one—Stinger. It can take a lot of different forms, but it's usually another weapon-focused class. The person finds a weapon or style they have an affinity with, usually by learning a style ability, and that guides them down the class. Like the Spear Warden, it's always a damage class.

"Then you've got Lonil and Nivian—Swarm Leaders. In *most* parties, they're both the tanks and the leaders."

"Except with you and Seeyela in the picture?" Hiral chuckled.

"What can I say? We like telling people what to do," Seena agreed.

"Luckily, you seem pretty good at it."

"Thanks. Swarm Leaders have a list of defensive and what we call taunting abilities."

"Why do I feel like Yanily got some of those taunting abilities too?" Hiral asked.

"Unfortunately, those aren't abilities. Just how he is. I *wish* he could use those in combat on somebody other than us."

"Wule and Cal are both the same class too, right?" Hiral asked, getting back on topic.

"Correct. Menders. They all have abilities focused on healing and restoration. Some of our highest-ranking Menders can even regrow lost limbs or cure diseases. It's a powerful class and very much in demand. Just need to get them enough experience down on the surface to gain some of those abilities." She grimaced a bit at that last part.

"You don't look happy about that," Hiral said.

"Remember how I talked about spontaneous ability evolution? That's usually what needs to happen to get those kinds of abilities. Which means…"

"Somebody needs to *lose* a limb for the Mender to gain the ability to regrow it," Hiral finished. "Ouch."

"Yeah. Part of me hopes Wule never gets that kind of skill," Seena said, looking over at her friends.

"You do a good job protecting them," Hiral said quietly. "I've only been with you all a short time, and even I can see it."

"Thanks," Seena said, eyes lingering on the other Growers a moment longer. "Fifth class is what me, Picoli, and Seeyela fall under. We're Callers. I'm what you'd name a Wood Caller. Picoli is a Light Caller, and Seeyela... Well, she's something special. A Gravity Caller. Maybe the first of her kind. Most of our abilities work around manipulating our focus. Wood, in my case."

"Which explains the roots and vines... Are vines actually wood?" Hiral asked, thinking about it.

"Don't get technical on me. We do actually have Plant Callers, but they use a much wider variety than I do, so I got wood."

"I'll take your word for it." Hiral chuckled, and Seena scowled at him. "Uh, so, sixth class?"

"Farmer," Seena said. "Kind of like your Academic. It's the catch-all class that non-combatants fall into. I hope that's what Favela gets. Farmers get to stay nice and safe up on the islands. If you get one of the other five, well, you have to come to the surface."

"Is Caaven a farmer?" Hiral asked.

"Yes, which is why I brought my party down looking for Seeyela. He wouldn't know the first thing to do if he came to the surface." Seena laughed. "I'd almost like to see it... if it wasn't so dangerous."

"Hah. Same with Arty. Did you see his face when I told him I wanted to come down with you? Actually, did you see your own? Complete shock."

"Gee, I wonder why? Crazy Islander jumps off the island, then tells me he wants to do it again? What did you expect my reaction to be?"

"Yeah, that's fair," Hiral said, looking away from Seena to find Seeyela stalking over. "Uh oh. Incoming."

Seena wiped the smile from her face just in time for Seeyela to plant her feet in front of them.

"You two don't look like you're training very hard," Seeyela said, crossing her arms.

"You kidding?" Seena looked up at her sister without standing. "Hiral here just gained two new abilities."

"And why aren't you trying them out to see what they do?" Seeyela asked, turning her attention on Hiral.

"The process drained all of my solar energy..." Hiral said, but the look on Seeyela's face told him just how weak of an answer that sounded. "But, hey, would you look at that? I've just now recovered enough to resummon Right and Left."

That was a lie; his solar energy was already past thirty percent. Really, he only needed three percent to use *Foundational Split*, but that would leave them all without enough energy to use any of their abilities.

"Then let's see what the light show was all about," Seeyela said, offering her hands to *help* them stand.

"Right," Hiral said. After getting pulled to his feet, he took a couple steps away and activated *Foundational Split*.

Right and Left peeled off of him on opposite sides, then each glanced at their upper arms.

"What is it?" Hiral asked them.

"It seems I have access to an additional tattoo," Left said. "*The Banner of Courage*." He pointed at the tattoo of a triangular flag planted in the ground on his left bicep.

"Reaaaaaaally?" Hiral said, unable to keep the excitement from his voice. "Right?"

"Ah, Meridian Line up to just under my shoulder now," the double said, the line glowing with solar energy along the back of his hand, up the side of his arm, and stopping just below his shoulder.

"When I got upper arm runes, you guys got access to your tattoos up to that point as well. So, for you to unlock more tattoos, I need to find more runes," Hiral mumbled.

"More abilities, huh?" Seeyela asked.

"Yeah… yeah!" Hiral said. "*The Banner of Courage* is a buff ability for anybody within a certain range. Versatile, and really well-suited for a party. Not many people get it in Fallen Reach, because they don't fight in groups usually, but my parents wanted me to have it to promote teamwork."

"Great story. Very moving," Vix said.

"Yup," Seeyela agreed. "And you know what more abilities means, don't you?"

Seena and Hiral looked at each other, then both spoke at the same time. "More training."

"Best get to it, then," Seeyela said.

43

THE VOTE

Two sleeps later, Hiral stepped out of the portal from their third and final run at *Splitfang Keep*, another pack of supplies over his shoulder.

"That was smooth," Seena said, the last of them to exit the dungeon. "Well done."

"Wish we could go in again. Another run and I'd be level twenty for sure," Yanily said. "That bonus experience from *Good Things Come in Threes* was legit. Almost got me there."

At the mention of it, Hiral took a quick look at the surprise notification he'd received when the group had cleared the dungeon for the third time.

> *Congratulations. Achievement Unlocked –*
> *Third Time's a Charm*
> *Reward: Class Modification – Good Things Come in Threes*
> *Good Things Come in Threes – Successfully completing a*
> *single dungeon three times results*
> *in significant bonus experience.*

And Yanily was right—the experience bonus had been pretty impressive. *Good reason to clear all the dungeons three times.*

"Yeah, but at least the rest of us are level nineteen now," Seena said. "Well, except for you, Hiral. What did you end up at?"

"Level seventeen," he said, checking his status window.

"Not bad. The teamwork in there was really good this time. You've all done a great job incorporating your new abilities—and Hiral—into the party. I'm proud of you."

"Aw, stop. You'll make me blush," Yanily said.

"All the way up to his silky-smooth scalp," Vix said.

"Don't start, you two," Seena interrupted. "We had the advantage knowing what was coming in *Splitfang Keep*, but I think we're as ready as we can be to head out to the next dungeon."

"Do you think your sister's party will come with us?" Nivian asked, and the whole group looked back to where the portal would open when they finished their third dungeon clear.

"Seeyela said they'd stay in the dungeon after they cleared it, to hold the vote. We'll know when they come out," Seena said.

"Don't want us affecting the vote with our opinions?" Wule asked.

"Probably. We're all friends, and nobody wants friction," Seena said.

"Won't there be friction no matter what?" Hiral asked. "I mean, if *anybody* votes differently than what's chosen?"

"And that's why not-thinking-and-following-the-boss is the best tactic," Yanily said… proudly?

"Knowing them all, even if one person votes differently, there won't be any hard feelings," Seena said. "They've all grown up together, like us. All close. Seeyela is more worried about friction between the two groups if we go and they don't."

"You really think there's a chance they'll stay behind?" Nivian asked.

"I don't know. Wule, you've been talking to Cal a lot lately. Any idea where she stands?"

"She was scared after the first time they went in," Wule said. "It was a lot more dangerous than she expected, and she was afraid she wouldn't be able to heal her friends if they got hurt."

"How about after the second clear?" Hiral prompted.

"Better. I think she's coming around. She knows she has to get stronger if she wants to protect her party. They can't hide in here until the islands come around again."

"Yanily, any word from Balyo?" Seena asked.

"She'll follow me wherever I go," Yanily said.

"Isn't it the opposite?" Vix asked.

"Details," Yanily said with a dismissive wave of his hand. "She's also pretty competitive. Doesn't want me getting ahead of her."

"Pretty sure she's also afraid to have you and your… spear… behind her," Vix muttered.

"Well, I know Seeyela wants to go," Seena said, ignoring Vix.

"If for no other reason than to keep you safe," Nivian said.

"There's that, but she's just as curious as I am about these dungeons and what they all mean. Our ancestors have been coming down to the surface for centuries—longer, maybe—and look how much we've learned already. This changes everything."

"Lonil wants to move to the next dungeon too," Nivian said. "He likes the challenge."

"Fitch will fight against anything Hiral suggests," Wule said. "But I think it's all for show. Underneath it, he wants the loot. Have you *seen* how he preens around with that sword?"

"It's kind of creepy how he strokes it," Yanily said.

"Have you ever seen yourself with your spear?" Vix asked.

"And what are you doing watching me during my private time?" Yanily shot right back.

Vix just shook his head and turned away.

"That just leaves Picoli," Seena said. "Despite the trail being lit up a bit, having her light would be useful."

"Especially if the trail leads to something like that lake we ran into before," Hiral said. "Who knows how the terrain has changed since they originally put in whatever those glowing roots are?"

"Do you think they even need to come with us?" Nivian asked. "I mean, if we clear the three dungeons, find the *Asylum,* then come back here to lead them there, would that work?"

Hiral was already shaking his head. "The image of Dr. Benza knew we hadn't cleared any dungeons when we got here. Probably something to do with our **PIMs**. How much you want to bet access to the *Asylum* is like access to a dungeon? Either through a door or portal keyed to our **PIMs**?"

"So, if they haven't cleared the dungeon, even if they know *where* the *Asylum* is, they won't be able to get in?" Seena finished. "I get the feeling that's likely."

"Why did Dr. Benza and his people make this so difficult?" Vix asked. "Why do we need to do dungeons? Gain experience and achievements? Unlock the *Asylum*? If they had the power and the magic to create our **PIMs**, why didn't they just make themselves S-Rank with maximum attributes? Couldn't they have beaten their *Enemy* with that?"

"There must be a reason," Hiral said, though, really, he could only shrug at the question.

"Add that to your list, Hiral," Seena said with a friendly wink.

"You're just saying that so *you* don't have to keep the list," Hiral accused.

"Absolutely correct."

"It's a good thing I have somebody with exceptional mental attributes, then," Hiral said. He activated **Foundational Split**, Left and Right peeling off his body. "Left, you know what to do?"

"Remember the questions so you don't have to?" Left asked.

"Exactly," Hiral said.

"Better you than me," Right said, elbowing Left gently in the side.

"By the way, now that you two are here, good job in the dungeon," Seena said.

"No problem. Like Hiral said up on the island, we've got your backs, if you'll let us," Right said.

"Wait, you guys know what I said up there?" Hiral asked. "I didn't have **Foundational Split** then."

"We're you, remember?" Right said.

"We know everything about you since the day you were born," Left said. "And no, you're not adopted," he added, tossing a glance at Seena.

"Thanks for the confirmation?" Hiral said, though he'd already been pretty sure about it.

"Great bonding moment," Yanily said. "But, where are they? Aren't they taking a long time?"

Hiral passed his hand over the interface crystal to bring up the menu. **Enter Dungeon** was noticeably absent, but that wasn't what he was looking for anyway. "**Help**," he said, and the image of Dr. Benza appeared. "**Time Records**."

Splitfang Keep Clear Times
Party (Seena) – 27:01
Party (Seeyela) – 28:16
Party (Seeyela) – 28:38

Hiral shared the window so everybody could see it, then pointed at the second spot. "They beat their previous record, so they must still be in there voting."

"Hah, but a full minute and a quarter behind us. Oh, yeah," Yanily said, sharing a fist-bump with Vix.

"We were *kind of* cheating," Wule pointed out. "Eight people when the limit was technically six. It's no wonder we got through faster."

"What is it with you folks and your details today?" Yanily complained, only to turn to Vix again and whisper, "Still number one."

Hiral closed the window while the two Growers yammered back and forth a bit, but then everybody quieted as the portal opened and Seeyela's party stepped out.

"Looks like you all made it through your final run without much trouble," Seeyela said. She passed her hand over the crystal and said, "**Help. Time Records**. Damnit. They beat us by over a minute."

"The Islander *did* cheat," Fitch said, echoing Wule's earlier words.

"What if we told you Hiral and his doubles sat at the entrance the whole time?" Yanily asked.

"What? Really?" Fitch asked, his head snapping from Yanily to Hiral so fast, it was a miracle he didn't get whiplash.

"No, I'm just asking what if," Yanily said.

"How did it go?" Seena loudly asked Seeyela to cut off any more arguing.

"We're leaving with you after we all get a good rest," Seeyela said. "Unanimous vote to go."

Hiral looked at Seeyela's party as she said that, and while the faces seemed to concur, there was also an undercurrent suggesting there had been a bit of discussion before the agreement.

Well, whatever. It'll be better for all of us if they come.

"That's great," Seena said. "I was hoping you would. I'll feel better having you with us. I think we have a few more hours before we should settle down for the night, so let's get our gear sorted and figure out if there's anything we don't need to take.

"The supplies from the dungeon are handy, but they could also slow us down in a fight."

"Agreed," Seeyela said. "Let's make sure everything is ready before we go to sleep. There were clothes in those supplies that looked like they might be better in the rain than what we have, so make sure you grab some of those. As soon as we get up, we're headed to the next dungeon."

44

PATH TO THE NEXT DUNGEON

HIRAL stood off to the side, Left and Right with him, as Seena stepped ahead of the group and looked at the **Spearing Roots** barricade set up in the doorway.

"Everybody ready?" she asked.

Hiral took a quick look at his buffs. The usual **Nature's Bulwark** was in place, along with a new buff from **Gourmand**. It wasn't terribly much—**End** increased by five percent—but considering it was from the dungeon rations they had tons of, it wasn't bad. And it lasted a full eight hours.

Wonder if multiple food buffs stack?

Lonil slapped his new club into his free hand, snapping Hiral's attention back to the real world, and the tank's skin hardened into matching stone. The plan was for Seeyela's group to go first in case there were any monsters waiting at the entrance, and the party readied themselves to rush out.

"Do it," Seeyela instructed.

With a wave of Seena's hand, the barricade vanished in a puff of slightly purple solar energy—*the infernal trait?*—and she stepped aside, Lonil and the others rushing past.

They gave them to the count of five, then Nivian led Seena's party through the door, around the turn, and out the short tunnel to find Seeyela and her group waiting for them in the rain.

"Clear," Fitch said as they arrived.

"You don't say?" Vix asked, but all eyes continued to scan the darkness as multiple *croaks* echoed somewhere deeper in the forest.

"Sounds like there are still lizards out there," Seena said. "Remember how we talked about dealing with them."

"They're in for a couple of nasty surprises if they try to get horny around me," Yanily said.

"Horned lizards. *Horned*," Vix repeated.

"Doesn't change my stance on this," Yanily shot back.

"Left, anything?" Hiral asked, blocking out the Growers and instead focusing his hearing on the sounds of the forest.

The rain, lighter than it'd been when they went into the dungeon, was a constant thrumming on the leaves and ground—easy enough to ignore—

but other, more inconsistent sounds filtered through. The faint buzzing and clicking of insects. Birds' wings flapping through the trees. The croaks of the giant lizards, of course, but also those of something smaller. Frogs?

"Nothing close, I think," Left responded. "A lot more life in the forest, though. Natural creatures emerging after the worst of the storm has passed."

"The rain is a lot better than before," Wule said. "And these clothes, whatever they're made of, are actually repelling most of the water. Do you think they're magic?"

Hiral looked at the sleeve of his jacket, the material smooth and light, and concentrated.

Raincoat – E-Rank

"I don't think it's magic," Hiral said. "Just a material we don't have up on the islands."

"Left, you sure you don't want one?" Seena asked the double.

"It would prevent me from quickly using my tattoos. Thank you anyway," Left replied, the rain pattering off his skin.

"Let me know if you change your mind," Seena said before turning her attention to the party as a group. "Time to get moving. Like we planned, Seeyela's party will take the lead, and we'll hang a bit back. Dr. Benza talked about moving in groups of six so as not to attract the *Enemy's* attention, and until we know for sure whether that *Enemy* is still around or not, we're going to take that advice."

"Do you want some **Light Darts**?" Picoli called over.

"Actually, no," Seena said. "Let's see if things are attracted to the light or kept away from it. Sis, we'll follow about fifty feet back."

"Sounds good," Seeyela said. "Shout if you get jumped by anything."

"I'm sure we'll hear Yanily's girlish screams," Balyo said out of the side of her mouth, though it was loud enough for everybody to hear, but Seeyela physically pushed her ahead before the usual banter could delay them.

"Right, hold the rear back here with me," Hiral said. "Left, you're up with Nivian. We're the lookouts."

"It would be handy if you could get a rune on your left ear so I could have access to the **Perfect Sense** tattoo," Left said.

"I'll add it to my list," Hiral said flatly, but Left nodded and jogged up to join Nivian at the front as the man started following after Seeyela's party.

True to his word, Hiral and Right waited until the others had gone, then started after them, though Hiral glanced back at the archway leading into the dungeon.

Those are definitely runes. I wonder if I could get more insights by studying them at the next dungeon. I should've thought of that before we left.

A tap on his shoulder from Right, and Hiral was moving again, attention back on the forest around him.

Thick roots, about as wide around as his leg, ran on both sides of them away from the archway, glowing a faint orange, and always exactly six feet apart. Their path. Even without Dr. Benza mentioning the existence of a trail, it would've been impossible to miss and hard to ignore following it to see where it led. Not to mention the faint emission of solar energy that was like water to a thirsty man in all this darkness.

Huh. I wonder if the solar energy is the cause of the roots glowing, or a result of it?

"There are other glowing plants," Right said, drawing Hiral's attention from the ground. "Up there."

Hiral followed Right's gesture, and, yes, faint though they were, it was like a root system *running up* the outside of the tree, also glowing a faint orange. And it wasn't just one tree. Dozens of them, just within his line of sight, sported one form of glowing plant or another. While there was that root system he'd spotted first, there was also another like a vine wrapped around and around the tree, while another came in the form of softly glowing flowers dotting the trunk.

"So many different shapes. Different kinds?" Hiral asked Right.

"Gauto would've loved this," Right said in reply, as if reading Hiral's next thoughts.

"He would've."

"Do you miss him? Them?" Right asked quietly.

"I thought you said you were me?" Hiral joked. "Shouldn't you know the answer?"

"I do, but a lot's happened. Thought you might want to *talk* about it," Right said, surprisingly seriously. "And with somebody who actually understands what you went through."

Hiral looked around the woods as they walked, as much to make sure they weren't going to get jumped by Troblins or lizards as to consider how to reply.

"I miss them," he admitted. "Gauto and Nat the most, but also Dad, Milly, and Loan. Even Arty and his nonsense. Do you think Nat is mad at me for not coming back?"

"Yes," Right said immediately, and Hiral couldn't stop the wince. "You aren't just her big brother, but also her role model, more than anybody else in the family."

"How could the *Everfail* be *her* role model?" Hiral asked, practically hissing at the hated nickname. "Shouldn't it be Mom or Dad? They're Artists like her, but even they don't have her skill. She's going to be the most talented Artist Fallen Reach has seen in hundreds of years. What could she possibly learn from me?"

"How to not give up. How to *work* for what she wants," Right said simply. "You know how easy it would've been for her to coast on her skill alone. She would've been as good as your... our... parents without trying. But she saw you striving for what you wanted, no matter what the obstacle was, and that taught her something."

"Yeah, taught her that her big brother was a failure," Hiral said.

"Do you really consider yourself a failure?"

"Of course I do!" Hiral practically shouted, only to look ahead as the others glanced back at the sudden sound. "Sorry, we're fine," he said with a wave of his hand. When they finally turned back to their own conversations, Hiral pulled the hood of his jacket further over his head. "You know how I feel."

"And, after everything we've learned, don't you think it's time to start reconsidering that?" Right asked. "You couldn't be a Shaper. You're not a Maker. Maybe it's time to stop beating yourself up over that?

"You've got a class now. A class nobody on Fallen Reach has ever seen. Not to mention Left and me. Isn't that something to be proud of?"

Hiral looked again at the glowing roots, trying to put his feelings into words. Right had a point. Several, in fact. But it wasn't that simple. He couldn't merely throw aside all the emotions and hurt from the last ten years. And, sure, he had a class now… but… but…

"I didn't *earn* the class," he finally said, teeth clenching. "It was just… an accident. How can I be proud of that? Just like my place with them." He gestured toward the party ahead of him. "They might only want me to come with them because they can't get into the dungeons without me. Fallen's balls, when we came down, they expected me to die, and they were okay with that—before they needed me.

"But me? I'm so desperate to be needed, finally—by anybody—that I ignore it. I know I'm doing it, but I can't stop, and I kind of hate myself for it."

"It's okay to want to be needed," Right said quietly. "We all do. Why do you think *they're* a party? Because they need each other, and in turn want to be needed. So what if they need you to get into the dungeons? Wule is the only healer, right? Do you think he holds it against the others when they need him because they're injured?

"Or Nivian? Does he think less of himself because Vix and Yanily need him to keep a monster's attention so they can do their thing? Hand in hand with that, it's not like Nivian and Wule could've cleared that last dungeon by themselves. You're all needed, even if it's for different reasons. So, don't begrudge other people—or yourself—for why they need you.

"And, Hiral, seriously, just because you got your role here a bit differently than you expected, don't think you didn't earn it with everything you've done up to this point. All the choices you've made, the work you've put in, the not giving up despite whatever everybody else thought—those are the things that brought you here. Sure, part of it was luck—everything is—but *you* worked to put yourself in a position for that luck to pay off."

"By jumping off an island?" Hiral asked to force a smile and take his attention off the pressure in his chest. *Is it really* okay *for me get my class like this? To become part of their party like this?*

"Part of it was by *recklessly* jumping off an island, yes," Right admitted. "And then by making friends with people who kind of hated you."

"Because I needed them to get me to… the dungeon…" Hiral said slowly, the whole conversation coming full circle.

"Give and take—that's what every relationship is," Right said. "With Nat, with Gauto, with Seena and the others. Nobody is selfless in it, so stop worrying about *why* they need you. In fact, if you let that go for just a minute, you might even realize some of them *want* you to be here with them."

"You really think they consider me a friend?"

"Well, not Fitch. Pretty sure he'd use your chest as a sword sheath if he thought he could get away with it," Right said, chuckling. "The others, though? Seena's party especially, yeah, I think they do."

"How do you know this if I don't?" Hiral asked, eyes looking over the backs of the party in the softly glowing light from the roots on both sides of the trail.

"You do know it; you're just not letting yourself admit it. Me? I can be objective because I'm on the outside. That's all."

Hiral nodded but didn't try to speak right away. Too many thoughts were spiraling through his head, and his chest was a mess of emotions. He actually *liked* most of the Growers—they seemed like good people—so why was it so difficult for him to accept they might like him too?

Because I've spent so long being hated and ridiculed by almost everybody.

They hadn't done that, though. *Fitch doesn't count.*

"Thanks, Right," Hiral finally said. "I think I needed to hear that."

"You did," Right agreed. "Now, back to the topic of Nat. You're going to need to find her one hell of a souvenir from down here if you don't want her to tattoo something obscene on your face in your sleep after you get back."

45

SHOWING OFF THE UPGRADES

H IRAL raised both **RHCs** in front of him and aimed as a name appeared to his **PIM**, floating above the monster's head. *That's got to be* **View** *kicking in.*

Giant Horned Lizard – High-E-Rank

No surprise there. He pulled the triggers, the weapons kicking up as the **Runes of Impact** activated and released bolts of pure force. Unlike his **Rune of Rejection**, which simply pushed things away, the **Runes of Impact** concentrated their energy on the instantaneous collision, resulting in a force much like Right punching something with his Meridian-infused fist.

Whomp. The twinned bolts smacked into the side of the *Giant Horned Lizard's* head, blasting off one of its namesake spines, and audibly fractured the skull. The lizard staggered to the side, distracted from Yanily as the man slid in beside it and unleashed a barrage of spear strikes. That wouldn't be enough to bring the beast down, though—the second that had made the mistake of attacking the party—and Hiral darted out to his side, weapons aimed again at the lizard's head.

Even in the relative dark and rain, the only light provided by the glowing roots and the slight purple flames from **Infernal Conjuration**, Hiral's **Dex** and **Atn** steadied his hands as he pulled the triggers. Alternating fire—the weapons had a one-second cooldown between shots—one then the other, Hiral peppered the head and shoulders of the lizard while the others struck from melee range.

Nivian, with his whip and shield sheathed in purple fire, held his ground as Hiral's shots zipped past him, visible only in how they displaced the rain. He then lashed out to drag the infuriating thorns across the lizard's face again. Angry eyes turned in his direction, and Nivian lowered his shoulder and charged in, **Spearing Roots** bursting out of the shield in his hand.

Pull after *pull,* Hiral kept up his barrage of shots, the combination of his attacks and Nivian's vicious shield strike twisting the lizard around on its back legs. From there, Vix danced in, his punches landing before he ever got close—projections of force shooting out with every strike—while Wule focused energy into his new rod and hurled a blast of icy energy at the lizard's back foot.

Suddenly unable to shift its foot—or its weight—the lizard overbalanced, and Right swerved around Vix to deliver a powerful uppercut, completely flipping the monster onto its back.

Another strike from Yanily scored a light wound across the exposed belly, and then the man's spear lit up with its final crude etching flaring purple light.

"Ready!" he shouted, shifting to the side and spinning the weapon in his hands.

That was Left's cue. The double leapt into the air, twisting his body into a powerful spin that surrounded him a bladed stream—now purple due to *Infernal Conjuration*—from his *Dagger of Sath*.

Yanily's spear struck with an eruption of purple flame at the same time Left's liquid dagger did, its trailing stream suddenly rushing to catch up to the blade and add an unparalleled explosive slice to the strike. *He's gotten better with the dagger if he can use that ability.*

The body of the huge lizard collapsed around the force of the two blows, bones and spines shattering, and bloody gore spilled across the ground in a wave. One of the thing's front legs shuddered, and Hiral pulled both triggers one more time at the thing's head.

Just to be sure.

And not a moment too soon, a *crooooooooak* and cascade of breaking branches swept in at the group from one side.

"Vix! Behind you," Hiral shouted, giving the pugilist just enough warning to dive to the side, though he still got clipped by the speeding lizard.

The new arrival, at least twenty percent larger than the original, skidded to a stop, claws digging into the ground for purchase, and its empty mouth clamped shut. The tail whipped hard in one direction, then snapped in the other, pulling the back end of the lizard around while it quick-stepped its feet to turn.

Too bad for it, Right caught the side of its head as it spun, snapping its body back in the other direction—right into a wall of *Spearing Roots* that burst out of the ground. Flickers of purple flames mixed with the green blood running down the roots, but they hadn't penetrated deeply enough to be fatal. The lizard's spines provided sufficient armor, and a great shudder along its body shattered the wood.

One of the lizard's eyes caught sight of Seena as she lowered her staff from using her ability, and the monster lunged forward to lash out, five-inch claws swiping across to disembowel her. Nivian appeared from out of nowhere, sliding smoothly in between Seena and their opponent, and brought his shield up to catch the claw.

Purple fire flashed and ran up the lizard's leg at the impact, doing little damage yet infuriating the beast, and it beat its claw a second time against the shield. Nivian fell back under the weight of the blow, then struck out with his whip, scoring one, two, three quick hits along the lizard's flank. Again, little damage was done, but that lizard wasn't going to be attacking anybody but the tank for at least several seconds.

And those several seconds gave the others time to get in position.

Hiral fell back a good thirty feet from the melee, still well within the optimal range for his **RHCs**, and pulled the triggers in quick succession. Bolts of force carved through the falling rain, leaving small tunnels in their wake, and passed over Nivian's shoulders and between his arms to smack the lizard head on, further drawing the monster's attention to the tank.

Between Nivian's and Hiral's tactics, the incensed monster roared ahead, claw after claw getting deflected by Nivian's shield, the tank methodically falling back along the glowing trail. And as the other damage dealers moved in from the sides, Hiral held his next shot, charging power into the runes, then dropped to one knee and unloaded both barrels through the space between Nivian's spread legs.

The empowered shots carved a six-inch tunnel through the rain, then struck the monster straight on in the face, bursting one eye entirely from the force and stopping its forward momentum cold. Just what Yanily and Left had been waiting for. Attacking with dagger and spear, the two chopped hard into the lizard from both sides, Yanily taking full advantage of the wounds already opened by Seena's **Spearing Roots**, Left winding his body around in a dance to extend the dagger's trailing stream before slamming it home with explosive results.

Sandwiched between the two onslaughts, the lizard's head snapped side to side with each new, flaring pain. Nivian, meanwhile, continued to lash it with his whip. Hiral peppered it with shots, never giving it a chance to settle on one target, and Wule began tossing balls of condensed cold at its tail.

Like Hiral's shots, Wule's attacks left a trail of falling icicles from the rain with every throw, and each hit coated the lizard's tough scales in ice. All together, the party was piling the damage on, though it still wasn't enough to completely put the creature down.

At least, not until Seena thrust her staff toward the sky. A fusillade of **Spearing Roots** burst straight up from the ground directly beneath the lizard's belly. Held in place from attacks on all sides, the lizard took the full brunt of Seena's attack in its most vulnerable area, the roots actually lifting the monster off its feet even as they buried themselves deep in the length of its body.

Hanging there, four feet off the ground, the lizard still feebly tried to pull it forward. Its claws couldn't reach the ground, and its lifeblood gushed out in great torrents.

"Fall back," Seena ordered. "It's dead, even if it doesn't know it yet. No need to risk it getting a lucky hit in."

Every party member took a few quick steps back, eyes still on the monster. Hiral signaled Left, and the two of them turned their attention back to the woods. Another of those things could come rushing out at any moment, and it was up to them to warn the party.

As each second passed, more and more blood fell from the lizard. Its movements slowed, then eventually completely stilled. And, at least for the moment, no more monsters appeared, though the sound of approaching footsteps reached Hiral's ears.

Looking up the path, he found Seeyela running in his direction, a pair of **Light Darts** over her shoulders for illumination.

"Well, guess we didn't even need to rush back this time," Seeyela said, her party just a few steps behind her as they ran up.

"Hiral spotted the first one coming at us from the side. Thought it could ambush us, I guess," Seena said, giving Hiral a thumbs-up.

"Hah, didn't work out so well for it. Or the other two," Yanily said, wiping the green blood from the blade of his spear. "Damn, that ability is good. Not as strong as what you can do, Balyo, but getting it for free every tenth hit? Loving it. Oh, and it looks like we got **Racial Growth** for these things up to level one. Five percent more damage against the next ones we fight!"

"You killed three of them in the time it took us to notice the fight was happening and run back?" Picoli asked.

"The new gear and abilities from the dungeon have made a huge difference already," Seena said. "Hiral's cannons there pack a mean punch, and finally give us a ranged option. Add in the new versatility Vix and Wule bring, we're a *much* stronger party than we were a few days ago.

"And, yes, Yanily, your new spear is great too. Don't pout," Seena finished.

"Wasn't pouting," Yanily said quietly.

"Do you think that first lizard let us pass and waited for your group?" Seeyela asked, turning to Hiral with the question.

"No, I only heard it because it was moving," Hiral said. "Maybe it was attracted by our sounds or the lights, and it just happened to find us when it arrived. I think it could've turned out much worse if it had been lying in wait for us."

"Still, only on the path for an hour, and already we've been attacked twice," Seeyela said. "That first lizard that attacked us was pretty small, but these three here look a little more intimidating. How do you think you would've done if they'd all come at once?"

"Not nearly as well," Seena said. "Takes all of us to bring one down. Their scales and spines are just too durable."

"You know, I was thinking about that after the first one we killed," Lonil said, standing beside the latest kill hanging from the **Spearing Roots**. "Cal, could you and Fitch make armor out of this?"

"Armor?" Hiral asked Seena quietly as the two aforementioned Growers moved closer to inspect the body.

"Fitch and Caleon have been learning how to tan hides and craft armor from them," Seena answered, her voice just barely above the sound of constantly falling rain. "Usually leather, like we're wearing, but they might be able to do something with the scales from these lizards."

"Fitch?" Cal asked. "Thoughts?"

"Maybe. It'll be a bit different than usual, but we could try attaching the scales, and maybe even some of these horns to leather. There's probably a way to make something directly out of the scales—would be lighter, but I don't know how to do it."

"Something Lonil could wear over his **Stone Form**?" Seeyela asked. "A few of those spikes would sure make anything attacking him regret it."

"You trying to steal my gimmick?" Nivian asked Lonil playfully.

"You know what they say about imitation and flattery," Lonil responded, his hand still running along one of the lizard's longer horns. "How long would it take?" he asked Fitch.

"Much longer than we want to spend out here in the open," Fitch answered. "When we get to the next dungeon and have a place out of the rain, we'll see what we can do."

"Sounds good," Lonil said, standing up. "Shall we keep going and see what else is stupid enough to attack us?"

46

NOT A DUNGEON, BUT...?

"This isn't the dungeon," Hiral said, almost ten hours—and just as many encounters—later. He pointed at the trail as it transformed into a paved street. "But it's definitely *something*."

The ruins of dozens of stone buildings filled the clearing in the forest. The tallest had to have been at least four stories tall in its prime, with thick walls, ornate windows—some of which still held glass—and stylized trim. Plants glowing faintly with solar energy crawled up the walls and draped through holes in the roofs, giving the whole place a multicolored aura in the falling rain.

But, despite the alien atmosphere created by the different hues of the plants, there was a familiarity to it. The way the roofs angled at the edges, the engravings around the windows, and even the spacing between the buildings.

This wasn't a city, like Fallen Reach, but the similarity in the architecture was unmistakable.

"There are differences, but I think the same people who built Fallen Reach must have built these buildings too," Hiral said.

"This place isn't floating," Vix pointed out.

"Okay, maybe not the *same* same people," Hiral admitted, unable to take his eyes off the buildings. His mind conjured images of people strolling down the streets in the afternoon sun. Even the look of the streets between the buildings was the same. "But, at least, people from the same time? Or, homeland? Or something. I could definitely imagine seeing these buildings in a corner of Fallen Reach.

"That one there; that would be a shop—a bakery, I think, by the size of the window in the front and the chimney in the back. That one over there; I think it's a blacksmith. And that cluster of buildings at the edge of the woods; those are homes. At the far end of this path; that *has* to be some kind of... inn? We don't have a lot of them in Fallen Reach, but the city is big enough we need places for people to stay if they're visiting different neighborhoods. That building looks just like them."

"Do you think we'll find any people here?" Yanily asked, though he still had his spear held firmly in both hands.

"I'd be shocked," Wule answered quietly. "Look at this place. It's falling apart."

"Worse than that," Nivian said. "Look at some of the damage to the buildings. Especially the roofs. I don't think it's all natural."

"You think the town was attacked?" Hiral asked, and the question had everybody turning their heads to make sure nothing was sneaking up on them from behind.

"It's one explanation," Nivian said.

"The *Enemy* Dr. Benza was talking about?" Seena asked.

"Could just be those lizards," Fitch replied.

"You guys never found anything like this before?" Hiral asked Seena, all the Growers more on edge than he'd seen them before.

"Never," she said. "At least, never that we were told about. This path we're on, I'm pretty sure it leads away from the EnSath River."

"Meaning it's taking us away from the jump points that would get us back up to the islands," Hiral reasoned.

"Exactly. This is outside the safe range of travel."

"Why didn't we ever notice it from above?" Hiral asked, looking up to the rain falling directly on his face.

"Maybe the angle? The trees are pretty tall all around the town. Or maybe we just never saw it because we didn't *expect* to see it?"

"It could be, but the glowing path to the next dungeon passes straight through the town and down the street like it was *meant* to be there," Wule said. "The roots, or whatever they are, practically look like part of the design." He pointed at the two glowing lines that spread out to each side of the street, then continued on through the town.

"Enough talk," Seeyela interrupted, her voice cutting through the sound of falling rain. "This looks as good a place as any to set up camp and get some sleep. We've pushed pretty hard since we left the dungeon. Let's check that inn at the end of the street and see if we can't find a dry corner."

"Can we look around the other buildings a bit?" Hiral asked, curiosity gnawing at the edges of his mind.

Seeyela didn't answer immediately, and when she did, there was obvious hesitance in her voice. "We'll see. These woods have been anything but safe, and I don't want to risk anybody if we don't have to."

"But, this could give us clues to what happened here. How Fallen Reach is connected," Hiral said. "Even what was going on before we were all on floating islands in the sky. Aren't you curious?"

"I said we'll see," Seeyela said, her voice rock-hard and leaving no room for argument. From the looks on the Growers' faces, they'd heard that tone before, and it wasn't promising.

"Sorry," Seena said quietly, for just his ears, and gave a small shrug.

Hiral just shook his head in the rain.

How can they just pass this by? Maybe I can send Left or Right to look around. That wouldn't be so dangerous, would it?

"Let's go," Seeyela said. "Keep an eye on side alleys and higher levels. No telling where something might attack from. If we're thinking of using this place to shelter from the rain, something else is too."

Lonil immediately moved forward, his skin hardening to stone, and the rest of the party fell in line without question.

Like before, Seena's group waited until the others had moved ahead, then started to form up.

"Seems like the kind of place where we'd find Troblins," Wule finally said, breaking the relative silence.

"You think so?" Vix asked. "Looks pretty different than ***Splitfang Keep***."

"Doesn't mean we won't find squatters," Wule said.

"He's right," Seena said. "Let's follow the others. If the inn is safe, we can talk about what comes next." Her last words came out as she looked at Hiral.

"Got it, boss," Nivian said, taking the lead with Left beside him. The rest fell in shortly after that, though Seena lingered back with Hiral and Right.

"Sorry about my sister," Seena said. "She has a good point, though."

"No, you're right. *She's* right. It's better to be safe than sorry. I just… it's such an opportunity to start learning about what we don't know. I can't imagine how you're not all fascinated by this." Hiral gestured around, taking the opportunity to check the higher levels for threats. Just because he was curious didn't mean he'd slack on his job.

"You sound like one of those Academics you were talking about before," Seena said. "Your people must know about these kinds of towns. Have records about before you were on the island."

"Not in the least—about the records, I mean. Sure, we have a class called Academics, but the title is kind of a misnomer. Learning and studying isn't all the class is good at. It allows specialization in a skillset, and the development of abilities particular to that skillset."

Hiral pointed at the large window of the bakery as they passed it. As he'd guessed, there was a counter and what looked like a large kitchen beyond, just the end of the oven visible.

"You're saying your Academics bake bread?" Seena asked.

"Some of them. Or make nails and horseshoes." He pointed at what he guessed was the smithy. "Er… have you ever seen a horse?"

"Just a drawing of one. Not the type of animal that would do well on our islands or the root systems we use to cross them. How many of them are up on Fallen Reach?"

"Just a few hundred. Some carriages in the city, then some out on the farms. That kind of thing. Anyway, only a few Academics *study*, because there just aren't a lot of records, and we don't come down to the surface. The infrastructure is the biggest resource for information, but people are worried about accidentally breaking it while studying it."

"And you don't know how to fix it if it breaks?"

"Exactly. But, after getting these"—Hiral pointed at the **RHCs** on his thighs—"I think I'm starting to understand more. Lots of the systems up in the city *just work*. We don't know how. Like the water being drawn up from the river."

"You think runes are responsible for that," Seena said, catching on.

"Or something related. What if it's just something like the **Rune of Rejection** keeping Fallen Reach in the sky? Or the **Rune of Attraction** pulling your islands along with it? If we could figure out how that all works, we might be able to make it so your islands don't fall anymore.

"Fallen's balls, we might be able to make it so you don't even *need* Fallen Reach anymore. You could travel on your own, if you wanted."

Seena stayed quiet at the declaration, the thoughts of it obviously working behind her eyes. "And there might be clues to that somewhere here in this town," she said. "I think I understand a bit of why you're so eager to get a look in these buildings."

"There might also be *nothing*," Hiral admitted. "But it's worth the time spent to at least check."

"Let me talk to my sister after we get settled. Explained like this, I think she'll agree it's worth the time. Assuming we don't find a Troblin horde waiting for us."

She actually saw my side? And agreed with me?

Hiral looked over to find Right looking back at him, then the double nonchalantly dropped back a few steps.

"Seena," Hiral started, "can… can I ask you something?"

Seena glanced at him sideways, something in his tone getting her attention. "Uh, sure."

"Why did you accept me into your party?"

"Why wouldn't I?" she asked right back.

"I didn't have a class."

"And I didn't know that."

"But I was keeping things from you. You had to know *that*," he said.

"And I was keeping things from you right back. Look, Hiral, you *jumped off the island* to save Favela. Jumped off! Everybody else just stood and watched. You saved my niece's life."

"I thought bringing me down to the surface made us even."

"Nah, nothing will ever make us even for what you did. Not really," she said. "But, if I'm being honest, that's not why you're part of the party."

"Ah," Hiral said, Seena's words confirming his suspicion.

"What's *ah*?"

"It's because you need me to get into the dungeons."

She slowly turned her head to look at him, one wet eyebrow up in the air, rainwater streaming down her face. "Is that what you think? We're only keeping you around for dungeon access?"

"You're not?"

"Well, it'd make sense, but that's not it. Okay, not the *only* reason."

"Then… why?"

"Jumped off the island!" she repeated, then chuckled. "Not just that, though. Hiral, even if I didn't know you didn't have a class, you knew. And you still jumped. You still fought the Troblins, and went in *alone* to face off against a group of Shapers. To save my sister and her party. Even after getting your class—your whole reason for coming down to the surface, if I understand things right—you still kept putting yourself at risk to help us.

"Back in **Splitfang Keep**, that time on the rope bridge, for example…"

"When you yelled at me."

"Damn straight I yelled at you! That was reckless. But I know you did it because you thought it was the only choice to keep us safe. I think I'm starting to understand you more, but *why* you did those things kind of doesn't matter. The *fact* you did them, on the other hand, makes me want you in this party. You're helping keep the people important to me safe."

"I… see," Hiral said, letting her words sink in.

Maybe Right was… right. Maybe I did earn this more than I was giving myself credit for.

"Is that it? Was it bugging you or something?" Seena asked.

"I've never… had a place I fit in," Hiral admitted. "The no-class thing. I just… I just wanted to know where we stood."

"Look, I'm not saying this because we're all trapped down on the surface, and there's only the twelve of us. Fourteen, I guess, if we count Left and Right, but whatever. You have a place with our party as long as you want it." Seena put a hand on Hiral's shoulder. "You're one of us now."

"Thanks, Seena. I needed to hear that."

"Good, but we're going to have to pick this up later. Looks like Seeyela is at the inn. Let's go see if they have any open rooms."

47

TROBLIN MIGHT

H IRAL looked up at the four-story building as lightning flashed high in the clouds above and the wind began to pick up.

"Rain's getting harder," Wule said, as if thinking about the same thing crossing Hiral's mind.

"Shouldn't we go in, then?" Yanily asked.

"Excuse me," Left said from further down the street, near the edge of the forest where the paved roadway once again gave way to mud and dirt. "I think I found some tracks."

"Let me see," Picoli said, jogging over and crouching down to look at the mud with her *Light Darts* hovering nearby. "Tri-Horns, from the looks of it. That's lucky."

"Tri-Horns?" Hiral asked Seena.

"Hooved animals—kind of like a horse, I guess. They have three horns on their heads, and more along their spines. *Very* tasty."

"You hunt them?"

"When we can find them," she said. "Any idea how old the tracks are?" she asked louder in Picoli's direction.

"Have to be recent for us to be able to see them in the rain. I'd say we just missed them." Picoli stood, looking up and down the line of buildings as if she'd catch sight of them.

"We going inside or going hunting?" Lonil asked Seeyela.

"We could split up," Seena offered. "One of us secures the building— and maybe those around it, just to be safe—and the other group could go get some fresh meat."

Seeyela looked up as another flash of lightning lit the street, and thunder rumbled behind it. "No," she finally said, drawing the word out slowly. "We don't know how bad this storm can get. We didn't pay enough attention around the dungeon. We'll all go in together. I'm sure we'll find more Tri-Horns later if they're around.

"Seena, my party will clear floor one while you find a way up to the second floor and clear it. When that's done, let us know and we'll move to three while you go to four. Questions?"

"None. After you," Seena said, and Lonil strode into the building at a nod from Seeyela.

"Say when," Nivian said.

Seena gave him the familiar shoulder tap to send him in.

"If this is like the buildings up on Fallen Reach, look for stairs in a back corner," Hiral instructed before following.

Glowing plants crawled along the floor, walls, and ceiling, providing a surprising amount of light to show how old furniture had been piled in front of the windows. Even the door they walked through had *stuff* piled in front of it, though it looked as if it had been bashed through. Windows on the far wall stood shattered, their stone frames pulled apart in many places, like something had ripped them open from the outside. The back-left corner of the building was missing entirely, rain pouring off the sides like small waterfalls.

There looked to be another room off to the left, which was where Lonil headed, and like Hiral had suggested, a staircase stood in the back-right corner.

"There," Seena suggested, and Nivian was already moving.

"What happened here?" Vix asked.

"Bad things, obviously," Yanily said as Nivian worked his way up the stairs, Wule right behind him, the others already climbing the steps as well.

Hiral ran his fingers along the wall on his right while he followed the others up the stairs, the stone cool under his touch. *Solid, and still in good shape despite all the years. And rain—wouldn't it ruin the mortar between the... hrm. No mortar,* he realized as he looked closer. Somehow, the stones fit together *so perfectly,* there was barely a seam, let alone need for mortar.

Just like Fallen Reach. This has to have been built by the same people.

"I think..." he started, but a commotion at the head of the line cut him off, something hitting Nivian's shield as the man tucked under it.

Whatever it was, it went right up and over the shield, then hit the line of Growers like a bowling ball through pins. People toppled forward or sideways in front of Hiral, until something caught him in the shins and pulled his legs right out from under him.

His chin hit a higher step with a painfully resounding *thwack* at the same time his chest did, knocking the air from his lungs and sending stars flashing in his eyes. He put one hand under himself to push up, but then something latched onto the back of his calf and, before he knew it, crawled up across his legs and back. A second later, his lungs still burning to take in air, powerful, bark-skinned limbs encased in glowing green bands of energy wrapped around his throat.

What little air he'd been pulling in cut off with brutal finality as the Troblin on his back squeezed. The others were still too busy trying to find their feet to even notice what was happening behind them. Hiral clawed at the arms with his bare hands, but even his 18 *Str* wasn't enough to dislodge the thing quickly choking him to death.

Those green bands are a powerful buff to make a Troblin that strong... Wait... buffs!

With a pulse of solar energy, Hiral activated his *Enraged* ability. Power flowed through his *PIM*, and the double-helix pattern on his arms flared. With a newly empowered *Str* of 27 filling his body, he grasped at the Troblin's arms around his neck, ready to pry them apart... but he didn't have the leverage. The Troblin's arms were too tight against his throat to squeeze his hands in, and he *still* wasn't strong enough to simply peel the arms open.

Just how strong is that buff? Fifteen strength? Twenty?

Analyzing the buff wasn't going to get him out of the situation, though. Darkness was already swarming in around the edges of his vision, so Hiral put his palm down to the step beneath him and activated his *Rune of Rejection*. Hiral—and the Troblin on his back—shot straight up to hit the ceiling with a violent *crack*, the arms around his neck slackening just a touch, then gravity took over.

"Ooof," Hiral groaned, releasing his sole precious breath as he crashed back down on the stairs.

He slid his left hand in between his neck and the Troblin's arms. It wasn't enough to break the thing's hold on him, but it did stop it from crushing his throat. Then, before it could wrestle for a better grip, Hiral twisted to the side and threw himself back-first toward the stone wall.

A breathy exhalation sounded in his ear at the impact, but the arms weren't letting go, and he didn't have the leverage from his position for another wall-slam. Worse, flaring green, the arms pulled tighter around him.

Need to do something about that buff.

Hiral's hand bent awkwardly as he fought against the crushing press of the arms, but he didn't have the angle to push them back, and even as he reached with his right hand, he couldn't get hold of the Troblin. With nothing more than a pinprick of light left to his eyes, Hiral desperately activated his *Rune of Absorption*. Green light tore off the Troblin's arms, then wrapped around Hiral's.

You have been buffed by Troblin Might.
Strength increased by 15 for 10 minutes
(540 seconds remaining).

With his newfound 42 *Str*, Hiral easily pried the arms away from his throat and gasped in a lungful of blessed air. Then, pulling the Troblin higher on his back, he finally found the front of its face with his right hand.

His *Rune of Impact* did the rest of the work. There was a sound like a club hitting a watermelon right behind his ear, and the arms went slack.

Shrugging off the body, Hiral pushed himself to hands and knees while he pulled deep breath after deep breath into his burning lungs. *The others?* They weren't on the stairs right in front of him, but the sounds of fighting from the top of the stairwell echoed as his own rushing blood quieted in his ears.

One more breath and he got to his feet, only looking briefly at the glowing green bands of energy around his biceps—*I absorbed the buff*—then dashed up the stairs. Two Troblins lay right at the head of the stairs, one of them getting back to its feet, so Hiral grabbed it by its ankle and hefted it into the air upside-down.

(Elite) Troblin Warrior – Mid-E-Rank

Elites? Explains why they're so tough, but why are they outside a dungeon?

The Troblin in his hand hissed at him, but that became a strangled yelp as Hiral whipped his arm up and around in a fast-pitch that sent the beast cartwheeling through the air to blast into another of its kind. The two Troblins vanished through a door and into an adjacent room, a loud crash signaling the end of their flight, and then there was silence.

Hiral drew both **RHCs** from his thighs and looked around the large room. Like below, glowing roots crawled along every surface, providing enough light to see by, and there were two hallways extending off the main room. Doors dotted the walls of both halls, and three Troblin bodies lay bleeding on the floor. Counting the one that'd tried to strangle him, then the two in the room, that made six.

"Yanily, Vix, make sure those two in there are dead." Seena pointed toward the room Hiral had tossed the Troblins into. "Be careful. Could be more."

"Got it, boss," Yanily said, then he and Vix disappeared into the room. A few quick *thuds* later, they came back out, Yanily wiping blood from the blade of his spear. "Taken care of. **Racial Growth** hit level four too. I pity the next Troblins we run into."

"Everybody okay?" Seena asked, turning as she spoke. She stopped when she got to Hiral, her eyes on the glowing green bands. "What's that?"

"Seems I can absorb buffs," Hiral said. "These things add fifteen strength."

"Fifteen?" Wule asked. "For a Troblin? That's a huge amount."

"And, I'm not sure if you noticed in all the chaos, but these were **Elites**," Hiral added.

The Growers' eyes flicked as they read notifications, but they were all nodding. Well, all but Yanily.

"Hah! Level twenty!" he said with a fist pump.

"Congratulations," Seena said, "but we'll celebrate later. We need to see if there are any more of these little bastards hiding in here."

"Good job," Nivian said, giving Yanily a pat on the shoulder. They then led the party down the hallway that didn't go to the stairwell.

Like Hiral had suspected, the building had to have been an inn, judging by the beds and dressers in the small rooms, though time had had its way with most of it. Little more than pieces of the wood furniture were left; the bedding and mattresses had long since rotted away. It wasn't until they got to the final room at the end of the hall they found more than wreckage.

There, in what was the largest room they'd seen so far—more a suite than anything else—they found an immaculately clean room. Six neatly rolled but small bedrolls, folded blankets, a small table with dinner precisely served, and even an easel in one corner of the room with an in-progress drawing on it.

A drawing of an uncomfortably suggestive Troblin.

"What… what did we just interrupt?" Yanily asked.

48

ENEMY

Wɪтн the building finally cleared—no more Troblins on the third or fourth floors—the party regrouped at the oddly neat room in the back of the inn.

"This can't possibly be the Troblins' room, can it?" Cal asked, her eyes wandering to the half-finished portrait in the back, then snapping away.

"You think maybe one of our missing groups stayed here?" Seena asked Seeyela. "When was the last time we lost a party in the area?"

"Not since we were little kids," Seeyela said. "This was the Troblins, as hard as that is to believe."

"Little bastards are neat-freaks," Yanily said. "This room is *spotless*."

"I'd avoid sampling what was for dinner, though," Nivian said. "Who knows what's in that soup."

"After **Splitfang Keep** and that smokehouse, you won't see me anywhere near Troblin food," Lonil said.

"I hate to say it," Hiral said, "but this room is the one in the best shape. If we're going to sleep somewhere, this is the place to do it. No windows to let the rain in, and it even has the best lighting." He pointed to the network of roots stretching across the ceiling.

"He's right," Seena said.

"I know, though it makes my skin crawl," Seeyela said. "Okay, folks. Left and Hiral, can you two keep watch? One of you watch the lower floor, and another go up to the fourth? The rest of us are going to clear out this room. We'll figure out a better watch rotation to give you a rest after that's done."

Hiral glanced at the portrait, shivered, then pushed himself up from where he'd been sitting to recover from using **Enraged**. "Sure." He nodded to Seeyela, then exited the room with Left. "Why don't you take the first floor? I want to get a better view of the town from the top."

"Sure," Left said, heading toward the stairs leading to the ground level while Hiral took the stairs up to the third, and finally the fourth floor.

Up there, the rain hammered against the roof, a constant drumming of lashing water and whipping wind. Cold air swirled through the halls from the missing section of the building, and Hiral went in that direction, sheets of water pouring down at the end of the hall.

It's amazing there's even a roof at all. I guess it makes sense, though; it's not like we do many building repairs up in Fallen Reach. Though… why is that? Some kind of magic keeping the buildings in good repair? Runes? Or, am I overthinking it now that I know runes exist?

Do I just want *to see the possible uses of them?*

Getting to the end of the hall, he tried looking through the deluge falling from the broken section of roof, but a violent gust of wind hurled water into the hall—and onto him—and he couldn't see through it anyway, so he turned into a nearby room. Like below, the window to this room had been ripped or blasted open, though there was no damage from anything like the infernal flames they'd seen in the *Troblin Keep*. No, it looked more like brute strength had peeled the stones out.

But how big did a thing have to be to rip apart windows on the fourth floor?

Hiral lifted his arm up to block some of the water spraying in, but then stepped back and instead pushed a trickle of energy into his *Rune of Rejection* while concentrating on the rain. This time, when he stepped forward, the cold wind still blew, but not a single drop of water touched him.

These runes have a lot of versatility.

Maintaining the slight shield of *Rejection*, he stepped up to the hole in the wall and peered out. Lightning cut across the sky, illuminating the buildings of the town like a snapshot of the end of the world. Roofs lay caved in, walls were little more than piles of rubble, and the rain was the only thing that moved. Another flash, and Hiral looked at the empty street, thunder cascading above him in a long, drawn-out series of booms that shook the building.

More flashes, and Hiral looked up, forks of wild lightning arcing between the clouds and toward the ground. On and on the display went, almost to the point there was constant light to show off the fury of the storm.

And to get a better look at the town.

Tearing his eyes away from the show in the sky, Hiral instead leaned further out the window, relying on his rune to keep him dry, and looked down the street. *Would Troblins go out in weather like this? Would anything else?*

To his left was the path leading to the next dungeon, winding between the enormous trees. *Bound to be more of those lizards that way…*

But that thought gave Hiral pause, and he focused on the spaces between the booming thunder. No *croaks*, not even one. He stayed still and listened, letting the seconds turn to minutes, and yet still nothing sounded. Those lizards had been making noise the entire trip between the dungeon and here, but now they were quiet? Did they not like the rain?

Maybe it would be safer to move when it's raining after all.

Putting the lizards out of his mind, Hiral turned his head to the right, down the street they'd just come. No sooner had he done that than lightning flashed overhead again, and huge red script exploded into his field of vision, startling him so much he fell back from the hole in the wall.

Warning! Warning! Warning!

The words repeated over and over again as Hiral's ass hit the floor and he scrambled back from the window.

What in the name of the…?

Warning! Warning! Warning!
Enemy Detected!
WARNING! WARNING! WARNING!

Hiral's breath caught in his throat as he stared at the words, the new sequence repeating rapidly in case he'd somehow missed it the first ten times.

Enemy detected? Dr. Benza's Enemy? *I have to tell the others!*

Pushing himself to his feet, Hiral didn't close the notification, but sprinted back to the stairs and down to the second floor. Around the corner, down the hall, he ran into the room. Grower heads snapped in his direction at the unexpected entrance.

"Hiral?" Seena started to ask, but Hiral silenced her by making his notification window visible to all of them.

Twelve heads stared at the large red text in the yellow status window, then turned back to him.

"Enemy?" Seena asked the question on everybody's lips. "As in *the Enemy*?"

"I don't know," Hiral said. "I was scouting out the town from one of the windows up on the fourth floor, and when I looked back down the street we'd come up, this exploded in my face."

"What did you see?" Seeyela asked.

"That's just it. Nothing," Hiral said. "Nothing but the rain."

"The *PIMs* must be extra sensitive to the *Enemy*," Wule theorized.

"If he isn't making it up," Fitch said. "Said himself he didn't see anything. Convenient."

"Don't think I could fake this if I tried," Hiral said, thumbing toward the flashing notification.

"You couldn't," Seeyela agreed, deep in thought. "Close that. The blinking is distracting."

"Sure," Hiral said, and concentrated on closing the notification. Oddly, it took more effort than a normal notification, like the *PIM* really, really wanted to make sure he saw it.

"What do we do?" Lonil asked Seeyela.

"I'm thinking," she said.

"We could make a run for it," Picoli suggested. "Use the rain as cover and keep going toward the next dungeon. The lighting of the path should make it so we don't get lost."

"We don't know how far it is," Cal countered. "It could be five minutes from here, or five days."

"Hole up here, then?" Nivian said, speaking to Seena. "Set up some kind of barricade at the top of the stairs to slow down anything coming up? Plenty of debris around to work with."

"Didn't work so well for whoever was here on the first floor," Yanily said.

"We don't even know *what* we're up against here," Wule said. "Does it need to come up the stairs, or will it come down from the fourth floor?"

"Then we set up more barricades at the stairs down as well," Nivian suggested.

"And how long do we hide in the building?" Lonil asked. "How long do we wait for something we don't know is actually even out there?"

"Pretty sure my **PIM** isn't lying about this," Hiral said.

"Did it see you?" Lonil asked. "Does it know we're here?"

"I don't even know what *it* is," Hiral said. "I have no idea what it knows or doesn't."

"If you bring something down on us…" Fitch threatened.

"I thought you didn't believe it was actually out there?" Right said. "Might want to pick a complaint and stick to it."

"Cool it, everybody," Seena said. "To be safe, we're going to assume *something* is out there. We're also going to assume it *might* have seen Hiral. I agree we have two main choices: stay or run."

"We could go out and kill it," Vix said.

Seena shook her head. "Not without knowing what we're up against. With how much Dr. Benza warned us about this *Enemy*, I don't want to run into it blindly. Sure, maybe the *Enemy* is Troblins, and we've been slowly wiping them out, or maybe it's something much worse. Stay or run, those are our choices. Both might involve fighting, but let's keep that as a last resort."

"We stay," Seeyela finally said. "Seena is right. We're not going looking for a fight until we know more. We set up barricades at the stairs and keep watch. If it comes in, we deal with it."

"How long do we stay hiding?" Picoli asked. "If we head for the dungeon now…"

"The storm is *bad*," Hiral said. "Even dealing with a lizard in that would be extra difficult. The thunder and lightning are distracting. The rain would make footing treacherous, and the wind would constantly be in our eyes, slowing our reaction time."

"He just wants more time to look around the town," Fitch accused.

"Do you ever give it a rest?" Hiral snapped at him. "That would require leaving this building, which I don't think is a good idea at all."

Seeyela held up her hand, palms out, as more mouths opened, but nobody else spoke. "You all have good points. Really. But we'll stay here for now. Better to have us all together and make a possible enemy come to us. If we go out there now and run, then we have the enemy at our back, and no idea where it'll strike.

"However! We can't stay here forever, and we won't. Once the storm calms down again, we'll make a break for the dungeon. Yes, we'll assume the *Enemy* saw Hiral, but there's also the chance it didn't, so I want us to be careful we don't do anything that could give away our presence to someone or something outside the building."

"Where are the Troblin corpses?" Hiral asked, realizing he hadn't jumped over any bodies when he'd returned from the fourth floor.

"We took them down to the first floor so they didn't stink up the place," Yanily said.

"Where did you put them?" Seena asked. "You didn't throw them outside, did you?"

"No! Give us a bit of credit," Yanily said, looking at Vix and Fitch. "Over in the corner by the hole in the wall. Figured the falling water would hide the bodies from the outside, and they would be out of our way."

"Not bad thinking, but maybe we want to make sure there is zero risk of them being seen from outside," Seena said.

"Left is down there. He'll give us warning if he spots anything," Vix said.

"Good," Seeyela said. "Okay, let's start getting chokepoints set up. If anything wants to come in here for us, we're going to make them work for it."

"I don't think we should leave Left down there alone," Hiral started, but then cut off as the tattoos reappeared on the left side of his body.

What the…?

"What did you do?" Fitch asked.

"I didn't *do* anything," Hiral said, pulling open his status window.

He noticed a 1/2 beside his **Foundational Split**. His solar energy capacity was still also at only twenty-eight percent. Since Right was standing next to him, that meant Left had somehow returned.

Returned? By choice, or…?

"You didn't cancel or… call him back? Or whatever it is you call it?" Seena asked.

"Of course not. But let's see if he can tell us," Hiral said, and activated **Foundational Split**.

Left peeled off Hiral's body and staggered for a moment, reaching for his throat, then looked around the room like he was confused to be there.

"You okay?" Hiral asked, reaching out and steadying his double.

"The last thing I remember was being on the first floor," Left said. "And now I'm here with you. I was… killed?"

"Look pretty good for a dead guy," Yanily murmured.

"Seems that way," Hiral said, ignoring the comment. "Do you remember anything before that?"

"Yes," Left said. "There was a sound over by where the Troblin bodies were, and I went to investigate. When I got there, the bodies were gone."

The Growers looked at each other at the comment, but then most of their eyes settled on Yanily.

"Uh…" he started.

"What kind of sound?" Seena asked, cutting off the comments before they could start.

"Like something moved through the falling water. The constant splashing was broken up for a brief second," Left said. "I suspect I only noticed it because of my higher attunement."

"There's something in the building with us already?" Nivian asked, moving to peek out the door into the hallway.

"I'm not sure," Left said. "I thought the same thing, so I turned back to look around the room."

"What happened after that?" Seeyela asked.

"I felt a brief touch on my shoulder," he said, reaching up to pat his right shoulder, and drew his hand across his neck. "Then, I assume I died. That's where my memory ends."

"When I summoned you back, you were reaching for your throat," Hiral said.

Left's eyes moved back and forth like he was thinking. His hand rubbed his throat, and he nodded. "Yes, whatever killed me happened around my neck, I think."

"You see anything, Nivian?" Seena asked.

"Nothing. Looks quiet," Nivian said. "No flashing warnings from my *PIM* either."

"We'll use the *PIMs* to our advantage," Seeyela said. "Even if Hiral didn't see whatever is out there, his *PIM* warned him. If anybody gets one of those notifications, speak up right away. In the meantime, let's secure this floor. Sorry, folks. Looks like nobody is getting any sleep tonight."

49

A CHANGE IN SCENERY

THE storm raged for hours as the two parties huddled in the room, weapons ready, and waited for something—anything—to come at them.

Nothing did.

But that didn't mean it was restful. Nobody slept, and they barely took the time to stuff one of the dungeon rations in their mouths.

Finally, as the hammering rain and howling wind receded from Hiral's ears, the group prowled out of the room, down the hall, and to the top of the stairs. Hiral held up a hand, urging silence as he concentrated on his hearing. When nothing caught his attention, he inched down the stairs, **RHCs** out, and kept his back to the solid stone wall.

The first floor was exactly as they'd left it, no sign of how or where Left had been killed, but Hiral turned his attention to the far corner. With the easing of the heavy rain, the sheets of water falling over the side of the building had lessened to smaller streamers of water, giving a better view of the alley outside. Wide as it was, it also appeared empty—with no evidence of what had happened to the Troblin corpses.

"I think it's clear," Hiral said, though he kept his voice down.

"Send Left next time," Seena said, joining him as the others filed down to the first floor. "Death is obviously less inconvenient for him."

"Not any less traumatic, though," Hiral said, glancing at the double who'd been unusually quiet.

"That's true. I shouldn't think of them like they're… disposable." Guilt crept onto Seena's face. "I'm sorry."

"Don't be. We're all coming to terms with everything happening since we came to the surface."

"Enough chatter," Seeyela scolded. "Get eyes out those windows. If you see anything, speak up. If not, we're getting back on the path to the dungeon. The sooner we get to the *Asylum*, the sooner we get to stop worrying about whatever that *Enemy* was."

"Talk later," Hiral whispered to Seena, then jogged quietly over to one of the torn-out windows looking onto the street.

The rain falling outside had lessened to little more than a gentle shower on the paved road, but he still softly pushed back the water with his **Rune of**

Rejection. A glance out the window didn't show anything out of the ordinary, or any flashing notification, so, inch by inch, Hiral leaned his head out the window and looked up and down the street.

Lightning flashed in the distance, back the way they'd come, along with the faint boom of thunder, but it did little to light up the town as it had earlier. All he had to rely on was the faintly glowing roots, and they didn't show him any signs of impending danger.

Moving slowly, Hiral ducked back into the room and stepped away from the window. "Looks clear," he said quietly, his opinion quickly getting echoed by Picoli and Balyo.

"Still moving as separate groups?" Seena asked her sister.

"Yes," Seeyela said after a second's thought. "Not as far, though. Thirty feet tops. Since the *Enemy* seems to be real, we might as well follow that small snippet of advice we got from Dr. Benza to move in groups of six. I know he said eighteen *could* get by under their notice, but no need to risk it. It killed Left without him even noticing it was there.

"On that note, Hiral," she said, turning to him.

"You sure you don't want more eyes watching?" Hiral asked, but he waved for Left and Right to come over to him.

"I'm sure," she said.

"Okay, but if we get into a fight, I need to bring them out. I can't do much with the Shaper tattoos on me."

"Agreed. If we're fighting, I want every advantage possible."

"We'll be ready if you need us," Right told Hiral.

"Thanks for everything, guys," Hiral said before taking his copies' hands and absorbing them into himself, the tattoos and Meridian Lines appearing on his skin.

"Can you still use your **RHCs** while combined?" Seena asked.

"Kind of?" he said. "They each hold enough solar energy for five shots, but I normally just recharge them on the fly. With the tattoos on me, I can't make the connection to do that."

"At least you're not defenseless. And didn't you say something about having bonus stats from Left and Right?"

"Yeah. It's not all bad, but I miss my runes already," he said, looking at the rain. "Not to mention Left and Right."

"It's comforting having them around," Seena agreed.

"Everybody ready?" Seeyela asked. "We don't know how far the dungeon is, and we're all tired, but I'd like to cover as much ground as we can before we rest."

Seena looked at her group, then to her sister. "We're ready."

Without another word, Lonil was out the door, and the other Growers followed. Hiral, the final one out to watch their backs, took one last look around the room—*no sign or clue of what the* Enemy *could be. Like it was never really here*—then followed after Seena.

The rain was cold on his scalp before he pulled the hood up. The water pattered on the thin material, and he jogged down the street. There were only two more buildings on each side of the road, the insides dark and quiet through broken windows, and soon his boots were squelching through mud again. He glanced down at his feet, curious about the supposed Tri-Horn tracks, but they'd long since been washed away by the rain.

Back on the narrow trail, the group quickly left the town behind, though that didn't stop Hiral from glancing over his shoulder every five seconds, half-expecting warning notifications to flash in front of his eyes. None came, and minutes of running turned to hours before the party ahead slowed to a walk.

What's going on?

The question didn't need to be asked out loud as Seena's party caught up, a change to the scenery around them being the obvious cause.

The towering trees they'd been surrounded by for almost the entire time Hiral had been on the surface stopped as if on a hard line or border, then suddenly gave way to short, stubby masses of scraggly branches. The ground, which had been firm—aside from the mud caused by the rain—changed into a boggy mess of small islands amidst watery pools of unknown depths. Glowing plants still wound around the trees and trailed off beneath the water's surface, creating strange, illuminated patterns. Even the air changed, becoming warm humidity like a wall as they crossed the threshold, and the smell of natural rot crawled up Hiral's nose.

"Ugh, that's nasty," Yanily said. "Do we have to go this way?"

"I think it's the only way we can go," Wule said, his voice muffled by how he held his arm up in front of his face. "Look at the path. Seems to avoid the worst of the pools."

"We could always go back," Cal said.

"Back isn't an option," Seeyela answered immediately. "And don't trust the path. There could still be deep pools hiding anywhere along it."

"Or something worse," Wule mumbled.

"The next dungeon was called *The Mire*, right?" Hiral asked, though he knew the answer. "Maybe this means we're getting close."

"I hope so," Seeyela said, and Lonil started down the path, his stone club at the ready.

Waiting behind with Seena and the others for Seeyela's party to get ahead, Hiral scanned left and right along the new terrain. He could still hear the faint *croaking* of the lizards—ahead as well as behind—but without the tall trees to hide them, where would they come from? Hiral's eyes settled on the surface of the many pools, water practically dancing from the raindrops hitting it.

Any threats are going to come from there. Nowhere else to hide. But, which one? When?

A ripple along the surface, disturbing the constant light, was Hiral's only warning, and he shouted ahead to the other party's tank. "Lonil, on your right!"

The tank turned as something burst out of one of the nearby ponds in a shower of water refracting the light. Up came his club, barely in time to block the jaws of the massive snake, but the thing had to be more than forty feet long—its entire body lined with spikes—and the power of its lunge, along with its weight, threw Lonil into the water behind him.

The swampy quagmire immediately erupted in a fury of splashing waves as the snake's body coiled and thrashed around Lonil. His party moved to assist, but another ripple tore Hiral's attention from the struggle.

"Another one coming for us," he shouted as he drew his **RHCs**, the weapons swinging up in a smooth motion.

Just like before, a huge snake's head breached the water, jaws splitting wide with vicious fangs. This time, though, it was met by twin bolts of **Impact**, the blasts smacking into its body just behind the skull.

The force of the attack stole most of the monster's momentum, and instead of careening into its target—Wule—like a runaway carriage, it flopped down onto the path, body twitching.

Barbed Swamp Snake – High E-Rank

The name floated above the gargantuan body, rings of hooked barbs running its entire length, and it dazedly lifted its head. Nivian was the first one to arrive. A backhand slam from his shield *cracked* into the side of its head and sent one of the long fangs spinning into the air, thorns ripping its skin as they tore across it.

The tank followed up with a quick one-two combo from his purple-enshrouded whip, small flames licking from within the wounds left by the thorns. The snake turned hate-filled eyes on him. With his feet planted, Nivian was ready for it when it lunged straight for him, and he caught the attack easily with his shield, hooking one edge of it behind the remaining large fang. Then, like it was a living thing, he snapped his whip out to coil around the snake's body, just behind the jaws, further holding it in place against his shield.

"Ready!" he shouted.

Ready for what?

Spearing Roots burst out of Nivian's shield, and directly into the inside of the snake's vulnerable mouth.

The snake's whole body spasmed as points of purple flame punched through the top of its head and bottom of its jaw from the inside, the back end churning the water in its death throes. Solid roots wrapping Nivian's feet and shins prevented him from getting catapulted deeper into the swamp from the fury of it, and also kept the head in one place.

Just what Vix and Yanily needed. They swept in from both sides, and their blows landed simultaneously at the nape of the monster's neck. Spear and fist hit with such force, they cleanly severed the head from the rest of the body, and Nivian ripped his shield away, tossing the decapitated head to the ground.

One second, two seconds more, the body thrashed, then finally fell still. Hiral kept his eyes on the surrounding water. Where they were two, there could be more, but his attention returned to the first attacker.

Water pulled aside by three *Gravity Wells*, the monster sat in a coiled mass, its barbed body wrapped in a crushing grip on Lonil. Anybody other than the stony tank would've been quickly ground into formless paste by the pressure and spikes—and from the looks of things, Lonil wasn't doing much better.

Red blood seeped from between the coils of the snake's body, and though he held back the deadly jaws, pain etched Lonil's face amidst his concentration.

Picoli and Balyo attacked where they could, though Picoli's abilities lacked the punch or accuracy to end the fight, and Balyo couldn't risk using her signature move with Lonil in the line of fire. That just left Fitch, and though his sword cut long scars along the snake's body, the way it writhed kept him from landing more than one hit in the same place. The damage would wear it down, eventually, but Lonil didn't have that long.

The head isn't moving as much, but he can't reach it!

Luckily, that wasn't a problem for Hiral. He took aim, fingers squeezing one trigger then the next in quick succession. One after another, the bolts carved narrow tunnels in the falling rain to slap into the back of the snake's skull. Though the first did little visible damage, scales blasted off with the second. The third drew blood, and the fourth tore off flesh big enough to stick a hand in. The fifth and sixth widened the hole to expose the white of bone, while the seventh and eighth echoed with *cracks* that sounded over the furious struggle.

But it wasn't enough. Even with the grievous wound, the snake squeezed tighter on Lonil, the man's head arching back from the pain, and Hiral was out of shots.

I'll need to split… even if it risks bringing the Enemy.

Before Hiral could activate his *Foundational Split*, though, pulsing *Light Darts* swarmed into the hole he'd dug in the back of the snake's head, alternating between purple and their usual white-yellow.

No damage? No, something is different with…

The *Darts* exploded in a concentrated blast, evaporating the rain in a small sphere and throwing the top of the snake's body in the opposite direction, where it slapped into the spongy ground with a wet *thud*. The head sagged, jaws caught on Lonil's club, and then, all at once, the strength left the coils wrapping his body.

"Ugh," he groaned as the long corpse uncoiled from around him, revealing dozens of bloody wounds.

"Wule, Cal," Seeyela ordered, and both healers immediately moved to his side, warm pulses of solar energy washing out of them and over the tank.

"Any more?" Seena asked as she came over to join Hiral, her gaze roving across the swamp.

"I don't see any," he said. "Doesn't mean they aren't there."

"It doesn't. Everybody keep your eyes open."

"If they were any more open, they'd fall out," Yanily responded.

"How is he?" Seeyela asked as Fitch and Vix helped carry a staggering Lonil back to the path.

"Not great," Cal said. "We can treat some of the wounds, but we're going to need time to deal with the worst ones. Those barbs tore him up pretty badly, even through his **Stoneform**."

"This doesn't seem like the best place to set up camp," Seeyela replied.

"I might have a better answer," Hiral offered, his eyes settling on something glowing distantly down the path. "I think I see one of the archways leading to the dungeons."

"How far?" Seeyela asked.

"Five hundred feet," he answered.

"You're sure it's the dungeon?"

"No. It could be more of those glowing plants, but from here, it looks like the runes on the arch."

"Can't hurt to go," Seena said. "If it's the dungeon, we found a place to treat Lonil. If not, it can't be worse than here."

"You're right. Nivian, you take the lead this time," Seeyela said, and the group set out for what was *hopefully* the dungeon entrance.

50

TUTORIAL 2

H IRAL eyed the arch as the party moved along the path, eyes open for more giant snakes hiding under the surface of the water. As before, faintly glowing runes ran the length of the stonework, though instead of being embedded in the side of the mountain, this one rested in something that couldn't be more than a mound of dirt, barely taller than the arch.

"Is there really a dungeon in there?" Wule asked.

"Path leading down," Nivian said, the first one to reach the archway. "Looks like forty feet or so. Careful, though—it's steep."

"Let us go in first to make sure it's secure," Seena suggested.

"No. If we get jumped by one of those snakes while you're down there and Lonil isn't in fighting shape, it wouldn't be good," Seeyela countered.

"I'm fine," Lonil said, one arm over each of Fitch's and Vix's shoulders, blood still seeping out of his wounds.

"Yeah, totally fine," Cal deadpanned. "Could you *please* stop bleeding, though? I just got that closed up."

"Whine, whine, whine," Lonil responded, then grimaced. "Okay, maybe I've had better days."

"Nivian, Wule, and Yanily, take the lead," Seena said. "Then Seeyela's party. Hiral and I will bring up the rear."

At the comment, Hiral turned his attention from the arch and back to the swampy surroundings. Only the two snakes had attacked them, but the *croaking* of lizards still echoed from within the darkness, and they likely weren't the only threats. As if on cue, a noise from one of the small islands in the swamp drew his attention, and he peered through the darkness while drawing his **RHCs.**

Damnit, they don't have a charge. Probably fine to summon Left and Right if I need to now.

"You see something?" Seena asked, eyes squinting as she peered in the same direction he did.

"Maybe... Yeah, there it is," he said, pointing with one of his weapons. "It looks like some kind of... pig? Hairy, though. Big tusks from its mouth, and of course it has curved spikes all over it."

"Sounds like a swamp boar," Seena said.

"Thought you said you haven't been here before?" Hiral asked.

"Not here, specifically, but there's another swamp half a rotation from here that has boars like what you're describing. They…" She trailed off and looked at the dungeon entrance. "They're kind of like the Quillbacks, in that we usually find them inside the dungeons."

"Should we hurry?" Hiral asked, but there didn't seem to be any in urgency in Seena's posture.

"Nah. They're surprisingly friendly," she said. "Not so cuddly with the spikes and all that, but they don't mind us in their space. Kind of tasty too."

"You hunt them?" Hiral asked.

"Not the ones we find in the dungeon, but there are always a few outside of it. We hunt those and bring the meat back up with us."

"I guess that makes sense. I mean, there would have to be something around for the snakes to hunt, or else why would they be here?"

Seena shrugged, then looked again at the arch as the last of Seeyela's party vanished within. "C'mon, our turn," she said, and Hiral followed her inside.

Like Nivian had said, there was a steep incline immediately beyond the arch, but something about it bugged Hiral enough that he stopped at the lip.

Something's wrong with this. What is it?

Glowing plants lined the walls down, providing more than enough ambient light to see by, and he couldn't hear any fighting even though Nivian and the others had already reached the bottom. So, what was bugging him?

Hiral crouched down and put his fingers to the earthy ramp, and his eyes widened.

It's dry. That's it. There's no rain running down the slope to flood the chamber inside, and the earth isn't wet even though it's in the middle of a swamp.

A splash somewhere behind Hiral reminded him that might not be the best place to get lost in thought, and he quickly stood, then passed through the arch, a slight shiver running across his skin. Despite the angle of the slope, the walking was surprisingly easy-going, with good traction for his boots, and he exited the tunnel only a few seconds after Seena had, to find her—and the rest of the party—staring at the herd of boars.

"Well," he said, "you're sure they're friendly?"

"They barely notice we're here," she said as one of the big animals—its head was easily at waist height—lumbered past Hiral and up the tunnel.

"Yeah, but it's tough to miss them," he said, doing a rough count. "There's, what, a hundred of them here? Where are we going to find space?"

"At the other dungeon, there's usually room by the interface… Yeah, look over there. They're avoiding that corner." Vix and Fitch were already carrying Lonil in that direction.

"The Quillbacks built their nest on the interface, though," Hiral said, walking beside Seena.

"Nah, they don't. Usually. I think that was because of the Shapers." Seena joined the group as they circled around Vix and Fitch, who were lowering Lonil to the ground. Wule and Cal immediately moved in and began working their healing abilities.

"This is going to take most of our solar energy to heal," Wule told Seena. "It'll take a while to absorb enough energy to safely go into the dungeon."

"It's fine. Lonil's life is far more important than getting into the dungeon," Seena said.

"Yeah, but I need to…" Yanily started, though he cut off at a look from Seena. "Right, evolution to D-Rank can totally wait. Not going to see me rushing you at all. Not a bit."

Hiral relaxed a little at the Grower jibes. If they could joke like that, it meant Lonil wasn't in any real danger anymore. Cal and Wule would take care of him and get him back into fighting shape, then they'd make their way into the second dungeon.

"Think I can bring Left and Right out?" Hiral quietly asked Seena.

"Yes. We might as well start getting a camp set up as well. Looks like we're going to be here a bit."

"Fine by me; I'd like to take a look at the runes on the arch anyway," Hiral said. He activated **Foundational Split**, Left and Right peeling off him. "Welcome back," he said to his doubles, and recharged the **RHCs** on his thighs before he forgot.

"Sure," Seena said. "But I don't want you going out there alone. Those snakes could be anywhere, even if we didn't run into another one."

Hiral turned his attention to what had to be the dungeon interface. "This is **The Mire**, right? How much you want to bet we'll have to deal with more of those snakes inside the dungeon?"

Seena groaned at the same time Nivian joined them.

"We'll need a plan before we go up against any more of them," the tank said. "If it'd been anybody other than Lonil getting caught like that, we'd be traveling with one less person. Even with the bonus I get from this amulet"—he held up his hand to show the amulet he'd gotten from **Splitfang Keep**—"I don't think I could survive that."

"Then I guess we need to make sure you don't get caught," Seena said. "You're right, though. We'll come up with something. We've got time while Wule helps Cal, and then recharges."

"In the meantime, how about we get some more answers from Dr. Benza?" Hiral asked, and pointed at the dungeon interface.

Seena looked over at Seeyela and her party, obviously wondering if they should all be present for it, but finally nodded instead. "We can always get it to repeat anything they miss," she said, then walked with Hiral over to the interface.

Hiral waved his hand above the crystal. The yellow and green rings formed under their feet, and the image of Dr. Benza sprang to life.

"Welcome, challengers, to *The Mire Dungeon*. Please choose an option," the image said, and a blue notification window sprang up beside him.

Tutorial
Enter Dungeon
Help

"Dr. Benza, *Tutorial*, please," Hiral said.

The image of the doctor shimmered briefly. "Accessing *PIMs*. Access complete," Dr. Benza said, his voice flat. "One dungeon clear detected. Introductory-two *Tutorial* loaded. Please complete further dungeons to access more advanced *Tutorials*.

"Welcome, challengers, to *The Mire Dungeon*," Dr. Benza continued, his voice more normal. "As this is your second dungeon attempt, I will enlighten you to the somewhat more advanced dungeon mechanics.

"As you may have realized from clearing"—the image flickered—"*Splitfang Keep*"—another flicker—"you will gain powerful equipment and achievements to increase your power. These incremental gains will allow you to clear more difficult dungeons, which will in turn further increase your power. I'm sure you have many questions about this whole process." He looked off to the side, then whispered, "Which I'm not allowed to tell you all about until more advanced *Tutorials*. Sorry." He winked.

"Oh, nothing, just talking to myself. Feel free to edit this all later. What do you mean there isn't a large budget for editing? First you tell me the memory crystals have limited space to download information, and now this? What is this? A B-Rank movie?"

"What's a movie?" Hiral whispered to Seena, and she shrugged, apparently just as confused about what Dr. Benza was saying as he was.

"Fine! I'll get back on topic," Dr. Benza said, his attention turning back to the party as everybody other than Lonil, Wule, and Cal came over to join. Even the two healers, however, got Lonil better positioned so they could all listen in while the healing abilities did their work. "For now, we will talk about the origins of the gear you're being provided upon successful completion of the dungeons, how you can reset the dungeons to allow entries beyond three, and how you can obtain further loot from cleared dungeons."

"I was hoping to find out more about our *PIMs*," Hiral said, "but I guess this is a start."

"We can go in more than three times?" Yanily asked, his eyes practically lighting up.

"And more loot?" Vix asked. "Sounds good to me."

"Before I talk about the origins of the loot," Dr. Benza said, his usually smiling face turning grave, "there is something you need to know. We are at war, and we're losing. No, maybe that's not even accurate. We've lost. Our people are being slaughtered, and our civilization is falling. It's only a matter of time, and there's nothing we can do.

"Nothing but this—entrusting our future to you.

"So, we've taken our greatest tools, weapons, and equipment away from the front line and put them in our *Vault* for safekeeping. As you clear each dungeon for the first time, a temporary link will be created between the dungeon instance and the *Vault*, and your *PIM* will be scanned. Based on the results of the scan—namely your race, class, rank and level—appropriate equipment will be selected and placed in a chest for you.

"This equipment is what the system, *PIMP*—or Personal Interface Magic Prime—will determine to be the best fit to help you grow. And your growth is paramount. It is *everything*. Without growth, the war will never end, the *Enemy* will win, and our people—all of them—will die.

"I don't know how long it's been between when we created these semi-interactive recordings and when you're watching them, but it may have even been a few years. In that time, I can only hope you've been training hard and that the war is turning in our favor. But, from the looks I'm getting"—Dr. Benza looked around the room at things Hiral couldn't see—"I have digressed. More information on the *PIM,* the war, and the *Enemy* will be in later *Tutorials*."

"Should anybody tell him that maybe we lost the war?" Vix asked.

"For now," Dr. Benza went on as if Vix hadn't spoken, "we shall continue on the topic of gear. As you may have noticed, the equipment and achievements you received after clearing your first dungeon possess powerful boons, but there are limits to how they can interface with your *PIM.* For example, you can only wear one ring per hand, or only one necklace. It is unlikely the *PIMP* will grant you equipment you cannot use, but you may discover such limits if you attempt to trade equipment. Keep these limits in mind as you grow as an individual and as a party, and as you delve deeper into more and more difficult dungeons.

"As you clear these dungeons of increased difficulty, you will also receive challenge-appropriate gear. Our analysts have determined this experiential cycle of challenge and growth will propel you faster to higher ranks and levels than any other alternatives. However, should you hit a roadblock in growth and need to return to a previously cleared dungeon to farm for experience… No, don't look at me like that. I *like* that term. Farm. It sounds wholesome. Seriously, which do you prefer? Farm the dungeon? Or commit wholesale slaughter of the dungeon inhabitants?

"Exactly. *Farm*. Yes, like they're vegetables.

"Ahem. As I was saying. Should you need to return to farm the dungeon, you will have that option upon reaching the *Asylum*. Using the *Asylum Interface*, you can reset dungeons in the associated area to allow re-entry. This will permit you to clear it an additional three times, as well as receive loot for the first clear.

"No new dungeon-specific achievements will be granted, however, though you could potentially gain random achievements depending on your actions. We tried to build this function into the dungeon interfaces, like the one you're using now, but I am afraid the power and memory requirements were just too large. Only the *Asylum Interface* had the necessary power." Dr. Benza's image shimmered.

"That brings us to the end of this ***Tutorial***. Should you require further information, please complete more dungeons and proceed to the next interface. Note, the ***Help*** section of this interface has only been uploaded with information pertaining to details found within this ***Tutorial***.

"Thank you for choosing…" Dr. Benza looked off to the side again and shrugged. "What? I thought it would be funny. Fine. You can edit that out too!" He stamped his foot, then walked off to the side, vanishing from the platform, only for his image to shimmer back into its standing position a second later.

"Isn't that the same thing he said last time? Even stomped his foot the same," Nivian said.

"He talked about a war, an *Enemy* they couldn't beat, and how important it is we get stronger, and his stomping foot is what caught your attention?" Balyo asked.

"Yeah. I mean… we can talk about that other stuff too," Nivian said.

51

HELP

"THAT... was a whole lot," Seena said to Hiral as most of them stood looking at the image of Dr. Benza. "I mean, I'm not surprised, in a way. *Something* had to have happened for us to be on the islands instead of down here on the surface, but how does it connect to the islands moving?"

"All our abilities are solar-powered," Nivian said. "If the islands don't chase the sun, we'll be without our source of power."

"Are we without solar energy now?" Hiral asked, and Nivian looked at him briefly before shaking his head. "Seena's right. There has to be more to it than that. Do you guys think the roots are natural?"

"Why don't we try asking Dr. Benza?" Vix asked.

"You think he'll tell us?" Yanily asked. "He seems pretty tight-lipped... other than when he's feeling talkative."

"Dr. Benza, *Help*," Hiral said.

The image on the pedestal shifted slightly.

"Dr. Benza, the roots glowing with solar energy—the path leading us between dungeons—did your people create those?" Hiral asked.

"We did not," Dr. Benza said. "The roots are a natural evolutionary step from the plants, creating a sort of symbiotic relationship with other creatures and plants that themselves need solar energy. As for the paths between dungeons, we simply directed the plants where we needed them to grow."

"Why couldn't we see them until we cleared the dungeon?" Hiral asked.

"Similar to the initial achievements you received for clearing the dungeon, your *PIM* did not have the ability to see the roots—and thus the path—until you completed your first dungeon. Other than the ones within the dungeon entrance rooms, of course."

"But why not?" Seena asked. "Why do we need to do any of these things? Why do our *PIMs* get stronger?"

"Unfortunately, information on the nature of the *PIM* and its growth is restricted to the Introductory-four *Tutorial*. To learn more, please clear your second and third dungeons, and access the *Asylum* interface."

"Told you. Tight-lipped," Yanily said.

"What else should we ask?" Hiral said to Seena. "I think he only told us about the roots because it was connected to the path statement from clearing the first dungeon."

"So, information about equipment? That's probably all he knows," Seena said.

"Dr. Benza, which dungeon has the most powerful weapons?" Yanily asked, then shrugged when the others looked at him.

"The most powerful equipment will be found in one of the six S-Rank dungeons," Dr. Benza said.

"S-Rank? Going to be a while before we get there," Yanily complained.

"However," Dr. Benza went on, "some of the most powerful artifacts were broken before we returned them to the *Vault* for safekeeping. These may be acquired from any dungeon, due to their reduced potency, if the **PIMP** judges it appropriate."

"Can we even use something S-Rank?" Yanily asked.

"If it's like a Shaper's tattoos, then yes," Hiral said.

"What do you mean?" Seena asked.

"Left, dagger, please," Hiral said, and Left shaped his ***Dagger of Sath***. "All of Left's tattoos are S-Rank, but he is only E-Rank. Because of this, when he shapes a tattoo, it is conjured at a… well, like Dr. Benza said, a reduced potency. Something around six percent, I think?"

"Approximately," Left said. "A bit less, technically. While I am at E-Rank, my tattoos are less than six percent of their maximum effectiveness. At D-Rank, that will double, to almost twelve percent. C-Rank will take it to around eighteen percent, B-Rank will be about thirty-five percent, and A-Rank will be sixty percent. When I finally reach S-Rank, my tattoos will have their full power."

"*If* you reach S-Rank," Fitch said. "Nobody has reached S-Rank in, well, ever."

"Nobody had access to dungeons before," Hiral said. "But, back to the point. Even though Left's tattoos are only operating at six percent of their maximum power, they are still more powerful than an E-Rank tattoo. Possibly even more powerful than many D-Rank tattoos. So, if we luck into getting an S-Rank artifact from a dungeon, it should still be quite impressive."

"Hold up a minute," Nivian interrupted, pointing at Left. "You're telling me *all* of his abilities… his tattoos… are S-Rank?"

"Yeah," Hiral said with a shrug.

"And he's had them from the beginning?" Nivian asked.

"Well, technically, *I* did, but they don't do me any good," Hiral said.

"And you just got them, without having to train or anything?"

"I guess?"

"How's that fair? You can just *get* S-Rank abilities without working for them." Nivian shook his head.

"It's not exactly that easy," Hiral said. "You need to find an Artist capable of inscribing S-Rank tattoos. Not just anybody can do that. I think there are only a few on the whole island. Maybe a dozen? My parents just happen to be two of them, so I had… would've had… a bit of an advantage."

"Why doesn't everybody go to your parents for their tattoos, then? Why would you get anything less than S-Rank?" Seena asked.

"Just because a Shaper has an S-Rank tattoo on their body, it doesn't mean they can use it," Hiral explained. "They need to have high ranks in absorption, capacity, and output to use them. At least an A-Rank in all three to use most S-Rank tattoos, and some, like the *Spear of Clouds,* needs an S-Rank in all three to successfully shape."

"A spear, you say?" Yanily asked, looking over at Hiral. "Do *you* have it?"

"Uh… yes…" Hiral said. "But I don't know if Left will ever be able to use it since it runs down the center of my spine. Left, can you turn around?"

"Sure," Left said, doing just that so the party could see half of the spear tattooed on his back.

"That… that thing is *gorgeous,*" Yanily said, walking over and leaning in uncomfortably close. "Don't get me wrong… my new spear is something special." He caressed the weapon. "But this? It's giving me chills."

"It's based off stories of a legendary weapon," Hiral said. "The spear is said to be what separated the clouds from the sky, so it should be pretty strong."

"Should be?" Wule asked.

"Nobody has even been able to successfully shape it," Hiral said. "My father hoped I'd be the first, which is why he gave me the tattoo. Just another disappointment for my mother, I guess."

Seena gave him a pat on the shoulder. "I'm sure she doesn't feel that way. And she definitely won't when she sees you the next time."

"Yeah, we'll see," Hiral said, forcing the resentment back down deep. "Anyway, most Shapers only actually get C- or B-Rank tattoos. A few can manage one or two A-Ranks, but that's not usually worth it."

"How come?" Seena asked, letting the comment about his mother go, but she still gave him another pat on the shoulder.

"Ah, a Shaper's tattoos are only as strong as the weakest tattoo on their body. So, even if they can use an A-Rank, if they have any B-Rank on them, that's the limit. But, hold on a second. Are you saying it's not the same for Growers? How do your ability ranks work?"

"They all start at Low-E-Rank," Wule said. "Kind of like we do, they gain experience, but only as we use them."

"And they cap at the high end of whatever rank we are," Seena continued. "So, Yanily there, his *Reed Spear Style* is High-E-Rank and is ready to evolve. As soon as he hits D-Rank, the ability will be able to start improving again."

"The more you use it, the faster it improves?" Hiral asked.

"Correct," Seena said with a nod.

"What about those ability evolutions you were talking about? What do they start at when you get them?"

"Right at the bottom. Low-E-Rank. But"—Seena held up a hand before Hiral could say anything else—"they seem to level up pretty fast until they catch up, so it's not too bad."

"Wow. I didn't think there were so many differences, but I guess both ways have advantages and disadvantages."

"I wouldn't say no to a few S-Rank abilities gifted to me," Yanily said, following Left's back as the double turned so he could continue looking at half of the *Spear of Clouds*.

"Dr. Benza, why do we need a Builder and a Grower to enter the dungeons?" Seena suddenly asked.

"Dungeon entry requirements and reasoning are found within the Introductory-three *Tutorial*. Please complete one more dungeon and proceed to the next interface for more information."

"Dr. Benza, can you tell us more about the four races?" she asked next.

"Class and race information is found within the Introductory-three *Tutorial*. Please complete one more dungeon and proceed to the next interface for more information."

"Hrm, doesn't seem like we're getting much more from him here," Seena said.

"That's fine," Seeyela said. "The goal was always to get to the *Asylum* for safety anyway. It just means we have more reasons to look forward to it."

"But, now, you want us to set up camp and get some rest before we clear this dungeon, right?" Seena said, and Seeyela gave a knowing smile.

"You know me so well. It's almost like we grew up together or something." Seeyela put a finger to her chin and looked up in thought.

"Har har, you're so funny," Seena said. Then, more quietly, "How's Lonil?"

"Worse than he admits," Seeyela said, only loud enough for Seena and Hiral to hear while the others chatted and dreamed about getting S-Rank loot. "I don't want to rush him into the dungeon before he's back at one hundred percent."

"Aren't Wule and Cal healing him?" Hiral asked.

"Magical healing treats the physical wounds, mostly, but with injuries as deep as his were, it'll take his body time to… how can I say this… reconnect?" Seeyela said. "All the flesh and muscle is back, but he needs some practice to get his reflexes back to where they were."

"Like rehabilitation?" Hiral asked, and Seeyela nodded.

"And the *PIM* is out of alignment as well. It needs time to fill in the holes where it was damaged. Might take twenty or thirty hours for him to be ready to go in."

"Twenty or thirty?" Seena asked, eyes widening. "The injuries were *that bad*? He's lucky to be alive."

"He is," Seeyela agreed. "If we didn't have two healers with us, I don't think he would've made it."

"And that was only one E-Rank snake," Hiral said.

"Exactly—there's a lot more dangerous stuff ahead of us," Seeyela said, looking at the interface. "Directly ahead of us. We need him at full strength."

"We'll go in first and scout it out," Seena said. "Take it slow and learn everything we can, then give you the information."

"Unless there's another summoning ritual," Hiral deadpanned. "Or something else forcing us to rush."

"Either way, we'll deal with it," Seena said. "With Left and Right joining us, we're better suited to go in first anyway, Seeyela."

"I know you are, and I think it's a good plan. Information on what to expect will make it so we don't have to push Lonil too hard, but maybe we also won't have to wait quite as long, so the others don't lose their edge. When will you go in?"

"We're going to get at least one good rest, then I'll see how everybody is feeling after that," Seena said. "I want to make sure we have a plan to deal with those snakes, though. Something more than the five-percent damage bonus we're getting from the *Racial Growth* ability. Don't get me wrong—it's great it only took two kills to get the first rank, but I don't think it's going to be enough to trivialize our next fight against them."

"That's something we can all work on together," Seeyela said. "I have an idea or two. Let's all sit down to eat in a couple of hours and talk then."

"I know, I know. Set up camp in the meantime. Come on, Hiral," Seena said, and led them over to where they'd set down the packs. "If you have any ideas for dealing with those snakes, I'd like to hear it while we set up tents. Hey, Vix, Yanily, Nivian. Get a couple tents set up, and maybe that pot we got from the last dungeon. Let's actually cook something."

Nivian looked from Seena to the herd of boars on the other side of the room. "Bacon?"

"As much as I'd love it," Seena said, then shook her head, "we'd have to hunt them outside the dungeon, and that'd put the whole party at risk. Take it easy until we go into the dungeon. We have some other ingredients we can use, right?"

"I've got a few things," Nivian said. "Was kind of wondering what buffs we'd get from them anyway, so it's fine either way."

"Great, get started on that. Can you make enough for everybody?"

"No problem," Nivian said, and got to work. "Er, maybe not if Fitch is eating. That guy can put it away."

"Do what you can. So, Hiral, snakes," Seena said, turning back to him. "How are we going to deal with them so they don't do the same thing to us they did to Lonil?"

"I'm not sure yet," Hiral admitted, "but something else has been on my mind. Those boars—they have spikes on their bodies, right?"

"Yeah, so?" Seena asked.

Before Hiral answered, he looked at one of the boars until a name appeared over its head.

Spined Great Tusk – Mid-E-Rank

Just like the others, it's right there in the name.

"So, the snakes have spikes," Hiral said. "The lizards have spikes. From the sounds of things, the Tri-Horns have spikes too. The Quillbacks have quills. Why is everything on the surface thorny? The boars I could see, to protect them from predators like the snakes. But, why do the predators have spikes too? What do they need protection from?"

Seena's hands stopped as she was unwinding a tent, and she looked up to meet Hiral's eyes. "The *Enemy*?"

"That's what I was thinking. Even the hunters are being hunted by whatever this *Enemy* is, and they've developed their own spikes as a kind of natural defense."

"It could be… but how does that help us with the snakes and the dungeon?" Seena asked, and Hiral couldn't help but chuckle.

"I don't know if it does, really," he said. "But, if we think about it, it could mean the *Enemy* is some kind of natural hunter. If it is, its prey is looking for protection from its physical hunting tactics. Do you know of any other animals in different regions that have these kinds of natural defenses?"

Seena sat back on her feet as her hands kept working. "Now that you mention it, several do. There's one region where a bunch of monsters have poisonous skin or blood. Real pain in the ass to deal with, by the way. There's another where the monsters have bladed hides, instead of spikes, and another where they're all like Lonil in his *Stoneform*."

"All things that protect against or dissuade a direct attack," Hiral said.

"Which is all we really have to offer," Seena replied. "There are Growers that have things like poison, abilities that do damage over time, instead of all at once. We aren't them."

"Sounds like the perfect time for a spontaneous ability evolution to me," Hiral said.

"If only we could count on that. We're going to need something a bit more concrete."

"Then we use the snake's strengths against it," Hiral said. "We know it's going to lunge and then try to constrict, right? Let's see if we can't come up with tactics that take that into account."

"My **Spearing Roots**?"

"Exactly. We just have to make sure the snakes focus on Nivian, though. His shield did a great job of blocking that last one we fought. The rest of us don't have one of those." Hiral glanced over at Left and Right. "And I know the topic will come up of using them as bait, but I'd really rather not."

Seena followed his look. "Are they... real? No, that's not the right way to put it."

"No, I get what you're saying. And, I don't know. I haven't really broached the subject with them... Kind of awkward. Left is acting a bit strange, though."

"He is," she agreed, "but he didn't hesitate against the snake."

"We can still count on them. It's just, like you said before, they aren't disposable. They even have different personalities."

"It's kind of a crazy ability."

"It is! I didn't even know things like this were possible. Which, actually, I guess I could say about a *lot* of things since we came to the surface."

"Me too. It's been... an adventure. We're still alive, though. And, when we get to the *Asylum*, we'll have a safe place to stay. Think about it, Hiral— we'll be the first ones to survive a full rotation down on the surface. And with everything we're learning about the dungeons—not to mention the fact we can get into them—we're going to have so much to tell when we get back."

"We... are..." Hiral said, his head tilting back so he was looking at the ceiling. But it wasn't the dirt above his head occupying his mind. No, it was something much, much higher above. "And we'll have to do something about the Makers killing Quillbacks. And planning to kill your people."

Seena nodded, the smile fading from her face. "Yeah. Do you think your people will handle it? Do you think they'll care enough to do anything about it?"

"Technically not my people," Hiral said, and he waved a hand before Seena could say anything. "No, don't worry, I'm not trying to dodge responsibility here. They wouldn't have listened to me before, but the fact the dungeons need two different races to get into them means we have to cooperate. We'll leverage *that*. Make people understand we need to work together.

"And that's not even taking into account this *Enemy* Dr. Benza keeps talking about. If this war really is still going on, we're all going to need to decide if we want any part of it."

"What's the alternative?" Seena asked.

"The status quo," Hiral answered. "We bury our heads back in the sand—or the clouds, I guess—and keeping circling the world on Fallen Reach. The *Enemy* obviously can't get to us there, so we keep running."

"Can we run forever?"

"We can try."

"What do *you* want to do, Hiral?"

"I honestly don't know. I've been working so hard—and for so long—to get a class and get stronger. The power we're gaining from the dungeons is almost addictive, but what's the point of it if we don't use it? I don't want to spend my days fighting exhibition matches up in the Amphitheatre of the Sun.

"If we're going to—what did he call it?—farm the dungeons for experience, does that mean we have an obligation to be part of this war? We don't even know who or what the *Enemy* is, and if Dr. Benza's people couldn't beat them, how could we? They created the **PIMs**. And they still lost.

"I just don't understand how we can succeed where they failed," Hiral went on. "And if we can't win, what's the point of fighting?"

52

THE MIRE

"Dr. Benza, **Enter Dungeon**," Hiral said, the party gathering around him as the portal opened to *The Mire*.

"Everybody has their food buffs?" Seena asked.

"Five percent increased critical hit chance, and twenty-five percent increased critical hit damage," Yanily said, one hand caressing his spear. "I didn't even know we could get buffs like that!"

"Sorry it doesn't do much for you two," Seena said to Wule and Nivian.

"Not as much as the rest of you," Wule admitted, holding up his icy rod, "but that doesn't mean it'll go to waste."

"Just don't forget to heal me when those snakes show up," Nivian said, his eyes going to Lonil, who stood nearby.

"Oh, you're such a worrier," Wule said.

"Seeyela, we'll be back in a few hours," Seena said, ignoring the banter between the brothers.

"Be careful in there," Seeyela said.

"We will. Don't worry. Nivian," Seena said. She tapped the tank on the shoulder, and he headed through the portal.

The others followed, Hiral going last, and as he passed through, the portal closed behind him with a soft *pop*. Like the last time, they appeared in a rather plain-looking room, though a blue notification quickly appeared in the center.

The Mire – Dungeon
E-Rank
Top Clear Times
XXX : --:--
YYY : --:--
ZZZ : --:--
Attempt Dungeon?
Yes / No

Seena gave the party one last look to make sure they were good, then tapped the *Yes* button, and the room dissolved around them in a puff of solar energy. A wave of humidity washed over them in an instant, practically drenching Hiral in sweat right away, while the familiar stench of the bog crawled up his nose.

"Never get used to that," Yanily said, his hand going to his nose reflexively.

"This place doesn't look any better in the light," Vix added, and the pugilist had a point.

A low, muggy haze hung above the ground and wound its way between scraggly tree trunks, hiding the surface of the water and making it impossible to tell where it was safe to walk. Larger fog banks stood off to their left and right, obscuring everything more than a hundred feet away. And, though the sunlight shone from above, a massive briar patch stood shrouded in darkness directly ahead of them. The walls of it had to be fifty feet tall, and the mist and shadows mixing with the foliage almost seemed to have a life of their own, their wisps reaching out like they were tasting the area before dissolving in the light.

"Who votes we don't go in there?" Wule asked, pointing his rod toward the briar.

"You kidding? There's *obviously* a boss in there," Yanily said. "And you know what bosses mean, right?"

"Means I have to heal you," Wule said.

"Besides that," Yanily said dismissively. "Loot and achievements!"

"I don't see a way in," Nivian said. "And I don't think we want to try climbing that."

Hiral activated **Foundational Split** while he looked around. Left and Right peeled off him, and he turned to them when they were fully formed. "You still have the food buffs?"

"We do," Right said. "Though, personally, I would've added more salt."

"I heard that," Nivian said.

"You were supposed to," Right responded.

"It looks like there are paths to either side of us," Hiral said to avoid another food critique—*am I that picky too?* "Each one is leading into the fog, but we have options."

"Or we could…" Yanily started.

"We're not climbing it," Seena said. "If we can find a way in around the sides, we'll go in then."

"Fine," Yanily said. "Either way, the sooner we get to the dungeon interface, the sooner I can evolve to D-Rank, so let's pick a direction and start the farming."

"Hiral, can you see any differences between the routes?" Seena asked him.

"Honestly, I can barely tell they're paths at all. So hard to make out with the fog, but the way the trees are spaced out… I'm *pretty* sure it's a path."

"You're only saying that because you don't have to go first," Nivian said before looking at Seena. "Which way, boss?"

She turned her head in both directions, then finally seemed to settle on one, pointing to the right. "Let's go that way. Hiral, you ready for your part in this?"

"Ready," Hiral said, pushing energy into his **Rune of Rejection** and holding it there.

"Counting on you," Nivian said.

He started in the direction Seena had pointed, while Wule hung back a few steps further than usual, Seena immediately behind him. Like Hiral, she was already gathering energy for her *Spearing Roots*, though she didn't activate the ability. Then came Vix and Yanily, eyes peeled on both sides of the group for any sort of movement.

Left and Right stayed with Hiral to escort him. His concentration was entirely on Nivian's surroundings.

They moved forward slowly, the water usually only up to their ankles, but often reaching up to their knees as they followed the apparent path between the trees. Every once in a while, Nivian would lash out with his whip to slap the still water. The splashes shattered the silence, and the infernal flames sizzled, but nothing else moved.

"Where are they?" Wule asked after they'd walked unmolested for almost five minutes, the fog thinning around them as they passed through the bank. "This dungeon can't be empty, can it?"

"Better not be," Yanily said. "I want the experience."

"Just keep your eyes peeled," Seena said softly, and the low-hanging mist off to her right shifted.

My imagination? No, there!

"Incoming!" Hiral shouted, thrusting out his arm and activating his *Rune of Rejection* at the same time a serpentine head erupted out of the fog.

The pre-charged pulse of *Rejection* shoved out like the palm of a giant hand. It pushed everything away from Hiral in a widening cone, creating a wave of water and fog that hit the lunging snake like a tsunami.

Shoved to the side, but too heavy to be carried away, the long body of the snake *thumped* to the ground, curved barbs digging through the soft ground, where it rolled once before righting itself. Its head shook in confusion, and then a thorned whip slapped into the side of its face, small purple flames dancing in the wound.

"Forget about me already?" Nivian shouted at the snake, catching it with another lash across its throat as it reared up and spread its jaws.

Though the ones they'd faced outside the dungeon had been almost forty feet long, this one was even bigger, easily approaching sixty feet, with fangs like curved swords and a maw that could swallow a man whole.

(Elite) Barbed Swamp Snake – High-E-Rank

"It's *Elite!*" Hiral warned, though it didn't change the fact they had to kill it.

"Wonderful news," Nivian said, a pulse of solar energy making the twisting vines of the shield on his arm grow to the size of a tower shield.

Vix activated his blur ability and sprinted past Nivian, the misty effects of it making him half-vanish amidst the thin fog in the area, while Yanily went in the opposite direction. The plan was for Nivian to keep the snake's attention—another lash across its face did just that—while Vix and Yanily prepared for an opening.

"It's much bigger than we expected," Hiral said to Left and Right, **RHCs** coming out in his hands at the same time. "They're going to need your help. Go. I'll support from back here and keep an eye out for more."

"And what'll you do if you *find* more?" Right asked.

"Improvise," Hiral said. "Go on, it's starting."

The two doubles dashed forward—Right easily outpaced Left with his higher physical stats—at the same time the snake lunged forward. It hit Nivian's shield like a battering ram, tearing apart the roots he'd wrapped around his feet and legs to drive him back in a splash of water. Somehow, the tank managed to stay on his feet, and he countered with a pair of lashing strikes as the snake retracted its head.

With fury practically sparkling in its eyes at the man in front of it, the snake reared up, tongue whipping side to side and its shadow spreading to encompass Nivian. Sitting there for a split second, it looked at him, like it wanted Nivian to know what was coming, and then it pounced down at him like a falling meteor. Scales and spines shot forward, practically whistling in the wind, and then **Spearing Roots** burst out of the ground in front of the tank, a spear-wall of purple-flaming spikes set to impale the charging snake.

Yes. Just like we planned!

Except the snake flexed its body, head jerking to the side then diving down to the surface of the water, before racing away and snapping around to charge behind the spikes from the side.

Not like we planned at all!

Seena couldn't get another **Spearing Roots** out in time to block the lightning-fast snake, but Vix's fists flashed out in a fury. Even from ten feet away, the flurry of blows *thwacked* along the snake's body as it raced by, his ability to project the force of his punches making it so he didn't have to worry about hitting the spikes. At the same time, Yanily dashed in at the serpent's rear, his spear striking like it was made of rubber to tear through scales.

Between the two of them, they distracted the snake just enough for Nivian to leap to the side, though the snake still clipped his shield and sent him spinning into the water. And then it was past them all, whipping back around for another pass even as Left and Right got into range to join the fight.

We can do this. We just have to…

Movement off to Hiral's right. The mist shifted like something was moving underneath—and heading right for a distracted Wule.

No time to warn him!

Hiral activated *Eloquent* and *Enraged* without hesitation, the double-helix pattern along his body flaring like the noonday sun, and the world practically slowed to a crawl as his *Atn* spiked. The movement of the water, the breeze on his skin, the way the scents carried through the air—he could feel each and every one, like all of his senses combined to become one super-sense.

And that sense told him a second snake swept just below the surface of the water.

Hiral's hands tightened around his *RHCs*, and he launched himself forward, his modified *Dex* of 55 allowing his body to keep up with the sensory input flowing into his mind. In a heartbeat, he devoured the distance, feet barely touching the water as he ran across its surface, then pulled both triggers at the same instant the snake's head burst free from the swamp.

Thuk thuk. The bolts of pure force slammed into the base of the serpent's jaw, blowing off scales and flesh, and sent the creature careening to the side in pain and surprise. Maybe Wule noticed, maybe he moved, maybe he even said something, but Hiral ignored everything but the snake in front of him as he charged in.

Step, step, leap. Hiral kicked his legs up to cartwheel over the snake's tail as it came whipping in from the side, pointing his *RHCs* straight down as if he hung frozen, upside-down. He fired both weapons, time snapping back to normal speed for his feet to slap back down to the water. With momentum pulling him onward, he dropped to his knees to skid across the surface of the water and kicked his left leg out, spinning him around while he slid backwards.

He shot off blast after blast at the snake; spines, scales, and chunks of flesh exploding with each hit.

Enrage and *Eloquent* must also be buffing the *RHCs* damage!

Finally, with the friction on the water slowing him, Hiral absorbed the last of the momentum by rolling over his shoulder backwards and getting his feet under him. *No time to stand still.* He dashed to the left, firing while the snake raised its front half into the air with blood leaking from its wounds.

Blast after blast smacked unerringly into the snake's body, each and every shot a hit. The monster seemed to have had enough, bursting ahead with its jaws wide to intercept Hiral's trajectory. Seeing, feeling, *knowing* it was coming, Hiral threw the *RHC* in his right hand into the air, and then leapt straight up, scissor-kicking his legs out to the sides.

The snake's body roared by just inches below him, gravity already pulling him toward the spines rushing past, and he thrust his right hand down at the same time he ignited the power of his *Rune of Rejection*. Hiral shot up into the air, flipping as he went and swapping his *RHC* from his left hand to his right.

Then, just as his upward movement came to a halt, upside-down once again, he threw out his left hand and activated his **Rune of Attraction**.

Slap. The second **RHC** hit his hand, and he took aim at the snake's speeding back, then fired repeatedly. His bolts tore holes in the scaley flesh, while gravity dragged him back to the surface. His feet splashed into the water at the same time the snake's head whipped around, and they launched themselves at each other once again.

The barbed spikes running the length of the snake's body shifted, signaling the flexing of the muscles underneath, and suddenly, the great beast sprang forward like some kind of giant corkscrew. It twisted in the air, completely defying physics, around and around, filling the space in front of Hiral. He wouldn't be jumping over this or leaping to the side in time; they were both moving too fast.

So, he did the only thing he could—he dove forward into the space left by the snake's corkscrewing movement. Powerful jaws snapped shut like a trap just behind him, and only the perfect combination of his **Dex** and **Atn** let him find the small space he could fit through. Even then, the tips of the spikes tore painful gouges along the entire length of his body. But he wasn't the only one taking damage from the exchange, as Hiral fired all the while.

In a second, maybe two, they were past each other, and Hiral hit the water to roll to his feet and spin while the snake crashed to the ground hard enough to throw up a huge wall of swamp muck.

He fired shot after shot into the water as it crashed back down, and not waiting for the snake to go back on the attack, he charged forward again. Out rolled a wave of water—Hiral vaulted it—and the snake struggled to rise just beyond, more shots tearing into its skin as it rose.

Then, already in close before the thing really knew where he was, Hiral swept in and around it, barrels at point-blank range as he pulled the triggers as quickly as he could. Chunk after chunk of the snake's neck blew off with each blast, and the pain-addled thing made the mistake of trying to follow him as he strafed around it. By the time it realized it was just lining up his shots for him, it was already too late. White bone lay exposed, and blood gushed like a waterfall from its neck.

Rearing back, the snake spread its jaws, though they hung crooked from a broken hinge. Hiral held his ground, pouring power into a charged shot.

This is it!

The beast lunged forward, just like the other had against Nivian, and Hiral dove straight ahead, spinning in the air and aiming his weapons straight up. The wide mouth skimmed past, and as the grievous wound passed above him, he pulled both triggers, their shots exploding out like true cannons.

Without any muscle, scales, or spikes to protect it, the twinned blast punched through the spine like kindling, and then completely annihilated the flesh beyond. Torn in two, the snake's head flipped end over end into the air, while its back half rose up to hang almost vertical before gravity pulled on it like a falling tree.

With no way to stop it, Hiral rolled to his feet to get out of the way, but then everything just… sort… of… slowed… down…

What… is… happening?

A yellow notification sprang up as the shadow of the serpent's body fell.

Self-Buff: Enraged has ended.
All physical attributes reduced by 50% for 180 seconds.

Self-Buff: Eloquent has faded.
All mental attributes reduced by 50% for 180 seconds.

53

I GOT THIS!

THE muck gripped at Hiral's boots—his legs were too weak to force them free—and his brain couldn't do anything but look at them as the shadow above him grew.

Should... move... maybe?

Something grabbed his left arm and yanked, the suction of the mud *popping* as his boots left 'it, and then he was rolling on the ground. A second later came the vibration of something large hitting, and a wave of mud and swamp water washed over him.

Coughing out the disgusting fluids from his mouth and noise, Hiral wiped his face with the back of his arm and pushed himself to a seated position. The fallen body of the large snake was barely a few feet away.

Somebody... pulled me out of the way. Who?

He looked to the side as the muck burst upward, and a pair of all-too-familiar eyes looked at him. "So, let me get this straight," Right said. "*Improvising* included you taking on the **Elite** snake solo?"

"Wasn't planned like that," Hiral said, the inside of his head feeling like the thick swamp fog had seeped in and slowed all his thoughts. "It just sort of happened. I wasn't..." He cut off as a pair of yellow notification windows popped into view.

> **Congratulations. Achievement unlocked – Water Walker**
> **You crossed more than 50 feet of water without sinking.**
> *Please access a Dungeon Interface to unlock class-specific reward.*

I did?

A thought dismissed the window—he wouldn't know what the reward was without the dungeon interface anyway—and a second achievement window sprang to life.

> **Congratulations. Achievement unlocked – I Got This!**
> **You defeated a High-Ranking Elite monster**
> **of your Rank without aid.**
> *Please access a Dungeon Interface to unlock class-specific reward.*

"Hey, Hiral, you okay?" Seena asked, jogging over with the rest of the party behind her.

Hiral closed his notification window and gave her a thumbs-up.

"Uh… did he hit his head? He's got a stupid grin on his face for being covered in mud," Yanily said.

"Used *Eloquent* and *Enraged*," Hiral said, doing his best to scowl at Yanily. "Just recovering from the backlash. Do we have a minute?"

"Doesn't look like there are any more of those snakes," Seena said. "Left, can you keep an eye out for us?"

"Of course," Left said, and he took a step back from the group to look around.

"I only caught the tail end of it, but that was pretty impressive, Hiral," Nivian said. "Can you do it again if we run into another pair of the snakes?"

"Not unless we wait an hour for the cooldown on the buffs to finish," Hiral said, the fog in his head finally starting to clear a bit. "Even then, I'd say there was a whole lot of luck involved in this. How about you guys? How'd it go with the other one?"

"Good, actually," Seena said. "Seems it had these, uh… these kind of weak spots? Maybe that's the best way to describe them. Vix, check the one Hiral killed. See if it has the same thing."

"Gotcha," Vix said, and moved to inspect the snake's corpse.

"Oh?" Hiral asked.

"Inside of its mouths, for one," Yanily said, pointing inside his own mouth with his spear like he was going to bite it. "Straight to the brain."

"Guess you don't have that weak point, then," Nivian mumbled.

"This one has them too," Vix said. "Not in exactly the same places, but the scales look the same. And, yeah, they're softer."

"Soft scales?" Hiral asked.

"It's like it's a spot where the spines broke off," Seena said. "The scales and flesh underneath are almost… rotten. Hit that and it seems to do big damage."

"Should make fighting more of those that much easier," Hiral said, then looked at Right beside him. "How about we get out of this mud?"

"Think you can stand on your own?" Right asked.

"Not sure. Give me a hand?" Hiral said.

"Sure." Right hefted himself up, then pulled Hiral to his feet as well.

"Thanks, and… there we go. Debuffs are gone. Phew, that feels better." Hiral slid his *RHCs* back into place on his thighs, and stretched his arms above his head. "Ready to keep going when you are."

"Unless we want to fight more snakes, I suggest we move," Left said. "I see at least two pairs moving out there, like patrols or something."

"We could fight them for experience," Yanily said. "Though, it looks like we need to kill eight more to get to the next level of **Racial Growth**. Man, ten of those things is a lot."

"Better than having them at our backs," Nivian agreed.

"Do you think we could get past them without fighting, Left?" Seena asked.

"Definitely. They're following the same pattern over and over. If we time it properly, we can get past without either pair noticing us."

"Past to where?" Hiral asked.

"I can see an actual path over there," Left said, pointing. "Dry ground."

"*Dry* sounds pretty nice right now," Hiral said.

"If this is anything like **Splitfang Keep**, we should expect a **Mid-Boss** around here somewhere," Seena said. "Let's find and deal with it, then we'll take care of those snake patrols after that for the experience."

"Works for me," Yanily said.

"Left, lead the way with Nivian," Seena instructed, and the group got moving again. "Hiral, keep your eyes peeled for anything Left might've missed."

"Sure thing, boss," Hiral said, and Seena raised an eyebrow as she looked at him. "What? They all call you that."

"I know. Just sounds strange to hear you say it. Anyway, seriously, good job with that other snake. Reckless, *again*, but I can't argue with the results."

"It was trying to sneak up on Wule," Hiral explained. "Believe me, taking it on solo wasn't what I wanted either. Did get a couple of achievements from the fight, though, so it was pretty worth it."

"Achievements? Anything we can get easily?"

"Uh… crossing fifty feet of water without sinking, and taking on a High-Level **Elite** of my own rank solo. Doable?"

"The first one is just… What? How did you do that? The second is risky, unless the reward is really good. Let me know what you get from that, and we'll see if we can't figure out a way for the others to get it. Maybe back at **Splitfang Keep**, if we decide to reset it."

"I'll let you know," Hiral said, his eyes tracing one of the patrols Left had identified.

Just like his copy had said, the two snakes seemed to follow the same path around and around. Left timed the group's movement for when the snakes were the furthest away, so the monsters never even noticed they were there.

With that, a few minutes later, they were back on solid ground. They quickly moved away from the edge of the marsh before pausing again.

"Hey, what's that in the trees there?" Hiral asked, pointing to what looked like bones tied together and hanging from a scraggly branch. "Some kind of… totem or something?"

"The snakes are craftsmen?" Vix asked.

"If the Troblins can be, why not?" Yanily asked right back.

"No opposable thumbs?" Vix said flatly.

"There's another one over there," Left said, pointing. "And there... and there."

"They're evenly spaced out, almost like a line straight across. A border?" Hiral suggested.

"Let's find out what's on the other side," Seena said at the same time a chorus of *croaks* echoed through the trees.

"Oh, good. I was wondering where the lizards were," Yanily said, actually licking his lips.

"You're addicted," Vix said, branches cracking on both sides of the path.

"Here they come," Hiral warned as his *RHCs* came out.

"On our left!" Nivian shouted, blurring and appearing in front of Wule as a lizard launched out of the woods like it was ejected.

Despite the monster's velocity, Nivian braced with his shield, roots crawling out of his legs to connect to the ground, and the lizard stopped like it'd hit a stone wall, bones popping from the force of the impact. With a subtle shift of his shield while the lizard crumpled against it, the monster flipped up and over the party to land hard on its back.

Yanily moved without hesitation, spearing a barrage of strikes at the lizard's exposed belly, then leapt back as two more lizards appeared on either side of the first. As soon as his feet touched down, he lunged in again at the monster on the left, stabbing until the spearhead glowed purple. His next strike splashed purple fire across the lizard's body.

Hiral, meanwhile, leveled his weapons at the lizard on the right. His first shot bounced off a head spike, but the second scored a direct hit against the beast's eye, exploding it like an overripe orange. *Croaking* in pain, the lizard lurched to the side, whipping its tail around in a vicious sweep as Hiral dashed in with Right at his side.

Both men leapt over the swinging tail like it was in slow motion. Hiral cut out wide to pepper the lizard's flank in shots while Right landed, then immediately jumped straight up into the air.

With its remaining eye searching out the source of the stinging blasts tearing scales and spikes off its side, the lizard didn't even see Right's arm burst alive with purple light above it. The man twisted in the air, lining up his shot, then brought his fist crashing down like a piledriver on the lizard's skull. A column of purple fire erupted from the impact, reaching for the sky, and left the lizard's head a smoking, charred husk.

Still, the beast wasn't dead, and though it was now blind in both eyes, it lashed out with one of its foreclaws. The five-inch blades hit nothing but air— Right was far too nimble to be caught by a blind strike—then two of Hiral's blasts smacked into its blackened head. Charcoal-like flesh blew off to reveal the white of cracked bone, and Right followed the blasts in for another combo.

A left hook sent the lizard staggering to the side, then a right uppercut lifted the front half of it off the ground. His body still twisting from the punch, Right snapped his hip around and drove a powerful kick into the lizard's exposed underside. Bone cracked from the blow, and the lizard somehow managed to backpedal without falling over—until a ball of ice caught its right leg.

The leg twisted then snapped, and the lizard collapsed over backwards, two more balls of biting cold from Wule's rod striking its exposed size. A pained *croak* wheezed from its scorched mouth, and it tried to right itself, claws grasping at the ground for purchase.

Hiral blasted one of the claws, shattering the finger-like toes and bending them at awkward angles while Right stalked in.

Holding his hand above his head, Right poured solar energy into it. The fist burst alight with purple flame, then purified itself until a corona like a purple sun surrounded it. Energy smoked out of the Meridian Line running along his arm, then Right brought his fist down like the hammer of an angry god.

BOOOM. The blow cratered the ground under the lizard and blasted the air away in a visible sphere, rattling the trees and tossing aside fallen leaves and debris. And the beast itself didn't fare much better—its insides ejected out through its mouth, spewing gore across the side of the last lizard still standing.

With that, the entire party focused their attention on the remaining monster, and it was dead less than a minute later.

54

QUEEN OF THE SWAMP

"**G**OOD teamwork," Seena said, eyeing the three lizard bodies. "Anybody hurt?"

"No, but I think I'm going to need new boots," Yanily said, pointing at what had to be a gallon of lizard blood coating him from the knees down.

"How did you even manage that?" Seena asked.

"Skill," Vix told them. "Path continues straight ahead, or we could go into the woods. What do you want to do, boss?"

"I think I see more of those totems in the woods ahead of us," Hiral said. "Bigger ones. More complicated."

"What kind of bones do you think they are?" Seena asked.

"Probably a question you don't really want to know the answer to," Nivian said.

Seena looked at the tank, then nodded. "Probably. Okay. Keep going, but be careful. Expect a *Mid-Boss* at any point now."

"Right," Nivian said, leading the party further down the path until they stopped at the lip of some kind of natural bowl in the ground. No, a bowl wasn't right; it was more seashell-shaped, with a snake bigger than any they'd seen before coiled at the far, narrow end.

"It's like some kind of theatre," Hiral said, staring at the snake.

(Mid-Boss) Queen of the Swamp – Unknown Rank

"Or maybe an audience hall," Hiral amended. "*Queen of the Swamp*, huh? There's your *Mid-Boss*."

"I don't like this. What does unknown rank even mean?" Seena said, crouching down and motioning for the others to do the same. "The smokehouse and the summoning ritual had tricks to them. Even the *Troblin Duke* had that *Enrage* ability. And this snake is just sleeping in the middle there? No, there has to be more to it."

"Only one way to find out," Yanily said.

"Do you see any of those weak spots you were talking about?" Hiral asked. "What did you say they looked like?"

"Spots where the spikes had been broken off," Vix said. "Usually a bit red, and you'll know when you hit one."

"Red, huh? Okay, I think I see a few of those."

"Can you hit it from here?" Seena asked. "Maybe even kill it?"

"Maybe, but at this range, the shots wouldn't do much damage, even if I hit those weak points. Need to be much closer," Hiral said. "We're going to have to fight it on its home turf."

"Fine. Watch out for whatever tricks it might have," Seena said. "Snake, so squeezing or venomous bite, I guess? And it's going to be tougher than the others."

"Yes, yes. Enough talking. Can we go kill it?" Yanily asked.

"Wule, let's do buffs," Seena said before quickly casting *Lashing Vines* on the party, while Wule did *Nature's Blade*. "Left, can you drop your banner when we get down there?"

"Right where the snake is?" Left asked. "Keep its fifty-foot range in mind."

"Yeah, let's fight it where it is, for now," Seena said, then gave Nivian his customary tap on the shoulder. "Take it to the *Queen*."

Nivian's body blurred then stretched as he activated his movement ability, rushing ahead while the rest of the group climbed over the lip of the audience hall and started after him. Crossing hundreds of feet in seconds, he arrived even as the *Queen of the Swamp* lifted her massive head, then activated his *Swarm Tactics*.

Yanily and Vix vanished from where they ran and appeared right next to Nivian, immediately moving to the sides to flank the huge snake. As soon as the two damage dealers began to spread out, Hiral and Seena did the same thing, arcing out wide to attack from range, while Right and Left escorted Wule into the melee.

The snake blinked as she watched them, her head lifting, lifting, lifting into the air. Then, in a burst of motion, she uncoiled, and a swarm of smaller snakes flooded out from where they'd hidden inside the coils of her body.

Even though each snake was *only* six or seven feet long, there were dozens and dozens of them, and the wriggling wave swarmed at the three closest targets.

Hiral skidded to a stop, his *RHCs* coming up, and he began to pull the triggers as fast as he could, bolts of *Impact* racing out to pick off the snakes rushing at Yanily. His first shot caught one snake in the face, blasting its lower jaw off as it lunged at Yanily, but his second only hit the snake in its body. Scales and blood flew off, and the body curled around the hit, but Hiral was still too far away for it to be an instant kill. Even the jawless one was still moving, and both were already heading toward Yanily again as Hiral pulled the trigger again.

Need to be closer!

Still firing as fast as the weapons' cooldowns allowed, Hiral dashed forward, though he spared a quick look to see how the others were doing.

Seena pulsed with energy as she summoned **Spearing Roots**, the flaming pikes erupting out of the ground just in front of Vix to intercept the rush of snakes. But the lithe bodies of the serpents simply wound around the dangerous spikes, suffering little more than mild burns for the effort, and then they were at Vix.

Not that the pugilist was defenseless—the man whipped himself around like a dervish, the blades on his knuckles, heels, and joints carving through snake flesh with every motion. And, even when it seemed he'd missed a snake, the **Lashing Vines** struck out with deadly accuracy.

Nivian, meanwhile, constantly struck out with his whip to pull more attention toward him, then backhanded the closing snakes with his thorned shield or left them to the **Lashing Vines**. Even the snakes that did get through found the tank's bark-like armor too tough to penetrate, and serpentine bodies were already piling up at his feet.

That just leaves us, Hiral thought, focusing his attention back on the swarm around Yanily.

The *laughing* Yanily.

The man hooted with joy as he pivoted in place, his feet never leaving a small circle about three feet wide, and he struck out with his **Reed Spear Style**. Unlike Seena's **Spearing Roots**, Yanily's spear seemed to know where the snakes were going to try to slither to avoid his strikes. *Stab, stab, stab*. His weapon cut the attacking snakes to ribbons, and then his tenth hit exploded in a sphere of flames to char a whole group of his enemies.

Dying by the drove, the snakes still pressed on, heedless of their own wellbeing, and Yanily kept up his onslaught, another ball of purple flame hurling small snake bodies aside. Hiral blasted at the few who looked like they *might* get through, but all in all, the swarm of snakes wasn't nearly as dangerous as it had first looked.

That's it? That's the trick?

But, no, that couldn't be it. Could it?

Still absently firing at the horde of small snakes, Hiral looked up at the **Queen of the Swamp**. Her head **Lord**ed above the party like the royalty in her name.

Wait, why isn't she attacking with the others? The little ones aren't a distraction? Trying to weaken us or tire us out? That's not working, though. Could it be something else?

Hiral watched as the **Queen's** head swivelled left and right, alternating focus on Vix, then Yanily, then back to Vix. Over and over her attention changed, slowing for a second as it passed over Nivian—Wule, Left, and Right joining him—then continuing on to the damage dealers.

Why? What's she looking for?

Another purple ball of flame from Yanily, and the **Queen's** head snapped toward the spear wielder, her eyes narrowing.

She's watching who is killing the most of her children. That look in her eyes… it's the same as when Nivian hits something with his whip!

"The **Queen of the Swamp**," Hiral shouted to the others. "She's going to attack whoever kills the most little snakes! She's going to go after Yanily!"

That warning was all the party had. The **Queen's** eyes narrowed as she sprang at the spearman, dozens upon dozens of feet uncoiling in an instant. Mouth opening wide with fangs like swords, she twisted her head to the side and slammed her jaw closed on Yanily like a giant mousetrap. The *snap* of it sent a shockwave out that lifted the smaller snakes off the ground. The **Queen's** body tore a divot in the dirt as her momentum carried her forward—straight toward Hiral—and he looked at her mouth in horror, expecting to find Yanily hanging broken and bloody between her teeth.

Except… he wasn't there.

Where?

A glance to his left—all he had time for—showed Yanily and Vix beside Nivian, the trio carving up smaller snakes and looking past them to the **Queen**.

*Nivian used **Swarm Tactics**! Smart man.*

But that left Hiral alone and in front of the charging **Mid-Boss**.

Hiral pulled the triggers on his **RHCs**, bolts slapping into the **Queen's** forehead to shear off a couple of scales—it wasn't nearly enough to slow her down—and then, suddenly, her huge body twisted around as she changed course. Dirt flung in Hiral's direction like a wave from her sudden maneuver, and he threw his arms around his head—only to get barreled over by the sheer amount of earth.

Letting go of the **RHC** in his right hand, a quick pulse of **Rejection** pushed the dirt off of him, and he sat up just in time to see the **Queen** crash into the party. Nivian tried to intercept her wild charge, but she twisted again at the last second, body-blocking the tank's shield and sending him flying into the air. Then she swept around and shot straight toward Yanily, mouth wide.

Yanily, to his credit, spread his hands wide along the spear's shaft. He brought the weapon up and then down in front of him just as the snake crashed into him. Driving the spear right through the **Queen's** lower jaw, the tip burst out of the bottom, gouging a line in the dirt, while Yanily shoved the shaft lengthwise into the giant snake's mouth, propping it open.

That didn't stop the **Queen's** momentum from tearing him off his feet. The spear shaft crunched into Yanily with a *crack*, and the other party members leapt out of the way to avoid the same fate.

Furious at the wedge in her mouth, the **Queen of the Swamp** reared up, her thick body stretching thirty feet in the air, then began to thrash her head back and forth. Yanily swung side to side as he held on for dear life, the spear blade tearing further through the **Queen's** mouth with every jerk. Then, all of a sudden, purple flames erupted out of her mouth, and the **Queen** jerked her head back in pain and surprise. Yanily somehow held on.

The spear counted the thrashing as attacks?

Hiral grabbed his dropped **RHC** from the dirt as the rest of the party rushed at the snake's lower half, taking advantage of her distraction due to the spearman in her mouth. He blasted shot after shot right into the spot where the **Queen's** body turned to lift her head into the air, while Vix and Left went to work on her coiled length.

"Seena, she's not moving much!" Hiral shouted, another pair of his blasts finally penetrating the **Queen's** thick skin enough to do some noticeable damage.

"I know," Seena said, solar energy gathering inside of her and building, building, building. "There!"

Energy flooded out of her, huge **Spearing Roots** erupting from the ground in a semicircle in front of the **Queen's** extended neck. Trailing lines of purple flame, the razor-sharp tips slammed into the serpentine body and jerked it back. Thin lines of blood dribbled down from the impact points.

But it wasn't enough. The tips barely penetrated more than an inch, the **Queen's** thick scales protecting her from the worst of the attack, and the damage looked like nothing more than a ruby necklace.

Another thrash of the **Queen's** head, then one more, and finally, Yanily lost his hold. The spearman sailed up through the air to thump down on the ground with a pained grunt fifty feet away.

"Wule!" Seena shouted, the healer already moving in the spearman's direction.

But, as Yanily forced himself to sit up, the snake's head snapped in his direction again.

"She won't give up until he's dead!" Hiral shouted, realizing the extent of her fury.

"Or, until this!" Nivian shouted, wading into a group of the smaller snakes that had grown oddly still since the **Queen** had attacked. Back and forth his whip lashed, thorns tearing open serpentine bodies as the **Lashing Vines** on his back also went to work. Then, noting how the snakes weren't even fighting back, Nivian expanded his shield to the size of a tower shield and slammed it down on the mass of thrashing snakes. "Seena!"

"Got it!" she said, channeling a **Spearing Roots** into Nivian's shield at the same time the **Queen** rushed toward Yanily and Wule.

She hadn't even gone ten feet when the roots burst out of Nivian's shield and instantly killed dozens of smaller snakes. Her head snapped around with the familiar fury in her eyes.

"That got her attention," Hiral shouted, firing off more blasts as the **Queen** focused on her new target.

Nivian got to his feet and readied himself. Left, meanwhile, dashed in beside the tank and put his right hand to his left bicep. Solar energy stretched from his arm to his fingers until a flapping banner appeared in his hands, the insignia of a glorious sun practically glowing with power. Thrusting the base of the banner into the ground, a dome of energy burst out to encompass a fifty-foot radius around the **Banner of Courage**, and both Nivian and Left's skin seemed to shine.

Not in the least dissuaded by the new buff, the **Queen of the Swamp** lowered her head and bull-rushed ahead—straight for Nivian and his lowered shield.

"Right," Hiral shouted, sheathing the **RHC** in his left hand, "she's coming your way."

"You sure about that?" Right asked as he ran into the shimmering dome, then set his feet as glowing energy began to gather in his right hand.

"Yes!" Hiral answered, reaching out his left hand and focusing his **Rune of Attraction** on Yanily's spear in the **Queen's** mouth.

While the serpent herself was *far* too large for Hiral to ever pull, the way the spear dug into the **Queen's** mouth turned her to the side as she instinctively moved to ease the pain. One eye flashed angrily in Hiral's direction, like she knew he was the cause of the tug, but then her body *whooshed* past Right.

Glowing like a purple sun, and buffed by the **Banner of Courage**, Right's fist hit the side of the speeding **Queen** like a wrecking ball. Scales and then blood gushed out of the side of the **Queen's** mass as she raced by, her own momentum dragging the growing wound the length of her body. Then, as her mouth widened in shock at the new and sudden pain, Hiral's pull on the spear in her jaw yanked the weapon free.

End over end, it sailed to slap into the palm of his hand, and he immediately spun it around and drove it into the ground. Then he drew his second **RHC** and raced ahead.

This is it. Our chance.

Blood and gore gushed out of the **Queen's** side. She writhed on the ground, tossing up chunks of dirt with every movement, and then let out a pained cry that echoed through the forest. Her head whipped around at the party closing in on her from all sides, the focus from earlier lost to the haze of pain.

Left arrived first, his **Dagger of Sath** trailing a purple river of flaming liquid. He ducked under a tail swipe aimed for his head, then spun and drove the dagger into the **Queen's** long flank. All at once, the hanging stream in the air from the dagger raced ahead and then caught up to the blade, exploding out the other side of the **Queen's** frame and nearly cutting her in half.

Another roar of pain as Right and Vix arrived, their fists hammering her from opposite sides. Nivian's whip lashed across her face, one of the thorns catching an eye. Back snapped her head, and that was it—all fight left the **Queen of the Swamp**, and she flexed her muscles and sprang over the party. More blood showered the ground as the desperate maneuver taxed her already severely injured body, and she let out a pained whine when she hit.

For a second, it looked like she wasn't going to move again, but one last burst of strength dragged her ragged body to the narrow end of the audience hall. Beaten and battered, the **Queen** weakly lifted her head into the air and let out one last cry, then toppled over sideways, her one good eye slowly blinking.

"Is that it? Did we win?" Nivian asked.

"Is that *it*?" Yanily asked, limping over and leaning on his spear. "Try getting tossed across the dungeon next time and see if you still feel the same way."

"Yeah, well, at least we…" Nivian started, but a massive *CROAAAAAAAK* echoed through the sky, followed by the violent cracking of wood. It wasn't the cracking of branches, though; it was the cracking of *trees*.

"And there's your trick, Seena," Hiral said as a gigantic lizard leapt out of the woods to land beside the **Queen**, the ground shaking with its arrival.

The monster had to be as big as the four-story inn they'd stayed in, and a name appeared above its head as Hiral stared at it.

(Mid-Boss) King of the Swamp – Unknown Rank

"Uh, I don't even want to know what their children look like…" Yanily said, but he managed to heft his spear up into a ready position.

The **Mid-Boss** fight wasn't over yet.

55

KING OF THE SWAMP

Dynamic Quest
You've trespassed on his land and slain his beloved queen.
He will now pass judgment.
Survive.

HIRAL slapped the notification aside as the ***King*** stalked over to his fallen queen, the ground shaking with each step. A low, long *croak* crawled up his throat and vibrated through the air, a combination of loss and anger building as he nudged the giant snake's body.

"Plan?" Nivian asked. "That's going to be like fighting a building. Are we even going to be able to hurt it? Its scales look like shields."

"I have a plan," Hiral said. "Left, Right, come here." As soon as the two doubles got to him, Hiral reabsorbed them into himself, and then immediately used ***Foundational Split***. "You guys got it?"

"You're crazy," Right said. "I like it."

"And just like that, you know his plan?" Wule asked.

"Faster and easier than explaining. It looks like our time out is finished." Hiral pointed to the giant lizard turning in their direction, its scales literally turning from normal green to a vibrant and violent red.

"Aaaaaand it looks pissed," Yanily said. "What's the plan?"

"Like the dynamic quest said—survive," Hiral said, pulling Left and Right back into himself, then sprinting forward as the lizard began to lumber in their direction. If it was anything like the smaller lizards, it would be capable of huge bursts of speed, so Hiral needed to get to it first.

Of course, even if I get to it, my plan could very well get me killed.

"Don't be reckless!" Seena shouted behind him, but then Nivian was beside him.

"You need to get close?" the tank asked.

"Yes," Hiral said.

Nivian's shape blurred and stretched ahead as he used his movement ability. Within a heartbeat, he was in front of the lizard, and a notification appeared in front of Hiral's eyes.

Nivian wishes to bring you to his position with Swarm Tactics
Accept? Yes / No

Hiral hit **Yes** without hesitation, and reality warped and then kind of burped around him, and he found himself right in front of the massive lizard as it took a step in his direction.

"I don't have enough solar energy to do that again, so make it count," Nivian said, running off to the side and lashing his whip up at the lizard's gigantic head.

"I will," Hiral promised, dashing toward the lizard's left side.

Like its smaller brethren, the beast was covered with hundreds of spikes, the ones down its legs and shoulders too close together to climb, and far too sharp to risk it. Even the usual softer underbelly looked heavily plated, and there was always the danger the lizard would simply fall on anything attacking it from below. No, the only area where it looked safe to attack from *and* there was space for something as big as Hiral to fit was up on its back.

"Here we go," Hiral said half to himself, and half to his doubles, even though they would know what he was thinking as soon as he thought it anyway.

The lizard's back was too high to reach even with the aid of his **Rune of Rejection**, so he was going to need to get a bit creative. Slowing just a half-step, Hiral activated his **Foundational Split**—only putting one percent into each copy—and his doubles peeled off him to sprint ahead. No more than a few feet in front of him, they skidded to a stop and then leaned in to lace their fingers together.

Hiral leapt forward, his foot landing perfectly in their cupped hands, and they launched him into the air.

Still not enough. Hiral pulled his legs up, aimed his right arm toward the ground, and triggered his **Rune of Rejection**. The burst pushed him even higher into the air, but the angle wasn't right—he'd miss the lizard—so he cancelled his summons of Right. The tattoos appeared on his right half immediately, and then Hiral initiated **Foundational Split** yet again.

This time, though, instead of Right peeling off to the side like he usually did, Hiral forced the separation down his back. The double practically rolled off him from the shoulders, across his back, and then his legs, until only the soles of their feet were touching, almost like Hiral was standing on a reverse mirror of himself.

Then they both *pushed*.

Right shot for the ground at the same time Hiral arced up and over the lizard's back. He had the momentum and the angle, but then the lizard changed direction to follow Nivian. And that left Hiral falling directly toward the pointy ends of all the spikes.

Using his *Rune of Attraction* would just hurtle him even faster into the waiting spikes, so Hiral quickly cancelled his summons of Left, then initiated *Foundational Split* as soon as the tattoos reappeared. This time, when Left formed, Hiral pushed him away to the side of the lizard with his *Rune of Rejection*, then subsequently activated his *Rune of Attraction.*

Focusing on his own movement, Hiral yanked himself toward Left, then twisted in the air and again used his *Rune of Attraction*, this time on the side of one of the *King's* biggest spines.

"Oof," he grunted, slamming into the side of the spike almost as big as he was. *Better than spearing myself on it.* With a thought, he cancelled both Left and Right, then called them to his side again with *Foundational Split*.

"That was crazy," Right said.

"And reckless," Left added. "Seena will be… annoyed."

"Not after we kill this thing," Hiral said, already moving through the forest of spikes toward the front shoulders of the beast. "You know what to do."

"You got it," Right said, his fist glowing with purple energy, and the *Lashing Vines* on his shoulders already slapping ineffectually at the lizard. Then, without another word, the double moved ahead of Hiral, toward the head.

"Cooldown time left on *Banner of Courage*?" Hiral asked.

"Just a few seconds," Left said.

"Make sure you can get both of us, so move ahead a bit," Hiral said.

Left nodded and moved off, leaving Hiral alone, just slightly back from the thing's shoulders.

This looks like a good place to…

Powerful muscles under the heavy scales shifted, and Hiral dropped to his knees and activated his *Rune of Attraction* just in time as the beast surged ahead like an arrow. The wind whistled past Hiral and lifted his legs from the lizard's back, his body flapping in the wind while he focused on keeping his left palm glued to one of the large scales.

Then, just as fast as the *King* had accelerated, it stopped, hurling Hiral forward. Shoulder screaming in pain at the treatment, he had no choice but to cancel the hold of his rune and slam into the side of one of the large spikes.

Falling to the *King's* back on his head with a grunt of pain, Hiral flipped himself over and again activated his *Rune of Attraction*. Judging by the movement of the beast under him, it was attacking the other party members on the ground—he didn't have time to dally.

I hope Left and Right are okay, but I can't worry about them. I need to do my part.

Taking his *RHC* in his right hand, Hiral pressed it against the back of the *King of the Swamp's* back and pulled the trigger. The scale beneath the weapon bent but didn't break, so he pulled the trigger again. And again.

Again. Again. Again. Again. Again.

Just how strong is this damn thing?

A dome of shimmering light rolled across the lizard's back—and Hiral—a moment later, and then a purple pillar of flame leapt toward the sky.

I guess Left and Right are okay after all.

> **You have been buffed by Banner of Courage**
> **Critical Strike Rate increased by 5% for 180 seconds.**
> **Critical Strike Damage increased by 25% for 180 seconds.**
> **Minor Healing Over Time for 180 seconds.**
> **Minor Shielding granted for 180 seconds.**
> **Immune to Fear and Fear-like effects for 180 seconds.**
> **Solar Absorption Rate increased by 1 Rank for 180 seconds.**

A quick check on his buffs showed the banner buff stacked with the food buff, and then Hiral pulled the trigger on his ***RHC*** again. The scale beneath the barrel *cracked* on the first shot, but he wasn't anywhere close to done.

Holding on with his ***Rune of Attraction*** while the lizard attacked his party, Hiral pulled the trigger as fast as the weapon's cooldown would allow. Four shots later, the scale blasted into small fragments, and he pushed the barrel of the weapon against the ***King's*** exposed flesh.

And then... he. Just. Kept. Pulling.

Blood geysered out like he struck oil with every blast, each successive shot drilling deeper and deeper into the back of the lizard. Occasionally, he got shifted around as the great beast moved, but all that did was widen the hole he was blasting open.

At the head of the beast, two more pillars of purple flame reached for the sky, but then the lizard jerked to the side. That didn't matter—Hiral was up to his elbow in the lizard's back, and he didn't dare spare the time to worry about his doubles. His party needed him. Without the protection of the thick scales, his ***RHC*** tore the lizard apart from the inside.

Six more shots and he was lying flat against the great ***King***, his arm all the way up to his shoulder inside the horrific wound, green blood shooting up with every pull of the trigger, and his face covered in it. Another shot, and the lizard staggered, then stumbled to the side.

Hit something important, huh?

CROAAAAAAK! The great lizard bucked its back end up. Hiral held on for dear life with his ***Rune of Attraction.*** The landing *whooshed* the air out of his lungs as he slammed down, and then the lizard's front end hopped into the air. Back down, and another smash against the lizard's back, sending black specks floating across Hiral's vision. But he was still holding on, so he did the only thing he could: He pulled the trigger.

Blood gushed up his arm as the lizard leapt straight up into the air, the speed of the jump pressing Hiral hard against its back and burying his face in the open wound. Thick, coppery liquid forced its way up his nose and into his mouth, and then there was a second of weightlessness.

Hiral floated atop the back of the *King of the Swamp*, one hand stuck inside the sucking wound, the other firmly attached via his rune. The sky stretched out to the sides, and he barely caught a glimpse of the insidiously dark briar patch off to the side before the lizard beneath him began to drop. Connected as he was to it, Hiral had no choice but to go along for the ride until the landing once again drove him hard into the lizard's back.

He coughed out the air in his lungs as his face smooshed into the open wound, blood bubbling and spattering from his body ejecting his breath. Consciousness was getting harder to hold on to, and even one more slam like that last one would definitely break his concentration on his rune. Frankly, it was a miracle he'd held on as long as he had. He needed to either end this now or do enough damage the party could finish things from the ground.

He started firing like mad.

The *King of the Swamp* let out a wet-sounding *croak*, then dropped down to the ground with a *thud* that compressed Hiral's already-punished lungs and rattled his bones. But, since the blood was still warm—still moving across his arm—Hiral kept pulling the trigger.

Time became an incoherent concept. It didn't slow down or speed up, or even stop. It just… didn't matter. The *Banner of Courage* faded somewhere along the way, but it wasn't like he needed the critical bonuses by that point anymore. There was only Hiral and the trigger of his *RHC*. He pulled and pulled and pulled until, finally, something tapped him on the shoulder. One more blast—just to be sure—and Hiral turned his blood-soaked head to the side.

Left stood beside him, one eyebrow raised, then pointed at the gaping hole in the *King's* back. "I think you missed a spot."

"Is it dead?" Hiral asked wearily, then checked his solar energy capacity.

Three percent. He'd used almost his entire reserve sticking to the lizard's back and firing his *RHC*.

"It's been dead a while," Left said. "Right and I both got knocked off, though, so it took us some time to get back up to tell you."

"The others?" Hiral asked, pulling his arm out of the thick, goopy blood with a sucking *pop*.

"Minor injuries. Wule is taking care of them. The **King** seemed to have a lot of health, and speed in a straight line, but the party used hit-and-run tactics. Not much damage done to the **King**, but they mostly stayed out of danger. Your plan worked."

Hiral looked down at himself where he sat—he was practically covered head to toe in green blood—then back up at Left. "That's great. Just wish I had planned *this* part of it a bit better."

56

INCOMING!

"Looks like I got an achievement, though," Hiral said, extending his hand for Left to help him to his feet.

His double just looked at the blood-covered arm and took a step *back*. "We all got an achievement for completing the *Dynamic Quest*. Or, do you mean something else?"

"Something else," Hiral said, shaking his hand again and looking at it as purposefully as possible.

"Oh, fine," Left finally said. He took Hiral's hand and helped pull him to his feet, the blood all across his body already congealing and making every movement stiff.

"Thanks, bud," Hiral said before pulling Left in for a sticky hug. He let him go almost immediately, taking a moment to savor the shocked expression—*is that really how I look?*—then closed the first achievement window for the next to take its place.

A thought closed that notification window as well, and Hiral shook his head at Left, who was still just standing there looking down at himself. "Oh, don't be a baby." Hiral reached out and reabsorbed the double. As soon as his tattoos appeared on himself again, he activated **Foundational Split**, and Left appeared without a drop of blood on him. "There. Better?"

"Much better," Left said. "Let's go—I'm sure the others are waiting."

"Sure," Hiral said, being careful of his footing with each step on the bloody back of the lizard. When he got to the shoulder, though, he simply leapt off and slowed himself down with a well-timed pulse of **Rejection**.

"Show-off," Left called as he climbed down the hard way between deadly spikes.

"What *happened* to you?" Seena asked as Hiral walked over, painted in green blood from head to toe.

"I killed the **King**," Hiral said, glancing over his shoulder at the absolutely massive beast. Green blood leaked from the sides of its mouth and in a long stream in front, as if it'd coughed it out. "And kind of made a mess doing it."

"You're not kidding about the mess part," Yanily said. "Still, better you than me. That's never going to come off."

Come... off? Could that work?

Hiral looked at the rune on the inside of his right forearm, then thought about the blood covering his body and activated his **Rune of Rejection**. In the blink of an eye, the green stuff burst off him in all directions, leaving him spotless.

"Ewwww," a voice said.

"Hiral..." Seena said, a dangerous edge to her words, and Hiral looked up from his arm to the group around him.

Now he was the only one *not* covered in lizard blood.

"That... that wasn't how it was supposed to work..." Hiral said.

"You mean you did that on purpose?" Nivian asked, shaking his hand to try to get some of the blood off.

"Uh... no..." Hiral said. "Look, I can fix this. Just... everybody turn around so you're not facing anybody else." Then, one by one, he went around and rejected the blood off them. "See? Just like new," he said when he'd finished.

"I'm traumatized," Yanily said.

"Your boots are clean now," Vix pointed out.

"Not sure that was worth it."

"Hey, folks, I found something over here," Right called from behind the body of the fallen **Queen**. "It seems like another totem of some kind, but this one is different."

"Oh? Found something? Great, coming!" Hiral jogged over to his double, happy to get away from the blood soaking the ground—and the dirty looks everybody was giving him.

"What is it?" Seena asked as the others caught up.

"Take a look for yourself," Right said, pointing at the totem tucked back in the narrowest part of the seashell-shaped area.

A skull sat perched in the center of an X formed from two bones. All that was atop three more of the long bones lashed together and driven into the ground. Tendrils of some kind of root extended out of the earth, then up around the bones to crawl into the skull's eyes. The entire thing was covered in a writhing, inky darkness.

"Kind of looks like a staff stuck in the ground, or maybe a banner," Wule said.

"A super creepy banner," Yanily said.

"Those roots—I think they lead to that huge briar patch we saw from the entrance," Left said, crouching down and pointing at a barely visible line of shadows leaking out of the ground.

"The totem connects to it?" Seena asked.

"Looks like it," Left said.

"If this place is anything like *Splitfang Keep*, there will be one more *Mid-Boss*, and then the actual boss," Nivian said. "How much you want to bet that *Boss* is hiding inside the briar patch? The other *Mid-Boss* is probably guarding the other totem."

"And we'll need to defeat both of them if we want to complete the dungeon," Seena said. "You think we need to destroy this?"

"It's the first thing that comes to mind," Nivian said.

"I can do that, if you'd like," Hiral said, hefting up one of his *RHCs*. "Might be best if nobody actually touched that thing."

Seena looked at the rest of the party, and when nobody had any other suggestions, she gestured for Hiral to go ahead.

A quick pull of the trigger shattered the skull and totem into a thousand small pieces, and the line of shadow running along the ground completely vanished. At the same time, the earth at the edge of the seashell-shaped bowl in the terrain where the shadow had led collapsed to reveal a new path.

"Guess we don't have to circle back by the entrance," Seena said. "Okay, let's take a few-minute break to give everybody a chance to recover some solar energy, then we'll move out. We're not here to rush this dungeon run. We can worry about getting our best time on the third run. For now, let's learn everything we can, as safely as we can."

"Sounds good, boss. That last fight completely drained me," Nivian said.

"Ditto," Hiral added, and everybody turned to the huge lizard corpse.

"And yet you still had enough left to give us a lizard-blood shower," Seena deadpanned.

"I think a rest is out of the question," Vix suddenly said, drawing everybody's attention before pointing over to the new path.

People were rushing through the break in the bowl, weapons drawn and wearing armor with strange helms. No, that wasn't armor—those were their actual heads, and they had long, spiked tails trailing behind.

Humanoid lizards? Lizardmen? What?

"Do you think they're friendly?" Wule asked.

"Judging by the weapons and angry shouting, I don't think so," Seena said, the Lizardmen's guttural voices carrying over the distance to reach the party.

"They're my people!" Yanily said, stepping forward with his spear to point at the spears they carried.

"I can see the resemblance," Vix deadpanned.

"Enough jokes," Seena said. "We're all low on solar energy, but form up. We don't know how strong they are."

(Elite) Lizardman Warrior – High-E-Rank

"Definitely not pushovers," Hiral said, drawing his *RHCs* and falling in behind Nivian with Seena. Right and Left couldn't have much more solar energy than he did, but at only ten percent himself, he couldn't afford to split what he had. "They're *Elite* and the same level as us."

"At least we outnumber them," Nivian said, lifting his shield in front of himself and beginning to stalk toward the five rushing Lizardmen.

The four in front had, like Yanily said, spears lowered as they charged, but it was the fifth and final one in the back that got Hiral's attention. Unlike the leather armor the others were wearing, this one was dressed in a long black robe, skulls adorning its shoulders, and it carried no weapon.

(Elite) Lizardman Sorcerer – High-E-Rank

"Sorcerer? What's a sorcerer?" Hiral asked as the four lead Lizardmen closed within one hundred feet. "Can I shoot them?"

"Yes! What are you waiting for?" Seena snapped back, solar energy gathering inside of her.

Deciding to skip the snarky reply for the time being, Hiral lifted his *RHCs* and took aim. There'd easily be time for a couple of shots before they arrived, so all he had to do was…

The four bodies blurred and then stretched, exactly like Nivian did when he used his movement ability, and suddenly, the Lizardmen were *right there*. The first crashed into Nivian's shield with enough force to push the tank back a step before he could settle himself, while the second and third spun off to deal with Yanily and Vix.

And *spun* wasn't an understatement. Where Yanily was all stabs and thrusts, the Lizardmen's spears were a nonstop, spinning dance of bladework. It would've almost been pretty, if Hiral had time to watch. The fourth Lizardman had actually *vaulted* over Nivian, landing behind the tank, and was now rushing right for Wule and Seena.

"Help Yanily and Vix," Hiral ordered Left and Right, moving to intercept the fourth Lizardman.

Fast as it was, Hiral was faster, and he landed two shots into his opponent's shoulder and abdomen as he raced to intercept. The blasts staggered the monster to the side, throwing off its charge, and it turned in his direction at the same time he leapt into the air and pivoted. Up Hiral went as he snapped his hip around to drive his heel into the Lizardman's long snout with a flying kick, sending the monster stumbling back while he dropped back to the ground and raised his pistols.

That should... uh... get its attention?

Where he'd half-expected that to end the fight, the Lizardman in front of him snorted a gob of blood out of its nose and took its spear again in both hands, beginning to casually spin it as it glared at Hiral. Then it burst forward, spear swinging like a headsman's axe for his neck.

A line of fiery pain crossed the front of Hiral's throat, as he wasn't *quite* fast enough to duck back—though he'd kept his head attached—then he had to dodge left, right, left, as the Lizardman stalked forward, spinning the spear from hand to hand in vicious diagonal slices. Just as Hiral got the timing down, the Lizardman changed it up again, whipping the spear around behind its back and then horizontally across at waist height.

The strikes were too fast to even give him time to counterattack. Hiral threw himself to the side, the blade of the spear passing just an inch above his back, then rolled to gain some distance. It wasn't enough; the Lizardman was in the air with the spear driving straight down for his chest. Hiral leapt straight back, the spear's blade stabbing in the space just between his legs as he spread them apart, then rolled back over his shoulders and to his feet, ready to dodge again.

But the Lizardman stood where it had landed, pulling the spear out of the ground, and looked at Hiral. Behind it, the rest of the party was doing everything they could to contain the other three warriors...

Wait, what's the sorcerer doing?

Hiral turned in the fourth Lizardman's direction just in time to see a ball of fire the size of a watermelon hurtling straight toward him.

57

THEY THROW FIRE?!

FLAT-FOOTED from the surprise of something throwing a literal ball of fire at him, Hiral let his instincts take over, dropping the *RHC* in his left hand and activating his *Rune of Absorption*. Searing pain burned Hiral's palm before the flaming ball vanished, the rune on his left bicep going from its usual yellow to a fiery orange.

I did it... Ugh...

But the pain was still there, like the fire had raced up the inside of his arm, scorching his veins, and he grimaced at the same time he caught movement out of the corner of his eye. Ducking back just in time, a spear blade whipped past his face, and he spun low under the follow-up horizontal slash. With a mounting pressure building in his arm, like a waterskin getting close to bursting, he dodged a third and then a fourth strike—suffering a gash across his chest for his effort—but the final attack took the spear out wide, and he finally had an opening.

With the Lizardman's eyes on the *RHC* in his right hand, Hiral instead slammed the palm of his left hand against its armored chest, then released the hold he'd unconsciously had on his rune. Flame erupted out in a *whomp* that tossed the two combatants in opposite directions.

The explosion sent Hiral skidding along the ground and seeing stars, but he didn't have the luxury of time to recover. Left hand still stinging from the initial burn, he hauled himself to his feet and looked directly ahead to see the Lizardman warrior struggling to get up. The front of its armor was completely gone, the scales and flesh underneath a charred mess, with the white of bone showing. The injury from the fireball was horrific—*that would've been me*—but the beast was already pulling its spear up like it intended to continue the fight.

And to Hiral's left, the sorcerer had another ball of fire building above its upraised hands.

Have to deal with that first.

Hiral snapped his *RHC* in the sorcerer's direction and pulled the trigger. The bolt of force hit it square in the chest and knocked it back a step, just enough to disrupt the flames above it. Hiral looked back at the warrior in front of him.

Now to finish you off before the sorcerer recovers.

Up came his ***RHC*** at the same time the Lizardman warrior launched itself forward. A snarl on its lips and heedless of its own injuries, the warrior charged in, spear spinning around to actually deflect the first shot Hiral sent its way. Then the second… and the third.

That's… new…

And then the lizard was at him, spear swinging in for his head, but Hiral smoothly ducked under it and aimed his ***RHC*** at the creature's knee. *Pull.* The blast slammed into the side of the creature's leg, cracking the bone, and threw off its return swing.

I've got the timing of it down when we're in close.

Hiral slapped the shaft of the spear safely past him on the next strike, then pressed the barrel of his weapon against the inside of the Lizardman's elbow. *Pull.* The bone broke, but still the monster held on to its weapon, so Hiral ducked low and twisted around his opponent, back to back. *Pull.* He hit the sorcerer with another blast to keep it off balance as he stepped over the Lizardman's tail, then sidestepped a rising slash as the warrior tried to catch him. With its bum leg and weakened arm, the blow easily went wide, and Hiral spun around while activating his ***Rune of Attraction.***

Pain flared in his hand as he caught his other ***RHC***, but he ignored it and hopped up and over a low swing of the spear. As soon as his feet touched down, he went down into a crouch to avoid the next high swing, then tucked the barrel of his ***RHC*** under his left arm. *Pull.* This blast hit the warrior right in the center of its injured chest, ribs crackling like dry paper, and the thing finally stumbled back in pain.

Not giving it a chance to recover, Hiral sped after it, sidestepping the first attack, then ducking under the second to come up inside its guard, his left shoulder practically right up against it. Before it could bring its weapon back again, he drove his right barrel into the center of its chest at the same time he slammed the left barrel into the bottom of its chin.

Then he pulled both triggers.

The Lizardman's back exploded out as its head snapped up, and the body toppled to the ground while Hiral spun and aimed both ***RHCs*** at the sorcerer. Except the thing hung in the air from the dozen or so ***Spearing Roots*** punching through its body.

With that one obviously taken care of, he turned his attention to the others. Yanily and Left were finishing off the last one engaged with Nivian.

"Did I really see that thing throwing fire?" Seena asked, jogging over to join Hiral.

In response, he sheathed his ***RHCs*** on his thigh plates and showed her his burned palm. "You definitely did. And it hurt. Think Wule can do anything about this? Or this?" He pointed at the blood running down his chest. It wasn't deep, but it stung.

"For sure. Come on. The others are all injured too, so he'll probably use his group heal. Hey, Wule," she called louder to the healer, "Hiral needs some healing too."

"Get over here, then," Wule called back from beside Vix, who had a nasty cut down the length of his right arm. Yanily and Nivian both had more than one wound as well, and even Wule had blood running down the front of his leg.

"Left, can you keep an eye out for more of those Lizardmen?" Hiral asked, the double looking no worse for wear.

"Sure," Left said, jogging off to the side to get a better view of the path the attackers had come down.

"They were tougher than I expected," Seena said. "Skilled fighters. Like, *really* skilled."

"Nah, not that good," Yanily said from where he sat. "Just a style we weren't expecting. Once me and Vix got used to what they were doing, they got real predictable, real fast."

"Yanily's right. As soon as I had a feel for what it was doing, it wasn't hard to avoid," Hiral said.

"Says the guy with… How much dexterity and attunement do you have now?" Seena asked. "I'm surprised you got hit at all."

Hiral thumbed toward the sorcerer hanging on the **Spearing Roots.** "The one throwing fireballs kind of distracted me," he said flatly. "But, you've never seen these things before?" He thankfully sat down beside Yanily as Wule came over and began to use his group-healing ability.

"Never," Seena said. "What were they called? Lizardmen? Any of you heard of these?"

"Nope," Nivian said. "Thought the only thing in these parts were Troblins."

"Do monsters in the dungeons have to be from *around here*?" Wule asked.

"They have been so far," Hiral said. "But, what did Dr. Benza call these dungeons? Snapshots of time and space or something? I guess that means they must be from somewhere on the world, so we should expect to encounter them at some point."

"I was hoping we could get a hint at what we'd find inside the dungeons based on what was *outside*," Seena said. "Now, it means we could be walking into *anything*. I don't really like that."

"On the other hand, it kind of answers something else I was worried about," Hiral said with a chuckle, then continued when the others looked at him. "The fourth race. I was half-worried it was Troblins, since they were the only other humanoid monster I'd seen. Though, I guess you did mention something called Duggers, so maybe there wasn't really a worry."

"Can't say I'd want a Troblin in the party," Yanily said.

"You kidding?" Vix responded. "Did you *see* how clean that room in the inn was? We'd never have to worry about tidying up."

"Sure, and you want to pose for the art we found there?" Yanily shot right back.

Vix's mouth opened, and then the man visibly shivered. "Agreed. No Troblin party members."

"How's everybody doing on solar energy?" Seena interrupted.

"Could use some more time," Nivian said. "Those last fights completely drained me."

Hiral slapped himself in the forehead. "Sorry, guys, I should've thought of this sooner. Left! Hey, Left. Can you drop a *Banner of Courage* for us?"

The Growers all looked at each other, then their eyes widened as they each remembered the solar absorption rate increase that came as one of the banner's buffs.

Left gave another look at the path, then jogged over to the group and shaped the banner for them, though he stayed holding on to it after he drove it into the ground.

"Oh, yeah, that's the good stuff," Yanily said.

"Hey, Left, what're you doing?" Hiral asked.

"It seems the time limit on the banner buff doesn't begin until I let go," Left said, looking at his hand around the banner pole. "I noticed it up on the back of the *King*, and it seems to be holding true now."

"What? Seriously?" Hiral asked, but he quickly opened his status window. Just like Left said, there wasn't a timer beside the buff notification. "That's amazing. Nice catch!"

"It makes sense," Left said. "The other tattoos don't have timers after being shaped."

"You didn't know about this, Hiral?" Seena asked.

"Not like anybody else on the island has the *Banner of Courage* tattoo, so this is news to me," Hiral said.

"Very good news," Wule said. "A full extra rank of absorption will really speed up downtime, even when we drain ourselves dry."

"Staying in one place during a fight may be too risky, though," Seena said. "Let's limit using it like this to between encounters."

"Good idea," Hiral said, then motioned for Right to come over. "I can't get above thirty-three percent while you two are out."

"I could use a nap anyway," Right said. He reached out and took Hiral's hand, quickly dissolving into solar energy, and the tattoos reappeared on Hiral's body.

"What about Left?" Seena asked.

"Once we start moving again, I'll reabsorb him to get closer to full," Hiral said.

"S-Rank absorption, even without the cheating banner, is seriously like *extra* cheating," Yanily said.

"It'll let you take a look at the entire **Spear of Clouds** tattoo in one piece," Hiral said.

"Don't hear me complaining about your cheating. Nope, not one bit," Yanily said, actually rubbing his hands together.

58

SKILL EVOLUTION

Nᴏᴛ even ten minutes after they'd defeated the group of Lizardmen, the party was back on their feet. Everybody had at least eighty percent solar energy, and Left had been reabsorbed back into Hiral.

"Expect more Lizardmen," Seena said, then looked over at Yanily. "And what are you doing?"

Yanily spun his spear around in front of himself from hand to hand, slowly at first, but building in speed as he went. "That Lizardman spear style—it got me to thinking. My **Reed Spear Style** is so straightforward. Having another option could really... hah!" He stopped spinning his weapon and gave a fist pump. "Skill evolution!"

"You just learned the Lizardman spear style?" Vix asked.

"**Dancing Spear Style**, it's called," Yanily said. "Going to have to try this out a bit and train it up. Balyo is going to be *so* jealous."

"We can use that," Seena said. "You can teach it to Balyo *and* help prepare them to deal with the Lizardmen. Give them an easier time than we had."

"Awww, do I have to?" Yanily asked.

Seena crossed her arms *very* slowly.

"I'll show her first thing when we get back. Was totally planning to even before you said anything," Yanily quickly amended. "Ah, shouldn't we be going? Only two and a half hours until the dungeon forcefully ejects us after all. Hop, hop. Let's move."

Seena just shook her head, gesturing for Nivian to take the lead, and the tank quickly fell into his familiar position.

"You're telling me all of your fighting styles are taught through abilities?" Hiral asked as he moved up beside Seena in the group formation.

"Taught? Not exactly," Seena said. "As soon as we get the ability, we gain all the knowledge to fight. Our **PIMs** even automatically condition our bodies with the necessary flexibility and muscle memory. It's like we always knew how to do it."

"So, Yanily and Vix... they never had to train to fight like they do? It literally comes naturally?" Hiral said, his eyes wide.

"Yup. That's not how it works for you?" Seena asked, raising an eyebrow as she looked at him.

"Fallen's balls, no. I've trained for *years* to fight. Since I couldn't shape my tattoos, I spent all my time learning every way to fight I could find. With every weapon we had."

This time, it was Seena's eyes that were wide when she looked at him. "You're saying you don't have an ability that taught you how to fight like that?"

Hiral just shook his head.

"The way you move… it's all…?" Seena couldn't even finish her sentence, apparently.

"All practice. Hours and hours and hours and more hours of practice."

"That's absurd," Seena said.

"Pretty sure that's my line."

"What about your **RHCs**? You don't have a proficiency ability for them or something?"

"No. I'm just using a hand-crossbow style I learned," Hiral said. "These are honestly way better than that. I mean, I don't have to stop to reload, but the basics are the same. Mostly."

Seena just shook her head, but by that point, Nivian had reached the newly created path. "We'll pick this up later. If you learned to fight like that, maybe you can teach the rest of us. We'll have the time when we get to the *Asylum*."

"Sure. Then you can get some spontaneous abilities and show me how to do it better," Hiral said jokingly, but he drew his **RHCs**. "Let's finish this dungeon first, though."

The group climbed the slight slope where the ground gave way to find a heavy stone road leading off through the swamp.

Hiral's eyes instinctively followed the road as it passed through the scraggly trees, around behind the dark briar patch towering on the left, and further, further, further, to what looked like a city sprawling on the side of a mountain. And there, carved into the peak of the mountain, was a giant lizard with a snake intimately wrapped around it.

"Yup, they're going to be pissed," Yanily said.

"I don't want to fight a whole city of them," Vix said. "Can we *please* not fight a whole city of them?"

"Think of the experience."

"A whole city? In two and a half hours? It'll never happen," Wule said.

"I don't think we could even *reach* the city in two and a half hours," Hiral said. "It's miles and miles and *miles* from here. Is it actually part of the dungeon?"

"That would make it massively bigger than **Splitfang Keep**," Seena said. "And Hiral's right. That's too far. We should expect a **Mid-Boss** way before that."

"We following the road, boss?" Nivian asked.

"Yes, but watch out for ambushes," Seena said. "Hiral, keep an eye on the water. Just because there's a road, that doesn't mean we won't have to deal with more snakes."

"Gotcha," Hiral said, and the party started down the road.

They didn't have to wait long for the first attack. Another group of five Lizardmen came running down the road toward them barely two minutes later. Just like before, a sorcerer trailed behind four warriors, and it stopped to lift its hands in the air, where fire started to rotate above.

"I've got the sorcerer. Hiral, bring out Left and Right," Seena barked. "Nivian, grab as much attention as you can, and Wule, blast them with your rod until somebody needs healing. Vix and Yan, you know what to do."

"Got it, boss," they all said, practically in unison.

Nivian blurred forward into the group of four running Lizardmen while Hiral activated **Foundational Split**. The tank caught the first warrior with a heavy shield-bash, slamming it to the side and off the road to fall into the swamp. The second and third took lashes from his whip and turned angry eyes in his direction. The fourth, well… Hiral shot it in the face while it was distracted, and it fell back, where it rolled on the ground in pain.

Vix and Yanily were at Nivian's side a moment later, and a ball of solid cold sailed over their shoulders to slam into one of the warriors. With the four-on-two advantage for the party, Hiral turned his attention to the Lizardman in the swamp.

Already getting up in the knee-deep water, the Lizardman hefted its spear to join the fray, but Hiral's blast to its shoulder staggered it to the side. It took another bolt to the chest as it turned toward him, and then it got its weapon spinning in front of it. The dancing spear blocked Hiral's third and fourth shots, but now that he'd seen it a few times, he simply aimed lower and drilled the warrior in the knee.

With Left and Right running ahead to join the front line, Hiral calmly walked toward the Lizardman off the side of the road, pulling his triggers one after the other as he went. Around and around went the warrior's spear, still blocking three out of four of Hiral's shots, but every one that got through hit it with enough force to push it back a step.

By the fifth hit, the spear wasn't spinning nearly as fast anymore, barely blocking half the shots, and the tenth hit finally dropped it dead into the water.

Durable bastards. How are the others doing?

Like the first sorcerer, this one dangled on **Spearing Roots** that had burst out of the swamp on both sides of the road and impaled it in several very uncomfortable places. Two of the three warriors were on the ground and didn't seem to be moving, though the final one was somehow holding off both Vix and Yanily.

A quick aim and a pull of the trigger blasted the warrior's ankle out from under it, toppling it to the ground, and the two damage dealers leapt in to finish it off. A stab and a punch, and that was the end of the fight.

"Any injuries?" Seena asked.

"No," Wule said. "I went full offense there."

"These lizard guys really don't like those cold blasts you're using," Nivian said. "I had to work to keep their attention. Maybe they have a weakness to it or something?"

"It *did* seem to hurt them quite a bit," Wule said. "One of you should play healer, and I'll be a damage dealer for the rest of the dungeon," he added with a laugh.

"Make Left do it," Yanily said. "He can walk around with that banner."

"In all seriousness," Seena said, "that was really well done. Much better than the first run-in we had with them. Good job, all. Hiral, did I see that one blocking your shots?"

"Yeah," Hiral said. "I got used to it, though. Their spear style is fast and versatile, but it's also pretty predictable. I won't have as much trouble with the next ones."

"Unless they change things up, I don't think those groups will pose much of a threat again," Nivian agreed.

"True, but..." Seena started.

"Don't get cocky," they all said in unison.

"We know," Nivian added with a smile.

"Oh, look. More experience is coming," Yanily said, pointing toward another distant group of five Lizardmen running down the road toward them.

"They won't get to us for a few minutes," Hiral said, looking at the distance. "Actually, it might even be around the same amount of time as between the first two groups."

"Like the endless Troblins we faced in **Splitfang Keep**?" Seena asked.

"Except these are **Elite**," Hiral said.

"**Elite** experience, you mean," Yanily corrected.

"Okay, team, time for a little farming," Seena said. "Let's find out if they'll just keep coming, or if there's a limit to them."

"Yes!" Yanily said, and the party took up positions to wait for the Lizardmen to arrive.

59
BOWS VS. RHCS

HALF an hour—and three more dead groups of Lizardmen—later, the party finally decided to move forward while they reviewed what they'd learned.

"Groups in ten-minute intervals, and always four warriors and a sorcerer," Left recounted. "The sorcerer's fireball ability is pretty powerful, but slow to activate."

"Even slower than my *Spearing Roots* was before I got this circlet," Seena said, pointing at the equipment she'd gotten from *Splitfang Keep*.

"Which makes it easy to deal with, if the warriors don't occupy our attention," Left agreed.

"Not much chance of that, now that we know their attack patterns and abilities," Nivian said. "Yan, what do you think of their spear style? Can you make use of it?"

"For sure," Yanily said. "And I think it'll mesh with Balyo's current style even better. She's mainly just got single, hard-hitting attacks. This'll give her something to work with while she's getting into position to set up. For me, I think it'll be a little better than my *Reed Spear Style* if we're dealing with multiple enemies."

"Good to know," Seena said. "Nivian, any trouble keeping their attention on you?"

"Other than Wule and how much they seem to hate the cold, not at all. A single hit with my whip or shield will keep them on me. I don't think Lonil will have any problem with it, if that's what you're asking about."

"It is, thanks. You all know my sister's party and their abilities. As we're finishing off this dungeon, keep them in mind. How can they make things easier? What are their strengths? Weaknesses? If Lonil is back at peak, it shouldn't be a problem. If he isn't, well, anything helps."

The group nodded while they continued jogging down the stone road.

Hiral could already see another Lizardman group running in their direction—right on schedule—but it would take several minutes for the two groups to meet in the middle. In the meantime, he looked to his left at the towering briar patch that stood only fifty feet away. The darkness crawling between the plants was anything but natural, stretching almost like thick webs to completely obscure what little space existed between the twists and thorns.

If the totem they'd destroyed before had something to do with the darkness, it was only partially responsible. There had to be at least one more. Probably with the second dungeon *Mid-Boss*. But, it was strange. The roots under the darkness looked almost… sick. Corrupted. Like the darkness was feeding on the life of the plants even as it reinforced them.

*Why would the dungeon protect the **Boss** like this? No, that's not the right question. This dungeon is a snapshot, which suggests it is, or was, real. So, why would the Lizardmen protect something like this? And if they worship the **King** and **Queen of the Swamp** like those statues on top of the mountain suggest, why weren't they protecting them more?*

I'm missing something. What is it?

"The road splits ahead," Left said, drawing Hiral's attention from the briar back to more immediate concerns. "Straight seems to go toward the city, while left wraps around the briar patch."

"Which way should we go?" Nivian asked.

"I'm all for the experience of taking on a whole city," Yanily said. "Buuuuuut…"

"Let's go left," Seena said. "Something about that city feels off. Does it actually look like it's getting closer at all? I swear it hasn't changed a bit. Even the clouds above the mountain look like they're in the same place."

"Now that you mention it, you're right," Hiral said. "It's almost like it's a painting."

"Maybe the city isn't actually real?" Wule suggested. "We don't know the boundaries of these dungeons. If *that* city and all its inhabitants were actually part of this, that would suggest the dungeon is bigger than Fallen Reach. I can't even imagine how much solar energy it would take to do something on that scale."

"All the more reason to go left," Seena said. "But… I've got an idea for after we finish this run."

"What's that?" Nivian asked.

"We'll talk about it later. For now, let's take out that next patrol, then we'll head down the other path and hope we don't get attacked from both sides at the same time."

"Speeding up?" Nivian asked.

"Speeding up," Seena confirmed, and the party went from a light jog to a spirited run. Within a minute, they met the Lizardman group and crashed into them like a battering ram.

During the last three fights, they'd worked out tactics that trivialized the encounters. Seena took care of the sorcerer in the back with her *Spearing Roots*, while Nivian made sure the four warriors were either focused on him or on the ground. Hiral and Wule supported from behind, their ranged attacks mainly intended to distract or disrupt the Lizardmen's concentration while the damage dealers did their jobs.

Working together like that, the fight was over before it ever really began, and within a minute, five Lizardmen bodies lay bleeding on the stone road.

"You seriously kept shooting them in the feet?" Yanily asked as Hiral and Wule caught up to the close-range fighters. "I almost feel bad for their little scaly toes. Lizardmen have toes, right?" he quietly asked Vix.

"It worked, didn't it?" Hiral pointed out, but Seena was already urging them to get moving again. "I can see the next group, but they're pretty far off."

"Let's keep the pace up to put some more distance between us," Seena said, pointing down the fork in the road just ahead. Like Left had said, it curved around to the other side of the briar patch.

"You got it, boss," Nivian said, running ahead and down the fork.

The group didn't have any trouble maintaining the pace, though Hiral kept an eye on the city in the distance and the Lizardmen running in their direction. Oddly, kind of like Seena had said, no matter how he looked at the city, it always appeared exactly the same.

Definitely something strange going on there. I wonder where it really was... and if it's still there. There's so much about this world we don't understand. Will these dungeons actually make us strong enough to get some of those answers?

A quick check of his status window showed he'd reached level 18 at some point since they'd entered the dungeon, and he quickly let his **PIM** auto-allocate points into **Dex** and **Atn** while he ran. That still left him with 18 unspent points.

Need to stop procrastinating and just spend those.

"After we get out of this dungeon," he mumbled to himself, then turned his attention ahead. "What's that?" he asked louder, stone walls now visible off to the right side of the road as it continued to curve around the briar.

"I see roofs over the tops of the walls... Oh... and Lizardmen manning those walls. A town?" Nivian asked, slowing down as the Lizardmen lifted bows to take aim at the approaching party.

"They aren't shooting at us?" Yanily asked.

"Still too far away to be accurate," Hiral said.

"What about for your **RHCs**?" Seena asked.

"Also too far," Hiral said. "I only count four archers. Two on each side of... Is that a gate?"

"It's seen better days," Vix said, and the pugilist wasn't wrong. Maybe it had been a gate at some point, but now it looked like something had torn the whole section of wall out to leave a thirty-foot gap.

"That hole in the wall is our entry point," Seena said. "***Mid-Boss*** must be in there."

"And the archers?" Wule asked.

RUNE SEEKER

"Worried you'll have to actually heal?" Yanily asked.

"Worried I'll get an arrow in the eye, thank you very much," Wule said.

"Would that be considered a debuff?" Yanily wondered aloud.

"Blindness?" Vix said.

"I'll do what I can about the archers," Hiral said to Wule before he whacked one of the damage dealers over the head with his rod.

"And I'll help with my **Splinter Storm**," Seena said. "Need to level it up anyway. But I'm sure they'll get a few shots off, so don't slow down once we get going."

"Probably more warriors inside as well," Nivian added.

"And the road continues on past the town, or whatever it is," Left said. "Back toward the entrance of the dungeon?"

"The left path from the beginning," Hiral said. "Makes sense."

"Everybody ready? Good on solar energy?" Seena asked.

The party members all nodded, and Seena gave Nivian the shoulder tap, setting the tank in motion.

Unlike the usual formation, Hiral hurried ahead to keep pace with Nivian, one **RHC** out in his left hand, but his right empty, and solar energy gathering in his **Rune of Rejection**. The tank raised an eyebrow in question at his presence there, though he didn't say anything. At about three hundred feet from the corner of the town wall, the first Lizardman let an arrow fly.

Hiral nudged the arrow in the air with his rune—easy from this distance—and it flew wide. The next arrow followed a few seconds later, also pushed aside, and then the third and fourth. One at a time, they were no problem, but now all four archers drew back their bows and lowered the angle of their shots at the much closer party.

The arrows would come all at once—and faster—so Hiral threw out his hand and released a constant cone of **Rejection**. With solar energy quickly draining at a rate of one percent per second, it was an expensive tactic, but the arrows jerked off in wild directions as soon as they hit the edge of the cone.

"I can't shoot and deflect the arrows at the same time," Hiral said, the constant application of his rune taking more concentration than he'd expected.

"On it," Seena said, a barrage of splinters shooting toward the nearest Lizardman.

Most of the small projectiles bounced off the archer's tough hide, but a ball of concentrated cold followed and splashed into the Lizardman's chest. *That* got its attention, and it staggered back while it swiped at the ice with its free hand.

Ignoring their comrade's pain, the other three archers let loose their arrows—easily deflected by the wall of **Rejection**—but then they did something strange. When they drew their bows again, they held the arrows back. Energy began to gather in the arrowheads as they strained to delay their release.

368

"Some kind of special attack," Yanily shouted.

"Can you block it?" Nivian asked.

"Don't want to risk it," Hiral said, sheathing his **RHC** and cancelling his **Rune of Rejection**.

Then he threw out his left hand to pull on the arrows with his **Rune of Attraction**. Already straining against the force of whatever they were doing, two out of the three arrows popped out of the archers' grips to clatter to the road below the wall. That still left one charging arrow—the furthest away—and a ball of energy as big as a watermelon coiled in front of the archer.

Hiral reached out for the final arrow, but he was too late. The projectile shot ahead, screaming through the air like the screech of a hundred dying cats—straight into a wall of **Spearing Roots** that burst out of both sides of the road to meet in the middle.

The arrow hit the roots with a cacophonous *BOOM*, shredding the wood and sending purple flaming splinters in every direction. Nivian, fast as always, shifted in front of the party with his shield now as big as he was, and absorbed the worst of the fallout.

With more likely on the way, Hiral dashed around the tank and through the smoke hanging in the air from the strange explosion, his **RHCs** coming out along the way. As soon as he broke through to clear air on the other side, he lined his barrels up with the second archer on the wall. One blast smashed the bow into two separate pieces, while the second shattered the archer's wrist.

One down.

A whistle through the air, and Hiral flipped himself to the side just in time to avoid the arrow that would've gone straight through his chest. The moment his feet touched the stone, he pivoted and went back the way he'd come. A second arrow was already blazing toward him. He aimed his weapons back at the furthest archer, who was once again gathering power in front of its bow.

His twinned bolts of **Impact** collided with the growing black ball of energy to release a *KA-BOOM*. Just like that, a massive explosion engulfed the entire far corner of the wall.

That just leaves you, Hiral thought as he shifted his **RHCs** to the lone remaining archer and pulled the trigger on the weapon in his right hand. His bolt of **Impact** met the archer's arrow midflight, shattering the arrowhead and the shaft behind. Then the bolt from his left weapon slammed into the center of the Lizardman's forehead.

The archer's eyes visibly crossed from the stunning blow to the head, and Hiral's next two shots hit it simultaneously in the center of the chest, knocking the Lizardman back and over the edge of the wall. With weapons still trained on the top of the wall for movement, and the pounding of feet on the stone behind him, Hiral skidded to a stop.

"Reckless!" Seena scolded him as the others caught up.

"The smoke from the explosion covered me, but we can talk about it later," Hiral said. "I don't think I finished more than one or two of them off."

The first archer that had been hit by Wule's cold blast stood up on the wall. With two trigger-pulls, Hiral shot the Lizardman in the arm and the side of its face, dropping it back to the ground.

"Warriors incoming," Nivian said, taking his position at the front of the group. Charging Lizardmen were visible through the gap.

And there, at the far end of the street in the small town, stood a thin Lizardman in shimmering black robes. A thick, dark tome floated in the air to its right, and it held its left hand out to the side, balls of flame roiling into existence in a line above its outstretched palm.

(Mid-Boss) Sssolasss the SsScholarly Sssealer –
Unknown Rank

60

THE SSSCHOLARLY SSSEALER

Dynamic Quest
The Ssscholarly Ssssealer plans to teach you a lesson.
Sssurvive.

T EN balls of fire, each as big as an apple, hung in a line in the air above the *Scholar's* open hand. The tome on his right opened, pages flipping in quick succession. The Lizardman's eyes watched the pages until they stopped, and it gave a slight nod, then turned its attention to the party standing at the breach in the wall.

"Punch through the warriors to get to the *Mid-Boss*," Seena instructed, reaching for Nivian's shoulder. "Hiral, you got a shot?"

"Not a good one. At two hundred feet, my *RHCs* won't do much more than annoy it," Hiral answered, but then the *Scholar* lifted its left arm in front of it, the balls of fire following. "What's it…?"

Balls of flame shot forward like meteors, the first tearing through the back of a Lizardman warrior like it was made of wet paper. Blood and viscera exploded out, but the other warriors didn't even flinch. The next flaming projectiles shot over their shoulders or between their running bodies, down the long street, and raced ahead with deadly intent.

"Look out!" Nivian shouted, stepping in front of the group as the first fireball arrived with an explosive *WHOMP* against his shield that sent the tank flying backwards into Seena and Wule.

Hiral tossed out a wave of *Rejection* in front of the trio as they hit the ground, but it had startlingly little effect on the fiery assault. Still, it was *just* enough. The nearest fireballs changed their angles to slam into the road ahead, against one of the walls, or shoot just barely over the party members' heads.

"Get to cover. Behind the wall," Hiral ordered them, pulling the trigger to blast the closest Lizardman.

He dove to the side as the next fireball whipped down the street. A glance back found Nivian, Wule, and Seena still getting untangled in the middle of the road, and Hiral poured power into his *Rune of Rejection*, unceremoniously sweeping them out of the way in a tangled mess of limbs and shouts.

And not a moment too soon. Explosions rocked the wall and crashed into the center of the road where the party had been, flames billowing ten feet in the air and sending out a wave of scorching heat with each impact.

He paused for one second, two, three… five, waiting for more explosions. When none seemed to be coming immediately, he blew out a breath and checked on the others.

"Sorry about that!" he shouted over at the rest of the party on the other side of the breach.

"It's fine," Seena shouted back, finally free of Wule and Nivian. "Thanks for the save. How often do you think it can do that?"

Another flaming barrage answered the question—ten explosions shook the ground in quicker succession than the first time.

As soon as the last sphere of fire faded, Hiral held up a finger to ask the others to wait, then peeked around the corner to see if the *Scholar* had moved. He almost got a spear in the face for his trouble.

Hiral fell back as the spear's blade scraped along the stone where his head had been, and hip-fired the *RHC* in his left hand as he hit the ground. The impact shoved the Lizardman warrior right back as it rounded the corner, but it recovered quickly and readied its spear to impale Hiral where he sat on the ground—until a thorned whip snapped around its neck. From across the gap, Nivian hauled on his weapon, tightening the noose on the warrior and hauling the monster into the road.

Too bad for it.

The first fireball took the warrior through the knee, completely shearing it off, while the next two went into its chest, leaving holes big enough to crawl through in their wake. The body dropped to the ground just in time for a concussive wave from another fireball to lift it into the air and toss it out of sight. Two seconds later, another Lizardman—burning like a torch from head to toe—staggered out of the breach between the walls, then collapsed to the ground, where it continued to twitch and burn.

"Note to self…" Yanily said, the entire party frozen while they looked at the burning Lizardman. His words carried clearly in the strange stillness between barrages of fire. "Don't take this guy's lessons."

"Plan, boss?" Vix asked.

"Wait for the next salvo," Hiral said, holding up his hands to make sure nobody looked around a corner. The next bombardment came seconds later— *thirty seconds between the first fireball of each barrage; that's a tight window*. He waited a few seconds to make sure there weren't any trailers, then glanced around the edge of the wall, ready for another spear. None this time. *Lucky?* Not for the closest Lizardmen—half a dozen bodies were burning in the street. Further down, another pack of warriors swept out of a side alley to rush mindlessly toward the gap.

As for the *Scholar* itself, balls of fire were forming over its left hand while Hiral watched. *One every three seconds. Does it need to wait for all ten to attack?* With only six formed, Hiral stepped out into the open and aimed both his *RHCs* toward the *Scholar*. Sure, they wouldn't do much damage from that range, but…

The *Scholar's* eyes narrowed at seeing Hiral standing so obviously. A seventh ball of fire appeared above its hand, yet it still didn't attack.

Perfect.

Hiral pulled both triggers, his bolts cutting through the air straight for the *Scholar's* chest… until one of the Lizardman warriors leapt in front of the attack. Chest caving in under the force of the dual blast, the monster fell back while the eighth ball of fire formed. There was still time, so Hiral pulled the triggers as soon as the cooldown on the weapons ended, aiming to do some damage to the *Scholar* before it could attack again.

Except another warrior jumped in front of the blasts, its body crumpling to the ground as the ninth fireball took shape above the *Scholar's* hand.

Hiral was already pulling the triggers again, this time alternating left and right firing so a steady stream of blasts raced down the street. And yet, somehow, there was always a warrior there to take the hit before the bolt got anywhere near the *Scholar*. Whether it was one of the ones standing up from where it had been on the ground, or another dashing out of the side alley, Hiral couldn't get a shot further than about halfway.

Then, with a cruel snarl of the *Scholar's* scaled lips, the tenth fireball appeared above its hand, and the whole line of them burst straight for Hiral, one after the other.

Hesitating just a heartbeat, Hiral watched the fireballs practically incinerate the line of Lizardman warriors racing down the street, then he dove back behind cover. The roaring spheres of fire shot past where he'd just been standing, exploding in great plumes in a line along the road and the swamp beyond, while waves of heat rolled outward.

As soon as the last lick of flame subsided, Hiral jumped to his feet and dashed across the gap in the walls to join the rest of the party.

"What was *that*?" Seena asked him.

"I had to test some theories," Hiral said. "Just one more thing I need to know, then I'll explain what I think we have to do."

"What do you need to know?" Wule asked.

"A few more seconds," Hiral said. "Shouldn't have any warriors coming through the gate, but watch out, just in case."

"A few seconds for what?" Nivian asked, sharing a look with his twin.

Hiral held up a hand for patience, and then a barrage of fireballs shook the walls and ground in answer.

"Every thirty seconds, no matter what, it does *that*," Hiral said. "It takes about three seconds for it to form one fireball, and for whatever reason, it won't—or can't—attack until it has all ten ready."

"I saw you shooting it—did you do any damage?" Seena asked. "Can you bring it down in those thirty-second intervals?"

"No. One of the Lizardman warriors always took the hit before the shot even got halfway. And the *Scholar* doesn't care if it hits its own kind, so we can't use them as a shield."

"Then, what? We need to get to the *Scholar* in the thirty seconds between attacks?" Nivian asked. "I can do that with my movement skill."

"Does your skill get cancelled if you hit anything?" Hiral asked.

"Yeah," Nivian said. "You think the warriors will block me?"

"I do. And, given the warriors on the street, I'm sure they'll do everything they can to slow us down, or maybe even *hold* us down for the *Scholar* to blast us. That said, there are alleys between the buildings on both sides of the street. I think our best bet is to aim for one of them during the thirty seconds between attacks…"

Hiral paused his idea while the next barrage of fireballs thundered against the wall and road. After it finished, he continued. "Side alleys. If we can get to one, we might be able to circle around behind the *Scholar* without having to deal with his attacks."

"And if we can't, do you think there are enough alleys for us to alternate between to get to the *Scholar*?" Seena asked.

"From all the warriors I saw, yes," Hiral said. "Like the road over there, or the Troblins on the top level of the keep, I don't know if there's a limit to how many warriors will come. We probably can't simply wait for them to run out."

"Okay, after the next…" Seena started, only to cut off as a pair of warriors rounded the corner and lunged at the party.

Nivian intercepted the first, parrying aside the spear with his shield, then straight-kicked the warrior in the chest. The blow didn't seem to do much damage, but it did knock the Lizardman prone to the ground in the middle of the road. Hiral hit it with a pair of blasts to keep it there.

Meanwhile, Yanily caught the second, fluidly redirecting the spear out to the side with his own, which opened it up to a vicious combo from Vix. Abdomen, chin, then temple. The three hits dropped the warrior down to its knees, where Vix grabbed it by the back of its head and pulled it into a rising knee of his own. The body tumbled to its side on the ground, and Yanily put his spear through it for good measure.

"Sorry for the interruption," Yanily said, giving a small bow to Seena. "You were saying?"

"Right. After the next…" she started, then a barrage of fireballs tore down the street, turning the Lizardman lying there to ash.

Seena sighed. "Oh, for the love of… After the next, next fireballs, we go. Hiral, you have the best eyes and you've watched the Lizardmen coming out of the alleys. Can you get us to one?"

"Absolutely," he said. "Left, Right, I'll take you back in with me. We don't know how much room we'll have."

The two doubles nodded, then took Hiral's hands to get reabsorbed.

"Wule, give us *Nature's Blade*," Seena said, then did *Lashing Vines* herself. "Okay, everybody, get ready."

The party members took their usual positions, other than Hiral stepping ahead of Nivian.

"Any second now," he said, and the predictable stream of fireballs exploded in a line down the road.

"Now!" Hiral shouted before the last flames even faded, dashing into the road and around the wall.

61

CLASSS ISSS NOW IN SSSESSSSION

HIRAL shot the two closest Lizardmen in the ankles, dropping them to the ground, then ran straight for the *Scholar* at the end of the street. Nivian appeared beside him, shield-slamming aside a warrior materializing from the darkness out of one of the alleys, and just like that, they were thirty feet closer.

A quick look at the *Scholar* showed five fireballs already formed above its hand, and a vicious scowl on its inhuman face.

Fifteen seconds. We'll never get all the way.

Left and right his head snapped, looking for an alley big enough to hold everyone and… There! He cut hard to the right, two more shots kneecapping a warrior barrelling down on them, then waved for the others to hurry over.

"Get in, as far back as you can," Hiral said, noting the eight fireballs above the *Scholar's* hand. "And watch out for lizards appearing in there!"

Nivian skidded to a stop beside Hiral while the party ran in, but the *clang* of metal on metal drew the tank inside right away.

That just left Hiral, who popped off a quick shot toward the *Scholar* only for it to get intercepted by a lunging warrior. The tenth fireball wound into place above the *Scholar's* hand, and Hiral didn't wait for what he knew was coming. He dashed into the alley behind the others.

Ahead of him, Yanily and Vix fought in close with a pair of warriors, the two Growers quickly gaining the advantage. Nivian charged in to completely turn the fight in their favor.

"Incoming!" Hiral said, a heartbeat before the barrage of fireballs smashed into the side of the building and ground where he'd just been standing.

The explosive force of the eruption lifted him off his feet and hurled him forward. The skin on his back singed, and then he hit the ground, rolling by reflex to absorb the impact. One, two, three times he rolled before hitting a wall and coming to a sudden stop.

Wule was already rushing over to him. "I've got you." Warm energy pulsed off him to heal the burns on Hiral's back, along with the small bruises, before the pain even really registered.

"Thanks," Hiral said, pushing himself up. He looked at the shadows in the far end of the alley as a Lizardman emerged.

"It's like they're coming out of thin air," Seena said, solar energy gathering. "Fall back!" she barked, and Nivian, Vix, and Yanily quickly hopped backwards a second before a barrage of **Spearing Roots** burst out between the shadows and the party. "That should buy us a minute or two. Hiral, you okay?"

"Wule fixed me up," Hiral said. "We'll wait a barrage or two, then head back out. Probably another alley."

"Nivian, I want you going in first next time," Seena instructed even as two more warriors formed out of the shadows, impaling themselves on the spikes before they even realized what they were doing.

"Ready when you are," Nivian said to Hiral.

"Okay, it should be just about time to…" Hiral started, then cut off as most of the wall of the building they hid behind exploded in a shower of fire and debris. Hiral twisted and got his arms up in front of his head to block the worst of the rain of battering rocks, but circles of pain erupted all along this right leg and side.

There was a sound like a blade whistling through the air, and Hiral ducked low just in time to evade the spear aimed for his neck, while a Lizardman leg appeared in his field of vision. He fired his **RHC** at the foot, shattering the bones, then shoulder-checked forward while his enemy was off balance. Hitting the Lizardman felt a lot like hitting a brick wall, but the bad foot gave under the pressure, and the two fighters tumbled to the ground.

Strong hands grabbed at Hiral's head and neck—the warrior had gotten much better positioning as they fell—so Hiral put the barrel of his **RHC** against a knee and pulled the trigger. The blast certainly wasn't a fatal wound, but the sudden pain bought him the second he needed to roll out of the warrior's grasp and off the Lizardman. Another roll, two more pulls of his triggers, and Hiral scrambled to his feet.

Three Lizardmen bodies sprawled across the alley, the blood on Yanily's spear and Vix's knuckles explaining the carnage. The two damage dealers hadn't escaped unscathed, though. They were covered in dust from the explosion, and blood ran down the right side of Yanily's face from a wound across his forehead.

"Can you all move? We can't stay here," Hiral said, just in time for another barrage of fireballs to tear apart more than half of the remaining wall. Another salvo like that would either kill them outright or completely expose them for the next. "We're going!" he shouted.

Without waiting to see if they'd follow, Hiral dashed out into the road. He ran into a warrior almost immediately, just barely twisting to the side to avoid the swinging spear, then popped off a shot into the side of its knee as he ran by. Three more Lizardmen charged at him from ahead, while the fifth fireball formed over the **Scholar's** hand, but Hiral didn't slow.

His first shot took the Lizardman on the right straight on in the knee, bending its leg in the wrong direction, which sent it tumbling to the ground. The second blast hit the one on the left in the gut, slowing its run and knocking the wind out of it, but it wasn't out of the fight. Worse, the one in the middle was almost on top of him, and thrust straight out with its spear.

With his weapons out of shots because he couldn't access his solar energy, he swerved to the side—the spear blade tore a gash across his chest, just above his central Meridian Node—then activated *Foundational Split*. Right peeled off him and into the surprised Lizardmen, delivering a punch to its face. Hiral cut out wide, and Left followed straight in to drive his *Dagger of Sath* into the center of the warrior's chest.

Leaving Right and Left to deal with the last warrior on the ground, Hiral recharged his *RHCs* and checked in on the *Scholar*. Eight fireballs! Just seconds until the next barrage, and the only option was a shallow alley immediately on his left.

"In here," he shouted, pointing, before he dismissed Right and Left. He'd only given them each three percent solar energy, just enough to activate an ability or tattoo, so he didn't lose much. Another look at the *Scholar*—the ninth ball had formed—and a smile split its face. "Seena, *Spearing Roots*, right here at the entrance," he told her as she rushed by, solar energy already building, likely in anticipation of warriors inside the alley.

The woman nodded as she passed, and Hiral followed her in as the tenth ball took shape.

He sheathed his *RHC* and spun, thrusting out his right hand along with a wave of *Rejection* at the same time the balls of fire shook the building on their left and the roots burst out of the ground. On their own, none of the three things would've stood up to the onslaught, but somehow, together, they weathered the fiery storm.

"No time to rest," Hiral said. He pointed at the burning roots, which Seena dismissed, then ran right back out into the street.

He dropped two lizards, then tossed two more shots in the direction of the surprised *Scholar*. Like before, the blasts didn't reach it, but it did take a step back in reflex.

Now halfway to the end of the street, Hiral spotted the next alley that would be their refuge. Two more stops and they'd be at the *Scholar*—except a new notification sprang to life in front of Hiral's eyes.

Dynamic Quest: Update
Class is now in session.
Sssurvive.

"What?" Hiral asked as he dismissed the notification and looked toward the *Scholar*.

The hanging line of fireballs stood paused at five flaming orbs, and the floating tome now hovered in front of the Lizardman, the pages once again flipping madly until they settled with a snap. Up went the *Scholar's* right hand, and then down to smack the open page. At the same time his hand connected with the book, two totems eerily similar to the one they'd found by the *King* and *Queen of the Swamp* rose out of the ground. Similar, but not the same.

Scorching red flames sat in the open jaws of these skulls, and embers flared to life in the eye sockets.

The *Scholar's* right hand jerked out, his finger pointing at the party, and suddenly, the two totems began spitting dart-like bolts of fire out in rapid succession. So fast they were almost a constant stream, the first wave of bolts smacked into a Lizardman ahead of Hiral, shuddering its body with the rapid-fire impacts and pushing the corpse forward despite the light leaving the warrior's eyes.

And that wasn't all. The *Scholar's* hand had returned to the hanging line of fireballs, the sixth one already forming while Hiral threw himself to the ground. Bolt after bolt after bolt seared through the air right above where Hiral slid along the ground, then backtracked toward the party, cutting a line of scorch marks along the buildings' walls.

Nivian hefted his shield in front of him as the stream of bolts swept past, lines of smoke rising from the impact, but doing no lasting damage. Beside him, Yanily set his spear spinning, even managing to deflect several of the lightning-quick fiery darts, but one, then two got through. The spearman grunted in pain as his skin blackened and his spinning spear faltered.

But then Nivian was there again, planting his feet while the totems spat their nonstop stream of flaming darts against his shield.

"Go! Go," Nivian shouted at the party, somehow knowing when to move to keep his shield directly in the line of fire.

"Ninth ball!" Hiral warned the others, back on his feet and waving madly at the closest alley with one hand while he fired off shots at the Lizardmen braving the crossfire.

Finally, as the tenth ball formed above the *Scholar's* hand, Nivian was the last one out in the street, and Hiral ducked back into the alley at the same time he activated *Foundational Split*. Left and Right peeled off of him in a heartbeat to aid against the Lizardmen pouring out of the shadows at one end of the alley, while Hiral reached for Nivian.

With ten balls of fiery death already in the air, Hiral pulled with his *Rune of Attraction* while Nivian activated his movement ability. The combination yanked the tank forward to crash into Hiral, and then the ground.

Orange and red bloomed into the air, the buildings and ground shook, and a wave of heat washed over Hiral with the impact of the latest salvo.

"No time to be lying down," Seena said to them, helping Nivian up despite burns on her arm and leg. "Wule, you've got thirty seconds to heal us, then we're getting back out there."

"I really need a buff that does something about fire damage," Wule mumbled. "For now, I'm going to use my *Terminal* ability. It will add a heal-over-time effect. Lasts thirty seconds per spell."

"Great," Seena said. "Less talking. More doing."

"Right. Sorry." Wule activated an ability, quickly followed by the group heal.

You have been buffed by Terminal: Swarm Healing.
Minor healing over time for 30 seconds.

The same refreshing energy from Wule's usual spells lingered on Hiral's skin and flowed through his veins, continuing to patch up his wounds even after the initial spell's effects ended.

"I'll do it again right before we run," Wule told them.

"We're toughing out one more barrage, then going. Nivian, you did a great job blocking those totems. Can you do it again?" Seena asked, bringing up a wall of *Spearing Roots* to try and shield them from the next wave of fireballs.

"I'll keep you all safe," Nivian promised while, at the back of the alley, Left and Right dealt with the Lizardmen as they appeared.

"Left, Right, I'm going to leave you guys here, then cancel as we get close to the next alley. Stay near the back," Hiral told the doubles, and they nodded their understanding. "Any second now…"

Wule refreshed his healing spell as the next barrage completely blew the roof off the building beside them, spinning it end over end to flip past the alley, and shook the walls. Flames leapt in the air on the other side of the thick wood Seena had summoned, but the party survived, and Seena dismissed her roots.

"Go!" Seena shouted.

Nivian dashed out with Hiral right beside him, and the others tightly packed behind.

Ember-glowing eyes in the totems zeroed in on Nivian, then the stream of fiery darts resumed.

"You've got this," Hiral told the tank, touching the edge of his shield. He activated his *Rune of Attraction* while focusing his mind on the fiery darts.

Actually curving in the air, the darts poured into Nivian's shield, one after another after another, flashing with each impact, but the group didn't pause. Across the street they went—Hiral picked off two more Lizardmen with his *RHC*—and got to the alley, just a bare thirty feet from the *Scholar* now.

"In, in," Nivian said, taking up position at the corner of the alley while the totems unloaded a seemingly endless stream of firebolts into his shield.

As soon as the last person passed them, Hiral canceled his *Attraction*, then slipped into the alley behind the tank, cancelling and reactivating *Foundational Split* in quick succession. Left and Right moved without being told, once again taking up the fight against warriors emerging from the shadows.

"We're heading straight for that *Scholar* right after the next barrage," Seena said.

"Stay as far back as you can," Hiral instructed. "From this angle, he might even be able to get one of his fireballs in here."

Not even a second later, the ten fireballs swept through the opening of the alley, crashing into the far wall and blowing through it. Waves of heat and stinging flames rolled over the party, stealing the breath from Hiral's lungs and making his eyes water.

A surge of refreshing energy pushed through the pain as Wule reused his ability, and then the group rushed out of the alley.

It was time for the student to become the teacher.

62

ANOTHER TOTEM? OF COURSE WE SHOULD SMASH IT

NIVIAN stepped out into the stream of firebolts, his shield absorbing hit after hit, then methodically stalked forward. Where he would've normally engaged his movement ability to get to the **Mid-Boss** immediately, the totems kept him contained for the moment, but they also gave Hiral cover to return fire.

Leaning out to the side, Hiral took a quick aim with his **RHC** and pulled the trigger. The bolt finally smacked into the center of the **Scholar's** chest. The monster snarled as it fell back a step, its hand coming away from the line of fireballs hanging in the air, and Hiral pulled the trigger again.

"I can hit it," Hiral told the others, who couldn't see from behind Nivian.

"And we've got incoming from behind," Seena said, pulsing with energy and activating an ability Hiral couldn't see without taking his eyes off the **Scholar**.

Another shot kept the **Scholar** back from his hanging fireballs, but those totems on the other side of it made it so Nivian couldn't...

The totems. Can I...?

Hiral shifted his **RHC** from the **Scholar** to the totem on the right, then took aim at the fire-spitting skull and fired. The totem exploded in a shower of bone fragments, while the **Scholar** leaned forward and screamed a wordless roar at the party.

"Get ready to charge," Hiral said, sliding around to the other side of Nivian and quickly picking off the other totem. "Go get him!"

"Why didn't you do that sooner?" Yanily asked from behind Hiral at the same time Nivian activated his movement ability and blurred forward.

"Lizardmen in the way," Hiral said as Nivian slammed shield-first into the **Mid-Boss**.

The force of the impact hurled the **Scholar** backwards to crash to the ground, its fireballs fizzling out, and its tome hanging in the air, motionless. Without the terrain advantage, it didn't seem like the **Scholar** would pose much of a threat—until the doorways of *every* building burst open in a flood of angry Lizardmen.

Hiral canceled and reactivated **Foundational Split** in quick succession, giving Left and Right each a full third of his solar energy, and the two doubles spread out to intercept some of the charging monsters.

"Yanily and Nivian, *Scholar* is yours," Seena said. "Make it dead. Rest of us, hold back the tide!" Her *Spearing Roots* erupted out of the ground to impale more than a dozen of the charging monsters.

After that, Hiral had no choice but to turn all his attention on the warriors rushing his way. There had to be a hundred of them, and more coming, so he lifted his *RHCs* and began pulling the triggers. His first shots went low, breaking ankles or kneecapping those in the front, tripping them up to slow the ones behind. As soon as they hit the ground, he raised the barrels of his weapons higher, shooting bolts of *Impact* into faces or chests.

Even with nonstop firing, though, the rush was going to reach him, so he dashed forward while he had the advantage of the Lizardmen being slightly spread out. Hiral leaped up and over the leading line of prone Lizardmen, pulling the triggers every time his *RHCs* were off cooldown, then landed and ducked under the first sweeping spear.

With his left *RHC* under his right arm, he pulled the trigger, then stood and dodged to the side to avoid a descending spear. Down and around, his leg sweep knocked the warrior from its feet, and his arms went out to each side as he rose. Spinning one hundred and eighty degrees, he fired in quick succession, then dashed into an opening between two Lizardmen, using their bulk against them to hide his movements.

After two shots into the backs of the legs on either side of him, he stopped short, a spear stabbing straight through where he would've gone, then ducked underneath and fired wildly at the source. A grunt of pain meant he hit, but he was already past and cutting hard to the left.

A spear lunged toward his face, but he avoided the worst of it with a tilt of his head, though the stinging pain on his left ear meant it didn't completely miss him. Then he leapt into the air. Using one of the moves he'd seen Vix perform, Hiral's knee collided with the warrior's face, dropping it to the ground as he flew past and landed in a roll. His fingers squeezed the triggers as he rose, bolts taking the legs out from a Lizardman in front of him, and he spun, sending two more shots directly into the faces of a pair of rushing warriors.

While the bodies fell, Hiral swept his weapons around for his next target, but nothing else was charging at him. In fact, the few Lizardmen still standing were running *away*. A look at the *Scholar* showed the black-robed Lizardman on its back, Yanily's spear straight through its chest and pinning it to the ground.

Dynamic Quest Complete: That is all for today's lesson.
Congratulations. Achievement unlocked – Trial by Fire
You've run the gauntlet and come out the other side.
Please access a Dungeon Interface
to unlock class-specific reward.

"Lizardmen are in full retreat," Wule said. "Please don't chase them. Yeah, I'm talking to you, Yanily."

"They're experience!" Yanily complained.

"So are the ones on the ground that're still moving," Seena said, her left arm hanging limply at her side and blood running down it from a nasty-looking shoulder wound. "Finish them off, then make sure our perimeter is secure."

"Left, *Banner of Courage*, please, and hold on to it. The small heal and solar energy absorption will help," Hiral said. "Right, you, me, and Yanily get the dirty work of putting these Lizardmen out of their misery."

"Just us? What about Vix?" Yanily asked, only to look over and find the pugilist sitting on the ground with a Lizardman spear still stuck in his gut. "Vix!? You let them hit you?"

"I didn't *let* them do anything," Vix said, grimacing while Wule inspected the injury.

"How bad?" Seena asked, joining the healer.

"I can fix it. Just need time," Wule said. "And you, Seena, sit down and put pressure on that wound to slow the bleeding."

"Come on, Yanily," Hiral said. "Let's get this over with."

Between Hiral, Right, and Yanily, the three picked their way through the bodies on the ground, finishing off any Lizardmen they found still alive. The work was gruesome, and without the adrenaline of the battle, Hiral had to fight to keep his stomach down.

He *knew* the enemies he was killing weren't actually real—just solar energy constructs of the dungeon—but that didn't change the look in their eyes when he met their gaze. When he pulled the trigger and had to watch their light fade.

"There's another totem over here," Nivian said several minutes later, the last of the Lizardmen finally dead. "The creepy, black kind. Not the fire-spitting kind. I think I see where it goes underground back to the briar too."

"The *Mid-Boss* was called some kind of sealer," Hiral said, but he went over to Seena instead of approaching the totem. He needed a *break*. Looking at the others, he wasn't the only one. "How's your arm?"

"The pain is fading," Seena said. "Wule's healing and the banner are helping a lot. A few more minutes and it'll be like it never happened."

"I didn't expect all those Lizardmen coming from behind," Hiral said. "I guess I should've."

"At least the stupid fireball Lizardman wasn't very strong once we got to it. If it was like the *Duke*, or even the *Butcher*, we could've been in trouble. His floating book thing was kind of neat, though. I wish I had something like that."

"Er… yeah, I guess? Anyway, the dungeons aren't designed to kill us. They're designed to make us stronger. To teach us to deal with different situations and adapt, right? This **Scholar**... encounter—if you want to call it that—was all about *getting* to it."

"Then why all the Lizardmen at the end?" Yanily asked.

"Because Dr. Benza was obviously a sadist," Hiral grumbled.

Seena smiled and gave Hiral a pat on the knee. "Help me up, would you?"

"Sure," Hiral said, getting to his feet and then helping pull Seena to hers.

"Wule, how's Vix?" Seena asked.

"I've done what I can with my healing, but I'd like him to get some actual rest when we get out of here. The wound was pretty deep, and I don't know if it's affected his **PIM**."

"I'm fine," Vix said, tentatively twisting and stretching. "Little stiff, but this won't be an issue. We can finish the dungeon."

"And everybody else?" Seena asked.

"The banner's aura fixed me up," Hiral said, reaching up to find a small chunk still missing from his ear. *Well, guess that isn't growing back.* "Nivian, how's your shield?"

The tank lifted his absolutely scorched shield to show the rest of the party, the entire thing barely more than thorny charcoal. "It's seen better days, but don't worry." He dropped the shield to the ground, where it crumbled into ash, then grew another one out of the palm of his left hand. "There. Good as new. Now, if I could just carry two of these, it would've made that whole encounter a lot easier."

"You can grow shields anytime you want? That's handy," Hiral said.

"Says the guy who literally grows two new entire versions of himself," Yanily said.

"I don't *grow* them," Hiral countered. "Anyway, are we ready to finish this dungeon?"

"Yes," Seena said. "Time to find out what kind of **Boss** they were protecting. Hiral, could you do the honors?"

"You bet," he said, following Nivian's gesture to the totem and pulling the trigger. Fragments of bone exploded in every direction, and the faint black line leaking up from the ground vanished. "Now what?"

ROOOOOOOOOOOOOOOOAR. The titanic bellow shook the entire dungeon from the center of the briar as the inky blackness within the plants faded and then disappeared entirely.

Dynamic Quest: The bound Prince of the Swamp awakens.
Time until it shakes off its lethargy: 10 minutes.
Defeat the Prince before it regains the terrible strength
that forced its parents to seal it away.

"Well... huh..." Yanily said as all heads turned toward the center of the dungeon.

A second roar, and the already-corrupted plants along the near side of the briar began to crumble and fall. Starting at the top, rigid branches snapped and gave way, tumbling down to take more with them, an avalanche in a thin line about ten feet wide all the way to the ground.

But, on either side of that gap, more and more branches looked to be weakening, and it wouldn't be long before the whole side came crashing down.

"That's our way in," Seena said. "Nivian, let's go. If it's anything like the summoning ritual from **Splitfang Keep**, we want to finish this before the timer reaches zero. Wule, re-buff while we move."

"On it," the healer said, reapplying **Nature's Blade** to the party while Seena did **Lashing Vines.**

"Watch those alleys," Seena instructed as the party jogged back down the street the way they'd come, Lizardman bodies—and parts of bodies—still littering the roadway.

Two hundred feet they jogged, Hiral looking left and right for an ambush from either side, but nothing came. In fact, other than the first two roars, the entire dungeon had gone deathly quiet. They reached the wall without trouble, checked both directions on the road, then crossed it to get to the swamp.

"Don't see a path," Nivian said. "Straight?"

"Nine minutes, so yeah, straight. Hiral, you see any snakes?" Seena asked while Nivian picked his way into the bog off the side of the road. He went up to his knees in the murky water, but that seemed to be as deep as it went.

"No snakes. No Lizardmen. No lizards. Nothing," Hiral said, the eerie quiet sending a shiver up his spine. "This must be the **Boss** of the dungeon, but it sounds like the **Scholar** sealed this thing away because it was too powerful."

"Let's hope *too powerful* is still E-Rank," Seena said, the whole party in the bog now.

"I'm going to be D-Rank as soon as we clear this dungeon," Yanily said. "It can't be too scary," he added as they reached the gap in the briar's outer layer, then worked their way inside.

Even with the inky shadows dispelled from the plants, the inside of the briar patch still lingered in darkness, like the sun directly above wasn't welcome, and broken stone ruins littered the ground. What had once been a temple of some kind now rested in shattered chunks, pillars knocked down or torn apart. Several Lizardman statues stood proud in a line, though the great claw marks rending across their bodies showed just what the supposed **Prince** thought of them.

And there, in the center of the destruction, stirred something that made even the **King of the Swamp** look *small*. Jet black and with long spines extending from its back, its body and tail were much like its father's. However, from its mother's side, it had three long, serpentine necks and heads, which weaved into the air in unison to look at the party.

Boss – Prince of the Swamp – Unknown Rank

63

THE PRINCE OF THE SWAMP

"**S**EVEN minutes," Vix said. "Plan?"

"That thing is *huge*," Nivian said. "Can we even hurt something like that?"

"Hiral, can you do the same thing you did to the **King of the Swamp**?" Seena asked.

"Doubt it. You see the way those heads are moving? It'd bite me right off its own back."

"So, we do it the old-fashioned way," Yanily said, making a few thrust feints with his spear.

"I don't think the old-fashioned way applies to something unlike *anything* we've ever fought," Wule said.

"Lots of terrain down there we can use for cover," Hiral said, pointing with one of his **RHCs** toward the ruins. "Nivian keeps its attention, and we wear it down."

"Lucky me," Nivian said quietly.

"Six forty-five," Vix said. "We're going to need every second we can get if that's the plan."

"It is," Seena said. "Wule, this may be tougher on you, but we're going to spread out. Hit it from all sides. I'm going for its belly with my **Spearing Roots**. Wule, I know you want to attack with your spheres, but keep an eye on how much attention you're getting. And stay close to Nivian.

"Good luck, people. Stay alive. If things go bad, meet up back here, and we'll find somewhere to ride out the two hours until the dungeon kicks us out. Go."

"Right, Left, with me," Hiral said, dashing down the slope and off to the side of the monstrous snake-lizard thing, while the rest of the party spread out to tackle it from other directions. One of the heads watched him until he broke line of sight by running behind a wall, then he reached out for his doubles. "Time for the plan," he said, taking their hands, cancelling and activating **Foundational Split** quickly. "Got it?"

"You hate me, don't you?" Right asked.

"Don't be like that," Hiral said.

He put his **RHCs** away and motioned for Left to go one way, then he and Right went the other. Without a lot of time until the countdown reached zero, he moved fast and low, occasionally catching a glimpse of the *Prince* as he went. Whether the monster saw him or not, it didn't give any indication, though suddenly a low growl vibrated the buildings, and Hiral looked between the ruins at his next chance.

Yanily and Vix had made it to the monster—*good luck, guys*—and its attention was firmly on them. Perfect.

Spotting a set of stairs leading up to a long wall left mostly intact, Hiral rushed up then along the walkway to the end, leaving him only twenty or thirty feet from the side of the beast. "Ready?" he asked Right.

"Like I have a choice," Right said.

"True," Hiral said with a smirk, then cupped his hands and motioned for Right to come over. A second later, Right's foot was in his hands, and they pushed off at the same time, though Hiral added a pulse of his *Rune of Rejection* at the last second.

Right soared up toward the *Prince's* back while the other party members attacked from the front, a glimpse of a thorned whip here, or the flash of purple flame from a spear there.

"You know what to do!" Hiral called to Right as his double nimbly avoided impaling himself on a spine, then dropped to the monster's back.

Right gave a thumbs-up, then vanished within the forest of black spikes. He would do his part as best he could, and now it was Hiral's turn to get to work.

Out came his *RHCs* as he looked over the side of the wall at the back leg of the great beast. Easily as thick as a tree, the heavy scales covered the gargantuan leg like a set of impenetrable armor. And while he couldn't do the same thing he'd done to the *King*, the same technique should still work to do *some* damage. Taking out the back legs would make it a lot easier to pound on it without it chasing them around—or give them an advantage if they had to run.

A quick check of the timer—already down to five minutes and thirty seconds—and Hiral aimed at the knee, then pulled both triggers. His first shots might as well have been him throwing pebbles for all the damage they did, but with the one-second cooldown on his weapons, he followed up pretty quickly. And again. And again… and again… and again.

On the far side of the *Prince*, Left would be going to work on the other rear leg with his *Dagger of Sath*. One of them would get through the plating sooner or later.

He kept firing, though he glanced at the three heads that rose into the air, their mouths opening wide like they were getting ready to lunge down and strike. He'd seen the *Queen of the Swamp* do the same thing, so Nivian and the others should be ready for it.

Except… the beast didn't lunge. Instead, something seemed to rise from within its throats to fill its mouths. Electricity sparked across the teeth of one mouth, fire leaked out between the teeth of the second, and a strange combination of the two—burning lightning—sparked in the middle mouth.

Then it leaned its heads forward and *breathed*. Fire, lightning, and flaming lightning cut terrible swathes through the ruins in front of the beast.

"NO!" Hiral shouted, constantly firing at the rear leg, but the huge beast took a ground-shaking step forward.

The heads shifted and looked, then lunged down at something moving between the buildings. The others were still alive. They had to be. Another ground-shaking step. The beast gave chase even as a barrage of *Spearing Roots* erupted from the ground underneath to slam into its huge stomach.

They didn't do any better than Hiral's *RHCs* against the heavy plate, the tips of the spears shattering as they hit the *Prince's* underbelly.

This isn't going to work. At least, not in the five minutes we have left before this monster stops feeling groggy. How in the Fallen's names are we expected to beat something like this?

Hiral pulled his triggers as the monster took another step forward, entire walls ahead of it toppling just from it walking. Like before, his blasts didn't even dent the thick plating around the leg. And if he couldn't get through—even when he was focusing his shots on one spot—how were any of them going to hurt it?

No, there has to be a trick to it. They wouldn't build this dungeon with a fight we can't win. So, what is it?

Turning his attention away from the *Prince*, Hiral focused instead on the ruins all around. If they were in the heart of an old temple—if the *Prince* had been sealed there—it was for a reason. More than just the briar patch. Just… what was it?

The ground shook, another step taken, and Hiral's eyes scoured the sides of the buildings: the broken pillars that'd once supported tall ceilings, and the Lizardman statues lying in shattered heaps. No, that would've all been there before the *Prince* had been sealed. He needed to look for something different. Something out of place. Something like…

His eyes landed on the skull of a bone totem, just barely visible inside an ancient archway.

Something like that!

Hiral sheathed his *RHCs* and leapt off the wall, slowing his fall with a pulse of *Rejection*, then sprinted over to the totem. Yes, it was the same as the ones the *Scholar* had been using. Small flickers of dark flames pulsed within the eye sockets, and… and its gaze was following the *Prince's* movements.

Creepy. Totally creepy. But, how does it work?

A glance at the countdown—four and a half minutes left—and Hiral got closer to the totem, a shiver running across his skin as if the air around the bone artifact was getting pulled toward it. No, it wasn't *air*; it was ambient solar energy. The totem needed a power source.

"This could be *such* a terrible idea," Hiral mumbled, but he didn't have time to hesitate.

He gingerly reached out to touch the totem's skull with just one finger. The second his skin touched bone, a yellow notification popped up in front of his eyes.

The Totem of Sealing requires power.
Supply that power? Yes / No
Note: If you agree, you must remain within thirty feet of the totem,
or the conduit will be broken.

Hiral slapped *Yes*, and a small stream of solar energy peeled off his skin like smoke, and then straight into the skull's mouth.

What happens now?

Totems of Sealing Activated: 1/6

One of six? Five more... Of course. Just like the summoning ritual. This is teaching us how to work together. I need to tell the others.

As soon as Hiral closed the latest notification, beams of black, inky light shot out of the totem's eyes to strike the side of the **Prince**. Tendrils of the darkness snaked up and over its body, then back around to connect like a noose.

Bellowing roars echoed from the **Prince's** three heads as its forward movement came to a sudden halt, and then those heads turned back around to glare at Hiral.

Uh oh.

Hiral dashed back behind a wall—the streamer of solar energy still connecting him to the totem—just in time as a wave of flames washed across the ground. *The totem?* Heat hung in the air like a physical thing even after the flames vanished, the ground just beyond the edge of the wall a scorched mess of melted stone, but he had to know. A pulse of *Rejection* with his mind on the heat, and Hiral risked a look around the corner.

The totem stood amidst the molten ground, a black corona of energy protecting it like a shield, and the eyebeams still wrapped around the monster's waist. It was using his solar energy to not only hold the beast, but also protect itself. As long as he stayed within thirty feet, it would be safe. And the solar energy drain? Manageable for the four minutes they had left.

Now, how to tell the others what we need to do?

A pillar of purple flames burst upward from where the three necks met the **Prince's** body, and Hiral had his answer. It was a shame to lose the solar energy he'd invested in them, but there was no other choice, and he cancelled his *Foundational Split*.

Wait—the totem's energy?

His eyes went to the totem as he realized he couldn't use any of his abilities with the tattoos on his skin, but he let out a sigh of relief when he saw the streamer still connecting him to the totem. Best not to risk it, though. He activated *Foundational Split*, and his doubles peeled off him, each with a third of his remaining energy. Eleven percent each—it'd have to be enough.

"You know what you need to do," Hiral said, and the doubles nodded, then dashed off.

Left, with the highest *Atn*, would find the five totems. Right, meanwhile, would have to explain this to the others and get them to the totems Left found. Hiral would just have to survive that long.

With that in mind, he looked from the totem back to the *Prince*. One of its heads still glared in his direction, but it wasn't breathing fire again. *Did it realize that wouldn't work?*

A growl rumbled out of its throat, and one of its other heads turned to look at the first. Another growl, then a nip at the second head's neck, and both heads turned in Hiral's direction again. When the second head seemed to notice the black binding around its body, it reared up in surprise, then narrowed its eyes and shifted its attention to Hiral.

They don't share thoughts. They're like three separate people.

Sparks danced in the mouth of the second head, and a strange tingling ran along Hiral's skin, the air itself charging. He dove for the cover of the wall a second before the air behind him *popped* and *sizzled*, electricity constricting his muscles just because he was close to the discharge, and he flopped to the ground like a fish out of water. His body twitched while he gasped for air, spikes of pain running up and down his limbs like they were asleep, but his eyes stayed locked on the streamer of solar energy. There was no way of telling if the totem would survive without it.

Another titanic roar shook the ruins, like all three heads shouted in fury at the same time, and Hiral forced his arms under himself, despite how little they wanted to cooperate.

"C'mon," he told his stiff limbs, but he finally got them where he wanted them, and reached his hands and knees.

A quick check on the countdown told him they only had three minutes left, so he reached out to the wall beside him. Fingers hooking on a ledge, he hauled himself to his feet, breathing deeply from the exertion, and took a glance back at where he'd been standing.

At the five-foot-wide crater in the stone flooring.

Right. Don't get hit by lightning. Noted.

Left hand still on the wall, he shakily drew his **RHC** in his right hand, then stumbled to the other end of the wall, careful to make sure he didn't get too far from the totem. Pausing at the corner, he took a deep breath, then peeked around the edge.

Black nooses wrapped two of the three heads in energy, and a third held the tail. Hiral looked at the minimized notification.

Totems of Sealing Activated: 4/6

Just two more!

Still free, though, the middle head reared back, then spat flaming lightning at a building on the other side of the monster from Hiral. Fire and debris exploded into the air, the tremor from the blast knocking Hiral from his feet. Another roar, and then the head snapped down at one of the black lines of energy. The jaws closed with enough force to send a shockwave blowing outward, but the stream of black didn't waver.

The head roared again, turning to the two other heads and snapping its jaws in their direction, but those heads hung limply, as if they were sleeping. Up and down, the front leg thrashed in frustration—then the monster flexed its legs. Claws dug deep divots through the stone as it tried to haul its weight forward, but the thin black streamers somehow held it back.

Two minutes left on the timer, and the monster turned its attention again to the buildings near where it had breathed its devastating attack.

One of the others must be over there!

Limbs under better control, Hiral pulled himself back to his feet, though he still needed the wall for balance, and aimed his **RHC** at the **Prince's** head.

Pull. The blast crossed the distance and slapped into the side of the behemoth's jaw as it spread its mouth wide, more fiery lightning forming inside. Whether through pain or surprise, the attack discharged from the **Prince's** mouth, searing the afterimage of red lightning into Hiral's eyes, then blew the top off one side of the briar patch.

Whipping its head around in his direction, the lizard's eyes narrowed as they found Hiral, so he pulled the trigger again. *Whap.* It hit the beast right between the eyes, causing the head to recoil and shake like somebody had just finger-flicked it in the forehead. No real damage done, though. The eyes focused again on Hiral, a snarl rippling across the monster's lips and promising a painful death to him.

Flaming lightning crackled along its teeth, smoke fumed out of its nose, and even its eyes seemed to take on an amber light. The legs shifted, tearing stones bigger than Hiral out of the ground as the beast tried to turn its body in his direction. *Pull.* He pinged another shot off the **Prince's** face to keep its attention, then it leaned in and opened its mouth.

Time seemed to slow as Hiral stared into the monster's maw, like looking down a vast tunnel. Fire and lightning coiled up its throat in a massive torrent, then combined when they met at the back of its teeth. The sheer energy of it was like looking at the sun, and there was no way the flimsy wall he leaned against could ever hope to blunt the blast.

It was over... unless... A fifth streamer of black energy shot out from the far side of the *Prince*, wrapping around its neck and hauling its whole head backwards. Time returned to normal speed as the powerful discharge of energy shot straight into the sky, blowing the clouds outward in an expanding circle of clear blue. The final head bucked and pulled, trying to get free of the insidious energy, but the eyelids blinked slowly, and it turned its attention once more in Hiral's direction.

A notification sprang up in his face.

Dynamic Quest: Update
**The Prince of the Swamp has promised terrible vengeance on you
(yes, you) should it fully awaken.
Time Remaining – 1:00
Time Remaining – 0:59
Time Remaining – 0:58**

Hiral slapped the notification to the side and shouted, "Less than a minute! Find that totem!"

**Time Remaining – 0:55
Time Remaining – 0:54**

A black leash of energy sprang out and over the *Prince's* body from the other side, finally looping around, and Hiral pulled up his notification window.

Totems of Sealing Activated: 6/6

Yes! They'd done it. Now all they needed was the quest complete window, and they could go find the dungeon interface.

**Time Remaining – 0:50
Time Remaining – 0:49
Time Remaining – 0:48**

The timer hadn't stopped. Why hadn't the timer stopped!?

Hiral looked at the great beast, the countdown continuing in his peripheral vision. What else did they have to do? The *Prince* was sealed.

Sealed. Not defeated.

Hiral lifted both **RHCs** and started pulling the triggers. The thick scales, seemingly indestructible before, exploded into shards as his blasts hit. Two more shots, and green blood flowed like a river. But the **Prince** was much bigger than the **King** had been. It would take far too long for him to dig through to something vulnerable.

If he was alone.

"Attack it! We have to kill it before the timer hits zero!" he shouted, pulling his triggers again and again. "Hurry!" The memory of the promised vengeance was a little too clear in his mind.

Purple flames leapt into the air up near the front, then orbs of cold lobbed in from the side.

Time Remaining – 0:30
Time Remaining – 0:29
Time Remaining – 0:28

Hiral charged energy into both pistols, then pulled the triggers. He hit it with everything he could, and silently prayed it was enough as the rest of the party did the same.

64

THE EMPEROR'S GREATSWORD

Time Remaining – 0:03

Dynamic Quest Complete
The Prince of the Swamp has been slain.
Congratulations. Achievement unlocked –
Sleepy Heads
You prevented a terrible power
from reawakening (for 3 hours).
Please access a Dungeon Interface
to unlock class-specific reward.

H IRAL dropped straight down to sit on the ground, the *RHCs* falling out of his hands as the drain of solar energy from the totem finally ended. In front of him, the bloody and torn body of the **Prince of the Swamp** lay unmoving. All three heads had been severed from the necks by Left, Yanily, and Seena, while Right and Vix had thrown everything they had into the far side of the body. Hiral, on the other hand, had done what he could on his side, which basically amounted to drilling a narrow hole right for the **Prince's** heart.

"We did it… We *actually* did it," he whispered to himself, ignoring the notification and looking at his current solar energy capacity. One percent. A few seconds longer wouldn't have just seen the resurrection of the **Prince** to full power; it also would've left him without any resources to continue the fight.

Still needing a minute to recover—not just his solar energy, but also emotionally—he swiped aside the quest notification, only for another to immediately take its place.

The Mire: Complete
New Record Time: 1:12:12
Congratulations. Achievement Unlocked –
Lizards, Snakes, and… Hydras? Oh, my!
You have conquered the horrors of The Mire
and prevented a terrible awakening.
Please access a Dungeon Interface
to unlock class-specific reward.
Time until The Mire instance closure: 59:43

"Hiral, you still alive?" Right called out, jogging over with Left beside him.

"The fact you're still around to ask that…" Hiral started, but just shook his head at the grin on his double's face. "Do I really smirk like that?" he asked Left.

"Absolutely do," Left said.

"All three of you do," Seena said, rounding a corner and coming to join the trio. "But Left only does it when he thinks nobody's looking. Yeah, I saw you." She gave the double a friendly punch in the shoulder.

"I'll have to be more careful in the future," Left said, his voice far too serious.

"You okay?" Hiral asked Seena before taking a breath and pushing himself up to his feet.

"Almost had at least five heart attacks during that fight there," Seena said while Hiral picked up his **RHCs** and sheathed them on his thighs.

"Don't think I can heal heart attacks," Wule said, the rest of the party coming over to join them.

Each of them had blood flowing freely from wounds, while Nivian looked like he'd had a fight with a barbeque and lost, practically dragging his left leg behind him with each step.

"We barely pulled that one out," Nivian said. "Hiral, how'd you figure out the totems?"

"Honestly? Luck," Hiral said. "Figured that thing was too tough to fight head on—er, heads on?— so I started looking for something else. Like Seena said before, a trick to the fight."

"Everybody remember where they found the totems?" Seena asked. "As soon as we get out of here, we're drawing up a map for my sister's group, and for our next run. I don't want any of us trying to take that thing straight up again."

"Yanily? Do you remember where your totem was?" Vix asked, cradling his left elbow like his arm was giving him trouble.

"Uh…" Yanily said, turning to look at the **Prince's** body, which was dissolving into inky black smoke even as they watched. "Is that normal?"

"Don't change the subject," Seena said, but her eyes were on the body that had already reduced to less than half its original size. "Do you know where your totem is?"

"Over… there?" Yanily said, pointing beyond the **Prince** with this spear. He then looked a little and shifted more to the left. "Or, over there? Maybe."

"I know where they all are," Left said. "I'll take care of the map."

"Thank you, Left. I'm glad *somebody* was thinking ahead," Seena said, glaring at the spearman.

"I *was* thinking ahead," Yanily said. "Thinking about getting to the dungeon interface to evolve."

"Speaking of which, where *is* the interface?" Wule asked.

"I think you're about to find out," Hiral said, pointing at the last few dregs of the **Prince's** large frame finally dissolving into nothingness. The interface stood where the body had been.

"Alright, let's do it," Yanily said, immediately starting for the interface, the rest of the party following quickly despite their injuries.

"I'll heal while we sort through the mess of notifications I know we're about to get," Wule said. "Left, could you do your **Banner of Courage** at the same time to help out?"

"Certainly," Left said.

"Who gets to do the honors?" Yanily asked, eying the pedestal, while Left placed the banner. The dome of light enveloped the party.

"Chests with loot will be first, right?" Nivian asked.

"Hiral, you spotted the totems," Seena said. "You do it."

"Sure," Hiral said, walking up to the pedestal then waving his hand over the inset crystal.

All at once, inky night burst from the briar patch, plunging the entire dungeon into absolute darkness, subduing even the banner's glowing dome. A few heartbeats later, the darkness eased, shrouding the party in foggy shadows. The ruins and everything beyond were hidden from sight—except for the six chests surrounding the party, and the large one in the center beside the pedestal.

"No torches this time," Nivian said while his brother worked on healing the tank's extensive burns. "How do we know who gets which chest?"

"The chests have gems on them," Seena said, looking at an ornate square chest. "Hiral, I think this one is yours. Yellow."

"This one is mine," Yanily said, standing in front of chest similarly shaped to Hiral's, but without the same trim. "Definitely not a spear this time."

"Maybe it's a really short one," Vix said, finding his own chest, not much larger than a breadbox. "Or a fishing rod. A collapsible one."

"Better not be," Yanily said, looking at his chest, then over at Hiral's, and back once more. "Hey, Hiral, how come yours is… fancier?"

"Fancier?" Hiral asked.

He took a closer look at the differences between the two boxes. While Yanily's chest was simple, a lot like a heavy trunk, Hiral's had filigree inscribed in the surfaces, a raised and curved lid, and some kind of golden metal around the edges. It really was a treasure chest. And it was the only one.

"Well, what are you waiting for?" Seena asked him. "Open it up."

Hiral shrugged and crouched down in front of his chest, hands coming up to run along the edges of the box. Was it his imagination, or was the box itself warm? Just what was inside?

Only one way to find out.

Hooking his fingers under the corners of the lid, Hiral lifted it up and flipped it back, then looked into the large chest. He blinked and looked again.

No way...

Hiral reached in and wrapped his fingers around the sword hilt—a good foot and a half long—and hefted the weapon out of the chest. The sword was *heavy*, really heavy, and made of solid crystal, its blade almost as wide as the hilt was long, two inches *thick*, and sharp on both edges. The crosspiece took the shape of spread wings, though it barely extended a few inches past the massively wide blade, and script similar to Hiral's double helix lined both sides. There looked to be runes embedded just above the winged crosspiece, but the most striking part about the whole thing was...

"It's broken?" Nivian asked, coming over to stand by Hiral with a small disc in his hand. "They gave you a broken sword?"

Hiral didn't respond immediately, laying the flat of the half-a-blade across his lap where he crouched, then ran his hand along it. True, just like Nivian said, there was only about two and a half feet of blade. Everything beyond the jagged break was completely missing, but there was no mistaking it. This was it.

> **The Emperor's Greatsword – Broken – S-Rank**
> **Effects: Unknown**
> **Dynamic Quest: Unfathomable Power**
> **You've discovered a rare—yet broken—S-Rank item.**
> **Find a way to restore it to its original state.**

"Is that what I think it is?" Left asked, and Right gave a low whistle.

"I don't get it," Nivian said. "Why do you look like you're happy about getting a broken sword?"

"This... this..." Hiral tried speaking, his voice getting stuck in his throat. "This is the **Emperor's Greatsword**. I'm sure of it. The *original*."

"And that's... what... exactly?" Yanily asked, coming over to join them, what looked like a suit of leather armor in his hands.

"A legendary S-Rank weapon," Hiral said. "Obviously broken, but it doesn't matter. And it gave me a quest to fix it."

"If it's *that* big broken, how long was it before?" Seena asked, a familiar-looking tome in her hands.

"Just over six feet, if you include the hilt," Hiral said. "Only two people in history are said to have wielded the weapon... and then it went missing. The Emperor and the Little Queen. I can't believe it." Hiral forced his eyes from the weapon to look back in the chest. Like his **RHCs**, there was a square of crystal, likely the equivalent of a sheath. It would have to go on his back—it wouldn't fit anywhere else. "What about you guys? What did you get?"

"The **Scholar's** tome," Seena said, holding up the book.

"Armor," Yanily said. "Made out of… hydra scales. What's a hydra?"

"I think the **Prince** was a hydra," Hiral said. "Didn't you read the dungeon's complete notification?"

"Uh…" Yanily said, one hand coming up to scratch his nose while his spear leaned in the crook of his elbow.

"Vix, how about you?" Seena asked.

"Goggles," Vix said. "They show weak points and give a critical hit damage bonus."

"Nice," Seena said. "And, Nivian, what've you got there?"

"*Orbital Shield*?" Nivian said, holding the disc up. "I've got a prompt to bond with it by giving it some solar energy."

"So, what are you waiting for?" Yanily asked.

Nivian shrugged, and a small streamer of energy wafted off his hand like glowing smoke, then into the disc. One second of this, two, three, and the disc pulsed and then hovered out of Nivian's hand. From there, it moved about three feet away from him, at about chest height, then slowly rotated completely around him, and around, and around…

"And what does *that* do?" Yanily asked.

Nivian's eyes moved side to side like he was reading, then he nodded. The disc shot out toward Yanily, and a dome of energy erupted out of the sides to form a barrier in front of him. The shield lasted for three seconds, then the disc shot back to resume its orbit around Nivian.

"A remote shield?" Seena asked. "Cooldown?"

"Only six seconds," Nivian said. "Requires a constant flow of solar energy, but it's not much, and I'll need to test how much punishment it can take."

"That'll be amazing when you need to be in two places at the same time," Seena said. "Wule, you're the last one—what's that you've got?"

Wule smirked as he lifted a simple-looking iron band up, then placed it on his head like a crown. As soon as the headpiece settled into place, three balls of energy formed and began to circle the crown of his head—a rolling ball of fire, a coiled ball of lightning, and a glowing ball combining the two.

"Each ball confers a buff," Wule said, the ball of fire darting away to circle around Nivian's head, where a red aura surrounded the tank's body. "Fire, lightning, and the combination of the two. They're mainly defensive—give resistances—but they also offer a small damage bonus."

"Hey, my new armor gives resistances to those too!" Yanily said. "Hah, I got the hydra's skin, and you got its balls. Pretty sure I know which is more badass."

Wule scowled at the spearman, but the ball of fire zipped back from his brother's head, and he held his tongue. With the three elemental balls from the crown, and the two glowing lanterns from an earlier achievement, the healer was practically a walking light show.

"Good haul," Seena said, looking again at Hiral. "Even if that is broken, the rest of us got items that'll definitely help the next time."

"Isn't it kind of odd?" Hiral asked, looking at the items in everybody's hands. "Seena, weren't you saying you wanted a floating book like that? And Wule said something about buffs to protect from fire. Nivian talked about a second shield... and this." He gestured at the sword. "We were just talking about S-Rank items before we came in."

"It's like the dungeon knew what we needed... or wanted, I guess," Seena said, nodding. "How do you think that works?"

"Something to ask Dr. Benza?" Hiral said.

"Speaking of which, let's see what's in the big box in the middle, get our achievements, and get out to tell my sister what's going on."

"I'm sure she's worried by now," Nivian said.

"Probably," Seena agreed, then shivered. "She gets angry when she gets worried."

"Well, we'll come bearing gifts," Vix said, throwing back the lid of the big central box, though he gave a slight wince and looked at his arm. "Nobody complains when you bring food."

"Except... where is the food?" Yanily asked, leaning over the chest and pulling a pack out. "This is... empty? Only two packs... and... yeah, both empty. What's going on?"

"Only two packs in there?" Seena asked, walking over to join them, and Hiral followed behind, the heavy sword in one hand and the backpiece in the other. "Nothing else?"

"There's a crate of something..." Nivian said, reaching into the chest, moving something around, and lifting out a board of solid crystal. "Same material as Hiral's sword?"

"Looks like it," Hiral said. Noticing both of his hands were full, he pushed a touch of solar energy into the backpiece, and pushed it against the sword. The two objects bonded immediately, and Hiral lifted it over his shoulder and pressed it against the center of his back. Like the thigh plates, it stuck comfortably, and despite the weight of the sword, he hardly noticed it. "Can I see that?" he asked Nivian, pointing at the crystal.

"Sure," Nivian said, handing over the piece.

Hiral took the piece of crystal and closely inspected it, running his fingers across the surface and peering at it from different angles. Despite the hard edges, something about it felt... malleable... and he easily bent it in his hands. Almost immediately, he got a flashing notification in the corner of his eyes.

Runic Artificer: Class Ability Unlocked – Mold Crystal
Mold Crystal – Shape and form crystal as needed for crafting.

"Huh. Unlocked a class skill without needing a dungeon interface," Hiral said, molding the crystal into a ball, pulling it apart into two pieces, and finally combining it back together and flattening it out. A circle of his thumb on the surface created a slot to put a runic slide—like in his **RHCs**—and he even had ideas popping into his head on what he could do with all of it.

Does the class skill even include basic schematics?

"How… how are you doing that?" Nivian asked, another piece of crystal in his hands as he obviously tried to bend it.

"I think I can make equipment with this stuff. I've even got a few ideas what I can do. I'll get to work on it as soon as we get out of here."

"Can you fix the sword with it?" Seena asked.

Hiral thought about it for a second but immediately shook his head. "No, this crystal isn't high enough quality. The sword is something special."

"Too bad. Load it up into the packs?" Seena suggested, and they did just that. Interestingly, the packs held *way* more than they looked like they would.

"That's everything from the big chest," Nivian said. "Time for achievements?"

"And evolutions!" Yanily said. "I've been very patient, but… it's finally time, right?"

"Almost," Seena said. "I was thinking. You all remember that stretch of road after the **King** and **Queen**? The Lizardmen that kept coming?"

"What about it?" Wule asked.

"We should farm it a bit," Seena said. "Come into the dungeon, kill the royalty, then just sit on the road and kill Lizardmen until the dungeon kicks us out. We're all getting closer to D-Rank, and those warriors were decent experience without being too challenging. If we can all get to D before going to the final dungeon…"

"I'm up for it," Nivian said. "We'll get bonus experience for completing the dungeon the third time too, won't we? We should keep that in mind. How many times do you think we'll need to run it?"

"A few times, at least. We'll see what Seeyela has to say about it," Seena said.

"Balyo will want to do it," Vix said. "She can't stand Yanily getting ahead of her, and this'll let her catch up."

"Means we delay getting to the *Asylum*, though," Wule pointed out. "Is it worth it?"

"Means we're stronger for the journey too," Hiral said. "If we run into more snakes, or groups of Troblins, or…"

"Or the *Enemy*," Seena said. "As soon as we leave the dungeon entrance, we're putting ourselves at risk. Might as well be a little stronger for it, right?"

Wule nodded. "Don't get me wrong. I agree with you. Just giving the other side of it."

"Speaking of a little bit stronger, could we *please* get our achievements?" Yanily asked.

"Yes, it's about that time," Seena said. "Hiral?"

"Sure," Hiral said, returning to the interface and swiping his hand across the crystal again.

Time Records
Achievement Rewards
Rank Evolution
Exit Dungeon

65

ONE MAN ARMY

"**A**chievement Rewards," Hiral said, and a slew of notification windows sprang to life in front of him—and the other party members, judging by the way their eyes went distant.

Achievement: Water Walker
Class Reward: Class Modification – Walk on Water
Walk on Water – You can move across water and many other liquid
surfaces as if they were solid.

Simple, yet effective. I wonder how that would work with something like the EnSath River and its rapids. Not sure I want to test it out. Still, as long as we're in the swamp, I won't have to worry about wet feet. Next.

Hiral dismissed the first notification window and went right on to the next.

Achievement: I Got This!
Class Reward: Class Modification (Conditional) –
One Man Army
One Man Army – When you have no allies within fifteen feet of you,
you deal additional damage to Elite or above enemies.
Note: Starting damage bonus is 10%
Note (2): Damage bonus can be increased
by defeating Elite or above enemies of your rank and level
(or higher) without any assistance.

*Any sort of damage bonus is good. I'll need to test to see how it interacts with something like **Nature's Blade**. Are they additive? The Lizardmen Seena is talking about farming will be a good chance. Hrm, no allies in fifteen feet of me? That's pretty easy to do with the **RHCs**. And it levels up! Assuming I want to fight·more **Elite** enemies by myself.*

Ugh. Do Left and Right count as "myself"?

Hiral's eyes lingered on the notification despite his curiosity to see what was next. Was there a way he could game the system to take on **Elites** without actually doing it by himself? Probably not. But, he could also give it a try and have the others handy to back him up if things went wrong. Seena would call it *reckless*—and she'd be right—but depending on the damage increase, it could be worth it. Something to talk about when they got out of there.

A flick of his hand closed the window, and he moved on to the one he got from killing the **King** from the inside, a shiver running down his spine at the memory of how yucky that had been.

> **Achievement: Belly of the Beast**
> **Class Reward: Class Modification – Internal Injuries**
> **Internal Injuries – Your attacks and abilities ignore**
> **some of an opponent's external defenses**
> **and inflict damage directly to their internals.**
> **Note: The amount of external defenses**
> **you ignore increases with Rank.**

*Okay, whoa. Ignoring armor? Obviously applies to something like the **King's** scales, but would it also work on worn body armor? Heh. I'll have to ask Nivian if I can test with him. Poor guy. Actually, it doesn't even specify "armor." It says defenses. Why? What else is there? The spines or quills? Or, is there something else? Something to do with the Enemy?*

We really need more information about them.

He pushed thoughts—and questions—about the *Enemy* out of his head. He wasn't getting any answers there in the dungeon anyway, so he closed the notification window for the next one to come up.

> **Achievement: In the Prescence of Royalty**
> **Class Reward: Class Modification – I Bow to No One**
> **I Bow to No One – Mid-Boss and above Rank enemies deal slightly**
> **less damage to you.**

*Slightly less damage? What's slightly? I guess any is better than none. Too bad it doesn't apply to **Elites** as well.*

Easy enough to understand. He closed the window and brought up the next one quickly.

> **Achievement: Trial by Fire**
> **Class Reward: Class Modification – Elemental Resistances**
> **Elemental Resistances – Damage based on the elements (natural or**
> **magic) is reduced by 10%.**

Another defensive improvement. That's good. We took a beating in the dungeon. And ten percent… is that good or bad? Ugh, I don't know if I prefer knowing the percentage or seeing "slightly less." Ten percent of what?

Hiral's fingers drummed against his arm as he read the notification a second and third time. It didn't do any good, so he swiped it aside and moved on to the next one.

Achievement: Sleepy Heads
Class Reward: Class Modification – Beauty Sleep
Beauty Sleep – Based on the amount of good rest
you get, you gain double experience from combat
for up to eight hours.

Bonus experience? Easy to understand and useful. Just one more reward left... and not a single active ability yet. Well, let's see what it is.
Hiral pushed aside the notification and opened the last one for the dungeon.

Achievement: Lizards, Snakes, and... Hydras? Oh, my!
Class Reward: Class Modification – View (upgrade) – Enemy Health
View (upgrade) – Enemy Health – Along with name and rank, View
now shows estimated health of opponents as a red bar above the
opponent's head. Damage inflicted to enemies will reduce the red
bar's length.

A passive upgrade to View, huh? These health bars could be useful to help us figure out how much damage we're doing, and how tough our opponents actually are. Nice.
"How'd you guys do?" Hiral asked, closing his last notification and looking up to see the others staring at him. "Uh… what's wrong?"
"Just how many achievements did you get?" Yanily asked. "We've all been done for ages."
"Uh… seven?" Hiral said. "You guys?"
"Four," Seena said. "The extras from that snake you killed at the beginning?"
"Two from that, and then one from how we killed the **King**," Hiral said. "Did you all only get passive class modifications? Did anybody get an actual new active ability?"
"All passives for me," Seena said. "Upgrade to **View**, elemental resistances, less damage from **Mid-Bosses** and above, and then an interesting upgrade to **Lashing Vines**. I can choose between how it normally is, or give it an element. Fire, lightning, or that fiery lightning. You guys?"
"Same first three," Nivian said. "My fourth was an upgrade to my **Thorn Whip**. Ah, just easier to show you."
He grew his whip out of his right hand. This time, however, instead of the single barbed whip, three connected lashes grew out of his hand, each sparking with one of the elements from the hydra, and the ends even snapping with small, plant-like mouths. As he held the weapon still, the whips writhed around as if seeking prey, jaws nipping at the air.

"Uh… do you need to feed them?" Yanily asked, gently poking at the lightning one with his spear. The plant-mouth snapped out to bite the spear blade, and Yanily jumped back, shaking his hand like he'd been shocked. "Ouch. Little bastard. I'll show you," he said, taking his spear in both hands.

"Down, boy," Seena said, chuckling. "You provoked it. What about the rest of you? Same passives?"

"I actually got an increase to the range of my healing abilities, and then the same first three as you," Wule said. "Nothing as creepy as what my brother got. Then again, I always was the good-looking one."

"What do looks have to do with anything?" Nivian asked, twisting to look at his twin. His three whips crawled along the ground toward the healer.

"I got some kind of damage-over-time effect added to my strikes," Vix said. "Starts out small, but the more I hit, the more it stacks up. Like your *Lashing Vines*, I can choose which element the damage is."

"That's good. We need more options for heavily armored enemies," Seena said. "Yanily, what about you?"

"A ranged attack I can use with either of my spear styles. Longer-range single strikes if I use it with *Reed Spear Style*, and more area of effect with *Dancing Spear Style*. Same as you guys, different elements."

"Also great. It can get pretty crowded up front with Left and Right in the mix as well," Seena said. "What about you, Hiral? Adding different elements to your shots or something from the *Prince* achievement?"

"Nothing like that at all," Hiral said. "I get bonus experience after getting a good sleep. No elements, and no modified abilities other than *View*."

"Hrm," Seena said. "Well, once we get back out, and after we explain the situation to Seeyela and the others, we'll take an inventory and get some practice in."

"I think you're forgetting something," Yanily said, standing right beside the dungeon interface. A wave of his hand over the crystal, and a smile lit up his face. "**Rank Evolution**."

A streamer of glowing smoke extended out of the interface crystal and connected to the center of Yanily's chest, right about the same place where Hiral had his crystal embedded. From there, the whole man's body pulsed with an internal light, a dark shadow within the glow like a series of roots growing through his limbs. As the light pulsed again and again, the roots grew longer, reaching more toward the surface of his skin, then stopped, and the light vanished in the blink of an eye.

"D-Rank!" Yanily said with a fist pump. "How's that? Huh. Bet you wish you were me right now." He gently elbowed Vix in the side.

"So, you guys really do have roots growing inside you?" Hiral asked Seena. "That's your *PIM*?"

"We do. You're probably the only Islander to see one of us evolve. Ever. I'm kind of relieved, though. I was worried we wouldn't be able to evolve without the Grandfather, despite what the interface suggested."

"The Grandfather?" Hiral asked.

"The big tree on the elders' island. It's where we get the seeds for our *PIMs*, and where we normally do evolutions."

"Like our Measure up in Fallen Reach," Hiral said, tapping the center of his chest. "It's where we get the crystal we embed in our chests."

"A crystal, huh?" Seena asked. "And then your *PIM* is the tattoos? No, those would be abilities."

"The Meridian Lines," Hiral said, pointing at Left and Right. "The thick lines connect to all parts of the body, and like the tattoos, they need to be inscribed by Artists. Pretty sure those are what you'd call a Shaper's *PIM*. For me, I think it's these." He ran a finger down the strange script making up the double-helix pattern on his skin.

"How are you two not even paying attention to this?" Yanily called at them.

"Yes, yes, you're D-Rank now. Congratulations," Seena said. "We'll ask Balyo to make you something special in celebration when we get back."

"Ugh, please no," Yanily said. "I'm pretty sure our *Gourmand* ability would give me a debuff from her cooking."

"Says the guy who's been chasing her since you were both kids," Vix said.

"Balyo is a lot of wonderful things, but a cook is not one of them," Yanily said. "It shows my true feelings for her that I don't only talk about her good qualities. Still, uh, maybe don't mention I said that?"

"Only if you behave yourself," Seena said. "Nobody else is ready to evolve yet, right? No, okay. Let's head back and start getting ready to farm this dungeon. We've got to catch up to Yanily before the power goes to his head."

With that, she passed her hand over the interface crystal. "**Exit Dungeon**."

66

WHAT COULD'VE DONE THAT?

HIRAL'S smile from successfully completing the dungeon vanished as soon as he stepped out of the portal. Something was wrong. It wasn't just the nervous energy he'd expected from Seeyela and her party at the lengthy dungeon run, though there was some of that almost physically hanging in the air as well.

The Great Tusks all huddled in one corner of the room, seemingly trying to get as far from the entrance and the pedestal both. Their *oinks* and huffs filled the small space with noise, while the largest of the beasts stood in a protective ring around the smaller, hooved feet scratching at the floor as if they'd need to charge.

"What's going on?" Hiral asked, but found at least part of the answer when he looked over at the entrance. At the bottom of the ramp lay half a Great Tusk body—just its head and front legs, really—with a thick line of blood leading back up the ramp. "Did you go hunting?"

Most of Seeyela's party looked over when Hiral and the others emerged from the portal, and the sisters shared a quick hug, but it was obvious even they'd been standing ready for a fight.

"That wasn't us," Seeyela said.

"Pigs started going crazy about thirty minutes ago," Lonil said. "All kinds of noise, then they all rumbled to that corner over there. That's when we saw… that," he finished, pointing at the remains.

"We were sitting over here, talking about our upcoming dungeon run and grabbing something to eat," Seeyela added. "Didn't see what happened."

"Have you gone over to inspect the corpse?" Hiral asked. "See if you can figure out what did it?"

"Every time we move a little closer, the pigs get even louder. It's eerie," Picoli said. "It's like they're trying to warn us it's dangerous."

"Or they expect you to eat their friend," Yanily said, but even he had both hands on his spear, and he hadn't once mentioned his evolution.

"That blood trail leading up the ramp—do you know if it's from the body coming in, or from the other half getting dragged out?" Hiral asked.

"Weren't you listening, Islander? We didn't see what happened," Fitch snapped.

"Whoa there, Fitch," Seena said, holding up a calming hand. "It's a good question, but we've got the answer now, thanks. Seeyela, since that we're all here, what do you want to do? Check it out?"

"It's probably just one of the snakes up there hunting," Seeyela said. "Caught a boar while it was coming back to shelter and... well... that happened," she said, gesturing over to the body.

"Probably," Seena said, but she looked over at Hiral and mouthed, "*Enemy?*"

He shrugged. The thought had crossed his mind too. The pigs' behavior wasn't normal—even if he'd never seen them before. "I'm going to go take a look. With my attunement and dexterity, I should be able to react fast enough if anything happens. Rest of you stay here for now."

"Be careful," Seena said.

"Not *too* careful," Fitch added in a whisper loud enough for everybody to hear.

Hiral ignored the expected comment and drew his **RHC** in his right hand. He could probably pull the body across the floor with his ***Rune of Attraction***, but there was no telling how the Great Tusks would react to that, or if it would damage any evidence of what had happened.

Like Picoli had said, as soon as Hiral started moving toward the remains, the other animals increased the volume of their *oinking*, their hooves slapping gently against the stone floor. They didn't look like they were going to charge, though. It really was like they were trying to warn him.

"It's okay," he said quietly to the herd of animals, patting the air before slowly continuing across the room toward the corpse. It wasn't like there was anything in his way, but the atmosphere in the room was pressing down on his shoulders like a weight. *Probably* just a snake, he told himself, but a few feet further, and he stopped cold.

The Great Tusks had stopped making any noise at all. Not an *oink*, a scratching hoof, or even a deep breath.

Hiral glanced back. Every single one of the pigs stood stone-still, barely shifting as their dark eyes watched him. Red health bars appeared above their heads beside their names as he stared—some longer than others—but that only added to the unnerving atmosphere. Holding their stares for a minute more, he looked from them over to the party. Seena shrugged in response—she had no idea either—and nobody else said a word. Then, there in that silence, another sound reached Hiral's ears.

Thunder.

The storm must've picked up outside. The others probably couldn't hear it—he barely noticed it with his higher **Atn**—but there was no mistaking it now. Thunder pealed like the beating of a drum, and as he looked closer at the entrance of the ramp, he could make out the faint flashes from lightning.

Another quick look at the Great Tusk remains by the ramp, and Hiral moved instead to the wall next to the ramp. From there, he got an unpleasantly good look at the garish wound that had no doubt killed the boar. He was no expert by any stretch, but it wasn't a clean cut. Not like a sword or spear. And there weren't the same kind of puncture wounds Lonil had from getting squeezed by the snake.

Bitten in half? No, that's not quite right either. It looks more like it was… pulled apart. The way it's… stretched.

Hiral turned away from the assessment, his stomach rolling as his imagination played out what could've caused the trauma. *Nothing good.* He looked over at Seena, shaking his head that he didn't know what had happened, then put his back firmly to the wall. The stone was surprisingly warm, considering the atmosphere in the room, and he took a deep breath, fingers tightening around the handle of his **RHC**. Sliding his feet quietly along the floor, he reached the edge of the doorway to the ramp, the thick line of gore almost perfectly center, then carefully, carefully, *carefully* leaned just his eye past the corner.

A bright flash made him leap back, **RHC** up and his finger on the trigger, breath caught in his throat.

"Hiral," Seena hissed, "you okay?"

His hand holding the **RHC** shook slightly, but he didn't lower it, and looked back at Seena. He opened his mouth to respond but wasn't quite able to get the words out, so he just held up a hand instead.

Just lightning. Nothing terrible and trying to eat me.

His brain showed him an image of the **Prince of the Swamp** to conveniently remind him lightning didn't necessarily mean something wasn't looking to put him on the menu. He took another look at the Great Tusk corpse—was that his imagination, or were those burns around the edges?

Could there be hydras in the swamp? Is that the Enemy? No, hydras would be too… simple. Not nearly enough to bring an entire world to its knees.

Hiral patted the air one more time, partly for Seena and partly for himself, then steeled his nerves and focused on steadying his hand. One breath, two… three. There… back under control. Lightning flashed, just barely reflecting on the trail of blood, and Hiral stalked up to the corner again. One more breath, and he peeked around the edge, managing not to flinch back at the next flash from the end of the tunnel.

Rain poured down like a sheet of water over the opening to the dungeon ramp, but not a drop of it seemed able to come in. With each flash of lightning, he could see the trail of blood running up the ramp, all the way to the top, and in an almost perfectly straight line. Straight didn't rule out one half coming in—or the other half going out.

No, Hiral, don't be an idiot. If it happened down here, there should be more…

Hiral looked at the pool of blood around the torn end of the Great Tusk. That *could* just be from the boar bleeding out, but… His eyes trailed along the floor, and even the wall beside him. There was blood there too. Spatters of it. Like a waterskin had popped.

Whatever happened to the boar happened *inside*.

Fallen's balls. But, what came inside? Seena said most monsters couldn't enter. Most…?

Hiral turned his attention away from the remains and again looked back up the tunnel. The heavy rain made it tough to see out, but the occasional flash of lightning gave him enough light to barely make out the silhouettes of the scraggly trees outside the entrance. Should he risk going up for a look? If he moved quickly and quietly…

Another flash of lightning, and a red bar appeared at the top of ramp where Hiral had been staring, a blinking notification screaming to life in front of his eyes.

Warning! Warning! Warning!
Enemy Detected!
WARNING! WARNING! WARNING!

Hiral yanked himself around the corner, back to the wall, and his breathing quickened. That had been a *long* health bar, and pretty high up for him to see it. Whatever the *Enemy* was… it was big. Really big. The question was—had it seen him too?

He dismissed the notification with some effort, then blew the air out gently between his lips. He waited for a crash of thunder and two more flashes of lightning before peeking around the corner. Nothing there.

Hiral backed away from the entrance to the ramp, but his eyes settled again on the Great Tusk corpse. If the *Enemy* was that big, how did it kill the boar down the ramp? Something didn't add up. Or, maybe he was just wrong about where it was killed. The splatter could've been from the corpse getting thrown down the ramp…?

Without an answer, or a real way to get one, he shook his head, then jogged back over to the group, thirteen sets of anxious eyes practically boring into him.

"Well?" Seena asked.

"The *Enemy*," Hiral said.

"You saw one?" Seeyela asked.

"Not exactly. I saw the health bar from ***View***, and it was really, *really* long, then I got the same warning notification I got last time."

"Convenient how it's just you who sees the *Enemy*," Fitch muttered.

"***View*** health bar?" Seeyela asked at the same time. "What's that?"

"Achievement reward for completing the dungeon," Seena explained quickly, though her attention stayed on Hiral. "Did it kill the boar?"

"I don't know," Hiral said with a shrug. "I thought maybe it did, but from where I saw the health bar in the rain, it had to be pretty big. I don't know how it could've gotten down here to do it."

"Either way, we need to be careful," Seeyela said. "Everybody stay away from the entrance."

"You're seriously going to trust his word on this?" Fitch asked. "Why is everybody so friendly with this guy? He's an *Islander*. They've basically treated us like pests our entire lives. You all know how they look at us when they come down to trade, like it *smells* just being around us. None of you have *ever* said a good word about one of them, not even that Arty guy."

"Caaven is just nice to him because he's the only Artist willing to come down and do the fertility glyphs. You all know it."

"Hiral isn't like the others," Wule said.

"Because he was a failure up in Fallen Reach? Because he didn't have a class? You think he's going to act the same when he gets back up with his people and suddenly he's one of them again?"

"I'm not one of them," Hiral pointed out. "They're Makers; I'm a Builder, apparently." The words sounded hollow, even in his ears.

"You'll still side with them over us," Fitch seethed, his hand actually going to the hilt of his sword. "Even after all the promises you made to Seena, once you get back, you'll tell them all about the dungeons."

Hiral's fingers tightened around his **RHC**, while Left and Right not so casually moved to his sides.

"This is *not* the time for this nonsense," Seeyela snapped, turning a glare at Fitch and then at Hiral. "Not the time at all. Once we get to the *Asylum*, we are going to sort out this shit between you two once and for all. Until then, stow it. Got it?"

Fitch's lips whitened in a tight line, but he didn't say anything else.

Hiral, for his part, sheathed his weapon on his thigh, then gave Left and Right a tap on the shoulders to make sure they didn't do anything rash. If he was thinking it, they both definitely were.

"Good," Seeyela said with one more glare for good measure—obviously where Seena had learned hers from—before looking at the others. "We can't go outside now, but that wasn't our plan anyway. Seena, tell us about the dungeon, and we'll get in there and clear it."

"Sure," Seena said, though there was still a tension in her shoulders, and in the others from her party.

Are they angry at me for causing trouble? Or angry at Fitch for making trouble with me?

"Left, could you get started on the locations of the *Prince's* totems?" Seena went on.

"Does anybody have something to write with? And on?" Left asked.

"I do. Just give me a minute," Cal said, going over to her pack and starting to root around.

Left turned to Hiral and asked quietly, so that only he and Right could hear, "You good?"

"Yeah," Hiral said. "Thanks for standing with me. Both of you."

Left and Right shared a look, then actually smiled.

"Who else would we stand with?" Right asked. "We're kind of biased."

"Still, thanks. Go on, Left. You're the only one who knows where all the totems are."

"I could lie about one," Left said seriously, eying the swordsman.

"Nah, that'd just hurt everybody," Hiral said.

"Yes, but thought I'd offer," Left said, then jogged over to join Cal.

At that point, Seena was already explaining the dungeon's encounters and mechanics to Seeyela and Lonil, with Nivian offering additional input. Vix and Yanily, meanwhile, were talking to the three other damage dealers, and Wule went over to talk to Cal.

"Doesn't look like they need us for anything," Hiral said to Right.

"Doesn't mean they're trying to exclude you, so stop thinking it," Right said.

"Could you blame them? I'm sure Fitch isn't the only one thinking it, even if he's the only one voicing it," Hiral said. "They all grew up together. I'll always be an outsider."

"Are you seriously still going on about that?" Right asked, but after a moment, he visibly sighed. "Sorry, that's not fair of me. I know you've had a lifetime of trauma related to not fitting in. Sure, I've got the memories of it, but it's not the same. Anyway, you obviously weren't watching the other people from your party when Fitch was talking.

"Yes, *your* party. They were ready to go to war for you, Hiral. If you'd looked away from Fitch for a second, you would've seen it. Childhood friends or not, you've been there for them in the dungeons. They weren't amused when he said the things he did. Stop doubting them, even if it's hard."

"A little voice in the back of my head agrees with you," Hiral said.

"That's literally my voice," Right said.

"But there's another big part of me that constantly says it's wrong. That I'll never fit in or be good enough."

"And that's why we don't let him out," Right said without missing a beat, and Hiral opened his mouth, then closed it.

"Pardon?" he finally said.

Right reached out and put a hand on Hiral's shoulder, then smiled. "Kidding. It's just me and Left. Nobody else in there. That voice is just an echo of the past. One that'll fade over time if you stop listening to it for a while."

Hiral blinked a few times, then blew out his breath. "You had me worried there for a second."

Right winked at him.

"Finished," Left told the group, holding out a piece of paper to Seena and Seeyela. "This is assuming they come from the *Scholar* like we did. These marks here are the totems. I've drawn in and labeled some of the notable landmarks nearby to make them easier to find."

"This is amazing, Left," Seena said. "I think we've gotten most of the major points explained, but let's go over a few of the details before you go in. Left, can you pull out your banner to top everybody off while we do it?"

"Planning to go back in?" Hiral asked, joining the group.

Seena looked at the huddled group of Great Tusks. "Maybe it's better we're in the dungeon than out here for the time being. We'll get started on the farming."

Left touched his right hand on the *Banner of Courage*, then pulled it away with a streamer of glowing smoke. The banner formed a second later, and he drove it into the ground, though he didn't let it go. The familiar golden dome grew out of the banner, filled the room, and then... vanished.

"That's... odd," Seena said, apparently noticing the same thing Hiral did.

A quick look at his status window showed he still had the banner's buff, so why wasn't...?

"The dome isn't constrained by walls," he said, his eyes widening. "How deep do you think we are? The ramp is what, thirty or forty feet? Which means the dome might be..."

"...visible from up above!" Seena said, catching on.

"Left, cancel it, hurry," Hiral said.

The double nodded, and the gently flapping banner faded into glowing smoke.

"Do you think anything above noticed?" Seena asked as everybody looked up.

"It was only for a second," Yanily said.

"A glowing second," Vix pointed out.

"I'm sure it's fine," Yanily countered.

WHAM. The entire room shook, dust and small rocks cascading down from the ceiling, and cracks suddenly split small lines along the far wall. Water splashed down from the ramp, along with chunks of chiseled stone, runes softly glowing in them. *WHAM.* More rocks bounced down the ramp and into the room while the Great Tusks went crazy.

"Something's coming in!" Wule said, weapons coming out in everybody's hands.

"And that's the only way *out*," Seena said.

417

"Not the only one." Hiral swept his hand over the interface crystal. "**Enter Dungeon**," he said. "Four hours. That's the maximum we can stay in there, if we include the time after the clear. I suggest we all do that, and hope whatever it is loses interest in the meantime."

"After you kill the *Scholar*, there will be a totem," Seena told her sister, shoving the totem map into her hands. "As soon as you destroy that, you have ten minutes to kill the *Prince*. Win or lose, wait until the last minute to do that. We'll see you in four hours."

WHAM!

"Good luck," Seeyela said, looking back at where more rocks and water rained down into the entrance room. Then she also waved her hand over the interface crystal and said, "**Enter Dungeon**."

"Zero of six party members have entered the current portal. Close portal and open a new one?" Dr. Benza asked.

"Only one can be open at a time?" Hiral asked, then pointed at Seeyela. "You guys go first. I need to be here to open the next one."

Seeyela looked briefly at her sister, then nodded and waved her party through.

As soon as the portal closed, Hiral said, "**Enter Dungeon**," and a second portal mercifully appeared.

With the portal open, Hiral reabsorbed Left and Right, and then the party fled the room before whatever was coming made it in.

I just hope there's a room to come back to.

67

DUNGEON FARMING

"H IRAL? You going to get a hit in on this one?" Seena shouted.

He looked up from where he sat cross-legged on the stone road, the *Emperor's Greatsword* perched across his knees.

"Hrm?" he said, noting only one of the five Lizardmen was still standing, its red health bar almost gone. "Right, sorry!"

He lifted his *RHC* off the ground beside him and promptly shot the monster in the face. The warrior dropped to the ground in a heap beside its comrades, and the next group was just barely visible in the distance. Right on schedule.

With his contribution to the battle complete, he put the weapon down on the ground, then went back to work studying the runes running in the shape of a diamond inside the sword's blade. Unlike his *RHCs*, these runes were a permanent part of the weapon, and couldn't be swapped in and out on slides. Some of them were also… far more complicated than the runes on his body.

Strangest yet, he could make out four distinct runes—the first four cardinal points of the diamond—but it also looked like there were several more that were blurred out.

"Thanks for your help on that one," Seena said flatly, coming over to sit beside him.

"Sorry," he said, a bit of heat running up his neck.

That was the third pack of Lizardmen they'd killed, and Hiral really hadn't done much, other than chip in to make sure he got experience. The rest of the group had done all the heavy lifting.

"Nah, I'm just kidding with you. We have it handled pretty readily. Actually, do you even need to shoot one? Do Left and Right count as you contributing to the fight?" Seena looked over at the doubles, who were joking with Yanily in his new armor.

Hiral blinked at the sword, then looked up at Seena. "That's a great question. Let's find out with the next group."

Seena groaned. "Did I just give you an excuse to pay even less attention?"

"I'm totally paying attention, just to something else," Hiral said, pointing at the sword, but his eyes trailed away from Seena to the small totem in the middle of the road, which suddenly crumpled into a pile. "Uh, your totem's duration ended again."

"Already?" she asked, following his gaze. "Stupid Low-E-Rank ability duration," she grumbled, then flipped a page on the tome floating beside her. "Still, I can't complain with how quickly it's leveling up."

She shrugged and tapped a finger on the page in front of her. Immediately below the debris left by the previous totem, a new one burst out of the ground. Unlike the ones used by the *Scholar*, Seena's summoned totem was made of carved wood wrapped in the usual thorny vines, and spat a mix of normal firebolts and infernal firebolts.

"How are the fireballs working out for you?" Hiral asked.

The woman beside him frowned slightly. "Taking some getting used to. Not sure how I feel about standing still for three seconds while they form."

"Better than thirty, like the *Scholar*," Hiral reminded her.

"True. Those ten it had each took longer—three seconds to my one—but they had a *lot* of power. Way more than what mine pack. Might almost be worth it, kind of like Balyo's big hit."

Hiral hesitated at the mention of Balyo. Since they'd entered the portal in a rush, they'd all been dancing around the topic of how the other party was doing. With their prior knowledge, Seena's team had raced through downing the *King* and *Queen*, and then the *Scholar*, all in short order. They'd left the *Scholar's* totem up, so as not to start the *Prince* encounter, and had come back to the road to farm some experience. Now that the rush from that was gone, well, everybody seemed to have something on their minds, though nobody talked about it.

And from the look on Seena's face, *not talking about it* was her way of dealing with the worry for the moment.

"Will you ever get to ten?" he asked instead of broaching the other subject.

"Just eight, I think," she said with a nod of her head, as though she knew what he'd been thinking, and was grateful he didn't ask. "One more fireball per rank on top of my current three. Not sure how the *Scholar* had ten, but it's fine. Eight will be plenty."

"And you get more totems per rank too?"

"Yes! That part I'm really looking forward to. Having six of those little guys around will add up to a lot of damage." Seena literally rubbed her hands together in front of herself. "Also, watch that guy. See how it's turning slowly?"

"You doing that?" Hiral asked.

"Nope. I noticed it earlier. The totems always seem to want to face the closest opponent. Even when it's not spitting out fire, it's watching. Aiming. And, right now, it's aiming at those Lizardmen waaaaaay over there."

"That could be really useful. How much solar energy does it cost you to drop one down?"

"Next to nothing. It's only when it starts spitting fire that it gets more costly. Uh, once I turn on the fire, I can't turn it off until the enemy is dead or the duration expires. That's out of my hands."

"Still, dropping those while we're worried about an ambush or something, it could warn us. We'll need to…"

"Let me guess," Seena interrupted. "Run some tests. I have no idea how you didn't become an Academic," she joked, elbowing him gently in the side.

"And I have no idea how you're not classified as a damage dealer," Hiral responded with a chuckle.

"Yeah, I dunno," Seena admitted. "Maybe it can change? How about you? You figure that thing out yet? We're all kind of waiting to see what it does."

"I feel like I'm getting close," Hiral said, running his fingers along the flat of the blade. "See this rune here, right beside the crosspiece?" He pointed at the bottom-most rune.

"Yeah, what about it?"

"It's far more complicated than the others. The two directly above it—these two that look like they're linked to it—are like a single stroke from a pen. I mean, you could make each one without leaving the page, if you were writing it. Like the runes on my arms. One clean stroke. Anyway, this one here… it's almost like three or four runes overlaid on each other. Maybe more."

"And you have no idea what it could mean?" Seena asked. "You didn't get a user manual with it or anything?"

"I wish," Hiral sighed. "When I got the **RHCs**, the notification told me what the **Rune of Impact** did. The notification for this? Told me it had unknown abilities. Gee, thanks."

"What's your best guess? You must have one."

Hiral looked at Seena out of the corner of his eyes, surprised by the sound of confidence in her voice. Confidence in him? Damn, maybe Right was… right. He really did need to get past his trauma.

"Well," Hiral started, turning his forearms up so they could both see the runes there, "notice how these are opposites of each other?"

"Yeah, we talked about that before. It was part of how you unlocked the other two, right?"

"Yes. When you look at these, and then you look at that rune in the sword, do you see any similarities?"

Seena leaned over, staring down at his arms, then at the sword. Back and forth her head turned as she looked, then she reached out and started tracing lines over the flat of the blade. "They're both there, aren't they? If I ignore some of the other lines, and *just* look for these, I feel like I see them crossing over each other here." She tapped a central point of the rune.

"That's what I was thinking too," Hiral said. "Though, maybe it's just because I *want* to see that?"

"Assuming it's not, what could it mean?"

"Best guess here," Hiral said, referring back to what she'd said earlier, "I think these *simple* runes—and I use 'simple' very loosely here—are kind of like foundational runes. Basic concepts. Rejection and attraction, for example. Almost like core, observable forces. Also, did I mention I never actually became an Academic? I don't have the right words to describe what I mean."

"You're doing great. Keep going," Seena said. "Attraction and rejection, like magnets, right?"

"Yes, like magnets. Simple to watch… to observe, but really difficult to explain. And this rune in the sword—it's like an equation of runes, but written all over each other, instead of in a line like we would do for math."

"I hate math," Seena said. "Don't get me wrong—I know how important it is, I'm just not very good at it. Back to the sword, though. You think it's like a magnet?"

Hiral shook his head before he even thought about the question. It was a good one, but that *idea* felt off. When he looked at the rune, it didn't make him think about magnets, though he did get a similar *impression* from it. "Not quite. I think actual magnetism, if done through runes, would be like this—some kind of an advanced concept rune. Argh, but that's not the right word for it either."

"That's okay; let's use it between us," Seena said.

"Thanks," Hiral said. "When I look at this rune, I don't think of magnetism, I think of… But never mind; that can't be right."

"What can't be right? Spit it out."

"It makes me think of gravity," Hiral said, even the words coming out of his mouth feeling *almost* correct—but not quite. "The attraction part, and some of these other runes. It makes me feel like I'm falling. That's mainly why I'm sitting here, actually," he said with a laugh. "But, this **Rune of Rejection** here? What would it be doing in a rune for gravity?"

"Hrm," Seena said, putting her finger to her lips in thought. "Are you looking at the runes individually, or as a group? Didn't you say your **RHC** had slots for you to add other runes? And… and that they'd interact with each other if you did that?"

Hiral's eyes widened at the question. "Individually," he said slowly, looking again at the sequence of runes. And the way they were *linked*.

"And this is a *weapon*," Seena went on. "Don't just think about gravity—think about how it could be applied to the sword. To combat."

"Seena… you're a genius," Hiral said, voice barely above a whisper, moving his finger from the advanced concept rune to the two linked runes. Runes that were just inverted versions of each other. "These two. They just apply an effect, a modifier, to this one…"

"And what's that modifier?" Seena asked.

"It's so simple. How did I not see it immediately?" Hiral lifted his hands from the blade in disbelief. "Increase and decrease."

Like before, as soon as the thought solidified in Hiral's mind, scripts of solar energy flowed from the double-helix patterns on his arms and chest, this time consolidating on his shoulder blades. The familiar yellow energy flared, power building as the scripts swirled into larger shapes. Left and Right vanished in a flash of light at the same time Hiral's solar energy dropped straight to zero.

"Oh," was all he had time to say before he collapsed straight back to the road, only Seena's quick reflexes catching his head before it bounced off the stone.

"Damn, Hiral, I guess you got it right?" she asked, gently lowering his head to the stone.

"Uh, yeah," he said, feeling like he'd just run a marathon.

"Left and Right…" Nivian started, rushing over, only to see Hiral on the ground. "Oh, this again? He got new runes?"

"I think so," Seena said. "Hiral?"

He pulled up his status window, then nodded from where he lay. "*Rune of Increase* and *Rune of Decrease.* On my shoulders… which means… Oh, wow. Left is going to be *happy.* Hrm. Or maybe really annoyed."

"Why? What's on your shoulders?" Wule asked, coming over and kneeling down beside Hiral. Refreshing energy flowed into him, soothing the very minor pains from toppling over.

"The *Wings of Anella,*" Hiral said. "With both, he'd be able to fly. With only one, though… we'll have to test. Help me sit up?"

"Sure," Nivian said, coming around and propping Hiral back into a seated position. "We've got a few minutes before the Lizardmen arrive. You going to be okay?"

"More than okay," Hiral said. "Thanks to Seena, I figured out what this is." He pointed at the complex rune on the sword. "There *is* a rune of gravity in here, these lines," he said, tracing the complex rune out on the flat of the blade, "and…" He cut off, energy suddenly exploding out of his body.

Party members shouted in surprise as they got thrown back from Hiral. The double-helix pattern burst out and surrounded him in a sphere of glowing lines of script, then lifted him to hover in the air. His arms and legs jerked out as though ropes wrapped his ankles and wrists, and a huge weight settled on his chest, crushing him down even though he lay unmoving several feet above the ground.

Beneath him, he heard the cracking of stone as the runic script expanded the sphere of influence, and he fought to force air into his lungs. Nothing came. Darkness clawed at the sides of his vision. Flashes of light and dark specks raced across in front of his eyes. His heart hammered in his chest, blood pounding through his veins, while his tattoos and Meridian Lines tore off his skin to hang an inch around his body.

The dungeon sky faded from sight as unconsciousness claimed him, though the glowing script continued to whirl within the darkness. And in that darkness, some of the script *made sense*. Like he had almost understood the gravity rune by looking at it. Knowledge of the foreign language etched across his body was right at his fingertips.

Another second, and…

…he thumped down to the ground, the impact shattering the moment of comprehension. Basic bodily needs—like breathing—quickly rushed to the forefront of his attention, and he curled up on the ground, coughing and gasping. Long seconds passed before he could take a real breath, and he rolled onto his back to look up at the sky. He lay in a curved indentation in the ground, the bottom-most point a good three feet deep, and he had to sit up to see over the lip.

"Everybody okay?" he asked weakly.

"Does soaking wet count as *okay*?" Yanily asked, sitting in the swampy muck on the side of the road.

"I thought your armor had elemental resistance," Vix asked, also standing up from the swamp.

"Apparently, water doesn't count as an element," Yanily said.

"Did the water hurt you?" Wule asked.

"Just my feelings," Yanily replied.

"Then the armor protected you just fine." Wule turned his attention to Hiral, but didn't approach. "You finished exploding?"

"Uh…" Hiral started, then held up his hands to keep everybody back. A quick check at his status window showed him back at three percent solar energy already, and he had a new **Rune of Gravity** listed. Unlike the last few runes, however, this one was listed immediately under the **Rune of Separation**.

*Hrm. Is this going to give me something like **Foundational Split**? Or… did I completely miss the fact I could use the **Rune of Separation** like I used the other runes? More testing…*

"Well?" Wule asked. "More exploding or not?"

"There actually might be one more," Hiral admitted, and Wule took a step back. "I think I figured out what that fourth rune on the sword is. And, if I'm right…"

"Exploding," Nivian said. "Got it. Could you get it over with? We've got Lizardmen coming."

"You're talking pretty casually about me exploding here…" Hiral said flatly.

"Not the first time it's happened," Nivian pointed out. "Seriously, get on with it. We're on a schedule."

"Fine. You might want to take an extra step back. This one was gravity, and you saw what it did to the ground around me." Hiral reached out to get the sword, then stood in the center of the small bowl in the ground.

"And what's this other one?" Seena asked.

Hiral looked at the rune on the sword, finally understanding how it worked in unison with the others he could see, and probably with the others that still appeared blurry. Those, he would figure out in time. For now, all that mattered was the fourth and final rune.

"Energy," he said, tracing the rune on the blade, and it was more than just his double helix that erupted from his body.

Pure yellow energy cascaded out of him in a column that stretched to the sky and blew the clouds away. Light filled his vision as the ground rumbled, and wind whipped around him like a tornado. On his status window, his solar energy capacity climbed and climbed, blowing past one hundred percent. Heat spread through him.

Two hundred percent, and it felt like he was standing in the sun.

Four hundred percent, and his skin ached like he'd gotten a sunburn.

Six hundred percent, a fever washed through his body, setting his limbs shaking.

Eight hundred percent, and fire ran through his veins instead of blood.

One thousand percent, and he *was* the sun, glowing like he was about to supernova…

Zero percent, and he collapsed back to the smoking ground, heat rising and shimmering the air, but still blessedly cool on his skin.

"That's your fault, Nivian!" Seena shouted somewhere above the lip of the depression in the ground.

"How is that *my* fault?" the tank asked.

"You just had to joke about him exploding," Seena shot back.

"Is anybody going to check on him?" Wule asked.

"You're the healer," Yanily said. "And… oh, look. Lizardmen are almost here. Guess we should go take care of those, right, Vix?"

"Safer than getting near the exploding Islander," Vix said.

"Didn't… explode…" Hiral said, pulling himself up by using the ***Emperor's Greatsword*** as a crutch. In his status window, the ***Rune of Energy*** appeared beneath the ***Rune of Gravity***, and there were even new labels beside them.

Rune of Separation – Primary
Rune of Gravity – Secondary
Rune of Energy – Tertiary

No idea what the primary, secondary, tertiary thing means, but that's for later.

"Hiral, you doing okay?" Seena asked. "You're... uh... done... exploding now, right?"

"Yeah, done," Hiral said, his solar energy climbing quickly. He hefted himself out of the depression in the ground. "And, if you don't mind, could you let me take the lead on the Lizardmen?"

"Sure. Why?" Seena asked.

"Because you wanted to see what it could do," he said, activating **Foundational Split** and pushing solar energy into the **Emperor's Greatsword**. A blade of solid energy extended out of the broken edge to bring the sword to its natural size. "Time to find out."

68
LET'S SEE WHAT THIS CAN DO

LEFT and Right peeled off to fall into step beside him as he started toward the approaching Lizardmen.

"Oh, somebody's confident," Right said.

"With good reason. That may not be the full power of the ***Emperor's Greatsword***, but it's nothing to scoff at," Left said.

"What's the plan, Hiral?" Nivian asked as Hiral walked up beside him, then strode past.

"Back me up if I get in trouble, but I want to see what this thing can do," Hiral said.

"Uh… did he hit his head?" Yanily asked Nivian, then looked at Hiral. "You do remember how to count, don't you? There are five of them and… three of you. Literally. Wow, that's still strange to say."

"I know, the odds aren't very good," Hiral said.

"For them," Right added, his entire right arm up to his shoulder flaring with purple flames along his Meridian Line.

"This shouldn't be a problem," Left added, his right hand going up to his left shoulder.

A blue, flaming wing erupted out to extend almost eight feet to his left, the air around it shimmering cold and dripping snowflakes. Another quick touch to his forearm, and the ***Dagger of Sath*** left a glowing trail like water behind him.

"Sorry you only got one wing," Hiral said.

"And half of the ***Spear of Clouds***," Left said.

"What!?" Hiral asked, looking at Left.

"Your new runes are on your back, which activated half of our back runes," Left said. "Unfortunately, that's not enough to shape the spear."

"Maybe not for you, but it got my Meridian Line on that side working," Right said.

"Damn," Hiral sighed, but he still turned his attention back to the Lizardmen charging at him. Just over five hundred feet away, they'd be activating their movement skills any second now, then the sorcerer would rush up and start preparing its fireball.

"We'll back you up if we see you getting in over your head," Right said, then he and Left stopped. "Let's see what you can do."

Hiral gripped the sword in both hands, the weapon practically thrumming with power, then lowered his shoulder and dashed forward at the same time the Lizardmen used their movement skills. Moving faster than they expected, he cut out wide and then in at the side of the right-most warrior just as it stopped. His sword arced out and around, a trail of energy hanging in the air behind it.

The Lizardman, no novice to battle, reacted quickly enough to start bringing its spear around to parry. Start—but not finish. Hiral's glowing blade struck it in the upper arm, then kept going right through the chest beyond. Completely cleaving the monster in two, Hiral couldn't help but be impressed at the sheer destructive power of the weapon, though that wasn't even its true strength, if he understood the runes properly.

Slamming his front foot to the ground, he halted the momentum of his swing, flipped his wrist, and pushed solar energy into the gravity rune in the crystal. A thought tethered the blade's gravity to the next Lizardman as he shifted to bring his trailing foot forward, and his backswing practically launched upward.

Even with the Lizardman's spear in the perfect position to parry, the strike lifted the monster right off its feet and hurled it backwards—and Hiral almost went with it before he severed the gravity tether. Still, that took him out of position as the next warrior in line moved at his exposed back. He could feel it coming straight for him, expecting the easy kill. There was no way Hiral could move such a huge sword around fast enough to stop it, after all.

Except, with a touch of solar energy, the massive greatsword suddenly weighed *nothing*, and Hiral pivoted around on his foot, bringing the weapon up and over for a vertical, downward strike.

The Lizardman's eyes widened in surprise, but its spear came up in a line to parry.

Another touch of solar energy removed the weightlessness of the sword, and instead multiplied the weight by a factor of over fifty. Hiral's fingers struggled to hold on to the weapon as it crashed down on the Lizardman like a falling building, the warrior's arms shattering as it tried to turn aside the unexpectedly heavy blow. As soon as its arms failed, the warrior's head was next, and the ground shook a heartbeat later from the sword slamming into it.

Hiral returned the sword's weight to normal as the Lizardman's two halves fell in opposite directions, then turned his attention to the fireball forming over the sorcerer's head. *Have to take care of that now.*

Tethering the sword's gravity to the sorcerer, Hiral turned and heaved, *throwing* the sword at the distant Lizardman, whose eyes widened in shock. Then, with a touch of **Rejection**, he adjusted the spinning weapon to cut the sorcerer clean in half from the waist down. That just left two more warriors, and his weapon sailing away from him.

The Lizardman he'd batted away earlier was the first to react, turning from the pieces of the sorcerer still falling—and the flying sword—to charge at Hiral.

Shouldn't have looked away... Hiral thought, then reached out with his left hand and activated his **Rune of Attraction**. With the momentum the sword had, it didn't stop and return to him, but instead arched like a boomerang, swinging end around end. The poor warrior never saw it coming, and his chest exploded in a shower of blood twenty feet away. Hiral caught the hilt in his hand, then turned his attention to the fifth and final warrior.

For the first time since he'd entered the dungeon, Hiral saw one of the monsters *hesitate*. Its spear came up, but its eyes went to Hiral's weapon—it'd seen how little good parrying had done its allies.

"What's it going to be?" Hiral asked the monster, shifting his own stance to comfortably take the weapon in both hands again.

He'd mostly trained with two weapons to build ambidexterity, but his instructor had insisted he get familiar with a single, heavier sword as well. Not that the **Emperor's Greatsword** was any heavier than Hiral wanted it to be at any given moment.

Still no movement from the Lizardman, so Hiral darted in, his **Dex** giving him a speed near the top end of E-Rank, and beyond what the warrior could handle. He swept his blade across from the right, letting the warrior get its spear up in time to parry, but didn't add any of the gravity-manipulated weight to the blow. As soon as the weapons touched, Hiral cocked the blade back and around to attack from the other side.

The warrior parried again as it stepped back, confusion on its face as to why it wasn't dead yet.

Because I need practice using the runes.

Again, as soon as the weapons hit, Hiral brought his sword back, up, and then straight down, this time pulsing solar energy into the rune. When the warrior brought its spear up to parry, the unexpected weight drove its weapon down, and the edge of Hiral's sword bit into its shoulder. Though he could've ended the fight right then and there, he quickly withdrew, a line of blood following his blade as he double-stepped back.

Free hand going to its shoulder wound, the Lizardman lifted its spear straight at Hiral in challenge, then charged in. The movement skill came first, trying to catch Hiral off guard, but he'd seen it more than a dozen times by this point, and he simply shifted his feet and brought his sword over beside his body to block the horizontal cut. Next was a withdrawal and quick stab, lightning fast with the warrior's natural strength, but an application of solar energy made Hiral's sword as light as a feather, and he easily slid it into place to block the thrust.

A feint, thrust, slash combo came next, aiming to catch Hiral's lead leg with the final blow. He neatly parried it all aside with his sword, each time adjusting how much solar energy he fed into the blade to see the effects. With the next one—a slash at his right shoulder—he pushed the sword's weight in the opposite direction, more than doubling it, and blew the warrior's attack away with his parry.

The instant the Lizardman shuffled off balance, Hiral readjusted the weight of the weapon in quick succession, going from heavy to light to *very* heavy, then tethered it to the Lizardman. Like the creature knew what was coming, it didn't even bother bringing its weapon up to try to parry, and its decapitated head fell to the ground a second later.

"You made that look easy," Right said, coming over to join him with Left.

Hiral dropped straight to a cross-legged seated position in response, the energy-half of his weapon vanishing. "This thing gulps up solar energy like you wouldn't believe," he said, his capacity barely at three percent after the fight.

"Not like you started at full," Left said.

"No, but I'll *never* be at full using it," Hiral said. "I'll need more practice to conserve energy as I fight."

"You sure you want to?" Seena asked as she walked over.

"And that's the power of an S-Rank weapon, folks," Yanily added as he followed.

Hiral was already shaking his head. "I wasn't using it at any more than E-Rank. That was maybe two percent of its power."

Yanily openly gaped at Hiral, then looked from his spear to Hiral's sword. "Not that I don't love you, baby, but when are you going to do that?" he asked the spear.

"Two percent, and it was that one-sided? *And* they were **Elites**," Seena said.

The mention of **Elites** reminded Hiral of his **One Man Army** achievement, and sure enough, the bonus now sat at fifteen percent.

One percent per solo kill?

"If we weren't sitting here farming enemies on a predictable schedule, I wouldn't want to be so low on energy. I would've had to fight differently. Don't worry, though. I'll figure it out with a bit more practice."

"Any chance we can help?" Yanily asked flatly. "I mean, yeah, we got experience for them, but no chance to improve our skills. I've gotta get all my skills to the top of D-Rank now!"

"Sorry," Hiral said. "That was selfish of me. Wait, you got experience without doing anything?"

"We did," Vix said.

"Well, that's good to know. In the dungeons, you get credit just for being here," Hiral said, filing away the interesting tidbit for later.

"Either way, it's fine," Seena said, glaring at Yanily. "At least he's already D-Rank himself."

"And now I've got to get to C-Rank. Do you have any idea how much experience I need for that?" Yanily shot back.

"Yes, you've only been telling us since you evolved," Vix said. "Or maybe unevolved is more accurate for you."

"Ouch," Yanily said, putting his hand over his heart. "You wound me."

"Wule, patch up Yanily's ego, would you?" Seena asked before turning her attention back to Hiral. "If you're going mix and match using your **RHCs** and that sword, we're going to need to work it into our tactics. Everybody, let's use these next few groups of Lizardmen to do that. We've still got more than ninety minutes before we need to go take care of the **Prince**."

"Unless Hiral solos it too," Yanily said, pouting.

"He's not going to solo the **Boss**," Seena deadpanned, then glanced at Hiral sideways. "Right?"

"Uh, no way," he said, though the image of leaping onto its back, driving the sword in, and maximizing its gravity did pop into his mind. *Would that work...?* "We've got to use the totems, after all," he said instead.

The looks on everybody else's faces told him they *knew* what he was thinking, and he gave them his best innocent smile.

Nobody believed it.

"Whatever," he grumbled.

Seena chuckled at them, then clapped her hands together. "Let's just get back to farming before we finish up in here."

Everybody looked at each other, the same worries about the other party passing through their heads, followed by the question of what they'd find when they got out. Like before, though, nobody voiced the concerns, and instead they turned their attention to the next group of distant warriors.

They couldn't leave the dungeon early, and worrying wouldn't do them any good. They'd deal with whatever was waiting for them on the outside when they left the dungeon. But first...

"Uh, actually," Hiral said, scratching his nose as they looked at him again.

"Hey, you said we could help," Yanily said.

"It's not that," Hiral said quickly. "I got an idea from the last fight. I need a few minutes to figure out if it'll work. So, could you...?"

"He wants to be lazy again," Seena said. "Solos one group and then he thinks he can just sit back and relax while the rest of us do the work."

"It's not like that at all!" Hiral said. "Okay, maybe *part* of it is! Shouldn't take long, though. One group, tops. I'll be ready for the next one."

"Not if you keep talking," Seena said, and led the party around to make sure they were between Hiral and the next Lizardman party approaching them in the distance.

"Thanks," Hiral said, then turned his attention to the sword across his lap. The way he'd tethered its gravity to the warriors and then later used his *Rune of Attraction* to pull it back after he'd thrown it—could he combine the two? With the idea in mind, he got to work experimenting.

69
CAN'T STAY HERE

HIRAL blinked water out of his eyes as he exited the dungeon portal, then looked up at the rain streaming down on top of him.

Rain? Am I outside?

No, that wasn't it. A huge chunk of the dungeon ceiling above him was simply missing, the pouring rain streaming through the gap and leaving water up to his ankles at his feet. A small step put him on top of the water—thanks to **Walk on Water**—and he looked around the room.

Carnage and devastation were the first words that came to mind. The entire herd of Great Tusks lay butchered in the water, most of the *pieces* filling the corner where they'd huddled before, but plenty more strewn about the floor like they'd been pulled apart. Huge blocks of the dungeon's roof lay collapsed on the other side of the room, and the original ramp down had been more than quadrupled in size, as if something massive had torn its way in.

"What… happened?" Nivian asked, holding his shield above his head to block some of the rain.

A flash of lightning and a boom of thunder overhead punctuated the question.

"Nothing good," his twin said quietly, just barely audible over the constant thrumming of rain.

"Seeyela and the others?" Seena asked.

"I don't see them," Hiral said, then turned to the dungeon pedestal. The *smashed* dungeon pedestal. "Damn."

He walked over to it and crouched to find the interface crystal. Maybe it'd still work if he could just… There! He pushed aside small pieces of rubble, then waved his hand over the crystal.

Nothing.

"Is that the crystal?" Seena asked.

"Yes, but it doesn't look like it works anymore," Hiral said. "No way to check the clear times."

"Or go back in," Yanily said.

"Now is not the time to think about experience," Nivian said, a slight reprimand in his voice.

"I wasn't," Yanily said. "At least, not entirely. Really. Look. We went in to escape something, right? Well, we don't have that option anymore."

"We need to get to the next dungeon," Vix said.

"One more and we can enter the *Asylum*," Wule agreed, then quickly turned to Seena. "Not that I'm suggesting we leave before Seeyela and the others get out."

"I know you aren't," Seena said.

"We finished a couple of minutes earlier than the four hours," Hiral said. "I'm sure they'll be out any minute now. We should see if our supplies survived while we wait, so we're ready to go as soon as they join us."

"We'll take care of it," Nivian said to Seena. "Vix and Yanily, check on our tents and sleeping bags. Wule and I will see about food and other supplies. Hiral, I know we just got more crystal from this run, but I'll leave it to you to find what we got from the first one, and get it ready to go."

"Sure thing," Hiral said, then he and the others moved off to work on their tasks. A pulse of solar energy brought Left and Right out to join him, and he headed for the back wall.

"I don't know if I agree with you," Left said quietly to Hiral.

"Which part?" Hiral asked.

"About thinking the pedestal was destroyed on purpose," Left said. "The entire room has been trashed, and the Great Tusks slaughtered. It could've just been collateral damage."

"It's possible," Hiral said. "But if it wasn't, that means we're dealing with something smart or knowledgeable enough to know about how we escaped."

"We don't know if whatever did this even knew we were down here," Right said.

"We do," Hiral countered, finding one of the odd bags that held way more than it looked like it should. There was some damage along the side, and one of the straps was broken, but the crystals inside seemed fine. "The Great Tusks have been living down here for how many years? Hundreds? More?

"It's not a coincidence this happened right after we showed up," Hiral went on. "It's safer to assume it was the *Enemy* who did this, and it knew we were here."

"If that's true, and they knew what the pedestals do, that would mean they might know about the four-hour time limit, then, too," Left said.

"Exactly, which is why we need to be ready to go as soon as..." Hiral cut off as the dungeon portal spiraled open, and Seeyela's party stepped out.

Like Hiral had, they all paused while their brains registered the fact they were getting rained on. Then Seena was there, wrapping her sister in a hug.

"How'd it go?" Seena asked, quiet enough that only Seeyela and Hiral—with his high *Atn*—heard the question.

"Rough," Seeyela said. "But we made it through. Those **Mid-Bosses** were no joke. What's the story here?"

"We're just about ready to go," Nivian said, carrying a pack in each hand. He handed one straight to Lonil. "Pedestal doesn't work anymore, so we need to get to the last dungeon as soon as possible."

"*The Troblin Throne*," Wule said before walking over to Cal. "Anything I can help with?"

Cal shook her head. "Got everybody patched up in the hour after we completed the dungeon."

"We've got all the crystals we managed to collect from our two runs," Hiral said, gesturing between himself and his doubles. "I've got some ideas what I can do with them when we get to the next dungeon. Should help make us stronger in the long run, assuming it works."

"Any chance it will explode?" Yanily asked.

"Not… likely…?" Hiral said with a shrug.

"Then we should let Vix try it first," Yanily said.

"Thanks," Vix said flatly.

"Vix, Yanily, do you have the tents?" Nivian asked, cutting off the banter.

"Salvaged what we could," Yanily said. "Half of them look like they got buried when the roof caved in."

"Same with the sleeping bags and a good amount of the food," Vix added.

"Even if the next dungeon doesn't give us supplies, we still have more than enough," Nivian said. "And maybe we can find some of those Tri-Horns that made the tracks."

"We'll worry about that after we get to the *Asylum*," Seeyela said. "Thanks for getting our stuff ready too. Since that's done, let's get going before whatever did this"—she slowly turned her head around the destroyed room—"thinks to come back and take another look."

Taking one of the packs with the crystals in them, Hiral jogged across the surface of the water to the entrance to the ramp. "Part of it caved in, but I think we can get through here. I'm going to head up first and make sure it's clear."

"Be careful," Seena said. "Just because you have a good attunement it doesn't make you any harder to spot."

"I know," Hiral said, drawing one of his **RHCs** and starting up the tunnel.

Water ran down the slope like a small river from the heavy rain, but his feet didn't move with it. If anything, he had better traction than he expected, and he jogged about halfway up before he got to the collapsed area. Some of the glowing roots were still visible, giving him enough light to see by, and he crouched down to look through the space.

It wasn't tight enough he'd need to crawl, but a shimmy was definitely in order.

"Maybe one of us should go first," Right offered.

"You're not expendable," Hiral said, dropping the pack off his shoulder into his hand and squeezing under the fallen slab of rock.

His arm brushed against the cool stone as he passed, his **RHC** leading the way. *Would it actually do any good against an* Enemy? The tunnel seemed to close around him with each step he took, forcing him to crouch lower and lower. The roots in the caved-in area themselves were crushed and lifeless, but light beckoned from not more than ten feet ahead. He slowed to gaze out at the storm.

Wind lashed the rain against the side of the tunnel, slapping against the rocks and spattering in all directions. Whatever magic had kept the elements out before had obviously been lost when the dungeon entrance had been destroyed. Lightning flashed, illuminating the scraggly trees littering the swamp, then again and again, their branches bent to the side by the fury of nature.

Was something out there waiting for him? For anything trying to leave the dungeon? Well, he wouldn't find out just crouching there, so he took another step forward. A second step, and the pack in his hand caught on something behind him. He half-turned in reflex to look, and at the same time, something darted past the entrance to the tunnel.

Hiral froze, his weapon aimed at the mouth of the ramp, waiting. One second, two, three… ten. He waited for something to come charging in at him.

"Everything okay?" Left asked quietly from just behind him.

"I think I saw something run past the entrance," Hiral said. "Might've been my imagination."

"Better to assume it wasn't," Left said. "Is there room ahead for more than one of us?"

"Yeah," Hiral said. "I'm going."

"And we're right behind you," Left said. "Because you're not expendable either."

"Fair," Hiral said. "The pack is caught. Think you could…?"

"Done," Left said, and the pack's weight settled in Hiral's hand again.

"Thanks." He moved as quickly as he could out of the tight space, his weapon trained on the tunnel entrance the entire time. As soon as he was out, he moved to the side, Left and Right following in quick succession.

"I told the others you might've seen something," Right said. "They're coming, but there isn't room for all of us here. If it's going to be a fight, we need more space."

"We're going out," Hiral said. "Left… uh… you've got the left side."

"Don't even bother telling me," Right deadpanned.

"Go," Hiral said, quick-stepping to the tunnel exit and out into the rain, his doubles fanning out to both sides beside him.

"Clear," Left said.

"Same here," Right added.

Hiral's eyes scanned the darkness ahead as lightning flashed. He quickly turned around to check and make sure nothing was waiting for them above the tunnel entrance. Clear.

"I guess it *was* my imagination," Hiral said.

"No, there are tracks here," Left said. "Another one of those Tri-Horns, I think."

"Could Tri-Horns be the *Enemy?*" Hiral asked.

"More likely the prey," Left said. "And if it was *running…*"

"We should be thinking about doing the same thing. That path there," he said, pointing off to one side. "That's the one to **Splitfang Keep**, yeah? Which means *that one*"—he pointed in the other direction, the opposite way the Tri-Horn had gone—"should lead to the **Troblin Throne**."

"Directly toward whatever the Tri-Horn was running from," Left pointed out.

"Any better suggestions?" Hiral asked him.

"No," Left admitted.

"Right, tell the others it's as clear as it's going to get. It's time to leave." Hiral looked down the path of glowing vines. Whether the *Enemy* was that way or not, they had to go in that direction.

Hiral glanced behind him at the ruins of the dungeon entrance.

Hopefully, the Asylum *is a bit sturdier…*

70

A FAMILIAR TOWN

T HE group made good time, Hiral insisting on being in the lead with Left and Right, Seena's party trailing fifty feet behind, and Seeyela's party a similar distance further back. Dr. Benza had said groups of six or less were more likely to avoid the *Enemy's* notice, and he wasn't willing to keep Left and Right inside him.

The more eyes watching for unknown threats, the better.

"Terrain is changing," Left said, his **Atn** just as high as Hiral's. "And, is it my imagination, or am I seeing a path between the trees over there?"

"I see it too," Hiral said, the spacing between the trees far too even to be natural. "Looks like our path will meet up with it ahead," he added, pointing along the twin glowing roots running on the ground. "Maybe that means the dungeon is close."

"We've barely been jogging two hours," Left said. "You really think they're that near each other?"

Hiral looked up at the rain—the worst of the storm had passed, for now—then back ahead. "We have to catch a break eventually."

"When did you get so optimistic?" Right asked.

"Trying something new," Hiral said as they reached the intersection between their path and the other one.

As soon Left's foot touched down, he slowed to a stop, then crouched down and ran his hand under the water.

"Find something?" Hiral asked, joining his double and dipping his fingers under the water.

There was muck there—of course there was, it was a swamp—but underneath that? No mistaking it… Stone. Worked stone.

"This is a road," Hiral said, looking up and down the new path. The roots they'd been following toward the next dungeon now ran on both sides of what had to be the edges of the stone road. It was only about twenty feet wide, so not a major causeway, but it was the first stone road he'd seen other than the small town.

Is it the same? Does it connect? Even if it does, we've come pretty far.

"Right, go tell the others what we've found," Hiral told his double while he wiped aside the muck to get a better look at the stone underneath. *Not the same as Fallen Reach… which means it's not the same as the town. Still, it feels like I've seen this somewhere before.* "Left, does this look familiar to you?"

Left pushed more of the mud aside to get a better look, peering at the stone in the dim light of the glowing roots. While they'd gotten used to seeing by it for most things, it wasn't made for close inspections of details.

"Yes," Left said. "It's the same as the road from the dungeon. The one where we were farming Lizardmen."

"I thought so," Hiral said, Seena and her party catching up to them by that point.

"Right said something about a road?" Seena asked.

"Yeah, and made by Lizardmen, I think," Hiral said.

"We haven't run into any yet," Yanily said, almost sadly. "Actually, we haven't fought a single thing since we left the dungeon. I'm never going to get to C-Rank like this."

"Everything was scared off by whatever destroyed the dungeon," Vix said.

"Which is pretty impressive when you think about the huge snakes," Nivian said. "And also means we shouldn't dawdle. The path is pretty clear, and a road means we're less likely to come across sinkholes, right?"

"I'm still going on ahead," Hiral said.

"Do any of Left's tattoos help with being sneaky?" Wule asked.

"Being… sneaky?" Hiral asked.

"Uh, stealthy? Our usual scout has abilities that make him tougher to notice. If you're going to be separated from the group, shouldn't you have something like that?"

"Maybe you missed the S-Rank weapon slung across his back?" Yanily said. "Don't think he needs to worry about it."

"It's powerful against other E-Ranks," Hiral said. "D and above… I'm not so sure. But, to answer your question, he has the **Way of Shadow**… if we can unlock it. Until then, not much else."

"What's the holdup?" Seeyela said, her party catching up and making the group uncomfortably large.

"Lizardman road," Hiral said. "Sorry for the delay, I'm going now."

"Be careful, since you can't be sneaky," Seena said before glancing in Wule's direction.

"Yeah, whatever," the healer said, pulling his hood further over his head to hide from the never-ending rain. "It was a valid question."

Hiral turned and left the group again, his eyes scanning between the trees for any health bars or flashing warning notifications. Nothing so far. Was it connected to the storms? Both times he'd seen the *Enemy*, the weather had been really bad. Were they safer when the rain was lighter?

No, he couldn't get complacent.

He jogged for another half an hour before he slowed again, the pattern of the roots ahead changing. For the most part in the swamp, they ran along the ground or wound around the trees. Further down the path, he could see them branching out as they climbed straight up something flat and ran off in both directions.

"A wall," Hiral said.

"More than a wall," Left said, pointing straight down the path.

Hiral pulled his attention from the sides and looked through what had to be the gate. "Another town," he said, unable to make out if it was a Lizardman town, or one like they'd found earlier.

"If it's a Lizardman town, we could run into trouble," Left said. "Around or through?"

"Through," Hiral said, drawing both his **RHCs**. "The dungeon could be in there, for all we know."

"And I think we're in pretty good shape to deal with *trouble*," Right said, cracking the knuckles of his right hand.

"You're spending too much time with Yanily," Left said dryly.

"And you sound too much like Vix," Hiral said with a shake of his head, then did a quick check behind him. Seena and the others had slowed when they saw him stop, so he gave them a wave—making it clear he had his weapons drawn—then took off down the road again. "Be ready for anything."

Hiral kept his eyes on the top of the wall for scouts as he ran, picking up speed in case they got spotted, but nothing moved other than the falling rain. As he got closer, he saw a missing chunk of wall there, the uneven top here, and the general disrepair of the thing as a whole.

"Same as usual," he said before the trio passed through the gate to the other side of the wall, Left and Right spreading out on his sides to cover his flanks, while he aimed his weapons straight down the street. The buildings on both sides were little more than ruins, nothing standing closer than a hundred feet to him.

Glowing roots wrapped the debris like small, illuminated hills, and climbed what looked to be still-standing buildings in the distance. The whole thing was almost surreal, with the layer of water covering the ground, reflecting the lines of light, but blurring in the falling rain.

"Clear on this side," Left said.

"Ditto over here," Right added. "No Lizardmen here for a long time, I'm thinking."

"Doesn't look like it," Hiral said, eying the sides of the street and what looked to be small alleys trailing off between the ruins of the buildings. *Wait, alleys?* Hiral pushed the image of the rain out of his mind and reconstructed the buildings, then overlaid a street that looked far too similar from his memory. The two images fit perfectly. One more touch, a fireball-tossing Lizardman at the end of the street, and there was no mistaking it. "This is the town from the dungeon."

"The original one, or are we back in the dungeon somehow?" Right asked.

"Probably the original. You see it too, don't you, Left?" Hiral asked.

"I do. And it's making me nervous we're about to get blasted," Left said.

"At least we know where the alleys are," Hiral said.

"We should wait for the others before we go any further in," Left said. "And…" he started, before a not-so-distant flash of lightning lit the sky.

One second, two, three, four… and thunder rumbled.

"Another storm," Hiral said.

"Or the same one. We don't actually know how they work," Left said.

"Seena," Hiral said, turning to the party as they jogged up, "this is the same town from *The Mire* dungeon. Or, at least, it looks like it."

"Any Lizardmen?" Yanily eagerly asked.

"Long since abandoned," Right said, breaking the news to him.

"That's not important now," Hiral said, pointing at the sky with his **RHC** at the same time another flash of lightning lit up in the distance. "Both times the *Enemy* has shown up, it's been in the storm. We need to hurry."

"What about finding shelter here?" Wule asked. "There's got to be at least one standing building that has an intact roof."

Hiral looked at Left. "They still found us back at the inn."

"And in the dungeon," Nivian said.

"Odds might be better than out in the open," Wule said. "We'll just stay still and quiet until the storm passes."

"Couldn't hurt to dry off for a bit," Seena admitted.

"I really think we should keep moving," Hiral said. "The sooner we get to *The Troblin Throne*, the sooner we can clear it and unlock the *Asylum*."

Seena wiped the water off her face while she thought. "Okay, here's what we're going to do. Find a building we can all fit in—our party and Seeyela's—then see what they have to say about it. No, Hiral, I know what you're going to say, but Wule does have a point. It might be safer to stay dry and quiet."

"That's fine," Hiral said, eyes back on the clouds as lightning flashed. "I want to keep moving, but you might be right. I don't know if that's the best thing to do any more than you do. Let's see what the others have to say."

"Thanks for not arguing about it," Seena said.

"He's not Fitch," Yanily said quietly.

"Fitch only argues if it's with Hiral," Vix pointed out.

"True."

"The building straight down this street looks like it might be intact," Hiral said, pointing in that direction with his weapon. "Right behind where the *Scholar* would've been. Why don't you try there?"

"And what are you going to do?" Seena asked.

"Check to see if there are any better options," Hiral said. "If we do decide to stay, I'd like to have a good roof over my head."

"Hiral…" Seena started.

"…don't do anything reckless," he finished for her. "I know. I won't. I'll see you before the storm hits."

With that, he jogged off into the town just as the lightshow in the sky grew more intense, lightning bolt after lightning bolt arcing across the dark clouds.

"I don't like the idea of staying," he said to Left and Right as they moved down an all-too-familiar alley. At least no Lizardmen jumped out of the shadows at them. "But… maybe they're right. Being out in the open wouldn't be any safer, even if we were moving."

"We could go on ahead, see if we can find the dungeon," Right suggested. "What? Don't look at me like that. If I'm thinking it, so are you."

"If Hiral died, the others wouldn't be able to get into the dungeon. It's too big a risk," Left said.

"Plus, we don't know how far it is," Hiral said. "And why are we even having this conversation? If we're all thinking the same thing, we've all come to the same conclusion."

"Because you needed to talk it out to agree with it," Right said. "That's just how you are."

"How *we* are," Left said.

"And we'll probably need to have the conversation five or six more times for it to stick in that head of yours," Right went on.

"Now you're just being mean," Hiral said as they slowed at the end of the alley. He peeked around the corner, looking up and down the new street.

"Am I wrong?" Right asked. "This way looks clear."

"No, you're not wrong, and that's the worst part," Hiral said. "What about that building over there? Looks like it's three stories, and…" He trailed off as lightning lit up the sky behind the stone building. "And there's no roof or floors," he said, the lightning visible even through the windows.

"I see a possibility down this way," Left said, pointing further down the street.

Thunder boomed again and again, each time sounding just a little bit closer, though maybe it was just his imagination.

"Uh… actually, maybe you *should* take a look in this direction," Right said, and Hiral turned to look at him.

"What is it?" he asked.

"Straight down the end of this street," Right said cryptically.

"The *Enemy?*" Hiral asked, gripping his weapons tighter.

"Just wait for it…"

"Wait for...?" Hiral started, but then lightning flashed to illuminate a break in the wall at the far end of the street. *What's so special about the breach?* Another flash, and Hiral saw what Right had to be talking about. A massive briar patch—shrouded in something like living darkness—towered out beyond the town.

"We must've walked right past it," Hiral whispered quietly, another streak of lightning illuminating the intimidating silhouette of the briar. "How did we not notice it?"

"No roots on it," Left pointed out. "We've gotten so used to using them to judge distances in the darkness."

"Do you think the **Prince** is still sleeping in there?" Hiral asked. "The real **Prince**?"

"Let's not find out," Right said. "We don't know if those totems in the dungeon actually exist, or if they were part of the encounter Dr. Benza built to test us."

"I agree with Right on this one," Left said.

"Of course you do; I'm right," Right said.

Hiral sighed. "I wondered how long it would take for you to make that joke," he said dryly, but another crash of thunder overheard reminded him he had more urgent problems to deal with. Still, his eyes lingered on the briar as the lightning lit it up again. Maybe his other problem was more urgent, but *that* could be bigger... if it woke up. Just another reason not to hang around the town too long.

"We'd better hurry," he said, and the trio ran down the street to check the building Left had pointed out earlier.

71

PART OF THE PARTY

HIRAL shook some of the water off his raincoat as he stepped into the building, the wind picking up outside and whipping the rain almost horizontally down the street. The storm had moved *fast*, charging the town like a runaway bull, and the visible wall of torrential rain was only a block away by the time he made it back to the building where the others should be waiting.

"That's almost as bad as the storm-wall out there," Hiral said, Left and Right dripping wet beside him.

"At least you have a raincoat," Right said, and ran a hand down his arm to skim off some of the water.

"Oh, come here, you big baby," Hiral said, absorbing and then resummoning his doubles in quick succession. "Better?"

"Much, thank you," Right said.

"I have to ask, though," Hiral started, pointing at Right's legs. "You have pants when I activate **Foundational Split**, the same ones I do. Why don't you have the raincoat?"

"Because we choose not to take a copy of it with us when we split," Left explained. "For me, it would interfere with reaching the tattoos. For him"—he pointed at Right—"it's about *image*."

"The glowing Meridian Lines and tattoos look pretty badass in the dark," Right said.

"Look badass?" Hiral asked. "So, let me get this straight. You've been complaining about being wet even though you're *choosing* not to take the raincoat with you?"

"I thought I heard you three arguing," Seena interrupted before Right could reply, poking her head out from behind the staircase. "Come on. The others are this way."

"We're not done with this conversation," Hiral said quietly to Right, then turned his attention to Seena. "Not upstairs?" He then noticed the floor in the building was higher than the road outside, saving it from being covered in a layer of water.

"Found a nice central room in here. Completely dry, and no Troblins!" Seena said. "Yanily was disappointed, but I'm pretty sure Wule was terrified we'd find another one of those paintings. He's still traumatized. How about you? Find anything else out there?"

"I checked a couple of buildings," Hiral said, following Seena toward the back. "Only one of them was in any shape to keep us out of the rain, and honestly, it was worse than this one."

He noted how well the stone walls around him had held up. The architecture was definitely different than what Fallen Reach had, with the Lizardmen using larger blocks that tended to be rougher around the edges. Still, whatever they used to fill in the cracks had stood the test of time and prevented even the slightest draft. The thick wood of the ceiling and braces had to have been brought in from somewhere else—no way it came from the twisting trees found in the swamps.

"No sign of Lizardmen, either," he went on. "Not for a long, long time. Maybe this is morbid, but I didn't even find bones. But…" He hesitated. Did she need to know about it? Yes, yes, she did. "I think I saw the briar patch the **Prince** was sealed in inside the dungeon. I don't know if it's still in there… but…" He trailed off, seeing something on Seena's face. "What is it? Did you find something?"

"Cutlery!" Yanily answered as Seena and Hiral entered the somewhat crowded room.

The two parties had moved a large table—somehow still in one piece—over next to one wall, and stacked their packs in the other corner. Dripping raincoats hung from hooks near a door on the far wall, and Cal was handing out rations to anybody who even looked in her direction. Seeing how cramped the room already was, he reached out and pulled Left and Right back into himself, the tattoos rising up to coat his skin again.

"*That* is cutlery?" Hiral asked, eying the almost foot-long knife Yanily was holding up. Then again, the fork he had in the other hand was just as absurdly large.

"Lizardmen and… are there lizardwomen?" Yanily asked. "Whatever. If they're the same size as the ones we fought in the dungeons, they had big hands. Need big spoons and stuff."

"Spoons?" Vix asked. "For what?"

"Soup," Yanily said knowingly.

"Back to the grown-up talk," Seena said with a shake of her head. "Follow me."

With a wave of her hand, she led him through the room and the door on the far side. The next room over wasn't in nearly as good of shape as the first, the far end of the building simply missing and the rain pouring outside, but Seena turned to the right instead of continuing.

"Stairs?" Hiral asked, noticing the stone steps descending into the foundation of the building. "Why not camp down there?"

"Uh… you'll see," Seena said, and Hiral had no choice but to follow her down. As soon as he got to the bottom, he understood her reluctance to spend more time than necessary in the small room.

His skin practically crawled, like it wanted to jump off his body and slink its way back up the stairs, and there was an aura of fear lingering like a bad smell. In the center of the room, a totem like those inside the dungeon stood propped in the dirt, leaning slightly to one side. Coiled shadows writhed in its eye sockets and loosely hanging jaw like a mass of worms. Looking at the base of the totem, Hiral found the corrupted roots and the expected line of shadows leading to the wall and beyond—in the same direction as the briar patch.

"The **Prince** is still in there," he said, shuddering slightly. "After all this time, it's still sleeping."

"And how annoyed do you think it'll be if we wake it up now?" Seena asked, then shooed Hiral back up the stairs, obviously having had enough of the small room.

"Very," Hiral said, turning and ascending the stairs. "I'm surprised Yanily didn't break the totem as soon as he saw it."

"Even he had better sense than that," Seena said, almost sounding impressed the experience-hungry spearman hadn't released a rampaging beast of unfathomable power.

"Wow. Other than that, find anything else?" he asked, eager to change the conversation and take his mind off the totem's aura.

"We didn't find much other than the cutlery in here," Seena said, leading him back into the room with the others. "Some dishes, though I'll point out not a single spoon or soup bowl, and that table. All of it in really good shape. You sure the Lizardmen have been gone that long?"

"Most of the other buildings are nothing more than a single wall, maybe two if they're in good shape," Hiral said. "This place is much better. Besides, look at the roots." His gaze went up to scroll along the ceiling and walls. No signs of a leak, even after all the rain, and all the glowing roots came in through the doors to spread out across the room. "It would've taken years for them to grow like this."

"Unless this is how it always was on the surface," Wule said. "There's a lot we don't know, but if we assume the sun has always moved around the world at the same speed, wouldn't it make sense these roots are part of the natural adaptation to that?"

"You may be right," Hiral said, thinking about it. "I'd just assumed they came around at the same time the dungeons did. But, Dr. Benza did mention repurposing them for the path. The more I think about it, the more that makes sense. How else would the trees grow as big as they did? They need sunlight."

"And those glowing roots provide it," Wule said. "They probably get some kind of nutrients from the other plants in return. A symbiotic relationship."

"You're probably right," Hiral went on, the puzzle of it scratching that curiosity that always made Gauto say he should've been an Academic. "Maybe they store the energy while the sun is overhead, then slowly release it the rest of the time."

"Why do you all keep encouraging him? Drop the façade already," Fitch interrupted from the side of the room. "What? You're *all* doing it. Sure, I expect it from the two clowns"—he looked at Yanily and Vix—"but you too, Wule? I thought you were better than that."

"Better…?" Wule asked, looking a bit like he'd been slapped.

"Yes. Better," Fitch said. "Pretending to like the Islander just because we need him to get into the dungeons. I'm so tired of this."

"Pretending?" Hiral asked, a dark voice in his head whispering *Everfail*. He looked toward Seena.

"No, we're not…" she started.

"You are," Fitch snapped. "You were talking about it right before he came back. Why don't we just get this out in the open? He needs us just as much as we need him, so let's quit it with the faux friendliness."

Now it was Seena's turn to look like she'd been slapped, her eyes wide as she looked at Hiral. "I wasn't… We weren't…" she started and stopped, and Hiral's stomach dropped.

Even after everything she'd said to him before… it wasn't true?

"Stop it, Fitch," Seeyela snapped. "Hiral"—she turned to him—"Seena didn't say anything before you got back. Fitch, for some reason, is just trying to cause trouble."

"Or maybe Seeyela is just saying that to make sure you open the next dungeon for us," Fitch said.

"Fitch!" Seeyela barked. "I'm not *just saying that*."

"Look at his face," Fitch said. "He doesn't believe you. And why would he? He's not one of us. Never will be. As soon as we get into the *Asylum*, you'll see, Islander. We won't need you anymore. Then what do you think will happen?"

"Fitch," Seeyela said once again, this time carrying an iciness that made everybody in the room pause. "I think you need to step out for a moment."

Fitch's mouth opened like he was going to ask "or what?", but the look on Seeyela's face made the answer pretty clear. "Fine," he finally said. "The room got too crowded anyway," he added, opening the door and walking out.

Hiral watched as Seeyela stepped over and gently closed the door behind Fitch, his stomach in knots, then turned to look at Seena. He almost activated **Foundational Split** for the support, but pushed down that urge. Right had said the party wasn't like everybody up in Fallen Reach. That they wanted him to be a member of their party. That they trusted him.

Well, then, he'd trust them too. That look on Seena's face… She was terrified either that Hiral had found out the truth or that he believed the lie. Time to find out which it was.

"Hiral, we weren't talking about you," Seena finally said, her mouth taking a few tries to get the words out of her mouth, and her eyes meeting his.

"Uh… yes, we were," Yanily said, and Seena snapped around to glare at him.

"What? We were," Yanily said, Hiral's stomach twisting more at every word.

"To be clear," Vix spoke up, "we were talking about your sword."

"My sword?" Hiral asked, his voice barely coming out past the lump in his throat.

"Yanily is jealous, but don't tell his spear," Vix said.

"Shhhh! She'll hear you," Yanily hissed.

Seena turned back to Hiral and took a step closer. "We weren't saying the things Fitch said we were," she said quietly. "We're not keeping you around just to get into the dungeons."

"It's one of the reasons," Yanily piped up.

"Not helping, Yanily," Seena seethed out of the side of her mouth without turning to look at the spearman.

"It's true, though," Yanily said. "And Hiral's doing the same thing too. Aren't you, Hiral? You want in the dungeons just as much as we do. What's wrong with that?"

"It's… not the only reason I'm with you," Hiral said, looking at Seena.

"And it's not the only reason we want you with us," she responded. "Sure, yes, maybe it's *one of the reasons*, if we're being completely honest about it. But you can't still think we secretly hate you or something."

"I… don't," Hiral said, fighting against his own inner demons rising up again. His rational mind *knew* it was just his own history making him even consider Fitch's words as possibly true. The setup—the active intent to hurt him—was so obvious, but he still couldn't just let it go.

"Good, because we don't. I told you, you're part of this party," Seena said, a bit of the fire back in her eyes. "And"—she turned to Seeyela—"if Fitch doesn't watch what he says, there's going to be a problem between us."

"Not just with Seena," Nivian said.

"I know," Seeyela said. "I'll talk to him after he cools down a bit. Hiral, you don't know me as well as the others do, but I hope you'll believe me when I say Fitch's opinion isn't everybody's. Has Seena told you what his problem with Islanders is?"

"No," Hiral said, still trying to silence the nagging doubt in his head. Could any reason really justify his behavior?

"It's a bit of a story, but the short of it is he blames a merchant from Fallen Reach for his sister's death," Seena said. "He's been angry for years and… then… here you are."

"It's a hard thing for him to get past, and you, coming down from Fallen Reach *with* a merchant…" Seeyela said. "You're like the perfect target for all his pent-up hate. But he's not a bad guy, if you can get past it." She shook her head and rubbed the bridge of her nose. "Sorry, I'm not trying to make excuses for him. Just… when we all get to the *Asylum*, give him a chance to get to know you as something other than an Islander. You might be surprised at what you find when you get past the hate."

"The merchant… was it Arty?" Hiral asked.

"No, it wasn't," Seena said. "And, really, we don't even know for sure what happened to his sister. Look, I'll give you the full story later. Now's not the time."

"I'll talk to him," Seeyela picked up. "If I can get him to stop being…"

"An asshole," Yanily filled in.

"Yes, that," Seeyela agreed. "If he can behave, can you give him a chance?" she asked Hiral.

"I'll think about it," Hiral said, part of him completely recoiling at the thought of spending more than five minutes with the infuriating man. And why did he have to be the one to give the other a chance? Hadn't he already been doing that?

"That's more than fair," Seeyela said. "Even if it doesn't work out between you and Fitch, you're still one of us, if you want to be. I don't know exactly what'll happen when we get back to the islands, but you're welcome to stay with us if you want to. And, no, before you even think it, I'm not *just saying that*."

"She isn't," Caleon said. "She's a terrible liar. Like, the absolute worst."

Hiral nodded while he watched Seeyela. The way she looked him in the eye, the steadiness of her voice, and the lack of fidgeting. His high **Atn** took it all in and told him she was telling the truth.

"I'm going to keep an eye on Fitch. Make sure he doesn't go too far," Lonil said, taking advantage of the small break in conversation to slip out the door.

"Are we good, Hiral?" Seena asked him, while everybody else looked on.

"We're good," he said. "I'm sorry I believed what he said, even for a second. I…"

"It's okay. We all have things we struggle with."

"For Seena, it's her cooking," Yanily said, and Seena rolled her eyes.

72

A TALK WITH MYSELVES

HIRAL sat in one corner of the room, a half-eaten ration in his hand. With the storm in full swing outside, the option of moving had vanished, and Fitch's words—even if he knew they weren't true, after some consideration— still rattled around in his head. It had just been in that moment, when all his old fears surfaced again, that he'd believed them, but they wouldn't go away so quickly.

Around him, the others made small talk, snacking like he was, and chatted about the skills they'd picked up in the last dungeon run before they'd been forced to flee. It was an odd break, a tension from feeling like they had to move, along with a relief that they *couldn't*.

For Hiral's part, he knew he should use the chance to test out that **Mold Crystal** skill he'd picked up—he even had a couple ideas for it—if he could just force the lingering doubt out of his head. Problem was, he couldn't. The things Fitch had said went round and round in his head, the words themselves discredited as bitter resentment, but leading to more genuine questions.

Namely—what *would* happen after they got to the *Asylum?*

There was no doubt things would change. They'd be safe.

There'd be no need to run dungeons anymore, or fight for experience to get stronger just so they could take another step toward that safety. So, what would they do? Wait out a rotation until Fallen Reach came back around, then head for a jump point? And then what?

Hiral would go back to being an Islander and they'd go back to being Nomads? He'd promised not to tell anybody else about the dungeons, and after his time with the party, the simple thought of breaking that promise clenched up his chest.

Or, would Seena and the others let him keep coming down to the surface with them to explore the mysteries of the dungeons and get stronger?

If they did *that*, somebody on Fallen Reach would take notice of his growth—even the fact he'd returned to the city would raise questions. How would he answer them? Then there was the whole issue of the *Enemy*, and what they'd do about it now that they knew.

Arrrrgh, it was just too much for him to think about all at once. Instead, he took a frustrated bite out of… whatever it was he had in his hand, and focused on the conversations around him.

"…and now my **Gravity Wells** have these snake heads that come out of them and constantly spit fire and lightning," Seeyela told Seena, making small snapping gestures with her hands like mouths.

"…no, no, you hold it like this, twist, and *then* lunge," Yanily instructed Balyo, both of them holding large forks like spears. "Think of it like the name suggests, a dance. An intimate, sexy dance."

"…needs salt," Vix said to Picoli and Wule.

"…and they've been gone a long time. Don't you think they've been gone a long time?" Cal asked Nivian, while the tank glared at the food complaints.

"I'm sure Lonil is just giving him time to cool off. It hasn't been that long," Nivian said, flattening out his scowl.

"At least half an hour. And I checked outside the door… they aren't in the building anymore," Cal said. "I'm getting worried."

Hiral dropped the half-ration in the pack beside him, then pushed himself to his feet and walked over to Nivian and Caleon. "Lonil and Fitch?"

"Yes. I'm not sure where they went," Cal said, her fingers twisting around each other as she wrung her hands.

"The storm is pretty bad," Nivian said. "I'm sure they didn't go far."

"I'll take a look for them," Hiral said.

"What's that?" Seena's voice cut over the low hum of conversation, then she came over to join the trio.

"Cal is worried about Lonil," Nivian told her.

"Yes… and… uh, Fitch too," Cal said, a little awkwardly.

"Yeah, so I'm going to just go check on them," Hiral said.

"Maybe you're not the best choice," Seena said slowly.

Why? Because without me you can't get into the dungeon? a voice in his head asked, but he stamped it out quickly.

"Seeing you again won't calm Fitch down," she went on.

"Maybe not, but I know the town the best since I was looking around. I have a couple ideas where they might've gone to get out of the rain." And, maybe, if he was being honest with himself, he just needed a few minutes alone.

"Somebody should go with you," Seena said, reaching for her hanging raincoat.

"Somebody will," Hiral said. "Left and Right. They'll watch my back. Don't worry, I won't do anything reckless or be gone long." He turned and exited the room before anybody could speak up.

Cool air washed over him the moment he left the crowded space, and the hammering of the rain echoed though the building. "Maybe they stayed out here just because it's so warm in there," Hiral mumbled to himself, and activated *Foundational Split*.

As soon as Right formed on his side, the double cuffed him on the back of the head.

"Seriously?" Right asked.

"I know," Hiral said. "I know I shouldn't have believed him even for a second. He just… pushed all the wrong buttons."

"You can't keep doubting them," Left said from his other side. "They *are* your friends."

"I know that too!" Hiral said, louder than he should have, before glancing back at the door and walking away from it. "Just need to clear my head."

He looked out at the pouring rain. Would they really have gone out in that? A hallway to his right was another option, so he turned that way to look before heading outside.

"And in case it needs to be said—again—we don't think they're using you to get into the dungeon," Right said. "Fitch was just being a jerk."

"I have to admit his barbs struck dangerously close to home. He's more intelligent than I gave him credit for," Left said.

"You're complimenting him now?" Hiral asked, glaring back at the double as he walked down the hall. The left wall had a couple of windows set in it— long since broken—and rain splashed on the sill and dripped into puddles on the floor. No wet footprints through them, but just as Hiral evaded the pools of water to get around them, the others could've done the same thing.

"Not so much a compliment as an observation," Left replied, likewise skirting the water.

"I'm kind of annoyed with him at the moment—could you maybe observe something more negative?" Hiral asked, reaching the end of the hall.

The remains of what had to have been a kitchen stood to his left, the large stone stove a pretty good clue, and rain poured in through a massive hole in the roof. Going that way would be just as good as going outside, and to the right was another hallway, with more rain falling at the far end.

"His nose is disproportionally large for his face," Left said.

"That somehow makes me feel better. Thank you." Hiral gestured in both directions. "Both ways lead to getting wet. Any ideas?"

"Maybe they went out before it got really bad?" Right offered.

"I don't know, it was pretty bad when we came in," Hiral said.

"We should split up and search," Left said. "We'll cover more ground that way. Right, you stay with Hiral."

"We should stick together," Hiral said immediately. "It's too risky for you to go off alone."

Left and Right exchanged a look, then both turned to Hiral. "Okay, I guess it's time to have *that* conversation," Right said.

"I know where babies come from," Hiral said, but the glares his doubles gave him told him they knew *he knew* that wasn't what they were talking about. "You're not expendable. I'm not going to put you at risk if I don't have to," he said, the words spilling out of his mouth in rush.

"And neither are you," Left pointed out. "Yes, dying was… unpleasant. But, as you can see, I got better. Can we say the same if it happens to you?"

"I…" Hiral started.

"As long as you're around for us to come back to, we'll be reborn again and again," Right said. "So, in a way, if you want us to survive, you need to take care of yourself first and foremost."

"But you *felt* yourself die," Hiral said. "You can get hurt, you can feel pain, and I saw the look in your eyes—it was traumatic."

"Yes, all of those things are true," Left said. "Getting hurt. Feeling pain. Trauma. You know what they call those things?"

"Life," Right answered. "Living does that to us just as much as dying does. What you felt when Fitch spoke back there, was it any less painful or traumatic?"

"It's not the same. Dying ends all that…" Hiral said, then cut off as both of his doubles smiled.

"Not for us, it doesn't. For us, it's just another part of living," Right said. "We *want* to keep living. To keep existing. Even though we *know* we're nothing more than concentrated solar energy." He looked down at his hands as he opened and closed his fingers. "We want to keep… being. To do that, we need you to keep living."

"Let us protect you," Left said. "Even if we're selfishly protecting ourselves at the same time."

Hiral reached out to the wall, the cool stone rough under his fingers, and let the sensation ground him. Let the image of the roiling emotions in his chest flow down through his arm and out his fingers. It wasn't perfect, but it gave him at least a moment of clear thoughts.

"I don't think of you just as concentrated solar energy," he said.

"We know you don't," Right said.

"You're just as much my friends as Seena and the others," Hiral went on.

"We are," Left said.

"But, I understand what you're saying, and I respect your opinions…"

"You should; they're ultimately *your* opinions," Right pointed out. "We're just better at expressing them."

"Why is that?"

"Less filters."

"Oh."

"Yeah."

"Wonderful," Left said. "Now that we're all on the same page, we really should get back to looking for Lonil and Fitch."

"You're right," Hiral said. "Like you suggested, we'll split up. Be careful, though."

"I will. However, before I go, I have too much solar energy. Resummon me with only about three percent."

"What? Why?"

"Because dying taught me a few things. The big one was that I remember what happened before I was killed, even if I don't know *how*. I kept my memory. Right and I can be used as scouts without putting you at unnecessary risk. By only giving us a small amount of solar energy, you're lowering the investment and making it more sustainable to keep summoning us."

"This still involves you dying," Hiral said flatly, not at all amused with this plan.

"Or," Left said, holding up a finger, "we can burn through all our solar energy and disperse ourselves. Either way, we come right back to you and can give a report on what we've learned. Another good reason to have very little energy."

"What if you run into something you need to fight?" Hiral asked.

"Have we fought anything since we left the dungeon?" Left asked. Before Hiral could answer, he said, "No. If there's anything out there, it's something I can't fight against and win by myself anyway. Better I get as much intel as I can and get back to you."

Hiral looked at his double, part of him wanting to contradict the reasoning, but he couldn't. It made sense. "Try not to do anything reckless," he said flatly, then absorbed and resummoned Left with just a tiny amount of solar energy.

"I'll be careful," Left said, starting back down the hall. "I'll go back and head out the front door, so to speak. Why don't you two head out from here?"

"Listen to him, trying to sound like he's the boss," Right said. "It's a good plan, though."

"It is. Good luck," Hiral said, waving at Left before turning to gaze out into the pouring rain.

73

LONIL

"READY?" Hiral asked his double.

"Wish I had one of those raincoats," Right complained, but then nodded. "Where to first?"

"With the rain this heavy, I can't imagine anybody would want to go far—even if they don't believe in the *Enemy*—so that's our first goal."

He pointed at what looked to be a mostly intact building just up the street. When Right didn't lodge any further complaints, Hiral did one more quick look up and down the roadway, then darted out into the rain.

The cold water hit him like a slap to the face, the rain far more frigid than before, and the wind lashed it down the street with painful ferocity. Even the raincoat Hiral had did little to shield him from the onslaught, the hood getting swept off his head, and he could feel the rain already running down his back.

"Raincoat doesn't help anyway," he told Right while he put his arm up in front of his face to try and block the worst of the deluge.

"I can see that," Right responded, doing the same thing, and the two of them pushed their way up the street against the rain, their above-average physical stats doing little to make it easier. What would've normally been a quick ten-second jog took three times as long, and when they finally ducked into the door, a shiver ran through Hiral's entire body.

"Was it that cold before?" Hiral asked, shaking himself to try and get some of the water off. Good thing he didn't have hair anymore…

"No, definitely not," Right said. "Let's hope they're in this place. I don't want to search the whole town."

"You'd think as soon as they felt how cold it was, they would've gone right back inside," Hiral mumbled, starting deeper into the building.

Left had said there probably wasn't anything to fight—and win against—but Hiral still drew one of his **RHCs** as he moved. Thunder boomed above them as they cautiously made their way down the hall, lightning flashing through the long-broken windows and drawing stretched outlines across the floor and wall.

The silhouettes of broken walls and buildings outside played out like a slideshow as Hiral walked the hall, each window a different scene. The first, a square building beside a twisted tree. The second, a broken and crooked wall.

Third, empty space except for a trio of thick, curving vines reaching down from *above*.

That last one was so different from the others that he paused and waited for the lightning to flash again.

Just empty space.

Another flash, and more empty space.

"Did you see that too?" Hiral asked Right quietly.

"I saw *something*," Right answered. "And I don't like it."

"Maybe Seena doing something?"

"Doubt it. Fitch might have vine powers we don't know about. Seems a common theme for them. The shiver crawling up my spine tells me that's not the case, though."

Another flash revealed a still-empty space, so Hiral stalked ahead, his eyes alternating between the hallway ahead of him and the blustering night outside. The near constant flashing of lightning provided a lot of light, but it also ruined his night vision for the intervals between. Whatever that had been, it was gone for the moment. Could it have just been his imagination if he and Right both saw it? That didn't seem likely, but then again, maybe they shared…

CRAAAAASH. The ground shook as a tremendous impact sounded from a block or two over. Silhouettes of flying rubble flashed on the wall from the lightning, and Hiral stumbled sideways. *Thunk… thunk… thunk. Thunkthunkthunk.* It came in quick succession, something pelting the roof and walls of the building, and stones the size of Hiral's fist shot through the windows. Only sheer luck saved him from taking a rock in the side of the head, and he dove for the wall between the windows as more and more debris came tumbling down.

"What is *that*?" Hiral asked Right, who just shrugged while ducking in another space between windows. "Whatever, we can't stay here." A second massive *CRASH* shook the ground—this one closer—and more rubble rained down on the building.

As soon as the worst of the deadly rain of debris subsided, Hiral was on his feet and dashing further down the hall, Right hot on his heels. The **RHC** went back on his thigh, and Hiral held a constant shield of minor **Rejection** right above them as they exited the hall into the next room. It wouldn't save them from the whole building falling on them, but it should at least stop a flying rock from conking him on the head.

"Where to?" Right asked.

"Debating whether I want to know what"—*CRASH*—"that is, or not," Hiral said, staggering to the side from the ground shaking.

"I'm voting for no," Right said. "But we may not have a choice in the matter. It's getting closer."

CRASH. This time, it came from practically the next building over, and suddenly, the wall right beside Hiral exploded inward as something hit it from the outside. Hiral leapt back into a roll, his **RHCs** coming out as he did a full rotation and found his feet, then leveled the weapons at the dust cloud. Rain poured in through the new space, lightning flashed, and a form took shape as the dust quickly settled

Fingers on his triggers, Hiral watched as the top half of a solid-stone figure started to push itself up and shake its head.

"Lonil?" Hiral asked, the red bar above the tank already below half. *What happened?*

The stone head snapped to the side, eyes widening as it recognized Hiral and Right.

"Get away! You have to…" Lonil started, lightning flashing, then something *yanked* him back outside so hard, his face clapped down on the floor before he vanished into the night.

Shit!

Hiral's weapons stayed trained on the space as he stood and carefully approached the hole in the wall. Thunder shook the building all around him while the constant thrum of rain pattered on the rubble next to his feet. His back to the cold, stone wall, he looked down at the line of blood from where Lonil's face had hit the ground as it quickly faded, diluted by the water. Then he carefully—oh so carefully—peeked just one eye past the edge of the wall.

There was nothing there.

No Lonil, and no sign of what had taken him.

Where did he…?

SLAAAAAM. Lonil hit the ground right in front of Hiral—like he'd fallen straight down after being tossed *very* high into the sky—his stone body cratering the alley between buildings even as the force of the impact threw out a shockwave that knocked Hiral back into the hallway. No sooner did he hit the floor than he found his feet and darted back to the opening. With a fall like that, Hiral had to get Lonil to Wule and Cal. It was the only chance the tank had.

Except when Hiral looked back outside, the alley was empty again except for the disturbingly man-shaped crater in the paved alley.

No, empty wasn't entirely true—there was a stone hand, from the elbow down, lying next to the crater.

Hiral *almost* reached out to the hand to bring it with him, but what good would that do? None, and the risk wasn't worth it, so he grimaced and turned away. A shake of his head to Right, then he dashed back down the hall, eyes glancing out the windows at every flash of lightning. Around a corner at the end of the hall, Hiral finally stopped and looked in both directions while Right caught up.

"Lonil is gone," Hiral said quietly. "That just leaves Fitch."

461

"And we could… just *leave* Fitch," Right said, then sighed. "Even as I say it, I know it isn't true. Part of me wishes we could leave him."

"Me too," Hiral said.

"Probably the Left part," Right grumbled. "Plan?"

"Sounds like the commotion outside has died down for the moment. Whatever it was… it must've been after Lonil. As long as we don't attract any more attention, we should be able to stay hidden. Let's see if we can find a way to move through the buildings instead of in the open down the street."

Right looked down the hallway they hadn't checked yet, back out the front door the way they'd come, then finally down the hallway they'd just run. "If Lonil came from that direction," he said, pointing in the third direction, "it's probably because Fitch is that way too."

"Great," Hiral said with a shake of his head, but he stopped when something other than the boom of thunder and patter of rain reached his ears. "Wait, do you hear that?" he asked quietly.

"Hear what?" Right said, though the double cocked his head to the side.

Hiral held up a finger for silence as he concentrated on his hearing. There it was again. Higher pitch than the rain, and only breaking through when the wind slowed down. It wasn't constant, but it was familiar…

A voice. A shouting voice.

"…il… r… r… ou…" the woman's voice said.

"Damnit, it's Cal," Hiral said. "She's shouting for Lonil."

"Why would they let her out of the room with all that crashing?" Right asked, and the two of them ducked over to the door, peering out into the pouring rain. "Do you see her?"

"No. She must be around front," Hiral said, the memory of Lonil face-down in the alleyway flashing in front of his eyes. He couldn't let that happen to another person. "We're going," he said without giving his brain time to talk him out of it, then ran out into the frigid rain.

The wind lashed at him immediately, like it was trying to throw him from his feet and beat him into the ground, but he raised his arms in front of his face and pushed himself forward. Caleon's voice danced between peals of thunder, carried along by that same brutal wind in a strange rising and falling that could've almost been his imagination. Lightning flashed overhead, long forks of it dancing across the sky first in one direction and then the other.

One foot, then the next, he headed for the intersection and then around to the front of the building, the route faster than working his way through the halls to the front door. He had to get to her before she attracted anything else's attention. He had to…

The building to his left exploded in his direction, and Hiral jerked his head that way just in time to see Right lunge in front of him before the shockwave hit. Right crashed into Hiral with the force of a runaway carriage, and then they were both in the air, wood and debris flying with them until Hiral hit something *hard*—stone-wall hard.

Mercifully, years and years of rain and wear had weakened the stone wall enough that Hiral went through it—instead of pasting onto the side of it—and crashed into the room beyond. He hit the ground, the weight of Right on top of him, then slid painfully along the floor. The ripping of fabric tore in his ear as his raincoat shredded, but he finally came to a stop before his skin started to do the same thing.

"Right… are you okay?" Hiral asked, the weight on top of him not moving. No response, so he shifted, pain blossoming in half a dozen places, and rolled Right off him as gently as he could. "Right, say something." A flash of lightning gave him a good look at the double.

Wounds covered the entire front of the man, solar energy leaking out of him like blood in massive streams. Everything from his left shoulder down was missing. Hiral's brain froze at the sheer severity of the wounds, only one simple sentence breaking through the shock of it—*that could've been me.*

"Right… I'll…" Hiral started, but an ominous creak of the building cut him off, and he looked straight up.

Then the roof collapsed.

74
THAT'S YOUR PLAN?

HIRAL groaned as he opened his eyes, something drip, drip, dripping on his forehead. At least, he thought he opened his eyes, but it was still pitch black. *Am I actually awake?* His body answered the question by informing him just how much it hurt. That, and there was a pressing weight covering him from head to toe, his arms and legs almost completely immobile from it.

That's right—the roof fell on me. Wow... yeah... that hurts.

He tried to shift, but there just wasn't any give to the debris on top of him. He had a little bit of breathing room—the worst of the rubble had to be propped on itself—but it wasn't nearly enough space to move. Still, he was alive, and despite the low, throbbing pain, it didn't feel like anything was broken or severed.

Right!

Hiral managed to shift his head to the side a bit, the unseen water now dripping on his temple, but he still couldn't see anything, let alone the body of his double. But, those injuries...

He pulled up his status window with a thought, and sure enough, ***Foundational Split*** was available to use. Right had vanished. No, not vanished. Died.

Died to save Hiral.

He'd have to thank his double next time he summoned him. Which... brought him to a bit of a problem. Hiral wiggled his fingers and toes—everything still worked—but when he tried to lift his arms or legs, he couldn't move them. The weight was just too much, even with the extra physical stats from Right being part of him again.

A quick look at his status window showed his ***Str*** at 18 (6) for a total of 24. That put him in the Low D-Rank of average strength, but if it wasn't enough to move the rubble on top of him... well... how much of the building had fallen? His best option—Right digging him out—was out of the question, so where did that leave him?

Foundational Split didn't show Left having been reabsorbed yet, so that double was still out there. Would he be able to find Hiral? Even if he did, his physical stats were lower than Hiral's, so he wouldn't be able to dig him out on his own. If he brought the others...

The others. Cal!

Hiral stopped thinking about his situation, about all the weight on his chest and limbs, and instead focused on his hearing. With his eyes completely useless in the dark anyway, it wasn't difficult. First, of course, there was the pattering of rain right above him, and the... *distant* boom of thunder. He couldn't hear any voices, and maybe it was his imagination or how much stuff was on top of him, but the wind seemed to have died down.

How long was I out? Are the others looking for me? Are they even okay?

Hiral couldn't answer those questions buried, and the possible answers to them meant he might not have any help coming. He needed to get himself out.

*Okay. Think. **Rune of Rejection**, obviously. It should be able to take care of this pretty easily. Except... I can't use it while Right is inside of me.*

Just in case, Hiral tried feeding solar energy to his rune. Nothing happened. Of course not.

He needed to activate **Foundational Split** to summon Right so he could use his runes. A shift of his right arm, maybe an inch at most, told him there was *definitely* not enough room for two of them down there. Still, without other options, he didn't have any choice but to try. Feeding just one percent—the bare minimum—of solar energy into the split, Hiral summoned Right.

The cramped area lit up briefly as the tattoos and Meridian Lines peeled off Hiral's skin, hovering just above his body as the solar energy seemed to look for a place to go and condense. Finding nowhere to spread, the ability collapsed with a jolt similar to static electricity, and the light faded.

Confirms I can't summon Right in here... but...

Hiral repeated the summons, again with just one percent, but instead of focusing on the solar energy and where it was trying to go, he turned his attention to his runes. Could he...? Yes—his **Rune of Rejection** was available to use—but the attempted split ability faded, another shock making his body twitch. *One more time*, he told himself, activating the ability again, and counted. One. Two. Three... The ability faded with another annoying shock.

Three seconds. That was how long it took for the ability to fail. Three seconds was how long he had to activate the **Rune of Rejection** and get the fallen debris off him. With the way it was propping itself up and *not* crushing him, he probably only had one chance at this.

Better make it count.

Priming his solar energy, Hiral pushed it toward his **Rune of Rejection**, building and building the amount of it right at the dam preventing him from using it. Then, while he kept most of his attention on that stream of solar energy, he fed another one percent into his **Foundational Split**. As soon as the ability activated, he turned his full focus on the energy rushing in his rune, and he *pushed*. Pushed as hard as he could.

The rubble on top of him didn't even shudder, no—it simply spewed off him in all directions like ten of the *Scholar's* fireballs had erupted under it.

Debris shot high up into the night sky, bouncing off the walls and pinballing away, while the sudden slight glow of roots was almost blinding to Hiral's sensitive eyes. But, as the energy from his rune faded, Hiral's thoughts turned quickly to another rune, and more importantly, the force it represented.

Gravity. What goes up…

Hiral forced himself into a sitting position, body complaining with every motion, then flipped over to hands and knees and crawled through a hole in one of the walls. *Probably the one I made coming in.* Light rain splashed on the ground all around him, and then pieces of wood and rock began to join it. After a small piece clipped his shoulder, he pushed himself up to his feet and then lunged under a leaning stone wall.

Rocks and chunks of wood—some as big as Hiral—slammed to the ground around him, deflecting off the wall he huddled under and making it shake ominously.

If I get buried under another wall…

And then it was over, the street in front of him covered in debris. He let out a breath. Doing a quick inspection of himself, he was covered in minor wounds, though nothing looked too serious for the moment. *Need to watch the bleeding. A lot of small injuries could add up.* Another check had both of his *RHCs* on his thighs, and the *Emperor's Greatsword* on his back, by some miracle. All in all, he was in pretty good shape, but that didn't mean the others were.

Rolling his left shoulder—a bit stiff from having a building fall on it—he stood up and activated *Foundational Split*.

"Hey, thanks. You saved my life," Hiral said as soon as Right formed beside him.

"No problem," Right said. "Sorry about the building falling on you."

"Nothing you could've done. Come on, we have to find the others. Any idea how long I was out?" Hiral ducked out from the leaning wall and confirmed it belonged to the building the parties had been in.

"None. Honestly, last thing I really remember is something sweeping through the building beside us. Uh… yeah. This building."

"Sweeping? It wasn't an explosion?" Hiral looked at the ruined building. "No, never mind… I see it. Like a giant hand hit it from the other side over there, then just slapped straight through it."

Just looking at the scope of the damage made Hiral gulp, and he glanced back up and down the street, even above the buildings. Something with the power to do that kind of damage had to be huge. And yet, there was nothing out there. With a shake of his head, he turned and stepped into the ruins of the building, quickly finding what was left of the hall he and his doubles had walked down, then came to the front.

"Cal had to be out there," he said, pointing where the font door had been. The whole street in front of it lay broken and shattered, with most of the stone torn up and tossed aside. "See if you can find anything," he told Right, then turned in the other direction and went into the room the others had been hiding in.

Though calling it a *room* was very generous. The ceiling and three of the walls were completely caved in, and the fourth didn't look like it would be standing much longer.

Are you all under there like I was?

Hiral immediately rushed forward and started picking up and throwing off the pieces he could move by himself. "Right!" he called. "Going to need your help in here."

"Didn't find anything out there. I mean, nothing other than everything being trashed," Right said a few seconds later, moving right away to help Hiral lift a massive crossbeam. "You think they're under here."

"I hope not," Hiral said, straining with his end of beam. "This is too slow…"

There had to be a better way. Attraction and rejection were too risky… They were too sudden. One of the others could be impaled under there, and if he shot the debris off like he did on himself… No. Just no. What else?

Hiral pulled up his status window and looked at his runes… then paused.

The runes of **Separation**, **Gravity**, and **Energy** were right there with the others, but **Gravity** and **Energy** hadn't given him anything like **Foundational Split.** What… what if he'd been wrong about them the whole time? He'd been expecting a specific ability like **Foundational Split** from the other advanced runes, but maybe **Separation** was an exception to that because it was his primary rune, whatever that meant.

Could he…?

Hiral reached out to the debris and pushed solar energy gently into his **Rune of Gravity**. Nothing happened. Was he wrong?

He slapped himself in the forehead, then pushed two streams of solar energy through his body. One to his **Rune of Gravity**, and the other to his **Rune of Decrease**. It was just like with his sword.

The debris in front of Hiral shifted—all of it—then began to rise off the ground, some pieces floating further and faster than others, but even the huge crossbeam he'd struggled with shuddered and rose. The rain, meanwhile, seemed to get caught in the gravity field as well, most of it stopping and forming something like a curved layer of water. The few drops that made it through that first coating halted midflight, then became the opposite of bubbles—little spheres of water floating in the air. Within seconds—his solar energy draining at an alarming rate the whole time—he could see the floor underneath, as well as the remains of the ruined packs floating above it.

Thankfully, bodies were noticeably absent, and the relief of it almost made Hiral lose his focus on his runes. Almost, but not quite. He caught himself before everything dropped back to the ground. "Right," he started.

"You're going to ask me to go under that floating death trap to get something, aren't you?" Right asked, practically glaring at Hiral. "Dying to save you and dying to save your lunch are two entirely different things."

Right… had a point, but Hiral was already using two runes at the same time. Could he do a third?

No harm in trying.

Keeping solar energy flowing into the **Runes of Gravity** and **Decrease**, he extended his left hand and gently pushed a thread of energy into his **Rune of Attraction**. The closest pack, one that held the crystals they'd gotten from **The Mire**, zipped over to his hand, and Hiral practically cheered.

Then he lost his control on the entire pile of debris, and the whole thing went tumbling to the ground with a large splash. Still, all things considered, he couldn't help but stare at the wreckage. If he could do that with the **Rune of Gravity**, what was the **Rune of Energy** capable of? Or even the **Rune of Separation**? Was there more to it than just **Foundational Split**?

"And that's why I didn't rush in," Right said, bringing Hiral's attention back to the present while he picked the pack up off the ground and flipped the top closed. "What's next? They weren't under there, fortunately."

"If I were them, I'd head for the next dungeon. **The Troblin Throne**. It's where we were all going anyway, so maybe they'll think of it as a rendezvous point. As for Left…"

As if it were a cue, the tattoos on Hiral's left side emerged from his skin, and **Foundational Split** became available. Hiral used it.

Left peeled off him, forming within a few seconds, then immediately stepped out into the street and pointed. "You were partially right. They started for the dungeon, but it seems like the *Enemy* caught up. They're hiding in some kind of watchtower on the border between this swamp and more forest."

"Did you see the *Enemy*?" Hiral asked, following Left out and looking in the direction he pointed, for whatever good it did—it was still dark and raining. "Did it kill you again?"

"No to both of those questions. I don't even know for sure it *is* the *Enemy*, but something seems to be waiting out in the rain for them, crashing around through the trees and searching. It won't be long until it smashes through the small watchtower like it did the buildings here. When I realized there was no easy escape for them, I burned off my solar energy in hopes of finding an option with you."

"How much of a head start do they have? How long was I out? Are Cal and Fitch okay?" Hiral loosed the rapid-fire questions while his brain worked through options.

"You were out about thirty minutes," Left explained. "Cal was badly injured when this building was attacked, though Nivian was able to pull her back just in time. They escaped through the back door and managed to mostly get away unnoticed until they left the town."

"If they have that much of a head start, shouldn't we get going?" Right asked, standing in the light rain with the other two.

Hiral shook his head. "What good would we do even if we caught up? Look at this." He gestured to the ravaged building. "And you saw what it did to Lonil…"

"I'm sorry about Lonil," Left said. "Don't beat yourself up over it. There's nothing you could've done to save him."

"Maybe," Hiral said, a spike of pain in his chest at the simple word. They'd been risking their lives nonstop since they'd arrived on the surface between the dungeons and the monsters. Still, somehow, it'd all almost felt like nothing more than one time trial after another. Like a game.

Seeing Lonil's body… what was left of it, though… no, it was all very real. And this *Enemy* wasn't something he could fight and win against. If he went to help the others, even with his increase in power, it wouldn't make a difference— other than the fact they'd all die together. This wasn't something having a class or their level of strength could solve.

"Hiral, you're not thinking of leaving them, are you?" Right asked.

"It's not a fight we can win," Hiral said slowly, eyes drifting back to the destroyed house.

"So, what? We give up and let them die?" Right asked.

"What? No," Hiral said, the pieces of a plan finally clicking into place. "It's not a fight *we* can win, so we need somebody else to fight in our place. At least long enough for us to get away."

"He has a plan," Left said.

"Somehow, I'm more concerned now than I was a few seconds ago," Right mumbled.

"I do, and you should be," Hiral answered.

He climbed over the rubble of the room and past the one wall still standing. There, on the other side, after tossing aside a bit of fallen wood from the ceiling, he found the stairs leading down into the basement.

"You're not thinking what I think you're thinking," Right said, but Hiral was already climbing down the stairs, an **RHC** coming out in his hand.

As soon as he got to the bottom of the steps, he took one look at the creepy totem, and then blasted it to smithereens with a bolt of impact. "You hear any angry roars?" Hiral called, climbing back up the stairs.

"Nothing but the rain," Left said. "What did you expect?"

"Was hoping the other totem was already destroyed," Hiral said. "I'll have to go do it myself."

Left was already shaking his head.

"If we can get the **Prince** to wake up, that'll get the *Enemy's* attention," Hiral said. "Buy us the time we need to escape."

"I agree," Left said.

"Not sure I do," Right interrupted. "Waking up the **Prince**—assuming it's still even there after all this time—might just create an even bigger problem."

"I don't see any other good choices," Hiral said. "We need to do something dramatic to get the attention off Seena and the others. This is it."

"But you're not going," Left said. "Right and I are."

"We are?" Right asked.

"Yes," Left said, and looked at Hiral before he could object. "When the **Prince** wakes up…"

"…if…" Right interjected.

"…you don't want to be anywhere close to that," Left went on like Right hadn't spoken. "If you're over in the **King's** court, or whatever it's called, you'll be too close. You might even lead the **Prince** right to the others. Right and I, we don't need to run back."

"You can just burn off your solar energy and you'll be right back with me," Hiral said, nodding. It would save the trip, and removed the risk of leading the **Prince** to the party. "Right, give me the pack."

"Here," Right said, handing over the pack full of crystal. The weight settled comfortably on Hiral's shoulders just behind the **Emperor's Greatsword**. "In the meantime, you go to the others and explain what's happening. As soon as the **Prince** gets the *Enemy's* attention, you make a run for the next dungeon. I suspect the border tower they're hiding in is a remnant from when Lizardmen and Troblins fought for territory. **The Troblin Throne** can't be too much further. And, if nothing else, at least you'll have the forest to hide from the *Enemy* in."

"Okay," Hiral said, nodding. "And this tower, how far?"

"They were carrying an injured Cal, so they didn't move as fast as normal. If you hurry, you should be able to get there in fifteen minutes, tops. As soon as you see the treeline, look to your right. There'll be a stone tower there. Almost impossible to miss."

"Any way I can get in without the *Enemy* spotting me?" Hiral asked.

Left just shrugged. "Before you go, leave us with less solar energy. Ten percent at most. I need to use the *Wings of Anella* to keep up with Right, but no more than that."

"You sure it's enough?" Hiral asked, and both doubles nodded. "Okay," he said, absorbing and then resummoning them, his own solar energy up at around seventy percent. "Good luck, you two."

"Don't die," Right said. "And watch out for exploding buildings."

"I'll do my best," Hiral said, and then all three turned and dashed off.

75

THE SLUMBERING PRINCE

HIRAL kept one **RHC** drawn while he ran down the street, hugging close to the buildings despite Right's warning. Something about standing out in the open in the cold rain sent shivers down his spine—and it wasn't just his lack of a raincoat. The *Enemy* only showed up when the weather was at its worst, but the lighter rain around the town didn't make him feel any safer, especially not when lightning still arced across the sky in the direction he was heading.

Still, he devoured the distance down the road to the wall surrounding the town, opposite where they'd come in—and where Left and Right had gone— and peeked out beyond. The twin glowing roots extended off into the night, continuing to follow the road, and the swamp spread around it on both sides. They hadn't run into any monsters between *The Mire* and the town, but that didn't mean there weren't some waiting for him out there.

If this is the town from the dungeon, does that mean that huge Lizardman city is around here somewhere? Could we hide there if we needed to? If we could even find it...

After a quick minute of watching, spotting nothing other than the falling rain, Hiral couldn't delay any more. With no telling how long it would take for his doubles to release the *Prince*, he gave the swamp one last look, then sprinted out and down the road. Left had said about fifteen minutes to the tower, a short enough distance Hiral could almost cover at a sprint due his higher *End*. With the water acting like a solid surface thanks to his *Walk on Water*, Hiral barely made a sound above the falling rain as he ran, and his head swivelled left and right, watching for any signs of movement.

If the *Enemy* attacked, where would it come from? They had to be huge to have the destructive power he'd seen, which meant he'd be able to see them coming out there in the swamp. *Unless they're under the water like the snakes.*

Could they even be snakes themselves? No, something about that didn't seem right, so Hiral discarded the questions and focused on watching his surroundings as he ran.

After five minutes, he hit a wall of heavier rain, somehow even colder than before, and immediately wished for his shredded raincoat. It wouldn't do *much* to block the rain, but anything was better than nothing.

Anything?

Hiral pushed a small, steady stream of energy into his **Rune of Rejection** while he thought of the rain, and just like that, the deluge ceased. Slowing to a jog in surprise, he looked around at the fifteen-foot diameter sphere of dry air around him, not a single drop of rain penetrating. As he watched, the rain seemed to rebound, doubling in intensity outside his sphere of influence. Made it a *bit* harder to see, but considering he was finally free of the chilling rain, it was well worth it.

"Why didn't I think of that sooner?" he asked himself. He'd done something similar back in the first town they'd visited… then completely forgotten about it after all the tension with the *Enemy* and Left dying. *Stupid. But, done is done.*

The self-deprecation finished, he picked up the pace, though he slowed again a few minutes later as the echoing thunder no longer sounded distant. If anything, it was right above him, and he narrowed his eyes while looking for the treeline Left had mentioned. With the sphere of **Rejection** around him, he couldn't quite make out much in the rain, so he cut power to the rune.

The cold rain shocked him alert, and he instinctively took a shivering step forward as his eyes widened, but there, straight ahead, was the unmistakable outline of glowing roots twisting around dozens and dozens of trees. That had to be the forest, which meant… There! That must be the fort Left was talking about.

Odd. Hiral hadn't heard any of that…

CRASH. Something slammed into the ground directly behind him, the impact blasting out a shockwave that sent him hurtling off the road and into the swamp. Ten, twenty feet he flew before he hit the surprisingly warm swamp water and plunged underneath. Barely closing his mouth in time, the water absorbed the worst of his momentum, and he paused, floating under the surface as the shock of what'd happened seeped out of his brain.

Something had snuck up on him… and very nearly flattened him. It had to be the *Enemy*. But, did it think he was dead? Forcing himself down deeper in the murky water, Hiral reached out and grabbed one of the thin, glowing roots gently floating up from the bottom. His weapons and the pack full of crystals on his back probably made the motion unnecessary, but it gave him a sense of control. With his **End**, he could hold his breath for a couple of minutes, so it might be best to just wait out…

No, this was the chance he'd needed. A way to the tower without being seen. Underwater. Assuming the swamp stretched all that way. Tactically, it would make sense for the tower to be mostly surrounded by water, especially if the Lizardmen were fighting Troblins.

As long as I don't run into an entire nest of Barbed Swamp Snakes.

Only one way to find out. Hiral gently pulled himself along, root by root, so as not to disturb the water above him as he moved. He headed in the direction where he thought he'd seen the tower. He'd need to surface to make sure he was going the right way, but first, he needed to get further from where he'd hit the water.

Finally, several minutes later, Hiral's lungs burning in his chest, he couldn't delay surfacing any longer. Finding a particularly long root—one that stretched almost all the way up from the swamp floor to the surface ten feet above—he used it to guide his ascent. Slowly, oh so slowly, his head breached the waterline and tilted back. Cold rain splashed his face as he took a deep breath.

Lightning and thunder flashed directly above him, crisscrossing the sky in its fury as it lit up the heavy clouds. Another deep breath, then one more, and Hiral gently pulled himself back down and tilted his head forward so only his eyes and smooth head were above the water. The road he'd been thrown away from was back... that way... and, of course, there was no sign of what'd attacked—and nearly killed—him. How did the *Enemy* move so quickly and quietly? It was a question he'd need to answer if he wanted to survive the surface, eventually, but for now...

Where's the tower?

He twisted in the water until he found it, barely a hundred feet away, then pulled himself back under the surface without making a sound. Just because he didn't see the *Enemy*, that didn't mean he'd gone unnoticed, so Hiral dragged himself back down to the swampy floor, then along it in the tower's direction.

The still water flowed over his skin as he went, somehow reassuring him that nothing else was hunting under there with him for the moment, and the glowing roots grew thicker and thicker as he went. Thirty seconds, a minute, a minute and a half later, and he found the swamp floor sloping upward, arm-thick roots climbing with it. This had to be the ground the tower was on.

Hiral reached out and wrapped his fingers around one of the thick roots, pulling himself forward at the same time the ground shook. Then, again, the vibrations sent ripples even under the water. *Something* was smashing around up there, but it didn't feel close enough to be the tower itself.

Hand over hand, Hiral pulled himself up the slope, faster than he'd moved across the swamp but urged on by the continued thumping that shook the ground. When his head breached the surface, there was one more titanic blow that set the top of the water rippling, and then silence.

That came from over near the trees.

Which put the tower between him and whatever was making that noise. This was his chance.

Hiral hauled himself out of the water, the cold rain washing away the modicum of warmth he'd gotten, and onto the muddy ground. Even though he sank almost up to his wrists as he pushed himself up, as soon as his feet touched down, it was like he was on solid stone again.

Mud counts for **Walk on Water***?*

Storing that useful bit of information away for later, Hiral quick-stepped over to the tower, easily finding a crack down the side of the two-story building, and slipped inside out of the rain. One more look outside to make sure nothing was around, and he turned toward the interior—only to come face to face with a spear at his nose.

"Uh, Yanily?" Hiral asked, the purple-black blade of the weapon unmistakable.

"Yes?" Yanily asked.

"Think you could lower the spear?"

"How do I know you're Hiral and not some kind of weird clone?"

"Like… Left or Right?"

"Yes. Exactly like that!" Yanily said, the spearpoint touching the tip of Hiral's nose.

"Yanily, put that down before I put a *Spearing Root* somewhere you wouldn't like," Seena's voice called from beyond Yanily, but Hiral didn't take his eyes off the spear.

"You're sure…?" Yanily asked.

"Yes!" Seena snapped loud enough Yanily jerked the spear away and left a nick of fiery pain on Hiral's nose.

"Not nice, Yanily," Hiral said, touching his nose with the tip of his finger, only for it to come away red.

"Sorry. But, look at it this way. I've gotten worse shaving."

"You shave your nose?" Vix asked, and the friendly banter was almost like a warm blanket on a cold day.

Except they didn't have time to sit around the proverbial fire.

"Hiral, how did you find us?" Seena asked.

"Left told me where you were," Hiral said, inspecting the group.

Like Left had said, Cal was the worst hurt of the bunch, even though Wule was still working on her. One of her arms was slung in front of her, and she was covered in drying blood. Nivian, also, had a fair amount of the stuff on him, but at least he was up and mobile, pacing back and forth quietly.

"Figured that's where he went," she said, half under her breath.

"Lonil and Fitch, did you find them? Where are they?" Seeyela asked, coming forward to join her sister.

Hiral's breath caught at the question, but of course she'd ask that. Wouldn't it be the first question out of Hiral's mouth if their roles were reversed? "I… couldn't find Fitch," Hiral said slowly. "I was hoping he'd somehow met up with you all. I guess not?"

Seeyela shook her head, but then her eyes narrowed, like she'd caught on to his omission. "Lonil?" she asked, voice low with a glance back at Cal, though the woman still appeared unconscious.

"Lonil… didn't make it," Hiral said with a soft shake of his head, unable to say more.

"What do you mean he didn't make it?" Picoli asked. "You mean you didn't find him, like Fitch?"

Hiral shook his head again. "I… I wish that was it. Lonil is… dead. I saw his body. Something caught him."

"Something?" Seeyela asked.

"I didn't see what it was, just what it did to him," Hiral said. "I'm sorry. I tried to get to him, to at least bring back his… To bring him back in case I was wrong, but…" He just shook his head yet again and shrugged.

"Damnit," Seeyela said, her curse coming out a hiss.

"At least Cal isn't awake to hear it," Balyo said. "She'll be devasted."

"That's not our only problem," Picoli said, then looked at the others. "I'm not trying to be heartless here, but without Fitch and Lonil, what does that mean for the rest of us? Not to mention the shape Cal is in. How are we going to clear the next dungeon to get into the *Asylum*?"

"We'll get you through," Seena said. "Rotate people in and out to make sure you get credit for the clear. We don't *need* to clear it three times, but we can use that to make sure everybody gets through at least once."

"I'll never be Lonil, but I'll take care of you," Nivian said.

"Thank you," Seeyela said. "Though there's still the small problem of even getting to the dungeon."

"Have any of you seen the *Enemy*?" Hiral asked. "Any hints on what it looks like or how it attacks?"

Seeyela and Seena both shook their heads. "It was all a blur when Cal got hurt," Seena said. "And then by the time we got here, the rain was so heavy, I could barely see my own hand in front of my face. We were lucky to find this tower to hide in, but we could hear it out there looking for us, smashing around."

"That seems to have stopped," Hiral said, glancing out the crack in the wall at the continuing downpour. "Rain hasn't let up at all. Is everybody ready to move? Left and Right are working on a distraction for us. As soon as it happens, that'll be our cue to get into the forest."

"What kind of distraction?" Seena asked.

"They're waking up the **Prince of the Swamp**," Hiral said, still peering out the crack. Had they done it already and he'd missed it? Or, worse, was the **Prince** long since dead like Right suggested?

"Shouldn't we be closer, then?" Yanily asked, and Hiral turned back to the group to see wide eyes on most of their faces.

"Don't you mean further away?" Wule said. "I seriously don't want to deal with the **Prince** and the *Enemy* at the same time."

"That's the plan, isn't it?" Seena said. "We won't deal with either of them, because they'll be busy with each other."

Hiral pointed at Seena and then gave her a thumbs-up. "That's exactly it. We just need to be ready to move."

"Cal is in as good a shape as I can get her here," Wule said. "She needs some dedicated rest, but we can move her as long as we're careful. I don't expect she'll wake up anytime soon, but she's also out of danger."

"I'll carry her," Nivian said, but Seena shook her head.

"We may need your shield," Seena said. "Vix, can you handle Cal?"

"She weighs next to nothing. I'll take care of her," Vix said.

"Good. That way, we can still move quickly, but say something if you need to swap off."

"I can help if you need a break," Hiral said. "And Right will be back by then as well."

"How much longer do you think it'll be?" Seena asked.

"Should be any minute now. They left the town the same time I did, unless they ran into trouble," Hiral said, but his tattoos hadn't emerged from his skin, so they were both still alive.

Just then, a tremendous *ROAAAAAAAR* echoed through the air, the whole building vibrating from the volume of it, and the distant sky lit up as arcs of fire and lightning sailed into the night.

"That's our cue," Hiral said.

76

ENEMY 2

IRAL peered out through the crack in the tower wall, thunder booming overhead as if in response to the challenge bellowed forth by the **Prince of the Swamp**. The frigid rain still came down in sheets, the wind whipping it back and forth and onto Hiral's face.

"Are they taking the bait?" Seena asked behind him.

"Can't tell," Hiral said, more fire and lightning arcing above the silhouette of the briar patch. "Though they might have an answer," he added, the tattoos emerging from his skin. **Foundational Split** brought Left and Right out to join the group, and Hiral turned his attention to them. "Good job, you two. Did the *Enemy* show up?"

"Something did," Right said. "Storm was still pretty bad over there, then the **Prince** sounded like it went crazy. Couldn't see it, but there is definitely a fight happening."

"Which means it's our chance to go," Left said, leading the way out into the rain.

Hiral followed his double out, while the others got Cal comfortably situated on Vix's back.

"Still didn't manage to see the *Enemy*?" Hiral asked while it was just him and Left.

"For a moment, I *thought* I saw something... but... no. It was just the wind playing havoc with the rain, I think. Whatever the *Enemy* actually is, it's fast, silent, and powerful." Left nodded toward where the battle continued to rage with the **Prince of the Swamp**.

"Do you think the ten-minute lethargy applies outside the dungeon?" Hiral asked, watching as the night sky lit up.

"I hope not. We need the **Prince** to buy more time than that," Seena said, coming out of the tower behind him. "Now, enough gawking. Didn't you say it was time to go?"

"It is... It definitely is," Hiral said.

The whole group jogged back to the root-lined path, then turned toward the forest. Barely a few hundred feet, and they left the swamp, the ground turning solid along an almost perfect line.

"Must've been some kind of magic involved in that," Left mumbled to Hiral as they passed under the boughs of the tall trees. The downpour of cold rain was lessened due to the cover, but the wind still howled between the tree trunks like a thing possessed.

Hiral turned back one last time at the flashes of the ongoing battle, more lightning and fire arcing up to paint the sky red and white, then left it behind and followed the curving path.

"I hope it isn't far," Picoli said, her fingers twitching like she wanted to summon her **Light Darts**, but the group limited themselves to the naturally growing roots. There was no telling what would draw the *Enemy* to them.

"At least the rain isn't as bad in here," Nivian said.

After that, they ran without talking, their focus on getting as far from the swamp and the *Enemy* as possible. One foot in front of the other, the exertion of the run warmed Hiral's body, fighting against the chill of the rain still falling, but nothing seemed to be chasing them.

"Hey, Vix, hold up—Cal looks like she's slipping," Nivian said to break the silence almost two hours later, the dense forest thinning and the trees growing more sparsely. The things still towered into the sky, each easily more than a hundred feet tall, but they also had that same distance between them.

"Harder when she's not awake to hold on," Vix said as they stopped to help him.

"You've done a good job so far," Seena said. "Need to trade off?"

"I can take her if you need a break," Hiral offered, walking over while the others looked around. Thanks to the glowing roots crawling along the ground, the terrain looked pretty flat in all directions, but the lack of cover meant they were getting wet—and cold—again.

"Just give me a second to stretch," Vix said after Nivian got Cal off his back, and he took a few steps away to reach up high on a tree trunk and stretch his back out. "Ah, that's the stuff."

"Let me know if you change your mind," Hiral said, running his hand along the top of his head to wipe away the water, though it got replaced by the cold rain as soon as his hand passed.

Is this stupid rain ever going to stop? He tilted his head back to look up along the tall trees, whose branches did little to stop the rain splashing straight down onto his face while small forks of lightning crossed the sky. What he wouldn't give to see the sun, even for just a few minutes. To feel the warmth of it on his skin and...

Hiral's brain paused as the wind twisted the rain off to the side directly above him, but... something about that wasn't right. He blinked and rubbed the water out of his eyes, the rain falling and falling and falling. *What's bothering me?*

He slowly lowered his gaze to look around at the others as Wule checked on Cal before they got her back on Vix. The rain was falling *straight* down. There was no wind. So why did it look like there was?

An image of the darkened briar patch floated into Hiral's mind, the gouts of flame and forks of lightning shooting up at the top of the **Prince's** prison. *Why would it be attacking up there? Because I've been looking in the wrong place the whole time.*

"I think we should get moving, right now," Hiral said, looking back up and then between the spread-out trees.

"Almost done here," Wule said.

"No time for that," Hiral said, his pulse quickening as he scanned along the ground... and then higher.

"I'm ready when you all are," Vix said, taking one last stretch against the side of a tree, but something about the rain above him was... wrong.

Next to the glowing roots winding around the tree, Hiral could see the individual drops falling—constant, steady—but the ones above Vix weren't dropping straight. They were... twisting, like they were running down something coiled and reaching.

"Vix, look out!" Hiral called at the same time the man stood straight with his arms above his head. Then Vix's head snapped up to look at his extended arm, where the water seemed to be pooling around his wrist.

Flashing warning notifications exploded in Hiral's vision.

Warning! Warning! Warning!
Enemy Detected!
WARNING! WARNING! WARNING!

He threw aside the window as the others turned toward him, and he instinctively reached out for Vix—and the long red health bar above him.

"What...?" Vix asked, and then he shot straight up at the same time the health bar vanished.

Hiral activated his **Rune of Attraction** to try and hold Vix down—to not lose him like he'd lost Lonil—but it instead yanked him into the air, the sudden shock of it breaking his concentration. Ten feet up in a heartbeat and then Hiral dropped back down, his head snapping up to look as soon as he got his balance.

"What the hell was that?" Seena shouted, the floating book appearing in the air beside her and opening up. "Vix?" she called.

No answer.

"There's an *Enemy* here," Hiral said, drawing his **RHCs** and aiming them higher up the tree. "Right, get Cal."

"Sure," Right said, rushing over and sweeping the unconscious healer into his arms.

481

"What about Vix?" Wule asked, looking around, everybody suddenly on edge.

"We can't leave him," Nivian said.

"We aren't," Seena answered. "Group up. Eyes out. We know it's here. Anybody see Vix?"

Part of Hiral wanted to tell them it wouldn't matter. That Vix was dead. The bigger part of him hoped he was wrong, and he joined the others in the circle around Right.

"It came from above him," Hiral said. "Down the side of the tree."

"What did it look like?" Nivian asked, his shield and whip out as he paced around the group like he was trying to protect them all at once.

"I... don't know," Hiral admitted. "I just saw something wrong with the rain, and then he was gone."

"We can't stay here," Balyo said, an unusual edge to her voice. "You saw what happened back in the town. Look at Cal."

The spearwoman wasn't wrong, but something was different about this than in the town. This *Enemy* had snuck up on Vix, instead of simply smashing him flat. Was it a weaker one? Maybe one they could fight? If they had a chance to...

Something smacked into the ground right in front of them with a wet *thud*, and every head snapped in that direction to find Vix lying there.

The top half of Vix—completely torn in half—with the white of his spine extending beyond the blood and gore that had been his stomach.

Somebody vomited as their brain processed what they were seeing, but nobody else moved.

Hiral's eyes locked on Vix's face, on the frozen expression of fear and pain. It hadn't been a quick or painless death.

"We're moving," Seeyela barked. "Nivian, lead the way!"

"But... Vix," Wule said woodenly, nobody moving despite the order.

"He's dead," Seeyela said. "Just like we'll be if we don't leave. Now."

Hiral took a step in Vix's direction, to at least close the man's eyes so he wouldn't have to stare up at the never-ending storm, but something about the rain shifted just beyond him. Up came Hiral's **RHCs** and he pulled both triggers, the invisible bolts of force carving small tunnels through the falling rain to rip chunks out of a distant tree.

Missed!

His head snapped left and right, looking, looking... There. He whipped his weapons around and fired. Two more tunnels of force carved through the rain and continued off until they vanished. *Missed again. Where are you?*

He watched for any changes in the falling rain, and when the wind shifted, he fired again. Two more misses, then again, and again, his **RHCs** spat their bolts of *Impact*, hitting nothing. Was it playing with him, or did it actually fear getting hit?

"What are you waiting for?" he called over his shoulder. "Go!"

"Here," Seena said, and a wooden totem popped out of the ground beside him, immediately rotating slightly to the left.

Of course—her auto-aim totems!

Hiral's *RHCs* followed the direction of the totem while the others started down the road, their footsteps splashing in the water behind him. Nothing there. A glance down at the totem revealed it was continuing to the left, like whatever it was tracking was following the party. Hiral narrowed his eyes, focusing on the rain… Still nothing. Why couldn't he see it in the storm?

Because the totem didn't turn on a vertical axis, only a horizontal one! He was looking too low!

Hiral shifted his attention up, but didn't pull the triggers. There was *something* moving through the rain in the air, eerily similar to how his bolts of *Impact* carved through it. Sleek and fast, it swept through the open air, over, around, then down toward the fleeing party.

Silent. Flying. And *invisible*!

Hiral's weapons came up. He fired repeatedly, shot after shot carving through the air, though he wasn't aiming at the absurdly fast target. Every time he blinked, he lost it in the rain. No, all he could do was put a barrier of shots between it and his friends. One after the other he fired, now running after the group as he did it.

Apparently, they noticed his shots firing overhead. Seena slowed and popped another totem, which instantly turned to the left, out of the ground. A gesture at her book, and firebolts began streaming out of the totem's mouth to zip through the air. Like Hiral's shots, they didn't hit anything, but they gave him an idea where to look.

He fired off bolts as quickly as he could, trying to predict where the totem would aim next. A wall of *Spearing Roots* likewise erupted from the ground off to the side of the party, the wood glowing with infernal fire, but still they didn't seem to hit anything.

"What are you even shooting at?" Yanily shouted. "I don't see anything!"

"It's invisible!" Hiral shouted, and suddenly, the totem darted left, the bolts of fire cutting off as the party crossed its path. "Look out!"

"You just said it's invisible!" Yanily complained, but Seeyela had apparently seen the totem's movements, as she threw out a *Gravity Well* on that side of the party.

No sooner had the *Gravity Well* formed in the air than three hydra heads lurched out of it, turning like the totem did to spit fire and lightning through the rain. Another totem quickly joined it on the ground on that side, the first collapsing into dust, and more firebolts tore through the rain with the hissing of evaporating water.

Hiral, meanwhile, kept his eyes on the way the rain moved. The others hadn't spotted the phenomenon yet—he'd have to explain it later, if there was a later—and he needed to use it to get ahead of the *Enemy*.

Why don't I see a health bar? Why could I see it before? Of course, because it takes a second or two to show up.

Throwing out the questions that weren't helping him, Hiral focused on the pattern set out by the totem's fire spitting. The way it moved, the constant stream, the speed… It was all consistent, which meant…

Hiral pulled both triggers at the same time, lining up his barrels with exactly where the speeding entity would move, and twinned bolts of force tore through the rain. And then the totem stopped spitting firebolts while Hiral's bolts shot off into the distance, hitting nothing.

What? Is it gone?

He watched the totem as it continued to rotate—*is the Enemy just out of range?*—but then he looked at the **Gravity Well** and, more importantly, the hydras. All three heads turned toward the sky and breathed out fire and lightning. Though the blasts didn't strike anything, Hiral aimed his weapons higher up and fired.

The *Enemy* was flying too high for the angle of the totem to hit it, and with the entire sky above him, Hiral didn't have a good place to aim. Instead, he fired almost wildly on the chance one of his random blasts would hit where his aimed shots had missed. Still no strikes, so he followed after the party as it continued to move down the road.

The old **Gravity Well** and totem vanished, new ones springing to life ahead of the people, and Hiral kept his shots zipping over his friends' heads. **Light Darts** burst to life and then swirled around above the group like a halo—a razor-sharp, saw-like halo.

How long could they keep this up? How far did they have to go?

Hiral passed the attacking hydra heads, one eye on them as they aimed toward the sky, then did a double take when the lightning-spitting head turned from the other two and breathed its deadly payload in a different direction. *What?* The **Gravity Well** vanished, then appeared again further ahead by the racing party—Seeyela was summoning it each time they got out of range.

And, again, one of the heads was aiming in a different direction. Was it broken? No, of course not…

"There's more than one *Enemy!*" Hiral shouted at the same time the lightning-spitting hydra head angled down to the opposite side of the party—and below the protective halo of **Light Darts**.

Picking up his speed as his words sank in, he aimed his weapons to the right of the group and pulled the triggers as fast as he could. Lines of impact tore through the rain—but so did something else.

A shimmer in the downpour, barely more than that, sliced through the air, and then Picoli rocketed out the side of the group. The woman's feet caught on a root, flipping her head over heels to tumble to the ground in a violent, rolling mess.

And then the screaming started.

77
ENEMY 3

PICOLI'S pained cry echoed between the sparse trees, crawling across the ground and over the roots like a living thing trying to flee the agony her body endured. The party ahead of Hiral was still looking around, trying to figure out what exactly had happened, but he cut hard to the left and sped toward the source of the screaming.

Arms pumping as he went, he deftly leapt across a series of glowing roots, darted around a tree, and then ran as fast he could. There, at the base of one of the trees ahead, he could vaguely make out Picoli leaning against the trunk, head tilted back as she screamed. Her hands groped at a garish wound in her stomach, blood flowing, while her legs kicked and stomped on the ground.

Up came Hiral's weapons in front of him, one aimed in Picoli's direction—her red health bar was already below half—while he scanned around for whatever had done *that* to the woman.

"Picoli?" Hiral said. "Where is it?"

The woman convulsed in response, her arms clenching up like hooked claws, and she fell sideways on the ground.

"Picoli!" Hiral shouted, sprinting the rest of the way over to find her seizing on the ground. "Wule will be here any second now," he told her, his head turning left and right. "Did you see where it went?"

"It… it…" she tried to force out of clenched jaws, her whole body rocking as tremors racked through her.

"It's where?" Hiral prompted, looking around once more and then crouching down beside her.

"It's… in… in… in… in… *insiiiiide* me!" she finally screamed, like the words themselves were ripping her apart, and her back arched up so violently, it was only her heels and crown of her skull still on the ground. Light, soft at first, and then suddenly blinding, burst out of her eyes and mouth, like she had the sun itself in her throat. Her screaming cut off just like that, replaced by the sizzling of a barbeque… coming from *inside* the woman.

Smoke curled out of the wound in her stomach, from her mouth and eyes, and red lines grew into burnt patches along her skin.

Hiral was forced to step back as the heat rose and rose, the falling rain turning to steam as soon as it touched her skin. Still, the heat continued to climb, the wet tree bark curling as it started to burn, and the falling drops of rain popping long before they ever reached her flesh.

He backed up five feet, ten, retreating until it didn't feel like he was standing next to a bonfire, and the others finally caught up to him.

"What is that?" Wule asked.

"That's Picoli," Hiral said.

"Is she exploding like you did?" Nivian asked, a thread of strained hope in his voice.

"I don't think so," Hiral said. "She said it was inside her, whatever that means. Then she started glowing like this." Even as he watched, her health bar plummeted, the red practically evaporating along with the rain.

"What's inside her?" Wule asked, taking a step forward, and then immediately retreating from the heat. A gesture from his hand pulled the orbiting ball of fire from his crown slightly down, a faint red aura surrounding him, and he tried moving toward Picoli again. "The buff isn't enough," he said, forced back to the others.

"We have to do something," Seeyela said, her eyes locked on her party member.

"Open to ideas," Yanily said, but then the glow vanished just as abruptly as it had started.

The sudden plunge into darkness, along with the cold rain, made some part of Hiral's brain think he'd been dunked underwater, and he reflexively gasped for air. Thankfully, his lungs filled, and he pushed aside the brief panic, then blinked his eyes rapidly.

"Picoli?" he asked, and something moved, the outline barely visible against the soft glow of the roots after the sun-like brightness before. His night vision had been completely destroyed by the light, and he squinted to try and make out what was moving. "Are you… okay?"

There came a *SNAP* like a branch breaking… No… something thicker. Harder. Like a *bone* breaking. Hiral raised both his weapons to point in Picoli's direction.

"Oh, enough with this," Seena said off to Hiral's right, and a ball of flame appeared above her hand. Then a second… and a third, finally bringing out enough light for Hiral to see Picoli standing next to the tree.

Another *SNAP* came at the same time something moved under her leather chestpiece. *Snap, snap, snap.* The sounds of breaking continued, everybody taking a step back as Picoli twitched and her chest… widened. Like something was making room inside, her ribs shattered and spread to the limits the armor would allow, and then she looked up at them.

Even under the flickering light of Seena's fireballs, Picoli's eyes looked burned out, seared to little more than charred black orbs. And yet… and yet, as Hiral looked closer, there was a pinprick of golden light right where her pupils would've been. Had she undergone something similar to Hiral? Some sort of powerful awakening?

One more *snap* from her ribs, and Picoli raised her head to peer directly at them.

Warning! Warning! Warning!
Enemy Detected!
WARNING! WARNING! WARNING!

The warning notification sprang to life so suddenly, Hiral jumped, and he wasn't the only one. Party members on both sides of him swiped aside the surprising notification window, and then everybody stood stone-still as they looked at the woman ahead of them. The *Enemy*?

"Picoli?" Seeyela asked gently, but she didn't step forward. There was something unnerving about the pinprick eyes.

"Did you all get the notification?" Yanily asked.

"Yes," Nivian said, his voice barely a hiss.

"What do we do?" Balyo asked, everybody practically frozen, though Hiral still had his weapons aimed at Picoli.

Guilt at pointing his weapons at a friend crawled up the back of his skull, but what he'd seen and heard—plus that notification—stopped him from lowering them. She barely had any health left, according to **View**, but, still… something primal in his brain screamed *threat*.

Seeyela, likewise, glanced at his **RHCs**, but didn't ask him to point them somewhere else.

"We figure this out—that's what we do," Seeyela said instead. "Picoli. Are you okay?"

Picoli's head tilted to the side, like Seeyela's question was strange. Or maybe she didn't even understand the words, from the way her lips moved, almost as if she was trying to copy the sounds. All that came out was a raspy wheeze.

"I feel like we should leave," Yanily said.

"We can't leave Picoli," Balyo snapped.

"Are you sure *that's* still Picoli?" Yanily asked, and Balyo opened her mouth to respond… but no words came out.

"Maybe we can learn something from her," Hiral said. "Or figure out how to get her back to normal."

He said the words even though no part of him believed it. That energy he'd seen, it had to have consumed her from the inside out. Burned her to charcoal inside. And now, whatever it was looking out at them through the woman's ruined eyes—it wasn't Picoli anymore.

Another twitch, and the woman hunched forward, *something* slithering out of her shoulders like Seena's **Lashing Vines** ability. Bereft of thorns, these

489

sinuous appendages coiled down around Picoli's arms, wrapping them like a snake until the tips stopped on the back of her hands.

Vines? No. Snakes? No. Those are… suction cups on the inside? Tentacles…

No sooner had the arms finished than more of the tenacles erupted out of her hips, two weaving their way down her legs, two more crossing up her chest, and a final, smaller pair cupping over the top of her skull. A moment later, the tentacles stopped moving, and a soft line of light ran along them, just like a…

"That looks a lot like a **PIM**," Seena said.

"Super creepy **PIM**," Yanily added.

"Look at her health bar…" Wule said, half wonder and half fear in his voice, as the red bar above the woman's head quickly filled back up—then more than *doubled* in size. Tripled. Quadrupled…

"Be ready," Hiral whispered, a shiver running up his spine as Picoli's eyes narrowed. He placed his fingers over his triggers.

Hunching forward, Picoli slowly lifted her right foot behind her, then placed it against the tree. Before Hiral could even wonder what she was doing—CRUNCH—she launched forward, the trunk shattering from the force, and shot toward Seeyela.

Nivian, faster than anybody else, slid in front of the other party leader, his thorny shield up, and braced his legs. A split second before Picoli struck, light formed around the front of her fist, and then her punch lifted Nivian from his feet and hurled him backwards, while the shockwave of the collision threw everybody else aside.

Hiral hit the ground and rolled to his feet, then aimed both weapons at Picoli. Instead of moving on the vulnerable Seeyela—who'd somehow managed to dive out of the way to avoid Nivian—the woman stared at her bloody fist, as if she was surprised by the crimson. Light flared along the tentacles, and the wounded knuckles sealed up even as Hiral watched.

We can't keep hesitating, his brain screamed at him, and he pulled the triggers. Bolts of force carved through the falling rain to slam into Picoli's shoulder and arm, knocking her to the side and carving chunks out of her health bar. Her pinprick eyes snapped up at him, more light flaring within, and she turned toward him in a crouch.

She's coming!

But a thorny whip lashed down her shoulder, tearing at the glowing tentacle, and Picoli's attention tore in Nivian's direction. Legs flexing, Picoli launched again at the tank where he stood, twenty feet away. She covered the distance in the single leap, rocketing straight at him, and once more, something flared in front of her knuckles as she swung her fist to meet his shield.

WHOMP. Rain burst outward in a sphere from the impact, but Nivian held his ground, roots wrapping his legs and holding him in place. Picoli's momentum carried her straight into the shield, her elbow snapping backwards from the force of her own blow, and she met the thorny barrier face-first. In the heartbeat it took her body to crumple against his shield, Nivian twisted and heaved, using Picoli's own momentum to deflect her off to the side with a shift of his balance.

Picoli hit the ground in a roll, bouncing up and over glowing roots, then sprang to her feet in an animalistic crouch—a quarter of her health bar gone from the collision. Her right arm, hanging awkwardly at her side, *snapped* as the tentacle flexed, straightening it out, and then light flared along its length. Picoli's hand opened and closed like the arm had never been injured—her entire red bar was fully restored—and then she leapt forty feet up toward the trunk of a nearby tree. Flipping midair, something glowed just below the soles her feet before she hit the tree… and then she kind of… stayed put.

Hiral fired at her, his first shot whizzing over her shoulder as she ducked under it with preternatural grace. She seemed to slap the other out of the air with her bare hand. No, *bare* wasn't right—something had glowed on her palm just before she intercepted the blast. So, he fired again and again.

"What are you doing, Hiral?" Seeyela shouted.

"What *aren't* you doing?" Hiral shouted back as he pulled his triggers. "That's *not* Picoli anymore."

Even as he spoke, his focus was on the woman somehow hanging on the side of the tree. Again and again, she either dodged or slapped aside his attacks, but the motions finally told him how she was doing it—even though the answer sent a shiver like ice water through his veins.

Another blast zipped right for Picoli, and her hand snapped out, a **Rune of Impact** forming on the palm of her hand a heartbeat before it blasted aside his own bolt of **Impact.** Then, as if she'd had enough of their little game, the tree cracked beneath her feet—where she must've been using the **Rune of Attraction**—and she blasted down in Hiral's direction.

He hit her while she dove at him with two blasts from his **RHCs**, but they hardly seemed to slow her down, and then her fist came around, the **Rune of Impact** glowing like a meteor. Far too fast—he'd never avoid her. Hiral instead poured as much energy as he could into his **Runes of Gravity** and **Increase**, right in front of him.

The ground fractured from the sudden shift, roots collapsing in on themselves and the rain speeding up, while Picoli slammed straight down. Just like that, Hiral was out of solar energy, the greedy rune having sucked it all up, and he staggered backwards, suddenly exhausted. The increased gravity faded immediately, and Picoli hauled herself to her feet, blood oozing out of dozens of wounds along her face and body.

If she even felt them, she gave no sign of it, and a flare of light along the tentacles made her injuries vanish. Runes glowed in front of her fists, and the seemingly unstoppable woman took a step toward Hiral.

He, in turn, lifted his **RHC** at her head and pulled the trigger.

The blast splattered Picoli's nose across her face in a grotesque shower of blood and cartilage, leaving a ghastly hole above her mouth, but it didn't slow the woman down one bit. Luminous energy glowed from within the wound, and a bloody smile split her lips. Up snapped her hand, bashing the **RHC** out of Hiral's grip to soar off into the woods, and then it stretched out to grasp his throat.

With strength *far* beyond Picoli's E-Rank, she lifted him off the ground with just the one arm, then cocked her other hand back, the **Rune of Impact** glowing ominously.

Down and around, a river cut through the air and into Picoli's extended arm. Then, in the blink of an eye, it rushed forward to explode at her wrist. Left's **Dagger of Sath** chopped through her arm, then the double twisted and lunged at Hiral, catching him in the gut with his shoulder and carrying him out of Picoli's reach.

Ten feet away, Left unhooked himself from Hiral, and the two squared up to look at Picoli. The woman was staring at the stump of her arm, like she was surprised the hand wasn't there anymore, then looked to where it lay on the ground. Picoli's shoulders gave a small shrug, and she raised her gaze to look at Hiral again.

"Get ready," Hiral whispered to Left without taking his eyes off the woman. Small flashes erupted in the corner of his view, as though his **PIM** was trying to bring up more warning windows.

Picoli's legs tensed at the same time Hiral swung his **RHC** up and pulled the trigger. Springing to the side, she dodged the first shot, then the second, lunging around like some kind of animal. After two more misses, Picoli hit the ground and bent hard at her knee, ready for another of her powerful leaps.

Sensing the same thing, Left put himself between her and Hiral, his blade up and ready to intercept. Except, when Picoli leapt, it wasn't toward Hiral.

She shot off to the side like a bolt from Hiral's **RHC**, cutting through the rain and leaving a void where she passed, and her fist came around with its glowing rune. WHAM. It collided with Balyo's spear shaft as the woman got it up just in time to block the blow. Something in her arms *snapped* at the impact, and without a buff like the roots Nivian had to brace himself, the blow hurled her backwards. Balyo hit the ground, bounced over a knobby root, and then slid along the ground.

Hiral took a shot at Picoli, but she was already moving, charging toward Balyo with a manic grin on her face. Light poured from her eyes, ruined nose, and mouth like a grinning skull. She dodged his shot, and then Yanily was there, finally running into action, his **Reed Spear Style** lashing out a dozen times in the span of a heartbeat.

Picoli's head bobbed and weaved, like his spear moved in slow motion, and then she was around Yanily, not paying him even another second of attention. Her eyes locked on Balyo as the spearwoman pushed herself to her feet. Hiral fired again and again, the first shot zipping over Picoli's ducking head, while the second simply got slapped out of the air, all without her even looking in his direction.

She can sense the shots somehow.

Balyo managed to stand and raise her spear, arms shaking like even the effort took everything she had. And yet, she planted her feet and took a stance, gathering her solar energy. Picoli smiled at the challenge, the glow from within her tracing lines across the night as she raced ahead.

Nivian appeared out of nowhere, sliding between the two of them, and raised his shield. Picoli had already seen that trick, though. She darted out, around, and back, completely avoiding the tank, who couldn't turn quickly enough with the roots bracing his feet. Her mocking grin as she passed told him just how useless his effort had been… until Nivian grinned back.

Picoli's glowing eyes narrowed at the expression, and she turned her attention back on Balyo, only to find a giant, glowing spear of light aimed straight at her.

Balyo lunged with everything she had, the amount of solar energy in her spear actually rippling the air and sending the falling rain cascading in wild directions. A sound like a giant sheet tearing bounced between the trees as Balyo thrust, her attack as inevitable as the rising sun.

As fast as she was, Picoli had too much momentum, and the spear filled the space in front of her. *WHAAAAAAM.* The collision dwarfed the earlier impact with Nivian, blasting out a shockwave that carried the rain like a wave.

The concussive force threw Hiral back a good ten feet, and he grunted as he hit the ground, the air getting knocked from his lungs. But breathing wasn't something he had time to worry about. He rolled to his hands and knees, lifting his **RHC** in a shaky hand. What he found could only make his jaw drop.

Picoli and Balyo stood directly opposite each other, cones of furrowed ground dug deep and extending out to the sides like an hourglass from the blast of the rune-empowered fist meeting solar-infused spear. Balyo had contested Picoli's absurd strength head on and held her ground!

Her spear couldn't say the same thing—it had been shattered to nothingness just inches above Balyo's forward hand.

And Picoli still had the same manic smile on her face. A twitch of her shoulders was all the warning anybody had before she burst forward, the rune glowing in front of her fist. Balyo tried to back up—to put some space between them—but from that close, she couldn't keep up.

Picoli's fist hit Balyo square in the chest, then went through it like it was a wet paper bag to burst out of her back.

"Balyo!" Yanily shouted, and he wasn't the only one. Voices cried out in shock all around.

Balyo, for her part, locked her eyes with Picoli, then reached out and grabbed the other woman's arm.

"No... more... jumping... around... now..." Balyo wheezed out, blood running down the sides of her mouth with every word, and from the obviously fatal wound in her chest. "Do it!"

"Balyo..." Seeyela said. "I... can't..."

Balyo didn't look away from Picoli when the other woman pulled experimentally on her arm. "You... can..." Balyo wheezed. "I'm... already... dead..."

"Wule can..." Seena started, but her words cut off, the truth of the injuries too clear to dispute.

"Fine... then..." Balyo said, solar energy gathering in her hands again as she held on to Picoli, then actually pulled the woman in *closer*, driving the arm further through her ruined chest.

The grin on Picoli's face finally faltered, and she tried to pull back, but something about Balyo's grip wouldn't let go.

"She's burning through the energy of her *PIM*," Left said. "Through her life."

"Let's... see... how... you... like... it..." Balyo said, releasing her left hand from Picoli's arm, then extending her fingers like a knife. Energy gathered around her hand as she cocked it back—just like it had around her spear—and Picoli seemed to realize the danger she was in.

Balyo thrust forward at the same time Picoli brought her other arm in to catch the blow, only to realize too late she didn't have *a hand* to catch it with. Still, Picoli's stump deflected Balyo's strike low, the blow piercing through her hip instead of her chest.

"Damnit..." Balyo wheezed. She dropped lifelessly to her knees, the two impaling arms the only things keeping her from toppling over, the last sliver of her red health bar vanishing.

Picoli stared down at the lolling spearwoman in front of her, and at her own injury. Then she swung her handless arm around so viciously, it took Balyo's head clean off.

"Noooo!" multiple voices shouted, Hiral's among them. Bolts of flame and a *Gravity Well* flared to life on both sides of Picoli and Balyo, the women vanishing in a wave of flame and lightning.

"Can you stand?" Left asked, joining Hiral and helping him to his feet.

"I... think so," Hiral said.

Deal with the shock later. Act now, while you can, he told himself, reaching out to his side. He activated his ***Rune of Attraction*** with the little solar energy he'd managed to recover. His lost ***RHC*** sailed through the air and into his hand, and he once again aimed both weapons at the center of the conflagration. Then he pulled the triggers, again and again, pouring his anger into each pull of the trigger.

Damnit. Damnit. Damnit!

"I don't think that will stop her," Hiral shouted, having seen firsthand her uncanny healing abilities. "Seena, can you do something to trap her? Your ***Spearing Roots***?"

"On it!" Seena said, hurling her next barrage of three fireballs before starting to prepare the necessary solar energy. "You need to keep her right there!"

"Leave that to me," Seeyela said, her face a tight scowl of anger and loss. A head-sized, pitch-black gravity well appeared near the ground in the center of the raging flames.

Why is it so small?

Hiral got the answer as *everything* got pulled toward the well. The flames and Picoli alike got hauled down, while the ground itself seemed to tear and rise up toward the veritable hole in space. At the same time, a dreadful tearing sound filled the air, howling like a hurricane through the eye of a needle.

"Can't... hold... this... long," Seeyela said, strained, her hands apart but squeezing together like she had an invisible ball between them.

"Few more seconds," Seena said, the solar energy continuing to build inside of her.

Despite the intense pressure of Seeyela's ***Gravity Well***, Picoli lifted her head to look at Hiral, their eyes meeting. Even with her missing nose still oozing blood, one arm through the headless husk that had been Balyo, much of her body blackened to charcoal, and her health bar below half, the woman smiled again.

"There!" Seena shouted, a dome of massively thick ***Spearing Roots*** bursting out of the ground to encompass Picoli. "I don't know how long that will hold."

"Then we need to go," Hiral said, his mind replaying the smile over and over. And how it seemed to promise him this wasn't finished.

78

RUN

Hiral ran.

He didn't try to speak, and he sure as hell didn't try to *think*. Thinking just conjured images of Balyo dying. Of the thing that had been Picoli *smiling* at him.

That was the *Enemy?* How were they supposed to ever beat that?

Hiral slapped himself in the face as he ran with the group, utterly failing at not thinking.

"You felt like you needed more abuse?" Right asked from beside him, Cal still cradled in his arms and mercifully unconscious. She was lucky she didn't have to see that... but maybe she wouldn't feel so lucky when she woke up to find *three* of her closest friends dead?

"Needed to stop thinking about what just happened," Hiral said.

"Is it going to come after us?" Wule asked from a few paces ahead where he ran with Nivian.

"Yes," Hiral said simply.

"We're not stopping again until we get to the dungeon," Seena said. "Then we're clearing it and getting right to the *Asylum*."

"Balyo..." Yanily said, his voice unusually lifeless.

"I'm sorry, Yan," Seena said.

Yanily glanced at Seeyela and Cal, the last two of the six party members, and shook his head. "She was... kind of badass, wasn't she?"

"She was," Seeyela said. "Always."

The simple words, forced out through the pain and grief on Seeyela's face, seemed to sum up what everybody was feeling—or at least forcing themselves to feel. The truth of it was just too much. After that, they ran in silence. Ran for hours, until finally, they came upon the ruins of a massive old building, made of thick logs that had somehow withstood the ravages of time. Their glowing root path led right in the front door.

"This isn't the same construction as the lizard town," Hiral said, the group slowing down to peer at the building. "Not same as Fallen Reach or that other town either. A Troblin castle?"

"Maybe," Seena said. "The dungeon is called **The Troblin Throne**, after all."

497

Hiral nodded—more out of habit than because he agreed with anything in particular—and ran his gaze up and down the building. Yes, the overall construction was very similar to the keep they'd found in the appropriately named *Troblin Keep* dungeon, though on a grander scale. Where the keep had been something more akin to a massive treehouse, this place was a very much a castle.

A castle made for war.

The wall that had once ringed the building stood in ruins, though the remnants were easily twenty feet thick, and Hiral spotted sections that were more than twice that in height. Beyond the outer wall, the castle itself was dotted with narrow windows and sheltered parapets, easy vantage points for those crossbow-wielding Troblins. The courtyard itself was oddly clear, but then again, those magic-enhanced warriors were formidable, and there would be plenty of places for the *Shamans* to direct a melee from. It was simple, but played to the Troblins' strengths.

"We going in?" Yanily said, glancing back the way they'd come.

"Hiral, see any signs of life?" Seena asked him.

"Nothing. This place looks abandoned, and I think I know why," he said, pointing at the ruined roof. Whatever had attacked had completely skipped the towering walls and killing ground beyond them. The *Enemy* had gone straight through the roof to the heart of the building.

"They must've put the dungeon interface in *after* the Troblins were attacked?" Wule asked.

"Not our problem," Seeyela said. "Keep an eye out, but we're going in. I'm tired of this damn rain."

Hiral drew his *RHCs* and started forward again with Nivian at his side, the man's lips a tight line.

"It wasn't your fault," Hiral said quietly so that only the tank could hear him.

"Maybe, but it was my *job*," Nivian said. "First Fitch and Lonil—nothing I could do about them, I guess. But Cal? Then Picoli and Balyo. I promised to keep them safe. I didn't."

"None of us did," Hiral said weakly. "I had the best chance, and I couldn't stop her." He thought back to his point-blank shot.

"At least you acted. The rest of us just stood there, frozen, until it was too late," Nivian growled, the anger at himself seething out through his clenched jaw.

"Picoli was a friend. I don't blame you for hesitating," Hiral said as they passed the outer wall and entered the courtyard. Glowing roots had long since overtaken the grounds, running haphazardly around, then up the walls and through the windows. "What the *Enemy* did—taking over her body like that— we had no idea they could do that."

"Something tells me that's not all they can do," Nivian said. "That thing Picoli... that *it* did with her punches... You know something about that, don't you?"

Hiral hesitated before answering, but then nodded. "Yes. She was using the **Rune of Impact** somehow. I think I saw **Attraction** too."

"How are they using your runes?" Nivian asked, glancing at Hiral.

"No idea," Hiral said, the pair leaving the courtyard and entering the building. The main entry wasn't anything fancy, but it was *big*, and their glowing route led toward the center of the structure. "I'm hoping Dr. Benza can tell me when we get to the *Asylum*, though."

"And I hope it's not far from here," Nivian said, glancing back to where Right carried Cal. "We're already going to have to run the dungeon twice to make sure everybody gets the clear. Is Cal even going to get credit if she doesn't wake up?"

"I think she will," Hiral said. "The interface scans our **PIMs** when we go in. I think that and being in the dungeon will be enough, like how you guys got experience when I killed those Lizardmen."

"And if you're wrong?" Nivian asked.

"Then we find another way," Hiral said as the pair reached a large intersection of hallways. The sound of falling rain came from straight ahead, where the *Enemy* had likely invaded, but the glowing path instead turned to the right. "Guess we're not going to the actual throne room."

"Maybe **The Troblin Throne** is actually a toilet reference?" Nivian suggested.

"I don't even want to imagine what kind of... monsters... we'd fight in there," Hiral said, sighing, as they turned down the hall and continued to follow the glowing path.

"Thought we'd be going to the center of the building," Seena said from behind them.

"The dungeon interface may not even be in the building," Hiral reasoned out loud. "The path might just be taking us through it."

"I hope that's not the case," she replied, and thunder boomed overhead, the echo through the building causing everybody to pause and look up and down the halls.

"I'm starting to think the movement of the storm isn't coincidental," Wule said.

"Pick up the pace," Seeyela instructed.

"Good idea," Hiral said, jogging further ahead to the top of a staircase leading down, their glowing root path clearly indicating that was the way to go.

"Basement?" Nivian asked.

Hiral just nodded, about to take the first step down when a tremendous crash and the sound of shattering wood echoed from the building behind them.

"What the…?" Seena started to ask, but the answer came almost immediately with another *CRASH*, and one of the hallway walls exploded inward. Wood bounced off the floor and ceiling at the same time as a figure skidded to a stop in the middle of the hall.

The woman stood up, light glowing from behind her eyes, her ruined nose, and the malicious grin on her face. What remained of Picoli's clothing—and flesh—was a charred mess, the sound of her skin cracking with each movement somehow carrying over the falling rain and peals of thunder outside. Only the tentacles looked untouched by the fire, and the woman took a step in their direction, a rune glowing to life in front of the knuckles of her one fist.

"Go!" Seena shouted to the others, a wall of **Spearing Roots** bursting from the ground and slamming into the ceiling, creating a thick wall between them and Picoli. "That won't hold her long…"

WHAM. The whole building shook from the impact, and cracks spread across the root wall from just the single blow.

Hiral didn't need to be told a second time, dashing down the stairs two at a time while a second *WHAM* shook the building. Cool air rushed up to meet him, the stairs narrowing to little wider than his shoulders, and the walls changing from wood to natural stone. Twenty steps, fifty steps, a hundred, and he finally reached the bottom. He glanced back to make sure the others were still with him, then ran down the slender hall ahead of him. The only light down there came from the two roots of their path, and every step of his run threw wild shadows along the wall, like the memories of dozens of other people running with him.

Two hundred feet and he reached the end of the hall, bursting out into a small room with the dungeon interface pedestal sitting in the middle.

"She's through the first wall!" Seena shouted from behind them, and Hiral rushed ahead, Nivian close at his heels. "I've put up another one, but it won't buy us much time."

As soon as two of the colored circles lit up on the pedestal, Hiral swiped his hand over the interface crystal, and an image of Dr. Benza sprang to life.

"Welcome, challengers, to *The Troblin Throne Dungeon*. Please choose an option," the image said, and a blue notification window sprang up beside him.

Tutorial
Enter Dungeon
Help

"**Enter Dungeon**!" Hiral snapped.

A portal formed as the others caught up, though everybody skidded to a stop, looking from one another to the glowing doorway.

"There's too many of us," Wule said.

"I'll stay and deal with Picoli," Seeyela said. "Somebody else will have to…"

"You can't!" Seena objected immediately.

"We don't have time to argue about this," Seeyela snapped.

"You're right—we don't," Hiral said, moving to stand in front of Seeyela. Then he winced. "Sorry," he said, hitting her with his **Rune of Rejection** and sending her straight through the open portal.

"What are you…?" Seena asked.

"She's gonna be pisssssssssed," Yanily said at the same time.

"All of you, go through *now*," Hiral ordered them. "I'll take Cal through a second portal as soon as you're gone. Hurry, before Picoli gets here. Maybe she won't know where we went." *Or be here when we finish.*

"Hiral, you can't clear…" Seena started.

"I won't try. We'll stay in the entry room until the dungeon kicks us out. Now, go!"

Seena's eyes narrowed like she was going to argue, but Nivian put a hand on her shoulder. "It's a good plan. Come on."

Seena forced her breath out between her clenched jaws. "We'll clear it with five, then get you two through it next. Don't die before that," she finally said, then spun on her heel and stomped through the portal.

"See you soon," Wule said, following Seena with Yanily close behind after a sharp wave.

Nivian, the last to go, let his eyes linger on Cal. "I'd take her with us if you didn't need her to open your own portal. Take good care of her."

"I will," Hiral said, then Nivian turned and went through the portal.

A *WHAM* echoed down the hall behind him, far too close for comfort, and Hiral swiped his hand over the interface crystal and said, "**Enter Dungeon**."

"Only five of six party members have entered the current portal. Close portal and open a new one?" Dr. Benza asked.

"Yes," Hiral practically snapped at the image, though the man just nodded, the first portal closing with a slight *pop*. A second later, a new portal opened to replace it. "Right, give me Cal, then you two need to rejoin me."

Right handed the woman over, then he and Left put their hands on Hiral's shoulders. Hiral absorbed them with a thought—another *WHAM* and *CRASH* signaled Picoli was through the final barricade—and he stepped into the portal.

As soon as he was through, he activated **Foundational Split**, Right and Left peeling off him, and turned around.

The portal was still open.

"Dr. Benza, close portal," he shouted through the portal at same time a blue notification window popped up in front of him.

The Troblin Throne – Dungeon
E-Rank
Top Clear Times
XXX : --:--
YYY : --:--
ZZZ : --:--
Attempt Dungeon?
Yes / No

Hiral ignored the window, pushing it aside, and shouted again at Dr. Benza when the portal remained open. "Close portal!" Nothing changed, so Hiral attempted to step back out, but he ran into something like an invisible wall, banging his head in the process.

"One-way portal," Left said. "Picoli will see it."

"And she might be able to come in," Right said. "Not good."

"No, not good at all," Hiral said.

Options. What are my options? The best thing would be that she didn't know we entered a portal at all.

Hiral's eyes went to the blue notification window, specifically at the **Attempt Dungeon** option.

Reckless, but what choice do I have?

He took a breath and slapped **Yes**.

79

THE TROBLIN THRONE

THE portal vanished with a soft *pop*, but so did the entry room, the walls dissipating to reveal a familiar intersection of hallways.

"That... may not have been the best plan," Right said, looking down the hallway on his side.

"Better than Picoli finding us," Left said, turning to face his hall.

"In the other dungeons," Hiral said, staring straight ahead with Cal in his arms, "we had to move forward before anything started happening. If we stay here, we might be safe."

"Or patrols will come at us from both sides," Right said.

"You think we should go try and clear the dungeon by ourselves?" Left asked.

"Would it count as soloing it?" Right asked, smirking. "Might be an achievement for it."

"Yes, *death* would be the achievement," Left said flatly.

"Shush," Hiral said, his attention firmly down the hall straight ahead of him.

There was something there, something waiting for them, its aura cascading out and reaching deeper into the building. For now, it was content to wait, but there was an edge to its patience, like a countdown. If they didn't move ahead eventually, it *would* come looking for them.

> **Dynamic Quest**
> **The Troblin Lord has noticed your presence**
> **and awaits your challenge.**
> **Move quickly and none shall obstruct you.**
> **Delay too long,**
> **and the entire Troblin army will scour the halls**
> **to drag you before their Lord.**
> **Note: The Lord is not known for its patience.**

"Of course," Right said with a shake of his head. "Come on, give me Cal."

"Why?" Hiral asked.

"Because I want you to be able to defend yourself and not die," Right pointed out.

"It looks like we have no choice but to advance," Left said. "I'm pretty sure this counts as being reckless."

"Maybe it won't be so bad," Hiral said, handing Cal over to Right and drawing his **RHCs.**

"There you go, being optimistic again," Right mumbled, but the group moved purposefully down the hall. They didn't have to go far before they came to what had to be the throne room, a large wooden chair dominating the center of the circular chamber.

The largest Troblin Hiral had ever seen—even bigger than the **Troblin Duke**—sat waiting for them in heavy armor seemingly made entirely from wood. In fact, there didn't even look to be joints in the armor, and Hiral thought for a moment it may have been a statue—until it shifted to look at them, the wood creaking with every movement.

Dynamic Quest: Update
The Troblin Lord accepts your challenge.
Send forth your warriors. Leave the spectators behind.
Entertain the Lord with your battle prowess and it shall spare your
lives. Defeat the Lord and earn powerful rewards.
Fail at both of these, and death will be your only achievement.

"More proof the notifications and reward systems listen to what we're saying," Hiral mumbled as he quickly read the final sentence, then closed the window. "Do you think it's safe to leave Cal here? Would she be a spectator?"

"If we're actually going to fight that thing, we can't afford to have one of us stay behind to protect her," Left said.

Hiral looked at the giant Troblin as it stood, towering above the throne. *That thing has to be at least nine feet tall.*

(Boss) Troblin Lord Zob – Unknown Rank

"I'd like to point out we didn't actually challenge it," Right said, gently putting Cal down off to the side of the hallway entrance to the room.

"If fighting it makes sure Cal stays safe, then that's what we're doing," Hiral said, **RHCs** in hand. He started toward the center of the room, Left and Right at his sides.

"This isn't going to be easy," Left said while he shaped the **Wing of Anella** from his left shoulder, and then brought forth his **Dagger of Sath**.

"Good thing we're here to keep you safe," Right added, purple light flaring up the Meridian Line of his right arm and down one side of his back.

"Yes, it is," Hiral said. "Thank you."

Then the time for speaking was over, and the three moved forward. Hiral went straight ahead, measured steps in time with his triggers as he pulled them, while his doubles went wide then cut in to flank the heavily armored **Lord**.

Bolts of *Impact* slapped into the huge Troblin with about as much effect as a gentle breeze, the wooden armor not even cracking, and the red bar above the *Troblin Lord* barely budging despite Hiral's **One Man Army** and **Internal Injuries** abilities.

The Troblin, for its part, simply held its right arm out to the side, hand extended. Not waiting to see what it had up its proverbial sleeve, Right and Left struck from opposite sides, while Hiral aimed both of his weapons at the Troblin's helmed head.

Flaring with purple infernal flames, Right's fist slammed into where the Troblin's kidney would be, the impact of the blow blasting a twenty-foot cone of fire in the opposite direction. Left, at the same time, spun and twisted in his approach, arm moving up, around, and then in, to drive his *Dagger of Sath* into the *Troblin Lord's* stomach. The instant the blade's momentum stopped, the long stream of water left hanging in the air by Left's movements rushed forward to magnify the force of the strike.

Troblin Lord Zob didn't even flinch.

All that, and he lost maybe two percent of his health?

Instead, green light flared in the palm of his open hand, and dark wood grew up and down, quickly forming into the nine-foot haft of a long weapon. Another pulse of green light, and a large, single leaf unfurled at the top, two feet long and serrated along the edges.

"Fall back," Hiral shouted, blasting two more shots into the Troblin's faceplate.

Left and Right darted back. Not a second too soon, either, as the **Lord** whipped its long spear around in front of itself for a dramatic flourish. It spun the weapon around and around in its hands, as if testing the weight, then spun it behind its back and forward again at the same moment it lifted a foot and stepped forward. As it dropped into an obvious fighting stance, the atmosphere around the room grew heavier. Some kind of battle intensity was pouring off the **Lord** and giving weight to the very air.

"It's like it gave us a free shot," Left said, twenty feet to the **Lord's** side.

"And we didn't impress it," Right added, the same distance on the other side.

"Maybe," Hiral admitted, his gaze landing on the **Lord's** stomach. "But Left... uh... left a mark. That's our focus."

He dropped his aim from the Troblin's face to the *tiny* crack in its armor. His bolts hit the crack with pinpoint accuracy, and maybe it was his imagination, but the crack spread. They could do this, and with that much heavy armor, the **Lord** couldn't be all that fast.

Right and Left, obviously coming to the same conclusion, dashed back in, weapons flaring with energy. Right got there first, but the **Lord's** spear came across to perfectly intercept Right's punch with the haft of its spear. Then, one-two, lightning fast, the **Lord** twisted and brought the bottom end of its spear up to slam into Right's gut, lifting the double off the ground. Before Right could even react to the blow, the second twist of the spear swung the bladed end around—and straight through Right's chest.

The double practically exploded in a puff of solar energy, and the **Troblin Lord** seamlessly spun around to intercept Left's dagger. Ignoring Hiral's shots the entire time, the **Lord** parried and blocked Left's dancing assault, its spear a whirling blur, though its feet barely moved an inch.

Hiral activated **Foundational Split**, then focused his blasts on the **Lord's** hands and arms to try and impair its defense. The momentum had shifted from Left attacking to defending, and he was already losing ground.

"That hurt," Right complained, only to charge directly in again as Left got caught flat-footed, his blade coming up in a last-ditch effort to parry.

The two weapons met, Left even putting his other hand behind his dagger to brace for the impact, and then the double hit the wall with a building-shaking impact fifty feet away. Something *CRACKED* from the collision, and Left dropped to the ground, a wing-shaped line of frost along the wall beside the shattered wood. Then he charged ahead again, ignoring his injuries and leaping into the air with the aid of his **Wing of Anella**.

Frosty snowflakes trailed in the air behind him along with the dagger's stream, and he drew back his weapon to strike at the same time the **Lord** parried the first of Right's attacks. Not even missing a beat, the **Lord** spun and brought his spear up to likewise bat aside Left's dagger, then turned back to deal with Right. Except the dagger was a feint, and Left let the dagger vanish at the slightest touch, instead twisting to slash his blue-flame wing across the **Lord's** shoulder.

Though the wing-strike did nothing to pierce through the **Lord's** substantial armor, ice spread in a long line as Left swept past, creeping up to encase the helm, and across to lock around the shoulder. Hitting the ground hands-first, Left crouched down like a cat as Right's glowing fist swung over him. With its shoulder wrapped in ice, the **Lord's** attempted parry fell short, and Right struck through the opening.

Right's punch hit like a Meridian-enhanced warhammer, crunching into the wooden armor to send chunks flying, and forced the **Lord** to take a step back. One step only. The ice over its shoulder shattered with a flex, and then around came the serrated spearhead. Spotting the racing weapon first, Left tried to intervene by blocking with his flaming wing, but his body moved too slow, and the long leaf bisected him in a flash of solar energy. Right didn't fare any better, noticing too late the oncoming attack, and he too burst apart.

With both doubles destroyed, the ***Lord*** lifted a hand up to its helm, a simple tap shattering the ice there, then fell again into its fighting stance. All that, and the exchange had only taken the ***Lord's*** health down another ten percent.

*Left can see the attacks coming, but his body isn't fast enough to keep up with it. Right is the opposite. Neither of them alone has what it takes to go toe to toe with the **Lord**.*

Hiral activated ***Foundational Split*** again, though he gave his doubles far less solar energy, then holstered the ***RHCs*** on his thighs. They weren't offering enough punch to get through the ***Troblin Lord's*** armor. Instead, he hefted the ***Emperor's Greatsword*** off his back and flared the energy-half of the blade to life.

"You think that will work?" Right asked, his Meridian Line only glowing weakly, but soft streamers of purple light wafting off it.

"I'm the only one who can both *see* and *react to* the ***Lord's*** attacks," Hiral said. "It has to be this way."

80

TROBLIN LORD

"Go," Hiral said, taking the greatsword in both hands, then dashing ahead behind Left and Right as they shot forward.

Crisscrossing as they went, their hanging streamers of light and water drew the **Lord's** eyes while Hiral lagged behind. Wider and wider the doubles went with each cross, forcing the **Lord** to turn his head, and Hiral activated the **Rune of Gravity** in the sword and tethered it to the **Lord's** chest.

The sword grew heavy in his hands, pulling ahead like it was falling in that direction, and Hiral waited until the copies made a final wide sweep, then poured energy into it. His feet left the ground as the force of gravity seemed to make *ahead* act like *down*, and he rocketed straight for the **Troblin Lord**.

Left and Right shot in like a closing pincer ahead, but the **Lord's** spear spun once, twice, knocking the doubles back, and it squared its stance to prepare for Hiral. Instead of hitting it head on, Hiral thrust his hand at the ground and activated his **Rune of Rejection**. Falling up and arcing over, Hiral's sword stayed aimed right at the **Lord**, but the momentum of his rush carried him past until he paused, hanging in the air, then started *falling* toward the **Lord's** back.

One foot coming ponderously up and down, the **Lord** began its turn as if in slow motion to block Hiral.

Its spear moves fast, but its body is slow!

Hiral pumped more solar energy into the **Rune of Gravity**, increasing his speed, wind whipping in his ears, and then slammed into the **Troblin Lord**. The glowing energy tip of the **Emperor's Greatsword** drove an inch into the **Lord's** armor, and then stopped, flipping Hiral over and past the **Lord**. A pulse of his **Rune of Rejection** kept him from faceplanting on the wooden floor, and a second pulse flipped him into the air to land on his feet, though he still skidded back toward the hall where he'd started.

Just how strong is that armor? I'll need to keep hitting the same spot like I planned after all.

Despite the massive sword jutting out of the **Lord's** back, the Troblin simply retook its fighting stance like nothing was out of the ordinary.

"Time for the other plan," Hiral shouted, then darted forward while he activated the connection between his **Rune of Attraction** and the **Emperor's Greatsword**. The sword twitched in the **Lord's** back, then twisted out and flipped through the air as Hiral got to within ten feet of the monster, whose spear was already sweeping out for him.

With plenty of warning, Hiral lowered the weight of the sword with a thought as soon as the hilt slapped into his hand, bringing it to his side, and then increased the weight again to parry the **Lord's** heavy blow. Sliding sideways from the impact, Hiral cancelled and resummoned Left in consecutive seconds, the double peeling off him within the **Lord's** guard. Around and in the **Dagger of Sath** went, stabbing into the earlier crack and then exploding with force, while Hiral raced past. Now behind the **Lord**, with its attention on Left, Hiral planted his foot and spun, increasing the weight of the greatsword mid-swing.

The six-foot-long sword slammed into the Troblin's shoulder where he'd hit before with ten times its usual weight, biting deeper into the armor and actually shattering a piece of it. No sooner had the wooden epaulet started to fall than the Troblin backhanded Left out of existence, and continued around with a one-armed swing of its spear.

Thanks to the **Lord's** slow body movement, Hiral had time to get his sword into a defensive position and increase the weight just in time to absorb the worst of the blow. Still, he didn't put enough power into the rune, and he launched backwards from the sheer heaviness of the **Lord's** swing. Readjusting the weight as he soared, he dropped it down to next to nothing, then quick-stepped back when he landed to absorb his momentum.

*I need to be able to adjust the weight faster and more accurately. Every time I don't put enough in, the **Lord** sends me flying. If I put in too much, it slows me down. Well, like every other time, since I don't have the natural talent, there's only one option—practice.*

A smile spread across Hiral's face as he lowered himself back down into a fighting stance, *practicing* in the life-or-death battle. Why did that somehow make him… happy? No, happy wasn't the right word. Comfortable. Nothing had come easy to him. Nothing had been given for free, even though he'd made progress. Testing. Training. Practicing. Improving. *Those* were his strengths. And now his life—and Cal's—depended on it.

It was almost poetic.

Hiral summoned Left as the Troblin finished its turn and dropped into its customary ready stance, spear pointed in Hiral's direction, then thought back to how he'd seen Picoli fighting. Well, the thing that Picoli had become, more specifically. The way she'd used the runes… Could Hiral do that too? Most of it would be too much to try right away while he was focused on the **Emperor's Greatsword**, but there was one thing she did that he might be able to replicate.

Turning his attention to the soles of his feet, Hiral leaned forward and gently pushed power into his **Rune of Rejection**. The wood cracked beneath his boots as he shot forward like an arrow, so fast he didn't even have time to alter the weight of his sword as he swung it around at the ***Troblin Lord***. Sword met spear, then Hiral was past, spinning in the air and putting energy into his rune again the second he touched down. His knees bent as momentum fought against the magic of the rune, but he flexed his muscles and practically ricocheted back toward the Troblin as it tried to follow his movement.

Except he was going to shoot wide—he'd angled his trajectory wrong—and would completely miss the opening on the ***Lord's*** exposed shoulder.

Unless...

Hiral brought his leg forward like he was taking a step, then activated his ***Rune of Rejection*** again on the air. It wasn't perfect—hell, it wasn't even *solid*—but he managed to push against a brief plane of rejection with his foot and hurl himself off. Again, overshooting, but if he'd done it once...

A second pulse of energy, and it was just like back in the ***Time Trial*** from Fallen Reach, kicking off the one triangular island and the next to correct his direction and keep moving forward.

Suddenly in the *perfect* position, Hiral swung the greatsword around, twisting his whole body as he went for maximum impact. He cut the top six inches of the blade through the Troblin's shoulder as he went past.

Damnit, forgot to increase the gravity!

Hiral sailed past the ***Troblin Lord***, his sword carrying a trail of green blood with it as he went, then hit the ground in a run before naturally slowing and turning.

One bloody hand coming away from its shoulder, the ***Troblin Lord*** looked from its fingers to Hiral, that same sense of presence washing out of it like a wave.

Dynamic Quest: Update
Congratulations. Achievement Unlocked: Kneel Before Zob
You have shown potential to entertain the Lord of the Troblins.
Continue to rise to the challenge.
Please access a Dungeon Interface to unlock class-specific reward.
...if you survive that long

"That last part wasn't necessary," Hiral mumbled, but then he snapped his attention from the notification window back to the ***Troblin Lord***, a visible ripple of green energy ballooning out from it.

The wave of energy passed over Hiral and his doubles before he even had time to react, but it didn't seem to be a kind of attack. No, it felt more like... like a release. Like taking the top off a boiling pot that was about to explode.

Hiral's eyes narrowed as the wound in the ***Lord's*** shoulder sealed up like it'd never even been there—the ***Lord's*** health bar also jumped back up to full—then pieces of its armor began to drop off. *Clunk... clunk... clunk. Clunkclunkclunkclunk.* They fell faster and faster, until the entire massive suit lay in chunks around the bare-chested Troblin. Rolling its neck, the absurdly muscular Troblin stepped lightly out of the ruins of its armor, a dangerous deftness to its movements that hadn't been there before. It turned left and right, stretching its arms and legs while the spear spun almost lazily from hand to hand.

But there was nothing casual about those motions, each and every one containing an almost palpable edge, the air whistling as the leaf-blade of the spear cut through it. The Troblin grinned, and then dropped down into the same fighting stance as before, indicating it was ready to resume.

"Be careful," Right said, coming over to join Hiral. "Something's different."

"You don't say?" Hiral deadpanned, but Right was correct. The *Lord* looked to have the same strength and speed with the spear, but from the way it moved, it wouldn't suffer from the lack of mobility anymore. The advantage he'd gained from using the runes was already gone…

Which is exactly how it should be. I haven't earned this yet.

That same smile from earlier crept back across Hiral's face, and he flushed power into his *Rune of Rejection* to launch himself forward. The *Troblin Lord* burst ahead at the same moment, spear a blur of motion as he attacked, and all thought of practicing with the runes fled from Hiral's mind as he was forced to focus every ounce of his attention on simply not getting skewered. Practically weightless, his sword turned aside the *Lord's* blows, but each contact sent painful reverberations through his body or sent him flying.

Parry, fly, land, set his feet, parry, fly, stumble, recover, parry… it was everything he could do to keep the spear from getting through his defense. Even alternating between long and short sword styles—possible only because of the weapon's negligible weight—didn't buy him any advantage, and he was left completely on his heels. Left and Right chased in, barely able to keep up with Hiral and the *Lord* darting around the room, but the Troblin hardly even acknowledged them. A casual swat or sweep kept them at bay before it was right back after Hiral, spear dancing through the air in a way that would make Yanily green with envy.

A minute that felt like an eternity later, after a low-left parry, Hiral was in the air again, feet skidding and quick-stepping as he landed, but the *Lord* didn't follow. Right and Left, who'd been charging in from behind, veered off as the Troblin set its feet. Another pulse of intent rolled off of it. It wasn't the same as earlier—this one contained impatience. Hiral wasn't living up to the Troblin's hopes for him.

"You're just too damn strong," Hiral muttered, but the words rang hollow in his ears.

The Troblin *was* strong, but Hiral was also keeping up. He could see the Troblin's attacks. Could parry them. He just needed to weave in the usage of the runes, and then he'd give the *Lord* the fight it wanted.

The *Troblin Lord's* head turned to look at Cal still lying unconscious by the entrance, its eyes lingering there, then it turned its attention back to Hiral. Another pulse of intent rolled off the *Lord*. The meaning was clear, along with the sensation of a countdown: Hiral had one minute to entertain the *Lord*, or it would go after Cal.

81

NO HOLDING BACK

Hiral burst forward with a ***Rune of Rejection***-enhanced step, already pushing energy into the ***Rune of Gravity*** in the ***Emperor's Greatsword*** as he went. Sword met spear, and Hiral went flying to the side, still not enough weight to his weapon, but kept his attention on his own feet. He couldn't afford to be on the defensive the whole time. The moment he landed, he pushed himself back, muscles straining and joints threatening to pop at the sudden change of direction, but change he did.

The ***Troblin Lord's*** lipless mouth twitched as Hiral came right back at it before it could even step forward. Hiral brought his sword across, and again their weapons met. And again, Hiral was thrown aside, but he was already charging back in.

Horizontal strike, parry, fly, rebound, horizontal strike, parry, fly, rebound. Hiral refused to slow down as he poured energy into his feet and used his ***Rune of Rejection*** to increase his speed. Ten seconds of the countdown passed within his fury of strikes, and in the eleventh second, Hiral changed his horizontal slash to a vertical uppercut, energy blade carving through the wood floor like a hot knife through butter.

No stranger to battle, the ***Lord*** had no problem adapting to the alteration, and instead brought its spear across to once again hurl Hiral away. Except the uppercut was a feint, and Hiral pulsed energy into his feet, flipping himself up and over the spear even as it swept in to strike the sword. A hand-numbing vibration shot up the blade, but Hiral managed to keep hold of the weapon as he completed his flip. The force of the ***Lord's*** strike actually *helped* Hiral's blade arc up and over.

Without the resistance of the previous exchanges, the ***Lord's*** weapon swept out further than anticipated, and Hiral twisted around, pouring energy into the sword's ***Rune of Gravity*** at the same time.

The sword swung like headman's axe with the weight of an entire building behind it—*WHOOSH*—and completely missed, the ***Lord*** deftly hopping forward.

"Damnit," Hiral swore, but a blue notification sprang up in front of him.

Dynamic Quest: Update
That was almost impressive. Almost.
Continue to grow to entertain the Lord.
Forty-five seconds remain until spectator involvement.

Hiral didn't even swear at the notification window as he closed it and charged ahead, running out of time to keep Cal out of danger. The sword became a blur in his hands as he kept on the attack, dancing and leaping around the *Troblin Lord* with his *Rune of Rejection*. The occasional pushes midair to change his direction quickly became second nature, and the *Lord's* eyes narrowed as he pressed it harder and harder.

A flip over, a spin around, then a duck under, and Hiral's sword finally slipped past the *Lord's* whirling spear—doing little more than scratching the *Lord's* muscular chest.

A vicious backhand in that moment of almost-triumph threw Hiral back, though he'd gotten his sword up to block the strike, and the *Lord* looked down at the wound. When it looked back up at him, a wave of disappointment rolled out.

Was that the best Hiral could do? All that effort for… a scratch?

The countdown hit thirty seconds, and the *Lord's* eyes went to Cal.

Hiral's hands clenched around the hilt of his sword, but he didn't charge right back in. His speed gave him an opening, but he needed a heartbeat longer to change the weight of the weapon. An opening. If he had a party with him…

Hiral almost punched himself. He'd been so focused on the sword and runes that he'd completely forgotten about his greatest assets. Left and Right hadn't been able to keep up with the fight, so he'd ignored them. *That* was his mistake.

"I hope you're ready," he shouted, twenty-five seconds left on the timer, and rushed forward.

Just like last time, Hiral built up speed as his weapon met the *Lord's*, the energy blade practically tracing lines in the air as the two danced around each other. Both relied heavily on their mobility for protection—even though Hiral's successful attack had barely wounded the *Lord*—but it also made for a chaotic fight. The two large weapons often obscured their views of each other, and it was more a sense from Hiral's high *Atn* that kept him aware of where the *Lord* was than just his eyes.

He kept the weapon's weight low, letting the *Lord* get used to how heavy his strikes were, and attacked in a fast-paced one-high-vertical, two-low-left, three-high-right-arc pattern, battering at the *Lord's* defenses. Once, twice, three times he repeated the pattern, and then started on the fourth, only ten seconds left now.

High-vertical, and the **Lord** parried, its eyes going ahead to where Hiral's sword moved predictably next to the low-left. *Wham.* Their weapons met, but the impact was different, the **Lord** only putting enough force into it to deflect Hiral's attack. Its eyes and spear were already powered in the other direction, predicting Hiral's third attack and aiming to blast him away in the process.

Hiral cancelled and activated **Foundational Split** in a heartbeat, Right peeling off him and swinging his glowing fist in to meet the oncoming spear while Hiral slipped off to the side and activated **Foundational Split** a second time. *WHAM.* Right's Meridian-enhanced fist exploded in a column of purple flame, completely consuming the double and washing over the **Troblin Lord**.

More out of surprise than pain, the **Lord** stepped back, head swivelling. It must've spotted movement out of the corner of its eye, because its spear came down like lightning.

Left took the spear through his chest in exchange for sweeping up and across the **Lord** with his **Wing of Anella**, a wide swath of ice creeping over and around the **Lord's** lead arm, along with most of its chest and face.

Which left it wide open for Hiral, standing behind it, as he poured energy into the sword's **Rune of Gravity** and swept it around. The timer ticked down to two seconds as the energy-blade ripped through the **Troblin Lord's** waist, cleaving the monster in two. A thick line of blood splashed through the air in its trail.

Hiral staggered two steps away from the weight of the blow, and a notification window sprang to life in front of him. He'd done it!

> **Dynamic Quest: Update**
> **Congratulations. Achievement Unlocked:**
> **This isn't even my final form!**
> **You have entertained the Troblin Lord enough to get serious.**
> **Please access a Dungeon Interface**
> **to unlock class-specific reward.**
> **Prepare yourself.**

"Seriously? I cut him in two!" Hiral shouted at the notification.

He activated **Foundational Split**, then spun back around to find the **Lord** clearly *not* in two pieces. Worse, as Hiral watched, green bands of energy began to wrap around its arms, legs, and chest.

Flexing its muscles, the **Troblin Lord** seemed to expand its body until its skin met the glowing bands of energy with a sizzle. One second, two, and the bands vanished, replaced with what looked eerily like tattoos or Meridian Lines on its skin.

"Son of a…" Hiral started, but then the **Troblin Lord** was right in front of him, spear swinging for his neck.

Pure instinct—or maybe it was his high *Atn*—brought his sword up to block, barely, as the *Lord's* spear became a blur of motion. Faster and faster it spun, straining the limit of what Hiral could keep up with, creeping ever closer to his flesh. It didn't take long for the first blow to get through, forming a searing line along Hiral's left bicep as the blade nicked him. He took a second hit across his thigh, and a third painful slash across his abdomen.

A fourth would've taken his head clean off, but Right and Left came in at the *Lord* from both sides, forcing its spear to intercept and giving Hiral the breather he needed to launch himself backwards. He could *almost* see and keep up with the *Lord's* enhanced attacks, but not quite. Gritting his teeth against the nagging pain of the minor wounds, Hiral popped open his status window and distributed the 18 points he'd been holding on to, 9 in *Dex* and 9 in *Atn*. Part of him winced at the unbalanced attributes, but he needed to play to his strengths.

That done, he slammed the window shut, his body feeling lighter and his senses razor sharp. Ahead of him, Left and Right fell back from the *Lord's* assault, so Hiral wasted no time racing forward. At under twenty percent solar energy, he couldn't afford to drag this out much longer.

Even after having been waylaid by the doubles, the *Lord* still got his weapon up perfectly to block Hiral's strike, but the added weight provided by the *Rune of Gravity* prevented a quick counter. Using the forward momentum, Hiral continued past the Troblin after the clash of blades, diving into a roll to avoid the delayed counterattack, then sprang to his feet and sprinted out in a wide arc. Step, step, *pull*, and his *RHC* was in his hand. The bolt of *Impact* zipped back and slapped the *Lord* square in the face.

Wincing from the bolt, the *Troblin Lord* didn't immediately give chase, and Hiral continued his run, firing every second as the weapon's cooldown allowed. He even scored another annoying hit before the *Lord* got its spear up and spinning to deflect the third and fourth shots. As soon as the fifth also got parried aside, Hiral cut hard toward the *Lord*, his turn and dash powered by his *Rune of Rejection*. He dropped his *RHC* to take his sword in both hands.

Hiral's arms screamed at him as he kept the weight of his weapon well above what he had during their previous exchanges, and he swung it around to slam into the *Lord's* parrying spear. Then, as soon as the weapons collided, Hiral released his grip on the hilt—the sword rebounded wildly away—and twisted down and inside the *Lord's* guard.

With a clench of his fist, he quickly cancelled and activated *Foundational Split*, Right peeling off his back and then flying forward to slam a Meridian-enhanced punch into the *Lord's* nose at the same time Hiral's *Impact*-enhanced fist hit its gut. The twinned assault blew the *Lord* backwards, quick-stepping to try to catch its balance—and right into Left's contribution.

The **Dagger of Sath** traced in the air ahead of a long stream of hanging water, and then stabbed into the **Lord's** back, the trail rushing forward to blow a hole out the **Troblin Lord's** stomach. Green blood spewed across the ground almost all the way to Hiral, and while the **Lord** staggered, it didn't fall.

Cutting it in two didn't finish it off—no way this is enough. And the **Lord's** red health bar agreed, nowhere even close to being empty.

Hiral and Right charged in as Left slashed low across the back of the **Lord's** knees with his **Wing of Anella**, freezing the legs at the joints. A hand out to the side summoned his sword back to him as he and Right crisscrossed in front of the **Lord**, and he swung the weapon for the **Lord's** neck.

Up came to the spear to block, though the movement wasn't as sharp. Hiral slid around the side while Right hammered a punch home directly against the **Lord's** wounded stomach. A gasp of pain escaped its lipless mouth, but it ignored Right's follow-up attack in favor of keeping its spear in front of Hiral. Again and again, it managed to parry, Hiral darting in with the blade spinning and slashing, high, low, overhead, low again, then twisting around the other way and infusing his sword with as much weight as he could manage.

The spear still snapped up in a perfect line, but this time, it was the **Lord** who got thrown back by the weight of the blow. Its feet dragged across the floor as it skidded back, the worst of the ice shattering from around its knees, and Hiral charged in for the kill. With less than ten percent of his solar energy left, he flooded his **Rune of Rejection** with power and practically flew through the air, arriving before the **Lord** could get his spear back up.

Speed came at the sacrifice of power, the sword back down to a more manageable weight, but the length of the blade dug deep into the **Lord's** muscular chest as Hiral dragged it across. Another spray of blood into the air, and Hiral completed his swing—unable to simply cleave through the **Lord's** tough body—then twisted his wrist around to follow up and end things.

A wave of bloodthirsty intent slammed into him from point-blank range. Outrage. Disbelief. Joy. The **Lord's** emotions hit like physical blows, staggering Hiral to the side, and then something slammed into his sword, hurling it from his hands. He reached out to summon it back with his **Rune of Attraction**, but the **Lord's** powerful arms reached around his chest and lifted him from the ground.

The air immediately fled Hiral's lungs as the **Lord** squeezed him in an impossible bear hug, threatening to shatter his ribs. His connection to the **Emperor's Greatsword** escaped his concentration, and though Left and Right raced in and hammered on the **Lord's** back, it seemed to completely ignore them, its intent flaring up as it crushed Hiral.

Panic rushed into Hiral's mind, and he slammed his fists against the **Lord's** face to no avail—he might as well have been punching solid rock. So, changing tactics, he grabbed the side of the **Lord's** head and unleashed twinned **Runes** *of Impact* from the palms of his hands. Again and again and again, he tried to crush the *Lord's* head with his blasts, but the monster just ignored the damage, the feeling of challenge climaxing.

Still not enough. He activated *Eloquent* and *Enraged*, regardless of the consequences, and slammed the empowered *Rune of Impact* into the side of the *Lord's* head.

The beast just gave him a lipless grin, then squeezed harder.

Hiral groaned in pain as something *snapped* in his chest, but he managed to let loose another blast of *Impact*.

Not… working…

He needed something with more power. He'd already used his buffs from his battle with the *Troblin Duke*—and it still hadn't even fazed the *Lord*. What… what was left? None of his other runes would… His memory flashed back to the *Disc of Passage* the crystal monster had destroyed. His *Rune of Separation*… Would it…?

Another snap—he didn't have time to wonder—and he closed his hands around the *Lord's* neck like he was trying to choke it. The *Rune of Separation* might do it… *might*… but he couldn't risk failing. Which meant it was time to gamble it all on the trump card he'd never used.

I am not *going to be Everfail forever!*

And then, with his paltry five percent solar energy, he activated *Terminal* and his *Rune of Separation*.

82

SOLO REWARDS

As soon as *Terminal* activated, pure potential lit up like the sun in Hiral's eyes, while his runes and the double helix written in on his skin flared with energy. If he'd had hair, it would've been standing straight above his head in the billowing force. Maximum rank. Full power. Everything he had.

And he put it into his *Rune of Separation.*

Energy flowed between his hands like an electric current—*sching*—and that was it. No big explosion. No Troblin ripping apart in front of him. And all the built-up potential drained out of his body in an instant. *Did it even work?*

Then the *Lord's* eyes rolled back in their sockets, followed by its head rolling back *off its body.* The arms around Hiral's chest slackened at the same time the glow from his body completely faded—the *Terminal* ability spent—and he pushed himself out of the lingering grip while the Troblin's body toppled to the side.

He landed with another grunt of pain, the jarring motion sending agony through his chest, and he reflexively wrapped his arms around himself. A quick look at his status window for the *System Shock* debuff—nothing. He'd managed to use it without suffering the penalties. This time.

"Left, banner," Right ordered as he rushed over to support Hiral.

"It's here," Left said, the familiar glow washing over them and slightly easing the sharp pain. Would it actually heal broken bones? Probably not.

"Did we do it?" Right asked, helping Hiral sit on the ground without falling to get there.

Dynamic Quest Complete
Congratulations. Achievement Unlocked: Oh, Lord!
You have entertained and defeated the Troblin Lord!
Please access a Dungeon Interface to unlock class-specific reward.

"We did it," Hiral confirmed, wincing as he settled on one of the few spots of the wooden floor not carved up by the battle with the *Lord*. He read the notification again just to make sure, then dismissed it.

> *Congratulations. Achievement Unlocked:*
> **Who Needs Friends with Enemies Like These?**
> **You have completed a Zone-Capping dungeon**
> **without the aid of others.**
> *Please access a Dungeon Interface to unlock*
> *class-specific reward.*

Hiral scanned the notification, then told Left and Right.

"Maybe something like **One Man Army**?" Left asked.

"Maybe," Hiral agreed, but a quick check showed the bonus already sitting at twenty percent. Five percent increase for defeating the **Boss**? Nice.

"Any other achievements?" Right asked.

"Hopefully, one that fixes ribs," Hiral said, dismissing the notification only for another to immediately spring into place.

> *Congratulations. Achievement Unlocked:*
> **Who Needs Enemies with Friends Like You?**
> **You have carried an injured party member**
> **through a dungeon without their aid.**
> *Please access a Dungeon Interface to unlock*
> *class-specific reward.*

Hiral explained it quickly, then looked over at Cal. The notification made it sound like she got credit for the dungeon, which was one less thing to worry about. Still, six achievements for one dungeon would be exciting, if it wasn't for what drove him into it in the first place. He'd need to collect his rewards, then... then what? Waiting out the hour was probably safest. Whatever. One thing at a time. He closed the window, and a seventh popped into his vision.

> *Congratulations. Achievement Unlocked:*
> **On to the Next Challenge!**
> **You have cleared all three dungeons in this zone. Congratulations!**
> *Please access a Dungeon Interface to unlock class-specific reward.*

"Zone?" Hiral asked after reading it out to Left and Right. "The geography for the three dungeons connected to the *Asylum*?"

The others shrugged, and when Hiral closed that notification, no more immediately popped up to replace it.

"Right, can you bring Cal over to join us under the banner? Maybe it'll help her," Hiral suggested.

"I... think I can bring... myself," Cal said, pushing herself up off the ground as Right jogged over to her. With his help, the limping healer woodenly sat down beside Hiral. "Looks like I got a couple of achievements while I was unconscious," she said with a forced smile.

"Glad to hear that," Hiral said. "How are you doing?"

She looked slowly around at who was with her, and clearly at who wasn't, then shook her head. "I... I don't... Please don't tell me where the others are. I don't think I can deal with it right now."

Hiral forced his face to stay neutral, his jaw clenching despite the pain it caused in his chest. Was it easier for her to believe the others were okay? Or that they weren't?

"Did I hear you say something about ribs?" she asked, taking a deep breath through her nose.

"Yeah, think the **Boss** broke a couple," Hiral said.

"I have an ability that can fix those," Cal said, and she chuckled slightly at Hiral's jaw dropping. "No, Wule doesn't have an ability like this, but it's got a long cooldown. Don't get hurt too badly again for a while."

"Deal," Hiral said.

"Give me your hand," she said, and he did.

As she closed her eyes, solar energy rolled off Cal, then roots made of sunlight grew out of her wrist. The glowing roots crawled from her hand to his, then up his arm and gently spread across his chest, warmth and relief following in their wake. They didn't just stop at his ribs either, extending along his entire body, washing away his pains and even partially restoring his solar energy.

"Wow," he said a moment later, the pain entirely gone, and his body feeling better than it had since they'd left *The Mire*.

"Like I said, long cooldown. Take it easy from now on," she said, gently patting his hand. "And, thank you for taking care of me."

"That's what friends do, right?" Hiral said, heat rising up his neck. "Uh, want to see what kind of rewards we got?"

"I'm not expecting much since I didn't do anything," she said, but she accepted Right's offer to help her up.

"Dungeon interface appeared in front of the throne," Left said.

"Still can't believe it was only one enemy," Right said as they all walked over.

"One was enough," Hiral pointed out, then waved his hand over the dungeon interface. As before, all light fled the room in the blink of an eye, then eerie torches sprang to life at the entrance hallway. Though their illumination felt like it wasn't nearly enough to cover the entire large room, Hiral didn't have any trouble spotting the three chests—a large one beside the pedestal, and two smaller ones. "Looks like there's something for you."

"Looks like it," Cal said, her voice sounding forced.

Don't push her too hard. She's been through a lot, and even if she doesn't want to talk about it, she has to suspect some of the others didn't make it.

Hiral watched her a moment longer while she opened her chest, then turned to his. Like in *The Mire*, it was far more like a treasure chest than the trunk Cal opened.

"Another special reward for all the work you did?" Left asked quietly, and Hiral could only shrug and open the lid.

"Uh… this looks more broken than the sword," Right said, looking at the pieces of crystal in the chest.

"It… does…" Hiral agreed, lifting the first curving piece of crystal out of the chest.

The edges weren't jagged, like the sword, but whatever this *had been*, it'd take some work to get it back into one piece. Oddly enough, *View* didn't give him any information on the object either. *Maybe something my* **Mold Crystal** *ability can help with?*

"I think I can fix it," Hiral said. "Whatever it is. Let's put the pieces in one of the packs and I'll figure it out when we get to the *Asylum*."

"Sure," Right said, fetching the pack they had and carefully sliding the new pieces inside as well.

"Oh, Left, what's in the central chest?" Hiral asked, his double already peering inside.

"I'm… not sure," Left said, lifting out a bag of something that *clinked*. "They look a lot like the crystal chips you use up on Fallen Reach as currency."

"Money? What do we need money for down here?" Hiral asked.

Left just shook his head and shrugged. "Should we bring it with us?"

"Definitely. If the dungeon gave it to us, there must be a reason. Put it with the other stuff?"

"The other stuff *I'm* carrying?" Right asked.

"It's a good thing you have all those physical stats," Hiral said, but he couldn't stop the grin from quirking his lips.

"I'm not a packhorse," the double mumbled. Still, he worked with Left to add the currency to the backpack.

"Cal, what did you get?" Hiral asked, turning his attention to the healer. "Cal?" he asked a second time, when she didn't respond immediately.

The healer jumped a little, then slowly turned, holding up a hand-mirror. "I guess Dr. Benza thinks I need to fix my hair," she said, another forced smile on her face.

Mirror of Memories popped up above the mirror as she held it, but Hiral didn't comment on the name—Cal was clearly hiding something about the strange object. There'd be plenty of time to ask about it later, and maybe it should be Seeyela who really talked to her. Who… told her about what had happened.

Just the *thought* of breaking the news to Cal had Hiral turning around and waving his hand over the dungeon interface again.

"**Achievement Rewards**," he said even before Dr. Benza fully materialized, and the first notification window mercifully sprang to life.

> **Achievement: Kneel Before Zob: Class Reward: Ability (Active) –**
> **Intimidate (60 second cooldown)**
> ***Intimidate (Active) – Your mere presence radiates how dangerous***
> ***you are. Successfully Intimidated opponents will flee or suffer***
> ***penalties for thirty seconds when fighting you.***

Sounds like some kind of debuff. Straight-up avoiding fights could be handy for weaker enemies, though it doesn't say if I can use it on a group or just one monster. Needs... yup... testing.

Knowing Right and Left would learn everything about his abilities as soon as he absorbed them, he skipped over explaining ***Intimidate***, then closed the window so the next one could pop up.

> **Achievement: This Isn't Even my Final Form!**
> **Class Reward: Class Modification – Inspirational Growth**
> ***Inspirational Growth – In extreme situations, your chance for***
> ***Spontaneous Ability Evolution is increased***
> ***by a factor based on your base Atn.***

*Spontaneous Ability Evolution? Like what the Growers have? Then again... I got **Mold Crystal** like that, so maybe I've always had it? Not something I can rely on, but it talks about extreme situations, so when I need it most. Could be handy.*

A mental swipe and the window vanished, the next replacing it right away.

> **Achievement: Oh, Lord!**
> **Class Reward: Class Modification –**
> **PIM Upgrade – Party Interface**
> ***Party Interface – Create a Party by linking your PIMs***
> ***to communicate over long distances and know***
> ***the direction of your allies.***
> ***Note: Requires initial setup after all members***
> ***have received the Party Interface Class Modification.***
> ***Note (2): Parties can only be created once every 240 hours.***
> ***Choose carefully.***

*Hrm. I wonder why it has the time restriction on it? And how long is long range? Either way, also really useful to coordinate. The battle with the **Prince** and the totems would've been way easier with this. I'll have to see if it applies to Right and Left... Next!*

> **Achievement: Who Needs Friends with Enemies Like These?**
> **Class Reward: Class Modification – Killing Spree**
> **Killing Spree – Each enemy defeated within sixty seconds of the previously defeated enemy grants the following stacking bonuses:**
> **+10% experience gained, +2% to all attributes (Duration: 60 seconds or until a new stack of Killing Spree is obtained), +2% solar energy instantly regained,**
> **and instant minor health recovery.**

Stacking attribute bonus? Even if it's only for a minute, that has potential. Not to mention the recovery aspects. They also stack... which means the more enemies I kill, the stronger I get? Crazy! If it applies just to contributing to fights, like experience, this could really get out of hand.

Hiral hesitated before closing the window, mind running over the numbers, but finally shook his head. He'd have to see how it worked in a fight before he got too excited. One minute between enemies like **Elites** wasn't very long. So, how about that next achievement?

> **Achievement: Who Needs Enemies with Friends Like You?**
> **Class Reward: Class Modification – The Life of the Party**
> **The Life of the Party – Simply being in a party with you (and nearby) grants the following buffs to your allies:**
> **+10% to all attributes, solar energy capacity, solar energy output, and solar energy absorption.**

Hiral's jaw practically dropped. Ten percent, just for being in a party with him? It didn't stack up like **Killing Spree**, but it also didn't have any ramp-up time. And *all* attributes? Wow. The only question was whether or not he would get the bonus. Probably not, but maybe Left and Right? Even if they didn't, that was a huge boon. Hiral's hand hesitated again, just imagining the look on Yanily's face when he saw this, then finally closed the window and moved on to the next.

> **Achievement: On to the Next Challenge!**
> **Zone Reward: The Asylum is unlocked for you, as is the path leading to it.**
> **Asylum – You've earned a rest, enjoy it, but remember—more challenges await.**

Hrm, nothing fancy, but probably the most important achievement of the bunch.

"You got the *Asylum* achievement?" he asked Cal, and the healer nodded. "That's a relief. So, here's what I'm thinking... Ah, I should explain something first. There was... there was an *Enemy* outside when we came into the dungeon," he said, skirting around the topic of Picoli. "That's why it's just you and me in here. Anyway, I think we should wait the full hour before we exit. Hopefully, it'll be clear by then."

"That... that sounds good to me," she said absently, still staring into the strange mirror she'd received. "I'm... uh... just tired," she added, seeing something on Hiral's face. "I'll be ready in an hour."

"I could use the rest too," Hiral said as he watched Cal slowly walk over to one of the walls and gently slide down it to sit on the floor, her eyes on the mirror the whole time.

"What do you think she's looking at?" Left asked quietly.

"I don't know," Hiral said. "We'll worry about it when we get to the *Asylum*. For now, let's join back up so we can recover more solar energy. And, guys, thanks. Couldn't have done it without you."

"We've always got your back," Right said. "'Cept when Troblins are hugging you, apparently. Sorry we couldn't get you out of that."

"It's okay—I handled it," Hiral said with a cough and a wink. Then he absorbed the two doubles and sat right there in the middle of the floor to recover his energy—no way to know what they'd face when they left the dungeon.

The hour passed in no time, and with just three minutes left on the countdown, Hiral stood and activated *Foundational Split*.

"Cal, you ready?" he asked, and the woman slowly pushed herself to her feet and ambled over.

"Is it just me, or does she look more tired now than before?" Right asked.

"You may need to carry her again," Hiral said. "We'll have to move quickly."

"No problem," Right said, and Hiral did a quick check to make sure he had everything.

Both **RHCs** were on his thighs, the greatsword across his back, and he had the pack with the crystal supplies and the broken dungeon reward.

As ready as they would be, he waved his hand over the dungeon interface crystal. *Ah, damn, I should've used the time to go through the tutorials. Oh, well, the Asylum is sure to have them too.* "Dr. Benza, **Exit Dungeon**," Hiral said.

However, instead of the portal appearing, Dr. Benza's image shimmered. "Warning," he said in a strange, almost metallic voice. "*Enemy* presence detected outside dungeon. Portal opening creates too great a risk.

"Calculating options. Calculations complete. Next best course of action chosen."

"*Enemy*? Next course of action?" Left asked. "Why don't I like the sound of this?"

"Exit request denied. Resetting dungeon," Dr. Benza said, then he and the portal vanished.

"Resetting...?" Hiral asked before looking toward the interface, which was also gone. In its place, though, sat the *Troblin Lord*, who slowly began to stand when it saw them. "Oh shi..."

As soon as the **Troblin Lord** reached to the side to summon his spear, Hiral ripped the **Emperor's Greatsword** off his back and charged in. Activating **Eloquent** and **Enraged**, and pouring his solar energy into the **Rune of Gravity** as fast as he could, he piled on the weight. Hundreds and hundreds of pounds with every inch, the blade arced around until it struck the **Lord** where its armored helm met its shoulders.

CRAAAACK. The sound of the impact was like a tree shattering, wood splinters exploding in all directions as the sword tore in one side and straight out the other. The **Lord's** whole body twitched, and Hiral reached out with his **Rune of Attraction** toward the head sailing away.

The armored head jerked in the air, then landed at Hiral's feet, at which point he flipped the greatsword around and drove it point-first straight down through the **Lord's** face. A twist for good measure, then he turned his attention to the still-standing body.

"Uh… why didn't you do that the first time?" Right asked, gently giving the body a push. The eight-foot monster toppled lifelessly over.

"Didn't know it would give us a free shot last time," Hiral said, eying the corpse just to make sure it wasn't going to still jump into phase two of the fight. When it didn't even twitch, he finally sheathed the sword on his back again and let out a breath.

"Well, with *that* out of the way," Left said, pointing at the Troblin, "an *Enemy* outside?"

"Guess we have no choice but to wait it out," Hiral said. "Which isn't bad since I just threw half of my solar energy into that one attack."

"Half?" Right asked. "You only gave us each ten percent."

"Yeah. The sword multiples its weight exponentially by how much solar energy I put in. One percent is doubled weight, two percent is four times the weight, three percent eight times the weight, and so on and so on." He plopped down on the ground. The drain of using that much solar energy all at once made him feel like he'd sprinted a marathon.

"So you basically hit it with…?" Right started.

"A *lot* of weight," Hiral finished. "It was worth it, though," he added, checking the experience he got from it and noticing a blinking buff notification.

Oh, **Killing Spree** *activates on the first kill.*

It'd fade long before they got into another fight, but that was handy to know for the future.

"Back to waiting for another hour?" Cal asked.

"Looks that way," Hiral said, then glanced at the throne. The interface hadn't reappeared, so they couldn't leave even if they wanted to.

Cal didn't seem to have the same reservations, her face slack, and she went back to her spot against the wall to sit down.

Just how long are we going to be stuck in here?

83

ASYLUM

IT turned out they needed to wait *five hours*—and four dungeon resets—for the portal to finally open, and Hiral let out a breath of minor disappointment when he didn't get to kill the ***Lord*** again. *Heh, I'm thinking too much like Yanily.*

"If the portal is open, that means P—the *Enemy*—isn't out there?" Right asked, changing what he was going to say after a brief look at Cal.

"Hope so," Hiral said. "Still, be ready for anything."

"I'll go first," Left said, shaping his ***Dagger of Sath*** and leading the way with Right and Hiral close behind, Cal bringing up the rear. "Clear," Left said as the others emerged.

Hiral still did a quick look around at the room and all the new chunks of wall, floor, and ceiling missing. Most notable was the new tunnel opposite the one they'd entered through, their glowing root path leading in that direction.

"Somebody was looking for us," Right said, running his finger along one of the gashes in the floor.

"And they weren't happy when they couldn't find us," Hiral muttered. Was Picoli down the new tunnel, or had she finally given up? Either way, they couldn't stick around. But, first, he spotted the dungeon interface and swiped his hand over it.

"**Clear Times**," Hiral said, as Dr. Benza appeared.

The Troblin Throne – Dungeon
E-Rank
Top Clear Times
Hiral: 5:57
Seena: 7:31
ZZZ : --:--
Close Window

"Whoa," Right said.

"A fast dungeon, one way or the other," Hiral said, nodding. "They must've done the same thing we did and went straight for the ***Lord***. It also means they should be out here any minute now, assuming they got stuck in the same reset loop we did. Left, keep an eye down the tunnel we entered from. Right, get the other one, please."

"Got it," they both said in unison, moving to take up positions.

This time, they didn't have to wait long. A portal opened, and the five Growers piled out, ready for a fight.

"Just us here," Hiral said quickly with his hands up.

"How do we know you're not…?" Yanily started, but cut off when Hiral subtly pointed to Cal standing in the corner of the room.

Seena, on the other hand, breathed out an obvious sigh of relief. "You got through."

"After being reckless," Right said helpfully from where he watched the tunnel.

"Thank you, Right," Hiral said flatly.

"Did you tell her?" Seena asked quietly, eyes zipping to Cal and back again. Hiral just shook his head. "Seeyela will talk to her, but she must've realized it when we came out."

"I think maybe she had an idea even before," Hiral said. "She got some kind of mirror from the dungeon, and she's been wrapped up in it. Maybe it's for the best. Either way, I think we should get out of here while we can. There's a new tunnel."

"I see that. Everybody ready to move?" Seena asked, though her lips tightened when she saw Cal fall into Seeyela's arms, shoulders shuddering. "Sis?"

"We're ready," Seeyela said, patting Cal on the back. The healer pulled away, tears still streaming down her face. She wouldn't be much help if it came to a fight, but at least she'd be walking on her own.

"Left, can you take the lead again?" Hiral said, pointing down the new tunnel, and the group quickly moved that way. Not even a hundred feet later, the tunnel widened significantly, and they found what looked like another dungeon interface. Twenty feet beyond the interface, the floor dropped off completely, only darkness below, though the tunnel continued off into the distance, the glowing roots running along the sides of the wall.

"They expect us to fly?" Wule asked.

"Or clear another dungeon?" Nivian said, eyeing the interface.

"Maybe not," Hiral said, joining Nivian. "Hey, everybody, stand close. I think I know what this is."

A *WHAM* echoed back from the way they'd come, small rocks and dust falling from the ceiling. Then, *WHAM* again.

"Maybe skip the explanation?" Seena suggested, the party drawing weapons and facing the tunnel.

Was that Hiral's imagination, or could he hear footsteps? Running footsteps, getting closer. Fast.

Hiral put his hands on the interface, and the image of Dr. Benza predictably appeared.

The image of the doctor shimmered briefly. "Accessing **PIMs**. Access complete," Dr. Benza said, his voice oddly flat. "All zone-dungeon clears detected. *Asylum* destination unlocked. Would you like to proceed to the *Asylum?*"

"Yes!" Hiral said, along with everybody else around the platform.

"Destination selected," Dr. Benza said, and a dome of soft blue light rose around the circular platform. Then it gently pulled ahead into the wide hallway so smoothly, Hiral couldn't even feel it moving under his feet.

At the same time, the sound of running steps grew louder and more frantic, glowing eyes and a manic grin appearing in the distance.

"Dr. Benza, faster, please," Hiral said, pushing back the rising panic. If Picoli got on the platform, would they take her right to the one place that was supposed to be safe?

"Speed increasing," Dr. Benza said, and the platform bolted away from the hall at the same time the thing that was Picoli arrived.

It skidded to a stop at the edge of the floor, nothing but emptiness immediately in front of it, then dropped down to hands and feet, a familiar glow appearing under the soles of her feet and the palms of her hands.

*She's going to try a **Rejection**-enhanced leap!*

Seena and Seeyela both recognized the threat at the same time, and all three raced back to the end of the platform. Hiral poured energy into his **Rune of Rejection** while a **Gravity Well** and a wall of **Spearing Roots** each filled half the hall. If Picoli jumped, they'd make her work for it.

But, as one second turned to two, to three, four… five, and the distance between them grew and grew, Picoli instead stood up. Her eyes narrowed, then she threw back her head and let out a raspy, keening howl, the sound quickly getting swallowed by the darkness as the platform accelerated away.

"Something tells me we haven't seen the last of her," Seeyela said, a note of sadness to her voice.

"Maybe we can find a way to bring her back," Seena said, the words forced, but Seeyela nodded her appreciation. "So, Hiral, what's this?" she asked, pointing at their feet.

"It's a **Disc of Passage**. But, a *real* one. Not a shaped tattoo. It makes sense, I guess. All our tattoos were based on actual items from history."

"Glad this is a bit more real than history," Seeyela said. "It's taking us to the *Asylum?*"

"Seems it," Hiral said.

"Doesn't even feel like we're moving," Seena said.

"The disc creates a protective shield around it—that's the blue dome, I think—to maintain a steady environment within. We could even go underwater, and we wouldn't notice. But, if you look at the roots along the walls, you can see just how fast we're going." Hiral pointed to the side in demonstration.

"I know how much you like testing things, but can we avoid the underwater bit?" Seena asked.

"Not up to me," Hiral said with a shrug.

"Since the travel is taken care of, I'm going to check on Cal," Seeyela said. "This is hitting her pretty hard."

"Sis… how are *you* doing? Cal isn't the only one who… who lost…" Seena started, but couldn't finish.

"Once we get to the *Asylum* and can finally relax, I'll deal with it. For now, I'm just not thinking about it. I can't. It'll be too much." A crack formed in her façade, but she quickly buried the emotion. "See. It's that close to the surface. Excuse me." She spun on her heel and went over to join Cal.

"I don't know how she's doing it," Seena said quietly for Hiral. "If that was me… would I be able to keep going?"

"You would," Hiral said. "You're both strong."

"I hope we never have to find out," Seena said. "Losing Vix was already hard enough. I couldn't bear to lose another one of you. Yes, I'm including you in that category, so stop being reckless," she added with a soft punch to his shoulder, then walked over to join the others.

Hiral, for his part, turned back the way they'd come, eyes trying to pierce the darkness to make sure Picoli didn't find a way to follow them. That *thing* inside of her could fly, couldn't it? So why didn't it burst out and give chase? A shake of his head, and he let it go—there were just too many questions he didn't have answers to.

Instead, he walked over to where Wule was handing out rations, and took one from the healer. "You guys have much trouble with the **Lord**?"

"Yes and no," Wule explained. "The fight was brutal, but relatively quick. We had a pretty good system by the fifth time we had to fight it, but it didn't get any easier. I can't believe you two made it through. You're lucky you didn't have to fight it multiple times."

"Uh…" Hiral said, then took a bite out of his ration.

"You *did* fight it five times? Just the two of you? Well, four, I guess. Maybe that's not so different than what we did."

"Except Hiral solo'd the **Lord** the last four times," Right said. "One swing. Boom. Dead."

"What!?" Wule exclaimed.

"Overpowered S-Rank weapons," Yanily grumbled, running a hand along the shaft of his spear. "Don't worry, baby. I know you're just working up to it."

"In all seriousness, you want to tell us how you managed?" Seena asked.

So, Hiral did, outlining the fight as the disc traveled. His story finished, and they took their turn. Then, from there, it became stories about Lonil, Balyo, Vix, and Fitch. They seemed to avoid talking about Picoli for the time being, but even Seeyela and Cal joined in. Minutes turned into an hour, then two, before the trip seemed to be nearing its end.

The **Disc of Passage** slowed to a stop when it ran out of tunnel, but then rose gently straight up. A moment later, the party found themselves in a wide, circular room seemingly cut from the stone itself, two more holes in the floor that looked like they'd fit their own discs, and a single tunnel leading out. More glowing roots ran along the walls and domed roof, and the air felt stale as Hiral breathed it in.

"It's been a long time since anyone was here," Nivian said, his voice barely above a whisper.

"Doesn't matter, as long as it's safe," Seeyela said, then strode toward the only exit.

The group walked down the narrow tunnel—just wide enough for two people to walk side by side—with their weapons drawn, the familiar roots their only light. This tunnel seemed to go on and on, so long, Hiral had trouble making out where they'd entered, and then further still. Ten minutes they walked in silence before somebody finally spoke.

"Why couldn't the disc thing just take us all the way?" Yanily complained, his voice echoing strangely off the stone around them.

"Shush," Seena scolded.

"Just saying..." Yanily mumbled, but they continued on in silence for another five minutes before emerging into another room.

Unlike the first room or the tunnel, the domed ceiling of this one was made from or covered in the same crystal as Hiral's weapons. Four more doorways branched off from this area, their own rooms visible beyond—so no more long tunnels, at least—and, of course, there was an interface pedestal in the middle.

"This *is* the *Asylum*, isn't it?" Wule asked as the group spread out around the room.

"This looks like some kind of training room over here," Nivian said from beside one of the doors. "It's huge."

"A kitchen here, and... a garden?" Seena said from beside another door.

Hiral veered over toward another door, peering in and finding what looked like workbenches, a forge, and tools lining the walls, among other things. "Some kind of workroom here. For trades or crafts?"

"This one looks like... a house?" Seeyela said, Cal close at her side. "Living quarters or a dorm or something. I see more doors further down, but it kind of reminds me of the inn we stayed at."

"Any Troblins and their inappropriate paintings?" Yanily asked.

"Don't even joke about that," Wule said. "Hey, I think I can activate this pedestal even though Hiral isn't close."

"Try it," Seena said, and Hiral made sure not to move closer despite his curiosity.

The healer waved his hand over the crystal, and Dr. Benza appeared beside the pedestal.

"Welcome to an *Asylum*," he said. "If you're here, that means you've cleared the three dungeons in the area. Congratulations. Within these walls, you will find safety, shelter, and a place to regain your strength before you push on to the next set of dungeons.

"The remote location, along with the rare materials used to craft the *Asylum* itself, reduces the chances of *Enemy* detection to almost zero. Though, this does limit the maximum occupancy to only eighteen," Dr. Benza added with a shrug. "Believe me, if we could've just built more *Asylums* to house our people, we would have. The dozen we've constructed around the world as waypoints for your journey through the dungeons will have to do, however.

"During your stay, please feel free to make use of the fully equipped training room, the well-stocked kitchen and garden—though watch out for the rabbits, they bite, little bastards—and the multi-purpose workroom. You will, of course, also have access to the **Tutorials** and **Help** sections equivalent to the number of dungeons you've cleared.

"With all that in mind, I'm sure you have many questions, and I would be happy to answer…" The image flickered, then vanished.

All at once, red lights came on within the crystal dome overhead, tinting the entire room the color of blood, and Dr. Benza's image reappeared, though this time, it looked… older. Tired. Ragged.

"If you're seeing this version of me, it can only mean one thing—the magic keeping Fallen Reach in the sky is failing.

"You need to act. You need to save it. If you don't, within one year, the island and everybody on it will be destroyed."

THE STORY WILL CONTINUE IN
RUNE SEEKER 2